Clarence Mulford

The Wild Bunch Boxed Set - 4 Westerns in One Volume
(Illustrated Edition)

OK Publishing 2021

Clarence Mulford

The Wild Bunch Boxed Set - 4 Westerns in One Volume (Illustrated Edition)

The Coming of Cassidy and Others, Buck Peters Ranchman, Tex & The Orphan

Published by

Books

- Advanced Digital Solutions & High-Quality book Formatting -

musaicumbooks@okpublishing.info

2021 OK Publishing

ISBN 978-80-272-7636-3

Contents

The Coming of Hopalong Cassidy and Others

Suddenly a rope . . . yanked him from the saddle

[Page 342]

Preface

It was on one of my annual visits to the ranch that Red, whose welcome always seemed a little warmer than that of the others, finally took me back to the beginning. My friendship with the outfit did not begin until some years after the fight at Buckskin, and, while I was familiar with that affair and with the history of the outfit from that time on, I had never seemed to make much headway back of that encounter. And I must confess that if I had depended upon the rest of the outfit for enlightenment I should have learned very little of its earlier exploits. A more secretive and bashful crowd, when it came to their own achievements, would be hard to find. But Red, the big, smiling, under-foreman, at last completely thawed and during the last few weeks of my stay, told me story after story about the earlier days of the ranch and the parts played by each member of the outfit. Names that I had heard mentioned casually now meant something to me; the characters stepped out of the obscurity of the past to act their parts again. To my mind's eye came Jimmy Price, even more mischievous than Johnny Nelson; "Butch" Lynch and Charley James, who erred in judgment; the coming and going of Sammy Porter, and why "You-Bet" Somes never arrived; and others who did their best, or worst, and went their way. The tales will follow, as closely as possible, in chronological order. Between some of them the interval is short; between others, long; the less interesting stories that should fill those gaps may well be omitted.

It was in the '70s, when the buffalo were fast disappearing from the state, and the hunters were beginning to turn to other ways of earning a living, that Buck Peters stopped his wagon on the banks of Snake Creek and built himself a sod dugout in the heart of a country forbidding and full of perils. It was said that he was only the agent for an eastern syndicate that, carried away by the prospects of the cattle industry, bought a "ranch," which later was found to be entirely strange to cattle. As a matter of fact there were no cows within three hundred miles of it, and there never had been. Somehow the syndicate got in touch with Buck and sent him out to look things over and make a report to them. This he did, and in his report he stated that the "ranch" was split in two parts by about forty square miles of public land, which he recommended that he be allowed to buy according to his judgment. When everything was settled the syndicate found that they owned the west, and best, bank of an unfailing river and both banks of an unfailing creek for a distance of about thirty miles. The strip was not very wide then, but it did not need to be, for it cut off the back-lying range from water and rendered it useless to anyone but his employers. Westward there was no water to amount to anything for one hundred miles. When this had been digested thoroughly by the syndicate it caused Buck's next pay check to be twice the size of the first.

He managed to live through the winter, and the following spring a herd of about two thousand or more poor cattle was delivered to him, and he noticed at once that fully half of them were unbranded; but mavericks were cows, and in those days it was not questionable to brand them. Persuading two members of the drive outfit to work for him he settled down to face the work and perils of ranching in a wild country. One of these two men, George Travis, did not work long; the other was the man who told me these tales. Red went back with the drive outfit, but in Buck's wagon, to return in four weeks with it heaped full of necessities, and to find that troubles already had begun. Buck's trust was not misplaced. It was during Red's absence that Bill Cassidy, later to be known by a more descriptive name, appeared upon the scene and played his cards.

C. E. M.

I

The Coming of Cassidy

The trail boss shook his fist after the departing puncher and swore softly. He hated to lose a man at this time and he had been a little reckless in threatening to "fire" him; but in a gun-fighting outfit there was no room for a hothead. "Cimarron" was boss of the outfit that was driving a large herd of cattle to California, a feat that had been accomplished before, but that no man cared to attempt the second time. Had his soul been enriched by the gift of prophecy he would have turned back. As it was he returned to the work ahead of him. "Aw, let him go," he growled. "He 's wuss off 'n I am, an' he 'll find it out quick. I never did see nobody what got crazy mad so quick as him."

"Bill" Cassidy, not yet of age, but a man in stature and strength, rode north because it promised him civilization quicker than any other way except the back trail, and he was tired of the coast range. He had forgotten the trail-boss during the last three days of his solitary journeying and the fact that he was in the center of an uninhabited country nearly as large as a good-sized state gave him no concern; he was equipped for two weeks, and fortified by youth's confidence.

All day long he rode, around mesas and through draws, detouring to avoid canyons and bearing steadily northward with a certainty that was a heritage. Gradually the great bulk of mesas swung off to the west, and to the east the range grew steadily more level as it swept toward the peaceful river lying in the distant valley like a carelessly flung rope of silver. The forest vegetation, so luxuriant along the rivers and draws a day or two before, was now rarely seen, while chaparrals and stunted mesquite became more common.

He was more than twenty-five hundred feet above the ocean, on a great plateau broken by mesas that stretched away for miles in a vast sea of grass. There was just enough tang in the dry April air to make riding a pleasure and he did not mind the dryness of the season. Twice that day he detoured to ride around prairie-dog towns and the sight of buffalo skeletons lying in groups was not rare. Alert and contemptuous gray wolves gave him a passing glance, but the coyotes, slinking a little farther off, watched him with more interest. Occasionally he had a shot at antelope and once was successful.

Warned by the gathering dusk he was casting about for the most favorable spot for his blanket and fire when a horseman swung into sight out of a draw and reined in quickly. Bill's hand fell carelessly to his side while he regarded the stranger, who spoke first, and with a restrained welcoming gladness in his voice. "Howd'y, Stranger! You plumb surprised me."

Bill's examination told him that the other was stocky, compactly built, with a pleasing face and a "good eye." His age was about thirty and the surface indications were very favorable. "Some surprised myself," he replied. "Ridin' my way?"

"Far's th' house," smiled the other. "Better join us. Couple of buffalo hunters dropped in awhile back."

"They 'll go a long way before they 'll find buffalo," Bill responded, suspiciously. Glancing around he readily picked out the rectangular blot in the valley, though it was no easy feat. "Huntin' or ranchin'?" he inquired in tones devoid of curiosity.

"Ranchin'," smiled the other. "Hefty proposition, up here, I reckon. Th' wolves 'll walk in under yore nose. But I ain't seen no Injuns."

"You will," was the calm reply. "You 'll see a couple, first; an' then th' whole cussed tribe. *They* ain't got no buffalo no more, neither."

Buck glanced at him sharply and thought of the hunters, but he nodded. "Yes. But if that couple don't go back?" he asked, referring to the Indians.

"Then you 'll save a little time."

"Well, let 'em come. I 'm here to stay, one way or th' other. But, anyhow, I ain't got no border ruffians like they have over in th' Panhandle. They 're worse 'n Injuns."

"Yes," agreed Bill. "Th' war ain't ended yet for some of them fellers. Ex-guerrillas, lots of 'em."

When they reached the house the buffalo hunters were arguing about their next day's ride and the elder, looking up, appealed to Bill. "Howd'y, Stranger. Ain't come 'cross no buffaler signs, hev ye?"

Bill smiled. "Bones an' old chips. But th' gray wolves was headin' southwest."

"What 'd I tell you?" triumphantly exclaimed the younger hunter.

"Well, they ain't much dif'rence, is they?" growled his companion.

Bill missed nothing the hunters said or did and during the silent meal had a good chance to study their faces. When the pipes were going and the supper wreck cleaned away, Buck leaned against the wall and looked across the room at the latest arrival. "Don't want a job, do you?" he asked.

Bill shook his head slowly, wondering why the hunters had frowned at a job being offered on another man's ranch. "I 'm headed north. But I 'll give you a hand for a week if you need me," he offered.

Buck smiled. "Much obliged, friend; but it 'll leave me worse off than before. My other puncher 'll be back in a few weeks with th' supplies, but I need four men all year 'round. I got a thousand head to brand yet."

The elder hunter looked up. "Drive 'em back to cow-country an' sell 'em, or locate there," he suggested.

Buck's glance was as sharp as his reply, for he could n't believe that the hunter had so soon forgotten what he had been told regarding the ownership of the cattle. "I don't own 'em. This range is bought an' paid for. I won't lay down."

"I done forgot they ain't yourn," hastily replied the hunter, smiling to himself. Stolen cattle cannot go back.

"If they was I 'd stay," crisply retorted Buck. "I ain't quittin' nothin' I starts."

"How many 'll you have nex' spring?" grinned the younger hunter. He was surprised by the sharpness of the response. "More 'n I 've got now, in spite of h —!"

Bill nodded approval. He felt a sudden, warm liking for this rugged man who would not quit in the face of such handicaps. He liked game men, better if they were square, and he believed this foreman was as square as he was game. "By th' Lord!" he ejaculated. "For a plugged peso I 'd stay with you!"

Buck smiled warmly. "Would good money do? But don't you stay if you oughtn't, son."

When the light was out Bill lay awake for a long time, his mind busy with his evening's observations, and they pleased him so little that he did not close his eyes until assured by the breathing of the hunters that they were asleep. His Colt, which should have been hanging in its holster on the wall where he had left it, lay unsheathed close to his thigh and he awakened frequently during the night so keyed was he for the slightest sound. Up first in the morning, he replaced the gun in its scabbard before the others opened their eyes, and it was not until the hunters had ridden out of sight into the southwest that he entirely relaxed his vigilance. Saying good-by to the two cowmen was not without regrets, but he shook hands heartily with them and swung decisively northward.

He had been riding perhaps two hours, thinking about the little ranch and the hunters, when he stopped suddenly on the very brink of a sheer drop of two hundred feet. In his abstraction he had ridden up the sloping southern face of the mesa without noticing it. "Bet there ain't another like this for a hundred miles," he laughed, and then ceased abruptly and started with unbelieving eyes at the mouth of a draw not far away. A trotting line of gray wolves was emerging from it and swinging toward the south-west ten abreast. He had never heard of such a thing before and watched them in amazement. "Well, I'm —!" he exclaimed, and his Colt flashed rapidly at the pack. Two or three dropped, but the trotting line only swerved a little without pause or a change of pace and soon was lost in another draw. "Why, they 're single hunters," he muttered. "Huh! I won't never tell this. I can't hardly believe it myself. How 'bout you, Ring-Bone?" he asked the horse.

Turning, he rode around a rugged pinnacle of rock and stopped again, gazing steadily along the back trail. Far away in a valley two black dots were crawling over a patch of sand and he knew them to be horsemen. His face slowly reddened with anger at the espionage, for he had not thought the cowmen could doubt his good will and honesty. Then suddenly he swore and spurred forward to cover those miles as speedily as possible. "Come on, ol' Hammer-Head!" he cried. "We're goin' back!"

The hunters had finally decided they would ride into the southwest and had ridden off in that direction. But they had detoured and swung north to see him pass and be sure he was not in their way. Now, satisfied upon that point, they were going back to that herd of cattle, easily turned from skinning buffalo to cattle, and on a large scale. To do this they would have to kill two men and then, waiting for the absent puncher to return with the wagon, kill him and load down the vehicle with skins. "Like h —l they will!" he gritted. "Three or none, you piruts. Come on, White-Eye! Don't sleep all th' time; an' don't light often'r once every ten yards, you saddle-galled, barrel-bellied runt!"

Into hollows, out again; shooting down steep-banked draws and avoiding cacti and chaparral with cat-like agility, the much-described little pony butted the wind in front and left a low-lying cloud of dust swirling behind as it whirred at top speed with choppy, tied-in stride in a winding circle for the humble sod hut on Snake Creek. The rider growled at the evident speed of the two men ahead, for he had not gained upon them despite his efforts. "If I 'm too late to stop it, I 'll clean th' slate, anyhow," he snapped. "Even if I has to ambush! Will you run?" he demanded, and the wild-eyed little bundle of whalebone and steel found a little more speed in its flashing legs.

The rider now began to accept what cover he could find and when he neared the hut left the shelter of the last, low hill for that afforded by a draw leading to within a hundred yards of the dugout's rear wall. Dismounting, he ran lightly forward on foot, alert and with every sense strained for a warning.

Reaching the wall he peered around the corner and stifled an exclamation. Buck's puncher, a knife in his back, lay head down the sloping path. Placing his ear to the wall he listened intently for some moments and then suddenly caught sight of a shadow slowly creeping past his toes. Quickly as he sprang aside he barely missed the flashing knife and the bulk of the man behind it, whose hand, outflung to save his balance, accidentally knocked the Colt from Bill's grasp and sent it spinning twenty feet away.

Without a word they leaped together, fighting silently, both trying to gain the gun in the hunter's holster and trying to keep the other from it. Bill, forcing the fighting in hopes that his youth would stand a hot pace better than the other's years, pushed his enemy back against the low roof of the dugout; but as the hunter tripped over it and fell backward, he pulled Bill with him. Fighting desperately they rolled across the roof and dropped to the sloping earth at the doorway, so tightly locked in each other's arms that the jar did not separate them. The hunter, falling underneath, got the worst of the fall but kept on fighting. Crashing into the door head first, they sent it swinging back against the wall and followed it, bumping down the two steps still locked together.

Bill possessed strength remarkable for his years and build and he was hard as iron; but he had met a man who had the sinewy strength of the plainsman, whose greater age was offset by greater weight and the youth was constantly so close to defeat that a single false move would have been fatal. But luck favored him, for as they surged around the room they crashed into the heavy table and fell with it on top of them. The hunter got its full weight and the gash in his forehead filled his eyes with blood. By a desperate effort he pinned Bill's arm under his knee and with his left hand secured a throat grip, but the under man wriggled furiously and bridged so suddenly as to throw the hunter off him and Bill's freed hand, crashing full into the other's stomach, flashed back to release the weakened throat grip and jam the tensed fingers between his teeth, holding them there with all the power of his jaws. The dazed and gasping hunter, bending forward instinctively, felt his own throat seized and was dragged underneath his furious opponent.

In his Berserker rage Bill had forgotten about the gun, his fury sweeping everything from him but the primal desire to kill with his hands, to rend and crush like an animal. He was brought to his senses very sharply by the jarring, crashing roar of the six-shooter, the powder blowing away part of his shirt and burning his side. Twisting sideways he grasped the weapon with one hand, the wrist with the other and bent the gun slowly back, forcing its muzzle farther and farther from him. The hunter, at last managing to free his left hand from the other's teeth, found it useless when he tried to release the younger man's grip of the gun; and the Colt, roaring again, dropped from its owner's hand as he relaxed.

The victor leaned against the wall, his breath coming in great, sobbing gulps, his knees sagging and his head near bursting. He reeled across the wrecked room, gulped down a drink of whisky from the bottle on the shelf and, stumbling, groped his way to the outer air where he flung himself down on the ground, dazed and dizzy. When he opened his eyes the air seemed to be filled with flashes of fire and huge, black fantastic blots that changed form with great swiftness and the hut danced and shifted like a thing of life. Hot bands seemed to encircle his throat and the throbbing in his temples was like blows of a hammer. While he writhed and fought for breath a faint gunshot reached his ears and found him apathetic. But the second, following closely upon the first, seemed clearer and brought him to himself long enough to make him arise and stumble to his horse, and claw his way into the saddle. The animal, maddened by the steady thrust of the spurs, pitched viciously and bolted; but the rider had learned his art in the sternest school in the world, the "busting" corrals of the great Southwest, and he not only stuck to the saddle, but guided the fighting animal through a barranca almost choked with obstructions.

Stretched full length in a crevice near the top of a mesa lay the other hunter, his rifle trained on a small bowlder several hundred yards down and across the draw. His first shot had been an inexcusable blunder for a marksman like himself and now he had a desperate man and a very capable shot opposing him. If Buck could hold out until nightfall he could slip away in the darkness and do some stalking on his own account.

For half an hour they had lain thus, neither daring to take sight. Buck could not leave the shelter of the bowlder because the high ground behind him offered no cover; but the hunter, tiring of the fruitless wait, wriggled back into the crevice, arose and slipped away, intending to crawl to the edge of the mesa further down and get in a shot from a new angle before his enemy learned of the shift; and this shot would not be a blunder. He had just lowered himself down a steep wall when the noise of rolling pebbles caused him to look around, expecting to see his friend. Bill was just turning the corner of the wall and their eyes met at the same instant.

"'Nds up!" snapped the youth, his Colt glinting as it swung up. The hunter, gripping the rifle firmly, looked into the angry eyes of the other, and slowly obeyed. Bill, watching the rifle intently, forthwith learned a lesson he never forgot: never to watch a gun, but the eyes of the man who has it. The left hand of the hunter seemed to melt into smoke, and Bill, firing at the same instant, blundered into a hit when his surprise and carelessness should have cost him dearly. His bullet, missing its intended mark by inches, struck the still moving Colt of the other, knocking it into the air and numbing the hand that held it. A searing pain in his shoulder told him of the closeness of the call and set his lips into a thin, white line. The hunter, needing no words to interpret the look in the youth's eyes, swiftly raised his hands, holding the rifle high above his head, but neglected to take his finger from the trigger.

Bill was not overlooking anything now and he noticed the crooked finger. "Stick th' muzzle *up*, an' pull that trigger," he commanded, sharply. "Now!" he grated. The report came crashing back from half a dozen points as he nodded. "Drop it, an' turn 'round." As the other obeyed he stepped cautiously forward, jammed his Colt into the hunter's back and took possession of a skinning knife. A few moments later the hunter, trussed securely by a forty-foot lariat, lay cursing at the foot of the rock wall.

Bill, collecting the weapons, went off to cache them and then peered over the mesa's edge to look into the draw. A leaden splotch appeared on the rock almost under his nose and launched a crescendo scream into the sky to whine into silence. He ducked and leaped back, grinning foolishly as he realized Buck's error. Turning to approach the edge from another point he felt his sombrero jerk at his head as another bullet, screaming plaintively, followed the first. He dropped like a shot, and commented caustically upon his paucity of brains as he gravely examined the hole in his head gear. "Huh!" he grunted. "I had a fool's luck three times in twenty minutes, —d —d if I 'm goin' to risk th' next turn. *Three* of 'em," he repeated. "I 'm a' Injun from now on. An' that foreman shore can shoot!"

He wriggled to the edge and called out, careful not to let any of his anatomy show above the sky-line. "Hey, Buck! I ain't no buffalo hunter! This is Cassidy, who you wanted to punch for you. Savvy?" He listened, and grinned at the eloquent silence. "You talk too rapid," he laughed. Repeating his statements he listened again, with the same success. "Now I wonder is he stalkin' *me*? Hey, *Buck!*" he shouted.

"Stick yore hands up an' foller 'em with yore face," said Buck's voice from below. Bill raised his arms and slowly stood up. "Now what 'n blazes do *you* want?" demanded the foreman, belligerently.

"Nothin'. Just got them hunters, one of 'em alive. I reckoned mebby you 'd sorta like to know it." He paused, cogitating. "Reckon we better turn him loose when we gets back to th' hut," he suggested. "I'll keep his guns," he added, grinning.

The foreman stuck his head out in sight. "Well, I'm d —d!" he exclaimed, and sank weakly back against the bowlder. "Can you give me a hand?" he muttered.

The words did not carry to the youth on the skyline, but he saw, understood, and, slipping and bumping down the steep wall with more speed than sense, dashed across the draw and up the other side. He nodded sagely as he examined the wound and bound it carefully with the sleeve of his own shirt. "'T ain't much-loss of blood, mostly. Yo 're better off than Travis."

"Travis dead?" whispered Buck. "In th' back! Pore feller, pore feller; didn't have no show. Tell me about it." At the end of the story he nodded. "Yo 're all right, Cassidy; yo 're a white man. He 'd 'a' stood a good chance of gettin' me, 'cept for you." A frown clouded his face and he looked weakly about him as if for an answer to the question that bothered him. "Now what am I goin' to do up here with all these cows?" he muttered.

Bill rolled the wounded man a cigarette and lit it for him, after which he fell to tossing pebbles at a rock further down the hill.

"I reckon it *will* be sorta tough," he replied, slowly. "But I sorta reckoned me an' you, an' that other feller, can make a big ranch out of yore little one. Anyhow, I 'll bet we can have a mighty big time tryin'. A mighty fine time. What you think?"

Buck smiled weakly and shoved out his hand with a visible effort. "We can! Shake, Bill!" he said, contentedly.

II
The Weasel

The winter that followed the coming of Bill Cassidy to the Bar-20 ranch was none too mild to suit the little outfit in the cabin on Snake Creek, but it was not severe enough to cause complaint and they weathered it without trouble to speak of. Down on the big ranges lying closer to the Gulf the winter was so mild as to seem but a brief interruption of summer. It was on this warm, southern range that Skinny Thompson, one bright day of early spring, loped along the trail to Scoria, where he hoped to find his friend, Lanky Smith, and where he determined to put an end to certain rumors that had filtered down to him on the range and filled his days with anger.

He was within sight of the little cow-town when he met Frank Lewis, but recently returned from a cattle drive. Exchanging gossip of a harmless nature, Skinny mildly scored his missing friend and complained about his flea-like ability to get scarce. Lewis, laughing, told him that Lanky had left town two days before bound north. Skinny gravely explained that he always had to look after his missing friend, who was childish, irresponsible and helpless when alone. Lewis laughed heartily as he pictured the absent puncher, and he laughed harder as he pictured the two together. Both lean as bean poles, Skinny stood six feet four, while Lanky was fortunate if he topped five feet by many inches. Also they were inseparable, which made Lewis ask a question. "But how does it come you ain't with him?"

"Well, we was punchin' down south an' has a li'l run-in. When I rid in that night I found he had flitted. What I want to know is what business has he got, siftin' out like that an' makin' me chase after him?"

"I dunno," replied Lewis, amused. "You 're sort of gardjean to him, hey?"

"Well, he gets sort of homesick if I ain't with him, anyhow," replied Skinny, grinning broadly. "An' who 's goin' to look after him when I ain't around?"

"That puts me up a tree," replied Lewis. "I shore can't guess. But you two should ought to 'a' been stuck together, like them other twins was. But if he 'd do a thing like that I 'd think you would n't waste no time on him."

"Well, he *is* too ornery an' downright cussed for any human bein' to worry about very much, or 'sociate with steady an' reg'lar. Why, lookit him gettin' sore on me, an' for nothin'! But I 'm so used to bein' abused I get sort of lost when he ain't around."

"Well," smiled Lewis, "he's went up north to punch for Buck Peters on his li'l ranch on Snake Creek. If you want to go after him, this is th' way I told him to go," and he gave instructions hopelessly inadequate to anyone not a plainsman. Skinny nodded, irritated by what he regarded as the other's painful and unnecessary details and wheeled to ride on. He had started for town when Lewis stopped him with a word.

"Hey," he called. Skinny drew rein and looked around.

"Better ride in cautious like," Lewis remarked, casually. "Somebody was in town when I left-he shore was thirsty. He ain't drinkin' a drop, which has riled him considerable. So-long."

"Huh!" grunted Skinny. "Much obliged. That's one of th' reasons I 'm goin' to town," and he started forward again, tight-lipped and grim.

He rode slowly into Scoria, alert, watching windows, doors and corners, and dismounted before Quiggs' saloon, which was the really "high-toned" thirst parlor in the town. He noticed that the proprietor had put black shades to the windows and door and then, glancing quickly around, entered. He made straight for the partition in the rear of the building, but the proprietor's voice checked him. "You needn't bother, Skinny-there ain't nobody in there; an' I locked th' back door an hour ago." He glanced around the room and added, with studied carelessness: "You don't want to get any reckless today." He mopped the bar slowly and coughed apologetically. "Don't get careless."

"I won't —it's me that's doin' th' hunting today," Skinny replied, meaningly. "Him a-hunting for me yesterday, when he shore knowed I was n't in town, when he knowed he could n't find me! I was getting good an' tired of him, an' so when Walt rode over to see me last night an' told me what th' coyote was doing yesterday, an' what he was yelling around, I just natchurly had to straddle leather an' come in. I can't let him put that onto me. Nobody can call me a card cheat an' a coward an' a few other choice things like he did without seeing me, an' seeing me quick. An' I shore hope he 's sober. Are both of 'em in town, Larry?"

"No; only Dick. But he's making noise enough for two. He shore raised th' devil yesterday."

"Well, I 'm goin' North trailin' Lanky, but before I leave I 'm shore goin' to sweeten things around here. If I go away without getting him he 'll say he scared me out, so I 'll have to do it when I come back, anyhow. You see, it might just as well be today. But th' next time I sit in a game with fellers that can't drop fifty dollars without saying they was cheated I 'll be a blamed sight bigger fool than I am right now. I should n't 'a' taken cards with 'em after what has passed. Why didn't they say they was cheated, then an' there, an' not wait till three days after I left town? All that's bothering me is Sam: if I get his brother when he ain't around, an' then goes North, he 'll say I had to jump th' town to get away from him. But I 'll stop that by giving him his chance at me when I get back."

"Say, why don't you wait a day an' get 'em both before you go?" asked Quigg hopefully.

"Can't: Lanky 's got two days' start on me an' I want to catch him soon as I can."

"I can't get it through my head, nohow," Quigg remarked. "Everybody knows you play square. I reckon they're hard losers."

Skinny laughed shortly: "Why, can't you see it? Last year I beat Dick Bradley out with a woman over in Ballard. Then his fool brother tried to cut in an' beat me out. Cards? H —l!" he snorted, walking towards the door. "You an' everybody else knows —" he stopped suddenly and jerked his gun loose as a shadow fell across the doorsill. Then he laughed and slapped the newcomer on the shoulder: "Hullo, Ace, my boy! You had a narrow squeak then. You want to make more noise when you turn corners, unless somebody 's looking for you with a gun. How are you, anyhow? An' how's yore dad? I 've been going over to see him regular, right along, but I 've been so busy I kept putting it off."

"Dad's better, Skinny; an' I'm feeling too good to be true. What 'll you have?"

"Reckon it's my treat; you wet last th' other time. Ain't that right, Quigg? Shore, I knowed it was."

"All right, here's luck," Ace smiled. "Quigg, that's better stock; an' would you look at th' style-real curtains!"

Quigg grinned. "Got to have 'em. I 'm on th' sunny side of th' street."

"I hear yo 're goin' North," Ace remarked.

"Yes, I am; but how 'd you know about it?"

"Why, it ain't no secret, is it?" asked Ace in surprise. "If it is, you must 'a' told a woman. I heard of it from th' crowd-everybody seems to know about it. Yo 're going up alone, too, ain't you?"

"Well, no, it ain't no secret; an' I am going alone," slowly replied Skinny. "Here, have another."

"All right-this is on me. Here's more luck."

"Where is th' crowd?"

"Keeping under cover for a while to give you plenty of elbow room," Ace replied. "He's sober as a judge, Skinny, an' mad as a rattler. Swears he 'll kill you on sight. An' his brother ain't with him; if he does come in too soon I 'll see he don't make it two to one. Good luck, an' so-long," he said quickly, shaking hands and walking towards the door. He put one hand out first and waved it, slowly stepping to the street and then walking rapidly out of sight.

Skinny looked after him and smiled. "Larry, there 's a blamed fine youngster," he remarked, reflectively. "Well, he ought to be-he had th' best mother God ever put breath into." He thought for a moment and then went slowly towards the door. "I 've heard so much about Bradley's gun-play that I 'm some curious. Reckon I 'll see if it's all true —" and he had leaped through the doorway, gun in hand. There was no shot, no sign of his enemy. A group of men lounged in the door of the "hash house" farther down the street, all friends of his, and he nodded to them. One of them turned quickly and looked down the intersecting street, saying something that made his companions turn and look with him. The man who had been standing quietly by the corner saloon had disappeared. Skinny smiling knowingly, moved closer to Quigg's shack so as to be better able to see around the indicated corner, and half drew the Colt which he had just replaced in the holster. As he drew even with the corner of the building he heard Quigg's warning shout and dropped instantly, a bullet singing over him and into a window of a near-by store. He rolled around the corner, scrambled to his feet and dashed around the rear of the saloon and the corral behind it, crossed the street in four bounds and began to work up behind the buildings on his enemy's side of the street, cold with anger.

"Pot shooting, hey!" he gritted, savagely.

"Says I 'm a-scared to face him, an' then tries *that*. *There*, d —n you!" His Colt exploded and a piece of wood sprang from the corner board of Wright's store. "Missed!" he swore. "Anyhow, I 've notified you, you coyote."

He sprang forward, turned the corner of the store and followed it to the street. When he came to the street end of the wall he leaped past it, his Colt preceding him. Finding no one to dispute with him he moved cautiously towards the other corner and stopped. Giving a quick glance around, he smiled suddenly, for the glass in Quigg's half-open door, with the black curtain behind it, made a fair mirror. He could see the reflection of Wright's corral and Ace leaning against it, ready to handle the brother if he should appear as a belligerent; and he could see along the other side of the store, where Dick Bradley, crouched, was half-way to the street and coming nearer at each slow step.

Skinny, remembering the shot which he had so narrowly escaped, resolved that he would n't take chances with a man who would pot-shoot. He wheeled, slipped back along his side of the building, turned the rear corner and then, spurting, sprang out beyond the other wall, crying: "Here!"

Bradley, startled, fired under his arm as he leaped aside. Turning while in the air, his half-raised Colt described a swift, short arc and roared as he alighted. As the bullet sang past his enemy's ear he staggered and fell, —and Skinny's smoking gun chocked into its holster.

"There, you coyote!" muttered the victor. "Yore brother is next if he wants to take it up."

* * * * *

As night fell Skinny rode into a small grove and prepared to camp there. Picketing his horse, he removed the saddle and dropped it where he would sleep, for a saddle makes a fair pillow. He threw his blanket after it and then started a quick, hot fire for his coffee-making. While gathering fuel for it he came across a large log and determined to use it for his night fire, and for that purpose carried it back to camp with him. It was not long before he had reduced the provisions in his saddle-bags and leaned back against a tree to enjoy a smoke. Suddenly he knocked the ashes from his pipe and grew thoughtful, finally slipping it into his pocket and getting up.

"That coyote's brother will know I went North an' all about it," he muttered. "He knows I 've got to camp tonight an' he can foller a trail as good as th' next man. An' he knows I shot his brother. I reckon, mebby, he 'll be some surprised."

An hour later a blanket-covered figure lay with its carefully covered feet to the fire, and its head, sheltered from the night air by a sombrero, lay on the saddle. A rifle barrel projected above the saddle, the dim flickering light of the green-wood fire and a stray beam or two from the moon glinted from its rustless surface. The fire was badly constructed, giving almost no light, while the leaves overhead shut out most of the moonlight.

Thirty yards away, in another clearing, a horse moved about at the end of a lariat and contentedly cropped the rich grass, enjoying a good night's rest. An hour passed, another, and a third and fourth, and then the horse's ears flicked forward as it turned its head to see what approached.

A crouched figure moved stealthily forward to the edge of the clearing, paused to read the brand on the animal's flank and then moved off towards the fitful light of the smoking fire. Closer and closer it drew until it made out the indistinct blanketed figure on the ground. A glint from the rifle barrel caused it to shrink back deeper into the shadows and raise the weapon it carried. For half a minute it stood thus and then, holding back the trigger of the rifle so there would be no warning clicks, drew the hammer to a full cock and let the trigger fall into place, slowly moving forward all the while. A passing breeze fanned the fire for an instant and threw the grotesque shadow of a stump across the quiet figure in the clearing.

The skulker raised his rifle and waited until he had figured out the exact mark and then a burst of fire and smoke leaped into the brush. He bent low to look under the smoke cloud and saw that the figure had not moved. Another flash split the night and then, assured beyond a doubt, he moved forward quickly.

"First shot!" he exclaimed with satisfaction. "I reckons you won't do no boastin' 'bout killin' Dick, d —n you!"

As he was about to drop to his knees to search the body he started and sprang back, glancing fearfully around as he drew his Colt.

"Han's up!" came the command from the edge of the clearing as a man stepped into sight. "I reckon —" Skinny leaped aside as the other's gun roared out and fired from his hip; and Sam Bradley plunged across the blanket-covered log and leaves.

"There," Skinny soliloquized, moving forward. "I knowed they was coyotes, *both* of 'em. Knowed it all th' time."

Two days north of Skinny on the bank of Little Wind River a fire was burning itself out, while four men lay on the sand or squatted on their heels and watched it contentedly. "Yes, I got plumb sick of that country," Lanky Smith was saying, "an' when Buck sent for me to go up an' help him out, I pulls up, an' here I am."

"I never heard of th' Bar-20," replied a little, wizened man, whose eyes were so bright they seemed to be on fire. "Did n't know there was any ranches in that country."

"Buck 's got th' only one," responded Lanky, packing his pipe. "He's located on Snake Creek, an' he 's got four thousand head. Reckon there ain't nobody within two hundred mile of him. Lewis said he 's got a fine range an' all th' water he can use; but three men can't handle all them cows in *that* country, so I 'm goin' up."

The little man's eyes seldom left Lanky's face, and he seemed to be studying the stranger very closely. When Lanky had ridden upon their noon-day camp the little man had not lost a movement that the stranger made and the other two, disappearing quietly, returned a little later and nodded reassuringly to their leader.

The wizened leader glanced at one of his companions, but spoke to Lanky. "George, here, said as how they finally got Butch Lynch. You did n't hear nothin' about it, did you?"

"They was a rumor down on Mesquite range that Butch was got. I heard his gang was wiped out. Well, it had to come sometime-he was carryin' things with a purty high hand for a long time. But I 've done heard that before; more 'n once, too. I reckon Butch is a li'l too slick to get hisself killed."

"Ever see him?" asked George carelessly.

"Never; an' don't want to. If them fellers can't clean their own range an' pertect their own cows, I ain't got no call to edge in."

"He 's only a couple of inches taller 'n Jim," observed the third man, glancing at his leader, "an' about th' same build. But he 's h —l on th' shoot. I saw him twice, but I was mindin' my own business."

Lanky nodded at the leader. "That 'd make him about as tall as me. Size don't make no dif'rence no more-King Colt makes 'em look all alike."

Jim tossed away his cigarette and arose, stretching and grunting. "I shore ate too much," he complained. "Well, there's one thing about yore friend's ranch: he ain't got no rustlers to fight, so he ain't as bad off as he might be. I reckon he done named that crick hisself, did n't he? I never heard tell of it."

"Yes; so Lewis says. He says *he 'd* called it Split Mesa Crick, 'cause it empties into Mesa River plumb acrost from a big mesa what's split in two as clean as a knife could 'a' done it."

There was a sharp report

"The Bar-20 expectin' you?" casually asked Jim as he picked up his saddle.

"Shore; they done sent for me. Me an' Buck is old friends. He was up in Montana ranchin' with a pardner, but Slippery Trendley kills his pardner's wife an' drove th' feller loco. Buck an' him hunted Slippery for two years an' finally drifted back south again. I dunno where Frenchy is. If it wasn't for me I reckon Buck 'd still be on th' warpath. You bet he 's expectin' me!" He turned and threw his saddle on the evil-tempered horse he rode and, cinching deftly, slung himself up by the stirrup. As he struck the saddle there was a sharp report and he pitched off and sprawled grotesquely on the sand. The little man peered through the smoke and slid his gun back into the holster. He turned to his companions, who looked on idly and with but little interest. "Yo 're d —d right Butch Lynch is too slick to get killed. I ain't takin' no chances with nobody that rides over my trail these days. An', boys, I got a great scheme! It comes to me like a flash when he 's talkin'. Come on, pull out; an' don't open yore traps till I says so. I want to figger this thing out to th' last card. George, shoot his cayuse; an' not another sound."

"But that's a good cayuse; worth easy —"

"Shoot it!" shouted Jim, his eyes snapping. It was unnecessary to add the alternative, for George and his companion had great respect for the lightning-like, deadly-accurate gun hands. He started to draw, but was too late. The crashing report seemed to come from the leader's holster, so quick had been the draw, and the horse sank slowly down, but unobserved. Two pairs of eyes asked a question of the little man and he sneered in reply as he lowered the gun. "It might 'a' been you. Hereafter do what I say. Now, go on ahead, an' keep quiet."

After riding along in silence for a little while the leader looked at his companions and called one of them to him. "George, this job is too big for the three of us; we can handle the ranch end, but not the drive. You know where Longhorn an' his bunch are holdin' out on th' Tortilla? All right; I 've got a proposition for 'em, an' you are goin' up with it. It won't take you so long if you wake up an' don't loaf like you have been. Now you listen close, an' don't forget a word": and the little man shared the plan he had worked out, much to his companion's delight. Having made the messenger repeat it, the little man waved him off: "Get a-goin'; you bust some records or I 'll bust you, savvy? Charley 'll wait for you at that Split Mesa that fool puncher was a-talkin' about. An' don't you ride nowheres near it goin' up-keep to th' east of it. So-long!"

He watched the departing horseman swing in and pass Charley and saw the playful blow and counter. He smiled tolerantly as their words came back to him, George's growing fainter and fainter and Charley's louder and louder until they rang in his ears. The smile changed subtly and cynicism touched his face and lingered for a moment. "Fine, big bodies-nothing else," he muttered. "Big children, with children's heads. A little courage, if steadied; but what a paucity of brains! Good G —d, what a paucity of brains; what a lack of original thought!"

Of some localities it is said their inhabitants do not die, but dry up and blow away; this, so far as appearances went, seemed true of the horseman who loped along the north bank of Snake Creek, only he had not arrived at the "blow away" period. No one would have guessed his age as forty, for his leathery, wrinkled skin, thin, sun-bleached hair and wizened body justified a guess of sixty. A shrewd observer looking him over would find about the man a subtle air of potential destruction, which might have been caused by the way he wore his guns. A second look and the observer would turn away oppressed by a disquieting feeling that evaded analysis by lurking annoyingly just beyond the horizon of thought. But a man strong in intuition would not have turned away; he would have backed off, alert and tense. Nearing a corral which loomed up ahead, he pulled rein and went on at a walk, his brilliant eyes searching the surroundings with a thoroughness that missed nothing.

Buck Peters was complaining as he loafed for a precious half hour in front of the corral, but Red Connors and Bill Cassidy, his "outfit," discussed the low prices cattle were selling for, the over-stocked southern ranges and the crash that would come to the more heavily mortgaged ranches when the market broke. This was a golden opportunity to stock the little ranch, and Buck was taking advantage of it. But their foreman persisted in telling his troubles and finally, out of politeness, they listened. The burden of the foreman's plaint was the non-appearance of one Lanky Smith, an old friend. When the second herd had been delivered several weeks before, Buck, failing to persuade one of the drive outfit to remain, had asked the trail boss to send up Lanky, and the trail boss had promised.

Red stretched and yawned. "Mebby he's lost th' way."

The foreman snorted. "He can foller a plain trail, can't he? An' if he can ride past Split Mesa, he's a bigger fool than I ever heard of."

"Well, mebby he got drunk an —"

"He don't get that drunk." Astonishment killed whatever else he might have said, for a stranger had ridden around the corral and sat smiling at the surprise depicted on the faces of the three.

Buck and Red, too surprised to speak, smiled foolishly; Bill, also wordless, went upon his toes and tensed himself for that speed which had given to him hands never beaten on the draw. The stranger glanced at him, but saw nothing more than the level gaze that searched his squinting eyes for the soul back of them. The squint increased and he made a mental note concerning Bill Cassidy, which Bill Cassidy already had done regarding him.

"I'm called Tom Jayne," drawled the stranger. "I 'm lookin' for Peters."

"Yes?" inquired Buck restlessly. "I 'm him."

"Lewis sent me up to punch for you."

"You plumb surprised us," replied Buck. "We don't see nobody up here."

"Reckon not," agreed Jayne smiling. "I ain't been pestered a hull lot by th' inhabitants on my way up. I reckon there 's more *buffalo* than men in this country."

Buck nodded. "An' blamed few buffalo, too. But Lewis did n't say nothin' about Lanky Smith, did he?"

"Yes; Smith, he goes up in th' Panhandle for to be a foreman. Lewis missed him. Th' Panhandle must be purty nigh as crowded as this country, I reckon," he smiled.

"Well," replied Buck, "anybody Lewis sends up is good enough for me. I 'm payin' forty a month. Some day I 'll pay more, if I 'm able to an' it's earned."

Jayne nodded. "I 'm aimin' to be here when th' pay is raised; an' I 'll earn it."

"Then shake han's with Red an' Bill, an' come with me," said Buck. He led the way to the dugout, Bill and Red looking after him and the little newcomer. Red shook his head. "I dunno," he soliloquized, his eyes on the recruit's guns. They were worn low on the thighs, and the lower ends of the holsters were securely tied to the trousers. They were low enough to have the butts even with the swinging hands, so that no time would have to be wasted in reaching for them; and the sheaths were tied down, so they would not cling to the guns and come up with them on the draw. Bill wore his guns the same way for the same reasons. Red glanced at his friend. "He 's a queer li'l cuss, Bill," he suggested. Receiving no reply, he grinned and tried again. "I said as how he 's a queer li'l cuss." Bill stirred. "Huh?" he muttered. Red snorted. "Why, I says he's a drunk Injun mendin' socks. What in blazes you reckon I 'd say!"

"Oh, somethin' like that; but; you should 'a' said he's a —a weasel. A cold-blooded, ferocious li'l rat that 'd kill for th' joy of it," and Bill moved leisurely to rope his horse.

Red looked after him, cogitating deeply. "Cussed if I hadn't, too! An' so he's a two-gun man, like Bill. Wears 'em plumb low an' tied. Yessir, he's a shore 'nuff weasel, all right." He turned and watched Bill riding away and he grinned as two pictures came to his mind. In the first he saw a youth enveloped in swirling clouds of acrid smoke as two Colts flashed and roared with a speed incredible; in the second there was no smoke, only the flashing of hands and the cold glitter of steel, so quick as to baffle the eye. And even now Bill practiced the draw, which pleased the foreman; cartridges were hard to get and cost money. Red roped his horse and threw on the saddle. As he swung off toward his section of the range he shook his head and scowled.

The Weasel had the eastern section, the wildest part of the ranch. It was cut and seared by arroyos, barrancas and draws; covered with mesquite and chaparral and broken by hills and mesas. The cattle on it were lost in the chaotic roughness and heavy vegetation and only showed themselves when they straggled down to the river or the creek to drink. A thousand head were supposed to be under his charge, but ten times that number would have been but a little more noticeable. He quickly learned ways of riding from one end of the section to the other without showing himself to anyone who might be a hundred yards from any point of the ride; he learned the best grazing portions and the safest trails from them to the ford opposite Split Mesa.

He was very careful not to show any interest in Split Hill Canyon and hardly even looked at it for the first week; then George returned from his journey and reported favorably. He also, with Longhorn's assistance, had picked out and learned a good drive route, and it was decided then and there to start things moving in earnest.

There were two thousand unbranded cattle on the ranch, the entire second drive herd; most of these were on the south section under Bill Cassidy, and the remainder were along the river. The Weasel learned that most of Bill's cows preferred the river to the creek and crossed his section to get there. That few returned was due, perhaps, to their preference for the eastern pasture. In a week the Weasel found the really good grazing portions of his section feeding more cows than they could keep on feeding; but suddenly the numbers fell to the pastures' capacity, without adding a head to Bill's herd.

Then came a day when Red had been riding so near the Weasel's section that he decided to go on down and meet him as he rode in for dinner. When Red finally caught sight of him the Weasel was riding slowly toward the bunkhouse, buried in thought. When his two men had returned from their scouting trip and reported the best way to drive, his and their work had begun in earnest. One small herd had been driven north and turned over to friends not far away, who took charge of the herd for the rest of the drive while the Weasel's companions returned to Split Hill.

Day after day he had noticed the diminishing number of cows on his sections, which was ideally created by nature to hide such a deficit, but from now on it would require all his cleverness and luck to hide the losses and he would be so busy shifting cattle that the rustling would have to ease up. One thing bothered him: Bill Cassidy was getting very suspicious, and he was not altogether satisfied that it was due to rivalry in gun-play. He was so deeply engrossed in this phase of the situation that he did not hear Red approaching over the soft sand and before Red could make his presence known something occurred that made him keep silent.

The Weasel, jarred by his horse, which shied and reared with a vigor and suddenness its rider believed entirely unwarranted under the circumstances, grabbed the reins in his left hand and jerked viciously, while his right, a blur of speed, drew and fired the heavy Colt with such deadly accuracy that the offending rattler's head dropped under its writhing, glistening coils, severed clean.

Red backed swiftly behind a chaparral and cogitated, shaking his head slowly. "Funny how bashful these gun-artists are!" he muttered. "Now has he been layin' for big bets, or was he —?" the words ceased, but the thoughts ran on and brought a scowl to Red's face as he debated the question.

* * * * *

The following day, a little before noon, two men stopped with sighs of relief at the corral and looked around. The little man riding the horse smiled as he glanced at his tall companion. "You won't have to hoof it no more, Skinny," he said gladly. "It's been a' awful experience for both of us, but you had th' worst end."

"Why, you stubborn li'l fool!" retorted Skinny. "I can walk back an' do it all over again!" He helped his companion down, stripped off the saddle and turned the animal loose with a resounding slap. "Huh!" he grunted as it kicked up its heels. "You oughta feel frisky, after loafin' for two weeks an' walkin' for another. Come on, Lanky," he said, turning. "There ain't nobody home, so we 'll get a fire goin' an' rustle chuck for all han's."

They entered the dugout and looked around, Lanky sitting down to rest. His companion glanced at the mussed bunks and started a fire to get dinner for six. "Mebby they don't ride in at noon," suggested the convalescent. "Then we 'll eat it all," grinned the cook. "It's comin' to us by this time."

The Weasel, riding toward the rear wall of the dugout, increased the pace when he saw the smoke pouring out of the chimney, but as he neared the hut he drew suddenly and listened, his expression of incredulity followed by one of amazement.

A hearty laugh and some shouted words sent him spinning around and back to the chaparral. As soon as he dared he swung north to the creek and risked its quicksands to ride down its middle. Reaching the river he still kept to the water until he had crossed the ford and scrambled up the further bank to become lost in the windings of the canyon.

Very soon after the Weasel's departure Buck dismounted at the corral and stopped to listen. "Strangers," he muttered. "Glad they got th' fire goin', anyhow." Walking to the hut he entered and a yell met him at the instant recognition.

"Hullo, Buck!"

"Lanky!" he cried, leaping forward.

"Easy!" cautioned the convalescent, evading the hand. "I 've been all shot up an' I ain't right yet."

"That so! How 'd it happen?"

"Shake han's with Skinny Thompson, my fool nurse," laughed Lanky.

"I 'm a fool, all right, helpin' *him*," grinned Skinny, gripping the hand. "But when I picks him up down in th' Li'l Wind River country I was a' angel. Looked after him for two weeks down there, an' put in another gettin' up here. Served him right, too, for runnin' away from me."

"Little Wind River country!" exclaimed Buck. "Why, I thought you was a foreman in th' Panhandle."

"Foreman nothin'," replied Lanky. "I was shot up by a li'l runt of a rustler an' left to die two hundred mile from nowhere. I was n't expectin' no gun-play."

"He's ridin' up here," explained Skinny. "Meets three fellers an' gets friendly. They learns his business, an' drops him sudden when he's mountin'. Butch Lynch did th' shootin'. Butch got his name butcherin th' law. He could n't make a livin' at it. Then he got chased out of New Mexico for bein' mixed up in a free-love sect, an' pulls for Chicago. He reckoned he owned th' West, so he drifts down here again an' turns rustler. I dunno why he plugs Lanky, less 'n he thinks Lanky knows him an' might try to hand him over. I 'm honin' for to meet Butch."

Buck looked from one to the other in amazement, suspicion raging in his mind. "Why, I heard you went to th' Panhandle!" he ejaculated.

Skinny grinned: "A fine foreman he'd make, less 'n for a hawg ranch!"

"Who told you that?" demanded Lanky, with sudden interest.

"Th' feller Lewis sent up in yore place."

"What?" shouted both in one voice, and Lanky gave a terse description of Butch Lynch. "That him?"

"That's him," answered Buck. "But he was alone. He 'll be in soon, 'long with Bill an' Red-which way did you come?" he demanded eagerly. "Why, that was through his section-bet he saw you an' pulled out!"

Skinny reached for his rifle: "I'm goin' to see," he remarked.

"I 'm with you," replied Buck.

"Me, too," asserted Lanky, but he was pushed back.

"You stay here," ordered Buck. "He might ride in. An' you 've got to send Bill an' Red after us."

Lanky growled, but obeyed, and trained his rifle on the door. But the only man he saw was Red, whose exit was prompt when he had learned the facts.

Down on the south section Bill, unaware of the trend of events, looked over the little pasture that nestled between the hills and wondered where the small herd was. Up to within the last few days he always had found it here, loath to leave the heavy grass and the trickling spring, and watched over by "Old Mosshead," a very pugnacious steer. He scowled as he looked east and shook his head. "Bet they 're crowdin' on th' Weasel's section, too. Reckon I 'll go over and look into it. He 'll be passin' remarks about th' way I ride sign." But he reached the river without being rewarded by the sight of many of the missing cows and he became pugnaciously inquisitive. He had searched in vain for awhile when he paused and glanced up the river, catching sight of a horseman who was pushing across at the ford. "Now, what's th' Weasel doin' over there?" he growled. "An' what's his hurry? I never did put no trust in him an' I 'm going to see what's up."

Not far behind him a tall, lean man peered over the grass-fringed bank of a draw and watched him cross the river and disappear over the further bank. "Huh!" muttered Skinny, riding forward toward the river. "That *might* be one of Peters' punchers; but I 'll trail him to make shore."

Down the river Red watched Bill cross the stream and then saw a stranger follow. "What th' h —l!" he growled, pushing on. "That's one of 'em trailin' Bill!" and he, in turn, forded the river, hot on the trail of the stranger.

Bill finally dismounted near the mesa, proceeded on foot to the top of the nearest rise, and looked down into the canyon at a point where it widened into a circular basin half a mile across. Dust was arising in thin clouds as the missing cows, rounded up by three men, constantly increased the rustlers' herd. To the northwest lay the mesa, where the canyon narrowed to wind its tortuous way through; to the southeast lay the narrow gateway, where the towering, perpendicular cliffs began to melt into the sloping sides of hills and changed the canyon into a swiftly widening valley. The sight sent the puncher running toward the pass, for the herd had begun to move toward that outlet, urged by the Weasel and his nervous companions.

Back in the hills Skinny was disgusted and called himself names. To lose a man in less than a minute after trailing him for an hour was more than his sensitive soul could stand without protest. Bill had disappeared as completely as if he had taken wings and flown away. The disgusted trailer, dropping to all-fours because of his great height, went ahead, hoping to blunder upon the man he had lost.

Back of him was Red, whose grin was not so much caused by Skinny's dilemma, which he had sensed instantly, as it was by the inartistic spectacle Skinny's mode of locomotion presented to the man behind. There was humor a-plenty in Red's make-up and the germ of mischief in his soul was always alert and willing; his finger itched to pull the trigger, and the grin spread as he pondered over the probable antics of the man ahead if he should be suddenly grazed by a bullet from the rear. "Bet he 'd go right up on his head an' kick," Red chuckled-and it took all his will power to keep from experimenting. Then, suddenly, Skinny disappeared, and Red's fretful nature clawed at his tropical vocabulary with great success. It was only too true-Skinny had become absolutely lost, and the angry Bar-20 puncher crawled furiously this way and that without success, until Skinny gave him a hot clew that stung his face with grit and pebbles. He backed, sneezing, around a rock and wrestled with his dignity. Skinny, holed up not far from the canyon's rim, was throwing a mental fit and calling himself outrageous names. "An' he's been trailin' *me*! H —l of a fine fool I am; I 'm awful smart today, I am! I done gave up my teethin' ring too soon, I did." He paused and scratched his head reflectively. "Huh! *This* is some populous region, an' th' inhabitants have pe-culiar ways. Now I wonder who's trailin' him? I 'm due to get cross-eyed if I try to stalk 'em both."

A bullet, fired from an unexpected direction, removed the skin from the tip of Skinny's nose and sent a shock jarring clean through him. "Is that him, th' other feller, or somebody else?" he fretfully pondered, raising his hand to the crimson spot in the center of his face. He did not rub it-he rubbed the air immediately in front of it, and was careful to make no mistake in distance. The second bullet struck a rock just outside the gully and caromed over his head with a scream of baffled rage. He shrunk, lengthwise and sidewise, wishing he were not so long; but he kept on wriggling, backward. "Not enough English," he muttered. "Thank th' Lord he can't massé!"

The firing put a different aspect on things down in the basin. The Weasel crowded the herd into the gap too suddenly and caused a bad jam, while his companions, slipping away among the bowlders and thickets, worked swiftly but cautiously up the cliff by taking advantage of the crevices and seams that scored the wall. Climbing like goats, they slipped over the top and began a game of hide and seek over the bowlder-strewn, chaparral-covered plateau to cover the Weasel, who worked, without cover of any kind, in the basin.

Red was deep in some fine calculations of angles when his sombrero slid off his head and displayed a new hole, which ogled at him with Cyclopean ferocity. He ducked, and shattered all existing records for the crawl, stopping finally when he had covered twenty yards and collected many thorns and bruises. He had worked close to the edge of the cliff and as he turned to circle back of his enemy he chanced to glance over the rim, swore angrily and fired. The Weasel, saving himself from being pinned under his stricken horse, leaped for the shelter of the cover near the foot of the basin's wall. Red was about to fire again when he swayed and slipped down behind a bowlder. The rustler, twenty yards away, began to maneuver for another shot when Skinny's rifle cracked viciously and the cattle thief, staggering to the edge of the cliff, stumbled, fought for his balance, and plunged down into the basin. His companion, crawling swiftly toward Skinny's smoke, showed himself long enough for Red to swing his rifle and shoot offhand. At that moment Skinny caught sight of him and believed he understood the situation. "You Conners or Cassidy?" he demanded over the sights. Red's answer made him leap forward and in a few moments the wounded man, bandaged and supported by his new friend, hobbled to the rim of the basin in time to see the last act of the tragedy.

The gateway, now free of cattle, lay open and the Weasel dashed for it in an attempt to gain the horses picketed on the other side. He had seen George plunge off the cliff and knew that the game was up. As he leaped from his cover Skinny's head showed over the rim of the cliff and his bullet sang shrilly over the rustler's head. The second shot was closer, but before Skinny could try again Red's warning cry made him lower the rifle and stare at the gateway.

The Weasel saw it at the same time, slowed to a rapid walk, but kept on for the pass, his eyes riveted malevolently on the youth who had suddenly arisen from behind a bowlder and started to meet him.

"It's easy to get him now," growled Skinny, starting to raise the rifle, a picture of Lanky's narrow escape coming to his mind.

"Bill's right in line," whispered Red, leaning forward tensely and robbing his other senses to strengthen sight. "They 're th' best in th' Southwest," he breathed.

Below them Bill and the Weasel calmly advanced, neither hurried nor touching a gun. Sixty yards separated them-fifty-forty-thirty —"G—d A'mighty!" whispered Skinny, his nails cutting into his calloused palms. Red only quivered. Twenty-five —twenty. Then the Weasel slowed down, crouching a little, and his swinging hands kept closer to his thighs. Bill, though moving slowly, stood erect and did not change his pace. Perspiration beaded the faces of the watchers on the cliff and they almost stopped breathing. This was worse than they had expected-forty yards would have been close enough to start shooting. "It's a pure case of speed now," whispered Red, suddenly understanding. The promised lesson was due-the lesson the Weasel had promised to give Bill on the draw. Accuracy deliberately was being eliminated by that cold-blooded advance. Fifteen yards-ten-eight-six-five-and a flurry of smoke. There had been no movement to the eyes of the watchers-just smoke, and the flat reports, that came to them like two beats of a snare drum's roll. Then they saw Bill step back as the Weasel pitched forward. He raised his eyes to meet them and nodded. "Come on, get th' cayuses. We gotta round up th' herd afore it scatters," he shouted.

Red leaned against Skinny and laughed senselessly. "Ain't he a d—d fool?"

Skinny stirred and nodded. "He shore is; but come on. I don't want no argument with *him*."

III
Jimmy Price

On a range far to the north, Jimmy Price, a youth as time measures age, followed the barranca's edge and whistled cheerfully. He had never heard of the Bar-20, and would have showed no interest if he had heard of it, so long as it lay so far away. He was abroad in search of adventure and work, and while his finances were almost at ebb tide he had youth, health, courage and that temperament that laughs at hard luck and believes in miracles. The tide was so low it must turn soon and work would be forthcoming when he needed it. Sitting in the saddle with characteristic erectness he loped down a hill and glanced at the faint trail that led into the hills to the west. Cogitating a moment he followed it and soon saw a cow, and soon after others.

"I 'll round up th' ranch house, get a job for awhile an' then drift on south again," he thought, and the whistle rang out with renewed cheerfulness.

He noticed that the trail kept to the low ground, skirting even little hills and showing marked preference for arroyos and draws with but little regard, apparently, for direction or miles. He had just begun to cross a small pasture between two hills when a sharp voice asked a question: "Where you goin'?"

He wheeled and saw a bewhiskered horseman sitting quietly behind a thicket. The stranger held a rifle at the ready and was examining him critically. "Where you goin'?" repeated the stranger, ominously. "An' what's yore business?"

Jimmy bridled at the other's impudent curiosity and the tones in which it was voiced, and as he looked the stranger over a contemptuous smile flickered about his thin lips. "Why, I 'm goin' west, an' I 'm lookin' for th' sunset," he answered with an exasperating drawl. "Ain't seen it, have you?"

The other's expression remained unchanged, as if he had not heard the flippant and pugnacious answer. "Where you goin' an' what for?" he demanded again.

Jimmy turned further around in the saddle and his eyes narrowed. "I 'm goin' to mind my own business, because it's healthy," he retorted. "You th' President, or only a king?" he demanded, sarcastically.

"I 'm boss of Tortilla range," came the even reply. "You answer my question."

"Then you can gimme a job an' save me a lot of fool ridin'," smiled Jimmy. "It 'll be some experience workin' for a sour dough as ornery as you are. Fifty per', an' all th' rest of it. Where do I eat an' sleep?"

The stranger gazed steadily at the cool, impudent youngster, who returned the look with an ironical smile. "Who sent you out here?" he demanded with blunt directness.

"Nobody," smiled Jimmy. "Nobody sends me nowhere, never, 'less 'n I want to go. Purty near time to eat, ain't it?"

"Come over here," commanded the Boss of Tortilla range.

"It's closer from you to me than from me to you."

"Yo 're some sassy, now ain't you? I 've got a notion to drop you an' save somebody else th' job."

"He 'll be lucky if you do, 'cause when that gent drifts along I 'm natchurally goin' to get there first. It's been tried already."

Anger glinted in the Boss's eyes, but slowly faded as a grim smile fought its way into view. "I 've a mind to give you a job just for th' great pleasure of bustin' yore spirit."

"If yo 're bettin' on that card you wants to have a copper handy," bantered Jimmy. "It's awful fatal when it's played to win."

"What's yore name, you cub?"

"Elijah-ain't I done prophesied? When do I start punchin' yore eight cows, Boss?"

"Right now! I like yore infernal gall; an' there's a pleasant time comin' when I starts again' that spirit."

"Then my name's Jimmy, which is enough for you to know. Which cow do I punch first?" he grinned.

"You ride ahead along th' trail. I 'll show you where you eat," smiled the Boss, riding toward him.

Jimmy's face took on an expression of innocence that was ludicrous.

"I allus let age go first," he slowly responded. "I might get lost if I lead. I 'm plumb polite, I am."

The Boss looked searchingly at him and the smile faded. "What you mean by that?"

"Just what I said. I 'm plumb polite, an' hereby provin' it. I allus insist on bein' polite. Otherwise, gimme my month's pay an' I 'll resign. But I 'm shore some puncher," he laughed.

"I observed yore politeness. I 'm surprised you even know th' term. But are you shore you won't get lost if you foller me?" asked the Boss with great sarcasm.

"Oh, that's a chance I gotta take," Jimmy replied as his new employer drew up alongside. "Anyhow, yo 're better lookin' from behind."

"Jimmy, my lad," observed the Boss, sorrowfully shaking his head, "I shore sympathize with th' shortness of yore sweet, young life. Somebody 's natchurally goin' to spread you all over some dismal landscape one of these days."

"An' he 'll be a whole lot lucky if I ain't around when he tries it," grinned Jimmy. "I got a' awful temper when I 'm riled, an' I reckons that would rile me up quite a lot."

The Boss laughed softly and pushed on ahead, Jimmy flushing a little from shame of his suspicions. But a hundred yards behind him, riding noiselessly on the sand and grass, was a man who had emerged from another thicket when he saw the Boss go ahead; and he did not for one instant remove his eyes from the new member of the outfit. Jimmy, due to an uncanny instinct, soon realized it, though he did not look around. "Huh! Reckon I 'm th' meat in this sandwich. Say, Boss, who's th' Injun ridin' behind me?" he asked.

"That's Longhorn. Look out or he 'll gore you," replied the Boss.

"'That 'd be a bloody shame,' as th' Englishman said. Are all his habits as pleasant an' sociable?"

"They 're mostly worse; he's a two-gun man."

"Now ain't that lovely! Wonder what he'd do if I scratch my laig sudden?"

"Let me know ahead of time, so I can get out of th' way. If you do that it 'll save me fifty dollars an' a lot of worry."

"Huh! I won't save it for you. But I wish I could get out my smokin' what's in my hip pocket, without Longhorn gamblin' on th' move."

The next day Jimmy rode the west section harassed by many emotions. He was weaponless, much to his chagrin and rage. He rode a horse that was such a ludicrous excuse that it made escape out of the question, and they even locked it in the corral at night. He was always under the eyes of a man who believed him ignorant of the surveillance. He already knew that three different brands of cattle "belonged" to the "ranch," and his meager experience was sufficient to acquaint him with a blotted brand when the work had been carelessly done. The Boss was the foreman and his outfit, so far as Jimmy knew, consisted of Brazo Charley and Longhorn, both of whom worked nights. The smiling explanation of the Boss, when Jimmy's guns had been locked up, he knew to be only part truth. "Yo 're so plumb fighty we dass n't let you have 'em," the Boss had said. "If we got to bust yore high-strung, unlovely spirit without killin' you, you can't have no guns. An' th' corral gate is shore padlocked, so keep th' cayuse I gave you."

Jimmy, enraged, sprang forward to grab at his gun, but Longhorn, dexterously tripping him, leaned against the wall and grinned evilly as the angry youth scrambled to his feet. "Easy, Kid," remarked the gun-man, a Colt swinging carelessly in his hand. "You 'll get as you give," he grunted. "Mind yore own affairs an' work, an' we 'll treat you right. Otherwise —" the shrugging shoulders made further explanations unnecessary.

Jimmy looked from one to the other and silently wheeled, gained the decrepit horse and rode out to his allotted range, where he saturated the air with impotent profanity. Chancing to look back he saw a steer wheel and face the south; and at other times during the day he saw that repeated by other cattle-nor was this the only signs of trailing. Having nothing to do but ride and observe the cattle, which showed no desire to stray beyond the range allotted to them, he observed very thoroughly; and when he rode back to the bunkhouse that night he had deciphered the original brand on his cows and also the foundation for that worn by Brazo Charley's herd on the section next to him. "I dunno where mine come from, but Charley's uster belong to th' C I, over near Sagebrush basin. That's a good hundred miles from here, too. Just wait till I get a gun! Trip me an' steal my guns, huh? If I had a good cayuse I 'd have that C I bunch over here right quick! I reckon they 'd like to see this herd."

When he reached the bunkhouse all traces of his anger had disappeared and he ate hungrily during the silent meal.

When Longhorn and Brazo pushed away from the table Jimmy followed suit and talked pleasantly of things common to cowmen, until the two picked up their saddles and rifles and departed in the direction of the corral, the Boss staying with Jimmy and effectually blocking the door. But he could not block Jimmy's hearing so easily and when the faint sound of hoofbeats rolled past the bunkhouse Jimmy knew that there were more than two men doing the riding. He concluded the number to be five, and perhaps six; but his face gave no indication of his mind's occupation.

"Play crib?" abruptly demanded the Boss, taking a well-worn deck of cards from a shelf. Jimmy nodded and the game was soon going on. "Seventeen," grunted the Boss, pegging slowly. "Pair of fools, they are," he growled. "Both plumb stuck on one gal an' they go courtin' together. She reminds *me* of a slab of bacon, she 's that homely."

Jimmy laughed at the obvious lie. "Well, a gal's a gal out here," he replied. "Twenty for a pair," he remarked. He wondered, as he pegged, if it was necessary to take along an escort when one went courting on the Tortilla. The idea of Brazo and Longhorn tolerating any rival or any company when courting struck him as ludicrous. "An' which is goin' to win out, do you reckon?"

"Longhorn-he 's bad; an' a better gun-man. Twenty-three for six. Got th' other tray?" anxiously grinned the Boss.

"Nothin' but an eight-that's two for th' go. My crib?"

The Boss nodded. "Ugly as blazes," he mused. "*I* would n't court her, not even in th' dark-huh! Fifteen two an' a pair. That's bad goin', very bad goin'," he sighed as he pegged.

"But you can't tell nothin' 'bout wimmen from their looks," remarked Jimmy, with the grave assurance of a man whose experience in that line covered years instead of weeks. "Now I knowed a right purty gal once. She was plumb sweet an' tender an' clingin', she was. An' she had high ideas, she did. She went an' told me she would n't have nothin' to do with no man what wasn't honest, an' all that. But when a feller I knowed rid in to her place one night she shore hid him under her bed for three days an' nights. He had got real popular with a certain posse because he was careless with a straight iron. Folks fairly yearned for to get a good look at him. They rid up to her place and she lied so sweet an' perfect they shore apologized for even botherin' her. Who 'd 'a' thought to look under *her* bed, anyhow? Some day he 'll go back an' natchurally run off with that li'l gal." He scanned his hand and reached for the pegs. "Got eight here," he grunted.

The Boss regarded him closely. "She stood off a posse with her eyes an' mouth, eh?"

"Didn't have to stand 'em off. They was plumb ashamed th' minute they saw her blushes. An' they was plumb sorry for her bein' even a li'l interested in a no-account brand-blotter like-him." He turned the crib over and spread it out with a sort of disgust. "Come purty near bein' somethin' in that crib," he growled.

"An' did you know that feller?" the Boss asked carelessly.

Jimmy started a little. "Why, yes; he was once a pal of mine. But he got so he could blot a brand plumb clever. Us cow-punchers shore like to gamble. We are plumb childish th' way we bust into trouble. I never seen one yet that was worth anythin' that would n't take 'most any kind of a fool chance just for th' devilment of it."

The Boss ruffled his cards reflectively. "Yes; we are a careless breed. Sort of flighty an' reckless. Do you think that gal's still in love with you? Wimmin' is fickle," he laughed.

"*She* ain't," retorted Jimmy with spirit. "She 'll wait all right-for him."

The Boss smiled cynically. "You can't hide it, Jimmy. Yo 're th' man what got so popular with th' sheriff. Ain't you?"

Jimmy half arose, but the Boss waved him to be seated again. "Why, you ain't got nothin' to fear out here," he assured him. "We sorta like fellers that 'll take a chance. I reckon we all have took th' short end one time or another. An' I got th' idea mebby yo 're worth more 'n fifty a month. Take any chances for a hundred?"

Jimmy relaxed and grinned cheerfully. "I reckon I'd do a whole lot for a hundred real dollars every month."

"Yo 're on, fur 's I 'm concerned. I 'll have to speak to th' boys about it, first. Well, I 'm goin' to turn in. You ride Brazo's an' yore own range for th' next couple of days. Good night."

Jimmy arose and sauntered carelessly to the door, watched the Boss enter his own house, and then sat down on the wash bench and gazed contentedly across the moonlit range. "Gosh," he laughed as he went over his story of the beautiful girl with the high ideals. "I 'm gettin' to be a sumptuous liar, I am. It comes so easy I gotta look out or I'll get th' habit. I'd do mor'n lie, too, to get my gun back, all right."

He stretched ecstatically and then sat up straight. The Boss was coming toward him and something in his hand glittered in the soft moonlight as it swung back and forth. "Forget somethin'?" called Jimmy.

"You better stop watchin' th' moonlight," laughed the Boss as he drew near. "That's a bad sign —'specially while that gal's waitin' for you. Here's yore gun an' belt —I reckoned mebby you might need it."

Jimmy chuckled as he took the weapon. "I ain't so shore 'bout needin' it, but I was plumb lost without it. Kept feelin' for it all th' time an' it was gettin' on my nerves." He weighed it critically and spun the cylinder, carelessly feeling for the lead in the chambers as the cylinder stopped. Every one was loaded and a thrill of fierce joy surged over him. But he was suspicious-the offer was too quick and transparent. Slipping on the belt he let the gun slide into the blackened holster and grinned up at the Boss. "Much obliged. It feels right, now." He drew the Colt again and emptied the cartridges into his hand. "Them 's th' only pills as will cure troubles a doctor can't touch," he observed, holding one up close to his face and shaking it at the smiling Boss in the way of emphasis. His quick ear caught the sound he strained to hear, the soft swish inside the shell. "Them 's Law in this country," he soliloquized as he slid the tested shell in one particular chamber and filled all the others. "Yessir," he remarked as the cylinder slowly revolved until he had counted the right number of clicks and knew that the tested shell was in the right place. "Yessir, them's The Law." The soft moonlight suddenly kissed the leveled barrel and showed the determination that marked the youthful face behind it. "An' it shore works both ways, Boss," he said harshly. "Put up yore paws!"

As the Boss leaped forward the hammer fell and caused a faint, cap-like report. Then the stars streamed across Jimmy's vision and became blotted out by an inky-black curtain that suddenly enveloped him. The Boss picked up the gun and, tossing it on the bench, waited for the prostrate youth to regain his senses.

Jimmy stirred and looked around, his eyes losing their look of vacancy and slowly filling with murderous hatred as he saw the man above him and remembered what had occurred. "Sand *sounds* like powder, my youthful friend," the Boss was saying, "but it don't *work* like powder. I purty near swallowed yore gal story; but I sorta reckoned mebby I better make shore about you. Yo 're clever, Jimmy; so clever that I dass n't take no chances with you. I 'll just tie you up till th' boys come back-we both know what they 'll say. I 'd 'a' done it then only I like you; an' I wish you had been in earnest about joinin' us. Now get up."

Jimmy arose slowly and cautiously and then moved like a flash, only to look down the barrel of a Colt. His clenched hands fell to his side and he bowed his head; but the Boss was too wary to be caught by any pretenses of a broken spirit. "Turn 'round an' hol' up yore han's," he ordered. "I 'll blow you apart if you even squirms."

Jimmy obeyed, seething with impotent fury, but the steady pressure of the Colt on his back told him how useless it was to resist. Life was good, even a few hours of it, for in those few hours perhaps a chance would come to him. The rope that had hung on the wall passed over his wrists and in a few moments he was helpless. "Now sit down," came the order and the prisoner obeyed sullenly. The Boss went in the bunkhouse and soon returned, picked up the captive and, carrying him to the bunk prepared for him, dumped him in it, tied a few more knots and, closing the door, securely propped it shut and strode toward his own quarters, swearing savagely under his breath.

An hour later, while a string of horsemen rode along the crooked, low-lying trail across the Tortilla, plain in the moonlight, a figure at the bunkhouse turned the corner, slipped to the door and carefully removed the props.

Waiting a moment it opened the door slowly and slipped into the black interior, and chuckled at the sarcastic challenge from the bunk. "Sneakin' back again, hey?" blazed Jimmy, trying in vain to bridge on his head and heels and turn over to face the intruder. "Turn me loose an' gimme a gun—I oughta have a chance!"

"All right," said a quiet, strange voice. "That's what I'm here for; but don't talk so loud."

"Who 're you?"

"My name 's Cassidy. I 'm from th' Bar-20, what owns them cows you been abusin'. Huh! he shore tied some knots! Wasn't takin' no more chances with you, all right!"

"G'wan! He never did take none."

"So I 've observed. Get th' blood circulatin' an' I 'll give you some war-medicine for that useless gun of yourn what ain't sand."

"Good for you! I'll sidle up agin' that shack an' fill him so full of lead he won't know what hit him!"

"Well, every man does things in his own way; but I 've been thinkin' he oughta have a chance. He shore gave you some. Take it all in all, he 's been purty white to you, Kid. Longhorn 'd 'a' shot you quick tonight."

"Yes; an' I 'm goin' to get him, too!"

"Now you ain't got no gratitude," sighed Cassidy. "You want to hog it all. I was figgerin' to clean out this place by myself, but now you cut in an' want to freeze me out. But, Kid, mebby Longhorn won't come back no more. My outfit's a-layin' for his li'l party. I sent 'em down word to expect a call on our north section; an' I reckon they got a purty good idea of th' way up here, in case they don't receive Longhorn an' his friends as per schedule."

"How long you been up here?" asked Jimmy in surprise, pausing in his operation of starting his blood to circulating.

"Long enough to know a lot about this layout. For instance, I know yo 're honest. That's why I cut you loose tonight. You see, my friends might drop in here any minute an' if you was in bad company they might make a mistake. They acts some hasty, at times. I 'm also offerin' you a good job if you wants it. We need another man."

"I 'm yourn, all right. An' I reckon I will give th' Boss a chance. He'll be more surprised, that way."

Cassidy nodded in the dark. "Yes, I reckon so; he 'll have time to wonder a li'l. Now you tell me how yo 're goin' at this game."

But he didn't get a chance then, for his companion, listening intently, whistled softly and received an answer. In another moment the room was full of figures and the soft buzz of animated conversation held his interest. "All right," said a deep voice. "We 'll keep on an' get that herd started back at daylight. If Longhorn shows up you can handle him; if you can't, there 's yore friend Jimmy," and the soft laugh warmed Jimmy's heart. "Why, Buck," replied Jimmy's friend, "he 's spoke for that job already." The foreman turned and paused as he stood in the door. "Don't forget; you ain't to wait for us. Take Jimmy, if you wants, an' head for Oleson's. I ain't shore that herd of hissn is good enough for us. We 'll handle this li'l drive-herd easy. So long."

Red Connors stuck his head through a small window: "Hey, if Longhorn shows up, give him my compliments. I shore bungled that shot."

" 'Tain't th' first," chuckled Cassidy. But Buck cut short the arguments and led the way to Jimmy's pasture.

At daylight the Boss rolled out of his bunk, started a fire and put on a kettle of water to get hot. Buckling on his gun he opened the door and started toward the bunkhouse, where everything appeared to be as he had left it the night before.

"It's a cussed shame," he growled. "But I can't risk him bringin' a posse out here. *What* th' devil!" he shouted as he ducked. A bullet sang over his head, high above him, and he glanced at the bunkhouse with renewed interest.

Having notified the Boss of his intentions and of the change in the situation, Jimmy walked around the corner of the house and sent one dangerously close to strengthen the idea that sand was no longer sand. But the Boss had surmised this instantly and was greatly shocked by such miraculous happenings on his range. He nodded cheerfully at the nearing youth and as cheerfully raised his gun. "An' he gave me a chance, too! He could 'a' got me easy if he didn't warn me! Well, here goes, Kid," he muttered, firing.

Jimmy promptly replied and scored a hit. It was not much of a hit, but it carried reflection in its sting. The Boss's heart hardened as he flinched instinctively and he sent forth his shots with cool deliberation. Jimmy swayed and stopped, which sent the Boss forward on the jump. But the youth was only further proving his cleverness against a man whom he could not beat at so long a range. As the Boss stopped again to get the work over with, a flash of smoke spurted from Jimmy's hand and the rustler spun half way around, stumbled and fell. Jimmy paused in indecision, a little suspicious of the fall, but a noise behind him made him wheel around to look.

A horseman, having topped the little hill just behind the bunkhouse, was racing down the slope as fast as his worn-out horse could carry him, and in his upraised hand a Colt glittered as it swung down to become lost in a spurt of smoke. Longhorn, returning to warn his chief, felt savage elation at this opportunity to unload quite a cargo of accumulated grouches of various kinds and sizes, which collection he had picked up from the Bar-20 northward in a running fight of twenty miles. Only a lucky cross trail, that had led him off at a tangent and somehow escaped the eyes of his pursuers, had saved him from the fate of his companions.

Jimmy swung his gun on the newcomer, but it only clicked, and the vexed youth darted and dodged and ducked with a speed and agility very creditable as he jammed cartridges into the empty chambers. Jimmy's interest in the new conditions made him forget that he had a gun and he stared in rapt and delighted anticipation at the cloud of dust that swirled suddenly from behind the corral and raced toward the disgruntled Mr. Longhorn, shouting Red's message as it came.

Mr. Cassidy sat jauntily erect and guided his fresh, gingery mount by the pressure of cunning knees. The brim of his big sombrero, pinned back against the crown by the pressure of the wind, revealed the determination and optimism that struggled to show itself around his firmly set lips; his neckerchief flapped and cracked behind his head and the hairs of his snow-white goatskin chaps rippled like a thing of life and caused Jimmy, even in his fascinated interest, to covet them.

But Longhorn's soul held no reverence for goatskin and he cursed harder when Red's compliments struck his ear about the time one of Cassidy's struck his shoulder. He was firing hastily against a man who shot as though the devil had been his teacher. The man from the Bar-20 used two guns and they roared like the roll of a drum and flashed through the heavy, low-lying cloud of swirling smoke like the darting tongue of an angry snake.

Longhorn, enveloped in the acrid smoke of his own gun, which wrapped him like a gaseous shroud, knew that his end had come. He was being shot to pieces by a two-gun man, the like of whose skill he had never before seen or heard of. As the last note of the short, five second, cracking tattoo died away Mr. Cassidy slipped his empty guns in their holsters and turned his pony's head toward the fascinated spectator, whose mouth offered easy entry to smoke and dust. As Cassidy glanced carelessly back at the late rustler Jimmy shut his mouth, gulped, opened it to speak, shut it again and cleared his dry throat. Looking from Cassidy to Longhorn and back again, he opened his mouth once more. "You-you-what'd'ju pay for them chaps?" he blurted, idiotically.

IV

Jimmy Visits Sharpsville

Bill Cassidy rode slowly into Sharpsville and dismounted in front of Carter's Emporium, nodding carelessly to the loungers hugging the shade of the store. "Howd'y," he said. "Seen anything of Jimmy Price —a kid, but about my height, with brown hair and a devilish disposition?"

Carter stretched and yawned, a signal for a salvo of yawns. "Nope, thank God. You need n't describe nothin' about that Price cub to none of us. *We* know him. He spent three days here about a year ago, an' th' town 's been sorta restin' up ever since. You don't mean for to tell us he 's comin' here again!" he exclaimed, sitting up with a jerk.

Bill laughed at the expression. "As long as you yearn for him so powerful hard, why I gotta tell you he 's on his way, anyhow. I had to go east for a day's ride an' he headed this way. He 's to meet me here."

Carter turned and looked at the others blankly. Old Dad Johnson nervously stroked his chin. "Well, then he 'll git here, all right," he prophesied pessimistically. "He usually gets where he starts for; an' I 'm plumb glad I 'm goin' on to-morrow."

"Ha, ha!" laughed George Bruce. "So 'm I goin' on, by Scott!"

Grunts and envious looks came from the group and Carter squirmed uneasily. "That's just like you fellers, runnin' away an' leavin' me to face it. An' it was you fellers what played most of th' tricks on him last time he was here. Huh! now I gotta pay for 'em," he growled.

Bill glanced over the gloomy circle and laughed heartily. Two faces out of seven were bright, Dad's particularly so. "Well, he seems to be quite a favorite around here," he grinned.

Carter snorted. "Huh! Seems to be nothin'."

"He ain't exactly a favorite," muttered Dawson. "He 's a —a —an event; that's what he is!"

Carter nodded. "Yep; that's what he is, 'though you just can't help likin' th' cub, he 's that cheerful in his devilment."

Charley Logan stretched and yawned. "Didn't hear nothin' about no Injuns, did you? A feller rid through here yesterday an' said they was out again."

Bill nodded. "Yes; I did. An' there 's a lot of rumors goin' around. They 've been over in th' Crazy Butte country an' I heard they raided through th' Little Mountain Valley last week. Anyhow, th' Seventh is out after 'em, in four sections."

"Th' Seventh is *a* regiment," asserted George Bruce. "Leastawise it was when I was in it. It is th' best in th' Service."

Dad snorted. "Listen to him! It was when he was in it! Lordy, Lordy, Lordy!" he chuckled.

"There hain't no cavalry slick enough to ketch Apaches," declared Hank, dogmatically. "Troops has too many fixin's an' sech. You gotta travel light an' live without eatin' an' drinkin' to ketch them Injuns; an' then you never hardly sometimes see 'em, at that."

"Lemme tell you, Mosshead, th' Seventh can lick all th' Injuns ever spawned!" asserted Bruce with heat. "It wiped out Black Kettle's camp, in th' dead of winter, too!"

"That was Custer as did that," snorted Carter.

"Well, he was leadin' th' Seventh, same as he is now!"

Charley Logan shook his head. "We are talking about ketchin' 'em, not fightin' 'em. An' no cavalry in th' hull country can ketch 'Paches in *this* country-it's too rough. 'Paches are only scared of punchers."

"Shore," asserted Carter. "Apaches laugh at troops, less 'n it's a pitched battle, when they don't. Cavalry chases 'em so fur an' no farther; punchers chase 'em inter h —l, out of it an' back again."

"They shore is 'lusive," cogitated Lefty Dawson, carefully deluging a fly ten feet away and shifting his cud for another shot. "An' I, for one, admits I ain't hankerin' for to chase 'em close."

"Wish we could get that cub Jimmy to chase some," exclaimed Carter. "Afore he gits here," he explained, thoughtfully.

"Oh, he 's all right, Carter," spoke up Lefty. "We was all of us young and playful onct."

"But we all war n't he-devils workin' day an' night tryin' to make our betters miserable!"

"Oh, he 's a good kid," remarked Dad. "I sorta hates to miss him. Anyhow, we got th' best of him, last time."

Bill finished rolling a cigarette, lit it and slowly addressed them. "Well, all I got to say is that he suits me right plumb down to th' ground. Now, just lemme tell you somethin' about Jimmy," and he gave them the story of Jimmy's part in the happenings on Tortilla Range, to the great delight of his audience.

"By Scott, it's just like him!" chuckled George Bruce.

"That's shore Jimmy, all right," laughed Lefty.

"What did *I* tell you?" beamed Dad. "He 's a heller, he is. He 's all right!"

"Then why don't you stay an' see him?" demanded Carter.

"I gotta go on, or I would. Yessir, I would!"

"Reckon them Injuns won't git so fur north as here," suggested Carter hopefully, and harking back to the subject which lay heaviest on his mind. "They 've only been here twict in ten years."

"Which was twice too often," asserted Lefty.

"Th' last time they was here," remarked Dad, reminiscently, "they didn't stop long; though where they went to I dunno. We gave 'em more 'n they could handle. That was th' time I just bought that new Sharps rifle, an' what I done with that gun was turrible." He paused to gather the facts in the right order before he told the story, and when he looked around again he flushed and swore. The audience had silently faded away to escape the moth-eaten story they knew by heart. The fact that Dad usually improved it and his part in it, each time he told it, did not lure them. "Cussed ingrates!" he swore, turning to Bill. "They 're plumb jealous!"

"They act like it, anyhow," agreed Bill soberly. "I 'd like to hear it, but I 'm too thirsty. Come in an' have one with me?" The story was indefinitely postponed.

An accordion wheezed down the street and a mouth-organ tried desperately to join in from the saloon next door, but, owing to a great difference in memory, did not harmonize. A roar of laughter from Dawson's, and the loud clink of glasses told where Dad's would-have-been audience then was. Carter walked around his counter and seated himself in his favorite place against the door jamb. Bill, having eluded Dad, sat on a keg of edibles and smoked in silence and content, occasionally slapping at the flies which buzzed persistently around his head. Knocking the ashes from the cigarette he leaned back lazily and looked at Carter. "Wonder where he is?" he muttered.

"Huh?" grunted the proprietor, glancing around. "Oh, you worryin' about that yearlin'? Well, you needn't! Nothin' never sidetracks Jimmy."

A fusillade of shots made Bill stand up, and Carter leaped to his feet and dashed toward the counter. But he paused and looked around foolishly. "That's his yell," he explained. "Didn't I tell you? He's arrove, same as usual."

The drumming of hoofs came rapidly nearer and heads popped out of windows and doors, each head flanked by a rifle barrel. Above a swirling cloud of dust glinted a spurting Colt and thrust through the smudge was a hand waving a strange collection of articles.

"Hullo, Kid!" shouted Dawson. "What you got? See any Injuns?"

"It's a G-string an' a medicine-bag, by all that's holy!" cried Dad from the harness shop. "Where 'd you git 'em, Jimmy?"

Jimmy drew rein and slid to a stand, pricking his nettlesome "Calico" until it pranced to suit him. Waving the Apache breech-cloth, the medicine-bag and a stocking-shaped moccasin in one hand, he proudly held up an old, dirty, battered Winchester repeater in the other and whooped a war-cry.

"Blame my hide!" shouted Dad, running out into the street. "It is a G-string! He 's gone an' got one of 'em! He 's gone an' got a 'Pache! Good boy, Kid! An' how 'd you do it?"

Carter plodded through the dust with Bill close behind. "*Where'd* you do it?" demanded the proprietor eagerly. To Carter location meant more than method. He was plainly nervous. When he reached the crowd he, in turn, examined the trophies. They were genuine, and on the G-string was a splotch of crimson, muddy with dust.

"What's in the war-bag, Kid?" demanded Lefty, preparing to see for himself. Jimmy snatched it from his hands. "You never mind what's in it, Freckle-face!" he snapped. "That's my bag, *now*. Want to spoil my luck?"

"How'd you do it?" demanded Dad breathlessly.

"*Where* 'd you do it?" snapped Carter. He glanced hurriedly around the horizon and repeated the question with vehemence. "Where 'd you get him?"

"In th' groin, first. Then through th' —"

"I don't mean where, I mean *where* —near here?" interrupted Carter.

"Oh, fifteen mile east," answered Jimmy. "He was crawlin' down on a bunch of cattle. He saw me just as I saw him. But he missed an' I did n't," he gloated proudly. "I met a Pawnee scout just afterward an' he near got shot before he signaled. He says hell's a-poppin'. Th' 'Paches are raidin' all over th' country, down —"

"I knowed it!" shouted Carter. "Yessir, I knowed it! I felt it all along! Where you finds one you finds a bunch!"

"We'll give 'em blazes, like th' last time!" cried Dad, hurrying away to the harness shop where he had left his rifle.

"I 've been needin' some excitement for a long time," laughed Dawson. "I shore hope they come."

Carter paused long enough to retort over his shoulder: "An' I hopes you drop dead! You never did have no sense! Not nohow!"

Bill smiled at the sudden awakening and watched the scrambling for weapons. "Why, there 's enough men here to wipe out a tribe. I reckon we 'll stay an' see th' fun. Anyhow, it 'll be a whole lot safer here than fightin' by ourselves out in th' open somewhere. What you say?"

"You could n't drag me away from this town right now with a cayuse," Jimmy replied, gravely hanging the medicine-bag around his neck and then stuffing the gory G-string in the folds of the slicker he carried strapped behind the cantle of the saddle. "We 'll see it out right here. But I do wish that 'Pache owned a better gun than this thing. It's most fallin' apart an' ain't worth nothin'."

Bill took it and examined the rifling and the breech-block. He laughed as he handed it back. "You oughta be glad it was n't a better gun, Kid. I don't reckon he could put two in the same place at two hundred paces with this thing. I ain't even anxious to shoot it off on a bet."

Jimmy gasped suddenly and grinned until the safety of his ears was threatened. "Would you look at Carter?" he chuckled, pointing. Bill turned and saw the proprietor of Carter's Emporium carrying water into his store, and with a speed that would lead one to infer that he was doing it on a wager. Emerging again he saw the punchers looking at him and, dropping the buckets, he wiped his face on his sleeve and shook his head. "I 'm fillin' everything," he called. "I reckon we better stand 'em off from my store-th' walls are thicker."

Bill smiled at the excuse and looked down the street at the adobe buildings. "What about th' 'dobes, Carter?" he asked. The walls of some of them were more than two feet thick.

Carter scowled, scratched his head and made a gesture of impatience. "They ain't big enough to hold us all," he replied, with triumph. "This here store is th' best place. An', besides, it's all stocked with water an' grub, an' everything."

Jimmy nodded. "Yo 're right, Carter; it's th' best place." To Bill he said in an aside, "He 's plumb anxious to protect that shack, now ain't he?"

Lefty Dawson came sauntering up. "Wonder if Carter 'll let us hold out in his store?"

"He 'll pay you to," laughed Bill.

"It's loop-holed. Been so since th' last raid," explained Lefty. "An' it's chock full of grub," he grinned.

They heard Dad's voice around the corner. "Just like last time," he was saying. "We oughta put four men in Dick's 'dobe across th' street. Then we'd have a strategy position. You see-oh, hullo," he said as he rounded the corner ahead of George Bruce. "Who 's goin' on picket duty?" he demanded.

Under the blazing sun a yellow dog wandered aimlessly down the deserted street, his main interest in life centered on his skin, which he frequently sat down to chew. During the brief respites he lounged in the doors of deserted buildings, frequently exploring the quiet interiors for food. Emerging from the "hotel" he looked across the street at the Emporium and barked tentatively at the man sitting on its flat roof. Wriggling apologetically, he slowly gained the middle of the street and then sat down to investigate a sharp attack. A can sailed out of the open door and a flurry of yellow streaked around the corner of the "hotel" and vanished.

In the Emporium grave men played poker for nails, Bill Cassidy having corralled all the available cash long before this, and conversed in low tones. The walls, reinforced breast high by boxes, barrels and bags, were divided into regular intervals by the open loopholes, each opening further indicated by a leaning rifle or two and generous piles of cartridges. Two tubs and half a dozen buckets filled with water stood in the center of the room, carefully covered over with boards and wrapping paper. Clouds of tobacco smoke lay in filmy stratums in the heated air and drifted up the resin-streaked sides of the building. The shimmering, gray sand stretched away in a glare of sunlight and seemed to writhe under the heated air, while droning flies flitted lazily through the windows and held caucuses on the sugar barrel. A slight, grating sound overhead caused several of the more irritable or energetic men to glance up lazily, grateful they were not in Hank's place. It was hot enough under the roof, and they stretched ecstatically as they thought of Hank. Three days' vigil and anxiety had become trying even to the most stolid.

John Carter fretfully damned solitaire and pushed the cards away to pick up pencil and paper and figure thoughtfully. This seemed to furnish him with even less amusement, for he scowled and turned to watch the poker game. "Huh," he sniffed, "playin' poker for nails! An' you don't even own th' nails," he grinned facetiously, and glanced around to see if his point was taken. He suddenly stiffened when he noticed the man who sat on his counter and labored patiently and zealously with a pocket knife. "Hey, you!" he exclaimed excitedly, his wrath quickly aroused. "Ain't you never had no bringin' up? If yo 're so plumb sot on whittlin', you tackle that sugar barrel!"

Jimmy looked the barrel over critically and then regarded the peeved proprietor, shaking his head sorrowfully. "This here is a better medjum for the ex-position of my art," he replied gravely. "An' as for bringin' up, lemme observe to these gents here assembled that you ain't never had no artistic trainin'. Yore skimpy soul is dwarfed an' narrowed by false weights and dented measures. You can look a sunset in th' face an' not see it for countin' yore profits." Carter glanced instinctively at the figures as Jimmy continued. "An' you can't see no beauty in a daisy's grace-which last is from a book. I 'm here carvin' th' very image of my cayuse an' givin' you a work of art, free an' gratis. I 'm timid an' sensitive, I am; an' I 'll feel hurt if—"

"Stop that noise," snorted a man in the corner, turning over to try again. "Sensitive an' timid? Yes; as a mule! Shut up an' lemme get a little sleep."

"A-men," sighed a poker-player. "An' let him sleep-he 's a cussed nuisance when he 's awake."

"Two mules," amended the dealer. "Which is worse than one," he added thoughtfully.

"We oughta put four men in that 'dobe —" began Dad persistently.

"An' will you shut up about that 'dobe an' yore four men?" snapped Lefty. "Can't you say nothin' less 'n it's about that mud hut?"

Jimmy smiled maddeningly at the irritated crowd. "As I was sayin' before you all interrupted me, I 'll feel hurt —"

"You *will*; an' quick!" snapped Carter. "You quit gougin' that counter!"

Bill craned his neck to examine the carving, and forthwith held out a derisively pointing forefinger.

"Cayuse?" he inquired sarcastically. "Looks more like th' map of th' United States, with some almost necessary parts missin'. Your geography musta been different from mine."

The artist smiled brightly. "Here 's a man with imagination, th' emancipator of thought. It's crude an' untrained, but it's there. Imagination is a hopeful sign, for it is only given to human bein's. From this we surmise an' must conclude that Bill is human."

"Will somebody be liar enough to say th' same of you?" politely inquired the dealer.

"Will you fools shut up?" demanded the man who would sleep. He had been on guard half the night.

"But you oughta label it, Jimmy," said Bill. "You 've got California bulgin' too high up, an' Florida sticks out th' wrong way. Th' Great Lakes is *all* wrong-looks like a kidney slippin' off of Canada. An' where's Texas?"

"Huh! It 'd have to be a cow to show Texas," grinned Dad Johnson, who, it appeared, also had an imagination and wanted people to know it.

"You cuttin' in on this teet-a-teet?" demanded Jimmy, dodging the compliments of the sleepy individual.

"As a map it is no good," decided Bill decisively.

"It is no map," retorted Jimmy. "I know where California bulges an' how Florida sticks out. What you call California is th' south end of th' cayuse, above which I 'm goin' to put th' tail —"

"Not if I'm man enough, you ain't!" interposed Carter, with no regard for politeness.

" —where I 'm goin' to put th' tail," repeated Jimmy. "Florida is one front laig raised off th' ground —"

"Trick cayuse, by Scott!" grunted George Bruce. "No wonder it looks like a map."

"Th' Great Lakes is th' saddle, an' Maine is where th' mane goes —*Ouch!*"

"Mangy pun," grinned Bill.

"Kentucky ought to be under th' saddle," laughed Dad, smacking his lips. "Pass th' bottle, John."

"You take too much an' we'll all be Ill-o'-noise," said Charley Logan alertly.

"Them Injuns can't come too soon to suit *me*," growled Fred Thomas. "Who started this, anyhow?"

The sleepy man arose on one elbow, his eyes glinting. "After th' fight, you ask *me* th' same thing! Th' answer will be ME!" he snapped. "I 'm goin' to clean house in about two minutes, an' fire you all out in th' street!"

Jimmy smiled down at him. "Well, you needn't be so sweepin' an' extensive in yore cleanin' operations," he retorted. "All you gotta do is go outside an' roll in th' dust like a chicken."

The crowd roared its appreciation and the sleepy individual turned over again, growling sweeping opinions.

"But if them Injuns are comin' I shore wish they 'd hurry up an' do it," asserted Dad. "I ought to 'a' been home three days ago."

"Wish to G—d you was!" came from the floor.

Bill tossed away his half-smoked cigarette, Carter promptly plunging into the sugar barrel after it. "They ain't comin'," Bill asserted. "Every time some drunk Injun gets in a fight or beats his squaw th' rumor starts. An' by th' time it gets to us it says that all th' Apaches are out follerin' old Geronimo on th' war trail. He can be more places at once than anybody *I* ever heard of. I 'm ridin' on tomorrow morning, 'Paches or no 'Paches."

"Good!" exclaimed Jimmy, glancing at Carter. "I 'll have this here carving all done by then."

There was a sudden scrambling and thumping overhead and hot exclamations zephyred down to them. Carter dashed to the door, while the others reached for rifles and began to take up positions.

"See 'em, Hank?" cried Carter anxiously.

"See what?" came a growl from above.

"Injuns, of course, you d—d fool!"

"Naw," snorted Hank. "There ain't no Injuns out at all, not after Jimmy got that one."

"Then what's th' matter?"

"My dawg's lickin' yore dawg. *Sic* him, Pete! Hi, there! Don't you run!"

"My dawg still gettin' licked?" grinned Carter.

"I 'll swap you," offered Hank promptly. "Mine can lick yourn, anyhow."

"In a race, mebby."

"H —l!" growled Hank, cautiously separating himself from a patch of hot resin that had exuded generously from a pine knot. "I 'm purty nigh cooked an' I 'm comin' down, Injuns or no Injuns. If they was comin' this way they'd 'a' been here long afore this."

"But that Pawnee told Price they was out," objected Carter. "Cassidy heard th' same thing, too. An' didn't Jimmy get one!" he finished triumphantly.

"Th' Pawnee was drunk!" retorted Hank, collecting splinters as he slipped a little down the roof. "Great Mavericks! This here is awful!" He grabbed a protruding nail and checked himself. "Price might 'a' shot a 'Pache, or he might not. I don't take him serious no more. An' that feller Cassidy can't help what scared folks tells him. Sufferin' *toads*, what a roof!"

Carter turned and looked back in the store. "Jimmy, you shore they are out? An' *will* you quit cuttin' that counter!"

Jimmy slid off the counter and closed the knife. "That's what th' Pawnee said. When I told you fellers about it, you was so plumb anxious to fight, an' eager to interrupt an' ask fool questions that I shore hated to spoil it all. What that scout says was that th' 'Paches was out raidin' down Colby way, an' was headin' south when last re —"

"*Colby*!" yelled Lefty Dawson, as the others stared foolishly. "*Colby*! Why, that's three hundred miles south of here! An' you let us make fools of ourselves for *three* days! I 'll bust you open!" and he arose to carry out his threat. "Where 'd you git them trophies?" shouted Dad angrily. "Them was genuine!" Jimmy slipped through the door as Dawson leaped and he fled at top speed to the corral, mounted in one bound and dashed off a short distance. "Why, I got them trophies in a poker game from that same Pawnee scout, you Mosshead! He could n't play th' game no better 'n you fellers. An' th' blood is snake's blood, fresh put on. You *will* drive me out of town, hey?" he jeered, and, wheeling, forthwith rode for his life. Back in the store Bill knocked aside the rifle barrel that Carter shoved through a loop hole. "A joke 's a joke, Carter," he said sternly. "You don't aim to hit him, but you might," and Carter, surprised at the strength of the twist, grinned, muttered something and went to the door without his rifle, which Bill suddenly recognized. It was the weapon that had made up Jimmy's "trophies"!

"Blame his hide!" spluttered Lefty, not knowing whether to shoot or laugh. A queer noise behind him made him turn, a movement imitated by the rest. They saw Bill rolling over and over on the floor in an agony of mirth. One by one the enraged garrison caught the infection and one by one lay down on the floor and wept. Lefty, propping himself against the sugar barrel, swayed to and fro, senselessly gasping. "They *allus* are raidin' down Colby way! Blame my hide, *oh*, blame my hide! Ha-ha-ha! Ha-ha-ha! They *allus* are raidin' down *Colby* way!"

"Three days, an' Hank *on* th' roof!" gurgled George Bruce. "*Three* days, by Scott!"

"Hank on th' roof," sobbed Carter, "settin' on splinters an hot rosim! Whee-hee-hee! Three-hee-hee days hatchin' pine knots an' rosim!"

"Gimme a drink! Gimme a drink!" whispered Dad, doubled up in a corner. "Gimme a ho-ho-ho!" he roared in a fresh paroxysm of mirth. "Lefty an' George settin' up nights watchin' th' shadders! Ho-ho-ho!"

"An' Carter boardin' us *free*!" yelled Baldy; Martin. "Oh, my G —d! He'll never get over it!"

"Yessir!" squeaked Dad. "*Free*; an' scared we 'd let 'em burn his store. 'Better stand 'em off in my place,' he says. 'It's full of grub,' he says. He-he-he!"

"An' did you see Hank squattin' on th' roof like a horned toad waitin' for his dinner?" shouted Dickinson. "I'm goin' to die! I'm goin' to die!" he sobbed.

"No sich luck!" snorted Hank belligerently. "I 'll skin him alive! Yessir; *alive*!"

Carter paused in his calculations of his loss in food and tobacco. "Better let him alone, Hank," he warned earnestly. "Anyhow, we pestered him nigh to death las' time, an' he 's shore come back at us. Better let him alone!"

Up the street Jimmy stood beside his horse and thumped and scratched the yellow dog until its rolling eyes bespoke a bliss unutterable and its tail could not wag because of sheer ecstasy.

"Purp," he said gravely, "never play jokes on a pore unfortunate an' git careless. Don't never forget it. Last time I was here they abused me shameful. Now that th' storm has busted an' this is gettin' calm-like, you an' me 'll go back an' get a good look at th' asylum," he suggested, vaulting into the saddle and starting toward the store. No invitation was needed because the dog had adopted him on the spot. And the next morning, when Jimmy and Bill, loaded with poker-gained wealth, rode out of town and headed south, the dog trotted along in the shadow made by Jimmy's horse and glanced up from time to time in hopeful expectancy and great affection.

A distant, flat pistol shot made them turn around in the saddle and look back. A group of the leading citizens of Sharpsville stood in front of the Emporium and waved hats in one last, and glad farewell. Now that Jimmy had left town, they altered their sudden plans and decided to continue to populate the town of Sharpsville.

V
The Luck of Fools

"Did you ever see a dog like Asylum?" demanded Jimmy, looking fondly at the mongrel as they rode slowly the second day after leaving Sharpsville.

Bill shook his head emphatically. "Never, nowheres."

Jimmy turned reproachfully. "Lookit how he 's follered us."

"Follered *you*," hastily corrected Bill. "He ought to. You feed an' scratch him, an' he 'll go anywhere for that. But he 's big," he conceded.

"Mostly wolf-hound," guessed Jimmy, proudly.

"He looks like a wolf-God help it-at th' end of a hard winter."

"Well, he ain't yourn!"

"An' won't be, not if I can help it."

"He ain't no good, is he?" sneered Jimmy.

"I wouldn't say that, Kid," grunted Bill. "You know there 's good *Injuns*; but he looks purty healthy right now. Why did n't you call him Hank? They look-Good G—d!" he exclaimed as he glanced through an opening in the hills. The ring of ashes that had been a corral still smoldered, and smoke arose fitfully from the caved-in roof of the adobe bunkhouse, whose beams, weakened by fire, had fallen under their heavy load.

"Injuns!" whispered Jimmy. "Not gone long, neither. Mebby they ain't all-ain't all—" he faltered, thinking of what might lie under the roof. Bill, nodding, rode hurriedly to the ruins, wheeled sharply and returned, shaking his head slowly. There was no need to explain Apache methods to his companion, and he spoke of the Indians instead. "They split. About a dozen in th' big party an' about eight in th' other. It looks sorta serious, Kid."

Jimmy nodded. "I reckon so. An' they 're usually where nobody wants 'em, anyhow. Would n't Sharpsville be disgusted if they went north? But let's get out of here, 'less you got some plan to bag a couple."

"I like you more all th' time," Bill smiled. "But I ain't got no plan, except to move."

"Now, if they ain't funny," muttered Jimmy. "If they only knowed what they was runnin' into!"

Bill turned in surprise. "I reckon I 'm easy, but I 'll bite: what are they runnin' into?"

"I don't mean th' Injuns; I mean that wagon," replied Jimmy, nodding to a canvas-covered "schooner" on the opposite hill. "Come here, 'Sylum!" he thundered. Bill wheeled, and smothered a curse when he saw the woman. "Fools!" he snarled. "Don't let *her* know," and he was galloping toward the newcomers.

"They shore is innercent," soliloquized Jimmy, following. "Just like a baby chasin' a rattler for to play with it."

Bill drew rein at the wagon and removed his sombrero. "Howd'y," he said. "Where you headin' for?" he asked pleasantly.

Tom French shifted the reins. "Sharpsville. And where in-thunder-is it?"

His brother stuck his head out through the opening in the canvas. "Yes; where?"

"You see, we are lost," explained the woman, glancing from Bill to Jimmy, whose spectacular sliding stop was purely for her benefit, though she knew it not. "We left Logan four days ago and have been wandering about ever since."

"Well, you ain't a-goin' to wander no more, ma'am," smiled Bill. "We 're goin' to Logan an' we 'll take you as far as th' Logan-Sharpsville trail," he said, wondering where it was. "You must 'a' crossed it without knowin' it."

"Then, thank goodness, everything is all right. We are very fortunate in having met you gentlemen and we will be very grateful to you," she smiled.

"You bet!" exclaimed Tom. "But where is Sharpsville?" he persisted.

"Sixty miles north," replied Jimmy, making a great effort to stop with the reins what he was causing with his shielded spur. His horse could cavort beautifully under persuasion. "Logan, ma'am," he said, indifferent to the antics of his horse, "is about thirty miles east. You must 'a' sashayed some to get only this far in four days," he grinned.

"And we would be 'sashaying' yet, if I had n't found this trail," grunted Tom. There was a sudden disturbance behind his shoulder and the canvas was opened wider. "*You* found it!" snorted George. "You mean, *I* found it. Leave it to Mollie if I did n't! And I told you that you were going wrong. Didn't I?" he demanded.

"Hush, George," chided his sister.

"But *did n't* I? Did n't I say we should have followed that moth-eaten road running-er-north?"

"Did you?" shouted Tom, turning savagely. "You told me so many fool things I couldn't pick out those having a flicker of intelligence hovering around their outer edges. *You* drove two days out of the four, did n't you?"

"Tom!" pleaded Mollie, earnestly.

"Oh, let him rave, Sis," rejoined George, and he turned to the punchers. "Friends, I beg thee to take charge of this itinerant asylum and its charming nurse, for the good of our being and the salvation of our souls. Amen."

Tom found a weak grin. "Yes, so be it. We place ourselves and guide under your orders, though I reserve the right to beat him to a pleasing pulp when he gets sober enough to feel it. At present he reclines ungracefully within."

"You mean you got a drunk guide, in there?" demanded Bill angrily.

"He feels the yearning right away," observed George. "We 'll have to take turns thrashing Bacchus, I fear."

"How long's he been that way?" demanded Bill.

"I have n't known him long enough to answer that," responded Tom. "I doubt if he were ever really sober. He is a peripatetic distillery and I believe he lived on blotters even as a child. The first day —"

" —hour," inserted George.

" —he became anxious about the condition of the rear axle and examined it so frequently that by night he had slipped back into the Stone Age-he was ossified and petrified. He could neither see, eat nor talk. Strange creatures peopled his imagination. He shot at one before we could get his gun away from him, and it was our best skillet. How the devil he could hit it is more than I know. At this moment he may be fleeing from green tigers."

"Beg pardon," murmured George. "At this moment I have my foot on his large, unwashed face."

"Why, George! You'll hurt him!" gasped Mollie.

"No such luck. He 's beyond feeling."

"But you will! It isn't right to —"

"Don't bother your head about him, Sis," interrupted Tom, savagely.

"Sure," grinned George. "Save your sympathy until he gets sober. He'll need some then."

"Now, George, there is no use of having an argument," she retorted, turning to face him. And as she turned Bill took quick advantage. One finger slipped around his scalp and ended in a jerky, lifting motion that was horribly suggestive. His other hand and arm swept back and around, the gesture taking in the hills; and at the same time he nodded emphatically toward the rear of the wagon, where Jimmy was slowly going. Across the faces of the brothers there flashed in quick succession mystification, apprehensive doubt, fear and again doubt. But a sudden backward jerk of Bill's head made them glance at the ruined 'dobe and the doubt melted into fear, and remained. George was the first to reply and he spoke to his sister. "As long as you fear for his facial beauty, Sis, I 'll look for a better place for my foot," and he disappeared behind the drooping canvas. Jimmy's words were powerful, if terse, and George returned to the seat a very thoughtful man. He took instant advantage of his sister's conversation with Bill and whispered hurriedly into his brother's ear. A faint furrow showed momentarily on Tom's forehead, but swiftly disappeared, and he calmly filled his pipe as he replied. "Oh, he 'll sober up," he said. "We poured the last of it out. And I have a great deal of confidence in these two gentlemen."

Bill smiled as he answered Mollie's question. "Yes, we did have a bad fire," he said. "It plumb burned us out, ma'am."

"But *how* did it happen?" she insisted.

"Yes, yes; how did it happen —I mean it happened like this, ma'am," he floundered. "You see, I —that is, *we-we* had some trouble, ma'am."

"So I surmised," she pleasantly replied. "I presume it was a fire, was it not?"

Bill squirmed at the sarcasm and hesitated, but he was saved by Jimmy, who turned the corner of the wagon and swung into the breach with promptness and assurance. "We fired a Greaser yesterday," he explained. "An' last night th' Greaser slipped back an' fired us. He got away, this time, ma'am; but we 're shore comin' back for him, all right."

"But is n't he far away by this time?" she asked in surprise.

"Greasers, ma'am, is funny animals. I could tell you lots of funny things about 'em, if I had time. This particular coyote is nervy an' graspin'. I reckon he was a heap disappointed when he found we got out alive, an' I reckon he 's in these hills waitin' for us to go to Logan for supplies. When we do he 'll round up th' cows an' run 'em off. Savvy? I means, understand?" he hurriedly explained.

"But why don't you hunt him now?"

Jimmy shook his head hopelessly. "You just don't understand Greasers, ma'am," he asserted, and looked around. "Does she?" he demanded.

There was a chorus of negatives, and he continued. "You see, he's plannin' to steal our cows."

"That's what he 's doin'," cheerfully assented Bill.

"I believe you said that before," smiled Mollie.

"Ha, ha!" laughed Bill. "He shore did!"

"Yes, I did!" snapped Jimmy, glaring at him.

"Then, for goodness' sake, are you going away and let him do it?" demanded Mollie.

Jimmy grinned easily, and drawled effectively. "We 're aimin' to stop him, ma'am. You see," he half whispered, whereat Bill leaned forward eagerly to learn the facts. "He won't show hisself an' we can't track him in th' hills without gettin' picked off at long range. It would be us that 'd have to do th' movin', an' that ain't healthy in rough country. So we starts to Logan, but circles back an' gets him when he 's plumb wrapped up in them cows he 's honin' for."

"That's it," asserted Bill, promptly and proudly. Jimmy was the smoothest liar he had ever listened to. "An' th' plan is all Jimmy's, too," he enthused, truthfully.

"Doubtless it is quite brilliant," she responded, "but I certainly wish *I* were that 'Greaser'!"

"Sis!" exploded George, "I'm surprised!"

"Very well; you may remain so, if you wish. But will someone tell me this: How can these gentlemen take us to Logan if they are going only part way and then returning after that dense, but lucky, 'Greaser'?"

"I should 'a' told you, ma'am," replied Jimmy, "that th' Logan-Sharpsville trail is about half way. We 'll put you on it an' turn back."

The strain was telling on Bill and he raised his arm. "Sorry to cut off this interestin' conversation, but I reckon we better move. Jimmy, tie that wolf-hound to th' axle-it won't make him drunk-an' then go ahead an' pick a new trail to Logan. Keep north of th' other, an' stay down from sky-lines. I 'll foller back a ways. Get a-goin'," and he was obeyed.

Jimmy rode a quarter of a mile in advance, unjustly escaping the remarks that Mollie was directing at him, her brothers, Bill, the dog and the situation in general. A backward glance as he left the wagon apprised him that the dangers of scouting were to be taken thankfully. He rode carelessly up the side of a hill and glanced over the top, ducked quickly and backed down with undignified haste. He fervently endorsed Bill's wisdom in taking a different route to Logan, for the Apaches certainly would strike the other trail and follow hard; and to have run into them would have been disastrous. He approached the wagon leisurely, swept off his sombrero and grinned. "Reckon you could hit any game?" he inquired. The brothers nodded glumly. "Well, get yore guns handy." There was really no need for the order. "There 's lots of it, an' fresh meat 'll come in good. Don't shoot till I says so," he warned, earnestly.

"O.K., Hawkeye," replied Tom coolly.

"We 'll wait for the whites of their eyes, *à la Bunker Hill*," replied George, uneasily, "before we wipe out the game of this large section of God's accusing and forgotten wilderness. Any *big* game loose?"

Jimmy nodded emphatically. "You bet! I just saw a bunch of copperhead snakes that 'd give you chills." The tones were very suggestive and George stroked his rifle nervously and felt little drops of cold water trickle from his armpits. Mollie instinctively drew her skirts tighter around her and placed her feet on the edge of the wagon box under the seat. "They can't climb into the wagon, can they?" she asked apprehensively.

"Oh, no, ma'am," reassured Jimmy. "Anyhow, th' dog will keep them away." He turned to the brothers. "I ain't shore about th' way, so I 'm goin' to see Bill. Wait till I come back," and he was gone. Tom gripped the reins more firmly and waited. Nothing short of an earthquake would move that wagon until he had been told to drive on. George searched the surrounding country with anxious eyes while his sister gazed fascinatedly at the ground close to the wagon. She suddenly had remembered that the dog was tied.

Bill drummed past, waving his arm, and swept out of sight around a bend, the wagon lurching and rocking after him. Out of the little valley and across a rocky plateau, down into an arroyo and up its steep, further bank went the wagon at an angle that forced a scream from Mollie. The dog, having broken loose, ran with it, eyeing it suspiciously from time to time. Jeff Purdy, the oblivious guide, slid swiftly from the front of the wagon box and stopped suddenly with a thump against the tailboard. George, playing rear guard, managed to hold on and then with a sigh of relief sat upon the guide and jammed his feet against the corners of the box.

"So he-went back for-his friend to-find the way!" gasped Mollie in jerks. "What a pity-he did-it. I could-do better myself. I 'm being jolted-into a thousand-pieces!" Her hair, loosening more with each jolt, uncoiled and streamed behind her in a glorious flame of gold. Suddenly the wagon stopped so quickly that she gasped in dismay and almost left the seat. Then she screamed and jumped for the dashboard. But it was only Mr. Purdy sliding back again.

Before them was the perpendicular wall of a mesa and another lay several hundred yards away. Bill, careful of where he walked, led the horses past a bowlder until the seat was even with it. "Step on nothing but rock," he quietly ordered, and had lifted Mollie in his arms before she knew it. Despite her protests he swiftly carried her to the wall and then slowly up its scored face to a ledge that lay half way to the top. Back of the ledge was a horizontal fissure that was almost screened from the sight of anyone below. Gaining the cave, he lowered her gently to the floor and stood up. "Do not move," he ordered.

Her face was crimson, streaked with white lanes of anger and her eyes snapped. "What does this mean?" she demanded.

He looked at her a moment, considering. "Ma'am, I was n't goin' to tell you till I had to. But it don't make no difference now. It's Injuns, close after us. Don't show yoreself."

"It's Injuns, close after us"

She regarded him calmly. "I beg your pardon-if I had only known-is there great danger?"
He nodded. "If you show yoreself. There's allus danger with Injuns, ma'am."
She pushed the hair back from her face. "My brothers? Are they coming up?"

Her courage set him afire with rage for the Apaches, but he replied calmly. "Yes. Mebby th' Injuns won't know yo 're here, Ma'am. Me an' Jimmy 'll try to lead 'em past. Just lay low an' don't make no noise."

Her eyes glowed suddenly as she realized what he would try to do. "But yourself, and Jimmy? Would n't it be better to stay up here?"

"Yo 're a thoroughbred, ma'am," he replied in a low voice. "Me an' Jimmy has staked our lives more 'n onct out of pure devilment, with nothin' to gain. I reckon we got a reason this time, th' best we ever had. I 'm most proud, ma'am, to play my cards as I get them." He bent swiftly and touched her head, and was gone.

Meeting the brothers as they toiled up with supplies, he gave them a few terse orders and went on. Taking a handful of sand from behind a bowlder and scattering it with judicious care, he climbed to the wagon seat and waited, glancing back at the faint line that marked the arroyo's rim. In a few minutes a figure popped over it and whirled toward him in a high-flung, swirling cloud of dust. Overtaking the lurching wagon, Jimmy shouted a query and kept on, his pony picking its way with the agility and certainty of a mountain cat. The wagon, lurching this way and that, first on the wheels of one side and then on those of the other, bouncing and jumping at such speed that it was a miracle it was not smashed to splinters, careened after the hard-riding horseman. A rifle bounced over the tailboard, followed swiftly by a box of cartridges and an ebony-backed mirror, which settled on its back and glared into the sky like an angry Cyclops.

Mr. Purdy, bruised from head to foot and rapidly getting sober, emitted language in jerks and grabbed at the tailboard as the wagon box dropped two feet, leaving him in the air. But it met him half way and jolted him almost to the canvas top. He slid against the side and then jammed against the tailboard again and reached for it in desperation. Another drop in the trail made him miss it, and as the wagon arose again like a steel spring Mr. Purdy, wondering what caused all the earthquakes, arose on his hands and knees in the dust and spat angrily after the careening vehicle. He scrambled unsteadily to his feet and shook eager fists after the four-wheeled jumping-jack, and gave the Recording Angel great anguish of mind and writer's cramp. Pausing as he caught sight of the objects on the ground, he stared at them thoughtfully. He had seen many things during the past few days and was not to be fooled again. He looked at the sky, and back to the rifle. Then he examined the mesa wall, and quickly looked back at the weapon. It was still there and had not moved. He closed his eyes and opened them suddenly and grunted. "Huh, bet a ten spot it's real." He approached it cautiously, ready to pounce on it if it moved, but it did not and he picked it up. Seeing the cartridges, he secured them and then gasped with fear at the glaring mirror. After a moment's thought he grabbed at it and put it in his pocket just before a sudden, swirling cloud of dust drove him, choking and gasping, to seek the shelter of the bowlders close to the wall. When he raised his head again and looked out he caught sight of a sudden movement in the open, and promptly ducked, and swore. Apaches! Twelve of them!

He had seen strange things during the last few days, and just because the rifle and other objects had turned out to be real was no reason that he should absolutely trust his eyes in this particular instance. There was a limit, which in this case was Apaches in full war dress; so he arose swaggeringly and fired at the last, and saw the third from the last slide limply from his horse. As the rest paused and half of them wheeled and started back he rubbed his eyes in amazement, damned himself for a fool and sprinted for the mesa wall, up which he climbed with the frantic speed of fear. He was favored by the proverbial luck of fools and squirmed over a wide ledge without being hit. There was but one way to get him and he knew he could pick them off as fast as they showed above the rim. He rolled over and a look of mystification crept across his face. Digging into his pockets to see what the bumps were, he produced the mirror and a flask. The former he placed carelessly against the wall and the latter he raised hastily to his lips. The mirror glared out over the plain, its rays constantly interrupted by Mr. Purdy's cautious movements as he settled himself more comfortably for defense.

A bullet screamed up the face of the wall and he flattened, intently watching the rim. Chancing to glance over the plain, he noticed that the wagon was still moving, but slowly, while far to the south two horsemen galloped back toward the mesa on a wide circle, six Apaches tearing to intercept them before they could gain cover. "I was shore wise to leave th' schooner," he grinned. "I allus know when to jump," he said, and then swung the rifle toward the rim as a faint sound reached his ears. Its smoke blotted out the piercing black eyes that looked for an instant over the edge and found eternity, and Mr. Purdy grinned when the sound of impact floated up from below. "They won't try that no more," he grunted, and forthwith dozed in a drunken stupor. A sober man might have been tempted to try a shot over the rim, and would have been dead before he could have pulled the trigger. Mr. Purdy was again favored by luck.

Leaving two braves to watch him, the other two searched for a better way up the wall.

The race over the plain was interesting but not deadly or very dangerous for Bill and Jimmy. Armed with Winchesters and wornout Spencer carbines and not able to get close to the two punchers, the Apaches did no harm, and suffered because of Mr. Cassidy's use of a new, long-range Sharps. "You allus want to keep Injuns on long range, Kid," Bill remarked as another fell from its horse. The shot was a lucky one, but just as effective. "They ain't worth a d —n figurin' windage an' th' drift of a fast-movin' target, 'specially when it's goin' over ground like this. It's a white man's weapon, Jimmy. Them repeaters ain't no good for over five hundred; they don't use enough powder. An' I reckon them Spencers was wore out long ago. They ain't even shootin' close." He whirled past the projecting spur of the mesa and leaped from his horse, Jimmy following quickly. Three hundred yards down the canyon two Apaches showed themselves for a moment as they squirmed around a projection high up on the wall and not more than ten feet below the ledge. The expressions which they carried into eternity were those of great surprise. The two who kept Mr. Purdy treed on his ledge saw their friends fall, and squirmed swiftly toward their horses. It could only be cowpunchers entering the canyon at the other end and they preferred the company of their friends until they could determine numbers. When half way to the animals they changed their minds and crept toward the scene of action. Mr. Purdy, feeling for his flask, knocked it over the ledge and looked over after it in angry dismay. Then he shouted and pointed down. Bill and Jimmy stared for a moment, nodded emphatically, and separated hastily. Mr. Purdy ducked and hugged the ledge with renewed affection. Glancing around, he was almost blinded by the mirror and threw it angrily into the canyon, and then rubbed his eyes again. Far away on the plain was a moving blot which he believed to be horsemen. He fired his rifle into the air on a chance and turned again to the events taking place close at hand. "Other way, Hombre!" he warned, and Jimmy, obeying, came upon the Apache from the rear, and saved Bill's life. At hide and seek among rocks the Apache has no equal, but here they did not have a chance with Mr. Purdy calling the moves in a language they did not well understand. A bird's-eye view is a distinct asset and Mr. Purdy was playing his novel game with delighted interest and a plainsman's instinct. Consumed with rage, the remaining Indian whirled around and sent the guide reeling against the wall and then down in a limp heap. But Bill paid the debt and continued to worm among the rocks.

There was a sudden report to the westward and Jimmy staggered and dived behind a bowlder. The other four, having discovered the trick that had been played upon them on the other side of the mesa, were anxious to pay for it. Bill hurriedly crawled to Jimmy's side as the youth brushed the blood out of his eyes and picked up his rifle. "It's th' others, Kid," said Bill. "An' they 're gettin' close. Don't move an inch, for this is their game." A roar above him made him glance upward and swear angrily. "Now they 've gone an' done it! After all we 've done to hide 'em!" Another shot from the ledge and a hot, answering fire broke out from below. "My G —d!" said a voice, weakly. Bill shook his head. "That was Tom," he muttered. "Come on, Kid," he growled. "We got to drive 'em out, d —n it!" They were too interested in picking their way in the direction of the Apaches to glance at Mr. Purdy's elevated perch or they would have seen him on his knees at the very edge making frantic motions with his one good arm. He was facing the east and the plain. Beaming with joy, he waved his arm toward Bill and Jimmy, shouted instructions in a weak voice, that barely carried to the canyon floor, and collapsed, his duty done.

Bill was surprised fifteen minutes later to hear strange voices calling to him from the rear and he turned like a flash, his Colt swinging first. "Well, I 'm d —d!" he ejaculated. Four punchers were crawling toward him. "Glad to see you," he said, foolishly.

"I reckon so," came the smiling reply. "That lookin' glass of yourn shore bothered us. We could n't read it, but we did n't have to. Where are they?"

"Plumb ahead, som'ers. Four of 'em," Bill replied. "There 's two tender feet up on that ledge, with their sister. We was gettin' plumb worried for 'em."

"Not them as hired Whiskey Jeff for to guide 'em?" asked Dickinson, the leader.

"Th' same. But how 'n h —l did Logan ever come to let 'em start?" demanded Bill, angrily.

"We did n't pay no attention to th' rumors that has been flyin' around for th' last two months. Nobody had seen no signs of 'em," answered the Logan man. "We did n't reckon there was no danger till last night, when we learned they had n't showed up in Sharpsville, nor been seen anywheres near th' trail. Then we remembers Jeff's habits, an', while we debates it, we gets word that th' Injuns was seen north of Cook's ranch yesterday. We moves sudden. Here comes th' boys back —I reckon th' job 's done. They 're a fine crowd, a'right. You should 'a' seen 'em cut loose an' raise th' dust when we saw that lookin' glass a-winkin'. We could n't read it none, but we didn't have to. We just cut loose."

"Lookin' glass!" exclaimed Bill, staring. "That's twice you 've mentioned it. What glass? We didn't have no lookin' glass, nohow."

"Well, Whiskey Jeff had one, a'right. An' he shore keeps her a-talkin', too. Ain't it a cussed funny thing that a feller that's got a hardboiled face like his'n would go an' tote a lookin' glass around with him? We never done reckoned he was that vain."

Bill shook his head and gave it up. He glanced above him at the ledge and started for it as Jimmy pushed up to him through the little crowd. "Hello, Kid," Bill smiled. "Come on up an' help me get her down," he invited. Jimmy shook his head and refused. "Ah, what's th' use? She 'll only gimme h —l for handin' her that blamed Greaser lie," he snapped. "An' you can do it alone-didn't you tote her up th' cussed wall?" It had been a long-range view, but Jimmy had seen it, just the same, and resented it.

Bill turned and looked at him. "Well, I 'm cussed!" he muttered, and forthwith climbed the wall. A few minutes later he stuck his head over the rim of the ledge and looked down upon a good-natured crowd that lounged in the shadow of the wall and told each other all about it. Jimmy was the important center of interest and he was flushed with pride. It would take a great deal to make him cut short his hour of triumph and take him away from the admiring circle that hedged him in and listened intently to his words. "Yessir, by G —d," he was saying, "just then I looks over th' top of a li'l hill an' what I sees makes me duck a-plenty. There was a dozen of 'em, stringin' south. I knowed they 'd shore hit that —"

"Hey, Kid," said a humorous voice from above. Jimmy glanced up, vexed at the interruption. "Well, what?" he growled. Bill grinned down at him in a manner that bid fair to destroy the dignity that Jimmy had striven so hard to build up. "She says all right for you. She 's done let you down easy for that whoppin' big Greaser lie you went an' spun her. She wants to know ain't you comin' up so she can talk to you? How about it?"

"Go on, Kid," urged a low and friendly voice at his elbow.

"Betcha!" grinned another. "Wish it was me! I done seen her in Logan."

Jimmy loosed a throbbing phrase, but obeyed, whereat Bill withdrew his grinning face from the sight of the grinning faces below. "He 's comin' ma'am; but he's shore plumb bashful." He looked down the canyon and laughed. "There they go to get Purdy off 'n his perch. I 'm natchurally goin' to lick anybody as tries to thrash that man," he muttered, glancing at George as he passed Jimmy on the ledge. George grinned and shook his head. "I 'm going to give him the spree of his sinful, long life," he promised, thoughtfully.

Far to the west, silhouetted for a moment against the crimson sunset, appeared a row of mounted figures. It looked long and searchingly at the mesa and slowly disappeared from view. Bill saw it and pointed it out to Lefty Dickinson. "There 's th' other eight," he said, smiling cheerfully. "If it was n't for Whiskey Jeff's lookin' glass that eight 'd mean a whole lot to us. We 've had the luck of fools!"

VI
Hopalong's Hop

Having sent Jimmy to the Bar-20 with a message for Buck Peters and seen the tenderfeet start for Sharpsville on the right trail and under escort, Bill Cassidy set out for the Crazy M ranch, by the way of Clay Gulch. He was to report on the condition of some cattle that Buck had been offered cheap and he was anxious to get back to the ranch. It was in the early evening when he reached Clay Gulch and rode slowly down the dusty, shack-lined street in search of a hotel. The town and the street were hardly different from other towns and streets that he had seen all over the cow-country, but nevertheless he felt uneasy. The air seemed to be charged with danger, and it caused him to sit even more erect in the saddle and assume his habit of indifferent alertness. The first man he saw confirmed the feeling by staring at him insolently and sneering in a veiled way at the low-hung, tied-down holsters that graced Bill's thighs. The guns proclaimed the gun-man as surely as it would have been proclaimed by a sign; and it appeared that gun-men were not at that time held in high esteem by the citizens of Clay Gulch. Bill was growing fretful and peevish when the man, with a knowing shake of his head, turned away and entered the harness shop. "Trouble's brewin' somewheres around," muttered Bill, as he went on. He had singled out the first of two hotels when another citizen, turning the corner, stopped in his tracks and looked Bill over with a deliberate scrutiny that left but little to the imagination. He frowned and started away, but Bill spurred forward, determined to make him speak.

"Might I inquire if this is Clay Gulch?" he asked, in tones that made the other wince.

"You might," was the reply. "It is," added the citizen, "an' th' Crazy M lays fifteen mile west." Having complied with the requirements of common politeness the citizen of Clay Gulch turned and walked into the nearest saloon. Bill squinted after him and shook his head in indecision.

"He wasn't guessin', neither. He shore knowed where I wants to go. I reckon Oleson must 'a' said he was expectin' me." He would have been somewhat surprised had he known that Mr. Oleson, foreman of the Crazy M, had said nothing to anyone about the expected visitor, and that no one, not even on the ranch, knew of it. Mr. Oleson was blessed with taciturnity to a remarkable degree; and he had given up expecting to see anyone from Mr. Peters.

As Bill dismounted in front of the "Victoria" he noticed that two men further down the street had evidently changed their conversation and were examining him with frank interest and discussing him earnestly. As a matter of fact they had not changed the subject of their conversation, but had simply fitted him in the place of a certain unknown. Before he had arrived they discussed in the abstract; now they could talk in the concrete. One of them laughed and called softly over his shoulder, whereupon a third man appeared in the door, wiping his lips with the back of a hairy, grimy hand, and focused evil eyes upon the innocent stranger. He grunted contemptuously and, turning on his heel, went back to his liquid pleasures. Bill covertly felt of his clothes and stole a glance at his horse, but could see nothing wrong. He hesitated: should he saunter over for information or wait until the matter was brought to his attention? A sound inside the hotel made him choose the latter course, for his stomach threatened to become estranged and it simply howled for food. Pushing open the door he dropped his saddle in a corner and leaned against the bar.

"Have one with me to get acquainted?" he invited. "Then I 'll eat, for I 'm hungry. An' I 'll use one of yore beds to-night, too."

The man behind the bar nodded cheerfully and poured out his drink. As he raised the liquor he noticed Bill's guns and carelessly let the glass return to the bar.

"Sorry, sir," he said coldly. "I 'm hall out of grub, the fire 's hout, *hand* the beds are taken. But mebby 'Awley, down the strite, can tyke care of you."

Bill was looking at him with an expression that said much and he slowly extended his arm and pointed to the untasted liquor.

"Allus finish what you start, English," he said slowly and clearly. "When a man goes to take a drink with me, and suddenly changes his mind, why I gets riled. I don't know what ails this town, an' I don't care; I don't give a cuss about yore grub an' your beds; but if you don't drink that liquor you poured out *to* drink, why I 'll natchurally shove it down yore British throat so cussed hard it 'll strain yore neck. Get to it!"

The proprietor glanced apprehensively from the glass to Bill, then on to the business-like guns and back to the glass, and the liquor disappeared at a gulp. "W'y," he explained, aggrieved. "There hain't no call for to get riled hup like that, strainger. I bloody well forgot it."

"Then don't you go an' 'bloody well' forget this: Th' next time I drops in here for grub an' a bed, you have 'em both, an' be plumb polite about it. Do you get me?" he demanded icily.

The proprietor stared at the angry puncher as he gathered up his saddle and rifle and started for the door. He turned to put away the bottle and the sound came near being unfortunate for him. Bill leaped sideways, turning while in the air and landed on his feet like a cat, his left hand gripping a heavy Colt that covered the short ribs of the frightened proprietor before that worthy could hardly realize the move.

"Oh, all right," growled Bill, appearing to be disappointed. "I reckoned mebby you was gamblin' on a shore thing. I feels impelled to offer you my sincere apology; you ain't th' kind as would even gamble *on* a shore thing. You 'll see me again," he promised. The sound of his steps on the porch ended in a thud as he leaped to the ground and then he passed the window leading his horse and scowling darkly. The proprietor mopped his head and reached twice for the glass before he found it. "Gawd, what a bloody 'eathen," he grunted. "'*E* won't be as easy as the lawst was, blime 'im."

Mr. Hawley looked up and frowned, but there was something in the suspicious eyes that searched his face that made him cautious. Bill dropped his load on the floor and spoke sharply. "I want supper an' a bed. You ain't full up, an' you ain't out of grub. So I 'm goin' to get 'em both right here. Yes?"

"You shore called th' turn, stranger," replied Mr. Hawley in his Sunday voice. "That's what I 'm in business for. An' business is shore dull these days."

He wondered at the sudden smile that illuminated Bill's face and half guessed it; but he said nothing and went to work. When Bill pushed back from the table he was more at peace with the world and he treated, closely watching his companion. Mr. Hawley drank with a show of pleasure and forthwith brought out cigars. He seated himself beside his guest and sighed with relief.

"I 'm plumb tired out," he offered. "An' I ain't done much. You look tired, too. Come a long way?"

"Logan," replied Bill. "Do *you* know where I 'm goin'? An' why?" he asked.

Mr. Hawley looked surprised and almost answered the first part of the question correctly before he thought. "Well," he grinned, "if I could tell where strangers was goin', an' why, I would n't never ask 'em where they come from. An' I 'd shore hunt up a li'l game of faro, you bet!"

Bill smiled. "Well, that might be a good idea. But, say, what ails this town, anyhow?"

"What ails it? Hum! Why, lack of money for one thing; scenery, for another; wimmin, for another. Oh, h—l, I ain't got time to tell you what ails it. Why?"

"Is there anything th' matter with me?"

"I don't know you well enough for to answer that kerrect."

"Well, would you turn around an' stare at me, an' seem pained an' hurt? Do I look funny? Has anybody put a sign on my back?"

"You looks all right to me. What's th' matter?"

"Nothin', yet," reflected Bill slowly. "But there will be, mebby. You was mentionin' faro. Here 's a turn you can call: somebody in this wart of a two-by-nothin' town is goin' to run plumb into a big surprise. There 'll mebby be a loud noise an' some smoke where it starts from; an' a li'l round hole where it stops. When th' curious delegation now holdin' forth on th' street slips in here after I 'm in bed, an' makes inquiries about me, you can tell 'em that. An' if Mr. —Mr. Victoria drops in casual, tell him I 'm cleanin' my guns. Now then, show me where I 'm goin' to sleep."

Mr. Hawley very carefully led the way into the hall and turned into a room opposite the bar. "Here she is, stranger," he said, stepping back. But Bill was out in the hall listening. He looked into the room and felt oppressed.

"No she ain't," he answered, backing his intuition. "She is upstairs, where there is a li'l breeze. By th' Lord," he muttered under his breath. "This is some puzzle." He mounted the stairs shaking his head thoughtfully. "It shore is, it shore is."

The next morning when Bill whirled up to the Crazy M bunkhouse and dismounted before the door a puncher was emerging. He started to say something, noticed Bill's guns and went on without a word. Bill turned around and looked after him in amazement. "Well, what th' devil!" he growled. Before he could do anything, had he wished to, Mr. Oleson stepped quickly from the house, nodded and hurried toward the ranch house, motioning for Bill to follow. Entering the house, the foreman of the Crazy M waited impatiently for Bill to get inside, and then hurriedly closed the door.

"They 've got onto it some way," he said, his taciturnity gone; "but that don't make no difference if you 've got th' sand. I 'll pay you one hundred an' fifty a month, furnish yore cayuses an' feed you. I 'm losin' more 'n two hundred cows every month an' can't get a trace of th' thieves. Harris, Marshal of Clay Gulch, is stumped, too. *He* can't move without proof; *you* can. Th' first man to get is George Thomas, then his brother Art. By that time you 'll know how things lay. George Thomas is keepin' out of Harris' way. He killed a man last week over in Tuxedo an' Harris wants to take him over there. He 'll not help you, so don't ask him to." Before Bill could reply or recover from his astonishment Oleson continued and described several men. "Look out for ambushes. It 'll be th' hardest game you ever went up ag'in, an' if you ain't got th' sand to go through with it, say so."

Bill shook his head. "I got th' sand to go through with anythin' I starts, but I don't start here. I reckon you got th' wrong man. I come up here to look over a herd for Buck Peters; an' here you go shovin' wages like that at me. When I tells Buck what I 've been offered he 'll fall dead." He laughed. "Now I knows th' answer to a lot of things.

"Here, here!" he exclaimed as Oleson began to rave. "Don't you go an' get all het up like that. I reckon I can keep my face shut. An' lemme observe in yore hat-like ear that if th' rest of this gang is like th' samples I seen in town, a good gun-man would shore be robbin' you to take all that money for th' job. Fifty a month, for two months, would be a-plenty."

Oleson's dismay was fading, and he accepted the situation with a grim smile. "You don't know them fellers," he replied. "They 're a bad lot, an' won't stop at nothin'.'"

"All right. Let's take a look at them cows. I want to get home soon as I can."

Oleson shook his head. "I gave you up, an' when I got a better offer I let 'em go. I 'm sorry you had th' ride for nothin', but I could n't get word to you."

Bill led the way in silence back to the bunk house and mounted his horse. "All right," he nodded. "I shore was late. Well, I 'll be goin'."

"That gun-man is late, too," said Oleson. "Mebby he ain't comin'. You want th' job at *my* figgers?"

"Nope. I got a better job, though it don't pay so much money. It's steady, an' a hull lot cleaner. So-long," and Bill loped away, closely watched by Shorty Allen from the corral. And after an interval, Shorty mounted and swung out of the other gate of the corral and rode along the bottom of an arroyo until he felt it was safe to follow Bill's trail. When Shorty turned back he was almost to town, and he would not have been pleased had he known that Bill knew of the trailing for the last ten miles. Bill had doubled back and was within a hundred yards of Shorty when that person turned ranchward.

"Huh! I must be popular," grunted Bill. "I reckon I will stay in Clay Gulch till t'morrow mornin'; an' at the Victoria," he grinned. Then he laughed heartily. "Victoria! I got a better name for it than that, all right."

When he pulled up before the Victoria and looked in the proprietor scowled at him, which made Bill frown as he went on to Hawley's. Putting his horse in the corral he carried his saddle and rifle into the barroom and looked around. There was no one in sight, and he smiled. Putting the saddle and rifle back in one corner under the bar and covering them with gunny sacks he strolled to the Victoria and entered through the rear door. The proprietor reached for his gun but reconsidered in time and picked up a glass, which he polished with exaggerated care. There was something about the stranger that obtruded upon his peace of mind and confidence. He would let some one else try the stranger out.

Bill walked slowly forward, by force of will ironing out the humor in his face and assuming his sternest expression. "I want supper an' a bed, an' don't forget to be plumb polite," he rumbled, sitting down by the side of a small table in such a manner that it did not in the least interfere with the movement of his right hand. The observing proprietor observed and gave strict attention to the preparation of the meal. The gun-man, glancing around, slowly arose and walked carelessly to a chair that had blank wall behind it, and from where he could watch windows and doors.

When the meal was placed before him he glanced up. "Go over there an' sit down," he ordered, motioning to a chair that stood close to the rifle that leaned against the wall. "Loaded?" he demanded. The proprietor could only nod. "Then sling it acrost yore knees an' keep still. Well, start movin'."

The proprietor walked as though he were in a trance but when he seated himself and reached for the weapon a sudden flash of understanding illumined him and caused cold sweat to bead upon his wrinkled brow. He put the weapon down again, but the noise made Bill look up.

"Acrost yore knees," growled the puncher, and the proprietor hastily obeyed, but when it touched his legs he let loose of it as though it were hot. He felt a great awe steal through his fear, for here was a gun-man such as he had read about. This man gave him all the best of it just to tempt him to make a break. The rifle had been in his hands, and while it was there the gun-man was calmly eating with both hands on the table and had not even looked up until the noise of the gun made him!

"My Gawd, 'e must be a wizard with 'em. I 'opes I don't forget!" With the thought came a great itching of his kneecap; then his foot itched so as to make him squirm and wear horrible expressions. Bill, chancing to glance up carelessly, caught sight of the expressions and growled, whereupon they became angelic. Fearing that he could no longer hold in the laughter that tortured him, Bill arose.

"Shoulder, *arms!*" he ordered, crisply. The gun went up with trained precision. "Been a sojer," thought Bill. "Carry, *arms!* About, *face!* To a bedroom, *march!*" He followed, holding his sides, and stopped before the room. "This th' best?" he demanded. "Well, it ain't good enough for me. About, *face!* Forward, *march!* Column, *left!* Ground, *arms!* Fall out." Tossing a coin on the floor as payment for the supper Bill turned sharply and went out without even a backward glance.

The proprietor wiped the perspiration from his face and walked unsteadily to the bar, where he poured out a generous drink and gulped it down. Peering out of the door to see if the coast was clear, he scurried across the street and told his troubles to the harness-maker.

Bill leaned weakly against Hawley's and laughed until the tears rolled down his cheeks. Pushing weakly from the building he returned to the Victoria to play another joke on its proprietor.

Finding it vacant he slipped upstairs and hunted for a room to suit him. The bed was the softest he had seen for a long time and it lured him into removing his boots and chaps and guns, after he had propped a chair against the door as a warning signal, and stretching out flat on his back, he prepared to enjoy solid comfort. It was not yet dark, and as he was not sleepy he lay there thinking over the events of the past twenty-four hours, often laughing so hard as to shake the bed. What a reputation he would have in the morning! The softness of the bed got in its work and he fell asleep, for how long he did not know; but when he awakened it was dark and he heard voices coming up from below. They came from the room he had refused to take. One expression banished all thoughts of sleep from his mind and he listened intently. "'Red-headed Irish gunman.' Why, they means me! 'Make him hop into h —l.' I don't reckon I 'd do that for anybody, even my friends."

"I tried to give 'im this room, but 'e would n't tyke it" protested the proprietor, hurriedly. "'E says the bloody room was n't good enough for 'im, *hand* 'e marches me out hand makes off. Likely 'e 's in *'Awley's.*"

"No, he ain't," growled a strange voice. "You 've gone an' bungled th' whole thing."

"But I s'y I did n't, you know. I tries to give 'im this werry room, George, but 'e would n't 'ave it. D'y think I wants 'im running haround this blooming town? 'E 's worse nor the other, *hand* Gawd knows 'e was bad enough. 'E 's a cold-*blooded* beggar, 'e is!"

"You missed yore chance," grunted the other. "Wish *I* had that gun you had."

"I was wishing to Gawd you did," retorted the proprietor. "It never looked so bloody big before, d —n 'is *'ide!*"

"Well, his cayuse is in Hawley's corral," said the first speaker. "If I ever finds Hawley kept him under cover I 'll blow his head off. Come on; we 'll get Harris first. He ought to be gettin' close to town if he got th' word I sent over to Tuxedo. He won't let us call him. He's a man of his word."

"He 'll be here, all right. Fred an' Tom is watchin' his shack, an' we better take th' other end of town-there 's no tellin' how he 'll come in now," suggested Art Thomas. "But I wish I knowed where that cussed gun-man is."

As they went out Bill, his chaps on and his boots in his hand, crept down the stairs, and stopped as he neared the hall door. The proprietor was coming back. The others were outside, going to their stations and did not hear the choking gasp that the proprietor made as a pair of strong hands reached out and throttled him. When he came to he was lying face down on a bed, gagged and bound by a rope that cut into his flesh with every movement. Bill, waiting a moment, slipped into the darkness and was swallowed up. He was looking for Mr. Harris, and looking eagerly.

The moon arose and bathed the dusty street and its crude shacks in silver, cunningly and charitably hiding its ugliness; and passed on as the skirmishing rays of the sun burst into the sky in close and eternal pursuit. As the dawn spread swiftly and long, thin shadows sprang across the sandy street, there arose from the dissipated darkness close to the wall of a building an armed man, weary and slow from a tiresome vigil. Another emerged from behind a pile of boards that faced the marshal's abode, while down the street another crept over the edge of a dried-out water course and swore softly as he stood up slowly to flex away the stiffness of cramped limbs. Of vain speculation he was empty; he had exhausted all the whys and hows long before and now only muttered discontentedly as he reviewed the hours of fruitless waiting. And he was uneasy; it was not like Harris to take a dare and swallow his own threats without a struggle. He looked around apprehensively, shrugged his shoulders and stalked behind the shacks across from the two hotels.

Another figure crept from the protection of Hawley's corral like a slinking coyote, gun in hand and nervously alert. He was just in time to escape the challenge that would have been hurled at him by Hawley, himself, had that gentleman seen the skulker as he grouchily opened one shutter and scowled sleepily at the kindling eastern sky. Mr. Hawley was one of those who go to bed with regret and get up with remorse, and his temper was always easily disturbed before breakfast. The skulker, safe from the remorseful gentleman's eyes, and gun, kept close to the building as he walked and was again fortunate, for he had passed when Mr. Hawley strode heavily into his kitchen to curse the cold, rusty stove, a rite he faithfully performed each morning. Across the street George and Art Thomas walked to meet each other behind the row of shacks and stopped near the harness shop to hold a consultation. The subject was so interesting that for a few moments they were oblivious to all else.

A man softly stepped to the door of the Victoria and watched the two across the street with an expression on his face that showed his smiling contempt for them and their kind. He was a small man, so far as physical measurements go, but he was lithe, sinewy and compact. On his opened vest, hanging slovenly and blinking in the growing light as if to prepare itself for the blinding glare of midday, glinted a five-pointed star of nickel, a lowly badge that every rural community knows and holds in an awe far above the metal or design. Swinging low on his hip gleamed the ivory butt of a silver-plated Colt, the one weakness that his vanity seized upon. But under the silver and its engraving, above and before the cracked and stained ivory handles, lay the power of a great force; and under the casing of the marshal's small body lay a virile manhood, strong in courage and determination. Toby Harris watched, smilingly; he loved the dramatic and found keen enjoyment in the situation. Out of the corner of his eye he saw a carelessly dressed cowpuncher slouching indolently along close to the buildings on the other side of the street with the misleading sluggishness of a panther. The red hair, kissed by the slanting rays of the sun where it showed beneath the soiled sombrero, seemed to be a flaming warning; the half-closed eyes, squinting under the brim of the big hat, missed nothing as they darted from point to point.

The marshal stepped silently to the porch and then on to the ground, his back to the rear of the hotel, waiting to be discovered. He had been in sight perhaps a minute. The cowpuncher made a sudden, eye-baffling movement and smoke whirled about his hips. Fred, turning the corner behind the marshal, dropped his gun with a scream of rage and pain and crashed against the window in sudden sickness, his gunhand hanging by a tendon from his wrist. The marshal stepped quickly forward at the shot and for an instant gazed deeply into the eyes of the startled rustlers. Then his Colt leaped out and crashed a fraction of a second before the brothers fired. George Thomas reeled, caught sight of the puncher and fired by instinct. Bill, leaving Harris to watch the other side of the street, was watching the rear corner of the Victoria and was unprepared for the shot. He crumpled and dropped and then the marshal, enraged, ended the rustler's earthly career in a stream of flame and smoke. Tom, turning into the street further down, wheeled and dashed for his horse, and Art, having leaped behind the harness shop, turned and fled for his life. He had nearly reached his horse and was going at top speed with great leaps when the prostrate man in the street, raising on his elbow, emptied his gun after him, the five shots sounding almost as one. Art Thomas arose convulsively, steadied himself and managed to gain the saddle. Harris looked hastily down the street and saw a cloud of dust racing northward, and grunted. "Let them go —*they* won't never come back no more." Running to the cowpuncher he raised him after a hurried examination of the wounded thigh. "Hop along, Cassidy," he smiled in encouragement. "You 'll be a better man with one good laig than th' whole gang was all put together."

The puncher smiled faintly as Hawley, running to them, helped him toward his hotel. "Th' bone is plumb smashed. I reckon I 'll hop along through life. It 'll be hop along, for me, all right. That's *my* name, all right. Huh! Hopalong Cassidy! But I didn't hop into h —l, did I, Harris?" he grinned bravely.

And thus was born a nickname that found honor and fame in the cow-country —a name that stood for loyalty, courage and most amazing gun-play. I have Red's word for this, and the endorsement of those who knew him at the time. And from this on, up to the time he died, and after, we will forsake "Bill" and speak of him as Hopalong Cassidy, a cowpuncher who lived and worked in the days when the West was wild and rough and lawless; and who,

like others, through the medium of the only court at hand, Judge Colt, enforced justice as he
believed it should be enforced.

VII

"Dealing the Odd"

Faro-bank is an expensive game when luck turns a cold shoulder on any player, and "going
broke" is as easy as ruffling a deck. When a man finds he has two dollars left out of more than
two months' pay and that it has taken him less than thirty minutes to get down to that mark,
he cannot be censored much if he rails at that Will-o'-the-wisp, the Goddess of Luck. Put him
a good ten days' ride from home, acquaintances and money and perhaps he will be justified in
adding heat in plenty to his denunciation. He had played to win when he should have coppered,
coppered when he should have played to win, he had backed both ends against the middle and
played the high card as well-but only when his bets were small did the turn show him what
he wanted to see. Perhaps the case-keeper had hoodooed him, for he never did have any luck
at cards when a tow-headed man had a finger in the game.

Fuming impotently at his helplessness, a man limped across the main street in Colby, constrained and a little awkward in his new store clothes and new, squeaking boots that were clumsy
with stiffness. The only things on him that he could regard as old and tried friends were the
battered sombrero and the heavy, walnut-handled Colt's .45 which rubbed comfortably with
each movement of his thigh. The weapon, to be sure, had a ready cash value-but he could
not afford to part with it. The horse belonged to his ranch, and the saddle must not be sold;
to part with it would be to lose his mark of caste and become a walking man, which all good
punchers despised.

"Ten days from home, knowin' nobody, two measly dollars in my pocket, an' luck dead agin
me," he growled with pugnacious pessimism. "Oh, I 'm a wise old bird, I am! A h —l of a
wise bird. Real smart an' cute an' shiny, a cache of wisdom, a real, bonyfied Smart Aleck with
a head full of spavined brains. I copper th' deuce an' th' deuce wins; I play th' King to win for
ten dollars when I ought to copper it. I lay two-bits and it comes right-ten dollars an' I see my
guess go *loco*. Reckon I better slip these here twin bucks down in my kill-me-soon boots afore
some blind papoose takes 'em away from me. Wiser 'n Solomon, I am; I 've got old Caesar
climbin' a cactus for pleasure an' joy. S-u-c-k-e-r is my middle name-an' I 'm busted."

He almost stumbled over a little tray of a three-legged table on the corner of the street
and his face went hard as he saw the layout. Three halves of English walnut shells lay on the
faded and soiled green cloth and a blackened, shriveled pea was still rolling from the shaking he
had given the table. He stopped and regarded it gravely, jingling his two dollars disconsolately.
"Don't this town do nothin' else besides gamble?" he muttered, looking around.

"Howd'y, stranger!" cheerfully cried a man who hastened up. "Want to see me fool you?"

The puncher's anger was aroused to a thin, licking flame; but it passed swiftly and a cold,
calculating look came into his eyes. He glanced around swiftly, trying to locate the cappers, but
they were not to be seen, which worried him a little. He always liked to have possible danger
where he could keep an eye on it. Perhaps they were eating or drinking-the thought stirred
him again to anger: two dollars would not feed him very long, nor quench his thirst.

"Pick it out, stranger," invited the proprietor, idly shifting the shells. "It's easy if yo 're right
smart-but lots of folks just can't do it; they can't seem to get th' hang of it, somehow. That's
why it's a bettin' proposition. Here it is, right before yore eyes! One little pea, three little
shells, right here plumb in front of yore eyes! Th' little pea hides under one of th' little shells,
right in plain sight: But can you tell which one? That's th' whole game, right there. See how
it's done?" and the three little shells moved swiftly but clumsily and the little pea disappeared.
"Now, then; where would *you* say it was?" demanded the hopeful operator, genially.

The puncher gripped his two dollars firmly, shifted his weight as much as possible on his sound leg, and scowled: he knew where it was. "Do I look like a kid? Do you reckon you have to coax like a fool to get me all primed up to show how re-markably smart an' quick I am? You don't; I know how smart I am. Say, you ain't, not by any kinda miracle, a blind papoose, are you?" he demanded.

"What you mean?" asked the other, smiling as he waited for the joke. It did not come, so he continued. "Don't take no harm in my fool wind-jammin', stranger. It's in th' game. It's a habit; I 've said it so much I just can't help it no more —I up an' says it at a funeral once; that is, part of it-th' first part. That's dead right! But I reckon I 'm wastin' my time-unless you happen to feel coltish an' hain't got nothin' to do for an age. I 've been playin' in hard luck th' last week or so-you see, I ain't as good as I uster be. I ain't quite so quick, an' a little bit off my quickness is a whole lot off my chances. But th' game's square-an' that's a good deal more'n you can say about most of 'em."

The puncher hesitated, a grin flickering about his thin lips and a calm joy warming him comfortably. He knew the operator. He knew that face, the peculiar, crescent-shaped scar over one brow, and the big, blue eyes that years of life had not entirely robbed of their baby-like innocence. The past, sorted thoroughly and quickly by his memory, shoved out that face before a crowd of others. Five years is not a long time to remember something unpleasant; he had reasons to remember that countenance. Knowing the face he also knew that the man had been, at one time, far from "square." The associations and means of livelihood during the past five years, judging from the man's present occupation, had not been the kind to correct any evil tendency. He laid a forefinger on the edge of the tray. "Start th' machinery —I 'll risk a couple of dollars, anyhow. That ain't much to lose. I bet two dollars I can call it right," he said, watching closely.

He won, as he knew he would; and the result told him that the gambler had not reformed. The dexterous fingers shifting the shells were slower than others he had seen operate and when he had won again he stopped, as if to leave. "When I hit town a short time ago I didn't know I 'd be so lucky. I went an' drawed two months' pay when I left th' ranch: I shore don't need it. Shuffle 'em again-it's yore money, anyhow," he laughed. "You should 'a' quit th' game before you got so slow."

"Goin' back to work purty soon?" queried the shell-man, wondering how much this "sucker" had left unspent.

"Not me! I 've only just had a couple of drinks since I hit town-an' *I* 'm due to celebrate."

The other's face gave no hint of his thoughts, which were that the fool before him had about a hundred dollars on his person. "Well, luck's with you today-you 've called it right twice. I 'll bet you a cool hundred that you can't call it th' third time. It's th' quickness of my hands agin yore eyes-an' you can't beat me three straight. Make it a hundred? I hate to play all day."

"I 'll lay you my winnings an' have some more of yore money," replied the puncher, feverishly. "Ain't scared, are you?"

"Don't know what it means to be scared," laughed the other. "But I ain't got no small change, nothin' but tens. Play a hundred an' let's have some real excitement."

"Nope; eight or nothin'."

He won again. "Now, sixteen even. Come on; I 've got you beat."

"But what's th' use of stringin' 'long like that?" demanded the shell-man.

"Gimme a chance to get my hand in, won't you?" retorted the puncher.

"Well, all right," replied the gambler, and he lost the sixteen.

"Now thirty," suggested the puncher. "Next time all I 've got, every red cent. Once more to practice-then every red," he repeated, shifting his feet nervously. "I 'll clean you out an' have a real, genuine blow-out on yore money. Come on, I 'm in a hurry."

"I 'll fool you *this* time, by th' Lord!" swore the gambler, angrily. "You've got more luck than sense. An' I 'll fool you next time, too. Yo 're quicker 'n most men I 've run up agin, but I can beat you, shore as shootin'. Th' game's square, th' play fair-my hand agin yore eye. Ready? Then watch me!"

He swore luridly and shoved the money across the board to the winner, bewailing his slowness and getting angrier every moment. "Yo 're th' cussedest man I ever bet agin! But I'll get you *this* time. You can't guess right all th' time, an' I know it."

"There she is; sixty-two bucks, three score an' two simoleons; all I 've got, every cent. Let's see you take it away from me!"

The gambler frowned and choked back a curse. He had risked sixty dollars to win two, and the fact that he had to let this fool play again with the fire hurt his pride. He had no fear for his money-he knew he could win at every throw-but to play that long for two dollars! And suppose the sucker had quit with the sixty!

"Do you get a dollar a month?" he demanded, sarcastically. "Well, I reckon you earn it, at that. Thought you had money, thought you drew down two months' pay an' hain't had nothin' more'n two drinks? Did you go an' lose it on th' way?"

"Oh, I drew it a month ago," replied the sucker, surprised. "I 've only had two drinks in this town, which I hit 'bout an hour ago. But I shore lost a wad playin' faro-bank agin a towhead. Come on-lemme take sixty more of yore money, anyhow."

"Sixty-*two*!" snapped the proprietor, determined to have those two miserable dollars and break the sucker for revenge. "Every cent, you remember."

"*All* right; I don't care! I ain't no tin-horn," grumbled the other. "Think I care 'bout two dollars?" But he appeared to be very nervous, nevertheless.

"Well, put it on th' table."

"After you put yourn down."

"There it is. Now watch me close!" A gleam of joy flashed up in the angry man's eyes as he played with the shells. "Watch me close! Mebby it is, an' mebby it ain't —th' game's square, th' play 's fair. It's my hand agin yore eye. Watch me close!"

"Oh, go ahead! I'm watchin', all right. Think I 'd go to sleep now!"

The shifting hands stopped, the shells lay quiet, and the gambler gazed blankly down the unsympathetic barrel of a Colt.

"Now, Thomas, old thimble-rigger," crisply remarked the supposed sucker as he cautiously slid the money off the table, to be picked up later when conditions would be more favorable. "Th' little pea ain't under *no* shell. *Stop*! Step back one pace an' elevate them paws. Don't make no more funny motions with that hand, savvy? But you can drop th' pea if it hurts them two fingers. Now we 'll see if I win; I allus like to be shore," and he cautiously turned over the shells, revealing nothing but the dirty green cloth. "I win; it ain't there-just like I thought."

"Who are you, an' how 'd you know my name?" demanded the gambler, mentally cursing his two missing cappers. They were drinking once too often and things were going to happen in their vicinity, and very soon.

"Why, you took twenty-five dollars from me up in Alameda onct, when I could n't afford to lose it," grinned the puncher. "I was something of a kid then. I remember you, all right. My foreman told me about yore bang-up fight agin th' Johnson brothers, who gave you that scar. I thought then that you were a great man-now I know you ain't. I would n't 'a' played at all if I had n't knowed how crooked you was. Take yore layout an' yore crookedness, find th' pea an' yore cappers, an' clear out. An' if anybody asks you if you 've seen Hopalong Cassidy you tell 'em I 'm up here in Colby makin' some easy money beatin' crooked games. So-long, an' *don't* look back!"

Hopalong watched him go and then went to the nearest place where he could get something to eat. In due time, having disposed of a square meal, Hopalong called for a drink and a cigar, and sat quietly smoking for nearly half an hour, so lost in thought that his cigar went out repeatedly. As he reviewed his disastrous play at faro many small details came to him and now he found them interesting. The dealer was not a master at his trade and Hopalong had seen many better; in fact the man was not even second class, and this fact hurt his pride. He had played a careful game, and the great majority of his small bets had won-it was only when he risked twenty or thirty dollars that he lost. The only big bet that he had been at all lucky on was one where doubles showed on the turn and he had been split, losing half of his stake. But when he had played his last fifty dollars on the Jack, open, the final blow fell and he had left the table in disgust.

Why weren't there cue-cards, so the players could keep their own tally of the cards instead of having to depend on the cue-box kept by the case-keeper? This made him suspicious; a crooked dealer and case-keeper can trim a big bet at will, unless the players keep their own cases or are exceptionally wise; and even then a really good dealer will get away with his play nine times out of ten. While he seldom played a system, he had backed one that morning; but he was cured of that weakness now. If the game were square he figured he could get at least an even break; if crooked, nothing but a gun could beat it, and he had a very good gun. When he thought of the gun, he reviewed the arrangement of the room and estimated the weight of the rough, deal table on which rested the faro layout. He smiled and turned to the bartender. "Hey, barkeeper! Got any paper an' a pencil?"

After some rummaging the taciturn dispenser of liquid forget-it produced the articles in question and Hopalong, drawing some hurried lines, paid his bill, treated, kept the pencil and headed for the faro game across the street.

When he entered the room the table was deserted and he nodded to the dealer as he seated himself at the right of the case-keeper, who now took his place, and opposite the dealer and the lookout. He was not surprised to find no other players in the room, for the hour was wrong; later in the afternoon there would be many and at night the place would be crowded. This suited him perfectly and he settled himself to begin playing.

When the deck was shuffled and placed in the deal box Hopalong put his ruled paper in front of him on the table, tallied once against the King for the soda card and started to play quarters and half dollars. He caught the fugitive look that passed between the men as they saw his cue-card but he gave no sign of having observed it. After that he never looked up from the cards while his bets were small. Two deals did not alter his money much and he knew that so far the game was straight. If it were not to remain straight the crookedness would not come more than once in a deal if the frame-up was "single-odd" and then not until the bet was large enough to practically break him. His high-card play ran in his favor and kept him gradually drawing ahead. He lost twice in calling the last turn and guessed it right once, at four to one, which made him win in that department of the game.

When the fifth deal began he was quite a little ahead and his play became bolder, some of the bets going as high as ten dollars. He broke even and then played heavier on the following deal. His first high bet, twenty dollars, was on the eight, open, only one eight having shown. Double eights showed on the next turn and he was split, losing half the stake.

It was about this time that the look-out discovered that Mr. Cassidy was getting a little excited and several times had nearly forgotten to keep his cases. This information was cautiously passed to the dealer and case-keeper and from then on they evinced a little more interest in the game. Finally the player, after studying his cue-card, placed fifty dollars on the Queen, open, and coppered the deuce, a case-card, and then put ten more on the high card. This came in the middle of the game and he was prepared for trouble as the turn was made, but fortune was kind to him and he raked in sixty dollars. He was mildly surprised that he had won, but explained it to himself by thinking that the stakes were not yet high enough. From then on he was keenly alert, for the crookedness would come soon if it ever did, but he strung small sums on the next dozen turns and waited for a new deal before plunging.

As the dealer shuffled the cards the door opened and closed noisily and a surprised and doubting voice exclaimed: "Ain't you Hopalong Cassidy? Cassidy, of th' Bar-20?"

Hopalong glanced up swiftly and back to the cards again: "Yes; what of it?"

"Oh, nothin'. I saw you onct an' I wondered if I was right."

"Ain't got time now; see you later, mebby. You might stick around outside so I can borrow some money if I go broke." The man who knew Mr. Cassidy silently faded, but did not stick around, thereby proving that the player knew human nature and also how to get rid of a pest.

When the dealer heard the name he glanced keenly at the owner of it, exchanged significant looks with the case-keeper and faltered for an instant as he shoved the cards together. He was not sure that he had shuffled them right, and an anxious look came into his eyes as he realized that the deal must go on. It was far from reassuring to set out to cheat a man so well known for expert short-gun work as the Bar-20 puncher and he wished he could be relieved. There was no other dealer around at that time of the day and he had to go through with it. He did not dare to shuffle again and chance losing the card beyond hope, and for the reason that the player was watching him like a hawk.

A ten lay face up on the deck and Hopalong, tallying against it on his sheet, began to play small sums. Luck was variable and remained so until the first twenty dollar bet, when he reached out excitedly and raked in his winnings, his coat sleeve at the same time brushing the cue-card off the table. But he had forgotten all about the tally sheet in his eagerness to win and played several more cards before he noticed it was missing and sought for it. Smothering a curse he glanced at the case-keeper's tally and went on with the play. He did not see the look of relief that showed momentarily on the faces of the dealer and his associates, but he guessed it.

He had no use for cue-cards when he felt like doing without them; he liked to see them in use by the players because it showed the game to be more or less straight, and it also saved him from over-heating his memory. When he had brushed his tally sheet off the table he knew what he was doing, and he knew every card that had been drawn out of the box. So far he had seen no signs of cheating and he wished to give the dealer a chance. There should now remain in the deal box three cards, a deuce, five and a four, with a Queen in sight as the last winner. He knew this to be true because he had given all his attention to memorizing the cards as they showed in the deal box, and had made his bets small so he would not have to bother about them. As he had lost three times on a four he now believed it was due to win.

Taking all his money he placed it on the four: "Two hundred and seventy on th' four to win," he remarked, crisply.

The dealer sniffed almost inaudibly and the case-keeper prepared to cover him on the cue-rack under cover of the excitement of the turn. If the four lay under the Queen, Cassidy lost; if not he either won or was in hock. The dealer was unusually grave as he grasped the deal box to make the turn and as the Queen slid off a five-spot showed.

The dealer's hand trembled as he slid the five off, showing a four, and a winner for Hopalong. He went white-he had bungled the shuffle in his indecision and now he did n't know what might develop. And in his agitation he exposed the hock card before he realized what he was doing, and showed another five. He had made the mistake of showing the "odd."

Hopalong, ready for trouble, was more prepared than the others and he was well under way before they started. His left hand swung hard against the case-keeper's jaw, his Colt roared at the drawing bartender, crumpling the trouble-hunter into a heap on the floor dazed from shock of a ball that "creased" his head. He had done this as he sprang to his feet and his left hand, dropping swiftly to the heavy table, threw it over onto the lookout and the dealer at the instant their hands found their guns. Caught off their balance they went down under it and before they could move sufficiently to do any damage, Hopalong vaulted the table and kicked their guns out of their hands. When they realized just what had happened a still-smoking Colt covered them. Many of Hopalong's most successful and spectacular plays had been less carefully thought out beforehand than this one and he laughed sneeringly as he looked at the men who had been so greedy as to try to clean him out the second time.

"Get up!" he snarled.

They crawled out of their trap and sullenly obeyed his hand, backing against the wall. The case-keeper was still unconscious and Hopalong, disarming him, dragged him to the wall with the others.

"I wondered where that deuce had crawled to," Mr. Cassidy remarked, grimly, "an' I was goin' to see, only it's plain now. I knowed you was clumsy, but my G —d! Any man as can't deal 'single-odd' ought to quit th' business, or play straight. So you had five fives agin me, eh? Instead of keepin' th' five under th' Queen, you bungled th' deuce in its place. When you went to pull off th' Queen an' five like they was one card, you had th' deuce under her. You see, I keep cases in my old red head an' I did n't have to believe what th' cue-rack was all fixed to show me. An' I was waitin', all ready for th' play that 'd make me lose.

"As long as this deal was framed up, we 'll say it was this mornin'. You cough up th' hundred an' ten I lost then, an' another hundred an' ten that I 'd won if it was n't crooked. An' don't forget that two-seventy I just pulled down, neither. Make it in double eagles an' don't be slow 'bout it. Money or lead-with *you* callin' th' turn." It was not a very large amount and it took only a moment to count it out. The eleven double eagles representing the mornin's play seemed to slide from the dealer's hand with reluctance-but a man lives only once, and they slid without stopping.

The winner, taking the money, picked up the last money he had bet and, distributing it over his person to equalize the weight, gathered up the guns from the floor. Backing toward the door he noticed that the bartender moved and a keen glance at that unfortunate assured him that he would live.

When he reached the door he stopped a moment to ask a question, the tenseness of his expression relaxing into a broad, apologetic grin. "Would you mind tellin' me where I can find some more frame-ups? I shore can use th' money."

The mumbled replies mentioned a locality not to be found on any map of the surface of the globe, and grinning still more broadly, Mr. Cassidy side-stepped and disappeared to find his horse and go on his way rejoicing.

VIII
The Norther

Johnny knew I had a notebook crammed with the stories his friends had told me; but Johnny, being a wise youth, also knew that there was always room for one more. Perhaps that explains his sarcasm, for, as he calmly turned his back on his fuming friend, he winked at me and sauntered off, whistling cheerfully.

Red spread his feet apart, jammed his fists against his thighs and stared after the youngster. His expression was a study and his open mouth struggled for a retort, but in vain. After a moment he shook his head and slowly turned to me. "Hear th' fool? He 's from *Idyho*, he is. It never gets cold nowhere else on earth. Ain't it terrible to be so ignorant?" He glanced at the bunkhouse, into which Johnny had gone for dry clothing. "So I ain't never seen no cold weather?" he mused thoughtfully. Snapping his fingers irritably, he wheeled toward the corral. "I 'm goin' down to look at th' dam-there 's been lots of water leanin' ag'in it th' last week. Throw th' leather on Saint, if you wants, an' come along. I 'll tell you about some cold weather that had th' *Idyho* brand faded. *Cold* weather! Huh!"

As he swung past the bunkhouse we saw Johnny and Billy Jordan leaning in the doorway ragging each other, as cubs will. Johnny grinned at Red and executed a one-hand phrase of the sign language that is universally known, which Red returned with a chuckle. "Wish he 'd been here th' time God took a hand in a big game on this ranch," he said. "I 'm minus two toes on each foot in consequence thereof. They can't scare me none by preachin' a red-hot hell. No, sir; not any."

He was silent a moment. "Mebby it ain't so bad when a feller is used to it; but we ain't. An' it frequent hits us goin' over th' fence, with both feet off th' ground. Anyhow, that Norther was n't no storm-it was th' attendant agitation caused by th' North Pole visitin' th' Gulf.

"Cowan had just put Buckskin on th' map by buildin' th' first shack. John Bartlett an' Shorty Jones, d —n him, was startin' th' Double Arrow with two hundred head. When th' aforementioned agitation was over they had less 'n one hundred. We lost a lot of cows, too; but our range is sheltered good, an' that rock wall down past Meeker's bunkhouse stopped our drifts, though lots of th' cows died there.

"We 'd had a mild winter for two weeks, an' a lot of rain. We was chirpin' like li'l fool birds about winter bein' over. Ever notice how many times winter is over before it is? But Buck did n't think so; an' he shore can smell weather. We was also discussin' a certain campin' party Jimmy had discovered across th' river. Jimmy was at th' bunkhouse that shift an' he was a great hand for snoopin' around kickin' up trouble. He reports there's twelve in th' party an' they 're camped back of Split Hill. Now, Split Hill is no place for a camp, even in th' summer; an' what got us was th' idea of campin' at all in th' winter. It riled Buck till he forgot to cross off three days on th' calendar, which we later discovered by help of th' almanac an' th' moon. Buck sends Hoppy over to scout around Split Hill. You know Hoppy. He scouted for two days without bein' seen, an' without discoverin' any lawful an' sane reason why twelve hard-lookin' fellers should be campin' back of Split Hill in th' winter time. He also found they had come from th' south, an' he swore there was n't no cow tracks leadin' toward them from our range. But there was lots of hoss tracks back and forth. An' when he reports that th' campers had left an' gone on north we all feel better. Then he adds they turned east below th' Double Arrow an' went back south again. That's different. It's plain to some of us they was lookin' us over for future use; learnin' our ways an' th' lay of th' land. There was seven of us at th' time, but we could 'a' licked 'em in a fair fight.

"In them days we only had two line houses. Number One was near Big Coulee, with Cowan's at th' far end of its fifteen miles of north line; th' west line was a twenty-five-mile ride south to Lookout Peak. Number Two was where th' Jumpin' Bear empties into th' river, now part of Meeker's range. From it th' riders went west twenty-five miles to th' Peak an' north from it twenty-five miles along th' east line. There was a hundred thousan' acres in Conroy Valley an' thirty thousan' in th' Meeker triangle, which made up Section Two. At that time mebby ten thousan' cows was on this section-two-thirds of all of 'em. When we built Number Three on th' Peak this section was cut down to a reasonable size. Th' third headquarters then was th' bunkhouse, with only th' east line to ride. One part, th' shortest, ran north to Cowan's; th' other run about seventeen miles south to Li'l Timber, where th' line went on as part of Number Two's. We paired off an' had two weeks in each of 'em in them days.

"When we shifted at th' end of that week Jimmy Price an' Ace Fisher got Number One; Skinny an' Lanky was in Number Two; an' me an' Buck an' Hoppy took life easy in th' bunkhouse, with th' cook to feed us. Buck, he scouted all over th' ranch between th' lines an' worked harder than any of us, spendin' his nights in th' nearest house.

"One mornin', about a week after th' campers left, Buck looked out of th' bunkhouse door an' cautions me an' Hoppy to ride prepared for cold weather. I can see he 's worried, an' to please him we straps a blanket an' a buffalo robe behind our saddles, cussin' th' size of 'em under our breath. I 've got th' short ride that day, an' Buck says he 'll wait for me to come back, after which we 'll scout around Medicine Bend. He 's still worried about them campers. In th' Valley th' cows are thicker 'n th' other parts of th' range, an' it would n't take no time to get a big herd together. He 's got a few things to mend, so he says he 'll do th' work before I get back.

"Down on Section Two things is happenin' fast, like they mostly do out here. Twelve rustlers can do a lot if they have things planned, an' 'most any fair plan will work once. They only wanted one day-after that it would be a runnin' fight, with eight or nine of 'em layin' back to hold us off while th' others drove th' cows hard. Why, Slippery Trendley an' Tamale Jose was th' only ones that ever slid across our lines with that many men.

"Three rustlers slipped up to Number Two at night an' waited. When Skinny opened th' door in th' mornin' he was drove back with a hole in his shoulder. Then there was h —l a-poppin' in that li'l mud shack. But it did n't do no good, for neither of 'em could get out alive until after dark. They learned that with sorrow, an' pain. An' they shore was het up about it. Ace Fisher, ridin' along th' west line from Number One, was dropped from ambush. Two more rustlers lay back of Medicine Bend lookin' for any of us that might ride down from the bunkhouse. An' they sent two more over to Li'l Timber to lay under that ledge of rock that sticks out of th' south side of th' bluff like a porch roof. Either me or Hoppy would be ridin' that way. They stacked th' deck clever; but Providence cut it square.

"Th' first miss-cue comes when a pert gray wolf lopes past ahead of Hoppy when he 's quite some distance above Li'l Timber. This gray wolf was a whopper, an' Hoppy was all set to get him. He wanted that sassy devil more 'n he wanted money just then, so he starts after it. Mr. Gray Wolf leads him a long chase over th' middle of th' range an' then suddenly disappears. Hoppy hunts around quite a spell, an' then heads back for th' line. While he's huntin' for th' wolf it gets cold, an' it keeps on gettin' colder fast.

"Me, I leaves later 'n usual that mornin'. An' I don't get to Cowan's until late. I 'm there when I notices how cussed cold it's got all of a sudden. Cowan looks at his thermometer, which Jimmy later busts, an' says she has gone down thirty degrees since daylight. He gives me a bottle of liquor Buck wanted, an' I ride west along th' north line, hopin' to meet Jimmy or Ace for a short talk.

"All at once I notice somebody 's pullin' a slate-covered blanket over th' north sky, an' I drag *my* blanket out an' wrap it around me. I 'm gettin' blamed cold, an' also a li'l worried. Shall I go back to Cowan's or head straight for th' bunkhouse? Cowan's the nearest by three miles, but what's three miles out here? It's got a lot colder than it was when I was at Cowan's, an' while I 'm debatin' about it th' wind dies out. I look up an' see that th' slate-covered blanket has traveled fast. It's 'most over my head, an' th' light is gettin' poor. When I look down again I notice my cayuses's ears movin' back an' forth, an' he starts pawin' an' actin' restless. That settles it. I 'm backin' instinct just then, an' I head for home. I ain't cussin' that blanket none now, an' I 'm glad I got th' robe handy; an' that quart of liquor ain't bulky no more.

"All at once th' bottom falls out of that lead sky, an' flakes as big as quarters sift down so fast they hurts my eyes, an' so thick I can't see twenty feet. In ten minutes everythin' is white, an' in ten more I 'm in a strange country. My hands an' feet ache with cold, an' I 'm drawin' th' blanket closer, when there 's a puff of wind so cold it cuts into my back like a knife. It passes quick, but it don't fool me. I know what's behind it. I reach for th' robe an' has it 'most unfastened when there 's a roar an' I 'm 'most unseated by th' wind before I can get set. I did n't know then that it's goin' to blow that hard for three days, an' it's just as well. It's full of ice-li'l slivers that are sharp as needles an' cut an' sting till they make th' skin raw. I let loose of th' robe an' tie my bandanna around my face, so my nose an' mouth is covered. My throat burns already almost to my lungs. Good Lord, but it *is* cold! My hands are stiff when I go back for th' robe, an' it's all I can do to keep it from blowin' away from me. It takes me a long time to get it over th' blanket, an' my hands are 'most froze when it's fastened. That was a good robe, but it did n't make much difference that day. Th' cold cuts through it an' into my back as if it was n't there. My feet are gettin' worse all th' time, an' it ain't long before I ain't got none, for th' achin' stops at th' ankles. Purty soon only my knees ache, an' I know it won't be long till they won't ache no more.

"I 'm squirmin' in my clothes tryin' to rub myself warm when I remember that flask of liquor. Th' cork was out far enough for my teeth to get at it, an' I drink a quarter of it quick. It's an awful load-any other time it would 'a' knocked me cold, for Cowan sold a lot worse stuff then than he does now. But it don't phase me, except for takin' most of th' linin' out of my mouth an' throat. It warms me a li'l, an' it makes my knees ache a li'l harder. But it don't last long-th' cold eats through me just as hard as ever a li'l later, an' then I begin to see things an' get sleepy. Cows an' cayuses float around in th' air, an' I 'm countin' money, piles of it. I get warm an' drowsy an' find myself noddin'. That scares me a li'l, an' I fight hard ag'in it. If I go to sleep it's all over. It keeps gettin' worse, an' I finds my eyes shuttin' more an' more frequent, an' more an' more frequent thinkin' I don't care, anyhow. An' so I drifts along pullin' at th' bottle till it's empty. That should 'a' killed me, then an' there-but it don't even make me real drunk. Mebby I spilled some of it, my hands bein' nothin' but sticks. I can't see more 'n five feet now, an' my eyes water, which freezes on 'em. I 've given up all hope of hearin' any shootin'. So I close th' peekhole in th' blanket an' robe, drawin' 'em tight to keep out some of th' cold. I am sittin' up stiff in th' saddle, like a soldier, just from force of habit, and after a li'l while I don't know nothin' more. Pete says I was a corpse, froze stiff as a ramrod, an' he calls me ghost for a long time in fun. But Pete was n't none too clear in his head about that time.

"Down at Li'l Timber, Hoppy managed to get under th' shelter of that projectin' ledge of rock on th' south side of th' bluff. Th' snow an' ice is whirlin' under it because of a sort of back draft, but th' wind don't hit so hard. He 's fightin' that cayuse every foot, tryin' to get to th' cave at th' west end, an' disputin' th' right of way with th' cows that are packed under it.

There 's firewood under that ledge an' there 's food on th' hoof, an' snow water for drink; so if he can make th' cave he 's safe. He 's more worried about his supply of smokin' tobacco than anythin' else, so far as he 's concerned.

"All at once he runs onto four men huddled half-froze in a bunch right ahead of him. He knows in a flash who they are, an' he draws fumblingly, an' holds th' gun in his two hands, they are so cold. One clean hit an' five clean misses in twenty feet! They're gropin' for their guns when a sudden gust of wind whirls down from th' top of th' hill, pilin' snow an' ice on 'em till they can't see nor breathe. An' a couple of old trees come down to make things nicer. Hoppy is blinded, an' when he gets so he can see again there's one rustler's arm stickin' up out of th' snow, but no signs of th' other three. They blundered out into th' open tryin' to get away from th' stuff comin' down on 'em, an' that means they won't be back no more.

"Hoppy manages to get to th' cave, tie his cayuse to a fallen tree, an' gather enough firewood for a good blaze, which he puts in front of th' cave. It takes him a long time to use up his matches one by one, an' then he pulls th' lead out of a cartridge with his teeth, shakes th' powder loose in it an' along th' barrel. Usin' his cigarette papers for tinder he gets th' fire started an' goin' good an' is feelin' some cheerful when he remembers th' three rustlers driftin' south. They was bound to hit a big arroyo that would lead 'em almost ag'in' Number Two's door. With th' wind drivin' 'em straight for it, Hoppy thinks it might mean trouble for Lanky or Skinny. He did n't think about 'em only havin' wool-lined slickers on, or he 'd 'a' knowed they couldn't live till they got halfway. They left their blankets in camp so they could work fast.

"People have called us clannish, an' said we was a lovin' bunch' because we stick together so tight. We 've faced so much together that us of th' old bunch has got th' same blood in our veins. We ain't eight men-we 're one man in eight different kinds of bodies. G —d help anybody that tries to make us less! It's one thing to stand up an' swap shots with a gunman; but it's another to turn yore back on a cave an' a fire like that an' go out into what is purty nigh shore death on a long chance of helpin' a couple of friends that was able to take care of themselves. That's one of th' things that explains why we made Shorty Jones an' his eleven men pay with their lives for takin' Jimmy's life. Twelve for one! That fight at Buckskin ain't generally understood, even by our friends. An' Hoppy crowns his courage twice in that one storm. Ain't he an old son-of-a-gun?

"He leaves that fire an' forces his cayuse to take him out in th' storm again, finds that th' arroyo is level full of snow, but has both banks swept bare. He passes them three rustlers in th' next ten minutes-they won't do no more cow-liftin'. Then he tries to turn back, but that's foolish. So he drifts on, gettin' a li'l loco by now. He 's purty near asleep when he thinks he hears a shot. He fights his cayuse again, but can't stop it, so he falls off an' lets it drift, an' crawls an' fights his way back to where that shot was fired from. G —d only knows how he does it, but he falls over a cow an' sees Lanky huggin' its belly for th' li'l warmth in th' carcass. An' he ought to 'a' found him, after leavin' his cayuse an' turnin' back on foot in that h —l storm! Th' drifts was beginnin' to make then-when th' storm was over I saw drifts thirty feet high in th' open; an' in th' valley there was some that run 'most to th' top of th' bluffs, an' they're near sixty feet high.

"Well, Lanky is as crazy as him, an' won't let go of that cow, an' they have a fight, which is good for both of 'em. Finally Lanky gets some sense in his head an' realizes what Hoppy is tryin' to do for him, an' they go staggerin' down wind, first one fallin' an' then th' other. But they keep fightin' like th' game boys they are, neither givin' a cuss for himself, but shore obstinate that he 's goin' to get th' other out of it. That's *our* spirit; an' we 're proud of it, by G—d! Hoppy wraps th' robe around Lanky, an' so they stagger on, neither one knowin' very much by that time. Th' Lord must 'a' pitied that pair, an' admired th' stuff He 'd put in 'em, for they bump into th' line house kerslam, an' drop, all done an' exhausted.

"Meanwhile Skinny's hoppin' around inside, prayin' an' cussin' by streaks, every five minutes openin' th' door an' firm' off his Colt. He has tied th' two ropes together, an' frequent he ties one end to th' door, th' other to hisself, an' goes out pokin' around in th' snow, hopin' to stumble over his pardner. He 's plumb forgot his bad shoulder long ago. Purty soon he opens th' door again to shoot off th' gun, an' in streaks somethin' between his laigs. He slams th' door as he jumps aside, an' then looks scared at Lanky's sombrero! Mebby he's slow hoppin' outside an' diggin' them out of th' drift that's near covered 'em! Now, don't think bad of Skinny. He dass n't leave th' house to search any distance, even if he could 'a' seen anythin'. His best play is to stick there an' shoot off his gun-Lanky might drift past if he was not there to signal. Skinny thought more of Lanky any time than he did of hisself, th' emaciated match!

"It don't take long to kick in a lot of snow with that wind blowin' an' he rubs them two till he 's got tears in his eyes. Then he fills 'em with hot stew an' whisky, rolls 'em up together an' heaves 'em in th' same bunk. It ain't warm enough in that house, even with th' fire goin', to make 'em lose no arms or laigs.

"It seems that Lanky, watchin' his chance as soon as th' snow fell heavy enough to cover his movements, slipped out of th' house an' started to circle out around them festive rustlers that held him an' his friend prisoners. He made Skinny stay behind to hold th' house an' keep a gun poppin'. Lanky has worked up behind where th' rustlers was layin' when th' Norther strikes full force. It near blows him over, an', not havin' on nothin' but an old army overcoat that was wore out, th' cold gets him quick. He can't see, an' he can't hear Skinny's shots no more! He does th' best he can an' tries to fight back along his trail, but in no time there ain't no tracks to follow. Then he loses his head an' starts wanderin' until a cow blunders down on him. He shoots th' cow an' hugs its belly to keep warm an' then he don't really remember nothin' 'till he wakes up in th' bunk alongside of Hoppy, both gettin' over an awful drunk. Skinny kept feedin' liquor to 'em till it was gone, an' he had a plenty when he began.

"Jimmy Price was at Number One when th' blow started, an' Buck was in th' bunkhouse, an' it was three weeks before they could get out an' around, on account of th' snow fallin' so steady an' hard they could n't see nothin'.

"Well, getting back to me explains how Pete Wilson came to th' Bar-20. He is migratin' south, just havin' had th' pleasure of learnin' that his wife sloped with a better-lookin' man. He was scared she might get tired of th' other feller an' sift back, so he sells out his li'l store, loads a waggin with blankets, grub, an' firewood, an' starts south, winter or no winter. He moves fast for a new range, where he can make a new beginnin' an' start life fresh, with five years of burnin' matrimonial experience as his valuablest asset. Pete says he reckoned mebby he would n't have so many harness sores if he run single th' rest of his life; heretofore he 'd been so busy applyin' salve that he did n't have time to find out just what was th' trouble with th' double harness. Lots of men feel that way, but they ain't got Pete's unlovely outspoken habit of thought. We used to reckon mebby he was n't as smart as th' rest of us, him bein' slow an' blunderin' in his retorts. We 've played that with coppers lots of times since, though. While he ain't what you 'd call quick at retortin', his retorts usually is heard by th' whole county. It ain't every collar-galled husband that's got th' gumption or smartness to jump th' minute th' hat is lifted. Pete had.

"He's drivin' across our range, an' when th' wind dies out sudden an' th' snow sifts down, he 's just smart enough to get out his beddin' an' wrap it around him till he looks like a bale of cotton. An' even at that he 's near froze an' lookin' for a place to make a stand when he feels a bump. It's me, fallin' off my cayuse, against his front wheel. He emerges from his beddin', lifts me into th' waggin, puts most of his blankets around me, an' stops. Knowin' he can't save th' cayuses, he shoots 'em. That means grub for us, anyhow, if we run short of th' good stuff. Nobody but Pete could 'a' got th' canvas off that waggin in such a gale, but he did it. He busts th' arches an' slats off th' top of th' waggin an' uses 'em for firewood. Th' canvas he drapes over th' box, lettin' it hang down on both sides to th' ground. An' in about five minutes th' whole thing was covered over with snow. Pete 's the strongest man we ever saw, an' we 've seen some good ones. Wrastlin' that canvas with stiff hands was a whole lot more than what he done to Big Sandy up there on Thunder Mesa.

"Pete says I was dead when he grabbed me, an' smellin' disgraceful of liquor. But th' first thing I know is lookin' up in th' gloom at a ceilin' that's right close to my head, an' at a sorta rafter. That rafter gives me a shock. It don't even touch th' ceilin', but runs along 'most a foot below it. I close my eyes an' do a lot of thinkin'. I remember freezin' to death, but that's all. An' just then I hears a faint voice say: 'He shore was dead.' I don't know Pete then, or that he talked to hisself sometimes. An' I reckon I was a li'l off in my head, at that. I begin to wonder if he means me, an' purty soon I 'm shore of it. An' don't I sympathize with myself? I 'm dead an' gone somewhere; but no preacher I ever heard ever described no place like this. Then I smell smoke an' burnin' meat-which gives me a clew to th' range I 'm on. Mebby I 'm shelved in th' ice box, waitin' my turn, or somethin'. I knew I 'd led a sinful life. But there wasn't no use of rubbin' it in-it's awful to be dead an' know it.

"Th' next time I opens my eyes I can't see nothin'; but I can feel somethin' layin' alongside of me. It's breathin' slow an' regular, an it bothers me till I get th' idea all of a sudden. It's another dead one, cut out of th' herd an' shoved in my corral to wait for subsequent events. I felt sorry for him, an' lay there tryin' to figger it out, an' I 'm still figgerin' when it starts to get light. Th' other feller grunts an' sits up, bumpin' his head solid against that fool rafter. No dead man that was shoved in a herd consigned to heaven ever used such language, which makes me all the shorer of where I am. But if hell's hot we 've still got a long way to go.

"He sits there rubbin' his head an' cussin' steadily, an' I 'm so moved by it that I compliments him. He jumps an' bumps his head again, an' looks at me close. 'D —d if you ain't a husky corpse,' he says. That settles it. I ain't crazy, like I was hopin', but I 'in dead. 'You an' me is on th' ragged edge of h —l,' he adds.

"But who tipped *you* off?' I asks. 'They just shoved me in here an' did n't tell me nothin' at all.'

"'Crazy as th' devil,' he grunts, lookin' at me harder.

"Yo 're a liar,' I replies. 'I may be dead, but d —d if I 'm crazy!'

"'An' I don't blame you, either,' he mused, sorrowful. 'Now you keep quiet till I gets somethin' to eat,' an' he crawls into a li'l round hole at th' other end of th' room.

"Purty soon I smell smoke again, an' after a long time he comes back with some hot coffee an' burned meat. I grab for th' grub, an' while I 'm eatin' I demands to know where I am.

"He laughs, real cheerful, an' tells me. I 'm under his waggin, surrounded by canvas an' any G —d's quantity of snow. Th' drift over us is fifteen foot high, th' wind has died down, an' it's still snowin' so hard he can't see twenty feet. It is also away down below freezin'.

"We stayed under that drift 'most three weeks, livin' on raw meat after our firewood gave out. We didn't suffer none from th' cold, though, under all that snow an' with all th' blankets we had. When it stopped snowin' we discovered a drift shamefully high about a mile northeast of us, an' from th' smoke comin' out of it I knew it was th' bunkhouse.

"Well, to cut it short, it was. An' mebby Buck wasn't glad to see me! He was worried 'most sick an' as soon as we could, we got cayuses and started out to look for th' others, scared stiff at what we expected to find."

He paused and was silent a moment. "But only Ace was missin'," he added. "We found him an' th' rustlers later, when th' snow went off."

He paused again and shook his head. "It shore was a miracle that we did n't go with 'em, all of us, except Buck. Pete was so plumb disgusted with travelin' in th' winter, an' had lost his cayuses, that when Buck offers him Ace's bunk he stays. An' he ain't never left us since. Huh! Cold? That cub don't know nothin' —mebby he will when he grows up, but I dunno, at that. *Idyho!*"

IX
The Drive

The Norther was a thing of the past, but it left its mark on Buck Peters, whose grimness of face told what the winter had been to him. His daily rides over the range, the reports of his men since that deadly storm had done a great deal to lift the sagging weight that rested on his shoulders; but he would not be sure until the round-up supplied facts and figures.

That the losses had not been greater he gave full credit to the valley with its arroyos, rock walls, draws, heavily grassed range and groves of timber; for the valley, checking the great southward drift by its steep ridges of rock, sheltered the herds in timber and arroyos and fed them on the rich profusion of its grasses, which, by some trick of the rushing winds, had been whirled clean of snow.

But over the cow-country, north, east, south and west, where vast ranges were unprotected against the whistling blasts from the north, the losses had been stupendous, appalling, stunning. Outfits had been driven on and on before the furious winds, sleepy and apathetic, drifting steadily southward in the white, stinging shroud to a drowsy death. Whole herds, blindly moving before the wind, left their weaker units in constantly growing numbers to mark the trail, and at last lay down to a sleep eternal. And astonishing and incredible were the distances traveled by some of those herds.

Following the Norther came another menace and one which easily might surpass the worst efforts of the blizzard. Warm winds blew steadily, a hot sun glared down on the snow-covered plain and then came torrents of rain which continued for days, turning the range into a huge expanse of water and mud and swelling the water-courses with turgid floods that swirled and roared above their banks. Should this be quickly followed by cold, even the splendid valley would avail nothing. Ice, forming over the grasses, would prove as deadly as a pestilence; the cattle, already weakened by the hardships of the Norther, and not having the instinct to break through the glassy sheet and feed on the grass underneath, would search in vain for food, and starve to death. The week that followed the cessation of the rains started gray hairs on the foreman's head; but a warm, constant sun and warm winds dried off the water before the return of freezing weather. The herds were saved.

Relieved, Buck reviewed the situation. The previous summer had seen such great northern drives to the railroad shipping points in Kansas that prices fell until the cattlemen refused to sell. Rather than drive home again, the great herds were wintered on the Kansas ranges, ready to be hurled on the market when Spring came with better prices. Many ranches, mortgaged heavily to buy cattle, had been on the verge of bankruptcy, hoping feverishly for better prices the following year. Buck had taken advantage of the situation to stock his ranch at a cost far less than he had dared to dream. Then came the Norther and in the three weeks of devastating cold and high winds the Kansas ranges were swept clean of cattle, and even the ranges in 'the South were badly crippled. Knowing this, Buck also knew that the following Spring would show record high prices. If he had the cattle he could clean up a fortune for his ranch; and if his herd was the first big one to reach the railroad at Sandy Creek it would practically mean a bonus on every cow.

Under the long siege of uncertainty his impatience smashed through and possessed him as a fever and he ordered the calf round-up three weeks earlier than it ever had been held on the ranch. There was no need of urging his men to the task-they, like himself, sprang to the call like springs freed from a restraining weight, and the work went on in a fever of haste. And he took his place on the firing line and worked even harder than his outfit of fanatics.

One day shortly after the work began a stranger rode up to him and nodded cheerfully. "Li'l early, ain't you?" Buck grunted in reply and sent Skinny off at top speed to close a threatened gap in the lengthy driving line. "Goin' to git 'em on th' trail early this year?" persisted the stranger. Buck, swayed by some swift intuition, changed his reply. "Oh, I dunno; I 'm mainly anxious to see just what that storm did. An' I hate th' calf burnin' so much I allus like to get it over quick." He shouted angrily at the cook and waved his arms frantically to banish the chuck wagon. "He can make more trouble with that waggin than anybody I ever saw," he snorted. "Get out of there, you fool!" he yelled, dashing off to see his words obeyed. The cook, grinning cheerfully at his foreman's language and heat, forthwith chose a spot that was not destined to be the center of the cut-out herd. And when Buck again thought of the stranger he saw a black dot moving toward the eastern skyline.

The crowded days rolled on, measured full from dawn to dark, each one of them a panting, straining, trying ordeal. Worn out, the horses were turned back into the temporary corral or to graze under the eyes of the horse wranglers, and fresh ones took up their work; and woe unto the wranglers if the supply fell below the demand. For the tired men there was no relief, only a shifting in the kind of work they did, and they drove themselves with grave determination, their iron wills overruling their aching bodies. First came the big herds in the valley; then, sweeping north, they combed the range to the northern line in one grand, mad fury of effort that lasted day after day until the tally man joyously threw away his chewed pencil and gladly surrendered the last sheet to the foreman. The first half of the game was over. Gone as if it were a nightmare was the confusion of noise and dust and cows that hid a remarkable certainty of method. But as if to prove it not a dream, four thousand cows were held in three herds on the great range, in charge of the extra men.

Buck, leading the regular outfit from the north line and toward the bunkhouse, added the figures of the last tally sheet to the totals he had in a little book, and smiled with content. Behind him, cheerful as fools, their bodies racking with weariness, their faces drawn and gaunt, knowing that their labors were not half over, rode the outfit, exchanging chaff and banter in an effort to fool themselves into the delusion that they were fresh and "chipper." Nearing the bunkhouse they cheered lustily as they caught sight of the hectic cook laboring profanely with two balking pintos that had backed his wagon half over the edge of a barranca and then refused to pull it back again. Cookie's reply, though not a cheer, was loud and pregnant with feeling. To think that he had driven those two animals for the last two weeks from one end of the ranch to the other without a mishap, and then have them balance him and his wagon on the crumbling edge of a twenty-foot drop when not a half mile from the bunkhouse, thus threatening the loss of the wagon and all it contained and the mangling of his sacred person! And to make it worse, here came a crowd of whooping idiots to feast upon his discomfiture.

The outfit, slowing so as not to frighten the devilish pintos and start them backing again, drew near; and suddenly the air became filled with darting ropes, one of which settled affectionately around Cookie's apoplectic neck. In no time the strangling, furious dough-king was beyond the menace of the crumbling bank, flat on his back in the wagon, where he had managed to throw himself to escape the whistling hoofs that quickly turned the dashboard into matchwood. When he managed to get the rope from his neck he arose, unsteady with rage, and choked as he tried to speak before the grinning and advising outfit. Before he could get command over his tongue the happy bunch wheeled and sped on its way, shrieking with mirth unholy. They had saved him from probable death, for Cookie was too obstinate to have jumped from the wagon; but they not only forfeited all right to thanks and gratitude, but deserved horrible deaths for the conversation they had so audibly carried on while they worked out the cook's problem. And their departing words and gestures made homicide justifiable and a duty. It was in this frame of mind that Cookie watched them go.

Buck, emerging from the bunkhouse in time to see the rescue, leaned against the door and laughed as he had not laughed for one heart-breaking winter. Drying his eyes on the back of his hand, he looked at the bouncing, happy crowd tearing southward with an energy of arms and legs and lungs that seemed a miracle after the strain of the round-up. Just then a strange voice made him wheel like a flash, and he saw Billy Williams sitting solemnly on his horse near the corner of the house.

"Hullo, Williams," Buck grunted, with no welcoming warmth in his voice. "What th' devil brings *you* up here?"

"I want a job," replied Billy. The two, while never enemies nor interested in any mutual disagreements, had never been friends. They never denied a nodding acquaintance, nor boasted of it. "That Norther shore raised h —l. There 's ten men for every job, where I came from."

The foreman, with that quick decision that was his in his earlier days, replied crisply. "It's your'n. Fifty a month, to start."

"Keno. Lemme chuck my war-bag through that door an' I'm ready," smiled Billy. He believed he would like this man when he knew him better. "I thought th' Diamond Bar, over east a hundred mile, had weathered th' storm lucky. You got 'em beat. They 're movin' heaven an' earth to get a herd on the trail, but they did n't have no job for *me*," he laughed, flushing slightly. "Sam Crawford owns it," he explained naïvely.

Buck laughed outright. "I reckon you did n't have much show with Sam, after that li'l trick you worked on him in Fenton. So Sam is in this country? How are they fixed?"

"They aims to shove three thousan' east right soon. It's fancy prices for th' first herd that gets to Sandy Creek," he offered. "I heard they 're havin' lots of wet weather along th' Comanchee; mebby Sam 'll have trouble a-plenty gettin' his herd acrost. Cows is plumb aggervatin' when it comes to crossin' rivers," he grinned.

Buck nodded. "See that V openin' on th' sky line?" he asked, pointing westward. "Ride for it till you see th' herd. Help 'em with it. We 'll pick it up t'morrow." He turned on his heel and entered the house, grave with a new worry. He had not known that there was a ranch where Billy had said the Diamond Bar was located; and a hundred miles handicap meant much in a race to Sandy Creek. Crawford was sure to drive as fast as he dared. He was glad that Billy had mentioned it, and the wet weather along the Comanchee-Billy already had earned his first month's pay.

All that day and the next the consolidation of the three herds and the preparation for the drive went on. Sweeping up from the valley the two thousand three- and four-year-olds met and joined the thousand that waited between Little Timber and Three Rocks; and by nightfall the three herds were one by the addition of the thousand head from Big Coulee. Four thousand head of the best cattle on the ranch spent the night within gunshot of the bunkhouse and corrals on Snake Creek.

Buck, returning from the big herd, smiled as he passed the chuck-wagon and heard Cookie's snores, and went on, growing serious all too quickly. At the bunkhouse he held a short consultation with his regular outfit and then returned to the herd again while his drive crew turned eagerly to their bunks. Breakfast was eaten by candle light and when the eastern sky faded into a silver gray Skinny Thompson vaulted into the saddle and loped eastward without a backward glance. The sounds of his going scarcely had died out before Hopalong, relieved of the responsibilities of trail boss, shouldered others as weighty and rode into the north-east with Lanky at his side. Behind him, under charge of Red, the herd started on its long and weary journey to Sandy Creek, every man of the outfit so imbued with the spirit of the race that even with its hundred miles' advantage the Diamond Bar could not afford to waste an hour if it hoped to win.

Out of the side of a verdant hill, whispering and purling, flowed a small stream and shyly sought the crystal depths of a rock-bound pool before gaining courage enough to flow gently over the smooth granite lip and scurry down the gentle slope of the arroyo. To one side of it towered a splinter of rock, slender and gray, washed clean by the recent rains. To the south of it lay a baffling streak a little lighter than the surrounding grass lands. It was, perhaps, a quarter of a mile wide and ended only at the horizon. This faint band was the Dunton trail, not used enough to show the strong characteristics of the depressed bands found in other parts of the cow-country. If followed it would lead one to Dunton's Ford on the Comanchee, forty miles above West Bend, where the Diamond Bar aimed to cross the river.

The shadow of the pinnacle drew closer to its base and had crossed the pool when Skinny Thompson rode slowly up the near bank of the ravine, his eyes fixed smilingly on the splinter of rock. He let his mount nuzzle and play with the pool for a moment before stripping off the saddle and turning the animal loose to graze. Taking his rifle in the hope of seeing game, he went up to the top of the hill, glanced westward and then turned and gazed steadily into the northeast, sweeping slowly over an arc of thirty degrees. He stood so for several minutes and then grunted with satisfaction and returned to the pool. He had caught sight of a black dot far away on the edge of the skyline that split into two parts and showed a sidewise drift. Evidently his friends would be on time. Of the herd he had seen no sign, which was what he had expected.

When at last he heard hoofbeats he arose lazily and stretched, chiding himself for falling asleep, and met his friends as they turned into sight around the bend of the hill. "Reckoned you might 'a' got lost," he grinned sleepily.

"G'wan!" snorted Lanky.

"What'd you find?" eagerly demanded Hopalong.

"Three thousan' head on th' West Bend trail five days ahead of us," replied Skinny. "Ol' Sam is drivin' hard." He paused a moment. "Acts like he knows we 're after him. Anyhow, I saw that feller that visited us on th' third day of th' round-up. So I reckon Sam knows."

Lanky grinned. "He won't drive so hard later. I 'd like to see him when he sees th' Comanchee! Bet it's a lake south of Dunton's 'cordin' to what we found. But it ain't goin' to bother us a whole lot."

Hopalong nodded, dismounted and drew a crude map in the sand of the trail. Skinny watched it, grave and thoughtful until, all at once, he understood. His sudden burst of laughter startled his companions and they exchanged foolish grins. It appeared that from Dunton's Ford north, in a distance of forty miles, the Comanchee was practically born. So many feeders, none of them formidable, poured into it that in that distance it attained the dignity of a river. Hopalong's plan was to drive off at a tangent running a little north from the regular trail and thus cross numerous small streams in preference to going on straight and facing the swollen Comanchee at Dunton's Ford. As the regular trail turned northward when not far from Sandy Creek they were not losing time. Laughing gaily they mounted and started west for the herd which toiled toward them many miles away. Thanks to the forethought that had prompted their scouting expedition the new trail was picked out in advance and there would be no indecision on the drive.

Eighty miles to the south lay the fresh trail of the Diamond Bar herd, and five days' drive eastward on it, facing the water-covered lowlands at West Bend, Sam Crawford held his herd, certain that the river would fall rapidly in the next two days. It was the regular ford, and the best on the river. The water did fall, just enough to lure him to stay; but, having given orders at dark on the second night for an attempt at crossing at daylight the next morning, he was amazed when dawn showed him the river was back to its first level.

Sam was American born, but affected things English and delighted in spelling "labor" and like words with a "u." He hated hair chaps and maintained that the gun-play of the West was mythical and existed only in the minds of effete Easterners. Knowing that, it was startling to hear him tell of Plummer, Hickock, Roberts, Thompson and a host of other gunmen who had splotched the West with blood. Not only did every man of that section pack a gun, but Crawford, himself, packed one, thus proving himself either a malicious liar or an imbecile. He acted as though the West belonged to him and that he was the arbiter of its destiny and its chosen historian-which made him troublesome on the great, free ranges. Only that his pretensions and his crabbed, irascible, childish temper made him ludicrous he might have been taken seriously, to his sorrow. Failing miserably at law, he fled from such a precarious livelihood, beset with a haunting fear that he had lost his grip, to an inherited ranch. This fear that pursued him turned him into a carping critic of those who excelled him in most things, except in fits of lying about the West as it existed at that time.

When he found that the river was over the lowlands again he became furious and, carried away by rage, shouted down the wiser counsel of his clear-headed night boss and ordered the herd into the water. Here and there desperate, wild-eyed steers wheeled and dashed back through the cordon of riders, their numbers constantly growing as the panic spread. The cattle in the front ranks, forced into the swirling stream by the pressure from the rear, swam with the current and clambered out below, adding to the confusion. Steers fought throughout the press and suddenly, out of the right wing of the herd, a dozen crazed animals dashed out in a bunch for the safety of the higher ground; and after them came the herd, an irresistible avalanche of maddened beef. It was not before dark that they were rounded up into a nervous, panicky herd once more. The next morning they were started north along the river, to try again at Dunton's Ford, which they reached in three days, and where another attempt at crossing the river proved in vain.

Meanwhile the Bar-20 herd pushed on steadily with no confusion. It crossed the West Run one noon and the upper waters of the Little Comanchee just before dark on the same day. Next came East Run, Pawnee Creek and Ten Mile Creek, none of them larger than the stream the cattle were accustomed to back on the ranch. Another day's drive brought them to the west branch of the Comanchee itself, the largest of all the rivers they would meet. Here they were handled cautiously and "nudged" across with such care that a day was spent in the work. The following afternoon the east branch held them up until the next day and then, with a clear trail, they were sent along on the last part of the long journey.

When Sam Crawford, forced to keep on driving north along the Little Comanchee, saw that wide, fresh trail, he barely escaped apoplexy and added the finishing touches to the sullenness of his outfit. Seeing the herd across, he gave orders for top speed and drove as he never had driven before; and when the last river had been left behind he put the night boss in charge of the cattle and rode on ahead to locate his rivals of the drive. Three days later, when he returned to his herd, he was in a towering fury and talked constantly of his rights and an appeal to law, and so nagged his men that mutiny stalked in his shadow.

When the Bar-20 herd was passing to the south of the little village of Depau, Hopalong turned back along the trail to find the Diamond Bar herd. So hard had Sam pushed on that he was only two days' drive behind Red and his outfit when Hopalong rode smilingly into the Diamond Bar camp. He was talking pleasantly of shop to some of the Diamond Bar punchers when Sam dashed up and began upbraiding him and threatening dire punishment. Hopalong, maintaining a grave countenance, took the lacing meekly and humbly as he winked at the grinning punchers. Finally, after exasperating Sam to a point but one degree removed from explosion, he bowed cynically, said "so-long" to the friendly outfit and loped away toward his friends. Sam, choking with rage, berated his punchers for not having thrown out the insulting visitor and commanded more speed, which was impossible. Reporting to Red the proximity of their rivals, Hopalong fell in line and helped drive the herd a little faster. The cattle were in such condition from the easy traveling of the last week that they could easily stand the pace if Crawford's herd could. So the race went on, Red keeping the same distance ahead day after day.

Then came the night when Sandy Creek lay but two days' drive away. A storm had threatened since morning and the first lightning of the drive was seen. The cattle were mildly restless when Hopalong rode in at midnight and he was cheerfully optimistic. He was also very much awake, and after trying in vain to get to sleep he finally arose and rode back along the trail toward the stragglers, which Jimmy and Lanky were holding a mile away. Red had pushed on to the last minute of daylight and Lanky had decided to hold the stragglers instead of driving them up to the main herd so they would start even with it the following morning. It was made up of the cattle that had found the drive too much for them and was smaller than the outfit had dared to hope for.

Hopalong had just begun to look around for the herd when it passed him with sudden uproar. Shouting to a horseman who rode furiously past, he swung around and raced after him, desperately anxious to get in front of the stampede to try to check it before it struck the main herd and made the disaster complete. For the next hour he was in a riot of maddened cattle and shaved death many times by the breadth of a hand. He could hear Jimmy and Lanky shouting in the black void, now close and now far away. Then the turmoil gradually ceased and the remnant of the herd paused, undecided whether to stop or go on. He flung himself at it and by driving cleverly managed to start a number of cows to milling, which soon had the rest following suit. The stampede was over. A cursing blot emerged from the darkness and hailed. It was Lanky, coldly ferocious. He had not heard Jimmy for a long time and feared that the boy might be lying out on the black plain, trampled into a shapeless mass of flesh. One stumble in front of the charging herd would have been sufficient.

Daylight disclosed the missing Jimmy hobbling toward the breakfast fire at the cook wagon. He was bruised and bleeding and covered with dirt, his clothes ripped and covered with mud; and every bone and muscle in his body was alive with pain.

The Diamond Bar's second squad had ridden in to breakfast when a horseman was seen approaching at a leisurely lope. Sam, cursing hotly, instinctively fumbled at the gun he wore at his thigh in defiance to his belief concerning the wearing of guns. He blinked anxiously as the puncher stopped at the wagon and smiled a heavy-eyed salutation. The night boss emerged from the shelter of the wagon and grinned a sheepish welcome. "Well, Cassidy, you fellers got th' trail somehow. We was some surprised when we hit yore trail. How you makin' it?"

"All right, up to last night," replied Hopalong, shaking hands with the night boss. "Got a match, Barnes?" he asked, holding up an unlighted cigarette. They talked of things connected with the drive and Hopalong cautiously swung the conversation around to mishaps, mentioning several catastrophes of past years. After telling of a certain stampede he had once seen, he turned to Barnes and asked a blunt question. "What would you do to anybody as stampeded yore stragglers within a mile of th' main herd on a stormy night?" The answer was throaty and rumbling. "Why, shoot him, I reckon." The others intruded their ideas and Crawford squirmed, his hand seeking his gun under the pretense of tightening his belt.

Hopalong arose and went to his horse, where a large bundle of canvas was strapped behind the saddle. He loosened it and unrolled it on the ground. "Ever see this afore, boys?" he asked, stepping back. Barnes leaped to his feet with an ejaculation of surprise and stared at the canvas. "Where'd you git it?" he demanded. "That's our old wagon cover!"

Hopalong, ignoring Crawford, looked around the little group and smiled grimly. "Well, last night our stragglers was stampeded. Lanky told me he saw somethin' gray blow past him in th' darkness, an' then th' herd started. We managed to turn it from th' trail an' so it did n't set off our main herd. Jimmy was near killed-well, you know what it is to ride afore stampeded cows. I found this cover blowed agin' a li'l clump of trees, an' when I sees yore mark, I reckoned I ought to bring it back." He dug into his pocket and brought out a heavy clasp knife. "I just happened to see this not far from where th' herd started from, so I reckoned I 'd return it, too." He held it out to Barnes, who took it with an oath and wheeled like a flash to face his employer.

Crawford was backing toward the wagon, his hand resting on the butt of his gun, and a whiteness of face told of the fear that gripped him. "I 'll take my time, right now," growled Barnes. "D —d if I works another day for a low-lived coyote that 'd do a thing like that!" The punchers behind him joined in and demanded their wages. Hopalong, still smiling, waved his hand and spoke. "Don't leave him with all these cows on his hands, out here on th' range. If you quits him, wait till you get to Sandy Creek. He ain't no man, he ain't; he 's a nasty lil brat of a kid that couldn't never grow up into a man. So, that bein' true, he ain't goin' to get handled like a man. I 'm goin' to lick him, 'stead of shootin' him like he was a man. You know," he smiled, glancing around the little circle, "us cowpunchers don't never carry guns. We don't swear, nor wear chaps, even if all of us has got 'em on right now. We say 'please' an' 'thank you' an' never get mad. Not never wearin' a gun I can't shoot him; but, by G —d, I can lick him th' worst he's ever been licked, an' I 'm goin' to do it right now." He wheeled to start after the still-backing cowman, and leaped sideways as a cloud of smoke swirled around his hips. Crawford screamed with fear and pain as his Colt tore loose from his fingers and dropped near the wheel of the wagon. Terror gripped him and made him incapable of flight. Who was this man, *what* was he, when he could draw and fire with such speed and remarkable accuracy? Crawford's gun had been half raised before the other had seen it. And before his legs could perform one of their most cherished functions the limping cowpuncher was on him, doing his best to make good his promise. The other half of the Diamond Bar drive crew, attracted by the commotion at the chuck wagon, rode in with ready guns, saw their friends making no attempt at interference, asked a few terse questions and, putting up their guns, forthwith joined the circle of interested and pleased spectators to root for the limping redhead.

Crawford's Colt tore loose from his fingers and dropped near
the wagon wheel

Red, back at the Bar-20 wagon, inquired of Cookie the whereabouts of Hopalong. Cookie, still smarting under Jimmy's galling fire of language, grunted ignorance and a wish. Red looked at him, scowling. "You can talk to th' Kid like that, mebby; but you get a civil tongue in yore head when any of us grown-ups ask questions." He turned on his heel, looked searchingly around the plain and mounting, returned to the herd, perplexed and vexed. As he left the camp, Jimmy hobbled around the wagon and stared after him. "Kid!" he snorted. "Grown-ups!" he sneered. "Huh!" He turned and regarded Cookie evilly. "Yo 're gonna get a good lickin' when I get so I can move better," he promised. Cookie lifted the red flannel dish-rag out of the pan and regarded it thoughtfully. "You better wait," he agreed pleasantly. "You can't run now. I 'm honin' for to drape this mop all over yore wall-eyed face; but I can wait." He sighed and went back to work. "Wish Red would shove you in with th' rest of th' cripples back yonder, an' get you off'n my frazzled nerves."

Jimmy shook his head sorrowfully and limped around the wagon again, where he resumed his sun bath. He dozed off and was surprised to be called for dinner. As he arose, grunting and growling, he chanced to look westward, and his shout apprised his friends of the return of the missing red-head.

Hopalong dismounted at the wagon and grinned cheerfully, despite the suspicious marks on his face. Giving an account of events as they occurred at the Diamond Bar chuck wagon, he wound up with: "Needn't push on so hard, Red. Crawford's herd is due to stay right where it is an' graze peaceful for a week. I heard Barnes give th' order before I left. How's things been out here while I was away?"

Red glared at him, ready to tell his opinion of reckless fools that went up against a gun-packing crowd alone when his friends had never been known to refuse to back up one of their outfit. The words hung on his lips as he waited for a chance to launch them. But when that chance came he had been disarmed by the cheerfulness of his happy friend. "Hoppy," he said, trying to be severe, "yo 're nothing' but a crazy, d —d fool. But what did they say when you started for huffy Sam like that?"

X
The Hold-Up

The herd delivered at Sandy Creek had traveled only half way, for the remaining part of the journey would be on the railroad. The work of loading the cars was fast, furious fun to anyone who could find humor enough in his make-up to regard it so. Then came a long, wearying ride for the five men picked from the drive outfit to attend to the cattle on the way to the cattle pens of the city. Their work at last done, they "saw the sights" and were now returning to Sandy Creek.

The baggage smoking-car reeked with strong tobacco, the clouds of smoke shifting with the air currents, and dimly through the haze could be seen several men. Three of these were playing cards near the baggage-room door, while two more lounged in a seat half way down the aisle and on the other side of the car. Across from the card-players, reading a magazine, was a fat man, and near the water cooler was a dyspeptic-looking individual who was grumbling about the country through which he was passing.

The first five, as their wearing apparel proclaimed, were not of the kind usually found on trains, not the drummer, the tourist, or the farmer. Their heads were covered with heavy sombreros, their coats were of thick, black woolens, and their shirts were also of wool. Around the throat of each was a large handkerchief, knotted at the back; their trousers were protected by "chaps," of which three were of goatskin. The boots were tight-fitting, narrow, and with high heels, and to them were strapped heavy spurs. Around the waist, hanging loosely from one hip, each wore a wide belt containing fifty cartridges in the loops, and supporting a huge Colt's revolver, which rested against the thigh.

They were happy and were trying to sing but, owing to different tastes, there was noticeable a lack of harmony. "Oh Susanna" never did go well with "Annie Laurie," and as for "Dixie," it was hopelessly at odds with the other two. But they were happy, exuberantly so, for they had enjoyed their relaxation in the city and now were returning to the station where their horses were waiting to carry them over the two hundred miles which lay between their ranch and the nearest railroad-station.

For a change the city had been pleasant, but after they had spent several days there it lost its charm and would not have been acceptable to them even as a place in which to die. They had spent their money, smoked "top-notcher" cigars, seen the "shows" and feasted each as his fancy dictated, and as behooved cowpunchers with money in their pockets. Now they were glad that every hour reduced the time of their stay in the smoky, jolting, rocking train, for they did not like trains, and this train was particularly bad. So they passed the hours as best they might and waited impatiently for the stop at Sandy Creek, where they had left their horses. Their trip to the "fence country" was now a memory, and they chafed to be again in the saddle on the open, wind-swept range, where miles were insignificant and the silence soothing.

The fat man, despairing of reading, watched the card-players and smiled in good humor as he listened to their conversation, while the dyspeptic, nervously twisting his newspaper, wished that he were at his destination. The baggage-room door opened and the conductor looked down on the card-players and grinned. Skinny moved over in the seat to make room for the genial conductor.

"Sit down, Simms, an' take a hand," he invited. Laughter arose continually and the fat man joined in it, leaning forward more closely to watch the play.

Lanky tossed his cards face down on the board and grinned at the onlooker.

"Billy shore bluffs more on a varigated flush than any man I ever saw."

"Call him once in a while and he 'll get cured of it," laughed the fat man, bracing himself as the train swung around a sharp turn.

"He 's too smart," growled Billy Williams. "He tried that an' found I did n't have no varigated flushes. Come on, Lanky, if yo 're playing cards, put up."

Farther down the car, their feet resting easily on the seat in front of them, Hopalong and Red puffed slowly at their large, black cigars and spoke infrequently, both idly watching the plain flit by in wearying sameness, and both tired and lazy from doing nothing but ride.

"Blast th' cars, anyhow," grunted Hopalong, but he received no reply, for his companion was too disgusted to say anything.

A startling, sudden increase in the roar of the train and a gust of hot, sulphurous smoke caused Hopalong to look up at the brakeman, who came down the swaying aisle as the door slammed shut.

"Phew!" he exclaimed, genially. "Why in thunder don't you fellows smoke up?"

Hopalong blew a heavy ring, stretched energetically and grinned: "Much farther to Sandy Creek?"

"Oh, you don't get off for three hours yet," laughed the brakeman.

"That's shore a long time to ride this bronc train," moodily complained Red as the singing began again. "She shore pitches a-plenty," he added.

The train-hand smiled and seated himself on the arm of the front seat:

"Oh, it might be worse."

"Not this side of hades," replied Red with decision, watching his friend, who was slapping the cushions to see the dust fly out: "Hey, let up on that, will you! There's dust a-plenty without no help from you!"

The brakeman glanced at the card-players and then at Hopalong.

"Do your friends always sing like that?" he inquired.

"Mostly, but sometimes it's worse."

"On the level?"

"Shore enough; they're singing 'Dixie,' now. It's their best song."

"That ain't 'Dixie!'"

"Yes it is: that is, most of it."

"Well, then, what's the rest of it?"

"Oh, them's variations of their own," remarked Red, yawning and stretching. "Just wait till they start something sentimental; you 'll shore weep."

"I hope they stick to the variations. Say, you must be a pretty nifty gang on the shoot, ain't you?"

"Oh, some," answered Hopalong.

"I wish you fellers had been aboard with us one day about a month ago. We was the wrong end of a hold-up, and we got cleaned out proper, too."

"An' how many of 'em did you get?" asked Hopalong quickly, sitting bolt upright.

The fat man suddenly lost his interest in the card-game and turned an eager ear to the brakeman, while the dyspeptic stopped punching holes in his time-card and listened. The card-players glanced up and then returned to their game, but they, too, were listening.

The brakeman was surprised: "How many did we get! Gosh! we didn't get none! They was six to our five."

"How many cards did you draw, you Piute?" asked Lanky.

"None of yore business; I ain't dealing, an' I would n't tell you if I was," retorted Billy.

"Well, I can ask, can't I?"

"Yes-you can, an' did."

"You didn't get none?" cried Hopalong, doubting his ears.

"I should say not!"

"An' they owned th' whole train?"

"They did."

Red laughed. "Th' cleaning-up must have been sumptuous an' elevating."

"Every time I holds threes he allus has better," growled Lanky to Simms.

"On th' level, we couldn't do a thing," the brakeman ran on. "There 's a water tank a little farther on, and they must 'a' climbed aboard there when we stopped to connect. When we got into the gulch the train slowed down and stopped and I started to get up to go out and see what was the matter; but I saw that when I looked down a gun-barrel. The man at the throttle end of it told me to put up my hands, but they were up as high then as I could get 'em without climbin' on the top of the seat.

"Can't you listen and play at th' same time?" Lanky asked Billy.

"I wasn't countin' on takin' the gun away from him," the brakeman continued, "for I was too busy watchin' for the slug to come out of the hole. Pretty soon somebody on the outside whistled and then another feller come in the car; he was the one that did the cleanin' up. All this time there had been a lot of shootin' outside, but now it got worse. Then I heard another whistle and the engine puffed up the track, and about five minutes later there was a big explosion, and then our two robbers backed out of the car among the rocks shootin' back regardless. They busted a lot of windows."

"An' you did n't git none," grumbled Hopalong, regretfully.

"When we got to the express-car, what had been pulled around the turn," continued the brakeman, not heeding the interruption, "we found a wreck. And we found the engineer and fireman standin' over the express-messenger, too scared to know he would n't come back no more. The car had been blowed up with dynamite, and his fighting soul went with it. He never knowed he was licked."

"An' nobody tried to help him!" Hopalong exclaimed, wrathfully now.

"Nobody wanted to die with him," replied the brakeman.

"Well," cried the fat man, suddenly reaching for his valise, "I 'd like to see anybody try to hold me up!" Saying which he brought forth a small revolver.

"You 'd be praying out of your bald spot about that time," muttered the brakeman.

Hopalong and Red turned, perceived the weapon, and then exchanged winks.

"That's a fine shootin'-iron, stranger," gravely remarked Hopalong.

"You bet it is!" purred the owner, proudly. "I paid six dollars for that gun."

Lanky smothered a laugh and his friend grinned broadly: "I reckon that'd kill a man-if you stuck it in his ear."

"Pshaw!" snorted the dyspeptic, scornfully. "You wouldn't have time to get it out of that grip. Think a train-robber is going to let you unpack? Why don't you carry it in your hip-pocket, where you can get at it quickly?"

There were smiles at the stranger's belief in the hip-pocket fallacy but no one commented upon it.

"Was n't there no passengers aboard when you was stuck up?" Lanky asked the conductor.

"Yes, but you can't count passengers in on a deal like that."

Hopalong looked around aggressively: "We 're passengers, ain't we?"

"You certainly are."

"Well, if any misguided maverick gets it into his fool head to stick *us* up, you see what happens. Don't you know th' fellers outside have all th' worst o' th' deal?"

"They have not!" cried the brakeman.

"They 've got all the best of it," asserted the conductor emphatically. "I 've been inside, and I know."

"Best nothing!" cried Hopalong. "They are on th' ground, watching a danger-line over a hundred yards long, full of windows and doors. Then they brace th' door of a car full of people. While they climb up the steps they can't see inside, an' then they go an' stick their heads in plain sight. It's an even break who sees th' other first, with th' men inside training their guns on th' glass in th' door!"

"Darned if you ain't right!" enthusiastically cried the fat man.

Hopalong laughed: "It all depends on th' men inside. If they ain't used to handling guns, 'course they won't try to fight. We 've been in so many gun-festivals that we would n't stop to think. If any coin-collector went an' stuck his ugly face against th' glass in that door he 'd turn a back-flip off 'n th' platform before he knowed he was hit. Is there any chance for a stick-up to-day, d'y think?"

"Can't tell," replied the brakeman. "But this is about the time we have the section-camps' pay on board," he said, going into the baggage end of the car.

Simms leaned over close to Skinny. "It's on this train now, and I 'm worried to death about it. I wish we were at Sandy Creek."

"Don't you go to worryin' none, then," the puncher replied. "It 'll get to Sandy Creek all right."

Hopalong looked out of the window again and saw that there was a gradual change in the nature of the scenery, for the plain was becoming more broken each succeeding mile. Small woods occasionally hurtled past and banks of cuts flashed by like mottled yellow curtains, shutting off the view. Scrub timber stretched away on both sides, a billowy sea of green, and miniature valleys lay under the increasing number of trestles twisting and winding toward a high horizon.

Hopalong yawned again: "Well, it's none o' our funeral. If they let us alone I don't reckon we 'll take a hand, not even to bust up this monotony."

Red laughed derisively: "Oh, no! Why, you could n't sit still nohow with a fight going on, an' you know it. An' if it's a stick-up! Wow!"

"Who gave you any say in this?" demanded his friend. "Anyhow, you ain't no angel o' peace, not nohow!"

"Mebby they 'll plug yore new sombrero," laughed Red.

Hopalong felt of the article in question: "If any two-laigged wolf plugs my war-bonnet he 'll be some sorry, an' so 'll his folks," he asserted, rising and going down the aisle for a drink.

Red turned to the brakeman, who had just returned: "Say," he whispered, "get off at th' next stop, shoot off a gun, an' yell, just for fun. Go ahead, it 'll be better 'n a circus."

"Nix on the circus, says I," hastily replied the other. "I ain't looking for no excitement, an' I ain't paid to amuse th' passengers. I hope we don't even run over a track-torpedo this side of Sandy Creek."

Hopalong returned, and as he came even with them the train slowed.

"What are we stopping for?" he asked, his hand going to his holster.

"To take on water; the tank 's right ahead."

"What have you got?" asked Billy, ruffling his cards.

"None of yore business," replied Lanky. "You call when you gets any curious."

"Oh, th' devil!" yawned Hopalong, leaning back lazily. "I shore wish I was on my cayuse pounding leather on th' home trail."

"Me, too," grumbled Red, staring out of the window. "Well, we 're moving again. It won't be long now before we gets out of this."

The card-game continued, the low-spoken terms being interspersed with casual comment; Hopalong exchanged infrequent remarks with Red, while the brakeman and conductor stared out of the same window. There was noticeable an air of anxiety, and the fat man tried to read his magazine with his thoughts far from the printed page. He read and re-read a single paragraph several times without gaining the slightest knowledge of what it meant, while the dyspeptic passenger fidgeted more and more in his seat, like one sitting on hot coals, anxious and alert.

"We 're there now," suddenly remarked the conductor, as the bank of a cut blanked out the view. "It was right here where it happened; the turn's farther on."

"How many cards did you draw, Skinny?" asked Lanky.

"Three; drawin' to a straight flush," laughed the dealer.

"Here 's the turn! We 're through all right," exclaimed the brakeman.

Suddenly there was a rumbling bump, a screeching of air-brakes and the grinding and rattle of couplings and pins as the train slowed down and stopped with a suddenness that snapped the passengers forward and back. The conductor and brakeman leaped to their feet, where the latter stood quietly during a moment of indecision.

A shot was heard and the conductor's hand, raised quickly to the whistle-rope sent blast after blast shrieking over the land. A babel of shouting burst from the other coaches and, as the whistle shrieked without pause, a shot was heard close at hand and the conductor reeled suddenly and sank into a seat, limp and silent.

At the first jerk of the train the card-players threw the board from across their knees, scattering the cards over the floor, and crouching, gained the center of the aisle, intently peering through the windows, their Colts ready for instant use. Hopalong and Red were also in the aisle, and when the conductor had reeled Hopalong's Colt exploded and the man outside threw up his arms and pitched forward.

"Good boy, Hopalong!" cried Skinny, who was fighting mad.

Hopalong wheeled and crouched, watching the door, and it was not long before a masked face appeared on the farther side of the glass. Hopalong fired and a splotch of red stained the white mask as the robber fell against the door and slid to the platform.

"Hear that shooting?" cried the brakeman. "They 're at the messenger. They 'll blow him up!"

"Come on, fellers!" cried Hopalong, leaping toward the door, closely followed by his friends.

They stepped over the obstruction on the platform and jumped to the ground on the side of the car farthest from the robbers.

"Shoot under the cars for legs," whispered Skinny. "That 'll bring 'em down where we can get 'em."

"Which is a good idea," replied Red, dropping quickly and looking under the car.

"Somebody's going to be surprised, all right," exulted Hopalong.

The firing on the other side of the train was heavy, being for the purpose of terrifying the passengers and to forestall concerted resistance. The robbers could not distinguish between the many reports and did not know they were being opposed, or that two of their number were dead.

A whinny reached Hopalong's ears and he located it in a small grove ahead of him: "Well, we know where th' cayuses are in case they make a break."

A white and scared face peered out of the cab-window and Hopalong stopped his finger just in time, for the inquisitive man wore the cap of fireman.

"You idiot!" muttered the gunman, angrily. "Get back!" he ordered.

A pair of legs ran swiftly along the other side of the car and Red and Skinny fired instantly. The legs bent, their owner falling forward behind the rear truck, where he was screened from sight.

"They had it their own way before!" gritted Skinny. "Now we 'll see if they can stand th' iron!"

By this time Hopalong and Red were crawling under the express-car and were so preoccupied that they did not notice the faint blue streak of smoke immediately over their heads. Then Red glanced up to see what it was that sizzed, saw the glowing end of a three-inch fuse, and blanched. It was death not to dare and his hand shot up and back, and the dynamite cartridge sailed far behind him to the edge of the embankment, where it hung on a bush.

"Good!" panted Hopalong. "We 'll pay 'em for that!"

"They 're worse 'n rustlers!"

They could hear the messenger running about over their heads, dragging and up-ending heavy objects against the doors of the car, and Hopalong laughed grimly:

"Luck's with this messenger, all right."

"It ought to be-he 's a fighter."

"Where are they? Have they tumbled to our game?"

"They're waiting for the explosion, you chump."

"Stay where you are then. Wait till they come out to see what's th' matter with it."

Red snorted: "Wait nothing!"

"All right, then; I 'm with you. Get out of my way."

"I 've been in situations some peculiar, but this beats 'em all," Red chuckled, crawling forward.

The robber by the car truck revived enough to realize that something was radically wrong, and shouted a warning as he raised himself on his elbow to fire at Skinny but the alert puncher shot first.

As Hopalong and Red emerged from beneath the car and rose to their feet there was a terrific explosion and they were knocked to the ground, while a sudden, heavy shower of stones and earth rained down over everything. The two punchers were not hurt and they arose to their feet in time to see the engineer and fireman roll out of the cab and crawl along the track on their hands and knees, dazed and weakened by the concussion.

Suddenly, from one of the day-coaches, a masked man looked out, saw the two punchers, and cried:

"It's all up! Save yourselves!"

As Hopalong and Red looked around, still dazed, he fired at them, the bullet singing past Hopalong's ear. Red smothered a curse and reeled as his friend grasped him. A wound over his right eye was bleeding profusely and Hopalong's face cleared of its look of anxiety when he realized that it was not serious.

"They creased you! Blamed near got you for keeps!" he cried, wiping away the blood with his sleeve.

Red, slightly stunned, opened his eyes and looked about confusedly. "Who done that? Where is he?"

"Don't know, but I'll shore find out," Hopalong replied. "Can you stand alone?"

Red pushed himself free and leaned against the car for support: "Course I can! Git that cuss!"

When Skinny heard the robber shout the warning he wheeled and ran back, intently watching the windows and doors of the car for trouble.

"We 'll finish yore tally right here!" he muttered.

When he reached the smoker he turned and went towards the rear, where he found Lanky and Billy lying under the platform. Billy was looking back and guarding their rear, while his companion watched the clump of trees where the second herd of horses was known to be. Just as they were joined by their foreman, they saw two men run across the track, fifty yards distant, and into the grove, both going so rapidly as to give no chance for a shot at them.

"There they are!" shouted Skinny, opening fire on the grove.

At that instant Hopalong turned the rear platform and saw the brakeman leap out of the door with a Winchester in his hands. The puncher sprang up the steps, wrenched the rifle from its owner, and, tossing it to Skinny, cried: "Here, this is better!"

"Too late," grunted the puncher, looking up, but Hopalong had become lost to sight among the rocks along the right of way. "If I only had this a minute ago!" he grumbled.

The men in the grove, now in the saddle, turned and opened fire on the group by the train, driving them back to shelter. Skinny, taking advantage of the cover afforded, ran towards the grove, ordering his friends to spread out and surround it; but it was too late, for at that minute galloping was heard and it grew rapidly fainter.

Red appeared at the end of the train: "Where's th' rest of the coyotes?"

"Two of 'em got away," Lanky replied.

"Ya-ho!" shouted Hopalong from the grove. "Don't none of you fools shoot! I'm coming out. They plumb got away!"

"They near got *you*, Red," Skinny cried.

"Nears don't count," Red laughed.

"Did you ever notice Hopalong when he 's fighting mad?" asked Lanky, grinning at the man who was leaving the woods. "He allus wears his sombrero hanging on one ear. Look at it now!"

"Who touched off that cannon some time back?" asked Billy.

"I did. It was an anti-gravity cartridge what I found sizzling on a rod under th' floor of th' express car," replied Red.

"Why did n't you pinch out th' fuse 'stead of blowing everything up, you half-breed?" Lanky asked.

"I reckon I was some hasty," grinned Red.

"It blowed me under th' car an' my lid through a windy," cried Billy. "An' Skinny, he went up in th' air like a shore-'nough grasshopper."

Hopalong joined them, grinning broadly: "Hey, reckon ridin' in th' cars ain't so bad after all, is it?"

"Holy smoke!" cried Skinny. "What's that a-popping?"

Hopalong, Colt in hand, leaped to the side of the train and looked along it, the others close behind him, and saw the fat man with his head and arm out of the window, blazing away into the air, which increased the panic in the coaches. Hopalong grinned and fired into the ground, and the fat man nearly dislocated parts of his anatomy by his hasty disappearance.

"Reckon he plumb forgot all about his fine, six-dollar gun till just now," Skinny laughed.

"Oh, he 's making good," Red replied. "He said he 'd take a hand if anything busted loose. It's a good thing he did n't come to life while me an' Hoppy was under his windy looking for laigs."

"Reckon some of us better go in th' cars an' quiet th' stampede," Skinny remarked, mounting the steps, followed by Hopalong. "They're shore *loco*."

The uproar in the coach ceased abruptly when the two punchers stepped through the door, the inmates shrinking into their seats, frightened into silence. Skinny and his companion did not make a reassuring sight, for they were grimy with burned powder and dust, and Hopalong's sleeve was stained with Red's blood.

"Oh, my jewels, my pretty jewels," sobbed a woman, staring at Skinny and wringing her hands.

"Ma'am, we shore don't want yore jewelry," replied Skinny, earnestly. "Ca'm yoreself; we don't want nothin'."

"*I* don't want that!" growled Hopalong, pushing a wallet from him. "How many times do you want us to tell you we don't want nothin'? We ain't robbers; we licked th' robbers."

Suddenly he stooped and, grasping a pair of legs which protruded into the aisle obstructing the passage, straightened up and backed towards Red, who had just entered the car, dragging into sight a portly gentleman, who kicked and struggled and squealed, as he grabbed at the stanchions of seats to stay his progress. Red stepped aside between two seats and let his friend pass, and then leaned over and grasped the portly gentleman's coat-collar. He tugged energetically and lifted the frightened man clear of the aisle and deposited him across the back of a seat, face down, where he hung balanced, yelling and kicking.

"Shut yore face, you cave-hunter!" cried Red in disgust. "Stop that infernal noise! You fat fellers make all yore noise after th' fighting is all over!"

The man on the seat, suddenly realizing what a sight he made, rolled off his perch and sat up, now more angry than frightened. He glared at Red's grinning face and sputtered:

"It's an outrage! It's an outrage! I'll have you hung for this day's work, young man!"

"That's right," grinned Hopalong. "He shore deserves it. I told him more 'n once that he 'd get strung up some day."

"Yes, and you, too!"

"Please don't," begged Hopalong. "I don't want t' die!"

Tense as the past quarter of an hour had been a titter ran along the car and, fuming impotently, the portly gentleman fled into the smoker.

"I 'll bet he had a six-dollar gun, too," laughed Red.

"I 'll bet he 's calling hisself names right about now," Hopalong replied. Then he turned to reply to a woman: "Yes, ma'am, we did. But they was n't real badmen."

At this a young woman, who was about as pretty as any young woman could be, arose and ran to Hopalong and, impulsively throwing her arms around his neck, cried: "You brave man! You hero! You dear!"

"Skinny! Red! Help!" cried the frightened and embarrassed puncher, struggling to get free.

She kissed him on the cheek, which flamed even more red as he made frantic efforts to keep his head back.

"Ma'am!" he cried, desperately. "Leggo, ma'am! Leggo!"

"Oh! Ho! Ho!" roared Red, weak from his mirth and, not looking to see what he was doing, he dropped into a seat beside another woman. He was on his feet instantly; fearing that he would have to go through the ordeal his friend was going through, he fled down the aisle, closely followed by Hopalong, who by this time had managed to break away. Skinny backed off suspiciously and kept close watch on Hopalong's admirer.

Just then the brakeman entered the car, grinning, and Skinny asked about the condition of the conductor.

"Oh, he 's all right now," the brakeman replied. "They shot him through the arm, but he 's repaired and out bossin' the job of clearin' the rocks off the track. He 's a little shaky yet, but he 'll come around all right."

"That's good. I 'm shore glad to hear it."

"Won't you wear this pin as a small token of my gratitude?" asked a voice at Skinny's shoulder.

He wheeled and raised his sombrero, a flush stealing over his face:

"Thank you, ma'am, but I don't want no pay. We was plumb glad to do it."

"But this is not pay! It's just a trifling token of my appreciation of your courage, just something to remind you of it. I shall feel hurt if you refuse."

Her quick fingers had pinned it to his shirt while she spoke and he thanked her as well as his embarrassment would permit. Then there was a rush toward him and, having visions of a shirt looking like a jeweler's window, he turned and fled from the car, crying: "Pin 'em on th' brakeman!"

He found the outfit working at a pile of rocks on the track, under the supervision of the conductor, and Hopalong looked up apprehensively at Skinny's approach.

"Lord!" he ejaculated, grinning sheepishly, "I was some scairt you was a woman."

Red dropped the rock he was carrying and laughed derisively.

"Oh, yo're a brave man, you are! scared to death by a purty female girl! If I 'd 'a' been you I would n't 'a' run, not a step!"

Hopalong looked at him witheringly: "Oh, no! You wouldn't 'a' run! You'd dropped dead in your tracks, you would!"

"You was both of you a whole lot scared," Skinny laughed. Then, turning to the conductor: "How do you feel, Simms?"

"Oh, I 'm all right: but it took the starch out of me for awhile."

"Well, I don't wonder, not a bit."

"You fellows certainly don't waste any time getting busy," Simms laughed.

"That's the secret of gun-fightin'," replied Skinny.

"Well, you 're a fine crowd all right. Any time you want to go any place when you 're broke, climb aboard my train and I 'll see't you get there."

"Much obliged."

Simms turned to the express-car: "Hey, Jackson! You can open up now if you want to."

But the express-messenger was suspicious, fearing that the conductor was talking with a gun at his head: "You go to h —l!" he called back.

"Honest!" laughed Simms. "Some cowboy friends o' mine licked the gang. Didn't you hear that dynamite go off? If they hadn't fished it out from under your feet you 'd be communing with the angels 'bout now."

For a moment there was no response, and then Jackson could be heard dragging things away from the door. When he was told of the cartridge and Red had been pointed out to him as the man who had saved his life, he leaped to the ground and ran to where that puncher was engaged in carrying the ever-silenced robbers to the baggage-car. He shook hands with Red, who laughed deprecatingly, and then turned and assisted him.

Hopalong came up and grinned: "Say, there 's some cayuses in that grove up th' track; shall I go up an' get 'em?"

"Shore! I 'll go an' get 'em with you," replied Skinny.

In the grove they found seven horses picketed, two of them being pack-animals, and they led them forth and reached the train as the others came up.

"Well, here 's five saddled cayuses, an' two others," Skinny grinned.

"Then we can ride th' rest of th' way in th' saddle instead of in that blamed train," Red eagerly suggested.

"That's just what we can do," replied Skinny. "Leather beats car-seats any time. How far are we from Sandy Creek, Simms?"

"About twenty miles."

"An' we can ride along th' track, too," suggested Hopalong.

"We shore can," laughed Skinny, shaking hands with the train-crew: "We 're some glad we rode with you this trip: we 've had a fine time."

"And we're glad you did," Simms replied, "for that ain't no joke, either."

Hopalong and the others had mounted and were busy waving their sombreros and bowing to the heads and handkerchiefs which were decorating the car-windows.

"All aboard!" shouted the conductor, and cheers and good wishes rang out and were replied to by bows and waving of sombreros. Then Hopalong jerked his gun loose and emptied it into the air, his companions doing likewise. Suddenly five reports rang out from the smoker and they cheered the fat man as he waved at them. They sat quietly and watched the train until the last handkerchief became lost to sight around a curve, but the screeching whistle could be heard for a long time.

"Gee!" laughed Hopalong as they rode on after the train, "won't th' fellers home on th' ranch be a whole lot sore when they hears about the good time what they missed!"

XI

Sammy Finds a Friend

The long train ride and the excitement were over and the outfit, homeward bound, loped along the trail, noisily discussing their exciting and humorous experiences and laughingly commented upon Hopalong's decision to follow them later. They could not understand why he should be interested in a town like Sandy Creek after a week spent in the city.

Back in the little cow-town their friend was standing in the office of the hotel, gazing abstractedly out of the window. His eyes caught and focused on a woman who was walking slowly along the other side of the square and finally paused before McCall's "Palace," a combination saloon, dance and gambling hall. He smiled cynically as his memory ran back over those other women he had seen in cow-towns and wondered how it was that the men of the ranges could rise to a chivalry that was famed. At that distance she was strikingly pretty. Her complexion was an alluring blend of color that the gold of her hair crowned like a burst of sunshine. He noticed that her eyebrows were too prominent, too black and heavy to be Nature's contribution. And there was about her a certain forwardness, a dash that bespoke no bashful Miss; and her clothes, though well-fitting, somehow did not please his untrained eye. A sudden impulse seized him and he strode to the door and crossed the dusty square, avoiding the piles of rusted cans, broken bottles and other rubbish that littered it.

She had become interested in a dingy window but turned to greet him with a resplendent smile as he stepped to the wooden walk. He noted with displeasure that the white teeth displayed two shining panels of gold that drew his eyes irresistibly; and then and there he hated gold teeth.

"Hello," she laughed. "I 'm glad to see somebody that's alive in this town. Ain't it awful?"

He instinctively removed his sombrero and was conscious that his habitual bashfulness in the presence of members of her sex was somehow lacking. "Why, I don't see nothin' extra dead about it," he replied. "Most of these towns are this way in daylight. Th' moths ain't out yet. You should 'a' been here last night!"

"Yes? But you 're out; an' you look like you might be able to fly," she replied.

"Yes; I suppose so," he laughed.

"I see you wear *two* of 'em," she said, glancing at his guns. "Ain't one of them things enough?"

"One usually is, mostly," he assented. "But I 'm pig-headed, so I wears two."

"Ain't it awrful hard to use two of 'em at once?" she asked, her tone flattering. "Then you 're one of them two-gun men I 've heard about, ain't you?"

"An' seen?" he smiled.

"Yes, I 've seen a couple. Where you goin' so early?"

"Just lookin' th' town over," he answered, glancing over her shoulder at a cub of a cowpuncher who had opened the door of the "Retreat," but stopped in his tracks when he saw the couple in front of McCall's. There was a look of surprised interest on the cub's face, and it swiftly changed to one of envious interest. Hopalong's glance did not linger, but swept carelessly along the row of shacks and back to his companion's face without betraying his discovery.

"Well; you can look it over in about ten seconds, from th' outside," she rejoined. "An' it's so dusty out here. My throat is awful dry already."

He had n't noticed any dust in the air, but he nodded. "Yes; thirsty?"

"Well, it ain't polite or ladylike to say yes," she demurred, "but I really am."

He held open the door of the "Palace" and preceded her to the dance hall, where she rippled the keys of the old piano as she swept past it. The order given and served, he sipped at his glass and carried on his share of a light conversation until, suddenly, he arose and made his apologies. "I got to attend to something" he regretted as he picked up his sombrero and turned. "See you later."

"Why!" she exclaimed. "I was just beginnin' to get acquainted!"

"A moth without money ain't no good," he smiled. "I 'm goin' out to find th' money. When I 'm in good company I like to spend. See you later?" He bowed as she nodded, and departed.

Emerging from McCall's he glanced at the "Retreat" and sauntered toward it. When he entered he found the cub resting his elbows on the pine bar, arguing with the bartender about the cigars sold in the establishment. The cub glanced up and appealed to the newcomer. "Ain't they?" he demanded.

Hopalong nodded. "I reckon so. But what is it about?"

"These cigars," explained the cub, ruefully. "I was just sayin' there ain't a good one in town."

"You lose," replied Hopalong. "Are you shore you knows a good cigar when you smokes it?"

"I know it so well that I ain't found one since I left Kansas City. You said I lose. Do you know one well enough to be a judge?"

Hopalong reached to his vest pocket, extracted a cigar and handed it to the cub, who took it hesitatingly. "Why, I'm much obliged. I —I did n't mean that-you know."

Hopalong nodded and rearranged the cigar's twin-brothers in his pocket. He would be relieved when they were smoked, for they made him nervous with their frailty. The cub lighted the cigar and an unaffected grin of delight wreathed his features as the smoke issued from his nostrils. "Who sells 'em?" he demanded, excitedly.

"Corson an' Lukins, up th' hill from th' depot," answered Hopalong. "Like it?"

"Like it! Why, stranger, I used to spend most of my week's pocket money for these." He paused and stared at the smiling puncher. "Did you say Corson an' Lukins?" he demanded incredulously. "Well, I 'll be hanged! When was you there?"

"Last week. Here, bartender; liquor for all hands."

The cub touched the glass to his lips and waved his hand at a table. Seated across from the stranger with the heaven-sent cigars he ordered the second round, and when he went to pay for it he drew out a big roll of bills and peeled off the one on the outside.

Hopalong frowned. "Sonny," he said in a low voice, "it ain't none of my affair, but you oughta put that wad away an' forget you have it when out in public. You shouldn't tempt yore feller men like that."

The cub laughed: "Oh, I had my eye teeth cut long ago. Play a little game?"

Hopalong was amused. "Didn't I just tell you not to tempt yore feller men?"

The cub grinned. "I reckon it 'll fade quick, anyhow; but it took me six months' hard work to get it together. It 'll last about six days, I suppose."

"Six hours, if you plays every man that comes along," corrected Hopalong.

"Well, mebby," admitted the cub. "Say: that was one fine girl you was talkin' to, all right," he grinned.

Hopalong studied him a moment. "Not meanin' no offense, what's yore name?"

"Sammy Porter; why?"

"Well, Sammy," remarked Hopalong as he arose. "I reckon we 'll meet again before I leave. You was remarkin' she was a fine girl. I admit it; she was. So long," and he started for the door.

Sammy flushed. "Why, I —I didn't mean nothin'!" he exclaimed. "I just happened to think about her-that's all! You know, I saw you talkin' to her. Of course, you saw her first," he explained.

Hopalong turned and smiled kindly. "You didn't say nothin' to offend me. I was just startin' when you spoke. But as long as you mentioned it I 'll say that my interest in th' lady was only brief. Her interest in me was th' same. Beyond lettin' you know that I 'll add that I don't generally discuss wimmin. I 'll see you later," and, nodding cheerily, he went out and closed the door behind him.

Hopalong leaned lazily against the hotel, out of reach of the spring wind, which was still sharp, and basked in the warmth of the timid sun. He regarded the little cow-town cynically but smilingly and found no particular fault with it. Existing because the railroad construction work of the season before had chanced to stop on the eastern bank of the deceptive creek, and because of the nearness of three drive trails, one of them important, the town had sprung up, mushroom-like, almost in a night. Facing on the square were two general stores, the railroad station and buildings, two restaurants, a dozen saloons where gambling either was the main attraction or an ambitious side-line, McCall's place and a barber shop with a dingy, bullet-peppered red-and-white pole set close to the door. Between the barber shop and McCall's was a narrow space, and the windows of the two buildings, while not opposite, opened on the little strip of ground separating them.

Rubbing a hand across his chin he regarded the barber shop thoughtfully and finally pushed away from the sun-warmed wall of the hotel and started lazily toward the red-and-white pole. As he did so the tin-panny notes of a piano redoubled and a woman's voice shrilly arose to a high note, flatted, broke and swiftly dropped an octave. He squirmed and looked speculatively along the westward trail, wondering how far away his outfit was and why he had not gone with them. Another soaring note that did not flat and a crashing chord from the piano were followed by a burst of uproarious, reckless laughter. Hopalong frowned, snapped his fingers in sudden decision and stepped briskly toward the barber shop as the piano began anew.

Entering quietly and closing the door softly, he glanced appraisingly through the windows and made known his wants in a low voice. "I want a shave, haircut, shampoo, an' anythin' else you can think of. I 'm tired an' don't want to talk. Take yore own time an' do a good job; an' if I 'm asleep when yo're through, don't wake me till somebody else wants th' chair. Savvy? All right-start in."

In McCall's a stolid bartender listened to the snatches of conversation that filtered under the door to the dance hall alongside and on his face there at times flickered the suggestion of a cynical smile. A heavy, dark complexioned man entered from the street and glanced at the closed door of the dance hall. The bartender nodded and held up a staying hand, after which he shoved a drink across the bar. The heavy-set man carefully wiped a few drops of spilled liquor from his white, tapering hands and seated himself with a sigh of relief, and became busy with his thoughts until the time should come when he would be needed.

On the other side of that door a little comedy was being enacted. The musician, a woman, toyed with the keys of the warped and scratched piano, the dim light from the shaded windows mercifully hiding the paint and the hardness of her face and helping the jewelry, with which her hands were covered, keep its tawdry secret.

"I don't see what makes you so touchy," grumbled Sammy in a pout. "I ain't goin' to hurt you if I touch yore arm." He was flushed and there was a suspicious unsteadiness in his voice.

She laughed. "Why, I thought you wanted to talk?"

"I did," he admitted, sullenly; "but there's a limit to most wants. Oh, well: go ahead an' play. That last piece was all right; but give us a gallop or a mazurka-anything lively. Better yet, a caprice: it's in keepin' with yore temperament. If you was to try to interpert mine you 'd have to dig it out of Verdi an' toll a funeral bell."

"Say; who told you so much about music?" she demanded.

"Th' man that makes harmonicas," he grinned. He arose and took a step toward her, but she retreated swiftly, smiling. "Now behave yourself, for a little while, at least. What's th' matter with you, anyhow? What makes you so silly?"

"You, of course. I don't see no purty wimmin out on th' range, an' you went to my head th' minute I laid eyes on you. *I* ain't in no hurry to leave this town, now nohow."

"I 'm afraid you 're going to be awful when you grow up. But you 're a nice boy to say such pretty things. Here," she said, filling his glass and handing it to him, "let's drink another toast-you know such nice ones."

"Yes; an' if I don't run out of 'em purty soon I 'll have to hunt a solid, immovable corner somewheres; an' there ain't nothin' solid or immovable about *this* room at present," he growled. "What you allus drinkin' to somethin' for? Well, here's a toast —I don't know any more fancy ones. Here's to —*you!*"

"That's nicer than-oh, pshaw!" she exclaimed, pouting. "An' you would n't drink a full glass to *that* one. You must think I 'm nice, when you renig like that! Don't tell me any more pretty things-an' stop right where you are! Think you can hang onto me after that? Well, that's better; why didn't you do it th' first time? You can be a nice boy when you want to."

He flushed angrily. "Will you stop callin' me a boy?" he demanded unsteadily. "I ain't no kid! I do a man's work, earn a man's pay, an' I spend it like a man."

"An' drink a boy's drink," she teased. "You 'll grow up some day." She reached forward and filled his glass again, for an instant letting her cheek touch his. Swiftly evading him she laughed and patted him on the head. "Here, *man*," she taunted, "drink this if you dare!"

He frowned at her but gulped down the liquor. "There, like a fool!" he grumbled, bitterly. "You tryin' to get me drunk?" he demanded suddenly in a heavy voice.

She threw back her head and regarded him coldly. "It will do me no good. Why should I? I merely wanted to see if you would take a dare, if you were a man. You are either not sober now, or you are insultingly impolite. I don't care to waste any more words or time with you," and she turned haughtily toward the door.

He had leaned against the piano, but now he lurched forward and cried out. "I 'm sorry if I hurt yore feelin's that way—I shore didn't mean to. Ain't we goin' to make up?" he asked, anxiously.

"Do you mean that?" she demanded, pausing and looking around.

"You know I do, Annie. Le's make up-come on; le's make up."

"Well; I'll try you, an' see."

"Play some more. You play beautiful," he assured her with heavy gravity.

"I'm tired of-but, say: Can you play poker?" she asked, eagerly.

"Why, shore; who can't?"

"Well, I can't, for one. I want to learn, so I can win my money back from Jim. He taught me, but all I had time to learn was how to lose."

Sammy regarded her in puzzled surprise and gradually the idea became plain. "Did he teach you, an' win money from you? Did he keep it?" he finally blurted, his face flushed a deeper red from anger.

She nodded. "Why, yes; why?"

He looked around for his sombrero, muttering savagely.

"Where you goin'?" she asked in surprise.

"To get it back. He ain't goin' to keep it, th' coyote!"

"Why, he won't give it back to you if he would n't to me. Anyhow, he won it."

"*Won* it!" he snapped. "He stole it, that's how much he won it. He 'll give it back or get shot."

"Now look here," she said, quickly. "You ain't goin' gunnin' for no friend of mine. If you want to get that money for me, an' I certainly can use it about now, you got to try some other way. Say! Why don't you win it from him?" she exulted. "That's th' way-get it back th' way it went."

He weighed her words and a grin slowly crept across his face. "Why, I reckon you called it, that time, Annie. That's th' way I 'll try first, anyhow, Li'l Girl. Where is this good friend of yourn that steals yore money? Where is this feller?"

As if in answer to his inquiry the heavy-set man strolled in, humming cheerily. And as he did so the sleepy occupant of the barber's chair slowly awoke, rubbed his eyes, stretched luxuriously and, paying his bill, loafed out and lazily sauntered down the street, swearing softly.

"Why, here he is now," laughed the woman. "You must 'a' heard us talkin' about you, Jim. I'm goin' to get my money back-this is Mr. Porter, Jim, who 's goin' to do it."

The gambler smiled and held out his hand. "Howd'y, Mr. Porter," he said.

Sammy glared at him: "Put yore paw down," he said, thickly. "I ain't shakin' han's with no dogs or tin-horns."

The gambler recoiled and flushed, fighting hard to repress his anger. "What you mean?" he growled, furiously.

"What I said. If you want revenge sit down there an' play, if you 've got th' nerve to play with a man. I never let no coyote steal a woman's money, an' I 'm goin' to get Annie her twenty. Savvy?"

The gambler's reply was a snarl. "Play!" he sneered. "I'll play, all right. It'll take more 'n a sassy kid to get that money back, too. I 'm goin' to take yore last red cent. You can't talk to me like that an' get it over. An' don't let me hear you call her 'Annie' no more, neither. Yo 're too cussed familiar!"

Her hand on Sammy's arm stopped the draw and he let the gun drop back into the holster. "*No!*" she whispered. "Make a fool of him, Sammy! Beat him at his own game."

Sammy nodded and scowled blackly. "I call th' names as suits me," he retorted. "When I see you on th' street I 'm goin' to call you some that I 'm savin' up now because a lady 's present. They 're hefty, too."

At first he won, but always small amounts. Becoming reckless, he plunged heavily on a fair hand and lost. He plunged again on a better hand and lost. Then he steadied as much as his befuddled brain would permit and played a careful game, winning a small pot. Another small winning destroyed his caution and he plunged again, losing heavily. Steadying himself once more he began a new deal with excess caution and was bluffed out of the pot, the gambler sneeringly showing his cards as he threw them down. Sammy glanced around to say something to the woman, but found she had gone. "Aw, never mind her!" growled his opponent. "She 'll be back-she can't stay away from a kid like you."

The woman was passing through the barroom and, winking at the bartender, opened the door and stepped to the street. She smiled as she caught sight of the limping stranger coming toward her. He might have found money, but she was certain he had found something else and in generous quantities. He removed his sombrero with an exaggerated sweep of his hand and hastened to meet her, walking with the conscious erectness of a man whose feet are the last part of him to succumb. "Hullo, Sugar," he grinned. "I found some, a'right. Now we 'll have some music. Come long."

"There ain't no hurry," she answered. "We 'll take a little walk first."

"No, we won't. We 'll have some music an' somethin' to drink. If you won't make th' music, I will; or shoot up th' machine. Come 'long, Sugar," he leered, pushing open the door with a resounding slam. He nodded to the bartender and apologized. "No harm meant, Friend. It sorta slipped; jus' slipped, tha's all. Th' young lady an' me is goin' to have some music. What? All right for you, Sugar! Then I'll make it myself," and he paraded stiffly toward the inner door.

The bartender leaned suddenly forward. "Keep out of there! You 'll bust that pianner!"

The puncher stopped with a jerk, swung ponderously on his heel and leveled a forefinger at the dispenser of drinks. "I won't," he said. "An' if I do, I 'll pay for it. Come on, Sugar-le's play th' old thing, jus' for spite." Grasping her arm he gently but firmly escorted her into the dance hall and seated her at the piano. As he straightened up he noticed the card players and, bowing low to her, turned and addressed them.

"Gents," he announced, bowing again, "we are goin' to have a li'l music an' we hopes you won't objec'. Not that we gives a d —n, but we jus' hopes you won't." He laughed loudly at his joke and leaned against the piano. "Let 'er go," he cried, beating time. "Allaman lef an' ladies change! Swing yore partner's gal —I mean, swing some other gal: but what's th' difference? All join han's an' hop to th' middle-nope! It's all han's roun' an' swing 'em again. But it don't make no difference, does it, Lulu?" He whooped loudly and marched across the room, executed a few fancy steps and marched back again. As he passed the card table Sammy threw down his hand and arose with a curse. The marcher stopped, fiddled a bit with his feet until obtaining his balance, and then regarded the youth quizzically. "S'matter, Sonny?" he inquired.

Sammy scowled, slowly recognized the owner of the imported cigars and shook his head. "Big han's, but not big enough; an' I lost my pile." Staggering to the piano he plumped down on a chair near it and watched the rippling fingers of the player in drunken interest.

The hilarious cowpuncher, leaning backward perilously, recovered his poise for a moment and then lurched forward into the chair the youth had just left. "Come on, pardner," he grinned across at the gambler. "Le's gamble. I been honin' for a game, an' here she is." He picked up the cards, shuffled them clumsily and pushed them out for the cut. The gambler hesitated, considered and then turned over a jack. He lost the deal and shoved out a quarter without interest.

The puncher leaned over, looked at it closely and grinned. "Two bits? That ain't poker; that's —that's dominoes!" he blurted, angrily, with the quick change of mood of a man in his cups.

"I ain't anxious to play," replied the gambler. "I 'll kill a li'l time at a two-bit game, though. Otherwise I 'll quit."

"A'right," replied the dealer. "I did n't expec' nothin' else from a tin-horn, no-how. I want two cards after you get yourn." The gambler called on the second raise and smiled to himself when he saw that his opponent had drawn to a pair and an ace. He won on his own deal and on the one following.

The puncher increased the ante on the fourth deal and looked up inquiringly, a grin on his face. "Le's move out th' infant class," he suggested.

The gambler regarded him sharply. "Well, th' other *was* sorta tender," he admitted, nodding.

The puncher pulled out a handful of gold coins and clumsily tried to stalk them, which he succeeded in doing after three attempts. He was so busy that he did not notice the look in the other's eyes. Picking up his hand he winked at it and discarded one. "Goin' to raise th' ante a few," he chuckled. "I got a feelin' I 'm goin' t' be lucky." When the card was dealt to him he let it lay and bet heavily. The gambler saw it and raised in turn, and the puncher, frowning in indecision, nodded his head wisely and met it, calling as he did so. His four fives were just two spots shy to win and he grumbled loudly at his luck. "Huh," he finished, "she 's a jack pot, eh?" He slid a double eagle out to the center of the table and laughed recklessly. The deals went around rapidly, each one calling for a ten-dollar sweetener and when the seventh hand was dealt the puncher picked his cards and laughed. "She 's open," he cried, "for fifty," and shoved out the money with one hand while he dug up a reserve pile from his pocket with the other.

The gambler saw the opener and raised it fifty, smiling at his opponent's expression. The puncher grunted his surprise, studied his hand, glanced at the pot and shrugging his shoulders, saw the raise. He drew two cards and chuckled as he slid them into his hand; but before the dealer could make his own draw the puncher's chuckle died out and he stared over the gambler's shoulder. With an oath he jerked out his gun and fired. The gambler leaped to his feet and whirled around to look behind. Then he angrily faced the frowning puncher. "What you think yo 're doin'?" he demanded, his hand resting inside his coat, the thumb hooked over the edge of the vest.

The puncher waved his hand apologetically. "I never have no luck when I sees a cat," he explained. "A black cat is worse; but a yaller one's bad enough. I 'll bet that yaller devil won't come back in a hurry-judgin' by th' way it started. I won't miss him, if he does."

The gambler, still frowning, glanced at the deck suspiciously and saw that it lay as he had dropped it. The bartender, grinning at them from the door, cracked a joke and went back to the bar. Sammy, after a wild look around, settled back in his chair and soothed the pianist a little before going back to sleep.

Drawing two cards the gambler shoved them in his hand without a change in his expression- but he was greatly puzzled. It was seldom that he bungled and he was not certain that he had. The discard contained the right number of cards and his opponent's face gave no hint to the thoughts behind it. He hesitated before he saw the bet-ten dollars was not much, for the size of the pot justified more. He slowly saw it, willing to lose the ten in order to see his opponent's cards. There was something he wished to know, and he wanted to know it as soon as he could. "I call that," he said. The puncher's expression of tenseness relaxed into one of great relief and he hurriedly dropped his cards. Three kings, an eight, and a deuce was his offering. The gambler laid down a pair of queens, a ten, an eight and a four, waved his hand and smiled. "It's just as well I did n't draw another queen," he observed, calmly. "I might 'a' raised once for luck."

The puncher raked in the pot and turned around in his chair. "I cleaned up that time," he exulted to the woman. She had stopped playing and was stroking Sammy's forehead. Smiling at the exuberant winner she nodded. "You should have let the cat stay —I think it really brought you luck." He shook his head emphatically. "*No*, ma'am! It was chasin' it away as did that. That's what did it, a'right."

The gambler glanced quickly at the two top cards on the deck and was picking up those scattered on the table when his opponent turned around again. How that queen and ten had got two cards too deep puzzled him greatly-he was willing to wager even money that he would not look away again until the game was finished, not if all the cats in the world were being slaughtered. One hundred and ninety dollars was too much money to pay for being caught off his guard, as he was tempted to believe he had been. He did not know how much liquor the other had consumed, but he seemed to be sobering rapidly.

The next few deals did not amount to much. Then a jackpot came around and was pushed hard. The puncher was dealing and as he picked up the deck after the cut he grinned and winked. "Th' skirmishin' now bein' over, th' battle begins. If that cat stays away long enough mebby I 'll make a killin'."

"All right; but don't make no more gun-plays," warned the gambler, coldly. "I allus get excited when I smells gun-powder an' I do reckless things sometimes," he added, significantly.

"Then I shore hopes you keep ca'm," laughed the puncher, loud enough to be heard over the noise of the piano, which was now going again.

The pot was sweetened three times and then the gambler dealt his opponent openers. The puncher looked anxiously through the door, grinning coltishly. He slowly pushed out twenty dollars. "There's th' key," he grunted. "A'right; see that an' raise you back. Good for you! I'm stayin' an' boostin' same as ever. Fine! See it again, an' add this. I 'm playin' with yore money, so I c'n afford to be reckless. All right; I'm satisfied, too. Gimme one li'l card. I shore am glad I don't need th' king of hearts-that was shore on th' bottom when th' deal *begun*."

The gambler, having drawn, cursed and reached swiftly toward his vest pocket; but he stopped suddenly and contemplated the Colt that peeked over the edge of the table. It looked squarely at his short ribs and was backed by a sober, angry man who gazed steadily into his eyes. "Drop that hand," said the puncher in a whisper just loud enough to be heard by the other over the noise of the piano. "I never did like them shoulder holsters —I carry my irons where everybody can see 'em." Leaning forward swiftly he reached out his left hand and cautiously turned over the other's cards. The fourth one was the king of hearts. "Don't move," he whispered, not wishing to have the bartender take a hand from behind. "An' don't talk," he warned as he leaned farther forward and shoved his Colt against the other's vest and with his left hand extracted a short-barreled gun from the sheath under the gambler's armpit. Sinking back in his chair he listened a moment and, raking in the pot, stowed it away with the other winnings in his pockets.

The gambler stirred, but stopped as the Colt leaped like a flash of light to the edge of the table. "Tin-horn," said the puncher, softly, "you ain't slick enough. I did n't stop you when you wanted that queen an' ten because I wanted you to go on with th' crookedness. Yaller cats is more unlucky to you than they are to me. But when I saw that last play I lost my temper; an' I stopped you. Now if you 'll cheat with me, you 'll cheat with a drunk boy. So, havin' cheated him, you really stole his money away from him. That bein' so, you will dig up six month's wages at about fifty per month. I 'd shoot you just as quick as I 'd shoot a snake; so don't get no fool notions in yore head. Dig it right up."

The gambler studied the man across from him, but after a moment he silently placed some money on the table. "It was only two forty," he observed, holding to three double eagles. The puncher nodded: "I 'll take yore word for that. Now, in th' beginnin' I only wanted to get th' boy his money; but when you started cheatin' against me I changed my mind. I played fair. Now here's your short-five," he said as he slid the gun across the table. "Mebby you might want to use it sometime," he smiled. "Now you vamoose; an' if I see you in town after th' next train leaves, I 'll *make* you use that shoulder holster. An' tell yore friends that Hopalong Cassidy says, that for a country where men can tote their hardware in plain sight, a shoulder layout ain't no good: you gotta reach too high. Adios."

He watched the silent, philosophical man-of-cards walk slowly toward the door, upright, dignified and calm. Then he turned and approached the piano. "Sister," he said, politely, "yore gamblin' friend is leavin' town on th' next train. He has pressin' business back east a couple of stations an' wonders if you 'll join him at th' depot in time for th' next train."

She had stopped playing and was staring at him in amazement. "Why didn't he come an' tell me himself, 'stead of sneakin' away an' sendin' you over?" she at last demanded, angrily.

"Well, he wanted to, but he saw a man an' slipped out with his gun in his hand. Mebby there'll be trouble; but I dunno. I'm just tellin' you. Gee," he laughed, looking at the snoring youth in the chair, "he got *that* quick. Why, I saw him less 'n two hours ago an' he was sober as a judge. Reckon I 'll take him over to th' hotel an' put him to bed." He went over to the helpless Sammy, shook him and made him get on his feet. "Come along, Kid," he said, slipping his arm under the sagging shoulder. "We'll get along. Good-by, Sugar," and, supporting the feebly protesting cub, he slowly made his way to the rear door and was gone, a grin wreathing his face as he heard the chink of gold coins in his several pockets.

XII
Sammy Knows the Game

A clean-cut, good-looking cowpuncher limped slightly as he passed the postoffice and found a seat on a box in front of the store next door. He sighed with relief and gazed cheerfully at the littered square as though it was something worth looking at. The night had not been a pleasant one because Sammy Porter had insisted upon either singing or snoring; and when breakfast was announced the youth almost had recovered his senses and was full of remorse and a raging thirst. Being flatly denied the hair of the dog that bit him he grew eloquently profane and very abusive. Hence Mr. Cassidy's fondness for the box.

Sounds obtruded. They were husky and had dimensions and they came from the hotel bar. After increasing in volume and carrying power they were followed to the street by a disheveled youth who kicked open the door and blinked in the sunlight. Espying the contented individual on the box he shook an earnest fist at that person and tried next door. In a moment he followed a new burst of noise to the street and shook the other fist. Trying the saloon on the other side of the hotel without success he shook both fists and once again tried the hotel bar, where he proceeded along lines tactful, flattering and diplomatic. Only yesterday he had owned a gun, horse and other personal belongings; he had possessed plenty of money, a clear head and his sins sat lightly on his youthful soul. He still had the sins, but they had grown in weight. Tact availed him nothing, flattery was futile and diplomacy was in vain. To all his arguments the bartender sadly shook his head, not because Sammy had no money, which was the reason he gave, but because of vivid remembrance of the grimness with which a certain red-haired, straight-lipped, two-gun cowpuncher had made known his request. "Let him suffer," had said the gunman. "It 'll be a good lesson for him. Understand; not a drop!" And the bartender had understood. To the drink-dispenser's refusal Sammy replied with a masterpiece of eloquence and during its delivery the bartender stood with his hand on a mallet, but too spellbound to throw it. Wheeling at the close of a vivid, soaring climax, Sammy yanked open the door again and stood transfixed with amazement and hostile envy. His new and officious friend surely knew the right system with women. To the burning indignities of the morning this added the last straw and Sammy bitterly resolved not to forget his wrongs.

Had Mr. Cassidy been a kitten he would have purred with delight as he watched his youthful friend's vain search for the hair of the dog, and his grin was threatening to engulf his ears when the Cub slammed into the hotel. Hearing the beating of hoofs he glanced around and saw a trim, pretty young lady astride a trim, high-spirited pony; and both were thoroughbreds if he was any judge. They bore down upon him at a smart lope and stopped at the edge of the walk. The rider leaped from the saddle and ran toward him with her hand outstretched and her face aglow with a delighted surprise. Her eyes fairly danced with welcome and relief and her cheeks, reddened by the thrust of the wind for more than twenty miles, flamed a deeper red, through which streaks of creamy white played fascinatingly. "Dick Ellsworth!" she cried. "When did you get here?"

Mr. Cassidy stumbled to his feet, one hand instinctively going out to the one held out to him, the other fiercely gripping his sombrero. His face flamed under its tan and he mumbled an incoherent reply.

"Don't you remember *me*?" she chided, a roguish, half-serious expression flashing over her countenance. "Not little Annie, whom you taught to ride? I used to think I needed you then, Dick; but oh, how I need you now. It's Providence, nothing else, that sent you. Father's gone steadily worse and now all he cares for is a bottle. Joe, the new foreman, has full charge of everything and he's not only robbing us right and left, but he 's —he 's bothering *me*! When I complain to father of his attentions all I get is a foolish grin. If you only knew how I have prayed for you to come back, Dick! Two bitter years of it. But now everything is all right. Tell me about yourself while I get the mail and then we 'll ride home together. I suppose Joe will be waiting for me somewhere on the trail; he usually does. Did you ever hate anyone so much you wanted to kill him?" she demanded fiercely, beside herself for the moment.

Hopalong nodded. "Well, yes; I have," he answered. "But you must n't. What's his name? We 'll have to look into this."

"Joe Worth; but let's forget him for awhile," she smiled. "I 'll get the mail while you go after your horse."

He nodded and watched her enter the post-office and then turned and walked thoughtfully away. She was mounted when he returned and they swung out of the town at a lope.

"Where have you been, and what have you been doing?" she asked as they pushed along the firm, hard trail.

"Punchin' for th' Bar-20, southwest of here. I wouldn't 'a' been here today only I let th' outfit ride on without me. We just got back from Kansas City a couple of days back. But let's get at this here Joe Worth prop'sition. I 'm plumb curious. How long's he been pesterin' you?"

"Nearly two years —I can't stand it much longer."

"An' th' outfit don't cut in?"

"They 're his friends, and they understand that father wants it so. You 'll not know father, Dick: I never thought a man could change so. Mother's death broke him as though he were a reed."

"Hum!" he grunted. "You ain't carin' how this coyote is stopped, just so he is?"

"No!" she flashed.

"An' he 'll be waitin' for you?"

"He usually is."

He grinned. "Le 's hope he is this time." He was silent a moment and looked at her curiously. "I don't know how you 'll take it, but I got a surprise for you —a big one. I 'm shore sorry to admit it, but I ain't th' man you think. I ain't Dick What 's-his-name, though it shore ain't *my* fault. I reckon I must look a heap like him; an' I hope I can *act* like him in this here matter. I want to see it through like *he* would. I can do as good a job, too. But it ain't no-wise fair nor right to pretend I 'm him. I ain't."

She was staring at him in a way he did not like. "Not Dick Ellsworth!" she gasped. "You are *not* Dick?"

"I 'm shore sorry-but I 'd like to play his cards. I 'm honin' for to see this here Joe Worth," he nodded, cheerfully.

"And you let me believe you were?" she demanded coldly. "You deliberately led me to talk as I did?"

"Well, now; I didn't just know what to do. You shore was in trouble, which was bad. I reckoned mebby I could get you out of it an' then go along 'bout my business. You ain't goin' to stop me a-doin' it, are you?" he asked anxiously.

Her reply was a slow, contemptuous look that missed nothing and that left nothing to be said. Her horse did not like to stand, anyway, and sprang eagerly forward in answer to the sudden pressure of her knees. She rode the high-strung bay with superb art, angry, defiant, and erect as a statue. Hopalong, shaking his head slowly, gazed after her and when she had become a speck on the plain he growled a question to his horse and turned sullenly toward the town. Riding straight to the hotel he held a short, low-voiced conversation with the clerk and then sought his friend, the Cub. This youthful grouch was glaring across the bar at the red-faced, angry man behind it, and the atmosphere was not one of peace. The Cub turned to see who the newcomer was and thereupon transferred his glare to the smiling puncher.

"Hullo, Kid," breezed Hopalong.

"You go to h—l!" growled Sammy, remembering to speak respectfully to his elders. He backed off cautiously until he could keep both of his enemies under his eyes.

Hopalong's grin broadened. He dug into his pockets and produced a large sum of money. "Here, Kid," said he, stepping forward and thrusting it into Sammy's paralyzed hands. "Take it an' buy all th' liquor you wants. You can get yore gun off 'n th' clerk, an' he 'll tell you where to find yore cayuse an' other belongings. I gotta leave town."

Sammy stared at the money in his hand. "What's this?" he demanded, his face flushing angrily.

"Money," replied Hopalong. "It's that shiny stuff you buys things with. Spondulix, cash, mazuma. You spend it, you know."

Sammy sputtered. He might have frothed had his mouth not been so dry. "Is it?" he demanded with great sarcasm. "I thought mebby it was cows, or buttons. What you handin' it to me for? I ain't no d—d beggar!"

Hopalong chuckled. "That money's yourn. I pried it loose from th' tin-horn that stole it from you. I also, besides, pried off a few chunks more; but them 's mine. I allus pays myself good wages; an' th' aforesaid chunks is plenty an' generous. Amen."

Sammy regarded his smiling friend with a frank suspicion that was brutal. The pleasing bulge of the pockets reassured him and he slowly pocketed his rescued wealth. He growled something doubtless meant for thanks and turned to the bar. "A large chunk of th' Mojave Desert slid down my throat las' night an' I 'm so dry I rustles in th' breeze. Let's wet down a li'l." Having extracted some of the rustle he eyed his companion suspiciously. "Thought you was a stranger hereabouts?"

"You 've called it."

"Huh! Then I 'm goin' to stick close to you an get acquainted with th' female population of th' towns we hit. An' I had allus reckoned lightnin' was quick!" he soliloquized, regretfully. "How 'd you do it?" he demanded.

Hopalong was gazing over his friend's head at a lurid chromo portraying the Battle of Bull Run and he pursed his lips thoughtfully. "That shore was some slaughter," he commented. "Well, Kid," he said, holding out his hand, "I 'm leavin'. If you ever gets down my way an' wants a good job, drop in an' see us. Th' clerk 'll tell you how to get there. An' th' next time you gambles, stay sober."

"Hey! Wait a minute!" exclaimed Sammy. "Goin' home now?"

"Can't say as I am, direct."

"Comin' back here before you do?"

"Can't say that, neither. Life is plumb oncertain an' gunplay 's even worse. Mebby I will if I 'm alive."

"Who you gunnin' for? Can't I take a hand?"

"Reckon not, Sammy. Why, I 'm cuttin' in where I ain't wanted, even if I am needed. But it's my duty. It's a h —l of a community as waits for a total stranger to do its work for it. If yo 're around an' I come back, why I 'll see you again. Meanwhile, look out for tin-horns."

Sammy followed him outside and grasped his arm. "I can hold up my end in an argument," he asserted fiercely. "You went an' did me a good turn-lemme do *you* one. If it's anythin' to do with that li'l girl you met to-day I won't cut in-only on th' trouble end. I'm particular strong on th' trouble part. Look here: Ain't a friend got no rights?"

Hopalong warmed to the eager youngster-he was so much like Jimmy; and Jimmy, be it known, could bedevil Hopalong as much as any man alive and not even get an unkind word for it. "I 'm scared to let you come, Kid; she 'd fumigate th' ranch when you left. Th' last twenty-four hours has outlawed you, all right. You keep to th' brush trails in th' draws-don't cavort none on skylines till you lose that biled owl look." He laughed at the other's expression and placed his hands on the youth's shoulders. "That ain't it, Kid; I never apologizes, serious, for th' looks of my friends. They 're my friends, drunk or sober, in h —l or out of it. I just can't see how you can cut in proper. Better wait for me here —I 'll turn up, all right. Meanwhile, as I says before, look out for tin-horns."

Sammy watched him ride away, and then slammed his sombrero on the ground and jumped on it, after which he felt relieved. Procuring his gun from the clerk he paused to cross-examine, but after a fruitless half hour he sauntered out, hiding his vexation, to wrestle with the problem in the open. Passing the window of a general store he idly glanced at the meager display behind the dusty glass and a sudden grin transfigured his countenance. He would find out about the girl first and that would help him solve the puzzle. Thinking thus he wandered in carelessly and he wandered out again gravely clutching a small package. Slipping behind the next building he tore off the paper and carefully crumpled and soiled with dust the purchase. Then he went down to the depot and followed the railroad tracks toward the other side of the square. Reaching the place where the south trail crossed the tracks he left them and walked slowly toward a small depression that was surrounded by hoofprints. He stooped quickly and straightened up with a woman's handkerchief dangling from his fingers. He grinned foolishly, examined it, sniffed at it and scratched his head while he cogitated. A decisive wave of his hand apprised the two spectators that he had arrived at a conclusion, which he bore out by heading straight for the postoffice, which was a part of the grocery store. The postmaster and grocer, in person one, watched his approach with frank curiosity.

Sammy nodded and went in the store, followed by the proprietor. "Howd'y," he remarked, producing the handkerchief. "Just picked this up over on th' trail. Know who dropped it?"

"Annie Allison, I reckon," replied the other. "She came in that way from th' Bar-U. Want to leave it?"

Sammy considered. "Why, I might as well take it to her —I'm goin' down there purty soon. Don't know any other ranch that might use a broncho-buster, do you?"

The proprietor shook his head. "No; most folks 'round here bust their own. Perfessional?"

Sammy nodded. "Yes. Here, gimme two-bits' worth of them pep'mint lozengers. Yes, it shore is fine; but it 'll rain before long. Well, by-by."

The bartender of the "Retreat" sniffed suspiciously and eyed the open door thoughtfully, holding aloft the bar-mop while he considered. Then he put the mop on the bar and went to the door, where he peered out. "Huh!" he grunted. "Hogin' that?" he sarcastically inquired. Sammy held out the bag and led the way to the bar. "Where's th' Bar-U? Yes? Do their own broncho-bustin'? Who, me? Ain't nothin' on laigs can throw me, includin' humans an' bartenders. What? Well, what you want to get all skinned up for, for nothin'? Five dollars? If you must lose it I might as well have it. One fall? All right; come out here an' get it."

The bartender chuckled and vaulted the counter as advance notice of his agility and physical condition, and immediately there ensued a soft shuffling. Suddenly the building shook and dusted itself and Sammy arose and stepped back, smiling at his victim. "Thanks," he remarked.

"Good money was spent on part of my education-boxin' bein' th' other half. Now, for five more, where can't I hit you?"

"Behind th' bar," grinned the other; "I got deadly weapons there. Look here!" he exclaimed hurriedly as a great idea struck him. "Everybody 'round here will back their wrastlin' reckless; le 's team up an' make some easy money. I 'll make th' bets an' you win 'em. Split even. What say?"

"Later on, mebby. What'd you say that Bar-U foreman's name was?"

The bartender's reply was supplemented by a pious suggestion. "An' if you wrastles *him*, bust his cussed neck!"

"Why this friendship?" queried Sammy, laughing.

"Oh, just for general principles."

Sammy bought cigars, left some lozenges and went out to search for his horse, which he duly found. Inwardly he was elated and he flexed his muscles and made curious motions with his arms, which caused the pie-bald to show the whites of its eyes wickedly and flatten its ragged ears. Its actions were justified, for a left hand darted out and slapped the wrinkling muzzle, deftly escaping the clicking teeth. Then the warlike pie-bald reflected judiciously as it chewed the lozenge. The eyes showed less white and the ears, moving forward and back, compromised by one staying forward. The candy was old and stale and the sting of the mint was negligible, but the sugar was much in evidence. When the hand darted out again the answering nip was playful and the ears were set rigidly forward. Sammy laughed, slipped several more lozenges into the ready mouth, vaulted lightly to the saddle and rode slowly toward the square. The pie-bald kicked mildly and reached around to nip at the stirrup, and then went on about its business as any well-broken cow pony should. Reaching the square Sammy drew rein suddenly and watched a horseman who was riding away from the "Retreat." Waiting a few minutes Sammy spurred forward to the saloon and called the bartender out to him. "Who was that feller that just left?" he asked, curiously.

"Joe Worth, th' man yo 're goin' to strike for that job. Why don't you catch him now an' mebby save yoreself a day's ride?"

"Good idea," endorsed Sammy. "See you later," and the youth wheeled and loped toward the trail, but drew rein when hidden from the "Retreat" by some buildings. He watched the distant horseman until he became a mere dot and then Sammy pushed on after him. There was a satisfied look on his face and he chuckled as he cogitated. "I shore got th' drift of this; I know th' game! Wonder how Cassidy got onto it?" He laughed contentedly. "Well, five hundred ain't too little to split two ways; an' mebby it is a two-man job. Mr. Joe Worth, who was once Mr. George Atkins, I would n't give a peso for yore chances after I get th' lay of th' ground an' find out yore habits. Yo 're goin' back to Willow Springs as shore as 'dogies' hang 'round water holes. An' you 'll shore dance their tune when you gets there."

Mr. Cassidy, arriving at the Bar-U, asked for the foreman and was told that the boss was in town, but would be back sometime in the afternoon. The newcomer replied that he would return later and, carefully keeping out of sight of the ranch house as well as he could, he wheeled and rode back the way he had come, being very desirous to have a good look at the foreman before they met. Arriving at an arroyo several miles north of the ranch he turned into it and, leaving his horse picketed on good grass along the bottom, he climbed to a position where he could see the trail without being seen. Having settled himself comfortably he improved the wait by trying to think out the best way to accomplish the work he had set himself to do. Shooting was too common and hardly justifiable unless Mr. Worth forced the issue with weapons of war.

The time passed slowly and he was relieved when a horseman appeared far to the north and jogged toward him, riding with the careless grace of one at home in the saddle. Being thoroughly familiar with the trail and the surrounding country the rider looked straight ahead as if attention to the distance yet untraveled might make it less. He passed within twenty feet of the watcher and went on his way undisturbed. Hopalong waited until he was out of sight around a hill and then, vaulting into the saddle, rode after him, still puzzled as to how he would proceed about the business in hand. He dismounted at the bunkhouse and nodded to those who lingered near the wash bench awaiting their turn.

"Just in time to feed," remarked one of the punchers. "Watch yore turn at th' basins-every man for hisself 's th' rule."

"All right," Hopalong laughed. "But is there any chance to get a job here?" he asked, anxiously.

"You 'll have to quiz th' Ol' Man-here he comes now," and the puncher waved at the approaching foreman. "Hey, Joe! Got a job for this hombre?" he called.

The foreman keenly scrutinized the newcomer, as he always examined strangers. The two guns swinging low on the hips caught his eyes instantly but he showed no particular interest in them, notwithstanding the fact that they proclaimed a gunman. "Why I reckon I got a job for you," he said. "I been waitin' to keep somebody over on Cherokee Range. But it's time to eat: we'll talk later."

After the meal the outfit passed the time in various ways until bed-time, the foreman talking to the new member of his family. During the night the foreman awakened several times and looked toward the newcomer's bunk but found nothing suspicious. After breakfast he called Hopalong and one of the others to him. "Ned," he said, "take Cassidy over to his range and come right back. Hey, Charley! You an' Jim take them poles down to th' ford an' fence in that quicksand just south of it. Ben says he 's been doin' nothin' but pullin' cows outen it. All right, Tim; comin' right away."

Ned and the new puncher lost no time but headed east at once with a packhorse carrying a week's provisions for one man. The country grew rougher rapidly and when they finally reached the divide a beautiful sight lay below them, stretching as far as eye could see to the east. In the middle distance gleamed the Cherokee, flowing toward the south through its valley of rocks, canyons, cliffs, draws and timber.

"There 's th' hut," said Ned, pointing to a small gray blot against the dead black of a towering cliff. "Th' spring's just south of it. Bucket Hill, up north there, is th' north boundary; Twin Spires, south yonder is th' other end; an' th' Cherokee will stop you on th' east side. You ride in every Sat'day if you wants. Don't get lonesome," he grinned and, wheeling abruptly, went back the way they had come.

Hopalong shook his head in disgust. To be sidetracked like this was maddening. It had taken three hours of hard traveling over rough country to get where he was and it would take as long to return; and all for nothing! He regarded the pack animal with a grin, shrugged his shoulders and led the way toward the hut, the pack horse following obediently. It was another hour before he finally reached the little cabin, for the way was strange and rough. During this time he had talked aloud, for he had the tricks of his kind and when alone he talked to himself. When he reached the hut he relieved the pack horse of its load, carrying the stuff inside. Closing the door and blocking it with a rock he found the spring, drank his fill and then let the horses do likewise. Then he mounted and started back over the rough trail, thinking out loud and confiding to his horse and he entered a narrow defile close to the top of the divide, promising dire things to the foreman. Suddenly a rope settled over him, pinned his arms to his sides and yanked him from the saddle before he had time to think. He landed on his head and was dazed as he sat up and looked around. The foreman's rifle confronted him, and behind the foreman's feet were his two Colts.

"You talks too much," sneered the man with the drop. "I suspicioned you th' minute I laid eyes on you. It 'll take a better man than you to get that five hundred reward. I reckon th' Sheriff was too scared to come hisself."

Hopalong shook his head as if to clear it. What was the man talking about? Who was the sheriff? He gave it up, but would not betray his ignorance. Yes; he had talked too much. He felt of his head and was mildly surprised to see his hand covered with blood when he glanced at it. "Five hundred 's a lot of money," he muttered.

"Blood money!" snapped the foreman. "You had a gall tryin' to get me. Why, I been lookin' for somebody to try it for two years. An' I was ready every minute of all that time."

Slowly it came to Hopalong and with it the realization of how foolish it would be to deny the part ascribed to himself. The rope was loose and his arms were practically free; the foreman had dropped the lariat and was depending upon his gun. The captive felt of his head again and, putting his hands behind him for assistance in getting up, arose slowly to his feet. In one of the hands was a small rock that it had rested upon during the effort of rising. At the movement the foreman watched him closely and ordered him not to take a step if he wanted to live a little longer.

"I reckon I 'll have to shoot you," he announced. "I dass n't let you loose to foller me all over th' country. Anyhow, I 'd have to do it sooner or later. I wish you was Phelps, d —n him; but he's a wise sheriff. Better stand up agin' that wall. I gotta do it; an' you deserve it, you Judas!"

"Meanin' yo're Christ?" sneered Hopalong. "Did you kill th' other feller like that? If I 'd 'a' knowed that I 'd 'a' slapped yore dawg's face at th' bunkhouse an' made you take an even break. Shore you got nerve enough to shoot straight if I looks at you while yo 're aimin'?" He laughed cynically. "I don't want to close my eyes."

The foreman's face went white and he half lowered the rifle as he took a step forward. Hopalong leaped sideways and his arm straightened out, the other staggering under the blow of the missile. Leaping forward Hopalong ran into a cloud of smoke and staggered as he jumped to close quarters. His hand smashed full in the foreman's face and his knee sank in the foreman's groin. They went down, the foreman weak from the kick and Hopalong sick and weak from the bullet that had grazed the bone of his bad thigh. And lying on the ground they fought in a daze, each incapable of inflicting serious injury for awhile. But the foreman grew stronger as his enemy grew weaker from loss of blood and, wriggling from under his furious antagonist, he reached for his Colt. Hopalong threw himself forward and gripped the gun wrist between his teeth and closed his jaws until they ached. But the foreman, pounding ceaselessly on the other's face with his free hand, made the jaws relax and drew the weapon. Then he saw all the stars in the heavens as Hopalong's head crashed full against his jaw and before he could recover the gun was pinned under his enemy's knee. Hopalong's head crashed again against the foreman's jaw and his right hand gripped the corded throat while the left, its thumb inside the foreman's cheek and its fingers behind an ear, tugged and strained at the distorted face. Growling like wild beasts they strained and panted, and then, suddenly, Hopalong's grip relaxed and he made one last, desperate effort to bring his strength back into one furious attack; but in vain. The battered foreman, quick to sense the situation, wrestled his adversary to one side long enough to grab the Colt from under the shifting knee. As he clutched it a shot rang out and the weapon dropped from his nerveless hand before he could pull the trigger. An exulting, savage yell roared in his ears and in the next instant he seemed to leave the ground and soar through space. He dropped ten feet away and lay dazed and helpless as a knee crashed against his chest. Sammy Porter, his face working curiously with relief and rage, rolled him against the wall of the defile and struck him over the head with a rifle butt, first disarming him.

Hopalong opened his eyes and looked around, dazed and sick. The foreman, bound hand and foot by a forty-five foot lariat, lay close to the base of the wall and stared sullenly at the sky. Sammy was coming up the trail with a dripping sombrero held carefully in his hands and was growling and talking it all over. Hopalong looked down at his thigh and saw a heavy, blood-splotched bandage fastened clumsily in place. Glancing at Sammy again he idly noted that part of the youth's blue-flannel shirt was missing. Curiously, it matched the bandage. He closed his eyes and tried to think what it was all about.

Sammy ambled up to him, threw some water in the bruised face and then grinned cheerfully at the language he evoked. Producing a flask and holding it up to the light, Sammy slid his thumb to a certain level and then shoved the bottle against his friend's teeth. "Huh!" he chuckled, yanking the bottle away. "You'll be all right in a couple of days. But you shore are one h —l of a sight-it's a toss-up between you an' Atkins."

* * * * *

It was night. Hopalong stirred and arose on one elbow and noticed that he was lying on a blanket that covered a generous depth of leaves and pine boughs. The sap-filled firewood crackled and popped and hissed and whistled under the licking attack of the greedy flames, which flared up and died down in endless alternation, and which grotesquely revealed to Hopalong's throbbing eyes a bound figure lying on another blanket. That, he decided, was the foreman. Letting his gaze wander around the lighted circle he made out a figure squatting on the other side of the fire, and concluded it was Sammy Porter. "What you doin', Kid?" he asked.

Sammy arose and walked over to him. "Oh, just watchin' a fool puncher an' five hundred dollars," he grinned. "How you feelin' now, you ol' sage hen?"

"Good," replied the invalid, and, comparatively, it was the truth. "Fine an' strong," he added, which was not the truth.

"That's the way to talk," cheered the Cub. "You shore had one fine séance. You earned that five hundred, all right."

Hopalong reflected and then looked across at the prisoner. "He can fight like the devil," he muttered. "Why, I kicked him hard enough to kill anybody else." He turned again and looked Sammy in the eyes, smiling as best he could. "There ain't no five hundred for me, Kid. I did n't come for that, did n't know nothin' about it. An' it's blood money, besides. We 'll turn him loose if he 'll get out of the country, hey? We 'll give him a chance; either that or you take th' reward."

Sammy stared, grunted and stared again. "What you ravin' about?" he demanded. "An' you didn't come after him for that money?" he asked, sarcastically.

Hopalong nodded and smiled again. "That's right, Kid," he answered, thoughtfully. "I come down to make him get out of th' country. You let him go after we get out of this. I reckon I got yore share of the reward right here in my pocket; purty near that much, anyhow. You take it an' let him vamoose. What you say?"

Sammy rose, angry and disgusted. His anger spoke first. "You go to h —l with yore money! I don't want it!" Then, slowly and wonderingly spoke his disgust. "He 's yourn; do what you want. But I here remarks, frank an' candid, open an' so all may hear, that yo 're a large, puzzlin' d —d fool. Now lay back on that blanket an' go to sleep afore I changes my mind!"

Sammy drifted past the prisoner and looked down at him. "Hear that?" he demanded. There was no answer and he grunted. "Huh! You heard it, all right; an' it plumb stunned you." Passing on he grabbed the last blanket in sight, it was on the foreman's horse, and rolled up in it, feet to the fire. His gun he placed under the saddle he had leaned against, which now made his pillow. As he squirmed into the most comfortable position he could find under the circumstances he raised his head and glanced across at his friend. "Huh!" he growled softly. "That's th' worst of them sentimental fellers. That gal shore wrapped him 'round her li'l finger all right. Oh, well," he sighed. "'Tain't none of my doin's, thank the Lord; I got sense!" And with the satisfaction of this thought still warm upon him he closed his eyes and went to sleep, confident that the slightest sound would awaken him; and fully justified in his confidence.

XIII

His Code

Mr. "Youbet" Somes, erstwhile foreman of the Two-X-Two ranch, in Arizona, and now out of a job, rode gloomily toward Kit, a town between him and his destination.

Needless to say, he was a cowman through and through. More than that, he was so saturated with cowmen's traditions as to resent pugnaciously anything which flouted them.

He was of the old school, and would not submit quietly to two things, among others, which an old-school cowman hated-wire fences and sheep. To this he owed his present ride, for he hated wire fences cordially. They meant the passing of the free, open range, of straight trails across country; they meant a great change, an intolerable condition.

"Yessir, bronch! Things are gettin' damnabler every year, with th' railroads, tourists, nesters, barb' wire, an' sheep. Last year, it was a windmill, that screeched till our hair riz up. It would n't work when we wanted it to, an' we could n't stop it when it once got started.

"It gave us no sleep, no peace; an' it killed Bob Cousins-swung round with th' wind an' knocked him off 'n th' platform, sixty feet, to th' ground. Bob allus did like to monkey with th' buzz saw. I shore told him not to go up there, because th' cussed thing was loaded; but, bein' mule-headed, he knowed more 'n me.

"But this year! Lord-but that was an awful pile of wire, bronch! Three strands high, an' over a hundred an' fifty miles round that pasture. That was a' insult, bronch; an' I never swaller 'em. That's what put me an' you out here, in th' middle of nowhere, tryin' to find a way out. G'wan, now! You ain't goin' to rest till I gets off you. G'wan, I told you!"

Mr. Somes was riding east, bound for the Bar-20, where he had friends. For a year or two, he had heard persistent rumors to the effect that Buck Peters had more cows than he knew what to do with; and he argued rightly that the Bar-20 foreman could find a place for an old friend, whose ability was unquestioned. Of one thing he was certain-there were no wire fences, down there.

It was dusk when he dismounted in front of Logan's, in Kit, and went inside. The bartender glanced up, reaching for a bottle on the shelf beside him.

Youbet nodded. "You got it first pop. Have one with me. I 'm countin' on staying over in town tonight. Got a place for me?"

"Shore have-upstairs in th' attic. Want grub, too?"

"Well, I sorter hope to have somethin' to eat afore I pull out. Here's how!" And when Mr. Somes placed his empty glass on the bar, he smiled good-naturedly. "That's good stuff. Much goin' on in town?"

"Reckon you can get a game most anywhere."

"Where do I get that grub? Here?"

"No-down th' street. Ridin' far?"

"Yes —a little. Goin' down to th' Bar-20 for a job punchin'. I hear Peters has got more cows than he can handle. Know anybody down there you wants to send any word to?"

"I 'll be hanged if I know," laughed the bartender. "I know a lot of fellers, but they shift so I can't keep track of 'em, nohow."

A man in a far corner pushed back his chair, and approached the bar, scowling as he glanced at Youbet. "Gimme another," he ordered.

"Why, hullo, stranger!" exclaimed Youbet. "I did n't see you before. Have one with me."

The other looked him squarely in the eyes. "Ex-cuse me, stranger —I 'm a sheepman, an' I don't drink with cowmen."

"Well, ex-cuse *me*!" retorted Youbet, like a flash. "If I 'd 'a' knowed you was a sheepman, I wouldn't 'a' asked you!"

The sheepman drank his liquor and, returning to his corner, placed his elbows on the table, and his chin in his hands, apparently paying no further attention to the others.

"If I can't get a job with Peters, I can try th' C-80 or Double Arrow," continued Youbet, as he toyed with his glass. "If I can't get on with one of them, I reckons Waffles, of th' O-Bar-O, will find a place for me, though I don't like that country a whole lot."

The bartender hesitated for a moment. "Do you know Waffles?" he asked.

"Shore-know 'em all. Why? Do you know him, too?"

"No; but I 've heard of him."

"That so? He 's a good feller, he is. I 've punched with both him an' Peters."

"I heard he wasn't," replied the bartender, slowly but carelessly.

"Then you heard wrong, all right," rejoined Youbet. "He's one of us old fellers-hates sheep, barb' wire, an' nesters as bad as I do; an' sonny," he continued, warming as he went on. "Th' cow country ain't what it used to be-not no way. I can remember when there war n't no wire, no nesters, an' no sheep. An', between you and me, I don't know which is th' worst. Every time I runs up agin' one of 'em, I says it's th' worst; but I guess it's just about a even break."

"I heard about yore friend Waffles through sheep," replied the bartender. "He chased a sheep outfit out of a hill range near his ranch, an' killed a couple of 'em, a-doin' it."

"Served 'em right-served 'em right," responded Youbet, turning and walking toward the door. "They ain't got no business on a cattle range-not nohow."

The man in the corner started to follow, half raising his hand, as though to emphasize something he was about to say; but changed his mind, and sullenly resumed his brooding attitude.

"Reckon I 'll put my cayuse in yore corral, an' look th' town over," Youbet remarked, over his shoulder. "Remember, yo 're savin' a bed for me."

As he stepped to the street, the man in the corner lazily arose and looked out of the window, swearing softly while he watched the man who hated sheep.

"Well, there 's another friend of yore business," laughed the bartender, leaning back to enjoy the other's discomfiture. "*He* don't like 'em, neither."

"He 's a fool of a mossback, so far behind th' times he don't know who 's President," retorted the other, still staring down the street.

"Well, he don't know that this has got to be a purty fair sheep town-that's shore."

"He 'll find out, if he makes many more talks like that-an' that ain't no dream, neither!" snapped the sheepman. He wheeled, and frowned at the man behind the bar. "You see what he gets, if he opens his cow mouth in here tonight. Th' boys hate this kind real fervent; an' when they finds out that he 's a side pardner of that coyote Waffles, they won't need much excuse. You wait-that's all!"

"Oh, what's th' use of gettin' all riled up about it?" demanded the bartender easily. "He did n't know *you* was a sheepman, when he made his first break. An' lemme tell you somethin' you want to remember-them old-time cowmen can use a short gun somethin' slick. They 've got 'em trained. Bet *he* can work th' double roll without shootin' hisself full of lead." The speaker grinned exasperatingly.

"Yes!" exploded the sheepman, who had tried to roll two guns at once, and had spent ten days in bed as a result of it.

The bartender laughed softly as he recalled the incident. "Have you tried it since?" he inquired.

"Go to th' devil!" grinned the other, heading for the door. "But he 'll get in trouble, if he spouts about hatin' sheep, when th' boys come in. You better get him drunk an' lock him in th' attic, before then."

"G'wan! I ain't playin' guardian to nobody," rejoined the bartender. "But remember what I said-them old fellers can use 'em slick an' rapid."

The sheepman went out as Youbet returned; and the latter seated himself, crossing his legs and drawing out his pipe.

The bartender perfunctorily drew a cloth across the bar, and smiled. "So you don't like wire, sheep, or nesters," he remarked.

Mr. Somes looked up, in surprise, forgetting that he held a lighted match between thumb and finger. "Like 'em! Huh, I reckon not. I 'm lookin' for a job because of wire. H —l!" he exclaimed, dropping the match, and rubbing his finger. "That's twice I did that fool thing in a week," he remarked, in apology and self-condemnation, and struck another match.

"I was foreman of my ranch for nigh onto ten years. It was a good ranch, an' I was satisfied till last year, when they made me put up a windmill that did n't mill, but screeched awful. I stood for that because I could get away from it in th' daytime.

"But this year! One day, not very long ago, I got a letter from th' owners, an' it says for me to build a wire fence around our range. It went on to say that there was two carloads of barb' wire at Mesquite. We was to tote that wire home, an' start in. If two carloads wasn't enough, they 'd send us more. We had one busted-down grub waggin, an' Mesquite shore was fifty miles away-which meant a whoppin' long job totin'.

"When I saw th' boys, that night, I told 'em that I 'd got orders to raise their pay five dollars a month-which made 'em cheer. Then I told 'em that was so providin' they helped me build a barb' wire fence around th' range-which did n't make 'em cheer.

"Th' boundary lines of th' range we was usin' was close onto a hundred an' fifty miles long, an' three strands of wire along a trail like that is some job. We was to put th' posts twelve feet apart, an' they was to be five feet outen th' ground an' four feet in it-which makes 'em nine feet over all.

"There was n't no posts at Mesquite. Them posts was supposed to be growin' freelike on th' range, just waitin' for us to cut 'em, skin 'em, tote an' drop 'em every twelve feet along a line a hundred an' fifty miles long. An' then there was to be a hole dug for every post, an' tampin', staplin', an' stringin' that hell-wire. An' don't forget that lone, busted-down grub waggin that was to do that totin'!

"There was some excitement on th' Two-X-Two that night, an' a lot of figgerin'; us bein' some curious about how many posts was needed, an' how many holes we was to dig to fit th' aforesaid posts. We made it sixty-six thousand. Think of it! An' only eight of us to tackle a job like that, an' ride range at th' same time!"

"Oh, ho!" roared the bartender, hugging himself, and trying to carry a drink to the narrator at the same time. "Go on! That's good!"

"Is, is it?" snorted Youbet. "Huh! You wouldn't 'a' thought so, if you was one of us eight. Well, I set right down an' writ a long letter-took six cents' worth of stamps-an' gave our views regardin' wire fences in general an' this one of ourn in particular. I hated fences, an' do yet; an' so 'd my boys hate 'em, an' they do yet.

"In due time, I got a answer, which come for two cents. It says: 'Build that fence.'

"I sent Charley over to Mesquite to look over them cars of wire. He saw 'em, both of 'em. An' th' agent saw him.

"Th' agent was a' important man, an' he grabs Charley quick. 'Hey, you Two-X-Two puncher-you get that wire home quick. It went past here three times before they switched it, an' I 've been gettin' blazes from th' company ever since. We needs th' cars.'

"'Don't belong to me,' says Charley. 'I shore don't want it. I 'm eatin' beans an' bacon instead.'

"'You send for that wire!' yells th' agent, wild-like.

"Charley winks. 'Can't you keep it passin' this station till it snows hard? Have a drink.'

"Well, th' agent wouldn't drink, an' he wouldn't send that pore wire out into a cold world no more; an' so Charley comes home an' reports, him lookin' wanlike. When he told us, he looked sort of funny, an' blurts out that his mother went an' died up in Laramie, an' he must shore 'nuff rustle up there an' bury her. He went.

"Then Fred Ball begun to have pains in his stomach, an' said it was appendix somethin', what he had been readin' about in th' papers. He had to go to Denver, an' get a good doctor, or he 'd shore die. He went.

"Carson had to go to Santa Fé to keep some of his numerous city lots from bein' sold off by th' sheriff. He went.

"Th' rest, bein' handicapped by th' good start th' others had made in corrallin' all th' excuses, said they 'd go for th' wire. They went.

"I waited four days, an' then I went after 'em. When I got to th' station, I sees th' agent out sizin' up our wire; an' when I hails, he jumps my way quick, an' grabs my laig tight.

"'You take that wire home!' he yells.

"'Shore,' says I soothingly. 'You looks mad,' I adds.

"'Mad! Mad!' he shouts, hoppin' round, but hangin' onto my laig like grim death. 'Mad! I 'm goin' *loco* —crazy! I can't sleep! There 's twenty letters an' messages on my table, tellin' me to get that wire off'n th' cars an' send th' empties back on th' next freight! You've got to take it —*got to!*'"

The bartender shocked his nervous system by drinking plain water by mistake, but he listened eagerly. "Yes? What then?"

"Well, then I asks him where I can find my men, an' team, an' waggin'. He tells me. Th' team an' waggin is in a corral down th' street, but he don't know where th' men are. They held a gun to his head, an' said they 'd kill him if he didn't flag th' next train for 'em. Th' next train was a through express, carryin' mail. He was n't dead.

"He showed me ten more letters an' messages, regardin' th' flaggin' of a contract-mail train for four fares; an' some of them letters must 'a' been written by a old-time cowman, they was that eloquent an' God-fearin'. Then I went.

"Why, Charley was twenty years old; an' we figgered that, when th' last staple was drove in th' last post, he 'd 'a' been dead ten years! Where did I come in, the —?"

"Oh, Lord!" sighed the bartender, holding his sides, and trying to straighten his face so that he could talk out of the middle of it. "That's th' best ever! Have another drink!"

"I ain't tellin' my troubles for liquor," snorted Youbet. "You have one with me. Here comes some customers down th' street, I reckon."

"Say!" exclaimed the bartender hurriedly. "You keep mum about sheep. This is a red-hot sheep town, an' it hates Waffles an' all his friends. Hullo, boys!" he called to four men, who filed into the room. "Where 's th' rest of you?"

"Comin' in later. Same thing, Jimmy," replied Clayton, chief herder. "An' give us th' cards."

"Have you seen Price?" asked Towne.

"Yes; he was in here a few minutes ago. What 'd you say, Schultz?" the bartender asked, turning to the man who pulled at his sleeve.

"I said dot you vas nod right aboud vat you said de odder day. Chust now I ask Clayton, und he said you vas nod."

"All right, Dutchy-all right!" laughed the bartender. "Then it's on me this time, ain't it?"

Youbet walked to the bar. "Say, where do I get that grub? It's about time for me to mosey off an' feed."

"Next building-and you'll take mutton if yo 're wise," replied the bartender, in a low voice. "Th' hash is awful, an' the beef is tough," he added, a little louder.

"Mutton be damned!" snorted Youbet, stamping out. "I eat what I punch!" And his growls became lost in the street.

Schultz glanced up. "Yah! Und he shoot vat I eat, tarn him, ven he gan!"

"Oh, put yore ante in, an' don't talk so much!" rejoined Towne. "He ain't going to shoot *you*."

"It 'll cost you two bits to come in," remarked Clayton.

"An' two more," added Towne, raising the ante.

"Goot! I blay mit you. But binochle iss der game!"

"I 'll tell you a good story about a barb' wire fence tomorrow, fellers," promised the bartender, grinning.

The poker game had been going for some time before further remarks were made about the cowman who had left, and then it was Clayton who spoke.

"Say, Jimmy!" he remarked, as Schultz dealt. "Who is yore leather-pants friend who don't like mutton?"

The bartender lifted a bottle, and replaced it with great care. "Oh, just a ranch foreman, out of a job. He's a funny old feller."

"So? An' what's so funny about him? Get in there, Towne, if you wants to do any playin' with us."

"Why, he was ordered to build a hundred an' fifty miles of wire fence around his range, an' he jumped ruther than do it."

"Yas-an' most of it government land, I reckon," interposed Towne.

"Pshaw! It's an old game with them," laughed Clayton. "Th' law don't get to them; an' if they 've got a good outfit, nobody has got any chance agin 'em."

"Py Gott, dot's right!" grunted Schultz.

"Shore, it is," responded Towne, forgetting the game. "Take that Apache Hills run-in. Waffles did n't have no more right to that range than anybody else, but that did n't make no difference. He threw a couple of outfits in there, penned us in th' cabin, killed MacKay, an' shot th' rest of us up plenty. Then he threatened to slaughter our herd if we did n't pull out. By God, I 'd like to get a cowman like him up here, where th' tables are turned around on th' friends proposition."

"Hullo, boys!" remarked the bartender to the pair who came in.

"Just in time. Get chairs, an' take hands," invited Clayton, moving over.

"Who's th' cowman yo're talkin' about?" asked Baxter, as he leaned lazily against the bar.

"Oh, all of 'em," rejoined Towne surlily. "There 's one in town, now, who don't like sheep."

"That so?" queried Baxter slowly. "I reckon he better keep his mouth shut, then."

"Oh, he 's all right! He 's a jolly old geezer," assured the bartender. "He just talks to hear hisself-one of them old-timers what can't get right to th' way things has changed on th' range. It was them boys that did great work when th' range was wild."

"Yes, an' it's them bull-headed old fools what are raisin' all th' hell with th' sheep," retorted Towne, frowning darkly as he remembered some of the indignities he had borne at the hands of cowmen.

"I wish his name was Waffles." Clayton smiled significantly.

"Rainin' again," remarked a man in the doorway, stamping in. "Reckon it ain't never goin' to stop."

"Where you been so long, Price?" asked Clayton, as a salutation.

"Oh, just shiftin' about. That cow wrastler raised th' devil in th' hotel," Price replied. "Old fool! They brought him mutton, an' he wanted to clean out th' place. Said he 'd as soon eat barb' wire. They 're feedin' him hash an' canned stuff, now."

"He 'll get hurt, if he don't look out," remarked Clayton. "Who is he, anyhow, Price?"

"Don't know his name; but he 's from Arizona, on his way to th' Pecos country. Says he 's a friend of Buck Peters an' Waffles. To use one of his own expressions, he 's a old mosshead."

"Friend of Waffles, hey?" exclaimed Towne.

"Yumpin' Yimminy!" cried Oleson, in the same breath.

"Well, if he knows when he's well off, he 'll stay away from here, an' keep his mouth closed," said Clayton.

"Aw, let him alone! He's one agin' th' whole town-an' a good old feller, at that," hastily assured the bartender. "It ain't his fault that Waffles buffaloed you fellers out of th' Hills, is it? He's goin' on early tomorrow; so let him be."

"You 'll get yoreself in trouble, Jimmy, m' boy, if you inserts yoreself in this," warned Towne. "It was us agin' a whole section, an' we got ours. Let him take his, if he talks too much."

"Shore," replied Price. "I heard him shoot off his mouth, an hour ago, an' he's got altogether too much to say. You mind th' bar an' yore own business, Jimmy. We ain't kids."

"Go you two bits better," said Clayton, shoving out a coin. "Gimme some cards, Towne. It 'll cost you a dollar to see our raises."

Baxter walked over to watch the play. "I 'm comin' in next game. Who 's winnin', now?"

"Reckon I am; but we ain't much more 'n got started," Clayton replied. "Did you call, Towne? Why, I 've got three little tens. You got anythin' better?"

"Never saw such luck!" exclaimed Towne disgustedly. "Dutchy, yo 're a Jonah."

"Damn th' mutton, says I. It was even in that hash!" growled a voice, just outside the door.

A moment later, Youbet Somes entered, swinging his sombrero energetically to shake off the water.

"Damn th' rain, too, an' this wart of a town. A man can't get nothin' fit to eat for love or money, on a sheep range. Gimme a drink, sonny! Mebby it 'll cut th' taste of that rank tallow out 'n my mouth. Th' reason there is sheep on this earth of our'n is that th' devil chased 'em out 'n his place-an' no blame to him."

He drank half his liquor, and, placing the glass on the bar beside him, turned to watch the game. "Ah, strangers-that's th' only game, after all. I 've dabbled in 'em all from faro to roulette, but that's th' boss of 'em all."

"See you an' call," remarked Clayton, ignoring the newcomer. "What you got, you Dutch pagan?"

"*Zwei Kaisers* und a bair of chackasses, mit a deuce."

"Kings up!" exclaimed Clayton. "Why, say-you bet th' worst of anybody I ever knew! You 'll balk on bettin' two bits on threes, and plunge on a bluff. I reckoned you did n't have nothin'. Why ain't you more consistent?" he asked, winking at Towne.

"Gonsisdency iss no chewel in dis game-it means go broke," placidly grunted Schultz, raking in his winnings.

His friend Schneider smiled.

"Coyotes are gettin' too numerous, this year," Baxter remarked, shuffling.

Youbet pushed his sombrero back on his head. "They don't get numerous on a cow range," he said significantly.

"Huh!" snorted Baxter. "They've got too much respect to stay on one longer than they 've got to."

"They'd ruther be with their woolly-coated cousins," rejoined the cowman quietly. It was beneath his dignity as a cowman to pay much attention to what sheepmen said, yet he could not remain silent under such a remark.

He regarded sheep herders, those human beings who walked at their work, as men who had reached the lowest rung in the ladder of human endeavors. His belief was not original with him, but was that of many of his school. He was a horseman, a mounted man, and one of the aristocracy of the range; they were, to him, the rabble, and almost beneath his contempt.

Besides, it was commonly believed by cowmen that sheep destroyed the grass as far as cattle grazing was concerned-and this was the chief reason for the animosity against sheep and their herders, which burned so strongly in the hearts of cattle owners and their outfits.

Youbet drained his glass, and continued: "The coyote leaves th' cattle range for th' same good reason yore sheep leave it-because they are chased out, or killed. Naturally, blood kin will hang together in banishment."

"You know a whole lot, don't you?" snorted Clayton, with sarcasm. "Yo 're shore wise, you are!"

"He is so vise as a —a gow," remarked Schultz, grinning.

"You 'll know more, when you get as old as me," replied the ex-foreman, carefully placing the empty glass on the bar.

"I don't want to get as old as you, if I have to lose all my common sense," retorted Clayton angrily.

"An' be a damned nuisance generally," observed Towne.

"I 've seen a lot of things in my life," Youbet began, trying to ignore the tones of the others. They were young men, and he knew that youth grew unduly heated in argument. "I saw th' comin' of th' Texas drive herds, till th' range was crowded where th' year before there was nothin'. I saw th' comin' of th' sheep-an' barb' wire, I 'm sorry to say. Th' sheep came like locusts, leavin' a dyin' range behind 'em. Thin, half-starved cattle showed which way they went. You can't tell me nothin' I don't know about sheep."

"An' *I* 've seen sheep dyin' in piles on th' open range," cried Clayton, his own wrongs lashing him into a rage. "*I* 've seen 'em dynamited, an' drowned and driven hell-to-split over canyons! I 've had my men taunted, an' chased, an' killed —*killed*, by God! —just because they tried to make a' honest livin'! Who did it all? Who killed my men an' my sheep? *Who did it?*" he shouted, taking a short step forward, while an endorsing growl ran along the line of sheepmen at his side.

"Cowpunchers-they did it! They killed 'em-an' why? Because we tried to use th' grass that we had as much right to as they had —*that 's* why!"

"Th' cows was here first," replied Youbet, keenly alert, but not one whit abashed by the odds, long as they were. "It was theirs because they was there first."

"It was not theirs, no more'n th' sun was!" cried Towne, unable to allow his chief to do all the talking.

"You said you knowed Waffles," continued Clayton loudly. "Well, he 's another of you old-time cowmen! He killed MacKay-murdered him-because we was usin' a hill range a day's ride from his own grass! He had twenty men like hisself to back him up. If we 'd been as many as them, they would n't 'a' tried it-an' you know it!"

"I don't know anything of th' kind, but I do know —" began Youbet; but Schultz interrupted him with a remark intended to contain humor.

"Ven you say you doand know anyt'ing, you know somedings; ven you know dot you doand know noddings, den you know somedings. Und das iss so-yah."

"Who th' devil told you to stick yore Dutch mouth —" retorted Youbet; but Clayton cut him short.

"So *yo 're* a old-timer, hey?" cried the sheepman. "Well, by God, yore old-time friend Waffles is a coward, a murderer, an' —"

"Yo're a liar!" rang out the vibrant voice of the cowman

"Yo 're a liar!" rang out the vibrant voice of the cowman, his gun out and leveled in a flash. The seven had moved forward as one man, actuated by the same impulse; and their hands were moving toward their guns when the crashes of Youbet's weapon reverberated in the small room, the acrid smoke swirling around him as though to shield him from the result of his folly —a result which he had weighed and then ignored.

Clayton dropped, with his mouth still open. Towne's gun chocked back in the scabbard as its owner stumbled blindly over a chair and went down, never to rise. Schultz fired once, and fell back across the table.

The three shots had followed one another with incredible quickness; and the seven, not believing that one man would dare attack so many, had not expected his play. Before the stunned sheepmen could begin firing, three were dead.

Price, badly wounded, fired as he plunged to the wall for support; and the other three were now wrapped in their own smoke.

Wounded in several places, with his gun empty, Youbet hurled the weapon at Price, and missed by so narrow a margin that the sheepman's aim was spoiled. Youbet now sprang to the bar, and tried to vault over it, to get to the gun which he knew always lay on the shelf behind it. As his feet touched the upper edge of the counter, he grunted and, collapsing like a jackknife, loosed his hold, and fell to the floor.

"*Mein Gott!*" groaned Schneider, as he tried to raise himself. He looked around in a dazed manner, hardly understanding just what had happened. "He vas mat; crazy mat!"

Oleson arose unsteadily to his feet, and groped his way along, the wall to where Price lay.

The fallen man looked up, in response to the touch on his shoulder; and he swore feebly: "Damn that fool-that idiot!"

"Shut up, an' git out!" shouted the bartender, standing rigidly upright, with a heavy Colt in his upraised hand. There were tears in his eyes, and his voice broke from excitement. "He wouldn't swaller yore insults! He knowed he was a better man! Get out of here, every damned one of you, or I 'll begin where he stopped. G 'wan —*get out!*"

The four looked at him, befuddled and sorely hurt; but they understood the attitude, if they did not quite grasp the words-and they knew that he meant what he looked. Staggering and hobbling, they finally found the door, and plunged out to the street, to meet the crowd of men who were running toward the building.

Jimmy, choking with anger and with respect for the man who had preferred death to insults, slammed shut the door and, dropping the bar into place, turned and gazed at the quiet figure huddled at the base of the counter.

"Old man," he muttered, "now I understands why th' sheep don't stay long on a cattle range."

XIV
Sammy Hunts a Job

Sammy Porter, detailed by Hopalong, the trail-boss, rode into Truxton three days before the herd was due, to notify the agent that cars were wanted. Three thousand three-year-olds were on their way to the packing houses and must be sent through speedily. Sammy saw the agent and, leaving him much less sweeter in temper than when he had found him, rode down the dismal street kicking up a prodigious amount of dust. One other duty demanded attention and its fulfillment was promised by the sign over the faded pine front of the first building.

"Restaurant," he read aloud. "That's mine. Beans, bacon an' biscuits for 'most a month! But now I 'm goin' to forget that Blinky Thompkins ever bossed a trail wagon an' tried to cook."

Dismounting, he glanced in the window and pulled at the downy fuzz trying to make a showing on his upper lip. "Purty, all right. Brown hair an' I reckon brown eyes. Nice li'l girl. Well, they don't make no dents on me no more," he congratulated himself, and entered. His twenty years fairly sagged with animosity toward the fair sex, the intermittent smoke from the ruins of his last love affair still painfully in evidence at times. But careless as he tried to be he could not banish the swaggering mannerisms of Youth in the presence of Maid, or change his habit of speech under such conditions.

"Well, well," he smiled. "Here I 'are' again. Li'l Sammy in search of his grub. An' if it's as nice as you he 'll shore have to flag his outfit an' keep this town all to hisself. Got any chicken?"

The maid's nose went up and Sammy noticed that it tilted a trifle, and he cocked his head on one side to see it better. And the eyes were brown, very big and very deep-they possessed a melting quality he had never observed before. The maid shrugged her shoulders and swung around, the tip-tilt nose going a bit higher.

Sammy leaned back against the door and nodded approval of the slender figure in spic-and-span white. "Li'l Sammy is a fer-o-cious cow-punch from a chickenless land," he observed, sorrowfully. "There ain't *no* kinds of chickens. Nothin' but men an' cattle an' misguided cooks; an' beans, bacon an' biscuits. Li'l Miss, have you a chicken for me?"

"No!" The head went around again, Sammy bending to one side to see it as long as he could. The pink, shell-like ear that flirted with him through the loosely-gathered, rebellious hair caught his attention and he leveled an accusing finger at it. "Naughty li'l ear, peekin' at Sammy that-a-way! Oh, you stingy girl!" he chided as the back of her head confronted him. "Well, Sammy don't like girls, no matter how pink their ears are, or turned up their noses, or wonderful their eyes. He just wants chicken, an' all th' fixin's. He 'll be very humble an' grateful to Li'l Miss if she 'll tell him what he can have. An' he 'll behave just like a Sunday-school boy.

"Aw, you don't want to get mad at only me," he continued after she refused to answer. "Got any chicken? Got any-eggs? Lucky Sammy! An' some nice ham? Two lucky Sammies. An' some mashed potatoes? Fried? Good. An' will Li'l Miss please make a brand new cup of strong coffee? Then he 'll go over an' sit in that nice chair an' watch an' listen. But you ought n't get mad at him. Are you really-an'-truly mad?"

She swept down the room, into the kitchen partitioned off at the farther end and slammed the door. Sammy grinned, tugged at his upper lip and fancy-stepped to the table. He smoothed his tumbled hair, retied his neck-kerchief and dusted himself off with his red bandanna hand-kerchief. "Nice li'l town," he soliloquized. "*Fine* li'l town. Dunno as I ought to go back to th' herd-Hoppy did n't tell me to. Reckon I 'll stick in town an' argue with th' agent. If I argue with th' agent I 'll be busy; an' I can't leave while I 'm busy." He leaned back and chuckled. "Lucky me! If Hoppy had gone an' picked Johnny to argue with th' agent for three whole days where would *I* be? But I gotta keep Johnny outa here, th' son-of-a-gun. He ain't like me-he *likes* girls; an' he ain't bashful."

He picked up a paper lying on a chair near him and looked it over until the kitchen door squeaked. She carried a tray covered with a snow-white napkin which looked like a topograph-ical map with its mountains and valleys and plains. His chuckle was infectious to the extent of a smile and her eyes danced as she placed his dinner before him.

"Betcha it's fine," he grinned, shoveling sugar into the inky coffee. "Blinky oughta have a good look at *this* layout."

"Don't be too sure," she retorted. "Mrs. Olmstead is sick and I 'm taking charge of things for her. I 'm not a good cook."

"Nothin 's th' matter with this," he assured her between bites. "Lots better 'n most purty girls can do. If Hopalong goes up against this he 'll offer you a hundred a month an' throw Blinky in to wash th' dishes. But he 'd have to 'point me guard, or you would n't have no time to do no cookin'."

"You 'd make a fine guard," she retorted.

"Don't believe it, huh? Jus' wait till you know me better."

"How do you know I 'm going to?"

"I 'm a good guesser. Jus' put a li'l pepper right there on that yalla spot. Say, any chance to get a job in this town?"

"Why, I don't know."

"Goin' to stay long?"

"I can't say. I won't go till Mrs. Olmstead is well."

"Not meanin' no harm to Mrs. Olmstead, of course-but you don't *have* to go, do you?"

"I do as I please."

"So I was thinkin'. Now, 'bout that job: any chance? Any ranches near here?"

"Several. But they want *men*. Are you a real cowboy?"

Sammy folded his hands and shook his head sorrowfully. "Huh! Want *men*! Now if I only had whiskers like Blinky. Why, 'course I 'm a cowboy. Regular one-but I can outgrow it easy. I 'm a sorta maverick an' I 'm willin' to wear a nice brand. My name's Sammy Porter," he suggested.

"That's nice. Mine is n't nice."

"Easy to change it. Really like mine?"

"Coffee strong enough?"

"Sumptious. How long's Mrs. Olmstead going to be sick?"

Her face clouded. "I don't know. I hope it will not be for long. She 's had *so* much trouble the past year. Oh, wait! I forgot the toast!" and she sped lightly away to rescue the burning bread.

The front door opened and slammed shut, the newcomer dropping into the nearest chair. He pounded on the table. "Hello, there! I want somethin' to eat, quick!"

Sammy turned and saw a portly, flashily dressed drummer whose importance was written large all over him. "Hey!" barked the drummer, "gimme something to eat. I can't wait all day!"

A vicious clang in the kitchen told that his presence was known and resented.

As Sammy turned from the stranger he caught sight of a pretty flushed face disappearing behind the door jamb, the brown eyes snapping and the red lips straight and compressed. His glance, again traveling to the drummer, began with the dusty patent leathers and went slowly upward, resting boldly on the heavy face. Sammy's expression told nothing and the newcomer, glaring at him for an instant, looked over the menu card and then stared at the partition, fidgeting in his chair, thumping meanwhile on the table with his fingers.

At a sound from the kitchen Sammy turned back to his table and smiled reassuringly as the toast was placed before him. "I burned it and had to make new," she said, the pink spots in her cheeks a little deeper in color.

"Why, th' other was good enough for me," he replied. "Know Mrs. Olmstead a long time?" he asked.

"Ever since I was a little girl. She lived near us in Clev —"

"Cleveland," he finished. "State of Ohio," he added, laughingly. "I 'll get it all before I go."

"Indeed you won't!"

"Miss," interrupted the drummer, "if you ain't too busy, would you mind gettin' me a steak an' some coffee?" The tones were weighted with sarcasm and Sammy writhed in his chair. The girl flushed, turned abruptly and went slowly into the kitchen, from where considerable noise now emanated. In a short time she emerged with the drummer's order, placed it in front of him and started back again. But he stopped her. "I said I wanted it rare an' it's well done. An' also that I wanted fried potatoes. Take it back."

The girl's eyes blazed: "You gave no instructions," she retorted.

"Don't tell me that! I know what I said!" snapped the drummer. "I won't eat it an' I won't pay for it. If you was n't so *busy* you 'd heard what I said."

Sammy was arising before he saw the tears of vexation in her eyes, but they settled it for him. He placed his hand lightly on her shoulder. "You get me some pie an' take a li'l walk. Me an' this here gent is goin' to hold a palaver. Ain't we, stranger?"

The drummer glared at him. "We ain't!" he retorted.

Sammy grinned ingratiatingly. "Oh, my; but we are." He slung a leg over a chair back and leaned forward, resting his elbow on his knee. "Yes, indeed we are-least-a-wise, *I* am." His tones became very soft and confiding. "An' I 'm shore goin' to watch you eat that steak."

"What's that you 're going to do?" the drummer demanded, half rising.

"Sit down," begged Sammy, his gun swinging at his knee. He picked up a toothpick with his left hand and chewed it reflectively. "These here Colts make a' awful muss, sometimes," he remarked. "'Specially at close range. Why," he confided, "I once knowed a man what was shot 'most in two. He was a moss-head an' would n't do what he was told. Better sorta lead off at that steak, *hombre*," he suggested, chewing evenly on the toothpick. Noticing that the girl still lingered, hypnotized by fear and curiosity, he spoke to her over his shoulder. "Won't you please get me that pie, or somethin'? Run out an' borrow a pan, or somethin'," he pleaded. "I don't like to be handicapped when I 'm feedin' cattle."

The drummer's red face paled a little and one hand stole cautiously under his coat-and froze there. Sammy hardly had moved, but the Colt was now horizontal and glowered at the gaudy waistcoat. He was between it and the girl and she did not see the movement. His smile was placid and fixed and he spoke so that she should get no inkling of what was going on. "Never drink on an empty stomach," he advised. "After you eat that meal, then you can fuss with yore flask all you wants." He glanced out of the corner of his eye at the girl and nodded. "Still there! Oh, I most forgot, stranger. You take off yore hat an' 'pologize, so she can go. Jus' say yo 're a dawg an never did have no manners. *Say* it!" he ordered, softly. The drummer gulped and muttered something, but the Colt, still hidden from the girl by its owner's body, moved forward a little and Sammy's throaty growl put an end to the muttering. "Say it plain," he ordered, the color fading from his face and leaving pink spots against the white. "That's better-now, Li'l Miss, you get me that pie-please!" he begged.

When they were alone Sammy let the gun swing at his knee again. "I don't know how they treats wimmin where you came from, stranger; but out here we 're plumb polite. 'Course you did n't know that, an' that's why you did n't get all mussed up. Yo 're jus' plain ignorant an' can't help yore bringin' up. Now, you eat that steak, *pronto!*"

"It's too cold, now," grumbled the drummer, fidgeting in the chair.

The puncher's left hand moved to the table again and when it returned to his side there was a generous layer of red pepper on the meat. "Easy to fix things when you know how," he grinned. "If it gets any colder I 'll fix it some more." His tones became sharper and the words lost their drawled softness. "You goin' to start ag'in that by yoreself, or am I goin' to help you?" he demanded, lifting his leg off the chair and standing erect. All the humor had left his face and there was a grimness about the tight lips and a menace in the squinting eyes that sent a chill rippling down the drummer's spine. He tasted a forkful of the meat and gulped hastily, tears welling into his eyes. The puncher moved a little nearer and watched the frantic gulps with critical attention. "'Course, you can eat any way you wants-yo're payin' for it; but boltin' like a coyote ain't good for th' stummick. Howsomever, it's yore grub," he admitted.

A cup of cold coffee and a pitcher of water followed the meat in the same gulping haste. Tears streamed down the drummer's red face as he arose and turned toward the door. "Hol' on, stranger!" snapped Sammy. "That costs six bits," he prompted. The coins rang out on the nearest table, the door slammed and the agonized stranger ran madly down the street, cursing at every jump. Sammy sauntered to the door and craned his neck. "Somebody 's jus' naturally goin' to bust him wide open one of these days. He ain't got no sense," he muttered, turning back to get his pie.

A cloud of dust rolled up from the south, causing Briggs a little uneasiness, and he scowled through the door at the long empty siding and the pens sprawled along it.

Steps clacked across the platform and a grinning cowpuncher stopped at the open window. "They're here," he announced. "How 'bout th' cars?"

Briggs looked around wearily. For three days his life had been made miserable by this pest, who carried a laugh in his eyes, a sting on his tongue and a chip on his shoulder. "They 'll be here soon," he replied, with little interest. "But there 's th' pens."

"Yes, there's th' pens," smiled Sammy. "They'll hold 'bout one-tenth of that herd. Ain't I been pesterin' you to get them cars?"

The agent sighed expressively and listened to the instrument on his table. When it ceased he grabbed the key and asked a question. Then he smiled for the first time that day. "They 're passing Franklin. Be here in two hours. Now get out of here or I 'll lick you."

"There 's a nice place in one of them pens," smiled Sammy.

"I see you 're eating at Olmstead's," parried the agent.

"Yea."

"Nice girl. Come up last summer when Mrs. Olmstead petered out. I ate there last winter."

Sammy grinned at him. "Why 'd you stop?"

Briggs grew red and glanced at the nearing cloud of dust. "Better help your outfit, had n't you?"

Sammy was thoughtful. "Say, that's a plumb favorite eatin' place, ain't it?"

Briggs laughed. "Wait till Saturday when th' boys come in. There 's a dozen shinin' up to that girl. Tom Clarke is real persistent."

Sammy forsook the building as a prop. "Who 's he? Puncher?"

"Yes; an' bad," replied the agent. "But I reckon she don't know it."

Sammy looked at the dust cloud and turned to ask one more question. "What does this persistent gent look like, an' where's he hang out?" He nodded at the verbose reply and strode to his horse to ride toward the approaching herd. He espied Red first, and hailed. "Cars here in two hours. Where 's Hoppy?"

"Back in th' dust. But what happened to *you?*" demanded Red, with virile interest. Sammy ignored the challenge and loped along the edge of the cloud until he found the trail boss. "Them cars 'll be here in two hours," he reported.

"Take you three days to find it out?" snapped Hopalong.

"Took me three days to get 'em. I just about unraveled that agent. He swears every time he hears a noise, thinkin' it's me."

"Broke?" demanded Hopalong.

Sammy flushed. "I ain't gambled a cent since I hit town. An' say, them pens won't hold a tenth of 'em," he replied, looking over the dark blur that heaved under the dust cloud like a fog-covered, choppy sea.

"I 'm goin' to hold 'em on grass," replied the trail boss. "They ain't got enough cars on this toy road to move all them cows in less 'n a week. I ain't goin' to let 'em lose no weight in pens. Wait a minute! You 're on night herd for stayin' away."

When Sammy rode into camp the following morning he scorned Blinky's food, much to the open-mouthed amazement of that worthy and Johnny Nelson. Blinky thought of doctors and death; but Johnny, noticing his bunkmate's restlessness and the careful grooming of his person, had grave suspicions. "Good grub in this town?" he asked, saddling to go on his shift.

Sammy wiped a fleck of dust off his boot and looked up casually. "Shore. Best is at the Dutchman's at th' far end of th' street."

Johnny mounted, nodded and departed for the herd, where Red was pleasantly cursing his tardiness. Red would eat Blinky's grub and gladly. Johnny was cogitating. "There 's a girl in this town, an' he 's got three days' head start. No wonder them cars just got here!" Red's sarcastic voice intruded. "Think I eat grass, or my stummick 's made of rubber?" he snapped. "Think I feed onct a month like a snake?"

"No, Reddie," smiled Johnny, watching the eyebrows lift at the name. "More like a hawg."

Friday morning, a day ahead of the agent's promise, the cars backed onto the siding and by noon the last cow of the herd was taking its first-and last-ride. Sammy slipped away from the outfit at the pens and approached the restaurant from the rear. He would sit behind the partition this time and escape his friends.

The soft sand deadened his steps and when he looked in at the door, a cheery greeting on the tip of his tongue, he stopped and stared unnoticed by the sobbing girl bent over the table. One hand, outflung in dejected abandon, hung over the side and Sammy's eyes, glancing at it, narrowed as he looked. His involuntary, throaty exclamation sent the bowed head up with a jerk, but the look of hate and fear quickly died out of her eyes as she recognized him.

"An' all th' world tumbled down in a heap," he smiled. "But it 'll be all right again, same as it allus was," he assured her. "Will Li'l Miss tell Sammy all about it so he can put it together again?"

She looked at him through tear-dimmed eyes, the sobs slowly drying to a spasmodic catching in the rounded throat. She shook her head and the tears welled up again in answer to his sympathy. He walked softly to the table and placed a hand on her bowed head. "Li'l Miss will tell Sammy all about it when she dries her eyes an' gets comfy. Sammy will make things all right again an' laugh with her. Don't you mind him a mite-jus' cry hard, an' when all th' tears are used up, then you tell Sammy what it's all about." She shook her head and would not look up. He bent down carefully and examined the bruised wrist-and his eyes glinted with rage; but he did not speak. The minutes passed in silence, the girl ashamed to show her reddened and tear-stained face; the boy stubbornly determined to stay and learn the facts. He heard his friends tramp past, wondering where he was, but he did not move.

Finally she brushed back her hair and looked up at him and the misery in her eyes made him catch his breath. "Won't you go?" she pleaded.

He shook his head.

"Please!"

"Not till I finds out whose fingers made them marks," he replied. The look of fear flashed up again, but he checked it with a smile he far from felt. "Nobody 's goin' to make you cry, an' get away with it," he told her. "Who was it?"

"I won't tell you. I can't tell you! I don't know!"

"Li'l Miss, look me in th' eyes an' say it again. I thought so. You mustn't say things that ain't true. Who did that?"

"What do you want to know for?"

"Oh, jus' because."

"What will you do?"

"Oh, I 'll sorta talk to him. All I want to know is his name."

"I won't tell you; you 'll fight with him."

He turned his sombrero over and looked gravely into its crown. "Well," he admitted, "he *might* not like me talkin' 'bout it. Of course, you can't never tell."

"But he did n't mean to hurt me. He 's only rough and boisterous; and he wasn't himself," she pleaded, looking down.

"Uh-huh," grunted Sammy, cogitating. "So 'm I. *I 'm* awful rough an' boisterous, *I* am; only I don't hurt wimmin. What's his name?"

"I'll not tell you!"

"Well, all right; but if he ever comes in here again an' gets rough an' boisterous he 'll lose a hull lot of future. I 'll naturally blow most of his head off, which is frequent fatal. What's that? Oh, he's a bad man, is he? Uh-huh; so 'm I. Well, I 'm goin' to run along now an' see th' boss. If you won't tell, you won't. I 'll be back soon," and he sauntered to the street and headed for Pete's saloon, where the agent had said Mr. Clarke was wont to pass his fretful hours.

As he turned the corner he bumped into Hopalong and Johnny, who grabbed at him, and missed. He backed off and rested on his toes, gingery and alert. "Keep yore dusty han's off'n me," he said, quietly. "I 'm goin' down to palaver with a gent what I don't like."

Hopalong's shrewd glance looked him over. "What did this gent do?" he asked, and he would not be evaded.

"Oh, he insulted a nice li'l girl, an' I 'm in a hurry."

"G'way!" exclaimed Johnny. "That straight?"

"Too d —n straight," snapped Sammy. "He went an' bruised her wrists an' made her cry."

"Lead th' way, Kid," rejoined Johnny, readjusting his belt. "Mebby he 's got some friends," he suggested, hopefully.

"Yes," smiled Hopalong, "mebby he has. An' anyhow, Sammy; you *know* yo're plumb careless with that gun. You might miss him. Lead th' way."

As they started toward Pete's Johnny nudged his bunkmate in the ribs: "Say; she ain't got no sisters, has she?" he whispered.

One hour later Sammy, his face slightly scratched, lounged into the kitchen and tossed his sombrero on a chair, grinning cheerfully at the flushed, saucy face that looked out from under a mass of rebellious, brown hair. "Well, I saw th' boss, an' I come back to make everythin' well again," he asserted, laughing softly. "That rough an' boisterous Mr. Clarke has sloped. He won't come back no more."

"Why, *Sammy!*" she cried, aghast. "What *have* you done?"

"Well, for one thing, I 've got you callin' me Sammy," he chuckled, trying to sneak a hand over hers. "I told th' boss I 'm goin' to get a job up here, so I 'll know Mr. Clarke won't come back. But you know, he only thought he was bad. I shore had to take his ol' gun away from him so he would n't go an' shoot hisself, an' when las' seen he was feelin' for his cayuse, intendin' to leave these parts. That's what I *done*," he nodded, brightly. "Now comes what I 'm goin' to do. Oh, Li'l Miss," he whispered, eagerly. "I 'm jus' all mixed up an' millin'. My own feet plumb get in my way. So I jus' gotta stick aroun' an' change yore name, what you don't like. Uh-huh; that's jus' what I gotta do," he smiled.

She tossed her head and the tip-tilt nose went up indignantly. "Indeed you 'll do nothing of the kind, Sammy Porter!" she retorted. "I'll choose my own name when the time comes, and it will not be Porter!"

He arose slowly and looked around. Picking up the pencil that lay on the shelf he lounged over to the partition and printed his name three times in large letters. "All right, Li'l Miss," he agreed. "I 'll jus' leave a list where you can see it while you 're selectin'. I 'm now goin' out to get that job we spoke about. You have th' name all picked out when I get back," he suggested, waving his hand at the wall. "An' did anybody ever tell you it was plumb risky to stick yore li'l nose up thataway?"

"Sammy Porter!" she stormed, stamping in vexation near the crying point. "You get right out of here! I 'll *never* speak to you again!"

"You won't get a chance to talk much if you don't sorta bring that snubby nose down a li'l lower. I 'm plumb weak at times." He laughed joyously and edged to the door. "Don't forget that list. I 'm goin' after that job. So-long, Li'l Miss."

"Sammy!"

"Oh, all right; I'll go after it later on," he laughed, returning.

XV
When Johnny Sloped

Johnny Nelson hastened to the corner of the bunkhouse and then changed his pace until he seemed to ooze from there to the cook shack door, where he lazily leaned against the door jamb and ostentatiously picked his teeth with the negative end of a match. The cook looked up calmly, and calmly went on with his work; but if there was anything rasping enough to cause his calloused soul to quiver it was the aforesaid calisthenics executed by Johnny and the match; for Cookie's blunt nature hated hints. If Johnny had demanded, even profanely and with large personal animus, why meals were not ahead of time, it would be a simple matter to heave something and enlarge upon his short cut speech. But the subtleties left the cook floundering in a mire of rage-which he was very careful to conceal from Johnny. The youthful nuisance had been evincing undue interest in early suppers for nearly a month; and judging from the lightness of his repasts he was entirely unjustified in showing any interest at all in the evening meal. So Cookie strangled the biscuit in his hand, but smiled blandly at his tormentor.

"Well, all through?" he pleasantly inquired, glancing carelessly at Johnny's clothes.

"I 'm hopin' to begin," retorted Johnny, and the toothpick moved rapidly up and down.

Cookie condensed another biscuit and gulped. "That's shore some stone," he said, enviously, eying the two-caret diamond in Johnny's new, blue tie. Johnny never had worn a tie before he became owner of the diamond, but with the stone came the keen realization of how lost it was in a neck-kerchief, how often covered by the wind-blown folds; so he had hastened to Buckskin and spent a dollar that belonged to Red for the tie, thus exhausting both the supply of ties and Red's dollars. The honor of wearing the only tie and diamond in that section of the cow-country brought responsibilities, for he had spoken hastily to several humorous friends and stood a good chance of being soundly thrashed therefor.

He threw away the match and scratched his back ecstatically on the door jamb while he strained his eyes trying to look under his chin. Fixed chins and short ties are trials one must learn to accept philosophically-and Johnny might have been spared the effort were it not for the fact that the tie had been made for a boy, and was awesomely shortened by encircling a sixteen-inch neck. Evidently it had been made for a boy violently inclined toward a sea-faring life, as suggested by the anchors embroidered in white down its middle.

"Lemme see it," urged Cookie, sighing because its owner had resolutely refused to play poker when he had no cash. This had become a blighting sorrow in the life of a naturally exuberant and very fair cook.

"An' for how long?" demanded Johnny, a cold and calculating light glinting in his eyes.

"Oh, till supper 's ready," replied Cookie with great carelessness.

"Nix; but you can wear it twenty minutes if you 'll get my grub quick," he replied. "Got to meet Lucas at half-past five." He cautiously dropped the match he had thoughtlessly produced.

The cook tried to look his belief and accepted the offer. Johnny's remarkably clean face, plastered hair and general gala attire suggested that Lucas was a woman-which Lucas profanely would have denied. Also, Johnny had been seen washing Ginger, and when a puncher washes a cayuse it's a sign of insanity. Besides, Ginger belonged to Red, who also had owned that lone dollar. Red's clothes did not fit Johnny.

"Goin' to surprise Lucas?" inquired the cook.

"What you mean?"

Cookie glanced meaningly at the attire: "Er-you ain't in th' habit of puttin' on war paint for to see Lucas, are you?"

Johnny's mental faculties produced: "Oh, we 're goin' to a dance."

"Where 'bouts?" exploded the cook.

"*Way* up north!" One's mind needs to be active as a flea to lie properly to a man like the cook. He had made a ghastly mistake.

"By golly! I 'll give th' boys cold grub an' go with you," and the cook began to save time.

Johnny gulped and shook his head: "Got a invite?"

Cookie caught the pan on his foot before it struck the floor and gasped: "Invite? Ain't it free-fer-all?"

"No; this is a high-toned thing-a-bob. Costs a dollar a head, too."

"High-toned?" snorted the cook, derisively. "Don't they know you? An' I thought Red was broke. Show me that permit!"

"Lucas 's got it-that's why I 've got to catch him."

"Oh! An' is *he* goin' all feathered up, too?"

"Shore, he 's got to."

"Huh! He wouldn't dress like that to see a *fight*. Has she got any sisters?" Cookie finished, hopefully.

"Now what you talkin' about?"

"Why, Lucas," answered the cook, placidly. "Lemme tell you something. When you want to lose me have a invite to a water-drinkin' contest. An' before you go, be shore to rub Hoppy's

boots some more; that's such a pasty shine it 'll look like sand-paper before you get to th' —
dance. You want to make it hard an' slippery. An' I 've read som'ers that only wimmin ought
to smell like a drug-store. You better let her do th' fumigatin'."

Johnny surrendered and dolefully whiffed the crushed violets he had paid two bits a pint for
at El Paso-it was not necessary to whiff them, but he did so.

"You ought to hone yore razor, too," continued the cook, critically.

"I told Buck it was dull, I ain't goin' to sharpen it for him. But, say, are you shore about
th' perfumery?"

"Why, of course."

"But how 'll I git it off?"

"Bury th' clothes," suggested Cookie, grinning.

"I like yore gall! Which clothes are best, Pete's or Billy's?"

"Pete's would fit you like th' wide, wide world. You don't want blankets on when you go
courtin'. Try Billy's. An' I got a pair of socks, though one 's green-but th' boots 'll hide it."

"I did n't put none on my socks, you chump!"

"How'd *I* know? But, say! Has she got any sisters?"

"No!" yelled Johnny, halfway through the gallery in search of Billy's clothes. When he
emerged Cookie looked him over. "Ain't it funny, Kid, how a pipe 'll stink up clothes?" he
smiled. Johnny's retort was made over several yards of ground and when he had mounted Cookie
yelled and waved him to return. When Johnny had obeyed and impatiently demanded the
reason, Cookie pleasantly remarked: "Now, be shore an' give her my love, Kid."

Johnny's reply covered half a mile of trail.

Johnny rode alertly through Perry's Bend, for Sheriff Nolan was no friend of his; and Nolan
was not only a discarded suitor of Miss Joyce, but a warm personal friend of George Greener,
the one rival Johnny feared. Greener was a widower as wealthy as he was unscrupulous, and a
power on that range: when he said "jump," Nolan soared.

The sheriff was standing before the Palace saloon when Johnny rode past, and he could not
keep quiet. His comment was so judiciously chosen as to bring white spots on Johnny's flushed
cheeks. The Bar-20 puncher was not famed for his self-control, and, wheeling in the saddle,
he pointed a quivering forefinger at Mr. Nolan's badge of office, so conspicuously displayed:
"Better men than you have hid behind a badge and banked on a man's regard for th' law savin'
'em from their just deserts. Politics is a h —l of a thing when it opens th' door to anything
that might roll in on th' wind. You come down across th' line tomorrow an' see me, without
th' nickel-plated ornament you disgraces," he invited. "Any dog can tell a lie in his kennel, but
it takes guts to bark outside th' yard."

Mr. Nolan flushed, went white, hesitated, and walked away. To fight in defense of the law
was his duty; but no sane man warred on the Bar-20 unless he must. Mr. Nolan was a man
whose ideas of necessity followed strange curves, and not to his credit. One might censure Mr.
Cassidy or Mr. Connors, or pick a fight with some of the others of that outfit and not get
killed; but he must not harm their protégé. Mr. Nolan not only walked away but he sought
the darkest shadows and held conversation with himself. If it were only possible to get the
pugnacious and very much spoiled Mr. Nelson to fracture, smash, pulverize some law! This,
indeed, would be sweet.

Meanwhile Johnny, having watched the sheriff slip away, loosed a few more words into the
air and went on his way, whistling cheerfully. Reaching the Joyce cottage he was admitted by
Miss Joyce herself and at sight of her blushing face his exuberant confidence melted and left
him timid. This he was wont to rout by big words and a dashing air he did not feel.

"Oh! Come right in," she invited. "But you are late," she laughed, chidingly.

He critically regarded the dimples, while he replied that he had drawn rein to slay the sheriff
but, knowing that it would cost him more valuable time, he had consented with himself to
postpone the event.

"But you must not do that!" she cried. "Why, that's terrible! You shouldn't even think of such things."

"Well, of course-if yo 're agin' it I wont."

"But what did he do?"

"Oh, I don't reckon I can tell that. But do you really want him to live?"

"Why, certainly! What a foolish question."

"But why do you? Do you —*like* him?"

"I like everybody."

"Yes; an' everybody likes you, too," he growled, the smile fading. "That's th' trouble. Do you like him very much?"

"I wish you wouldn't ask such foolish questions."

"Yes; I know. But do you?"

"I prefer not to answer."

"Huh! That's an answer in itself. You do."

"I don't think you 're very nice tonight," she retorted, a little pout spoiling the bow in her lips. "You 're awfully jealous, and I don't like it."

"Gee! Don't like it! I should think you 'd want me to be jealous. I only wish you was jealous of *me*. Norah, I 've just got to say it now, an' find out —"

"Yes; tell me," she interrupted eagerly. "What *did* he do?"

"Who?"

"Mr. Nolan, of course."

"Nolan?" he demanded in surprise.

"Yes, yes; tell me."

"I ain't talkin' about him. I was goin' to tell you something that I 've —"

"That you 've done and now regret? Have you ever-ever killed a man?" she breathed. "Have you?"

"No; *yes*! Lots of 'em," he confessed, remembering that once she had expressed admiration for brave and daring men. "Most half as many as Hopalong; an' I ain't near as old as him, neither."

"You mean Mr. Cassidy? Why don't you bring him with you some evening? I 'd like to meet him."

"Not *me*. I went an' brought a friend along once, an' had to lick him th' next day to keep him away from here. He 'd 'a' camped right out there in front if I had n't. No, ma'am; not any."

"Why, the idea! But Mr. Greener's very much like your friend, Mr. Cassidy. He 's very brave, and a wonderful shot. He told me so himself."

"What! He told you so hisself! Well, well. Beggin' yore pardon, he ain't nowise like Hoppy, not even in th' topics of his conversation. Why, he 's a child; an' blinks when he shoots off a gun. Here-can he show a gun like mine?" and forthwith he held out his Colt, butt foremost, and indicated the notches he had cut that afternoon. A fleeting doubt went through his mind at what his outfit would say when it saw those notches. The Bar-20 cut no notches. It wanted to forget.

She looked at them curiously and suddenly drew back. "Oh! Are they —*are* they?" she whispered.

He nodded: "They are. There is plenty of room for Nolan's, an' mebby his owner, too," he suggested. "Can't you see, Norah?" he asked in a swift change of tone. "Can't you see? Don't you know how much I —"

"Yes. It must be terrible to have such remorse," she quickly interposed. "And I sympathize with you deeply, too."

"Remorse nothin'! Them fellers was lookin' for it, an' they got just what they deserved. If I had n't 'a' done it somebody else would."

"And *you* a murderer! I never thought that of *you*. I can hardly believe it of you. And you calmly confess it to me as though it were nothing!"

"Why, I —I —"

"Don't talk to me! To think you have human blood on your hands. To think —"

"Norah! Norah, listen; won't you?"

" —that you are that sort of a man! How dare you call here as you have? How dare you?"

"But I tell you they were tryin' to get *me*! I just *had* to. Why, I didn't do it for nothin'. I 've got a right to defend myself, ain't I?"

"You *had* to? Is that true?" she demanded.

"Why, shore! Think I go 'round killin' men, like Greener does, just for th' fun of it?"

"He doesn't do anything of the kind," she retorted. "You know he does n't! Did n't you just say he blinks when he shoots off a gun?"

"Yes; I did. But I didn't want you to think he was a murderer like Nolan," he explained. Even Cookie, he thought, would find it hard to get around that neat little effort.

"I 'm so relieved," she laughed, delighted at her success in twisting him. "I am so glad he does n't blink when he shoots. I 'd hate a man who was afraid to shoot."

Johnny's chest arose a little. "Well, how 'bout me?"

"But you've killed men; you've shot down your fellow men; and have ghastly marks on your revolver to brag about."

"Well-say-but how can I shoot without shootin' or kill without killin'?" he demanded. "An' I don't brag about 'em, neither; it makes me feel too sad to do any braggin'. An' Greener's killed 'em, too; an' he brags about it."

"Yes; but he doesn't blink!" she exclaimed triumphantly.

"Neither do *I*."

"Yes; but you shoot to kill."

"Lord pity us-don't *he*?"

"Y-e-s, but that's different," she replied, smiling brightly.

Johnny looked around the room, his eyes finally resting on his hat.

"Yes, I see it's different. Greener can kill, an' blink! I can't. If he kills a man he's a hero; I 'm a murderer. I kinda reckon he 's got th' trail. But I love you, an' you 've got to pick my trail-does it lead up or down?"

"Johnny Nelson! What are you saying?" she demanded, arising.

"Something turrible, mebby. I don't know; an' I don't care. It's true-so there you are. Norah, can't you see I do?" he pleaded, holding out his hands. "Won't you marry me?"

She looked down, her cheeks the color of fire, and Johnny continued hurriedly: "I 've loved you a whole month! When I 'm ridin' around I sorta' see you, an' hear you. Why, I talk to you lots when I 'm alone. I 've saved up some money, an' I had to work hard to save it, too. I 've got some cows runnin' with our'n —in a little while I 'll have a ranch of my own. Buck 'll let me use th' east part of th' ranch, an' there 's a hill over there that 'd look fine with a house on it. I can't wait no longer, Norah, I 've got to know. Will you let me put this on yore finger?" He swiftly bent the pin into a ring and held it out eagerly: "Can I?"

She pushed him away and yielded to a sudden pricking of her conscience, speaking swiftly, as if forcing herself to do a disagreeable duty, and hating herself at the moment. "Johnny, I 've been a —a flirt! When I saw you were beginning to care too much for me I should have stopped it; but I did n't. I amused myself-but I want you to believe one thing, to give me a little credit for just one thing; I never thought what it might mean to you. It was carelessness with me. But I was flirting, just the same-and it hurts to admit it. I 'm not good enough for you, Johnny Nelson; it's hard to say, but it's true. Can you, *will* you forgive me?"

He choked and stepped forward holding out his hands imploringly, but she eluded him. When he saw the shame in her face, the tears in her eyes, he stopped and laughed gently: "But we can begin right, now, can't we? I don't care, not if you 'll let me see you same as ever. You might get to care for me. And, anyhow, it ain't yore fault. I reckon it's me that's to blame."

At that moment he was nearer to victory than he had ever been; but he did not realize it and opportunity died when he failed to press his advantage.

"I *am* to blame," she said, so low he could hardly catch the words. When she continued it was with a rush: "I am not free —I haven't been for a week. I 'm not free any more-and I 've been leading you on!"

His face hardened, for now the meaning of Greener's sneering laugh came to him, and a seething rage swept over him against the man who had won. He knew Greener, knew him well-the meanness of the man's nature, his cold cruelty; the many things to the man's discredit loomed up large against the frailty of the woman before him.

Norah stepped forward and laid a pleading hand on his arm, for she knew the mettle of the men who worked under Buck Peters: "What are you thinking? Tell me!"

"Why, I 'm thinking what Nolan said. An', Norah, listen. You say you want me to forgive you? Well, I do, if there's anything to forgive. But I want you to primise me that if Greener don't treat you right you 'll tell me."

"What do you mean?"

"Only what I said. Do you promise?"

"Perhaps you would better speak to him about it!" she retorted.

"I will-an' plain. But don't worry 'bout me. It was my fault for bein' a tenderfoot. I never played this game before, an' don't know th' cards. Good-by."

He rode away slowly, and made the rounds, and by the time he reached Lacey's he was so unsteady that he was refused a drink and told to go home. But he headed for the Palace instead, and when he stepped high over the doorsill Nolan was seated in a chair tipped back against one of the side walls, and behind the bar on the other side of the room Jed Terry drummed on the counter and expressed his views on local matters. The sheriff was listening in a bored way until he saw Johnny enter and head his way, feet high and chest out; and at that moment Nolan's interest in local affairs flashed up brightly.

Johnny lost no time: "Nolan," he said, rocking on his heels, "tell Greener I 'll kill him if he marries that girl. He killed his first wife by abuse an' he don't kill no more. Savvy?"

The sheriff warily arose, for here was the opportunity he had sought. The threat to kill had a witness.

"An' if you opens yore toad's mouth about her like you did tonight, I 'll kill you, too." The tones were dispassionate, the words deliberate.

"Hear that, Jed?" cried the sheriff, excitedly. "Nelson, yo 're under ar —"

"Shut up!" snapped Johnny loudly, this time with feeling. "When yo 're betters are talkin' you keep yore face closed. Now, it ain't hardly healthy to slander wimmin in this country, 'specially *good* wimmin. You lied like a dog to me tonight, an' I let you off; don't try it again."

"I told th' truth!" snapped Nolan, heatedly. "I said she was a flirt, an' by th' great horned spoon she is a flirt, an' you —"

The sheriff prided himself upon his quickness, but the leaping gun was kicked out of his hand before he knew what was coming; a chair glanced off Jed's face and wrapped the front window about itself in its passing, leaving the bar-tender in the throbbing darkness of inter-planetary space; and as the sheriff opened his eyes and recovered from the hard swings his face had stopped, a galloping horse drummed southward toward the Bar-20; and the silence of the night was shattered by lusty war-whoops and a spurting .45.

When the sheriff and his posse called at the Bar-20 before breakfast the following morning they found a grouchy outfit and learned some facts.

"Where 's Johnny?" repeated Hopalong, with a rising inflection. "Only wish I knowed!"

A murmur of wistful desire arose and Lanky Smith restlessly explained it: "He rampages in 'bout midnight an' wakes us up with his racket. When we asks what he 's doin' with *our* possessions he suggests we go to h —l. He takes *his* rifle, Pete's rifle, Buck's brand new canteen, 'bout eighty pounds of catridges an' other useful duffle, *all* th' tobacco, an' blows away quick."

"On my cayuse," murmured Red.

"Wearin' my *good* clothes," added Billy, sorrowfully.

"An' *my* boots," sighed Hopalong.

"I ain't got no field glasses no more," grumbled Lanky.

"But he only got one laig of my new pants," chuckled Skinny. "I was too strong for him."

"He yanked my blanket off'n me, which makes me steal Red's," grinned Pete.

"Which you didn't keep very long!" retorted Red, with derision.

"Which makes us all peevish," plaintively muttered Buck.

"Now ain't it a h —l of a note?" laughed Cookie, loudly, forthwith getting scarce. He had nothing good enough to be taken.

"An' whichever was it run ag'in' yore face, Sheriff?" sympathetically inquired Hopalong. "Mighty good thing it stopped," he added thoughtfully.

"Never mind my face!" snorted the peace officer hotly as his deputies smoothed out their grins. "I want to know where Nelson is, an' d —d quick! We 'll search the house first."

"Hold on," responded Buck. "North of Salt Spring Creek yo 're a sheriff; down here yo 're nothin'. Don't search no house. He ain't here."

"How do I know he ain't?" snapped Nolan.

"My word 's good; or there 'll be another election stolen up in yore county," rejoined Buck ominously. "An' I would n't hunt him too hard, neither. We 'll punish him."

Nolan wheeled and rode toward the hills without another word, his posse pressing close behind. When they entered Apache Pass one of them accidentally exploded his rifle, calling forth an angry tirade from the sheriff. Johnny heard it, and cared little for the warning from his friend Lucas; he waited and then rode down the rocky slope of the pass on the trail of the posse, squinting wickedly at the distant group as he caught glimpses of them now and again, and with no anxiety regarding backward glances. "Lot's wife 'll have nothing on them if they look back," he muttered, fingering his rifle lovingly. At nightfall he watched them depart and grinned at the chase he would lead them when they returned.

But he did not see them again, although his friends reported that they were turning the range upside down to find him. One of his outfit rode out to him with supplies and information every few days and it was Pete who told him that six posses were in the hills. "An' you can't leave, 'cause one of th' cordon would get you shore. I had a h —l of a time getting in today." Red reported that the sheriff had sworn to take him dead or alive. Then came the blow. The sheriff was at the point of death from lockjaw caused by complete paralysis of the curea-frend nerve just above the phlagmatic diaphragm, which Johnny had fractured. It was Hopalong who imparted this sad news, and withered Johnny's hope of returning to a comfortable bunkhouse and square meals. So the fugitive clung to the hills, shunned sky-lines and wondered if the sheriff would recover before snow flew. He was hungry most of the time now because the outfit was getting stingy with the food supplies-and he dared not shoot any game.

Four weeks passed, weeks of hunger and nervous strain, and he was getting desperate. He had learned that Greener and his fiancée were going down to Linnville soon, since Perry's Bend had no parson; and his cup of bitterness, overflowing, drove him to risk an attempt to leave that part of the country. He had seen none of Pete's "cordon" although he had looked for them, and he believed he could get away. So he rode cautiously down Apache Pass one noon, thoughtfully planning his flight. The sand, washed down the rock walls by the last rain, deadened all sounds of his progress, and as he turned a sharp bend in the cut he almost bumped into Greener and Norah Joyce. They were laughing at how they had eluded the crowd of friends who were eager to accompany them-but the laughter froze when Johnny's gun swung up.

"'Nds up, Greener!" he snapped, viciously, remembering his promise to Sheriff Nolan. "Miss Joyce, if you make any trouble it 'll cost him his life."

"Turned highwayman, eh?" sneered Greener, keenly alert for the necessary fraction of a second's carelessness on the part of the other. He was gunman enough to need no more.

"Miss Joyce, will you please ride along? I want to talk to him alone," said Johnny, his eyes fastened intently on those of his enemy.

"Yes, Norah; that's best. I 'll join you in a few minutes," urged Greener, smiling at her.

Johnny had a sudden thought and his warning was grave and cold. "Don't get very far away an' don't make no sounds, or signals; if you do it 'll be th' quickest way to *need* 'em. He 'll pay for any mistakes like that."

"You coward!" she cried, angrily, and then delivered an impromptu lecture that sent the blood surging into the fugitive's wan cheeks. But she obeyed, slowly, at Greener's signal, and when she was out of sight Johnny spoke.

"Greener, yo 're not going to marry her. You know what you are, you know how yore first wife died-an' I don't intend that Norah shall be abused as the other was. I 'm a fugitive, hard pressed; I 'm weak from want of food, and from hardships; all I have left is a slim chance of gettin' away. I 've reached the point where I can't harm myself by shooting you, an' I 'm goin' to do it rather than let any trouble come to her. But you'll get an even break, because I ain't never going to shoot a man when he 's helpless. Got anything to say?"

"Yes; yo 're th' biggest fool I ever saw," replied Greener. "Yo're locoed through an' through; an' I 'm goin' to take great pleasure in putting you away. But I want to thank you for one thing you did. You were drunk at the time an' may not remember it. When you hit Nolan for talking like he did I liked you for it, an' I 'm goin' to tell you so. Now we 'll get at th' matter before us so I can move along."

Neither had paid any attention to Norah in the earnestness and keen-eyed scrutiny of each other and the first sign they had of her actions was when she threw her arms around Greener's neck and shielded him. He was too much of a man to fire from cover and Johnny realized it while the other tried to get her to leave the scene.

"I won't leave you to be murdered —I *know* what it means, I *know* it," she cried. "My place is here, and you can't deny your wife's first request! What will I do without you! Oh, dear, let me stay! I *will* stay! What woman ever had such a wedding day before! Dear, dear, what can I do? Tell me what to do!"

Johnny sniffled and wished the posse had taken him. This was a side he had never thought of. His wife! Greener's wife! Then he was too late, and to go on would be a greater evil than the one he wished to eliminate. When she turned on him like a tigress and tore him to pieces word by word, tears rolling down her pallid cheeks and untold misery in her eyes, he shook his head and held up his hand.

"Greener, you win; I can't stop what's happened," he said, slowly. "But I 'll tell you this, an' I mean every word: If you don't treat her like she deserves, I 'll come back some of these days and kill you *shore*. Nolan got his because he talked ill of her; an' you 'll get yours if I die the next minute, if you ain't square with her."

"I don't need no instructions on how to treat my wife," retorted the other. "An' I 'm beginnin' to see th' cause of yore insanity, and it pardons you as nothing else will. Put up yore gun an' get back to th' ranch, where you belong-an' *keep away from me*. Savvy?"

"Not much danger of me gettin' in yore way," growled Johnny, "when I 'm hunted like a dog for doing what any man would 'a' done. When th' sheriff gets well, if he ever does, mebby I 'll come back an' take my medicine. How was he, anyhow, when you left?"

"Dead tired, an' some under th' influence of liquor," replied Greener, a smile breaking over his frown. He knew the whole story well, as did the whole range, and he had laughed over it with the Bar-20 outfit.

"What's that? Ain't he near dead?" cried Johnny, amazed.

"Well, purty nigh dead of fatigue dancin' at our weddin' last night; but I reckon he 'll be driftin' home purty soon, an' all recovered." Greener suddenly gave way and roared with laughter. There was a large amount of humor in his make-up and it took possession of him, shaking him from head to foot. He had always liked Johnny, not because he ever wanted to but because no one could know the Bar-20 protégé and keep from it. This climax was too much for him, and his wife, gradually recovering herself, caught the infection and joined in.

Johnny's eyes were staring and his mouth wide open, but Greener's next words closed the eyes to a squint and snapped shut the open mouth.

"That there paralysis of th' cure-a-friend nerve did n't last; an' when I heard why you licked him I said a few words that made him a wiser man. He didn't hunt you after th' first day. Now you go up an' shake han's with him. He knows he got what was coming to him and so does everybody else know it. Go home an' quit playin' th' fool for th' whole blamed range to laugh at."

Johnny stirred and came back to the scene before him. His face was livid with rage and he could not speak at first. Finally, however, he mastered himself and looked up: "I 'm cured, all right, but *they* ain't! Wait till my turn comes! What a fool I was to believe 'em; but they usually tell th' truth. 'Cura-a-friend nerve'! They 'll pay me dollar for cent before I 'm finished!" He caught the sparkle of his diamond pin, the pin he had won, when drunk, at El Paso, and a sickly grin flickered over the black frown. "I 'm a little late, I reckon; but I 'd like to give th' bride a present to show there ain't no hard feelin's on my part, an' to bring her luck. This here pin ain't no fit ornament for a fool like me, so if it's all right, I 'll be plumb tickled to see her have it. How 'bout it, Greener?"

The happy pair exchanged glances and Mrs. Greener, hesitating and blushing, accepted the gift: "You can bend it into a ring easy," Johnny hastily remarked, to cut off her thanks.

Greener extended his hand: "I reckon we can be friends, at that, Nelson. You squared up with me when you licked Nolan. Come up an' see us when you can."

Johnny thanked him and shook hands and then watched them ride slowly down the canyon, hand in hand, happy as little children. He sat silently, lost in thought, his anger rising by leaps and bounds against the men who had kept him on the anxious seat for a month. Straightening up suddenly, he tore off the navy blue necktie and, hurling it from him, fell into another reverie, staring at the canyon wall, but seeing in his mind's eye the outfit planning his punishment; and his eyes grew redder and redder with fury. But it was a long way home and his temper cooled as he rode; that is why no one knew of his return until they saw him asleep in his bunk when they awakened at daylight the following morning. And no one ever asked about the diamond, or made any explanations-for some things are better unmentioned. But they paid for it all before Johnny considered the matter closed.

Buck Peters, Ranchman

Chapter I
Tex Returns

Johnny Nelson reached up for the new, blue flannel shirt he had hung above his bunk, and then placed his hands on hips and soliloquized: "Me an' Red buy a new shirt apiece Saturday night an' one of 'em 's gone Sunday mornin'; purty fast work even for this outfit."

He strode to the gallery to ask the cook, erstwhile subject of the Most Heavenly One, but the words froze on his lips. Lee Hop's stoop-shouldered back was encased in a brand new, blue flannel shirt, the price mark chalked over one shoulder blade, and he sing songed a Chinese classic while debating the advisability of adopting a pair of trousers and thus crossing another of the boundaries between the Orient and the Occident. He had no eyes in the back of his head but was rarely gifted in the "ways that are strange," and he felt danger before the boot left Johnny's hand. Before the missile landed in the dish pan Lee Hop was digging madly across the open, half way to the ranch house, and temporary safety.

Johnny fished out the boot and paused to watch the agile cook. "He 's got eyes all over hisself-an' no coyote ever lived as could beat him," was his regretful comment. He knew better than to follow-Hopalong's wife had a sympathetic heart, and a tongue to be feared. She had not yet forgotten Lee Hop's auspicious initiation as an *ex-officio* member of the outfit, and Johnny's part therein. And no one had been able to convince her that sympathy was wasted on a "Chink."

The shirtless puncher looked around helplessly, and then a grin slipped over his face. Glancing at the boot he dropped it back into the dish water, moved swiftly to Red's bunk, and in a moment a twin to his own shirt adorned his back. To make matters more certain he deposited on Red's blankets an old shirt of Lee Hop's, and then sauntered over to Skinny's bunk.

"Hoppy said he 'd lick me if I hurt th' Chink any more; but he did n't say nothin' to Red. May th' best man win," he muttered as he lifted Skinny's blankets and fondled a box of cigars. "One from forty-three leaves forty-two," he figured, and then, dropping to the floor and crawling under the bunk, he added a mark to Skinny's "secret" tally. Skinny always liked to know just how many of his own cigars he smoked.

"Now for a little nip, an' then th' open, where this cigar won't talk so loud," he laughed, heading towards Lanky's bunk. The most diligent search failed to produce, and a rapid repetition also failed. Lanky's clothes and boots yielded nothing and Johnny was getting sarcastic when his eyes fell upon an old boot lying under a pile of riding gear in a corner of the room. Keeping his thumb on the original level he drank, and then added enough water to bring the depleted liquor up to his thumb. "Gee —I 've saved sixty-five dollars this month, an' two days are gone already," he chuckled. He received sixty-five dollars, and what luxuries were not nailed down, every month.

Mounting his horse he rode away to enjoy the cigar, happy that the winter was nearly over. There was a feeling in the air that told of Spring, no matter what the calendar showed, and Johnny felt unrest stirring in his veins. When Johnny felt thus exuberant things promised to move swiftly about the bunk-house.

When far enough away from the ranch houses he stopped to light the cigar, but paused and, dropping the match, returned the "Maduro" to his pocket. He could not tell who the rider was at that distance, but it was wiser to be prudent. Riding slowly forward, watching the other horseman, he saw a sombrero wave, and spurred into a lope. Then he squinted hard and shook his head.

"Rides like Tex Ewalt-but it ain't, all right," he muttered. Closer inspection made him rub his eyes. "That arm swings like Tex, just th' same! An' I did n't take more'n a couple of swallows, neither. Why, d —n it! If that ain't him I 'm going' to see *who* it is!" and he pushed on at a gallop. When the faint hail floated down the wind to him he cut loose a yell and leaned forward, spurring and quirting. "Old son-of-a-gun 's come back!" he exulted. "Hey, Tex! Oh, Tex!" he yelled; and Tex was yelling just as foolishly.

They came together with a rush, but expert horsemanship averted a collision, and for a few minutes neither could hear clearly what the other was saying. When things calmed down Johnny jammed a cigar into his friend's hands and felt for a match.

"Why, I don't want to take yore last smoke, Kid," Tex objected.

"Oh, go ahead! I 've got a hull *box* of 'em in th' bunk-house," was the swift reply. "Could n't stay away, eh? Did n't like th' East, nohow, did you? Gosh, th' boys 'll be some tickled to see you, Tex. Goin' to stay? How you feelin'?"

"You bet I 'm a-stayin'," responded Tex. "Is that Lanky comin'?"

"Hey, Lanky!" yelled Johnny, standing up and waving the approaching horseman towards them. "*Pronto*! Tex 's come back!"

Lanky's pony's legs fanned a haze under him and he rammed up against Tex so hard that they had to grab each other. Everybody was talking at once and so they rode towards the bunk-house, picking up Billy on the way.

"Where's Hopalong?" demanded Tex. "Married! H —l he is!" A strange look flitted across his face. "Well, I 'm d —d! An' where 's Red?"

Johnny glanced ahead just in time to see Lee Hop sail around a corner of the corral, and he replied with assurance, "Red 's th' other side of th' corral."

"Huh!'" snorted Lanky, "You 've got remarkable eyes, Kid, if you can see through-well, I 'm hanged if he *ain't!*"

After Red came Pete, waving a water-soaked boot. They disappeared and when Tex and his friends had almost reached the corral, Lee Hop rounded the same corner again, too frightened even to squeal. As he started around the next corner he jumped away at an angle, Pete, still waving the boot, missing him by inches. Pete checked his flow of language as he noticed the laughing group and started for it with a yell. A moment later Red came into sight, panting heavily, and also forgot the cook. Lee Hop stopped and watched the crowd, taking advantage of the opportunity to gain the cook shack and bar the door. "Dlam shirt no good-sclatchee like helle," he muttered. White men were strange-they loved each other like brothers and fought one another's battles. "Led head! Led head!" he cried, derisively. "My hop you cloke! Hop you cloke chop-chop! No fliend my, savee?"

Skinny Thompson, changing his trousers in the bunkroom, heard Lee's remarks and laughed. Then he listened-somebody was doing a lot of talking. "They 're loco, plumb loco, or else somethin's wrong," and he hopped to the door. A bunched crowd of friends were tearing toward him, yelling and shooting and waving sombreros, and a second look made him again miss the trousers' leg and hop through the door to save himself. The blood swept into his face as he saw the ranch house and he very promptly hopped back again, muttering angrily.

The crowd dismounted at the door and tried to enter *en masse*; becoming sane it squirmed into separate units and entered as it should. Lee Hop hastily unbarred his door and again fled for his life. When he returned he walked boldly behind his foreman, and very close to him, gesticulating wildly and trying to teach Hopalong Cantonese. The foreman hated to chide his friends, but he and his wife were tired of turning the ranch house into a haven for Chinese cooks.

As he opened the door he was grabbed and pushed up against a man who clouted him on the back and tried to crush his hand. "Hullo, Cassidy! Best sight I've laid eyes on since I left!" yelled the other above the noise.

"Tex!" exclaimed Hopalong. "Well, I'm d —d! When did you get here? Going to stay? Got a job yet? How'd you like the East? Married? *I* am-best thing I ever did. You look white-sick?"

"City color-like the blasted collars and shirts," replied the other, still pumping the hand. "I 'm goin' to stay, I 'm lookin' for a job, an' I 'd ruther punch cows for my keep than get rich in th' East. It 's all fence-country —can't move without bumping into somebody or something-an' noise! An' crooked! They 'd steal th' fillin's out of yore teeth when you go to talk-an' you won't know it!"

"Like to see 'em fool *me!*" grunted Johnny, looking savage.

"Huh! Th' new beginners 'd pick you out to practise on," snorted Red. "That yore shirt or mine?" he asked, suspiciously.

"They 'd give you money for th' fun of taking it away from you," asserted Tex. "Why, one feller, a slick dresser, too, asks me for th' time. I was some proud of that ticker-cost nigh onto a hundred dollars. He thanks me an' slips into th' crowd. When I went to put th' watch back I did n't have none. I licked th' next man, old as he was, who asks me for th' time. He was plumb surprised when I punched him-reckon he figured I was easy."

"Ain't they got policemen?" demanded Red.

"Yes; but *they* don't carry watches-they 're too smart."

"Have a drink, Tex," suggested Lanky, bottle in hand. When the owner of it took a drink he looked at his friends and then at the bottle, disgust pictured on his face. "This liquor's shore goin' to die purty soon. It's gettin' weaker every day. Now I wonder what in h —l Cowan makes it out of?"

"It *is* sort of helpless," admitted Tex. "Now, Kid, I 'll borrow another of them cigars of yourn. Them Maduros are shore good stuff. I would n't ask you only you said you had a —"

"D'ju see any shows in th' East?" demanded Johnny, hurriedly: "Real, good, bang-up shows?"

Skinny faded into the bunk-room and soon returned, puzzled and suspicious. He slipped Tex a cigar and in a few moments sidled up close to the smoker.

"That as good as th' Kid's?" he asked, carelessly.

Tex regarded it gravely: "Yes; better. I like 'em black, but don't say nothin' to Johnny. He likes them blondes 'cause he 's young."

It was not long before Tex, having paid his respects to the foreman's wife, returned to the bunk-house, leaned luxuriously against the wall and told of his experiences in the East. He had an attentive audience and it swayed easily and heartily to laughter or sympathy as the words warranted. There was much to laugh at and a great deal to strain credulity. But the great story was not told, the story of the things pitiful in the manner in which they showed up how square a regenerated man could be, and how false a woman. It was the old story-ambition drove him out into a new world with nothing but a clean conscience, a strong, deft pair of hands, and a clever brain; a woman drove him back, beaten, disheartened, and perilously near the devious ways he had forsaken. He could not stay in the new surroundings without killing-and he knew the woman was to blame; so when he felt the ground slip under his hesitating feet, he threw the new life behind him and hastened West, feverish to gain the locality where he had learned to look himself in the face with regret and remorse, but without shame.

In turn he learned of the things that had occurred since he had left: of the bitter range-war; of his best friend's promotion and marriage; and of Buck Peters' new venture among hostile strangers. The latter touched him deeply-he knew, from his own bitter experiences, the disheartening struggle against odds great enough to mean a hard fight for Buck and all his old outfit. Something that in Tex's heart had been struggling for weeks, the vague uneasiness which drove him faster and faster towards the West, now possessed him with a strength not to be denied. He knew what it was-the old lust for battle, the game of hand and wits with life on the table, could not be resisted. The southern range was now peaceful, thanks to Buck and his men, thanks to Meeker's real nature; the Double Arrow and the C80 formed a barrier of lead and steel on the north and east, a barrier that no rustler cared to force. Peace meant solitude on the sun-kissed range and forced upon him opportunities for thought-and insanity, or suicide. But up in Montana it would be different; and the field, calling insistently for Tex to come, was one where his peculiar abilities would be particularly effective. Buck needed friends, but stubbornly forbade any of his old outfit to join him. Of course, they would disregard his commands and either half or all of the Bar Twenty force would join him; but their going would be delayed until well after the Spring round-up, for loyalty to their home ranch demanded this. Tex was free, eager, capable, and as courageous as any man. He had the cunning of a coyote, the cold savagery of a wolf, and the power of a tiger. In his lightning-fast hands a Colt rarely missed-and he gathered from what he heard that such hands were necessary to make the right kind of history on the northern range.

Finally Hopalong arose to go to the ranch house for the noon meal, taking Tex with him. The foreman and his wife did not eat with the outfit, because the outfit would not allow it. Mary had insisted at first that her husband should not desert his friends in that manner, and he stood neutral on the question. But the friends were not neutral-they earnestly contended that he belonged to his wife and they would not intrude. Lanky voiced their attitude in part when he said: "We 've had him a long time. We borrow him during workin' hours-we never learned no good from him, so we ain't goin' to chance spottin' our lily white souls." But there was another reason, which Johnny explained in naive bluntness: "Why, Ma'am, we eats in our shirt sleeves, an' we grabs regardless. We has to if we don't want Pete to get it all. An' somehow I don't think we 'd git very fat if we had to eat under wraps. You see, we 're free-an'-easy-an' we might starve, all but Pete. Why, Ma'am, Pete can eat any thin', anywheres, under any conditions. So we sticks to th' old table an' awful good appetites."

So Hopalong and Tex walked away together, the limp of the one keeping time with that of the other, for Tex's wounded knee had mended a great deal better than he had hoped for. Hopalong stopped a moment to pat his wolf hounds, briefly complimenting them to Tex, and then pushed open the kitchen door, shoving Tex in ahead of him.

"Just in time, boys," said Mary, "I hope you 're good an' hungry."

They both grinned and Hopalong replied first: "Well, I don't believe Pete can afford to give us much of a handicap to-day."

"Nor any other time, as far's I 'm concerned," added Tex, laughing. "We 'll do yore table full justice, Mrs. Cassidy," he assured her.

Mary, dish in hand, paused between the stove and the table. She looked at Tex with mischievous eyes: "Billy-Red tells me you love him like a brother. Is he deceiving me?"

Hopalong laughed and Tex replied, smiling: "More like a sister, Mrs. Cassidy —I can't find any faults in him, an' we don't fight."

Mary completed her journey to the stove, filled the dish and carried it to the table; resting her hands on the edge of the table, she leaned forward in seeming earnestness. "Well, you must know that we are one, and if you love Billy-Red —" finishing with an expressive gesture. "Those who love me call me Mary."

Tex's face was gravely wistful, but a wrinkle showed at the outer corner of his eyes. "Well," he drawled, "those who love me call me Tex."

"Good!" exclaimed Hopalong, grinning.

"An' I 'm thankful that my hair 's not th' color to cause any trustin' soul to call me by a more affectionate name," Tex finished. He ducked Hopalong's punch while Mary laughed a bird-like trill that brought to her husband's face an expression of idolizing happiness and made Tex smile in sympathy. As the dinner progressed Tex shared less and less in the conversation, preferring to listen and make occasional comments, and finally he spoke only when directly addressed.

When the meal was over and the two men started to go into the sitting-room, Mary said: "You 'll have to excuse me, Mr. —er-Tex," she amended, smiling saucily. "I guess you two men can take care of each other while I red up."

"We 'll certainly try hard, Mrs. —er-Mary," Tex replied, his face grave but his eyes twinkling. "We watched each other once before, you know."

As soon as they were alone Hopalong waved his companion to a chair and bluntly asked a question: "What's th' matter, Tex? You got plumb quiet at th' table."

The other, following his friend's example, filled a pipe before he replied.

"Well, I was thinkin' —could n't help it; an' I was drawin' a contrast that hurt. Hoppy, I 'm not goin' to stay here longer 'n I can help; you don't need me a little bit, an' if you took me in yore outfit it 'd be only because you want to help me. This ain't no place for me —I need excitement, clean, purposeful excitement, an' you fellows have made this part of th' country as quiet as a Quaker meetin'. I 've been thinkin' Buck needs somebody that 'll stick to him-an' there ain't nothin' I won't do for Buck. So I 'm goin' to pull my freight north, but *not* as Tex Ewalt."

"Tex, if you do that I 'll be able to sleep better o' nights," was the earnest reply. "We 'd like to have you. You know that, but it might mean life to Buck if he had you. Lord, but could n't you two raise h —l if you started! He 'll be tickled half to death to see you-there will be at least one man he won't have to suspect."

Tex considered a moment. "He won't see me-to know me. I 'm one man when I 'm known, when I 've declared myself; I can be two or three if I don't declare myself. One fighting man won't do him much good-if I could take th' outfit along we would n't waste no time in strategy. Th' rest of th' population, hostile to Buck, would move out as we rode in-an' they would n't come back. No, I 'm playing th' stranger to Buck. Somebody 's goin' to pay me for it, too. An' th' pay 'll not be in money but in results. I won't starve, not as long as people like to play cards. I quit that, you know; but if I do play, it 'll be part of my bigger game."

"I feel sorry for th' card-playin' population if you figger you ought to eat," smiled Hopalong, reminiscently.

"If I 'd 'a' knowed about Buck, I 'd 'a' gone to Montana 'stead of comin' here, an' saved some valuable time," Tex observed.

"But as far as that goes, Tex, they can't do much before Spring, anyhow," Hopalong remarked, thoughtfully. "An' it's yore own fault," he added. "We wanted to send you th' news occasionally, but you never let us know where you was. We 'd 'a' liked to hear from you, too."

"Yes, I reckon I 've got time enough; besides, I need th' exercise," agreed Tex.

"How is it you never wrote?" asked Hopalong, curiously.

Tex left his seat and walked to the door. "Take a walk with me-this ain't no place to tell a story like that."

"I 've got somethin' better 'n that —I want to go down to th' H2 an' see my father-in-law for a couple of minutes. Never met him, did you? We can ride slow an' have lots of time. Be with you in a minute," and Hopalong hastened to ask his wife if she had any word to send to her father. He joined Tex at the bunkhouse, now deserted except for Lee Hop, and in a minute they left for the H2. As they rode, Tex told his story.

"This is going to be short an' meaty. When I left here I struck Kansas City first, then Chicago, spending a few days in each of them. I 'd heard a lot about New York, an' headed for it. I had n't been there very long before I met a woman, an' you know they can turn us punchers into fool knots. Well, I courted her four days an' married her-oh, I was plumb in love with her, all right. She was one of them sweet, dreamy, clingin' kind-pretty as h —l, too. I had a good job by then, and for most a year I was too happy to put my feet on this common old earth. I never gambled, never drank, and found it not very hard to quit cussing, except on real, high-toned occasions. But I never could get along without my gun. Civilization be d —d! There 's more crooks an' killers in New York than you an' me ever saw or heard of. Once I was glad I had it-did n't have to shoot, though. Th' man got careless an' let his gun waver a little an' was lookin' at th' works in *mine* before he knowed it. He did n't want no money-what he needed was a match, an' he was doin' it to win a bet-or so he palavers. I takes his stubby .32 an' kicks him so he 'd *earn* that bet, an' lets him go. I had to laugh-him stackin' agin *me* at that game!

"Well, I got promoted, an' had to travel out of town every two weeks. I 'd be gone two days an' then turn up bright an' smilin' for my wife to admire. Once I was wired to come back quick on account of somethin' unexpected turnin' up, an' I lopes home to spend that second night in my own bed. I remember now that I wondered if th' wife would be there or at her mother's.

"She was there, but she was n't admirin' *me*. I saw red, an' th' fact that I did n't go loco proved that I ain't never goin'. But th' trigger hung on a breath an' *he* knowed it. He was pasty white an' could n't hardly stand up. Then th' shock wore off an' he was th' coolest man in town.

"'What are you goin' to do about it?' he asks, slowly. 'Yore wife loves *me*, not you. She 's allus loved me-you never really reckoned she was in love with *you*, did you?'"

"*I* was shocked then, only I was wearin' my poker face an' he could n't see nothin'. 'Why, I did think, once in a while, that she loved me,' I retorts. 'I certainly kept you hangin' 'round th' gutter an' *sneakin'* in, anyhow. When I get through with you they 'll find you in that same gutter.'

"'Goin' to shoot me? I *ought* to have a chance. I ain't got no gun-you see, I ain't wild an' woolly like you,' an' he actually grinned!

"'What kind of a chance did *I* have, out of town an' not suspectin' any thin'?' I asks.

"'But she *loves* me; don't you understand? She was *happy* with me. What good will it do *you* if you kill me an' break her heart? She 'll never look at you again.'

"'I reckon she won't anyhow,' I retorts. 'Leastwise not if I can help it. Look here: Don't you know you deserve to die?'

"'That's open to debate, but for brevity I 'll say yes; but I want a chance. I gave *you* a chance every time I came here-you did n't take it, that's all.'

"'I 'll get you a gun, d —d if I won't,' I replied, an' backed towards th' valise where my big old Colt was. But he stops me with a sneer.

"'I said a *chance*! You was *born* with a gun in your hand, an' it 'd be pure murder.'

"'I 'm glad somethin 's pure,' says I. Then I remembered that old valise again. Remember th' last thing I did for you an' Peters before I quit, Hoppy?"

Hopalong thought quickly. "Yes, you an' Pete put in two days settin' poisoned cows in th' brush on th' west line. Did a good job, too. Ain't been bothered none by wolves since."

Tex chuckled. "There was a bottle of yore stuff in that war-bag an' it was half full. I don't remember puttin' it there, but there she was. So I takes it an' holds it up for him to look at, readin' th' label out loud. That was th' only time my wife says a word, an' she says *his* name, sorrowful; then she goes on lookin' from him to me an' from me to him.

"He laughs at me an' sneers again. 'Think I 'm go in' to eat that?' he says.

"I don't answer. I 'm too busy workin' with one hand an' watchin' him. I knowed he did n't have no gun, but there was chairs an' bottles a-plenty. I got down a bottle of bitters an' poured some of it in a couple of glasses. Then I drops in some pain-killer an' stirs it up. It does n't mix very well, so I pushed th' remains of their supper to one side an' slips th' two glasses under th' table cloth, holdin' one edge of it in my teeth so it would n't touch th' glasses an' let him follow 'em. If they 'd been cards I 'd 'a' spread 'em monte-fashion under his nose-but they was n't.

"'Now, you skunk-take your pick an' don't wrangle no more about yore chances. An' you drink it before I drink mine, or I 'll blow yore cussed ribs loose!'

"I had given him credit for havin' a-plenty nerve, but now I sees it was n't nerve at all-just gall. He was pasty white again, almost green, an' his little soul plumb tried to climb out of his eyes. I was a whole lot surprised at how he went to pieces an' I was savagely elated at th' way he was a-starin' at that cloth. He looks at me for an instant and then back at th' little shell game on th' table' an' he says in a weak, thin voice: 'How 'd I know-you 'll drink-yourn?'

"'You ain't supposed to be knowin' anythin' about my habits while I 've got this gun-an' it's gettin' plumb heavy, too,' I retorts. 'You 've been yellin' about an even break, an' there it is. An' if it 'll hurry things any I 'll pick up my glass now an' drink it as soon as I see yore glass empty, an' yore Adam's apple bob enough. We won't have to wait very long before we get results. You 'll pick yore glass an' drain it or you 'll stop lead.' An' I did n't care, Hoppy, which one he got —I was worse'n dead then-what th' h —l did I care about livin'?

"I reached out to get my glass as soon as he had his'n an' I laid th' gun on my knee, knowin' he did n't have no weapon, an' that I could get th' drop before he could swing a bottle or chair. But I knowed wrong. He was a liar. As I touched my glass his hand streaks for his hip pocket. I gave him th' liquor in his eyes an' lunged for his gun hand just in time. Then I lets loose all th' rage that was boilin' in me an' when I gets tired of punishin' him, I throws him at th' feet of th' woman, picks up both guns, gets what personal duffle I need, an' blows th' ranch. His face was even all over, his nose was busted, his teeth stuck in his lips, an' he had a broken gun-wrist that gave somebody a whole lot of trouble before it worked right again, if it ever did. I 'm glad I did n't shoot him-there was a lot more of satisfaction doin' it with my naked hands. It was man to man an' I played with him, with all his extra twenty pounds. By G —d, I can feel it yet!"

During the short pause Hopalong looked steadily ahead with unseeing eyes, his face hard, his eyes narrowed, and a tightness about his lips that told plainly what he felt. To come home to that! He realized that his companion was speaking again and gave close attention.

"I don't know where I put in th' next week, but when I got rational I found myself in a cell in a Philadelphia jail, along with bums and crooks. I found that I 'd beat up a couple of policemen when I was drunk. When I got ready to leave th' town I didn't have a whole lot of money, so I played cards with what I had an' left th' town as soon as I had my fare-which did n't take long. That bunch never went up agin' such a well trained deck in their lives."

This time Hopalong broke the silence that ensued, his hand dropping unconsciously on his friend's arm in warm, impulsive sympathy. "By G —d, what a deal! It's awful, Tex; awful!"

"Yes, it was-an' it ain't exactly what you 'd call a joke right now. But I ain't worryin' none about th' woman-she killed my love stone cold that night. But when I think of how things *might* 'a' turned out if she 'd been square, of th' home I 'd 'a' had-but h —l, what's th' use, anyhow? Now what hurts me most is my pride an' conceit-an' th' way I turned to th' drink an' cheatin' so easy. It makes me mad clean through to think of what a infant I was, how I played th' fool for th' Lord knows how long; an' sometimes I want to kill somebody to sort of get square with myself. Up north I 'll be too busy tryin' to make fools out of other people to do much in th' line of sympathizin' with myself-an' too busy an' cautious to break back to drink an' cards. That was one of th' things drove me back here-there 's a whole lot more temptation facin' a man back East, an' 'specially a feller that's totin' a big load of trouble."

"Don't it beat all how different luck will run for different people?" marvelled Hopalong, thinking of his portion.

"That was runnin' in my mind while I was eatin'," replied Tex. "Reckon I *did* get sort of quiet. But I 'm plumb glad th' right kind of luck came yore way, all right."

They rode on for a short time, each busy with his own thoughts, and then Hopalong looked up. "We 're goin' up to see Buck just as soon as I feel th' ranch is in proper shape. I 've got to get th' round-up out of th' way first. You see, we ain't had no honeymoon trip yet."

"Yo 're lucky again; I never could see no joy in hikin' over th' country changin' trains, livin' in hotels, sleepin' in a different bed every night, each one worse'n th' one before, lookin' after baggage, an' workin' hard all th' time. I 've often wondered why it is that two people jump into all that trouble just as soon as they get into their own little heaven for th' first time." Then Tex's face grew earnest. "Now, look here, Hoppy: You ain't goin' up to see Buck till I tell you to come. I know you, all right; just as soon as you land you 'll be out gunnin' for th' bunch that's tryin' to bust Buck's game. You ain't single no more-yo're a married man, an' when a man 's got a wife like yourn he naturally ain't got no cussed business runnin' 'round puttin' hisself in th' way of gettin' killed. You let yore gun get plumb dusty an' when you want any excitement, go out an' try to make water run up hill, or somethin' simple like that. You handle th' trouble that comes to you, an' don't go off a-lookin' for it."

They spent the rest of the time in discussing the status of the married man, and when Mary afterward learned of the stand Tex took she shared more of her husband's affection for him. After a short stay at the H2 they turned homeward and went thoroughly into the matter of Tex's ride north. It was agreed that extra precaution would do no harm, and in order to have no blunder on the part of any one, they decided that it was best not to say anything about where he was going. Hopalong was greatly pleased and relieved now that he knew that his old foreman would have some one to help him fight his battles on that cold, distant range; but he did not appear to be as cheerful about it as was his companion. Tex looked forward to the trip with all the eagerness and impatience of a boy and it showed in his conversation and actions.

When they reached the ranch house at dusk they found Mary cooking a very small meal, and she waved them off. "You an' Billy-Red can't eat here to-night: yo 're goin' to eat with th' boys in th' bunk-house. I would n't spoil your fun for anything. Now you get right out —I mean just what I say!"

"But, girl —" began Hopalong.

"Now I 've made up my mind, an' that's all there is about it. I can get along without you this once —I won't do it again, you know-an' I want you boys to have a rousin' good time all by yoreselves. I want th' boys to like me, Billy-Red, to feel that I ain't changed *everythin'* by bein' here. Now you clear out-Lee knows all about it, an' I cooked some goodies this afternoon for th' feast. Johnny cleaned out th' cake tins an' scraped th' bowls I mixed th' fillin' in —I had to drive him away. Look! There he is, leanin' up against that tree watchin' for me to set somethin' out to cool. He purty near got away with a pie-oh, he 's terrible! But he 's a good boy, just th' same."

Tex turned, emitted a blood-curdling yell and started for the anxious Johnny, Hopalong close behind, while Mary stood in the door and watched the fun, laughing with delight. The outfit piled out of the bunk-house, caught sight of Johnny pounding towards them, and joined in, much to the Kid's disgust. They did not know anything about the affair, but they did not have to know-Johnny was legitimate prey for all, at any time and under any conditions. The fleeing youngster was nearly caught twice as he dodged and doubled, but once past them, he drew away with ease. When the winded and laughing pursuers finally stopped, he circled around to the nearest corral, found a seat on the gate and watched them straggle back to the bunk-house, deriding them with cheerful abandon, dissecting them with a shrewd and cutting tongue. He took them up in rotation and laid bare their faults and weaknesses until they leaned against the wall and laughed at each other until the tears came. Then he turned to ridicule.

"An' there's Skinny," he continued, slowly and gravely, while he rolled a cigarette. "Th' only way you can see him, except at noon, is to look at him in front, or at his feet. Why, I grabbed a broom in th' dark one time an' shore apologized before I realized that it was n't him at all. When he sits down he looks like a figger four, an' I 'm allus a-scared he 'll get into one pant's laig by mistake. When he eats solid stuff he looks like a rope with a knot in it-it's scary watchin' them knots go down-looks like he was skinnin' hisself. You can't tell whether he 's comin' or goin' —th' bumps is all alike. His laigs is so long he looks like a wishbone an' I 'm holdin' my breath most of th' time for fear he 'll split. When he goes huntin' all he has to do is to stand still so th' game won't see him; it wanders up to see what's holdin' up th' hat. He put Pete's pants on once when he fell in th' crick-after he fell in-an' I lifts my hat when I saw th' ridin' skirts. His laigs are beautiful-except for them knobs half way down where they hinge. An' when he swallers a mouthful of water he looks like a muscle dance. Why, I got into his bunk one night by mistake an' spent five minutes a-tryin' to smooth out a crease in th' blanket. Then he wakes up an' tells me to go over an' scratch Red for a change. Tells me to git off 'n him, 'cause I 'm flattenin' him out. That can't be did, an' he knew it, too.

"What *you* laughin' at, Red? You ain't got no laugh comin'. Every mornin' you sit on th' bunk an' count yore clothes an' groan. You put yore hat on first an' yore boots next. Then you takes off th' boots so yore socks can get on. Then th' boots go on again. Then they come off again to let yore pants go on, after which on go th' boots again. Then you take yore hat off to let th' shirt slip over yore head an' it goes right back on again. I 've seen you feel around for yore suspenders for five minutes before you remembered they was under th' shirt."

"Yo 're another! I don't wear no suspenders!"

"No, you don't. Not now, but you did. You quit 'em 'cause they cost a dollar a pair an' kept gettin' lost under th' shirt. Now when you dress up you lift my suspenders. Tex never saw you in love. I did; lots of times; about twice a month. You put th' saddle on th' corral wall, close th' horse, an' mount th' gate. You eat coffee with a knife an' sugar th' water. When I wake up first I see you huggin' th' pillow, which is my old coat wrapped around my old pants. If anybody says 'patience,' you bust yore neck a-lookin' for her. What did you do up to Wallace's that time when his niece came on to visit at his ranch? Wallace told me all about it, an' all about th' toothbrush, too. Lemme see if you remember good. Did n't you —"

"You never mind about me rememberin'," Red shouted, grabbing up a bucket of water off the wash bench and starting for his tormentor. Johnny leaped down and backed off, dodging behind the corral wall. As Red made the turn he fell sprawling, the water affectionately clinging to him. When he arose and looked around Johnny was entering the bunk-house door and the rest of the outfit clung together trying to hold themselves up, and voiced its misery in wails. At that moment Lee Hop buck-jumped around the corner on his trip from the cook shack to the corral, his favorite place of refuge when the ranch house was cut off from him, and he saw Red too late. When he was able to think he was minus a shirt and Red was carrying him under one arm and the shirt under the other.

"Now, you heathen-get that grub on th' table or I 'll picket you an' Johnny to th' same stake!" Red threatened, grimly.

"Him get clake. Him stealie pie. Alle same in klitchen. Eat chop-chop!" wailed the cook. He was promptly dropped and looked up in time to see a rush for the cook shack. But Johnnie was placing the delicacies on the table and close scrutiny failed to discover anything wrong with them, notwithstanding the suspicious manner in which his tongue groomed his teeth.

The supper was a howling success, and unlike the usual Bar-20 meals, was prolonged, and fun seasoned every dish. Even Lee Hop, incapable as he was of grasping most of the points in their rapid flight, and not wholly in sympathy with certain members of the outfit-even his countenance lost its expression of constant watchfulness; his mouth widened into a grin whose extremities were lost somewhere in the region of his back hair; his eyes gleamed like jet buttons in a dish of mush; and his moisture-laden skin shone until, altogether, his head resembled nothing so much as a pumpkin-bogie, a good-natured one, with an extra large candle lighted inside. He was tempted now and again to insert a remark in the short openings, but experience checked him in time. When the crowd filed into the living-room it was to tell tales of men living and dead; stories that covered a great range of human action, from the foolishness of "Aristotle" Smith to the cold ferocity and cruelty of Slippery Trendley and Deacon Rankin. The hours flew past with astonishing speed and when Tex looked at his watch he stared for a moment and returned it to his pocket with a quick, decisive movement.

"It's past midnight, fellows, an' I 'm riding' on in the mornin'," he remarked, arising.

The crowd looked its amazement and then vociferously announced its regret. These men held it a breach of etiquette to question, and because there were no "whys" or "wherefores," Tex felt impelled to explain. He was going on to see old friends, but he would return. The Bar-20 was his range and he would get back as soon as he could. In deference to his wishes and to let him get as much sleep as possible, the outfit quietly prepared for rest, and Hopalong, bidding them good-night, departed for the ranch house.

Breakfast over the next morning, Tex rode north, followed by an escort of friends of which any man would have been proud. Hopalong and Mary rode at his side and behind in a compact bunch came the boys. They stopped when the river trail was reached and Tex shook hands all around.

"I 'm sorry to leave you, Hopalong," he said earnestly; "but you know how it is: I 've been away quite a spell and things happen quick out here. You 'll see me again this Summer an' I 'll come to stay if you want me. Mary, I 'm mighty glad to see he 's got such a good foreman-he 's needed one a long time; an' I can see a big improvement in him already."

"Reckon you might profit by the example-must be girls a-plenty out in this country who 'd make good foremen," she replied, laughing.

Tex's face showed no trace of hurt as the chance arrow sped to the mark; he laughed, pointing at Johnny. "I reckon there are; but the Kid would n't give me no show."

"We 'll answer for him, Tex," chuckled Red. "We cured him once before an' we 'd be shore glad to do it again."

"Yep-kept him in the hills, starvin' an' freezin' for a whole month," sweetly added Skinny.

Johnny flushed and squirmed but had no time to retort, Pete and the others being too busy talking to Tex to let him be heard. Finally Tex backed off, raised his hat, and with a bow and a smile to Mary, wheeled and loped off along the trail to run Spring a race to Montana. Every time he looked back he waved in answer to his friends, and then, swiftly mounting a rise, was silhouetted for an instant against the white clouds on the horizon and as swiftly dropped from sight, a faint chorus of yells reaching him.

The outfit turned slowly to return to their ranch and when they missed their foreman, they saw him sitting silent where they had left him, his wife's hand on his arm. He could still see Tex against the sky, clear cut, startlingly strong and potent, and he nodded his head slowly. "He 's needed up there, an' he 's the best man to go." Turning, he was surprised to find his wife so near and he smiled joyously: "Wouldn't go an' leave me all alone, would you, Honey? Yo 're shore a thoroughbred an' I 'm plumb proud of you. Race you to th' bunch!"

Chapter II
H. Whitby Booth is Shown How

If any man of the Bar-20 punchers had been brought face to face with George McAllister he would have suffered the shock of his life. "Frenchy?" he would have hesitated, "What in —? Why, Frenchy?" And the shock would have been mutual, since Frenchy McAllister had been dead some months, a fact of which his brother George was sorrowfully aware. Yet so alike were they that any of Frenchy's old friends would have thought the dead come to life.

A distinguishing feature was the eye-glasses which George had long found necessary. He took them off and laid aside his book as the butler announced Mr. Booth.

H. Whitby Booth entered the room with the hesitating step of one who has a favor to ask. A tall, well-set-up man of the blonde type of so many of his countrymen, his usual movements were slow when compared with the nervous action of those in the hustling city of Chicago. Hesitation gave him the appearance of a mechanical figure, about to run down. Mr. McAllister's hearty welcome did not seem to reassure him.

"Ah-Miss McAllister-ah-is not at home," he volunteered, rather than questioned.

The other man eyed him quizzically. "No," he agreed, "she and Mrs. Blake are out somewhere; I am not just sure where. Shall I inquire?"

"No, oh no. I rather wanted to talk to you, you know-that is-ah —"

"Sit down, Whitby, and relieve your mind. Cigars on that table there, and some whiskey and fizz. Shall I ring for brandy?"

"Awfully good of you, really. No, I —I think I 'll go in as I am. The fact is I want Margaret-Miss McAllister-and I thought I 'd ask if you had any objections."

"Margaret has."

"Oh, I say!"

"Fact, she has. Might as well face the music, Whitby. The truth is just this: It's less than a week ago since Margaret was holding you up as a horrible example. Margaret comes from a line of hustlers; she has not had common sense and national pride bred out of her in a fashionable school; and she looks with extreme disfavor on an idler."

"But I say, Mr. McAllister, you don't think —"

"No, my boy, I don't think where Margaret is concerned-Margaret thinks. Don't misunderstand me. I like you, Whitby. Confidentially, I believe Margaret does, too. But I am quite sure she will never marry a man who does nothing and, as she expressed it herself, lives on an allowance from his father."

"Then I understand, sir, you have no objections?"

"None in the world-because I believe you will strike your gait before long and become something of a hustler yourself. But let me tell you, Margaret does n't deal in futures —I 'm used to it-but she insists on a fact, not a probability."

Whitby drew a breath which was largely expressive of relief. "In that case, sir, I 'll try my luck," and he arose to say good-night.

"You know where to find them?"

"Rather! I was going there when I had spoken to you."

"I see," said Mr. McAllister, somewhat grimly, remembering the other's greeting. "Sit down, Whitby. The night is young, you can't miss them, and I am so sure of the badness of your luck that I should like to give you a little encouragement to fall back on." Whitby resumed his seat and Mr. McAllister puffed thoughtfully at his cigar for a few moments before speaking.

"Not to go too far back," he began, "my grandfather was a boy when his father took him from Ireland, the birthplace of the family, to France, the birthplace of liberty, as the old man thought. Those were stirring times for that boy and the iron of life entered into him at an early age. He married and had one son, my father, who thought the liberty of this country so much better than that of France, that he came here, bringing his young wife with him; the wife died in giving birth to my younger brother, John. All that line were hustlers, Whitby. They had to be, to keep alive. Margaret knows their history better than I do and glories in it. You see?"

Whitby nodded mournfully. He was beginning to lose confidence again.

"My father would have been alive to-day but for an unfortunate accident which carried off both him and my mother within a few days. My brother and myself were found pretty well provided for. My share has not decreased. In fact I have done very well for a man who is not avaricious. But I had to fight; and more than once it was a close call, win or lose. Margaret knows all that, Whitby, and the dear girl is as proud of her father, I do believe, as of any who went before him. Her mother left us very soon and Margaret has been my companion ever since she could talk. Are you beginning to understand?"

"I am, indeed," was the reluctant acknowledgment.

"Very good. Then here is where you come in." His face clouded and he was silent so long that Whitby looked up inquiringly. The motion aroused McAllister and he continued:

"My brother was queer. I have always thought his birth had something to do with it; but however that may be, he was, in my opinion, peculiar in many of his ways. The choice of his path in life was quite on a par with his character: he invested every dollar he had in land out West, he and a partner whom I have never seen; bought and paid for land and stock at a time when Government land was used by any one without payment of any kind and when live-stock raising was almost an unknown industry, at least in that part of the country. But that was n't all. He went out to the ranch and took his delicate young wife with him, a bride, and lived in a wild region where they saw only Indians, outlaws, and those who were worse than either." His face hardened and the hand he laid on the table trembled as he turned to face to his listener. "Worse than either, Whitby," he repeated. "The Indians were bad enough at times, God knows, but there is excuse for their deviltry; there could be no excuse for those others.

"One reason John gave for going West was that the life would bring health to his wife. It did so. A few months' time saw her a robust woman. And then John returned to the ranch one day to come upon a scene that drove him crazy, I verily believe. No need to go into it, though I had the details from his partner at the time-John did not write me for years. They both started out after the murderers and wandered over a great part of this country before finding the chief fiend. Even his death brought no peace to John. He would never go back to the old place nor would his partner, out of feeling for him. After much persuasion I got them to put matters into my hands, but so many years had passed that I found the ownership in dispute and it is but lately that I have succeeded in regaining title. It was too late for John, who died before I came into possession, but his partner, a man named Peters, has gone up there from a Texan ranch to run the place. He is half owner and should be the best man for the job. But-and my experience with those Westerners places emphasis on that 'but' —I do not really know just what kind of a man he is. I am putting quite a large sum of money in this venture, relying upon Peters' knowledge and hoping for a square deal. And if he is the best man for the place, you are the best man I know to show me that. Don't interrupt.

"I know right well what Margaret will tell you to-night, and if you want to make her change her mind, you could have no better opportunity than I offer. My brother's history is an abiding grief with Margaret, and if you go out there and make good you will surely make good with her.

"That's all. If I 'm right, come and see me to-morrow at the office. I will have everything noted down for you in writing. Commit it to memory and then destroy the notes; because you would be valueless if any one interested discovered you were acting for me. And don't see Margaret after to-night before you go."

He arose and held out his hand. Whitby grasped it as he stood up and looked frankly at him. "It's awfully good of you, Mr. McAllister," he declared. "You 've left me deuced little hope, I must say, but there 's no knowing where you are if you don't ask, is there? And if I come a cropper I 'll try your way and chance it."

"You 'll find my way is right. I 've made mistakes in my life but never any where Margaret was concerned. Good-night."

* * * * *

Whitby stood at the top of the steps, slowly drawing his right-hand glove through his gloved left hand, time after time, casting a long look before he leaped. The driver of his hired *coupé* eyed him with calculating patience, observing to himself that if this were a specimen of the average Englishman, England must be a cinch for a cabman. Whitby had not yet arrived at the leaping stage when another *coupé*, a private one with a noticeably fine team, stopped in passing the house, and a voice hailed him: "Hello, Whit! What are you mooning there for?"

Whitby smiled: for all his consideration he had been pushed in at the last. He slowly descended the steps while he replied: "Evenin', Wallie. I was just going to drop in on the Sparrows."

"Good enough! Me, too. Jump in here and let your wagon follow. Do you hear, you driver? Trail in behind-unless you won't need him, Whit."

"Oh, let him come along. I —ah —I may be leaving rather early, don't you know."

"That so? Me, too. I'm darned glad I met you, Whit. I 'm in a regular blue funk-Brown is sulky as a bear. He 's been driving me about for an hour, I should say, and he does n't understand it. Fact is, Whit, I 'm going to ask a girl to marry me to-night, and I don't want to, not a little bit; but if I don't, some other fellow will, and that would be-well, worse."

"By Jove! Marry you *to-night*! Do you fancy she will?"

"No, you 'bloomin' Britisher.' *Ask* her, not marry her, to-night. For the love of Moses! Do you think it's an elopement?"

"Well, I did n't know, you know," and his tone was one of distinct disappointment. "You seem to be pretty certain she 'll have you."

"Oh! She 'll have me right enough, but I 've got to ask first and make sure. There 're too many others hanging around to suit me."

"I say, old chap, I hope you won't mind my asking but-it is n't Miss McAllister, by any chance, is it?"

Wallie turned in his seat and stared at the anxious face of Whitby for a few moments, then he broke into shouts of laughter. "You, too," he managed to say; and at last: "No, you trembling aspirant, it isn't, by any chance, Miss McAllister. Margie and I are good friends, all right, but not in that way. Oh, you sly Johnnie! Why, I 'll bet a hundred you 're up to the same game, yourself. Own up, now."

"I think a great deal of Miss McAllister, a very great deal. If I thought she 'd have me I 'd ask her the first opportunity."

"And that will be in a few minutes. She 's bound to be there-and here we are. Wish me luck, Whit."

"I do, with all my heart, Wallie," and he was very serious in his earnestness.

"Same to you, Whit, and many-no, not that, of course." They were in the rooms by this time, both pairs of eyes wandering, searching this way and that as they moved toward their pretty hostess whose recent marriage seemed to have increased, if possible, her popularity with the male sex; she stood so surrounded by a chaffing crowd of men that they found difficulty in getting near her. They did not linger, however, as each caught sight of the object of his pursuit at the same time, and their paths parted from that moment.

The maturity of Margaret McAllister's mind would never have been suspected from her appearance. The pale green satin gown, overhung with long draperies of silk-fringed tulle, the low round satin corsage being partly veiled by a diagonal drapery of the same transparent material, and ornamented-as was the skirt-with a satin scarf, tied with knots of ribbon and clusters of water-lilies —this formed a creation that adorned a perfect figure of medium height, whose symmetry made it seem smaller than it really was. The Irish temperament and quickness of intelligence were embodied in a brunette beauty inherited from her French ancestry; but over all, like the first flush of morning's light on a lovely garden, lay the delicate charm of her American mother. One of a group of girls, with several men hovering on the outer circle, she detached herself upon Whitby's approach and advanced to meet him.

"Good-evening, Mr. Booth. Are n't you late?"

"Yes, rather." Whitby drew comfort from the fact that she had chosen to notice it.

"Aunt Jessie is over this way. She is complaining of the heat already. Perhaps you would better mention it."

"Mrs. Blake? I will. I 've a favor to ask of Mrs. Blake. Let's join her."

Mrs. Blake was of that comfortable age, size, and appearance which expressed satisfaction with the world and its ways. She affected black at all times with quite touching consistency; doubly so, since gossip hinted at a married life not altogether happy. However, her widowhood did not permit derogatory remarks concerning the late Mr. Blake, who made up to her in dying all his short-comings when alive; and she had proven a discreet chaperon for Margaret from the assumption of that position. Her most conspicuous weakness was endeavoring to overcome a growing embonpoint with corsets, and the tight lacing undoubtedly had much to do with her susceptibility to heat. Whitby was a favorite with her and she greeted him warmly, closing her waving fan to tap him with it now and again in emphasis.

But Whitby's purpose would not wait; as soon as the chance offered he begged free, and arose to the occasion with a daring that surprised himself. "I am going to hide up with Miss McAllister for quite a time, Mrs. Blake. If any one comes bothering, just put him off, will you? That is, if Miss McAllister doesn't mind."

"Mind? Of course she doesn't mind. Run along, Margie, and for Heaven's sake, don't sit in a draft-though I don't believe you can find one in this house," and the fan was brought into more vigorous action at the reminding thought.

"Well, I don't know, Mr. Booth," remonstrated Margaret as they moved away. "They will begin to dance very soon and I promised Wallie Hartman the opening. You came in together, didn't you?"

"Oh, Wallie! Yes, he was pretty keen on getting here but I rather fancy he's forgotten about that dance, you know."

"What makes you say that? What mischief are you two brewing?"

"Ah-it's Wallie's secret, you know, —that is, his part of it is —I say, here 's the very spot."

They had made the turn behind the stairs, where a punch bowl stood; the space immediately behind the stairs being too low in which to stand comfortably upright, a mass of foliage was banked in a half circle, outside of which the stand and punch bowl were placed; inside, a thoughtful hostess had arranged a *tête-à-tête*, quite unnoticeable from without. Whitby's attention had been drawn to it by the couple who had emerged upon their approach, the girl radiant and the man walking on air, of which details Whitby was entirely oblivious. Margaret was more observing and she looked after Wallie with a dawning look of understanding and then at Whitby with a quick glance of apprehension. There was no time to protest, even if she would, as Whitby had led her behind the leafy screen before she fully realized the import of his action.

Like many slow starters, Whitby, when once in movement, set a rapid pace. He came to the point now with promptitude:

"Miss McAllister, I arrived late because I called on your father before coming here, to ask his permission to address you. I must say he rather dashed my hopes, you know. He does n't think I 'm such a bad sort-he does n't object in the least-but he seemed to fancy his daughter Margaret would. I —I hope he is mistaken."

She turned to him a face in which the eyes were slowly filling with tears, nor did she remove the hand upon which his rested, on the curving back of the seat. It was not her first proposal, by several, but there was a vibrating earnestness, an unexpected tenderness in this big, slow Englishman which told her she was going to hurt him seriously when she spoke. And she did not want to hurt him; with all her heart and soul she wished she did not have to hurt him.

"I 'm not worthy of you, Margaret. I don't think any man is worthy of a good woman, and I 'm just an ordinary man. But I 'll *be* worthy of you, from to-night. —and that whether you say yes or no.

"You know I love you. You must know I left London and came over here to follow you. But you don't know how much I care for you-and I can't tell you. I 'm a duffer at this sort of game-like everything else —I never did it before-and 'pon my word, I don't know how. But if I could say what I feel, then perhaps, you might know better. What is it to be, Margaret? Wait a bit! If you feel doubtful, I 'll wait as long as you want me to. But-but —I 'm afraid it's no go." He sat looking dumbly at her, hoping for some sign of encouragement, but there was no misreading the answer in her face.

It was a long minute before she spoke. She was unnerved by the hysterical desire to put her arms around him and soothe him as she might a hurt child. Something of her embarrassment was conveyed to him and with the wish to save her the pain of refusing in words he started as if to rise. She stopped him with a gesture.

"Wait. I *will* say what I want you to know. I like you-no! not in that way; not the way a woman should-the man she expects to marry. Perhaps if you had been —I am not sure-but I could *not* marry a drone. Oh! why don't you wake up! How *can* you go on from day to day with no thought but self-indulgence? You say you love me. Ask yourself: Is not that merely a form of self-indulgence? Oh, I know you would take care of me and defer to me and let me have my way in everything-you are that kind of a man-but to what end? That I might be the more pleasing to you. Is it your purpose to dawdle through life, taking only such pains as shall make things more pleasing to you?"

"Is that all, Margaret? Is it only because you fancy I'm a loafer?"

"But you are! You are! Oh! I don't know —I 'm not sure —"

"I 'm sure!" the exulting certainty in his voice startled her. "I 'm sure!" he repeated. "I may be a bit of an ass in some things but no woman would care as you care, what a man was or what he did unless she loved him. You love me, Margaret, thank God! Give me a chance. You 're only a girl, yet. Give me a year and if I go under, or you find I 'm wrong, I 'll thank you for the chance and never blame you. Will you?"

Her heart was pounding in suffocating throbs and she trembled like a leaf in the wind before the eager intensity of his gaze. A strong will held her in check, else she had given way then and there, but she faced him with a fine bravery. "Yes," she promised, "I will. Go away and make good."

"Make good! By Jove, that's what your father said. Make good —I 'll not forget it." His head bent low in an old-fashioned but becoming salute while her free hand rested unfelt for an instant upon the yellow hair, a gesture that was at once a blessing and a prayer.

Chapter III

Buck Makes Friends

The town of Twin River straggled with indifferent impartiality along the banks of the Black Jack and Little Jill branches where they ran together to form the Jones' Luck River, two or three houses lying farther north along the main stream. The trail from Wayback, the nearest railway point, hugged the east bank of Jones' Luck, shaded throughout its course by the trees which lined the river, as they did all the streams in this part of the country: cottonwoods mostly, with an occasional ash or elm. Looking to the east, the rolling ground sloped upward toward a chain of hills; to the west, beyond the river, the country lay level to the horizon. On both sides of the trail the underbrush grew thick; spring made of it a perfect paradise of blossoms.

Boomerang, pet hobo of Twin River and the only one who ever dared to come back, left Little Nell's with his characteristic hurried shuffle and approached the wooden bridge where the Wayback trail crossed the Jill, and continued south to Big Moose. Boomerang was errand boy just now, useful man about the hotel or one of the saloons when necessity drove, at other times just plain bum. He was suspected of having been a soldier. A sharp "'tention" would startle him into a second's upright stiffness which after a furtive look around would relax into his customary shambling lack of backbone. He had one other amusing peculiarity: let a gun be discharged in his vicinity and there was trouble right away, trouble the gunner was not looking for; Boomerang would fly into such a fury of fighting rage, it was a town wonder that some indignant citizen had not sent him long ago where he never could come back.

Coming to the bridge he looked casually and from habit along the trail and espied a horseman riding his way. He studied him reflectively a few seconds and then spat vigorously at something moving on one of the bridge planks, much as the practised gun-man snaps without appearing to aim. "Stranger," he affirmed; "Cow-punch," he added; "Old man," he shrewdly surmised, and shook his head; "Dunno 'im" and he glanced at the stain on the plank to see what he had bagged. Among his other pleasing human habits "Boom" used tobacco-as a masticant-there was the evidence of the fact. But he had missed and after a wistful look for something to inspire him to a more successful effort, he shuffled on.

The horseman came at a steady gait, his horse, a likely-looking bay with black spots, getting over the ground considerably faster than the cow-ponies common to the locality; approaching the bridge he was slowed to a walk while his rider took in the town with comprehensive glance. A tall man, lean and grizzled, with the far-seeing, almost vacant eye of the plainsman, there was nothing, to any one but such a student of humanity as "Boom," to indicate his calling, much less his position in it. The felt hat, soft shirt and rough, heavy suit, the trousers pushed into the tops of his boots, were such as a man in the town might wear and many did wear. He forded the stream near the bridge at a walk. Pop Snow, better known as Dirty, cleverly balancing himself within an inch of safety in front of the "I-Call" saloon, greeted him affably: "Come a long way, stranger?" asked Dirty.

"From Wayback," announced the other and paused in interested suspense. Dirty had become seized with some internal convulsion, which momentarily threatened disaster to his balance. His feet swung back and forth in spasmodic jerks, the while his sinful old carcass shook like a man with the Chagres fever. Finally a strangled wheeze burst from his throat and explained the crinkle about his eyes: he was laughing.

"Wayback ain't fur," he declared, licking his lips in anticipation of the kernel of his joke about to come. "You can a'most see it frum here through the bottom uv —"

"How d' you know it ain't?" the horseman abruptly interrupted.

Dirty was hurt. This was not according to Hoyle. Two more words and no self-respecting "gent" could refuse to look toward Wayback through a glass-and certainly not alone. The weather was already too cold to sit fishing for such fish as this; and here was one who had swallowed the bait, rejecting the hook.

"Why, stranger, I been there," explained Dirty, in aggrieved remonstrance.

"How long since you been there? Not since two-at-once, was you? Didn't it used to be at Drigg's Worry? Didn't it?"

Snow lost his balance. He nodded in open-mouthed silence.

"Course it was-at Drigg's Worry-and now it's way back," and with a grim chuckle the stranger pressed in his knees and loped on down the trail to the Sweet-Echo Hotel.

Dirty stared after him. "Who in hell's that?" he asked himself in profane astonishment. "It 's never Black Jack-too old; an' it ain't Lucky Jones-too young. He sure said 'two-at-once.' Two-at-once: I ain't heard that in more 'n twenty years." His air-dried throat compelled inward attention and he got up from his box and turned and looked at it. "Used to be at Drigg's Worry, did n't it?" he mimicked. "Did n't it? An' now it's way back." He kicked the box viciously against the tavern wall. "D —n yer! This yer blasted town 's gettin' too smart," and he proceeded to make the only change of base he ever undertook during the day, by stamping across the bridge to the "Why-Not."

The door of the I-Call opened and a man appeared. He glanced around carelessly until he noticed the box, which he viewed with an appearance of lively interest, coming outside and walking around it at a respectful distance. "Huh!" he grunted. Having satisfied himself of its condition he drawlingly announced it for the benefit of those inside. "Dirty 's busted his chair," he informed, and turned to look curiously after Pop Snow, who was at that moment slamming the door of the Why-Not behind him.

Through the open door three other men came out. They all looked at the box. One of them stopped and turned it over with his thumb. "Kicked it," he said, and they all looked across at the Why-Not, considering. A roar from behind them smote upon their ears like a mine blast: "Shut that door!" With one accord they turned and trooped back again.

The rider meanwhile was talking to his horse as he covered the short distance to the Sweet-Echo Hotel. "Wonderful climate, Allday. If twenty years don't wear you down no more 'n old Snow you 'll shore be a grand horse t' own," and he playfully banged him alongside the neck with his stirrup. Allday limited his resentment to a flattening of the ears and the rider shook his head sorrowfully. "Yo 're one good li'l hoss but yore patience 'd discourage a saint." He swung off the trail to ride around the building in search of a shelter of some kind, catching sight of Boomerang just disappearing through the door of the bar-room. "Things has been a-movin' 'round Twin River since Frenchy an' me went after Slippery an' his gang: bridges, reg'lar hotels, an' tramps. An' oblige me by squintin' at th' stable. If Cowan 'd wake up an' find that at th' back door, he 'd fall dead."

He dismounted and led his horse through the stable door, stopping in contemplation of the interior. He was plainly surprised. "One, two, three, four," he counted, "twenty stalls-twenty tie-'em-by-th'-head stalls-no, there 's a rope behind 'em. Well, I 'm d —d! He ain't meanin' to build again in fifty years; no, not never!"

Allday went willingly enough into one of the stalls-they were nothing new to him-and fell to eating with no loss of time. Buck watched him for a few moments and then, throwing saddle and bridle onto his shoulder, he walked back the way he had come and into the hotel bar. No one noticed him as he entered, all, even the bartender, being deeply intent on watching a game of cards. Buck grunted, dropped his belongings in a corner, and paused to examine the group. A grand collie dog, lying near the stove in the middle of the room, got up, came and sniffed at him, and went back and lay down again.

The game was going on at a table close to the bar, over which the bartender leaned, standing on some elevation to enable him to draw closer. Only two men were playing. The one facing Buck was a big man, in the forties, his brown hair and beard thickly sprinkled with gray; brown eyes, red-rimmed from dissipation, set wide apart from a big, bold nose, stared down at the cards squeezed in a big hand. The other man was of slight build, with black hair, and the motions of his hands, which Buck had caught as he entered, were those of a gambler: accurate, assured, easy with a smooth swiftness that baffled the eye. He was dressed like a cowpunch; he looked like a cow-punch —all but the hands; these, browned as they were, and dirty, exhibited a suppleness that had never been injured by hard work. Buck walked up to the bar and a soft oath escaped him as he caught sight of the thin, brown face, the straight nose, the out-standing ears, the keen black eyes-Buck's glance leaped around the circle of on-lookers in the effort to discover how many of the gambler's friends were with him. He was satisfied that the man was playing a lone hand. There was a tenseness in the air which Buck knew well, but from across the hall came a most incongruous sound. "Piano, by G —d!" breathed Buck in amazement. The intentness on the game of those in the room explained why he had seen no one about the place and he was at a loss to account for the indifference of the musician.

At the big man's left, standing in the corner between the bar and the wall, was a woman. Her blonde hair and blue eyes set off a face with some pretensions to beauty, and in point of size she was a fitting mate for the big man at whom she stared with lowering gaze. Close to her stood the hobo, and Buck rightly concluded he was a privileged character. Surrounding the table were several men quite evidently punchers, two or three who might be miners, and an unmistakable travelling salesman of that race whose business acumen brings them to the top though they start at the bottom. Buck had gauged them all in that one glance. Afterward he watched the gambler's hands and a puzzled expression gradually appeared on his face; he frowned and moved uneasily. Was the man playing fair or were his eyes getting old? Suddenly the frown disappeared and he breathed a sigh of relief: the motion itself had been invisible but Buck had caught the well-remembered preliminary flourish; thereafter he studied the faces of the others; the game had lost interest, even the low voices of the players fell on deaf ears. His interest quickened as the big man stood up.

"I 'm done," he declared. "That lets me out, Dave. You 've got th' pile. After to-night I 'll have to pound leather for forty a month and my keep." He turned to the woman, while an air of relief appeared among the others at his game acceptance of the loss. "Go on home, Nell. I won't be up yet a while."

"You won't be up at all," was the level-voiced reply.

"Eh?" he exclaimed, in surprised questioning.

She pushed past him and walked to the door. "You won't be up at all," she repeated, facing him. "You 've lost your pile and sent mine after it in a game you don't play any better than a four-year-old. I warned you not to play. Now you take the consequences." The door slammed after her. "Boom" silently opened the door into the hall and vanished.

The big man looked around, dazed. No one met his eye. Dave was sliding the cards noise-lessly through his fingers and the rest appeared fascinated by the motion. The big man turned to the bartender.

"Slick, gimme a bottle," he demanded. Slick complied without a word and he bore it in his hand to the table behind the door, where he sat drinking alone, staring out morosely at the gathering darkness.

Buck dropped into the vacated chair and laid his roll on the table. "The time to set in at a two-hand game of draw," he remarked with easy good nature, "is when th' other feller is feelin' all flushed up with winnin'. If you like to add my pile to that load you got a'ready, I 'm on." He beamed pleasantly on the surrounding faces and a cynical smile played for a moment on the thin lips of the man facing him. "Sure," he agreed, and pushed the cards across the table.

"Bar-keep, set 'em up," said Buck, flicking a bill behind him. Slick became busy at once and Buck, in a matter-of-fact manner, placed his gun on the table at his left hand and picked up the pack. "Yes," he went on with vacuous cheerfulness, "the best man with a full deck I ever saw told me that. We crossed trails down in Cheyenne. They was shore some terrors in that li'l town, but he was th' one original." He shook his head in reminiscent wonder, and raised his glass. "Here 's to a growin' pile, Bud," and nodding to the others, who responded with indistinct murmurs, the drink was drained in the customary gulp. "One more, bar-keep, before we start her," he demanded. "I never drink when I 'm a-playin'." Here he leaned forward and raised his voice. "Friend, you over there by th' winder, yo 're not drinkin'."

The big man slowly turned his head and looked at Buck with blood-shot eyes, then at the extra glass on his table. "Here 's better luck ner mine, friend-not wishin' you no harm, Dave," and he added the drink to the generous quantity he had already consumed. Buck waved his hand in acknowledgment, then he smiled again on his opponent.

"Same game you was playin', Bud?" he asked, genially.

"Suits me," was the laconic reply.

Buck raised the second drink. "Here's to Tex Ewalt, th' man who showed me th' error of my ways." The tail of his eye was on Dave.

The name of Tex must have shocked him like a bucket of ice water but he did not betray it by so much as the flicker of an eyelid. Ewalt and he had been friends in the Panhandle and both had escaped the fate of Trendley and his crowd more by luck than merit. Buck knew Dave's history in Texas, related by Ewalt himself, who had illustrated the tell-tale flourish with which Dave introduced a crooked play; but he did not know that Dave Owens was Black Jack, returned after years of wandering, to the place of his nativity.[1]

Buck shuffled the cards slowly and then with a careful exaggeration of the flourish, dealt the hand in a swift shower of dropping units. A sigh of appreciation escaped the observant group and this time Buck got results: at sight of the exaggerated flourish an involuntary contraction of the muscles hardened the deceptively boyish form and face of the younger man and the black eyes stared a challenging question at the smiling gray ones opposite before dropping to the cards he had unconsciously gathered up.

Luck smiled on Buck from the start. He meant that it should. Always a good player, his acquaintance with Tex, who had taught him all he knew of crooked plays, had made him an apt pupil in the school in which his slippery opponent was a master. With everything coming his way Buck was quite comfortable. Sooner or later the other would force the fighting. Time enough to sit up and take notice when the flourishing danger signal appeared.

It came at last. Dave leaned forward and spoke. "Cheyenne, how'd jack-pots strike yer? I got ter hit th' trail before six an' it's pretty nigh time to feed."

"Shore!" assented Buck, heartily.

The pot grew in a manner scandalous to watch. "Double the ante," softly suggested Dave.

"Shore," agreed Buck, with genial alacrity.

"Double her ag'in."

"Double she is," was Buck's agreeable response.

Pass after pass, and Slick stretched out over the bar and craned his neck. At last, with a graceful flourish a good hand fell to Buck, a suspiciously good hand, while Dave's thin lips were twisted into a one-sided smile. Buck looked at him reproachfully.

"Bud, you should oughter o' knowed better 'n that. I got six cards."

The smile faded from Dave's face and he stared at the cards like a man who sees ghosts. The stare rose slowly to Buck's face, but no one could possibly suspect such grieved reproach to be mere duplicity. It was too ridiculous-only Dave knew quite well that he had not dealt six cards. "Funny," he said. "Funny how a man 'll make mistakes."

"I forgive you this once, but don't do it no more," and Buck shuffled the cards, executed a particularly outrageous flourish, and dealt.

"Ha! Ha!" barked Bow-Wow Baker. "D—n if they ain't both makin' th' same sign. Must belong to th' same lodge."

Chesty Sutton dug him in the ribs with an elbow. "Shut up!" he hissed, never taking his eyes from the game.

Dave passed and Buck opened. Dave drew three cards to two high ones. Buck stood pat. Dave scanned his hand; whatever suspicion he might have had, vanished: he had never seen the man who could deal him a straight in that fashion. He backed his hand steadily until Buck's assurance and his own depleted cash made him pause, and he called. Buck solemnly laid down four aces. Four! —and Dave would have taken his oath the diamond ace had been on the bottom of the deck before the deal-and Buck had not drawn cards.

"They 're good," said Dave shortly, dropping his hand into the discard. "If you 're goin' to stay around here, Cheyenne, I 'll get revenge to-morrer." He started to rise.

"Nope, I guess not, Bud. I never play yore kind of a game with th' same man twice."

Dave froze in his position. "Meanin'?" he asked, coldly.

"I don't like th' way you deal," was the frank answer.

"D —n you!" cursed Dave. His hand flew to his gun-and stopped. Over the edge of the table a forty-five was threatening with steady mouth.

"Don't do it, Bud," warned Buck.

Dave's hand slowly moved forward. "A two-gun man, eh?" he sneered.

"Shore. Never bet on th' gun on th' table, Bud. You got a lot to learn. Hit her up or you 'll be late-an' down where I came from it's unhealthy to look through a winder without first makin' a noise."

"Yore argument is good. But I reckon it 'd be a good bet as how you 'll learn somethin' in Twin River you ain't never learned nowhere else." Dave sauntered carelessly to the front door.

"You ain't never too old to learn," agreed Buck, sententiously. The front door closed quietly after Dave and half a minute later his pony's hoofs were heard pounding along the trail that led toward Big Moose.

"Cheyenne, put her there! I like yore style!" Chesty Sutton, late puncher for the Circle X, shoved his hand under Buck's nose with unmistakable friendliness. "I like th' way *you* play, all right."

"Me, too," chimed in Bow-Wow. "Dave Owens has got th' lickin' of his life. An' between you an' I, Cheyenne, I ain't never seed Dave get licked afore-not reg'lar."

The chorus of congratulations that followed was so sincere that Buck's heart warmed toward the company. Chesty secured attention by pointing his finger at Buck and wagging it impressively. "But you hear me, Cheyenne," he warned. "Dave ain't no quitter. He 's got it agin' you an' he 's h —l on th' shoot. I ain't never heerd of his killin' nobody but he 's right handy spoilin' yore aim. Ain't he, Bow-Wow?"

"Look a-here. How often have I told you? You sez so. He is. Don't allus leave it to me." Bow-Wow's tone was indignant as he rubbed his right arm reflectively.

"Gentlemen, I 'm not sayin' a word against anybody, not one word," and Slick glanced from man to man, shaking his head to emphasize his perfect belief in the high standard of morality prevalent in Twin River. "But I begs leave to remark that *I* like Cheyenne's game-which it is th' first time in my brief but eventful career that I seen five dealt cards turn into six. You all seen it. It sure happened. Mr. Cheyenne, you have my joyous admiration. Let's celebrate. An' in th' meantime, might I inquire, without offence, if Cheyenne has a habit of complainin' of too many cards?"

They had lined up before the bar and all glasses were filled before Buck answered. Slick stood directly before him and every face, showing nothing beyond polite interest, was turned his way. But Buck well knew that on his reply depended his position in the community and the gravity of the occasion was in his voice when he spoke.

"Gentlemen, Mr. Slick has called. There's two ways of playin'. When I plays with any gentleman here, I plays one way. Dave Owens played th' other way. I played his game."

He glanced at the silent figure by the window, set down his glass, and started to cross the room. Chesty Sutton put out his hand and stopped him. "I would n't worry him none, Cheyenne. Ned Monroe 's th' best boss I ever worked for but hard luck has been pilin' up on him higher 'n th' Rockies since he lost his ranch. Better let him fight it out alone, friend."

Lost his ranch-Ned Monroe-Buck's intention was doubly strengthened. "Leave it to me," was his confident assurance, and he strode across the room and around the table in front of the window. The sombre eyes of the big man were forced to take notice of him.

"Friend, it's on th' house. Mr. Slick is a right pleasant man, an' he 's waitin'." A rapid glance at the bottle told him that Monroe, in his complete oblivion, had forgotten it. Ned eyed him with a puzzled frown while the words slowly illumined his clouded mind. At length he turned slowly, sensed the situation, and rose heavily to his feet. "Sure," was the simple reply.

At the bar significant looks were exchanged. "I 'm beginnin' to *like* Cheyenne," declared Slick, thoughtfully, rubbing the palm of his left hand against the bar; "which his persuadin' language is fascinatin' to see."

"It sure is," Chesty Sutton endorsed promptly, while the others about him nodded their heads in silent assent.

"Well, gentlemen," said Slick, "here 's to th' continued good health of Mr. Cheyenne." Down the line ran the salutation and Buck laughed as he replaced his empty glass.

"I shore hope you-all ain't tryin' to scare me none," he insinuated; "because I 'm aimin' to stop up here an' —who in h —l's poundin' that pie-anner?" he broke off, turning to glare in the direction of the melancholy sound.

"Ha! Ha!" barked in his ear, and Buck wheeled as if he had been kicked. "That's Sandy," explained Bow-Wow Baker. "He thinks he 's some player. An' he is. There ain't nothin' like it between here an' Salt Lake."

"Oh, yes; there is," contradicted Buck. "You an' him 's a good team. I bet if you was in th' same room you 'd set up on yore hind laigs an' howl." Bow-Wow drew back, abashed.

"Set 'em up, Mr. Slick," chuckled the salesman.

"Don't notice him, Cheyenne," advised Chesty in a disgusted aside. "He don't mean nothin' by it. It's just a habit. It's got so I 'm allus expectin' him to raise his foot an' scratch for fleas," and he withered the crestfallen Bow-Wow with a look of scorn.

"You was sayin' as how you was aimin' to stop here," suggested Ned Monroe, his interest awakened at thought of a rising star so often following the fall of his own.

"Yes," acknowledged Buck. "If I find —"

Crash! Ding-dong! Ding-dong! The noise of the bell was deafening. Buck set down his glass with extreme care and looked at Slick with an air of helpless wonder, but Bow-Bow was ready with the explanation. "Grub-pile!" he shouted, making for the side door, grasping hold of Chesty's hand as he went out and dragging that exasperated puncher after him by strength of muscle and purpose. "Come on, Cheyenne! No 'angel-in-th'-pot,' but a good, square meal, all right."

Chesty Sutton cast behind him at Buck a glance of miserable apology, seized the door-frame in passing, and delivered to Bow-Wow a well-placed and energetic kick. Relieved of the drag of Chesty's protesting weight and with the added impetus of the impact of Chesty's foot, Bow-Wow shot across the wide hall, struggling frantically to regain his equilibrium, and passed through the door of the dining-room like a quarter-horse with the blind staggers. The bell-ringing ended in a crash of broken crockery, succeeded by a fearful uproar of struggling and profanity.

The collie bounded to his feet, his hair bristling along his spine, and rushed at the door with a low growl. Ned caught him by the collar and held him. "Down, Bruce, down!" he commanded, and the dog subsided into menacing growls.

Chesty, at the door, snorted in derision. "D —n fool!" he informed those behind him. "He 's tryin' to climb th' table. Hey, Ned; let th' other dog loose," he suggested, hopefully.

By the time the highly entertained group had gathered about the dining-room door, the oaths and imprecations had resolved themselves into a steady railing. Bow-Wow sat sprawled in a chair, gazing in awed silence along the path of wreckage wrought by the flying bell; opposite him, waving a pair of pugnacious fists in close proximity to Bow-Wow's face, stood Sandy McQueen, proprietor of the Sweet-Echo. It appeared that he was angry and the spectators waited with absorbed expectancy on what would happen next.

"Ye gilravagin' deevil!" he shouted, "canna ye see an inch afore yer ain nase? Gin ye hae nae better manners na a gyte bull, gang oot to grass like thae ither cattle. Lord preserv's," he prayed, following the strained intensity of Bow-Wow's gaze, "look at the cheeny! A 'm ruined!" He started to gather up the broken crockery when the roar of laughter, no longer to be restrained, assailed his outraged ears. He looked sourly at his guests. "Ou, ay, ye maun lauch, but wha's to pay for the cheeny? Ou, ay! A ken weel eneuch!"

The hilarious company pushed into the dining-room and began to help him in his task, casting many jocose reproaches on the overburdened Bow-Wow. Slick returned to the bar-room to clean off the bar before eating, and Buck went after him. "Hey, what have I struck?" he asked, with much curiosity. "He sounds worse 'n a circus."

"He 's mad," explained Slick. "Nobody on God's green earth can understand him when he 's mad. Which a circus is music alongside o' him. When he 's ca'm, he talks purty good American."

"You shore relieves my mind. What is he-Roosian?"

"Claims to be Scotch. But I dunno —a Scotchman 's a sort of Englishman, ain't he?"

"That was allus my opinion," agreed Buck.

"Well—I dunno," and Slick shook his head doubtfully as he hung the towel onto a handy hook and stooped to come under the bar. "Sounds funny to me, all right. 'Tain't English; not by a h—l of a sight."

"Sounds funny to me," echoed Buck. "I 'm *shore* it ain't English. But, say, Slick; gimme a room. I 'm stoppin' here an' I 'd like to drop my things where I can find 'em."

"Right," said Slick, and he led the way into the hall and toward a bedroom at the rear. Chesty Sutton stood in the doorway of the dining-room. "Better git in on th' jump, Cheyenne," he advised, anxiously. "Bow-Wow 's that savage, he's boltin' his grub in chunks an' there ain't goin' to be a whole lot left for stragglers."

"Muzzle him," replied Buck, over his saddle-weighted shoulder, while Slick only grinned, "If I goes hungry, I eats Bow-Wow. Dog ain't so bad." Chesty chuckled and returned to the sulky Bow-Wow with the warning.

Despite Chesty's fears, there was plenty to eat and to spare. Little talking was done, as every one was hungry, with the possible exception of Ned, and even he would have passed for a hungry man. Sandy McQueen and the cook officiated and the race was so nearly a dead heat that the first to finish was hardly across the hall before the last pushed his chair back from the table.

An immediate adjournment to the bar-room was the customary withdrawal, and Buck, doing as the others, found Ned in his former seat beside a table. Buck joined him and showed such an evident desire for privacy that the others forbore to intrude.

"Ned," said Buck, leaning towards him across the table, "it ain't none of my business, an' it ain't as I 'm just curious, but was that straight, what you said about bein' broke?"

"That's straight," Ned assured him, gloomily.

"An' lookin' for a job?" asked Buck, quietly.

"You bet," was the emphatic reply.

"Chesty said as how he used to work for you. Was you foreman?"

"I was foreman an' boss of the NM ranch till them blood-suckers back East druv me off 'n it —d —n 'em."

"Boss, was you? Then I reckon you wouldn't refuse a job as foreman, would you?"

Ned's interest became practical. "Where 's yore ranch?" he asked, with some show of eagerness.

"Why, I was aimin' to stop 'round here some'rs."

"H —l! There ain't a foot o' ground within eighty mile o' where yo 're sittin' as ain't grazed a heap over, less 'n it's some nester hangin' on by his fingers an' toes-an' blamed few o' them, neither. Leastaways, none but th' NM an' Schatz's range, which they says belongs to th' old Double Y, both of 'em."

"What's keepin' them free?"

"'Bout a regiment o' deputies, I reckon." He smiled grimly. "It's costin' 'em somethin' to keep th' range free o' cattle. Mebby you could lease it. That McAllister feller ain't never goin' to get a man to run it for long. Some o' th' boys is feelin' mighty sore an' Schatz is a tough nut. It's goin' to be a mighty big job, when he starts, an' that's certain."

"I 'd like to see it. We 'll go t'morrow."

Buck's careless defiance of the situation pleased Ned. With the first evidence of good humor he had shown he hit Buck a resounding slap on the back. "That's you," was his admiring comment.

The door opened to admit the short, broad figure of a man who, after a glance around the room, made his bow-legged way to their table. His tone betrayed some anxiety as he asked: "Ned, haf you seen mein Fritz?"

"Nope," answered Ned, "I have n't, Dutch. Hey, boys!" he called, "Anybody seen Pickles?"

A chorus of denials arose and Chesty sauntered over to get details. "W'y, you durned ol' Dutch Onion, you ain't gone an' lost him again, have you?"

"Ach! Dot leetle *Kobold*! Alvays ven I looks, like a flea he iss someveres else."

"How 'd you lose him?" demanded Chesty.

Dutch stole a look askance at Ned and turned on Chesty a reproachful face. He laid a glove on the edge of the table. "Dot's Fritz. I turn 'round, like dot," suiting action to word, in a complete turn, his right hand reaching out, taking up the glove and whirling it behind his back as he faced the table again. He looked at the empty spot with vast surprise, in delicious pantomime.

The glove, meanwhile, had fallen against the nose of Bruce, who sniffed at it and then picked it up and carried it to Slick behind the bar, returning to his resting place with the air of a duty accomplished.

Dutch continued to stare at the table for several seconds. Then he glanced around and called: "Fritz! Fritz! *Komm' zu mir* —und Fritz iss gone," he finished, turning to those at the table an expression of comical bewilderment. He took a couple of steps in the direction where he supposed the glove to be. Bruce was just lying down. Dutch looked more carefully, stooping to see along the floor. A light broke in on him. He straightened up and excitedly declared: "Yoost like dot! Yoost like der glove iss Fritz: I know ver he iss bud I can't see him."

"Dutch, come here." Ned's voice was stern and Dutch approached with hanging countenance. "Where was you when you 'turn 'round like dot'?" asked Ned.

"Only a minute, Ned; yoost a minute!"

"Where?"

"In Ike's I vas; yoost a minute."

"Ain't I told you to keep out o' there?"

Dutch moved his feet, licked his lips, and cleared his throat; words seemed to fail him.

While he hesitated the door opened again, something more than six inches, and Boomerang squeezed through. He shuffled up to Dutch and touched him on the shoulder. "Hey, Dutch, I been chasin' you all over. Pickles went home wit' Little Nell, see? An' she sent me ter tell you."

"Vat! mit dot —" he broke off and turned to Ned. "I begs your pardon, but Fritz, he iss leetle-he learn quick. Right avay I go." He was at the door when Slick hailed him.

"Hey, Dutchy, this yourn?" The other caught the tossed glove, and nodded.

"Yah, first der glove, soon iss Fritz," and the door closed behind him.

"Good as a circus," laughingly declared Buck. "About pay now-how would eighty a month hit you, for a starter?"

"Fine," declared Ned.

"Then here she is, first month," and Buck handed it over. "Will that be enough to square up what you owe?" he added.

"W'y, I don't owe nothin'," declared Ned.

"Well-now —I was just a-thinkin' 'bout th' lady as seemed right vexed when you dropped yore roll to Dave." He looked casually at Slick, behind the bar, while he was saying it.

"Little Nell? I don't owe her nothin', neither. It was my pile, —all of it."

Buck heaved a sigh of relief. "I 'm right glad to hear it. Then you 'll be all ready to hit th' trail with me in th' mornin'?" he asked.

"Shore; but s'pos'n you can't get th' ranch?" suggested Ned.

"I 'll get it. An' when I get it I 'll run it, too, less'n they load me with lead too heavy to sit a horse-then you 'll run it." His smile was infectious.

"Cheyenne, I like yore style. Put 'er there," and he shoved a huge, hairy fist at Buck. "'Nother thing," he went on, "Chesty an' Bow-Wow was a-goin' over to th' Bitter Root. I 'll tell 'em to hang 'round for a spell. Them 's two good boys. So 's Dutchy-when he ain't a-runnin' after Pickles."

"All right; you talk to 'em. See you in th' mornin'," and with a general good-night, Buck went to his room.

Chesty and Bow-Wow joined Ned to have a "night cap" and say good-bye, intending to start early next morning. "No, boys, I 've had enough," said Ned. "I 've took a job with Cheyenne, an' you boys better hang 'round. Find Dutch in th' mornin' an' tell him. An' I 'm a-goin' to turn in, too. I 'm cussed sleepy." The other two sat staring across the table at one another. The news seemed too good to be true.

"Ha! Ha!" barked Bow-Wow, "I never did like them d —n Bitters, not nohow."

Chesty nodded his head. "Me, too," he agreed. "Son, there 's a big time due in these parts: I feel it in my bones."

Seized with a common impulse they sprang to their feet and began a war-dance around the stove, chanting some Indian gibberish that was a series of grunts, snarls, and yells. Their profane demands for information meeting with no response, the others one by one joined them, until a howling, bobbing ring of men circled the stove, and, growling and barking at their heels, the dog danced with them. Slick looked on with an indulgent grin and the row did not cease until Sandy stuck his head in at the hall door. "Deil tak' ye!" he shouted. "Canna ye let a body sleep?"

A minute later the room had settled down into its customary decorum and Bruce, with a wary look about, now and then, was preparing to resume his rudely interrupted doze.

Chapter IV
The Foreman of the Double Y

Buck cinched up his saddle on Allday and led him out of the stable. "Ned, this is shore one scrumptious hotel," he observed as he swung into his seat.

"It certainly is. Nothin' to beat it in Montany, I reckon," was Ned's hearty endorsement.

Buck shook his head as they passed through the gate together. "Most too good," he suggested.

"I dunno," Ned doubted, "th' branch from Wayback 's shore to come down th' Jones' Luck, an' then Sandy 'll rake in."

They had just turned into the trail when a rider passed them at speed, causing Ned's cayuse to shy and buck half way to the Jill. The evener-tempered Allday only pointed his ears and pulled on the bit. "Reckon you could catch that feller, eh? Well, you could n't," was Buck's careless insult. "If Hoppy could see that horse he 'd give all he 's got for him-bar Mary."

The horse merited his criticism. A powerful black, well over fifteen hands, he showed the sloping thigh bones and shoulder of a born galloper, while the deep chest gave promise of long-sustained effort. His rider had pulled up at the general store just beyond the hotel and Ned joining him, Buck expressed his admiration. A moment later he added to it: "By th' Lord, Ned, that 's a woman." The rider had dropped from the saddle and paused to wave her hand to Ned before she entered the store. Buck caught the glance from a pair of beautiful dark eyes that rested on him a moment before it fleeted past to his companion. The grave smile was well suited to the wonderfully regular features and when she turned and entered the store it was with the swinging step of perfect movement. Buck faced about with a jerk when he realized that he had actually turned in his saddle to gaze after her.

"Best horse in these parts an' th' finest woman," agreed Ned, "an' honest," he added, gruffly.

Buck stared at him, surprised. "Why, o' course! Anybody says different?" He unconsciously stiffened at the thought.

"Um-no, not as I knows of. Her daddy 's a nester; got a quarter-section 'tother side o' Twin River, off th' trail a piece. Rosa LaFrance-pretty name, ain't it? Th' boys calls her the French Rose."

"Yes, 'tis pretty," drawled Buck. "What I'm askin' about is this recommendation o' character to me."

It was Ned's turn to feel surprised. He pondered as he looked at Buck. "I reckon I warn't exactly speakin' to you, Cheyenne," he explained; "more to myself, like. You see, it's this way: Dave Owens, he won that horse from McReady of the Cyclone, one night in Wayback. I was n't there but I hears it's a regular clean up. McReady was in a streak o' bad luck and would a' lost ranch an' all but his friends hocussed his liquor an' Mac, he drops out of his chair like somebody hit him with an axe. Next day Rose rides into Twin River on that same horse. John, that's her daddy, he never bought him; he could n't. Then how did she come by it? That's her business, I says. That's one thing. For another, Dave Owens travels that way considerable, an' Dave ain't no company for the French Rose. I 'm too old to interfere or I durn soon would."

Buck brooded on this situation for some time and then burst into a laugh. Ned eyed him with stern disapproval. "I was thinkin' of a cow-punch I know," explained Buck, in apology. "He 'd interfere so quick, there would n't be time to notify th' mourners."

Ned smiled in sympathy. "That 'd do," he admitted, "but you can't jump in an' shoot up a fellow if a girl's sweet on him, can you? It 'd be just nacheraly foolish."

"That 's so," agreed Buck, "but if the French Rose can look at that son of a thief and like him, then Hopalong Cassidy has no call to be proud o' *hiss*elf."

"Eh?" questioned Ned.

"Th' name slipped out. But now 's as good a time as any to tell you. Did you ever hear o' Frenchy McAllister?"

"Owner o' the Double Y?"

"Half owner-leastways, he was. Frenchy 's dead. You was cussin' his brother last night. I want to tell you about Frenchy."

Buck told the story in terse, graphic sentences, every one a vivid picture. He painted the scene of Trendley's crime to the accompaniment of a low-voiced growl of lurid profanity from Ned, who was quite unconscious of it. The relentless hunt for the criminals, extending through many months; the deadly retribution as one by one they were found; the baffling elusiveness of Slippery Trendley and the unknown manner of his fate when run to earth at last-one scene followed another until Buck left the arch devil in his story, as he had left him in fact, bound and helpless, looking up at the pitiless face of the man he had injured beyond the hope of pardon, their only witnesses the silent growths of Texas chaparral and the grieving eye of God.

It was a terrible story, even in the mere telling of it. Buck's level voice and expressionless face hid the seething rage which filled him now, as always, when his thoughts dwelt upon the awful drama. Ned's judgment was without restriction: "By the Eternal!" he swore, "that h —l-hound deserved whatever he got. D —d if you ain't made me sick." They rode in silence for several minutes and then: "Poor fellow! poor fellow!" he lamented. "Did you say he's dead?"

"Yes, Frenchy's gone under," answered Buck gravely. "You 'd 'a' liked him, Ned."

"Yes, I reckon I would," agreed Ned. He looked at the other, considering. "Where do you come in?" he asked. Buck's narrative had failed to connect the new-born "Cheyenne" as "Frenchy's pardner."

"I 'm Buck Peters," was the simple explanation.

Ned pulled his horse back onto its haunches and Buck wheeled and faced him. So they sat, staring, Ned inarticulate in his astonishment, Buck waiting. The power of coherent thought returned to Ned at last and he rode forward with outstretched hand. "Th' man as stuck to Frenchy McAllister through that deal is good enough for me to tie up to," he declared, and the grip of their hands was the cementing of an unfailing friendship. "An' I 'd like for Buck Peters to tell Frenchy's brother as I takes back what I said agin' him."

Their way led through an excellent grass country. The comparatively low ground surrounding Wayback rose gradually to Twin River and more rapidly after leaving that town. The undulating ground now formed in higher and more extensive mounds, rising in places to respectable-sized hills; usually the sides reached in long slopes the intervening depressions, but not infrequently they were abrupt and occasionally one was met which presented the broad, flat face of a bluff. The air was perceptibly colder but the bunch grass, hiding its wonderfully nourishing qualities under the hue it had acquired from the hot summer sun, was capable of fattening more cattle to the acre than any but the best lands of the Texan ranges with which Buck was familiar. Snow had not yet swept down over the country, though apt to come with a rush at any time. Even winter affected the range but little as a general rule; disastrous years were luckily few and far separated, so that the average of loss from severity of weather was small. The talk of the two naturally veered to this and kindred topics and Buck began stowing away nuggets of northern range wisdom as they fell from the lips of the more experienced Ned.

Studying the trail ahead of him, Buck broke the first silence by asking: "Ain't we near the boundary of the Double Y?"

"You 'll know, soon enough. Th' first big butte we come to, some cuss 'll be settin' there, hatchin' out trouble."

"That's him, then," and Buck pointed to the right where a solitary horseman showed dark against the sky-line.

"Yep, that's one of 'em. Reglar garjun, ain't he?"

"Beats me how you let 'em stand you off, Ned," wondered Buck.

"Well, when we made good and sure you owned the range, Buck, there were n't no use in fighting. That McAllister would 'a run in th' reglar army next, d —d if he would n't."

Buck chuckled. "He 's sure a hard man to beat. I don't mind fighting when I have to, but I 'm mighty glad it looks peaceful."

"We 'll have fightin'. When I was turned off my ranch, it just about foundered me. I sold th' stock, every head, an' you saw where th' last o' th' cash went. But don't forget Smiler Schatz. He 's a bigger man an' a better man nor I ever was, an' he 's a-layin' low an' a-waitin'. He calculates to get you —I dunno how."

"An' I dunno how," mused Buck. "Say, Ned, I thought th' stage line ran through to Big Moose: there ain't no tracks?"

"'Cause it crosses th' ford at th' Jack an' goes to th' Fort; then it swings round to Big Moose, an' back th' same road. Wonder who 's that pointin' this way?"

Buck glanced ahead to see a moving speck disappear behind a knoll far along the trail. "Dunno; maybe another deputy," he suggested.

The distant rider came into sight again and Ned stared steadily at him. "No," he declared, "think I know that figger. Yessir! It's Smiler. I kin tell him 'most as far as I kin see him."

"That's the feller gave us the fight, ain't it?"

"Did his share—some over, mebbe. He 's a hard nut."

"Well, I 'm not bad at a pinch, myself, Ned; mebbe I can crack him." Ned smiled grimly at the jest and hoped he would be cracked good. Evidently there was no great liking between the quondam owners of the Double Y.

However, this was not apparent in their greeting. The steady approach had been uninterrupted and Buck looked with interest at the "hard nut" as they met.

In a land of dirty men—dirty far more frequently from necessity than from choice—Schatz was a by-word for slovenliness nearly approaching filth. If he washed at all it left no impression on the caked corrugations of his smiling countenance. His habit of smiling was constant, so much a part of him that it gave him his name. And it had been solemnly affirmed by one of his men that he never interfered with his face until the dirt interfered with his smile; then he chipped it off with a cold chisel and hammer. This must have been slander: no one had ever seen him when it looked chipped. A big man, with a fine head, he sat in his saddle with the careless ease of long practice. "Hello, Ned!" he called, with a gay wave of the hand. *"Wie geht's?"*

"Howdy, Karl!" replied Ned. "How's sheep?"

"Ach! don't say it, der grasshoppers. Never vill dey reach Big Moose. Also, I send East a good man to talk mit dat McAllister to lease der range yet. Before now he say a manager come from Texas, soon. Vat iss Texas like Montana? Nodding. Ven der snow come —"

"Hol' on! This is th' manager, Mr. Buck Peters, half owner o' the Double Y, an' he 's put me in as foreman."

"So-it pleases me greatly, Mr. Buck. Ned iss a good man. If you haf Ned, that iss different." He shook hands with Buck who took note of the blue eyes and frank smile of the blonde German, at a loss to discover where he hid that hardness Ned had referred to.

"Sorry I can't offer you a job," said Buck, matching the other's smile at the joke, "but from what I hear, one foreman will be a-plenty on the Double Y."

"It iss a good range-eggselent-und der iss mooch free grass ven you haf der Double Vy for der hard years; but dere iss not enough for you und for me, too, so I turn farmer. Also some of der boys, dey turn farmer. I take oud quarter-section alretty."

"Quarter-section! Turn farmer! You! Sufferin' cows! give me a drink," and Ned looked wildly around for the unattainable.

"Donnerwetter! Somet'ing I must do. To lend money iss good but not enough. Also my train vill not vait. So I say good-morning und vish you luck."

Ned wheeled his horse to gaze after the departing figure and Buck sat laughing at his expression. "Luck," echoed Ned; "bad luck, you mean, you grinnin' Dutchman. H —l of a farmer you 'll be. Now I wonder what's his little game."

"Aw, come on, Ned. 'Pears to me he 's easy," and Allday sprang away along the trail.

"Easy, eh!" growled Ned, when he caught up, "he 's this easy: him and me started even up here, 'bout th' same time. 'T was n't long before he begun crowdin' me. Neither of us had nuthin' at first but when we quit he could show five cows to my one. How 'd he do it?"

"Borrowed th' money and bought yearlin's," answered Buck.

"Yes, he did," Ned grudgingly admitted. "But I kep' a-watchin' him an' he allus branded more than th' natural increase, every round-up —an' I could never see how he done it."

"You-don't —say," was Buck's thoughtful comment, "Well, down our way when a man gets to doin' miracles on a free range we drops in on him casual an' asks questions-they don't do it twice"; and he unconsciously increased Allday's pace.

"Here, pull up," urged Ned; "this bronc 's beginnin' to blow. That's a bang-up horse you 've got there. No good with cattle, is he?"

"No," agreed Buck. "I got this horse because 'discretion is sometimes better than valler,' as Tex Ewalt said when somebody asked him why he did n't shoot Hoppy. Most times I finish what I start, but once in a while, on a big job, it's healthy to take a vacation. An' I naturally expected to leave some hasty an' travel fast."

"Ain't nothin' could catch you, in these parts, not if you got a good start, less'n it's French Rose an' Swallow."

"Well, I was n't aimin' to run far nor yet to stay long. That seems like it 'd be th' ranch."

"That's her," agreed Ned.

The ranch house, rectangular and of much greater dimensions than Buck expected to find it, presented two novel features, one of which he noticed at once. "What's th' idea of a slopin' roof, Ned?" he asked.

"That's Karl's notion. See that upside down trough runs along th' high part at th' back? There ain't a foot o' that roof you can't slosh with a bucket o' water. An' you can shoot along th' walls from them cubby holes built out at each corner. Th' house is a heap bigger 'n th' old one was; it used to set over yonder in that valley, but th' wipin' out o' Custer put th' fear o' God in Smiler an' he raised this place soon after. Five men could stand off five hundred Injuns."

"Where 's th' water?"

Ned chuckled. "Wait till you see it. There 's a well sunk at th' side an' you can pull it in without goin' out-door if you wants to. Karl is one o' them think-of-everything fellers. He put th' ranch house on a knoll an' th' bunk-house on another. Then, he figgers, if they wants to rush me they 'll be good an' winded when they gets here. My shack is a pig-pen 'long side o' this un', but I got it figgered out I need n't to stop if I don't want."

"How's that, Ned?"

"I could cut an' run any time-come night. I 'll show you when we goes over there."

Bare as was the interior, the ranch house gave promise of comfort and the bunk-house and the stable with its adjacent corral proved equally satisfactory. The fire-place of the bunk-house was built over the bare earth and there they repaired to make a fire and eat the food they had brought with them. The added warmth was a distinct comfort but the smoke brought company on the run. They had scarcely begun their meal when a faint sound led Buck to saunter to the door and look out. Down the steep side of a high butte dropped a horseman with considerably more speed and no more care than a dislodged boulder; arriving at the bottom, his horse straightened out into a run that showed he was expected to get somewhere right away. Buck gravely bit into a sandwich the while he admired the rider's horsemanship; an admiration that was directed into another channel when the object of it slipped rifle from holster, pumped a cartridge into the barrel, and threw it forward in business-like attitude. "'Spects to have use for it, right soon," mused Buck, and then, over his shoulder: "Better hide, Ned. Here comes a garjun an' he 's got his gun out."

"Th' h —l he has!" rumbled Ned. "Come an' push me up th' chimley, Buck; I 'm a-scared."

Buck strolled back to the fire and half a minute later the horse pounded up to the house, his rider sprang off and came through the door, gun first. He continued across the room with solemn countenance, set his gun against the wall, and went to the fire where he extended his hands to the blaze. "Howdy, Ned; howdy, stranger," was his easy greeting.

Ned, sitting cross-legged, smirked up at him. "Howdy, Jack. You were n't going to run me off'n th' range, was you?"

"Nope. Saw Cheyenne Charley headin' this way 'bout an hour since. Thought mebbe he 'd burn her up-Pipes o' peace!" His eyes widened as he gazed at Ned's upturned mouth. "Bottled beer, or I 'm a Injun. You lives high," and he swallowed involuntarily as the inspiring gurgle stimulated his salivary glands.

"I 'm taperin' off on beer," explained Ned. "Got three bottles, one for Buck and two for me. I 'm biggest. But you can have one o' mine. Buck, this is Jim's Jack, head garjun an' a right good sort. Buck Peters has come to take charge of his own ranch, Jack."

"Shake," said Jack. He glanced over the papers Buck handed him and passed them back. All three turned to look at the open door.

"Hang up a sign, Buck," advised Ned. "If we stops here long enough we can start a hotel. Come in, Charley."

The Indian stepped slowly in. "Cheyenne Charley, Buck," said Ned; "off the Reservation for a drunk at Twin River. You 'd think he 'd stop in Big Moose. Reckon he 's hungry, too; he —" Ned paused and his eyes sought the object of Charley's steady and significant gaze. "Oh, that be d —d!" he exclaimed, swooping onto the third bottle of beer beside him and holding it out to Buck. "He wants your beer. Charley is a good Injun —I *think* —but 'lead us not into temptation'"—and with the other hand he proceeded to put his share of temptation out of sight, an example that Jim's Jack emulated with dignified speed.

"Let him have it," said Buck, good naturedly. "I never hankered much for beer, nohow." He passed the bottle to the Indian, not in the least suspecting what "an anchor he had cast to windward." The other two exchanged a look of regretful disapproval.

Half an hour later they had separated, Buck and Ned going on to the more distant NM ranch, Jack to gather up his fellow deputies, and the Cheyenne hitting the trail for Twin River with a thirst largely augmented by the sop he had thrown to it.

Chapter V
"Comin' Thirty" has Notions

Up from the south, keeping Spring with him all the way, rode Tex. The stain of the smoke-grimed cities was washed out of him in the pure air; day by day his muscles toughened and limbered, his lightning nerves regained their old spontaneity of action, each special sense vied with the others in the perfection of service rendered, and gradually but surely his pulse slowed until, in another man, its infrequency of beat would have been abnormal. When he rode into Twin River, toward the end of a glorious day, he had become as tireless as the wiry pony beneath him, whose daily toll of miles since leaving the far-off Bar-20 was well nigh unbelievable.

Tex crossed the ford of the Black Jack behind the Sweet-Echo Hotel. Dirt had bespattered him from every angle; it was caked to mud on his boots, lay in broad patches along his thighs, displayed itself lavishly upon his blue flannel shirt, and had taken frequent and successful aim at his face; but two slits of sun-lit sky seemed peering out from beneath his lowered lids, the pine-tree sap bore less vitality than surged in his pulsing arteries, his lounging seat was the deceptive sloth of the panther, ready on the instant to spring; and over all, cool as the snow-capped peaks of the Rockies, ruled the calculating intelligence, unscrupulous in the determination to win, now that it was on the side of the right, as when formerly it fought against it.

One glance at the imposing Sweet-Echo and Tex turned his pony's head toward the trail. "No, no, Son John, you 'll not sleep there with your stockings on-though I shan't ask you to go much farther," Tex assured him. "I 've seen prettier, and ridden cleverer, but none more willing than you, Son John. Ah, this begins to look more like our style. 'I-Call' —sweet gamester, I prithee call some other day; I would feed, not play. 'Ike's' —thy name savors overly much of the Alkali, brother. Ha! 'By the prickling of my thumbs, something wicked that way bums.'" He had turned to cross the Jill and saw Pop Snow basking in the failing sunlight. "'Why-Not' —well, why not? I will."

"Come a long way, stranger?" asked Dirty, his gaze wandering over the tell-tale mud. He had come the wrong way for profit, but Dirty always asked, on principle: he hated to get out of practice.

Tex swung his right leg over his pony's neck and sat sideways, looking indolently at the pickled specimen who sat as indolently regarding him. "Plucked from a branch of the Mussel Shell," murmured Tex, "when Time was young"; and then drawled: "Tolerable, tolerable; been a-comin' thirty year, just about."

Dirty looked at him with frank disgust, spat carefully, and turning on his seat no more than was absolutely necessary, stuck his head in at the open door and yelled: "Hey, boys! Come on out an' meet Mr. Comin' Thirty. Comin' is some bashful 'bout drinkin' with strangers, so get acquaint."

Scenting a tenderfoot half a dozen of the inmates strolled outside. When they saw the sun-tanned Tex they expressed their opinion of Dirty in concise and vitriolic language, not forgetting his parents; after which they invited Tex to "sluice his gills." One of them, a delicate-featured, smooth-faced boy, added facetiously: "Don't be afraid; we won't eat you."

Tex released his left foot from the stirrup and slid to earth. "I was n't afraid o' bein' et, exactly," was his slow response; "I was just a-wonderin' if it would bite. I notice it 's slipped its collar."

"Go to h —l! Th' lot o' you!" screeched Pop, bouncing to his feet with surprising alacrity. "Wait till I buy th' nex' one o' you a drink-wait! That's all."

"Lord, Dirty, we *has* been a-waitin'. Since Fall round-up, ain't it?" appealing to the others who gave instant, vigorous, and profane endorsement.

"Pah!" exploded Pop. He faced about and executed a singular and superlatively indecent gesture with a nimbleness unexpected and disgracefully grotesque in so old a man; and then without a backward glance, he stamped off across the bridge to the I-Call. The others watched him in fascinated silence until he plumped down on his inevitable box, when the smooth-faced first speaker turned to his nearest neighbor and asked in hushed tones: "What do you think of him, Mike?"

"Fanny, me boy, if I thought I 'd ever conthract Dirty's partic'lar brand o' sinfulness, I 'd punch a hole in th' river-with me head," and he solemnly led the way in to the bar.

"Gentlemen, it's on me," declared Tex, " —for good and special reasons," he explained, when they began to expostulate. "Give me a large and generous glass," he requested of the barkeeper, "and fill it with 'Water for me, water for me, and whiskey for them which find it agree.' You see, gentlemen, liquor an' I don't team no better 'n a lamb an' a coyote. I must either love it or leave it alone an' I 'm dead set agin' spiritual marriage. Here 's how."

"If I 'd begun like that I 'd be a rich man this day," observed Mike, when his head resumed the perpendicular.

"If I 'd begun like that I would n't be here at all," responded Tex.

"Well, ye 'll have a cigar with me, anyhow. Putt a name to it, boys, an', Fred, whisper: Pass up that wee little box ye keep, in th' locker. Me friend, Comin', will take a good one, while he 's at it."

A blue-shirted miner next him interposed: " 'T is my trate. He 'll hev a cigar with me, he well. Das' thee thenk I be goin' to drenk with thee arl the time, and thee never taake a drenk 'long o' me? Set un up, Fred, my son, and doan't forget the lettle box."

Tex gazed curiously at the speaker. It was his first meeting with a Cornishman and Bill Tregloan was a character in more than speech. Wherever gold, or a rumor of gold, drew the feet of miner, there sooner or later would be Bill Tregloan. He had crossed the continent to California on foot and alone at a time when such an attempt was more than dangerous. That he escaped the natural perils of the trip was sufficiently wonderful; as for the Indians, there is no doubt they thought him mad.

Bill had his way in paying for the order and turned to lounge against the bar when his eye caught sight of that which drew from him a torrent of sputtering oaths and a harsh command. The only one who had failed to join the others at the bar was Charley, the Cheyenne Indian. He lay sprawled on the floor against the opposite wall, very drunk and asleep, and about to be subjected to one of the pleasing jokes of the railroad towns, in this instance very crudely prepared. The oil with which he was soaked, had been furnished far too plentifully, and he stood an excellent chance of being well roasted when the match, then burning, should be applied.

The man holding the match looked up at the Cornishman's shout. He did not understand the words but the meaning of the action that followed was plain; and when the miner, growling like a bear, started to rush at him, his hand dropped to his gun with the speed of a hawk. Fanny promptly stuck out his foot. Tregloan went down with Fanny on top of him but it takes more than one slight boy, whatever his strength, to hold down a wrestling Cornishman. The flurry that followed, even with the added weight of numbers, would have been funny but for the scowling face of the olive-skinned man who stood with ready gun until assured the struggle had gone against his opponent. Then he slipped gun in holster and felt for another match. "Take him away," he said, with a sneering smile, "he make me sick."

"What did they do that for?" asked Tex of Mike. Neither had moved during the excitement. The rest were pushing and pulling Tregloan out of the saloon.

"That's Guinea Mike," was the explanation. "He 'd murder his mother if she crossed him. First fair chanst I mane to break his d —d back-an' if ye tell him so he 'll kill me on sight."

"Interestin' specimen," observed Tex. Guinea Mike found another match and calmly lit it. Those not engaged in soothing Bill were looking in at the door and windows. Dutch Fred, behind the bar, was swearing good American oaths regarding the unjustified waste of his kerosene. Tex stepped away from the bar. "Blow that out," he said, dispassionately.

Guinea Mike looked up with a snarl. The two stares met and grappled. Guinea slowly raised the match to his lips and puffed it out, flipping it from him with a snap of one finger so that it fell almost at the feet of Tex. They watched each other steadily. A solitary snore from the Indian sounded like the rumble of overhead thunder. Slowly the hand of Guinea descended from before his lips and in unison with it descended the head of Fred until his eyes just cleared the top of the bar. Guinea's hand rested in the sagging waist of his trousers, a second, two —

The roar of the explosion was deafening. Guinea Mike's right shoulder went into retirement and his gun dropped from his nerveless fingers. Screaming with rage he stooped to grasp it with his left hand and pitched forward at full length, both knee-caps shattered, at the mercy of this stranger who shot as if at a mark.

The noise awakened Cheyenne Charley who opened his eyes and smiled foolishly at the distorted face which had so unexpectedly reached his level. "D —n drunk," he observed, and immediately went to sleep again.

Tex walked over and kicked the gun across the floor. Irish Mike picked it up and handed it to Fred. "I could a' killed you just as easy as I didn't, Guinea," said Tex. "I don't like you an' yore ways. It's just a notion. So don't you stop. An' don't send any o' yore friends. 'No Guineas need apply.' That goes, if I has to Garibaldi yore whole d —n country."

The spectators had filed back to the room and were engaged in audible comments on the justification and accuracy of the shooting, while they busied themselves in the rough surgery which had to serve. To the suggestion that he ought to be taken to the doctor at Wayback, Fred interposed the objection: "No, dake him to Nell's. Mike is a friend mit her."

Pop Snow, attracted by the excitement, stood peering in a window. Twin River crowded the room but Pop's resentment was still warm. A man rode up and stooped from the saddle to look over his shoulder. "Who 's that? What's up?" he asked.

"'T aint nothin'; *only* Guinea Mike. See th' feller Fanny 's hangin' onto? Well, that's him: Comin' Thirty has notions-an' I ain't never seen better shootin'."

Dave swung down, tied his pony to the rail and went inside to see the new bad-man of Twin River. It had been growing steadily colder during the past few hours; the wind, sweeping in from the west, held a sinister threat, the air a definite chill, and Dave felt he would be none the worse for a little fire-water. Dirty felt it also, but his senile annoyance had merely simmered down, not subsided, and he scurried back to the I-Call for cover until such time as he thought it fitting to go home.

* * * * *

It was very late when Dave turned a tired pony to pasture and entered the three-room cabin of Karl Schatz. The rough exterior gave no indication of the comfort with which the German had surrounded himself. Fur rugs covered the floor of the living-room; the chairs and table had travelled many miles before landing here; a fine sideboard showed several pieces of fair china; mounted horns of various kinds were on the walls, one group being utilized as a gun rack, and between them hung several good paintings. A stove had been removed but in its place smouldered a wood fire, the fireplace jutting out from the wall. When Dave came in Karl sat smoking; on the table beside him lay an open volume of poems. "Vell?" he asked, as Dave dropped into a chair and stretched his legs wearily before him.

"Double Y has got a new bunch o' cattle. Hummers. Bought 'em out of a drove come up last Fall on Government contract; the Government went back on th' deal an' they was wintered up here. Got th' pick o' th' lot, I hear." Dave fell into silence and stared at the fire. Karl puffed thoughtfully while he looked at the black head whose schemes seemed coming to nought.

"Cameron 's got back," continued Dave; "he 's brought his money with him; took up his note at the bank; paid full interest." Another pause, with no comment from Karl. Dave continued to display his items of information in sections. "I met One-eye Harris at Eccles'.

"Th' Cyclone ranch has got some with th' itch. It 'll mean a lot o' work-an' then some.

"LaFrance wants to bleed you for two hundred. Don't you. He 'll get too rich to have me for a son-in-law."

Karl nodded his head. "Farming iss goot," he murmured, " —mit vasser." Dave glanced at him.

"Them new steers o' th' Double Y oughta fetch forty in th' Fall. Will, too."

"Farming iss goot," repeated Karl, " —mit vasser. Also, to lend money. But Camerons, dey pay und der money lies idle. Ven do ve eat up der Double Y, Dave?"

Dave glanced at him sullenly. "Why don't you let me kill that d —n Peters? Are you afraid I 'll get hurt?"

"Alvays I fear. I haf no one bud you, *du Spitzbub*. But kill him? Ach! Soon anoder manager come. Killing iss not goot, Dave. You must plan besser, *aber* I do id. Dat make you feel sheep, *du Schwarzer Spitzbub, vas?*"

"I 'll get 'em. Guinea Mike 's shot up."

"Vell, he iss anoder von likes killing. Who vas id?"

"Stranger. Reminded me of a feller, somehow-an' then, again, he did n't. Deals a slick hand at cards."

"Ach, cards! Alvays der cards! Who know dem besser as me? Who pay for dem so much? Cards und killing, dey are no goot."

"Well, let's roost," suggested Dave, and led the way to the inner room. Karl fastened doors and windows, put out the light, and followed him.

Chapter VI
An Honest Man and a Rogue

How to do it? That was the question that hammered incessantly at Dave's brain until he actually dreamed of it. Dreaming of it was the only satisfactory solution, for in his dreams matters arranged themselves with the least possible effort on his part and with little or no danger-though, to do him justice, danger was the consideration which had the least weight. But the dreams presented lamentable gaps which Dave, in his waking moments, found it impossible to bridge. Winter had given way to Spring and Buck Peters, aided by the indefatigable Ned, was rounding the ranch into a shape that already cut a figure in the county and would do so in the Territory before long.

The Double Y owed nothing to Dave. His animosity was confined strictly to Buck; but he knew that Karl was resolved to usurp ownership of the range he had come to look upon as his own. And Dave had become imbued with the idea that his own interests demanded the realization of Karl's wishes.

Why the German had become interested in this handsome idler, so many years younger than himself, Karl could not have explained. True, he was alone in the world, he was a red fox where the other was a black one, while Dave's present sinfulness and inclinations were such as the elder man understood and sympathized with. Yet these were hardly reasons; Karl himself never would have advanced them as such. Perhaps he had it in mind to use him as a cat's-paw. Few of our likes or dislikes have their origin in a single root.

If only they could "eat up" the Double Y! Dave cursed the obsession which threatened his fortunes; he cursed the energetic Buck who was rearing obstacles in his way with every week that passed; and he cursed his own barren imagination which balked at the riddle.

No heat of the inward furnace showed in the cool gravity of his face. Sitting at a table in the crowded bar-room of the Sweet-Echo, he seemed intent on mastering the difficulties of a particularly intricate game of solitaire. From time to time some of those at the same table would become interested, only to turn away again, baffled by their lack of knowledge.

The usual class of patrons was present, augmented in number, since the spring round-up was at hand and strangers were dropping in every day. Later in the evening, most of those present would gravitate to the lower end of the town where forms of amusement which Sandy McQueen did not countenance, were common. To none of these did Dave give any attention, though he looked with interest at Tex Ewalt when he entered; the increased hum of voices and several loud greetings had taken his mind momentarily from his thoughts. Tex's reputation had lost nothing in force since the excitement of his advent.

Suddenly and for the first time Dave hesitated in his play. He looked fixedly at the Jack of Spades and removed it from the pile where it lay. He paused with it in his hand. The Jack of Spades was in doubt-so was Dave.

A querulous voice was damning Buck Peters. *"Donner und Blitzen*! Vas it my fault *der ver-ruchter* bull break loose *und ist hinaus gegangen*? 'Yah!' says Buck, 'Yah!' loud, like dat. Mad? — *mein gracious*! Vot for is a bull, anyhow? 'Gimme my time,' I say; 'I go.' 'Gif you a goot kick,' says Buck; 'here, dake dis und get drunk und come back *morgen*.' I get drunk und go back und break his d—n neck-only for leetle Fritz."

"Leetle Fritz" sat swinging his legs, on the bar. He looked at his father with plain disapproval. "Ah, cheese it, Pap!" was his advice. "What's th' good o' gittin' drunk? Why can't you hol' y' likker like a man?"

A roar of laughter greeted this appeal, at which even Gerken smiled gleefully. He was glad that Fritz was smart, *"une seine Mutter."*

Dave pushed the Jack of Spades back into the pack. He arose and sauntered over to the bar. "That's th' way to talk, Pickles," he endorsed, tickling the boy playfully in the ribs. "Yo 're a-going to hold yore likker like a man, ain't you?"

"No sirree! Ther' ain't goin' to be any likker in mine. I promised mother."

"Bully for you!" Dave's admiration was genuine and the boy blushed at the compliment. Like many other rascals, Dave was easily admitted into the hearts of children and simple folk and women and dogs. Bruce, the collie, was nuzzling his hand at that moment and the broad, foolish face of Gottlieb was beaming on him. "Hi, Slick! Pickles 'll have a lemonade. I 'll have a lemonade, too; better put a stick in mine, I 'm a-gettin' so 's I need one. An' Pap 'll have a lemonade, too-oh! with a stick, Pap, with a stick —I would n't go for to insult your stomach."

They drank their lemonades, Gottlieb's face expressive of splinters, and a minute later Pickles sat alone while his father endeavored to win some of Dave's money and Dave endeavored to let him. Tex tilted his chair and with a fine disregard for alien fastidiousness, stuck his feet on the edge of the table and smiled. He almost crashed over backward at sight of a figure that entered the room from the hall. "God bless our Queen!" murmured Tex, "he 's a long way from 'ome. Must be a remittance man come over the line to call on Sandy."

H. Whitby Booth swept an appraising glance over the company and, without a pause, chose a seat next to Tex. "Surprisin' fine weather, isn't it?" he observed, taking a cigar-case from his pocket.

"My word!" agreed Tex, succinctly.

Whitby looked at him with suspicion. "Try a weed?" he invited.

"I don't mind if I do, old chap," and Tex selected one with a gravity he was far from feeling.

Whitby looked hard at him while Tex lit the cigar. It was a good one. Tex noted it with satisfaction.

"I say, are you chaffing me?" asked Whitby, smilingly.

It was a very good cigar. Tex had not enjoyed one as good in a regrettably long time. He blew the smoke lingeringly through his nostrils and laughed. "I 'm afraid I was," he admitted, "but you must n't mind that. It's what you 're here for, the boys 'll think-that is, if you don't stop long enough to get used to it."

"Oh, I don't mind in the least. And I expect to stop if the climate agrees with me."

"What's the matter-lunger? You don't look it."

"Not likely. But they tell me it's rather cold out here in winter."

"Some cold. You get used to it. You feel it more in the East, where the air 's damp."

"I 'm delighted to hear it. And the West is becoming quite civilized, I believe, compared with what it was."

"Oh, my, yes!" Tex choked on a mouthful of cigar smoke in his haste to assure Whitby of the engaging placidity of the population. "Why, no one has been killed about here since-well, not since I came to Twin River." Tex did not consider it necessary to state how short a time that had been. "Civilized! Well, I should opinionate. Tame as sheep. Nowadays, a man has to show a pretty plain case of self-defence if he expects to avoid subsequent annoyance."

"Ah, so I was informed. They seem quiet enough here."

"Yes, Sandy won't stand any disturbance. He's away to-night but Slick's got his orders. Know Sandy?"

"No. Is he the proprietor?"

"That's him: Sandy McQueen, proprietor, boss, head-bouncer, the only —"

"I say, what's the row?"

Tex's feet hit the floor with a bang. Gottlieb Gerken was shaking his fist in Dave's face, Dave sitting very still, intently watchful. *"Du verdammter Schuft!"* shouted Gerken, *"Mein Meister verrathen, was!"* He sent the table flying, with a violent thrust of his foot: "I show you!"

Watchful as he was, Dave did not anticipate what was coming. As the table toppled over he sprang to his feet, the forward thrust of his head in this action moving in contrary direction to the hurtling fist of Gottlieb, which stopped very suddenly against his nose. Dave staggered backward, stumbled over his chair and went crashing to the floor, where he lay for an instant dazed.

"By Jove! that was a facer," cried the appreciative Whitby. The others were ominously quiet.

The next moment Dave was on his feet, white with murderous rage. There was more than fallen dignity to revenge: Gottlieb knew too much. Without the least hesitation his gun slanted and the roar of the discharge was echoed by Gottlieb's plunging fall. A frenzied scream, feminine in shrillness, rang through the room. Dave's gun dropped from his hand and he sank to the floor; a whiskey bottle, flying the length of the room, had struck him on the head, and Boomerang, struggling with maniacal fury in the arms of several men, strove to follow his missile. At the other end of the bar the numbed Pickles suddenly came to life and leaped to the floor. Caught and stopped in his frantic rush across the room he kicked and struck at his captor. "Lemme go!" he shrieked, "lemme go! I 'll kill the —— ——" The men holding Boomerang ran him to the open hall door and gave him forcible exit and the stern command to "Git! an' keep a-goin'."

A sullen murmur swelling to low growls of anger formed an undertone to the boy's hysterical cries, as the men looked on at Tex's efforts to revive the stunned culprit. "Lynch him!" growled a voice. "Lynch him!" echoed over the room. "Lynch him!" shouted a dozen men, and Tex ceased his efforts and came on guard barely in time to stop a concerted rush. Straddling the recumbent figure, his blazing eyes shocked the crowd to a stand-still. With a motion quicker than a striking rattler a gun in either hand threatened the waverers. "Dutchy 's got a gun," he rebuked them; "he was a-reachin' for it when he dropped."

"That's correct," agreed a backward member. "Sure. I seen him a-goin' for it," affirmed another. They gathered about Gottlieb to look for the proof.

Suddenly the door was flung open and Rose LaFrance stood in the opening. "What are you doing?" she questioned. "What is the matter with Fritz? Come here, Fritz."

The boy, released and subsiding into gasping sobs, staggered weakly toward her. She drew him close and folded him in her arms. The men, silent and abashed, in moving to allow the boy to pass, had disclosed to her the figure of the prone Gottlieb and she understood. "Oh-h!" she breathed and looked slowly from one to another, her gaze resting last on Tex, the fallen table hiding from her the man he was protecting. Utter loathing was in her look and the innocent Tex was stung to defiance by it, throwing back his head and returning stare for stare.

"You wolf!" she accused, in low, passionately vibrant tones. "Kill, kill, kill! You and your kind. Is it then so great a pleasure to you? Shame to you for mad beasts! And greater shame to the cur dogs who let you do it." Her glance swept the averted faces with blasting scorn. "Come, Fritz." She led the boy out and the door was closed carefully after her by a sheepish-looking individual whose position behind it and out of sight of those scornful eyes had been envied by every man in the room.

"Well — I 'm — d — d!" said Tex, recovering his voice.

"'They that touch pitch will be defiled,'" observed Whitby, sententiously. Tex looked his resentment. He felt a touch on his leg and glanced down. Dave had recovered consciousness. "Get off me, Comin'," he requested. "Who hit me?"

"Boomerang flung a bottle at you," informed Tex. "How you feeling?"

"All serene. Head 's dizzy," he added, swaying on his feet. He walked to the nearest chair and sat down. "Must 'a' poured a pint o' whiskey into me."

"Boom passed you a quart bottle," replied Tex.

Dave glanced at the inert form of Gerken as it was carried out into the hall. "Sorry I had to do it," he said, "but I had to get him first or go under. He oughtn't to said I cheated him."

"I say, that's a bally lie, you know." Whitby's drawling voice electrified the company. Those behind him hastily changed their positions. Dave, with a curse, reached again for his gun-it lay on the floor against the wall, where it had fallen.

"Drop it, Dave," came Slick's grating command. "Think I got nothin' to do but clean up after you? Which yo 're too hot to stay indoors. Go outside and cool off."

"You tell me to git out?" exclaimed Dave, incredulously.

"That's what," was Slick's dogged reply. "The Britisher wants to speak his piece an' all interruptions is barred entirely. An' don't let Sandy see you for a month."

Dave walked over and picked up his gun. "To h — l with Sandy," he cursed. The door slammed open and he was gone.

Slick slid his weapon back onto the shelf and proceeded to admonish Whitby. "See here, Brit, don't you never call a man a liar 'less yo 're sure you can shoot first."

"But dash it all! the man is a liar, you know. The German chap said 'you d — n scoundrel! Traitor to my master, eh!' There 's nothing in that about cheating, is there?"

"Well, mebbe not," agreed Slick, "but comparisons is odorous, you don't want to forget that. Which we 'll drink to the memory of th' dead departed. What 'll it be, boys?"

Chapter VII
The French Rose

The home of Jean LaFrance, a small cabin built principally of the ever-ready cottonwood, was located in a corner of his quarter-section, farthest from the Jones' Luck River, which formed one boundary of his farm. He had designs upon more than one quarter-section, not at that time an unusual or impossible ambition, in so far as homestead laws went. His simple plan regarding residence was to move the cabin or build against it as occasion arose. The rolling country sloped steadily upward from the river to the chain of hills farther to the east. These sent down several tributary streams, all unreliable during the warm weather with the exception of one which passed close to the cabin. The conformation of the land gave a view from the cabin of one long stretch of the trail from Twin River and several short ones; opposite the house, continuing to Wayback, the trail was lost sight of.

Thus Buck was plainly visible as he loped along the trail on the morning following the Sweet-Echo tragedy, only no one happened to be observing him. As he disappeared behind the first rise, a pair of inquisitive young eyes, half closed in the effort of the mouth below to retain possession of far more than its capacity, arose above the level of the window sill and looked eagerly for an invitation to mischief. Seeing nothing that particularly called him, Pickles went out and into the barn.

Buck struck off the trail and rode along the path to the house. Spring had returned in force after its temporary retreat before the recent cold and the air bore whisperings of the mighty wedlock of nature; all about him the ecstatic song of the meadow-lark held a meaning that escaped him, vague, intangible, but thrillingly near to suggestion; the new green of the prairie melted into the faint purple of the distant hills, beneath a sky whose blue depths touched infinity. It was a perfect day and Buck, on his errand of aid to the helpless, forgave the fences and the evidence of land cultivation which threatened the life of the range. Riding close to the door he raised his quirt-and paused.

Rivalling the meadow-larks there flowed the music of a mellow contralto roice in song. His hand dropped to his side. That the language was strange made little difference: the meaning of life almost was discovered to him as he listened.

> "Earth has her flowers and Heaven her sun —
> But I have my heart.
> Winter will come, the sweet blossoms will die —
> But warm, ah! so warm
> Is my heart.

> "When the White King makes his truce with the Gold —
> How dances my heart!
> All the sweet perfumes that float in the Spring
> Rest close, ah! so close
> In my heart.

> "One day when Love like a bee, buzzing past,
> Wings close to my heart,
> Deep he shall drink where no winter can chill,
> Content, ah! content
> In my heart."

The low voice died away into silence; from afar came the soft cooing of a dove, soothingly insistent as the croon of a lullaby; the riotous call of the larks arose in gleeful chorus; within the cabin were the sounds of movement: footsteps, the pushing of a pan across the table, and then a subdued pounding which sent Buck's thoughts whirling back into the distant past to hover over one of his most sacred memories. He sat perfectly still. How many years had gone by since he had heard a good woman singing over her household tasks! How very long ago it seemed since his mother had made bread to the tune of that same 'punch, punch, slap-punch, punch'! His stern face softened into a tenderness that had not visited it since he was a boy. Mother-The French Rose-it was a pretty name.

Buck was not in the least aware of it but when a man thus links the name of a woman with that of his mother, it has a significance.

The faint nicker of a horse aroused Allday from his apathetic interest in flies; he raised his head and sent forth a resounding whinny in response; the blare of it was yet in the air when Rose stood in the open doorway.

I despair of picturing her to you, so difficult it is to portray in words the loveliness of a woman's beauty; and the charm of the French Rose was as many-hued as the changing sky at sunset; the modulations of her voice ranged from the grave, rich tones of an organ to the melting timbre of a flute, pitched to the note of the English thrush; her very presence was as steadfastly delightful as the fragrance of a hay field, newly mown. In a long life I have known but one such woman and this was she.

First, then, she harmonized. The simple gown, turned in at the throat, with sleeves rolled high on the arms for greater freedom in her work, the short skirt impeding but little her activity of movement, covered a form meant by God to be a mother of men; and the graceful column of her neck supported a head that did honor to her form. Lustre was in every strand of the black hair, against which the ears set like the petals of a flower; the contour of the face, the regularity of the features, were flawless, unless for an overfulness of the lips in repose; the natural olive complexion, further darkened by the sun-tan from her out-door life, could not conceal the warm color of the blood which glowed in her cheeks like the red stain on a luscious peach; and the mystery of her dark, serious eyes had drawn men miles to the solving-in vain.

So she stood, silently regarding Buck, who as silently regarded her. When she had first come upon him, in those few moments of unaccustomed softness when the hard mask of assertive manhood had been slipped aside, her questioning gaze had probed the depths of him, wondering and warming to what it found there. Her smile awoke Buck to a sense of his rudeness and he swept off his hat with the haste of embarrassment. "I 've come for Pickles," he blurted out, anxious to excuse his unwarranted presence.

"Is it-is it M'sieu Peters?" she questioned.

"That's me," admitted Buck. "Can I have him?" He smiled at the absurdity of his question. Of course she would be glad to get rid of such a mischievous little "cuss."

Rose considered. "Enter, M'sieu Peters. We will speak of it," she invited.

"I shore will," was the prompt acceptance. Buck's alacrity would have called forth hilarious chaffing from the Bar-20 punchers. It surprised himself. She set out a cup and a bottle on one end of the table and hastened to the other with an exclamation of dismay: *"Hélas, mon pain!"* and forthwith the "punch, punch!" was resumed, while Buck stared at the process and forgot to drink.

"Why do you take Fritz from me?" asked Rose.

Buck resumed his faculties with a grunt of disgust. "What's th' matter with me?" he asked himself. "Am I goin' loco or did Johnny Nelson bite me in my sleep? What was that: *'Take Fritz?'*"

This was seeing the matter in a different light. Buck ran his fingers through his hair and looked helpless. He poured himself a drink. "Take Fritz? Take anything she wants? Why, I'd give her my shirt. There I go again —" and he savagely, in imagination, kicked himself.

"You see —I sort o' reckoned," he faltered, "Dutch bein' one o' my boys-Pickles-Fritz-ought to be taken care of, an' —"

"So-and you think I will not take care of him?"

"Oh, no; ma'am. Never thought nothin' o' th' kind. You stick yore brand on him an' we 'll say no more about it. Yore health, ma'am."

Rose packed the dough into the pan and set it aside. Buck watched her with rueful countenance. "Now you 've gone an' made her mad," he told himself. "Guess you better stick to cows, you longhorn!"

She returned to her place and sat opposite him, her flour-stained arms lying along the table. "You shall take him, M'sieu Peters," she declared.

To Buck's remonstrance she nodded her head. *"Mais oui* —it is better," she insisted. "He grow up a man, a strong man-yes. Only a strong man have a chance in this so bad country. Yes, it is better, I call him."

"Let me," Buck interposed, and stepping to the door he cried out a yodelling call that brought Fritz scampering into the cabin with scared face: it was his father's well-known summons. Rose called him to her and put her arms about his shoulders.

"M'sieu Peters have come to take you with him, Fritz. You will go?" she asked him.

"Betcher life," said Pickles.

Buck grinned and Rose laughed a little at the callous desertion. *"Eh, bien, m'sieu* —you hear?" she said to Buck, and then, to the boy: "It please you more to go with M'sieu Peters than stay with me-yes?"

"Betcher life," repeated Pickles. "Yo 're all right, but I want to be a cow-punch an' rope an' shoot. Some day I 'll get that d —d ol' Dave Owens for killin' dad."

"*Dieu!*" Rose was on her feet, gripping Fritz so hard that he squirmed. "Dave kill-Dave —"

"Sure, he done it! Who'd yeh s'pose?" Fritz wriggled loose and stood rubbing his shoulder. Rose stood staring at him until Buck pushed him out of the room, when she sank back into her chair, covering her eyes with one shaking hand.

Outside Buck was questioning Pickles. "You rid yore daddy's bronc over, didn't you? Can you rope him? Bully for you. Get a-goin', then. We want to pull out o' here right smart." Pickles was off on the run and Buck slowly entered the cabin. He went over and stood looking out of the window. "I would n't take it so hard," he ventured. "These sort o' mistakes is bound to happen. An' it might a' been worse. It might a' been Dave went under."

Rose flung out a hand towards him. "I wish —" she began passionately and then caught back the words, horrified at her thought.

"Course you wish he had n't done it. He had n't oughter done it. Dutchy was a good man-an' a square man-an' Dave ain't neither-though I shore hates to hurt yore feelin's in sayin' so."

"*I* know him. He is bad-bad. No one know him like me." The deep voice seemed to hold a measureless scorn. Buck wondered at this.

"Well, if you know him I 'm right glad. I figgered it out you did n't."

"I know him," she repeated, and this time she spoke with a weariness that forbade further remark.

They remained thus silent until Fritz rode up on the Goat, shouting out that he was ready and long since forgetful of a scene he had not understood. Buck turned from the window. "Good-bye, ma'am, I reckon we 'll drift."

Rose came forward with extended hand. "Good-bye. You will guard him? But certainly. When you ride to town, maybe you ride a little more and tell me he is well and good. It is not too far?"

"Too far! Th' Double Y ain't none too far. I reckon you forget I come from Texas."

They waved to her just before they dropped from sight down the last dip to the trail. She was watching when they came into view again at the first gap and watched them out of sight at the end of the long stretch before the bend. Then she turned back into the room and removing the demijohn and cup from the table, she stood looking at the chair where Buck had sat. "*Voilà, un homme,*" she declared, patting gently the rough back of the chair: "a true man. They are not many-no."

Chapter VIII
Tex Joins the Enemy

Tex slung a leg over Son John and ambled away from Wayback, in the wake of Dave. His adroit and unobtrusive observance of Dave had been without results unless there were something suspicious in the long conversation held with a one-eyed puncher who rode away on a Cyclone-brand pony. Tex, however, was by no means cast down; he could not hope to pick up something every day and he already had learned the only quarter from which trouble might come to Buck. He delayed action in the hope that something tangible might turn up; and he fervently hoped that it might be before Hopalong found himself foot-loose from the Bar-20. Tex was quicker with his gun than most men but he possessed a real artist's love for a reason why action should occur in a certain way; if he were also able to show that it could have occurred in no other way, he found all the more satisfaction in the setting.

A loud splash in the nearby river brought his head around in the direction of the sound; through a break in the foliage a broad patch of water, seen dimly in the dusk of the evening, showed rapidly widening circles. "Walloper," commented Tex, immediately resolving to emulate that fish in the morning. "Though I certainly hope old Smiler won't come to the water below

me for a drink: nice mouthful of mutton I'd make for his wolf fangs. What in thunder! —"
his pony had plunged forward as if spurred. Tex got him in hand and whirled to face the
unknown danger. The rush of the river, the steady wind through the trees, the elusive chirp
or movement of some bird—only familiar sounds met his ear and there was still light enough to
show only familiar objects. "Why, you white-legged, ghost-seeing plug-ugly!" remonstrated
Tex. "Who do you think is riding you? Johnny Nelson? Then you must be looking for a lesson
on behavior about now. Get along."

He rode slowly, not wishing to overtake Dave before he settled in Twin River. Tex had as
much right as Dave to be riding from Wayback but he wished to avoid arousing the faintest hint
of suspicion. There was no other place along the trail for Dave to stop, except the LaFrance
cabin. Queer how opinions differed regarding the French Rose: from the extreme of all-bad
to that of all-good. Judicious Tex, summing up, concluded her to be neither —"Just like any
other woman: half heart, quarter intellect, and the balance angel and devil; extra grain of angel
and she 's good; extra grain of devil and she 's bad." Tex, not knowing Rose personally, gave
her the benefit of the doubt.

"If he stops in there I 'll miss him," said Tex. "But he 's bound to go on to Twin from
there. If we come together in the trail, it's no harm done: Dave will never suspect me until
he looks into my gun. Bet a hat he thinks I 'm a pretty good friend of his." He chuckled,
recalling the arguments for and against Gerken on the night of the shooting. The consensus
of opinion seemed to be that Dave had been within his rights but "some hasty." This was not
Tex's opinion. He chuckled again as he recalled the lurid out-spokenness of Sandy McQueen's
opinion which had turned the perfunctory trial into a farce and had kept Twin River on the
grin for two days. "And all is gay when Sandy comes marching home," he hummed. "I 'm glad
they found the gun on Dutch. Peck of trouble if he had n't been heeled. There 's me, just
naturally obliged to pull out Dave. If he goes under I lose touch with the old thief who stops
at home. Funny they don't get at it. There 's enough material in Twin River alone to wipe
three Double Y's off the map, good as Buck is. Give him six months more and half Montana
could n't do it-because the other half would be fighting *for* him, Lordy! The old-times! Folks
have grown most surprising slow these days."

He had left the foot of the farm road half a mile in the rear when he heard the sound of a horse
coming up behind him. The darkness hid Tex until the other was nearly abreast, when he hailed.
"He did turn off to see Rose," reflected Tex, as he returned the greeting and Dave rode up.

"That you, Comin'?" said Dave. "I been wantin' to see you. Goin' anywhere particular?"

"No," drawled Tex. "I was just considerin' which of them shanties in Twin 'd have th' most
loose money."

"Bah!" scornfully exclaimed Dave, drawing alongside him. "There ain't no money in Twin
River. You an' me could make a good haul over in Wayback but I got somethin' better 'n that.
Let's go into Ike's. Ike never hears nothin' an' all th' rest is deaf, too. I want to talk to you."

Ike's was primitive to a degree but once removed from a tent. The log walls of the low, single
room were weather-proofed in several ingenious ways, ranging from mud to bits of broken
boxes. The bar was a rough, home-made table, the front and both ends shut in by canvas
on which was painted: "Don't shoot here." Ike was careful either of his legs or his kegs. A
big stove stood in a shallow trough of dirt midway between the bar and the door, accepting
salival tributes in winter which developed into miraculous patches of rust in summer. Several
smaller tables, likewise home-made, a number of boxes, and a few very shaky chairs completed
the furnishings. It was the reverse of inviting, even in the bitter cold of winter, but Ike never
lacked for customers of a sort and probably made more money than any one in Twin River. Ike
himself was a grizzled veteran of more than fifty years, sober, taciturn, not given to cards but
always ready to "shake-'em-up." Dice was his one weakness at any time of the day or night. To
be sure, he always won. He had them trained.

The regular *habitués* were a canny lot, tight-lipped, cautious, slow in speech and in movement,
except at a crisis. The opening door was a target for every eye and not a straight glance in the

crowd; each seemed trying, like the Irishman when he bent his gun-barrel, to make his eyes shoot around a corner. And they all took their liquor alike, squeezing the glass as if it were a poker hand and they were afraid to show the quality or quantity of the contents. It was usually easy to pick out an occasional caller or a stranger: he was drunk or on the way to it; Ike's regulars were never drunk.

The entry of Dave and Tex was noted in the usual manner. Dave had long been recognized as one of their kind. Tex, since his dramatic entry into Twin River, had shown no displeasing partiality for hard work. Both were welcomed therefore, silently or laconically, not to be confounded with sullenly. As they sauntered over to an unoccupied corner table, Tex noticed Fanny sitting in a game with Bill Tregloan, both of them much the worse for liquor, while their three companions showed the becoming gravity of sober winners. Fanny closed one of his wide, woman's eyes and nodded to them with a cheerful grin, but Bill was too far gone to notice anything but his persistent bad luck. "D —n this poker game," he bellowed, banging a huge fist on the table, "If 't was Nap I might win something, but here I 've been sittin' all night, scatting my money in the say."

Fanny laughed uproariously but the others eyed him in silent disapprobation. What "Nap" might be they did not know, but poker was good enough for them.

"What 'll you drink, Comin'?" asked Dave as a preliminary.

"I ain't drinkin', Dave, not never. But I 'm right ready an' anxious to hear o' that somethin' good you 've got to deal out."

"Y-e-e-a —well, it's this way," began Dave, sampling his liquor in the customary gulp. He set down his glass to ask abruptly: "Got any friends in Twin River?"

"Nary friend-nor anywhere else," replied Tex, indifferently. "Don't need 'em-can't afford 'em."

Dave looked hard at Tex. "What about that bunch Fanny travels with?" he suggested.

"You said friends," was the significant answer.

"All right-all th' better. I seen you play a mighty good game o' cards."

Tex snorted. He could not restrain it. Was it possible Dave was aiming to milk him? "I'm allus willin' to back my play," he declared, drily.

"You won't have to back it. If yo 're as good as I hopes, I 'll back it. It's this way: I want to back you agin' a man as thinks he can play. He 's considerable of a dealer-considerable-an' he won't play me because he beats me once an' thinks I 'm no good. He 's got money, a-plenty, an' I don't want a dollar. You keeps what you wins-an' I wants you to get it all." He turned and called across the room: "Ike, flip us a new deck." The pack in his hands, he faced Tex again. "Suppose we plays a few hands an' you gimme a sample o' yore style."

Tex thrust his hands in his pockets and tipped back in his rickety chair. "Lemme get this right," he demanded. "You backs me to play, pockets th' losses, gives up th' winnin's, all to best th' other feller-on'y he must n't win."

"You got it."

"On'y he must n't win."

"That's what I said."

"Must be a friend o' yourn."

"Y-e-s," drawled Dave, with a sardonic smile.

"Who is it?"

"Peters o' th' Double Y."

"Ah! I 've heard o' him."

"An' you an' me an' a lot more 'll hear too d —d much o' him if we don't run him out. He 's a heap too good for Twin River."

"How 'll you rope him?"

"I got a bait-best kind. They allus fall for a woman." Dave's sneering tones, as he broke open the pack, sorely taxed his companion's self-control. "What'll we play?" he continued. "Better make it 'stud.' Th' gamer a man is th' quicker he goes broke at stud an' Peters is game enough."

Tex dropped back into position and took his hands from his pockets. "I shine at stud," he remarked softly, taking the deck Dave offered him. The joker was sent spinning across the room to glance from the nose of Fanny who sat sprawlingly asleep, nodding to an empty table; the Cornishman, swearing strange oaths, had gone off some time previously; two of the others were renewing the oft-defeated attempt to dice Ike to the extent of a free drink; the rest of the inmates were attending strictly to business and if an occasional oblique glance was aimed at Tex and Dave it did not show the curiosity which may have directed it.

"He must n't win," murmured Tex. The cards rustled in the shuffle. Dave grunted. "An' you must n't win?" Tex inquired.

"I 'm a-goin' to do all I know how to win," warned Dave.

"Oh, that o' course," sanctioned Tex. "Shift this table. I likes to see th' door," he explained.

Dave complied, looking sharply for some other reason. The lamp on the wall divided its light fairly between them. Dave was satisfied.

"Is it for love or money?" asked Tex.

"Might as well make it interestin'," suggested Dave.

Tex thought for a moment. "No," he dissented, "'Dog eat dog' ain't no good. But we 'll keep count so you can see how bad you make out."

It was no game. Tex won as he liked with the deck in his hand and his remarks on Dave's dealing were neither complimentary nor soothing. "Duced bad form, as the Britisher would say," was his plaintive remonstrance at Dave's first attempt; "you palms th' pack like a professional." Sometime later, as he ran his finger nail questioningly along the edge of the cards, he shook his head in sorrow: "You shore thumbs 'em bold an' plenteous, Dave," was his caustic comment. And then, querulously: "D —n it, Dave! don't deal me seconds. Th' top card is plenty good enough for me."

It required very little of this to cross Dave's none too easy temper. He pushed the cards away from him, pleased and annoyed at the same time. "You 'll do," he declared, "if you can't clean up Peters there ain't a man in th' country as can." A sudden suspicion struck him. Tex had reached out with his left hand to pick up the deck. "Where 'd you get that ring, Comin'? I never seen it afore."

A swift movement of the fingers under the idly held pack and Tex extended his hand, palm up. The band of dark metal, almost unnoticeable on the brown hand, was as plain on the palm side as Dave had seen it to be on the back of the hand. "Belonged to my wife," said Tex, the cynical undertones in his voice bearing no expression in his face. "I wear it on our wedding anniversary."

"Excuse *me*," was Dave's hasty apology. He pushed back from the table. "Keep in trainin', Comin'. I 'll see Rose an' start things rollin'. Jean will take you in as an old friend when we 're ready. We must n't be too thick; Peters might hear of it. Good-night. I 'm goin' to roost."

"Night, Dave." Tex sat fingering the cards with something very like wonder on his face. "What sort of a babe-in-arms is this for deviltry? He used to have better ideas. The cold weather up here must have congealed his brains. Break Buck Peters at stud! Maybe he plans to get us shooting. I 'll bet a hat old Schatz never hatched that scheme." He took the cards over to Ike and strolled out, unseating Fanny with one sweep of his foot as he went.

Fanny arose to his feet, looking for trouble. He was sober in his legs but his ideas crossed. No one being near him, he surveyed his backless, up-ended chair with blinking ferocity. "Cussed, buckin' pinto! Think I can't ride you, huh? Watcher bet?" He righted the chair and took a flying seat, all in one movement. "Huh! Ride anythin' on four laigs," he boasted. Lulled by this confidence in his horsemanship, his head began to nod again, in sleep.

Tex ambled over to the Why-Not where his entry was greeted with boisterous invitations to a game. Four bright boys had come over from the Fort and were cleaning up the crowd. Tex was ashamed of them, and said so, refusing to go to the assistance of such helpless tenderfeet. He borrowed paper and pencil of Dutch Fred and rapidly composed a note to Buck. Much adroit manoeuvring secured the services of Cheyenne Charley, not yet too drunk to understand the repeated instructions of Tex. Thus it came about that Buck, without knowing how it got there, found on his table a communication of absorbing interest, signed: "A Friend." It read:

Buck Peters: Don't play cards with strangers, especially stud poker. Dave Owens aims to have Rose rope you into a frame-up. John is in it, too. Mighty easy to plug you in a row.

"A Friend," mused Buck. "An' Rose is to rope me into a crooked game. I 'm d —d if I believe it." He made as if to tear the paper but changed his mind. "No, I 'll just keep this. Mebby there 'll be more of 'em. Jake!" he roared.

"—lo!" came the answering roar.

"Who's been here this mornin'?"

"Where?"

"At th' ranch."

A huge, slouching figure with a remarkable growth of hair appeared in the doorway. Jake was a cook because he was too big to ride and too lazy to dig. He ran his fingers through his hair, considering. "At th' ranch?" he repeated. "There was Pickles an' Ned, o' course; and Cock Murray come over to ask —"

"I don't mean them, I mean some stranger."

"Stranger? Where?"

"Right here in this room."

"Ther' ain't been no stranger. What'd he do?"

"Do? Why-why, he stole all th' silver, that's what. It's gettin' so I 'll have to lock up all th' valuables every time I go out, yo 're that interested in yore cookin'. Course, you need th' practice, I agree. Sling on th' chuck, you blind, deaf elephant. I got to get."

Jake rapidly retreated. In the kitchen he paused and ran his fingers through his hair. He looked scared. "Stole th' silver! Lock up th' valuables! He must be loco." Whereupon he stole out of the back door and concealed two stones in his clothes, where they would be handy. At close quarters he was a very grizzly for strength but if Buck should start to shoot him up from a distance, he did not purpose to be altogether at a disadvantage. Thus fortified he prepared to serve the meal.

Chapter IX
Any Means to an End

Jean LaFrance carefully cleaned his boots and stepped into the cabin. *"Bon jour, ma belle Rose. Breakfast is ready, eh? But for why you make three to eat?"*

"Did you not see, on the trail?"

"No." He took up a bucket of water and a tin basin, going to a bench outside, to wash. In a few moments a horseman loped into view and disappeared again, hidden by an intervening rise. At sight of the rider a look of fear flashed across the face of Jean and he smothered a curse, hastily re-entering the cabin to dry his hands. "Dave!" he exclaimed.

"Yes," assented Rose, impassively.

"You know he come?"

"No," as expressionless as before.

"For why he come some early? But yes! Schatz, he send the money, eh? Eh?"

Rose shrugged her shoulders doubtfully and answered the consequent look of anxiety on Jean's face by placing her hands on his shoulders and gently shaking him. "Wait till he comes, *mon père,*" she encouraged him.

He nodded his head, unconsciously squaring his shoulders in response to the subtle appeal to his manhood. At the sound of the horseman's feet he went outside. Dave's smiling cheerfulness relieved his mind and he returned the greeting with newborn good humor, leading the horse off to the stable while Dave went indoors.

The handsome animal glowed with the health of youth; not a trace of his evil nature showed in the sparkle of his eyes, and the clear red of his cheek still stood proof against the assaults of a life of reckless debauchery. "Hello, Rose," he cried, "I could n't stay away no longer. I come up last night but you 'd turned in." Encircling her waist he drew her to him to kiss her on the cheek, laughing good-naturedly at the interposed hand. "All right, have it your own way. But I wants you to know I never aims to kiss a girl yet, as I don't kiss her, come kissin'-time."

"It is not kissing-time for me, Dave-no. Not for any man. Why you stay away so long?" she asked-and could have bitten her tongue for it the next instant.

"Missed me, did you?" commented Dave, delighted. "Well, you see I—" he hesitated.

"You do not want to tell for why you kill that unoffensive man and leave Fritz without a father." The contempt in her voice cut like a whip.

"Unafensive!" he repeated, the color ebbing from his face to leave it the dangerous white of the fated homicide. "He was that unafensive he knocked me off my feet an' started to pull a gun on me. It was an even break. That's more 'n yore dad allows when anybody tries to rush him."

She winced as if struck. "Is it not promise you speak nothing of this?"

"I ain't a-speakin' of it. Nobody knows 't was him. Leastwise nobody but me. I would n't 'a' dug it up on'y you go accusin' me o' killin' when I has to protect myself."

Jean was heard approaching and Rose made a weary gesture of submission. *"Eh, bien.* Me, I know nothing but what I hear. Do not be angry when father comes."

"Peters, I suppose. D—n him for a liar." His face cleared as Jean entered. "Well, I got bad news for you, Jean. Schatz says he can't let you have that money just now, but he 'll remember you."

"Good! Soon, I hope," and Jean rubbed his hands in pleased anticipation as he drew up to the table.

* * * * *

Dave sat silently watching Rose, after Jean had left them to go to his work. She went about her daily duties, patiently waiting. Something in Dave's manner told her he had come for more than the mere pleasure of seeing her.

"Rose, sit down," he said at last. "I want to talk to you." She seated herself obediently and faced him.

"Allons," she prompted him.

"You see, it's this way: Here 's me, errand boy for Schatz. I draws my time, same as I 'm a-punchin' for him, but what is it? Not enough to live on. I can make more with th' cards, a whole lot more, on'y you says no. An' there ain't nothin' reglar 'bout gamblin', anyhow. Schatz is honin' for his ranch. He 's bound to get it an' I 'm bound to help him. 'Cause why? I strike it rich. Schatz will put me on as foreman or mebby better. Now, how do we get th' ranch? Break that McAllister-Peters combine, that's how. An' how do we break 'em? You."

"Me?"

"You. It's pie. You get him here-Peters-an' I got a man as 'll clean him out like a cyclone lickin' up a haystack. You get him here, that's all. You know how. I ain't a-goin' to be jealous of a girl as breaks off a kiss in th' middle an' han's me back my end of it. You ain't woke up yet, Rose, an' when you do, I 'll be there."

"You will be there."

"You bet-with aces-four of 'em." He nodded with confident assurance. "You get Peters a-comin' here an' then some night Comin' Thirty drops in casual to see yore daddy. That 'll be all. Comin' knows his business."

"Who is Comin'?"

"Who is he?" Dave grinned. "Well, he's th' on'y man can deal a deck between th' Mississip' an' th' Rockies. When Peters gets through with him he won't think so much o' that feller he met in Cheyenne —H —l!" He sprang to his feet, consternation on his face. Rose gazed at him in mute wonder. "It can't be!" he muttered, "he went out long ago." He was silent in

165

troubled speculation for a while. "Rose," he continued abruptly, "you ask Peters, first time you see him-when 'll you go? To-day?"

"Go where?"

"Over to th' ranch," he explained, impatiently. "You 've got to set her rollin'. Go over to see Pickles, can't you?"

"Yes, if you say go."

"All right. Go to-day. An' ask Peters when he 's seen Tex Ewalt. Don't forget th' name: Tex Ewalt."

"Tex Ewalt. I go now. It may be difficult. Men do not come here like before —"

"Before I showed 'em th' way. You 'll get Peters, if you try right."

"And you? Is it to Big Moose you ride?"

"No, I got to go to Wayback. Will I throw th' leather onto Swaller?"

"No, Swallow come when I call."

"All right. Then I'll hit th' trail. What, you won't? Wait till you wake up." He went off laughing and in a minute more swung past the house with a rattle of harness and shout of farewell. Rose stood in the doorway, motionless, looking after him.

"If I try right. You beast!" The words came through her lips laden with unutterable loathing. She put her hands before her eyes to shut out the sight of him and turned back into the room, throwing out her arms in despair. "What can I do?" she asked passionately; and again: "What can I do?"

* * * * *

To Tex, grimly watchful in the bar-room of the Why-Not, her coming brought a shock. He remembered her as she appeared when publicly denouncing him for a crime he had not committed, a memory that ill prepared him for the all-pervading charm of her beauty. Approaching rapidly, a glorious figure, sitting the powerful black with unaffected grace, her grave loveliness smote him with a sort of wonder. Plunging through the ford in a series of magnificent leaps, the rifted spray flashed about her in the sunlight like bursting clouds of jewels. The solid ground once more under his feet, the black settled into his stride and they were away, the blue sky above the distant hills set wide for them, a gateway of the gods. "When she had passed it seemed like the ceasing of exquisite music," murmured Tex.

Dutch Fred laughed genially at his companion's interest. They two were alone in the room. "Der French Rose, a fine voman, yes," he remarked, with open and honest admiration. "You like her?"

Tex stared steadily out of the window as he answered:

>"'Had she been true
>If Heaven had made me such another world
>Of one entire and perfect chrysolite
>I 'd not have sold her for it.'"

"Sold her! Sold her for a —vot? Vot you talk, anyvay?"

"That, my friend, is what the nigger said when the shoe pinched. There 's a h —l of a lot of tight shoes in th' world, Fred."

Fred walked to the door and gazed solemnly after Tex as he rode away; then he walked back to the bar and solemnly mixed himself a fancy drink, which he compounded with the judgment of long experience. He set down the glass and admonished it with a pudgy forefinger: "How *he* know she vear tight shoes, vat?"

But the glass had already given up all it contained.

Swallow, meanwhile, was putting the trail behind him with praiseworthy speed, and brought Rose within hailing distance of the ranch house just as Jake, with his carefully concealed stones, re-entered the kitchen. As she dropped from her horse Buck appeared at the door and sprang forward to greet her, his stern face aglow with pleasure. "Why, ma'am, I 'm right glad to see you," he declared, appreciative of the firm clasp of the hand she gave him. "Honest as a man's," was his thought. "Jake! O-o, Jake!" he called.

Jake tip-toed to the door and peered cautiously forth, heaving a huge sigh of relief at the new development. "Better run him in the stable, Jake," advised Buck. "An' take some o' th' sweat off 'n him. Take yore time. We 'll wait. You see," he went on to Rose, "none of th' boys is up; but Ned ought to be here right soon. An' Pickles, Pickles 'll be that pleased he won't eat nothin'. Pickles says yo 're a brick an' he likes you 'most as well as Whit."

Her bubbling laughter set Buck to laughing in sympathy and they stood, one at either side the table, looking at each other like two happy children, moved to mirth by they knew not what.

"It is a disappointment I have not come before, M'sieu Peters," said Rose, "you make me so very welcome. But Whit-who is Whit?"

"Whit? Oh, he's th' Britisher we took on when-when we went short a hand. He 's willin' an' strong an' learns quick, though he shore has some amazin' ideas about cows."

The momentary clouding of her face as she recalled how he had "gone short a hand," he allowed to pass without comment and went gayly on. "Pickles, he likes to hear him tell stories; fairy stories, you might call them, but they ain't like no fairy stories I ever heard. An' he tells 'em like he believes 'em. I ain't right certain he don't. Pickles does. You would n't think a kid like that would take to fairy stories, would you, ma'am?"

"No-o. Always he is for the grand minute-to be a man, to ride, to throw the rope, —like that. And to shoot-he must not shoot, M'sieu Peters."

"Well, you see, ma'am, he-you —I —" he was clearly embarrassed, but Truth and Buck were Siamese twins and always moved in pairs. Hot and uncomfortable as it made him, he had to confess. "Why, he 's just naturally boun' to shoot. Yesterday I give him a rifle an' a big bunch o' cartridges. He won't hurt nothin', ma'am."

"*Mais non* —I hope not. Make him to be-to be good. A strong man can be good, M'sieu Peters?"

Buck frowned in thought. "Yes," he declared. "But there 's more ways than one o' bein' good. Our way 'd never do for some places, an' their way 'd never do for us. Th' quickest man with a short gun I ever knowed an' one as has killed considerable few, first an' last, he 's a good man, ma'am. He would n't lie, nor steal, nor do a mean act. An' he never killed a man 'less he was driven to it. I say it an' I know it. I 'd trust him with my life an' my honor. An' there 's more like him, ma'am, a-plenty." He stood tensely upright, an admirable figure, deep in earnest thought. And she stood watching him, silent, studying his face, absorbing his words with a thirsty soul: the firm conviction of a man who, intuition told her, was sound to the core. "This is a rough country," he continued, "with rough ways. There 's good men an' bad men. Th' bad men are th' devil's own an' it seems like th' good men are scattered soldiers with a soldier's work to do. If a bad man takes offence an' you know he means to get you if he can, it's plumb foolish to wait till yo 're shot before you begin shootin'. He did n't begin with you an' he shore won't stop with you, an' it's your plain duty to drop him at th' first threatenin' move. Mebby you won't have to kill him, but if you must, you must. I don't say it's right but it's necessary. That's all, ma'am."

He turned to her with a whimsical smile. Her face was alight with a heartfelt gratitude, for Buck, all unknowingly, had exonerated her father, in showing her a new aspect of his doubtful matter from the view-point of a man among men. She passed her hand across her eyes in a swift gesture, then laid it for an instant firmly upon his shoulder. "*Merci, mon ami,*" she said quietly. That shoulder, whenever he thought of it, tingled for days after, in a way that to Buck was unaccountable.

A moment later Jake appeared. "Ready in two shakes," he promised, referring to the meal.

"Can't you rustle up somethin' extra, Jake?" asked Buck. "You know we got company."

Jake assumed an air of nonchalant capability. "Well, now, I reckon," he answered; in spite of himself a hint of boasting was in his voice. "What do you say to aigs?"

"Aigs?" repeated Buck, his eyes widening.

"Aigs!" reiterated Jake, complacently.

Rose looked on in much amusement while Buck's astonished stare wandered down half the length of Jake's lofty height and stopped. "Are you carryin' 'em in yore pockets?" asked Buck.

"In my pockets!" exclaimed Jake. He glanced down. What in blazes did he have in his pockets? A hasty investigation brought forth two large stones.

"What in-what are you carryin' *them* for?" asked Buck, with lively curiosity.

Jake turned to Rose with his explanation: "You see, ma'am, it's th' cyclone. I got a' almanac as says a cyclone is a-comin' an' due to-day, an' I did n't want to be blown onto th' top o' one o' these yer mountains an' mebby freeze to death." Rose's responsive peal of laughter repaid him, and, withering Buck with a look, he retired to the kitchen to cook his magically acquired eggs.

The meal was nearly finished when Pickles appeared, late as usual. Ned had been given up by Buck, who explained his absence as probably due to the development of some unexpected duty. Rose, awaiting a more favorable opportunity to introduce the real object of her visit, had deliberately prolonged the enjoyment of listening to his conversation. His friends would not have known the usually taciturn Buck. Quite equal to the production of a flow of language when language was desirable, his calling and environment seldom found it necessary. Indeed, if brevity were the sole ingredient of wit, few men had been wittier. But to-day he surpassed himself in eloquence; and it was in the midst of an unconsciously picturesque narrative that he was interrupted.

There came a scramble of hoofs, the slam of a door, a rapid padding of moccasined feet, followed by a yell from Jake and the taunting treble of a boyish voice, and Pickles sped into view, clutching the door frame as he ran, and swinging himself out of range. His back toward them and his head craned in the direction of Jake to insure the full effect of a truly hideous grimace, he jeered that worthy for his bad marksmanship: "Yah! you missed me ag'in! W'y don't you use a gun like a man?" and by way of emphasis he shook the light rifle he was carrying. As Jake directed a missile with unerring skill at anything short of a bird on the wing, it is to be presumed that, with Pickles as a mark, he did not try very hard. It is certain that he was chuckling gleefully as he went to pick up the dishcloth, a large remnant of what looked suspiciously like the passing of a blue flannel shirt.

Satisfied there was no immediate danger from the rear, Pickles wheeled about. "Buck, I near got —" he stopped short. "Rose!" he exclaimed and looked sharply from her to Buck and back again. "You ain't a-goin' to take me back?" he asked, doubtfully.

Rose shook her head as she looked at him. It was a new Pickles she saw. The roguish mischief had gone from the eyes which, when he faced them, had been alive with eager intensity; the air of precocious anxiety, tribute to a happy-go-lucky father (oftener "happy" than lucky) had vanished completely; motionless as he stood in his hopeful expectancy, he was aquiver with life. "No, Fritz," she assured him, "M'sieu Peters, he need you-more than me-yes."

Pickles was at the table in a moment. "Betcher life he does," he agreed. "You don't want a boy, anyhow. I 'd have a girl if I was you. Say, Buck," he informed between bites, "I seen Ned an' he says that d —n bull's broke out again. He 's gone after him. An' Cock Murray says: Can you lend him a hat. That wall-eyed pinto o' his made b — out o' his 'n."

"You young scallywag! You must n't swear afore a lady-not never. An' you must talk polite, besides. Don't you never forget it."

Pickles looked straight into Buck's stern eyes, without fear. "I won't," he promised, earnestly. "Gosh! I 'm hungry," and he proceeded to prove it. And Rose knew then that Pickles would grow up a "strong man" —and a good man, after the ideas of M'sieu Peters, which, she had become convinced, were very good ideas, indeed.

Pickles had long since departed with a hat for the far-distant Murray; the boys had straggled in and gone again from the bunk-house, where Jake ministered to their amazing appetites; and the afternoon sun was casting shadows of warning before Rose remembered the long ride home which was to come. A silence, longer than usual, had fallen upon them, which neither seemed to find embarrassing. Buck's inscrutable face, as he looked upon her, told nothing of his thoughts; but on hers was a soft wistfulness that surely sprang from pleasant imaginings. She pushed back her chair at last with a murmur of regret. Jake was glad to hear it. He had begun to have anxious misgivings regarding his job. Buck glanced through the window and really saw the outside world for the first time in two hours. He sprang to his feet and exclaimed in bewilderment. "First time in my life I ever did it," he declared. Rose looked an inquiry. "First time th' sun ever stole a march on me that way," he explained. "Reckon I must a' been some interested in your talk, ma'am," and his humorous smile was deliciously boyish. The sparkle in her eyes and the flush on her cheeks told that Rose discerned a compliment higher than the spoken one. She began to draw on her thick man's gloves with an air almost demure.

"It is very selfish that I have make you waste so much time, M'sieu Peters," she apologized, her eyes intent upon the gloves.

Buck stared. There was a certain grimness in his humor as he answered: "Hm! Well, I 'm a-goin' to waste some more. That is, I will if you don't run away from Allday. He 's good, but that black o' yourn has got th' laigs of him, I reckon."

She watched him as he strode away for the horses, deciding how best to approach the object of her visit. True to her nature it was less an approach than a direct appeal. As they set off together she spoke abruptly: "What time did you see Tex Ewalt last? I think —I am sure-it is better if you have not see him for a long time-so."

"Well, I ain't seen him in a long time." He was plainly surprised. "Do you know Tex?" he asked, wonderingly.

She shook her head. "No. Some one ask me-but you have not seen him. That is good. Once I tell you I am glad if you come to see me about Fritz."

"Shore I 'll come," he promised heartily.

"You must not," she warned him. "In the morning, a little while, yes; at night or to stay long-no."

A light broke in upon Buck, who recalled the mysteriously delivered letter of that morning. The wholesome admiration for a lovely woman, the natural pleasure in an experience infrequent in his man-surrounded life, began to concentrate and take definite shape in his mind at the promised vindication of his judgment. He tested her shrewdly: "You don't want to see me," was his brusque comment.

She looked reproachfully at his set profile. "*Mais, quelle folie!* I am glad to see you always," she assured him, "but it must be like that. It is better." She hesitated a moment and continued: "It is better *aussi*, if you will not play cards. I —I like it, much, if you will not play cards." Her heightened color and diffident manner showed what it cost her to make it a personal request.

"By G—d! I knew it," cried Buck. He whanged Allday over one eye with his hat, and that sedate animal executed a side jump that would have done credit to a real bad pony. There are limits to all things and Allday was feeling pretty good just then, anyway.

Rose was startled. "What is it you know?" she asked, doubtfully.

Buck's face was alight with smiling gratification. Oblivious of the fact that at last he had stung Allday into remonstrance, he answered by the card, "I knowed that gamblin' habit 'd grow on me so my friends could see it. An' I hereby swears off. I never touches a deck till you says so, ma'am. That goes as it lays."

Still doubtful as to his meaning-such exuberance of feeling could scarcely be induced by swearing off anything-she questioned him in some embarrassment. "Is it I ask too much, that you will not play?"

"Too much! There ain't nothin' you can't ask me, nothin' —" he paused. "It's time I was hittin' th' back trail 'fore I say mor'n I ought. Just one thing, ma'am: I can't never know you better than I do right now. An' I want to say I 'm right proud to know you." He drew Allday down to a walk and halted as she stopped and faced him, sweeping her a salute as eloquent in gesture as were his words in speech.

The color came and went in her cheeks as she regarded him. "I am glad," she said at last, "Oh, I am very glad," and turning, she left him at a speed that vied with her racing thoughts.

Buck watched her go, the definite shape in his mind assuming a seductiveness that fascinated while it scared him. "If I was only ten years younger," he muttered. He jerked Allday's head around. "Get away, boy," he cried, and the horse struck his gait at a bound.

Buck was riding wide of the ranch house when a suspicion pricked him and he headed for home. At the door he shouted for Jake.

Jake lounged out. "What's th' noise?" he asked, languidly.

"Say, Jake, where 'd you get them aigs?"

Jake looked pained. "I got 'em off Cheyenne Charley," he asserted.

"Cheyenne Charley? Where 'n blazes did he get 'em," wondered Buck.

"Well, now, I can't rightly say," drawled Jake, "but I'm certain shore o' one thing: he never laid 'em."

"No," agreed Buck, reflectively. "Did he give 'em to you?" he added.

Jake yawned elaborately to hide the weakness of his position. "Not exactly," he admitted. "I got him drunk."

"Oh," commented Buck. He turned to ride off when another question obtruded itself, but Jake had disappeared. Buck slid to the ground and entered quietly by another door, going to where he kept his private stock. A rapid inspection showed where Jake had obtained his supply. He had appropriated Buck's whiskey to pay for eggs which it was very evident he had meant to eat himself. Only his vanity had led to their disclosure. "Th' d —n scoundrel!" said Buck, and he hurriedly secured the demijohn in the one place in the house that locked.

Chapter X
Introducing a Parasite

In the northeast corner of the Cyclone ranch, not far from the Little Jill, and in a hollow, well screened by hills and timber, One-Eye sat on his horse, smoking a brown cigarette and keeping a satisfied watch over a dozen mangy-looking cattle as they grazed intermittently in a restless, nervous way. They were a pitiful-looking handful, weak, emaciated, their skins showing bald patches and scabs, and they continually licked themselves and rubbed against the trees. While they were restless, it was without snap or vim; they were spiritless and drooping, enduring patiently until death should end their misery.

One-Eye beamed upon them, his good optic glowing with satisfaction. He had gone to some trouble and risk to cut these miserable animals cut of the herd collected by the hasty round-up, and now that he was about to have them taken off his hands he sighed with deep content. To run infected cattle onto the Cyclone's non-infected northern range was very dangerous, for his foreman was direct and unhesitating in his methods. Discovery might easily mean a bullet above One-Eye's blue-red nose-and this accounts for that puncher's satisfaction. Some men will do a great deal for ten dollars.

"D —n if they ain't beauts," he chuckled. "When it comes to pickin' out th' real, high-toned wrecks, th' constant scratchers, why I reckon I 'm some strong. He says to me 'Get th' very wust, One-Eye,' —an' I shore has obeyed orders. That two-year-old tryin' to saw through that cottonwood is a prize-winner when it comes to scabs-his tail looks like a dead tree in a waste of sand, th' way th' hair 's gone. Wait till he gets rubbin' hisself through th' brush across th' river, where Peters' cows like to hang out. He 'll hang mites on every twig; an' this kind o' weather will boom things. I heard tell that Peters examined that new herd extra cautious afore he bought it-well, boxcars an' pens can hand out itch a-plenty, so he can't prove they got it from us." He pulled out a battered brass watch and gauged where the broken hands would be if they were all there to point. "He 's due in ten minutes an' he 's usually on time. Yep: here he comes now. I 'll get my ten afore I do any more work-wish I could get ten dollars as easy every day."

Dave cantered up, his eyes fastened intently on the cattle, and he laughed cynically as he turned and regarded the puncher. "Well," he grinned, "I reckon you got th' wust that could stand bein' drove. Come on; we 'll get 'em off our hands as quick as we can —I don't want to answer no questions right now. It 'll be like puttin' a match to dry grass, th' way this dozen will cut down Peters' cows."

"It shore will," replied One-Eye. "Got that ten handy?" he inquired, carelessly.

"Why, they ain't across th' river yet," replied Dave, frowning.

"They 'll get across when I gets my ten," smiled One-Eye.

"Here 's th' money!" snapped Dave, angrily, as he almost threw the gold piece at his companion. "Fust time I was ever told I could n't be trusted for ten dollars."

"Oh, I trust you, all right-on'y I worked plumb hard for that coin, an' I want to feel it, like. Come on-take th' south side —I 'll handle th' rest."

The herd moved slowly forward into a dry ravine and finally came to the river bank. They hadn't life enough to give trouble until they understood what they were expected to do. Then the everlasting, thick-headed obstinacy, the perverse whims which all cows have to an outrageous extent, asserted itself in a manner wholly unexpected in such tottering hulks of diseased flesh. They did everything but get wet, even showing a returning flash of spirit in the way they swung their heads and kicked up their heels. Time and time again they broke and ran along the bank, and always in Dave's direction, who, until now, had nursed the belief that he was something of a cow-puncher. When half-dead cows unhesitatingly picked him out, time after time, for an easy mark, and simply walked through his defence, it was time to exchange ideas on some things.

At first One-Eye was greatly amused. He liked Dave well enough but he hated Dave's conceit-and to be present at his companion's discomfiture was very gratifying. But gradually One-Eye grew restless unto peevishness and a vast contempt settled upon him, edging his temper with a keenness rare to him. He had been trying to get one dozen imitation cows to cross an ordinarily wide river, and neither coldness nor unusual depth had any bearing on the matter. As he wondered how long he had been engaged in watching Dave's blunders and jerked out the brass watch to see, his voice rumbled and boomed with a jarring timbre and suddenness that make Dave jump.

"What th' h —l d' you think yo're doin'?" demanded One-Eye. "'Allamanleft' an' 'Ladies chain' is all right for a dance, but it 's some foolish out here. An' somebody 's goin' to lope along this way an' see us, if you don't quit makin' a jackass out er yo'rself."

Stung to the quick, Dave wheeled to face his critic, his pent-up rage almost hysterical. He had held it in, choked it back, and forced himself to be calm, but now-his purpose was never disclosed, for at the instant he wheeled, the watchful cattle leaped through the opening he had made and headed for the hills, their heads down and tails up. Dave hesitated, glancing from One-Eye to the cattle and back again, his face white and pinched. One-Eye's anger melted under his impelling sense of the ridiculous and, slapping his thigh a resounding smack, he burst into roars of laughter, until he was bent in his saddle like a man drunk or sorely wounded.

"This yer 's a circus," he finally managed to cry. "Don't get mad, Dave: we 'll make 'em cross this time or they 'll float down like logs. Come on."

When they rounded up the bunch and started it toward the river again the cows were surprisingly docile and the two drivers exchanged wondering glances. At the river edge the dozen hesitated for a moment while they nosed the water and at One-Eye's wondering command, pushed into the stream, scrambled out on the farther bank, and walked slowly into the brush. Dave's hypnotized senses were all in his eyes and he barely heard his companion speak.

One-Eye prefaced his remarks with a fluent burst of profanity, and cogitated aloud: "Cows is worse than wimmin! They *is*! Of all th' crazy hens what ever a man drove, them dozen mangy critters has got 'em all roped an' tied! What in h —l do you *think* of 'em?"

"I ain't thinkin', One-Eye," softly replied Dave. "I 'm prayin' for strength an' fortitude. I figgers I can drop th' last six from where I 'm sittin', an' it's some temptation!"

One-Eye ironed out his grin. "I'm some tempted myself, Dave. There 's things in a cowman's life to drive him plumb loco. I 've been part loco more 'n once. Mum? You bet I 'll keep mum. You don't reckon I 'm hankerin' for to collect no cold lead, do you?"

Dave scarcely heard him. He was looking across the river, a smile on his face. Before him was the Rocking Horse, and south of it, so close as to appear a part of it from that angle, lay the Hog Back. He had planned well, he told himself, when he had decided to turn infected cattle on the Double Y at that point.

"Now, they ain't goin' fur to be found while they stops near ol' Hog Back, Dave," One-Eye was saying. "Nobody hardly ever rides that way, an' they 'll drift down where th' grass is better, soon as they finds out what they 're up agin. Wonder if it was true about that feller ridin' th' Rockin' Horse all day long?" he asked, curiously.

He would have talked all day if given half a chance, but his companion, knowing One-Eye's inability to gracefully terminate a conversation, or effect a parting, mercilessly performed the operation himself. "I 'm goin' south, One-Eye. See you in town, some night," and Schatz' *protégé* cantered away, and became hidden by the brush and hills of the rough country skirting the river.

One-Eye looked after him. "Black devil!" he scowled. "If anybody gets plugged for this, you can bet it won't be little Davy. I wonder what th' Dutch Onion knowed that Dave didn't want told? Well, when me an' him is together my gun hand ain't never far from home-but I 'm surprised he did n't pump lead into me when I laughed like I did. I plumb forgot, then. Come on, boss; home for us, an' sudden. I ain't hankerin' none to be seen 'round here, *now*."

Chapter XI
The Man Outside

Dave loped through Twin River in no amiable mood. An unreasoning irritability tormented and blinded him to everything but the trail ahead. But if Dave failed to notice his friends, one of them at least bore him no ill-feeling for the oversight; this one was so solicitous for Dave's welfare that he followed all the way to the LaFrance cabin; when Dave went indoors he still lingered, hugging the cabin wall close to a window, while he listened with much interest to the talk that went on inside.

"Where 's Jean?" asked Dave, briefly, as he entered.

Rose glanced at him. The even, metallic tones meant temper and she was painfully anxious to avoid crossing him when in this mood. Her voice was soothing as a summer breeze through tree branches when she answered. "He go to the station," she explained; "something about a harrow. He will be late."

"See Peters?"

"Yes."

"What 'd he say about Tex Ewalt?"

"He have not see him for many months. He ask me if I know him."

"Well?"

"You forget to tell me what to say. I forget to answer."

"Hm! Beats th' Dutch how a woman 'll crawl out of a hole. When 's he comin' to see you?"

"I do not know. He-he is very droll, that M'sieu Peters. Always he look at me strange like he suspect something."

"He ain't got nothin' to suspect. Did n't try to kiss you, did he?"

"He never come near me one time-no; only he look at me, straight, without any smile."

"Bah! I knowed you did n't take th' right way with him. You got t' tempt them gray-eyed galoots. They 'll follow you easy enough if you show 'em there's somethin' at the end o' th' trail. You go ag'in. Make him glad to see you. Won't be long afore he 's hangin' round, then."

"*Quel jour* —when I must go?"

"Oh, whenever you get th' chanst. Soon as you kin. You got Pickles for an excuse, ain't you?"

At this point the solicitous caretaker outside risked a look through the window. His glance travelled over the shoulder of Dave, sitting with his back to the window, and rested on the face of Rose. Wrhat he saw there was a revelation: scorn, contempt, loathing, the expression any good woman might bear toward a man with a mind considerably lower than the nobler beasts; it lasted but a moment; placidity swept over the regular features as she replied. *"Mais oui,"* she admitted, "Fritz is excuse."

"Well, you won't need any excuse if you play th' game right. You 'll be excuse enough, yourself."

Enthralled by the contradiction between the expression and speech of Rose, the watcher prolonged his stare beyond safety. Rose's level gaze lifted from the unnoting eyes of Dave and rested full on the face in the window. The watcher changed instantly to the listener with one hand on his gun, but not so quickly that he failed to see the brilliant smile that flashed across the face of Rose. The alert tenseness of his attitude relaxed as he realized the significance of that smile and his shoulders heaved in strangling a laugh at the way Dave was being fooled.

Dave's moodiness persisted. He sat glowering at the point of his boot, switching it venomously with his quirt, a thing he had not carried since his experience with the Cyclone cattle at the Hog Back. It reminded him of his proven lack of ability as a driver of cows; but it was "out of this nettle, Chagrin, that he plucked the flower, Complacence"; a cynical laugh announced recovery from the black mood. "Well, there 's some as help me better 'n you do," he declared. "If I can't get Peters here, I give him somethin' that 'll keep him busy at home."

"Bien, but how?" Rose's interest had just the proper amount of congratulatory warmth and a faint wheeze escaped the listener outside as he choked back a laugh of admiration.

"I give him the itch," replied Dave, with dramatic brevity.

"Itch?" repeated Rose, in perplexity.

"Yes-itch, mange, scab! His d —n cows 'll be scratchin' their hides off afore he knows it. Th' Cyclone had it an' I got One-Eye Harris to save me out some. Mangiest lot o' cows ever *I* saw. We put 'em across th' Jill, up by th' Rocking Horse, a while back."

"But the range-is it not bad?" asked Rose, wonderingly.

"Shore is. What do I care? Makes 'em trouble, don't it? An' it 'll spoil some o' their cows, you bet."

"M'sieu Schatz, he tell you do this?"

"Smiler! The cussed ol' bear! He 's been a-layin' up all winter like a bear in a hole an' he ain't woke up yet. Poetry! an' Philosophy! an' some shifty *I*talian named Mac-Mac somethin' or other. Smiler sets a heap by Mac. Jus' sits an' reads an' hol's out his han's an' says: 'Gimme th' Double Y, Dave.' Mus' think I carry it in m' hat."

"But you will get it, Dave-yes."

"You bet yo' boots I 'll get it. Peters 'll be so sick o' that range afore I 'm done with him he 'll be glad to quit. But if you get him comin' here, it 'll be done quicker."

"I will try," murmured Rose.

The flush that went with the words was wrongly interpreted by Dave. "That's you!" he exclaimed, admiringly, and was at her side before she realized it, bending over her in a swift movement that almost caught her by surprise. He laughed easily at his defeat, in no wise discomfited. "Ain't come kissin'-time yet, eh, Rose?"

She looked up coolly, careful not to give way an inch from the nearness of him. Nothing tempts a man so much as a retreat. *"Mais non, m'sieu.* When the day, then the hour-you go too far unless," was her calm warning.

"All right. Time enough," he rejoined carelessly. "Guess I 'll drift back to Twin. Have to see Comin' an' keep him on edge, or he 'll get tired o' waitin' for that good thing I promised him. He ain't a feller as you can ask questions or I 'd cussed quick find out who he is an' where he come from."

Rose stood in the doorway until the sound of his horse's feet assured her that he was certainly on his way to Twin River. Then she went in, closed the door behind her, darkened the front windows and going to the window at the back called out clearly: "Enter. I want to talk to you, Tex Ewalt."

Tex lounged forward a step, bringing himself into view, his face the picture of mischievous amusement. He rested his arms on the sill and smiled at her. "You are a good guesser," he admitted.

"Enter," she insisted. "Not the door, no; the window-hurry."

He slipped through with the suppleness of a naked Indian and she at once shut out the night at this and the other windows. "We must beware more eaves-droppers," she explained. She motioned to a bench and seated herself near him, looking at him intently.

"I think you kill Fritz' father that night," she began. "I am sorry."

Tex bowed, as if such unjust suspicions were his daily portion, and waited.

"You are M'sieu Peters' friend?" she questioned.

Tex carefully poked two depressions in the crown of his hat and carefully poked them out again, thinking swiftly. "Yes," he replied, meeting her eyes again.

"You are Tex Ewalt. Dave call you Comin'. M'sieu Peters not know you are here. You spy for M'sieu Peters, yes?"

"Buck told you, eh? Did you tell him I was in Twin River?"

She shook her head. "But no. I guess, when I see you at the window."

Tex looked incredulous. "How did you guess?" he asked.

Rose reviewed the incidents from which she had drawn her conclusion. Tex was impressed. "That's not guessing. That's pure reason," he declared.

"You will tell M'sieu Peters about the itch?" she inquired eagerly.

"Why don't you tell him? I can't risk going out to the ranch."

"No! No! Dave must not suspect. You tell him quick so Dave not think it is me."

"Why, Dave is in a hole. Harris will squeal the minute I put my fingers on him."

"He will suspect. He must not-Oh! you do not understand."

Tex indented his hat on the left side; that was Dave: then on the right side; that was Buck: then, with careful precision, in the middle of the crown; that was Rose. He studied the result with thoughtful attention. "Like Dave?" he inquired, casually.

"I —" she began with passionate intensity but paused. "No," she answered, more calmly.

"No," repeated Tex. He smoothed out the left-hand depression with an air of satisfaction. "That 's good," he continued, "because I shall have to put a crimp, a very serious crimp, in his anatomy one of these days. I can feel it coming. What do you think of Buck?"

"M'sieu Peters is a good man —a good man," she repeated, dreamily. Tex glanced at her and back at his hat, which he eyed malevolently. Then he sighed. "Oh, well, every man has to find it out for himself," was his irrelevant comment. "Where does Schatz stand in this?"

"Dave say he try to get back the range. But Dave he is so much a liar."

"Yes, I should say he was a pretty good liar. Well, I 'll be going."

"But no!" she exclaimed. "You must eat supper," and she began hastily to make preparations.

"You did n't offer Dave any," suggested Tex, with a ghost of a grin.

"No," she admitted, seriously. "Sometimes I must, but to-night it is not necessary. I am glad, always, to see him go."

"Well, so am I," agreed Tex. "Here, let me do that."

Tex learned much during the meal that went to confirm the suspicions he had already formed. Also his opinions in regard to women-kind in general seemed less plausible than before. But though shaken, they were not routed; and when he took up his hat in leaving, the two dimples in it looked at him mockingly. "Oh, well, what's the use?" he said. "Good-night, Miss LaFrance," and he threw the hat on his head as it was.

Chapter XII
A Hidden Enemy

Cock Murray had an engagement to meet Schatz at the point where the Double Y's north line touched the Black Jack, and after he had ridden up to the south line to see how the cows were doing, as Buck had ordered, he swung west to the Black Jack to follow it down to the meeting place. As he rode he neared the Hog Back, a vast upheaval of rock, not high enough to be called a mountain, flat on the top except for hollows and gullies, scantily covered with grass and stunted trees. The Hog Back would have been called a mesa in the South, for want of a better name, though it was no more a mesa than it was a mountain. A mile long and a third of that across at its widest point, it made an effective natural barrier between the Double Y and the river, hiding a pasture of great acreage which lay between it and the precipitous cliff which frowned down upon the rushing, swishing Black Jack eighty feet below. While the round-up would, of course, comb this poor-grass part of the range for outlaws and strays, the outfit never gave it any attention because cattle seldom were found upon it.

Cock Murray, knowing that he had an hour to spare, and fond of hard riding where his skill was called into play, suddenly decided to ascend the Hog Back. Antelope were still to be found even on the range itself, along the wildest part of the south line, and he might get a shot at one if he made the climb. It was an easy task to go up the northern end, where the trail arose in a succession of steep grades; but he had no time for that and guided his pony up the rough, rocky east wall. As he gained the top he rested the horse while he looked around. It was a favorite view of his; below him lay the range and the river; he could see, on a clear day, the dot that represented his ranch house; and to the west and south lay the wild, rolling range of the Cyclone. Gradually his gaze sought nearer objects and he thought of antelope. Moving forward cautiously he kept keen watch on all sides, intending if he caught sight of one, to dismount and stalk it on foot. He had ridden nearly to the northern end when he jerked his pony to a stand, and then, gazing earnestly ahead a short distance, went on as rapidly as the broken ground would permit.

"Dead cows! What 'n h —l killed 'em? Wolves would clean 'em to the bone. G'wan, you fool!" he growled at his mount. "Scared of dead cows, are you! If you are, I 've got the cure for it right here on my heel."

The horse went on, picking its footing, and soon Murray whistled in surprise: "Cyclone brand! Bet they 've got the itch, too. Yep! Died from it, by G —d! Now, how the blazes did they get over here! Cows, and sick ones especially, don't hanker to swim the Jack. Well, that will hold over a little-let 's see how many are up here" —and he began the search. Four were all he could find, two alive and two dead. The two that still stumbled weakly in search of food, dropped as if struck by lightning as the acrid gray smoke sifted past Murray's head. "Wonder how many more there was and where they went to? Must have been here some time, judging by the carcasses. Holy smoke! If any cows gone as bad as these are loose on our range may the Lord pity *us*! Come on, bronc; we 'll see what Schatz thinks about it. Wish I had time to build a fire over these itch farms."

He was careful to guide his horse on ground barren of vegetation and not let brush or grass touch the animal when he could avoid it. As he plunged down the steep northern trail, a dried water course, he reined up hard, looking closely at the tracks in the soft alluvial soil washed down by the last rain. "Must have been about a dozen; perhaps a few less-then some did get where we don't want them-holy cats! as if we have n't got enough with our regular calf round-up!"

When he galloped up to the north line he found Schatz waiting for him. "Schatz," he shouted, "I just found four itch cows on the Hog Back. Six or eight are loose on th' ranch. They was Cyclone, an' they never crossed th' Jack by themselves."

"*Mein Gott*! Did you drive dem back?"

"Two was dead; th' other two was so near it I just dropped 'em. They could n't stand a drive even to th' river. Shall I tell Peters?"

"Shall you tell him? *Gewiss*! Vat you t'ink —I vant itch on de Double Vy? How dey come?"

"I don't know. But they must 'a' been driven. Th' Jack is cold as ice an' she runs strong by th' Rocking Horse. That's where th' tracks led to. Cows ain't goin' to swim that for fun. Why, these was all et up with th' itch-wonder they did n't drown."

"*Dank Gott*! Sick cows ain't made vell mit ice vater und schwimmin'. Dey don't lif so long like de vater vas varm. Der shock help kill dem quick."

Murray nodded, his hand resting on his gun, and Schatz noticed it. "*Gewiss*, if dey vas too veak to drive in der river, it vas besser to shoot dem. But ven dey drop dey stay mit all dem parasites. Drivin' dem off de range is besser. *Aber*, you stopped dem de best vay you could."

Murray nodded again. "Yes, yo're right-but I was n't thinkin' of shootin' no cows," he asserted calmly. "I know all about that. But I was just a-wonderin' if I should ketch some skunk of a cow-punch drivin' itch cattle on us, an' shoot him, if he 'd drop any parasites when *he* fell."

"*Ach Gott*! Alvays you shoot, like Dave! Shoot, shoot, shoot! Vy in *Himmel* should you alvays grab dot gun? Brains are in your head, and *besser* as lead in dot Colt. Brains first, and if dey don't do it, den der gun. But alvays der gun should be last. *Verstanden?*"

Murray did not reply and his companion, exchanging a few terse sentences with him, waved him towards the ranch house while he followed the line towards the Little Jill.

Buck was washing for supper when Murray arrived and kept right on with his ablutions as the puncher told his tale. Murray quite expected to see some signs of its effect on the owner, but he met with surprise and looked it. Buck Peters almost made an ally when he turned, after Murray's last word. "Murray, that's good work. Prepare for *hard* work. Send Ned here right away," he said, quietly, no trace of emotion in his voice.

Murray went out, thinking hard. When a man could take such a blow as that one had been taken, then he was clean grit all through. To smile as Buck had done —"By G —d, he 's a man!" swore the puncher. "I can't *help* liking him; wish I did n't have to help throw him. And I wish he did n't trust me like he does-ah, h —l!" he growled, savagely. "He 's a range thief, after all!"

When Monroe entered the ranch house he found his employer looking out of the window in the direction of the Hog Back, but he turned at Ned's entry. "Got work ahead, Ned. Murray found some Cyclone cows dead and wobbly on th' Hog Back. Bad case of itch. He killed th' wobblers but says th' tracks show that about a dozen was in th' herd. That means eight of 'em are on our range among the cattle. Tell th' boys we start th' round-up at daylight. If we can, we 'll make this do for the spring round-up, too; if not, then th' calves 'll have to wait till we can go for 'em. Th' north range won't have no itch cows on it yet, so take th' south first. As fast as we can cut out th' cattle that are free from it, we 'll throw 'em over on th' north range. Begin in th' Hog Back country an' clean up. Drive everything out of it."

"It's d —d funny Cyclone cows swum th' Jack," commented Monroe, a black look on his face. "By G —d, let *me* ketch anybody at that game!"

"That's th' whole thing, Ned," and Buck smiled: "To ketch 'em. I know a man who 'd clean up th' mystery if he was here, an' was told he did n't have nothin' else to do." He smiled again quietly and turned to his supper. "But he ain't here, so what's th' use."

"Mebby I —" suggested Ned, nervously.

"No, yo 're goin' to help me most by curing th' evil on th' table; never mind th' dealer, nor th' game. We 've got as many cards as we 're goin' to get-use 'em, Ned. Help me lick th' itch first-th' hows an' whys can wait."

"Yo 're right, Peters; an' we *will* lick it! But it makes me fightin' mad, a thing like this. I 'll get everything all ready to-night an' th' round-up starts with th' comin' of th' sun to-morrow. Good-night."

Buck ate slowly, his thoughts far more occupied with the problem than with the food. This was the firing of the first cannon in the fight Monroe had predicted. Who was responsible? His suspicions, guided by Monroe's warning, were directed towards Schatz, but in his present absence of knowledge they could advance no farther than suspicions. Dave's half-closed eyes sneered at him as he recalled the ambiguous threat made that first night in the Sweet-Echo: still remained suspicion only. McReady, of the Cyclone, might have designs for the Double Y, but he doubted it. They had yet free grass a-plenty, though the time was not far distant when the private ownership of the Double Y would be an invaluable asset. Still, it might be any other cowman in that part of the country-or none of them. Well, he had met problems as great as this one on the Texan range-but he had fought them with an outfit loyal to the last man, every unit of it willing and eager to face all kinds of odds for him. He now recalled those men to his mind's eye, and he never loved them more than he did now, when he realized how really precious unswerving loyalty is. Hopalong, Red, Johnny and the others of the old Bar-20 outfit, made an honor roll that held his thoughts even to the temporary exclusion of the bitterness of his present situation. If only he had that outfit with him now! Even his neighbors and acquaintances on that southern range were to be trusted and depended upon more than his present outfit. His vision, knocking patiently at first upon the door of his abstraction, at this point kicked its way in and demanded attention. Buck became aware that for some time he had been staring unseeingly at a folded paper, tucked partly under his bunk blanket. With a smothered oath he sprang from his seat, strode to the bunk and snatched up the paper. The warning it contained was better founded than the first. It read:

> "Buck Peters: Itch on the YY. Crossed the Jack at the Rocking Horse. A Friend."

"If you told me who sent it across, you 'd be more of a friend," muttered Buck-in which he was less wise than Tex, who did not see the sense in having the servant removed while the master remained.

Hoofbeats rolled up in the darkness and stopped at the door of the house and a moment later Whitby entered the room, his pink, English complexion aglow with the exercise and wind-beating of his ride.

Buck was glad to see him; he needed a little of the other's cheerful optimism and after a few minutes of random conversation, Buck told him of the latest developments. Whitby's surprise was genuine, and the practicability of his nature asserted itself. This was ground upon which he was thoroughly at home.

"I say, Buck, we can show these swine a thing or two they don't know," he began. "They don't know it in the States, I 'll lay, nor north of the line either, for that matter. My Governor is a cattle man, you might say; on the other side of the pond, of course. And I 've knocked about farm land a good bit, you know. Now a chap in the same county had a lot of sheep with this what-d'you-call it-scab, they said. He used a preparation of arsenic but a lot of the beggars died, poisoned, you know. He had tried a number of other things and he got jolly well tired of the game; so he wrote to a cousin, chemist or something, and told him about it; and this chap sent him a recipe, after a bit, that killed off the parasites like winking, without injuring a single sheep."

"That ain't goin' to help us none, Whit. You ain't got th' receipt an' you don't know how to make th' stuff."

"Ah! But I do though. I gave him a hand with the silly beggars and bally good fun it was, too. We passed them through a long trough and ducked their heads under as fast as they came along. But it was work, no end, mixing the solution. There was nothing funny about that part of it."

"See here, Whit, are you really in earnest? Do you think you can make the stuff and show us how to use it?"

"Absolutely certain, dear boy. Cattle are n't sheep, but I 'll be bound it 'll do the trick."

"How fast can you run 'em though?"

Whitby reflected. "We could do a thousand a day, perhaps more. It depends on how many you do at once, you know." And Whitby went into a detailed description to which Buck gave close attention. At the end he shook his head. "Reckon we 'll have to stick to th' old way," he adjudged, regretfully. "There ain't that quantity of lime and sulphur in all Montana."

"Ah, yes; your point is good," drawled Whitby, smiling. "But your partner lives in Chicago where there is any quantity of it. If we wired him to-morrow to get the stuff and ship it at once he would do it, don't you know."

"Take it too long to get here," replied Buck, gloomily.

"Don't you think the railroad will see that such an important consignment gets off and comes through quickly, especially if the consignor is willing to pay the damage? I 'll bet you a good cigar it will be here within a week after we wire. Let *me* send the wire and I 'll bet you a box. I 'm bally good at wires. I used to get money out of the Governor by wire when I could get it no other way."

"Let her go," said Buck. "If it's all you say we 'll show them coyotes we know a few tricks ourselves."

"Yes, I fancy we shall," replied Whitby. "But isn't this a rummy game? They act like savages, you know. It is all very refreshing to a sated mind-and their justice is so deuced direct, right or wrong. Fancy Blackstone in the discard, as you Americans say, and a Colt's revolver sovereign lord of the realm!"

"King Colt is all right, Whitby, when you *know* who to loose him at," declared Buck, turning toward the door to the kitchen. "Jake! Jake!" he called.

The sharp, incisive tones told their story and brought buoyancy to the cook, for he was on his feet, across the kitchen, and into the dining-room in apparently one movement, which astounded the soul of that culinary devotee when leisure gave time for reflection.

"Why, Jake, I believe yo 're gettin' to be almost a human, livin' creature," remarked Buck. "I never saw you move so fast before. It ain't pay day now, you know."

"Shore I know, but next *week is*," grinned Jake, not quite catching the meaning.

"Oh, I 'm glad you do," sighed Buck with relief. "Now as long as you ain't sufferin' no hallucernations, suppose you tell Ned to come in here. You need n't tell *him* —he knows it ain't, too."

"Knows what ain't?" demanded Jake, his fingers slowly ploughing through his mass of hair. "If I need n't tell him, what do you want me to tell him for?"

"Be calm, Jake, be calm," replied Buck, raising a warning finger. "There are *two* tells in this; one you must, th' other you need n't."

"Ah, go to h —l an' tell him yourself," retorted Jake, backing toward a handy chair so as not to be without a weapon.

"You tell Ned I want to see him —I 'll explain th' second tell later. Now —*Will* y'u tell?"

Jake backed into the kitchen, slammed shut the door behind him, and lost no time in getting to the bunkhouse.

"Hey, Ned," he blurted out, "th' boss says to tell you he wants to see you. Th' second tell can wait till later. William Tell?"

"What t'ell!" snorted Bow-Wow, arising.

"You another?" demanded the cook; then he fled, Ned following more leisurely.

Bow-Wow looked at Murray inquiringly: "What did he mean by William Tell?"

Murray put down his mended riding gear. "Why, don't you know?"

"Shore; what is it?" sarcastically responded Bow-Wow. "If I knew, do you think I 'd tell?"

"Well I know, all right. It's what he was brought up on, Bow-Wow."

"Huh! Did you know him when he was a kid?"

"Shore! He used to live in th' next street in th' same town, or was it in some other town?" he mused, thoughtfully. "H —l, that don't make no difference, 'cause he lived in th' next street. See?"

"No; I don't; not a d —d bit!"

"Bow-Wow, if I was as thick as you get sometimes, I 'd drink lots of water an' thin down a bit. This is th' story of William Tell, an' I 'll tell it to you if you won't tell: When he was a kid he had a awful yearnin' for apples, like you has for cheap whiskey, Bow-Wow. Nothin' else suited him an' th' bigger he got th' more apples he had to eat. All th' farmers was a-layin' for him with guns, so what did li'l Willie do? Why, he shot 'em down with a bow an' arrer. An' that's why he can throw a stone so straight to-day. *Now* do you see?"

Bow-Wow threw a shoe after Murray's departing figure and suggested a place to go to. Then he scowled and muttered: "If I was shore of what I suspects I 'd give you a sample of *my* shootin', *six* samples so you 'd appreciate the real thing." He grinned at the memory of Jake's message.

"You 'll say somethin' with sense in it some day if you gropes long enough, Jake. Yo 're gettin' warmer all th' time."

When Monroe reached the ranch house Buck met him with some sharp orders: "Send Bow-Wow to Twin River and Wayback first thing to-morrow. Tell him to leave word we want two dozen more punchers for our round-up —fifty dollars a month an' a full month's work guaranteed. Jake 's goin' to dig some big holes in th' ground in th' next few days-he ain't fit for nothin' else, not even cookin'."

A crash in the kitchen interrupted him. "Jake!" he called. There was a scramble and the cook appeared, much excited. "What's th' fuss about?"

"Fell off my chair," replied Jake. "An' it hurts, too."

"Yo 're gettin' too soft, Jake. A little exercise 'll toughen you so a chair would n't dare to tackle you. I 'm goin' to let you dig some holes first thing to-morrow."

Jake had visions of extensive excavations, dug by him, into which thousands of dead cows were being piled for burial. "Would n't it be better to burn 'em, or push 'em into th' river an' shoot 'em there?"

"I never saw holes you could handle that way, Jake," gravely replied Buck.

"Why, no," supplemented the foreman. "Most holes would ruther be slit up th' middle an' salted. That's th' way we allus used to get rid of 'em."

"I don't mean holes —I mean *cows*!" explained Jake.

"Oh, then it 's all right," responded Buck. "I ain't goin' to ask *you* to dig no cows, Jake. But yo 're goin' to dig some nice ditches to-morrow; long, deep ones, an' good an' wide."

"I ain't never dug a ditch in my life," hastily objected Jake.

"Why, did n't you tell me how you dug that railroad cut down there in Iowa, an' got a hundred dollars extra 'cause you saved th' company so much money?" inquired Buck.

"Oh, but that was a steam shovel!"

"All right; you 'll steam afore yo 're at it very long."

Jake backed out again, slipped out of his kitchen, and stood reflective under the stars. He would quit and flee to Twin River if it was n't such a long walk. "D —n it!" he growled, and forthwith threw two stones into the darkness by way of getting rid of some of his anger.

"Sa-a-y!" floated a voice out of the night. "You jerk any more rocks in *this* direction an' I 'll beat you up so you 'll wipe your feet on yoreself, thinkin' yo 're a doormat! What 'n h —l you mean, anyhow?"

"Mebby they 's *apples*!" jeered Bow-Wow from the bunk-house. "Hello, William Tell!"

The cook softly closed the door and propped a chair against it. "Gee whiskers! I ain't goin' to stay *here* much longer! *Every*body 's gettin' crazy!"

" 'If a body meets a body, comin' through th' rye,'" quavered a voice from the corral and a voice in the darkness profaned the song: "Ever meet yoreself goin' t'other way, after surroundin' th' rye?"

"Never had that pleasure after you 'd been at th' booze."

Chesty Sutton entered the bunk-house and stared at Bow-Wow. "What's eatin' you?" he demanded, curiously.

"I dunno; I 've been itchin' ever since Murray told us. Wonder if I 've got it?"

Chesty considered: "Well, now I remember that chickens, cats, and dogs don't get cattle itch. You ain't got it, Bow-Wow. It 's yore imagination that's got it. But if you 're bound to scratch, do it somewhere else-you make me nervous, keepin' on one spot so long. Wait till I asks th' boys about it."

"Stop!" snapped Bow-Wow, his hand on a bottle of harness oil: "You never mind about askin' anybody! I 'll take yore word for it-remember, I 'll bust yore gizzard if you gets that pack o' coyotes barkin' at my heels!"

"Holy Smoke! We 'll have our hands full a while," growled Chesty, dropping onto a box. "Let any o' this crowd ketch anybody throwin' mangy cows over on us! An' right after it comes th' Spring combin' —this is shore a weary world."

"Jake 's got to dig some ditches," remarked the foreman, entering the house, and immediately the misery of future hours was forgotten in the merriment and satisfaction found in this news. Jake would have a lot of advisers.

In the ranch house Whitby was laughing gently and finally he voiced a wish: "I say, Peters, what a wealth of character there is out here. I wish Johnnie Beauchamp were here-what a rattling good play he could make. You know, Johnnie's last play was almost a success-and I 'm very much interested in him. I backed him to the tune of two thousand pounds."

Invited to spend the night in the ranch house, Whitby accepted with alacrity. In carrying out McAllister's wishes he could not be too near headquarters, he concluded; but added to this, he entertained a sincere admiration for Buck Peters which increased as the days went by.

Some few minutes after the lights were out, Buck was brought back from the shadowy realm of sleep by Whitby's voice coming from the other room. "I say, Peters, did you keep those calculations?"

"Yes," answered Buck. "Why?"

"There 's the lumber, you know. It might be a good idea to have McAllister send it on."

"Shore would. You tell him."

"I will," promised Whitby. A few seconds later he broke out again: "Do you know, Buck, the railroad companies of America are cheerful beggars. They take your luggage and then play ducks and drakes with it, in a very idiotic way. Why, mine was lost for two weeks and I was in a very devil of a fix. So it would not be a bad idea, you know, if I tell your partner to send a man with the consignment. He can sit on the barrels and see that they are n't placed on a siding to prove the theory that loss of movement results in inertia. Am I right?"

Buck laughed from his heart. "If there 's anything you don't think of make a note of it an' let me see it," he commended.

"What a rummy remark. I say, how-ha! ha!" and Whitby's bunk creaked to his mirth. "That's rather a neat one, you know! I did n't know you were Irish, Peters, blessed if I did! I must tell that to your man Friday-it will keep the bally ass combing his frowsy locks for a week."

Buck had one foot on the Slumberland boundary when he heard the voice again, seeming to have travelled a long distance: "And I believe I should be rewarded for my brilliancy. I 'll ask your partner to send some brandy and a box of *good* cigars with the rest of it as my fee. I 'll have to learn to smoke all over again," he complained drowsily. A raucous snore bounced off the partition and Whitby opened his eyes for a moment: "My word, if Friday could only cook as well as he snores!"

Chapter XIII
Punctuation as a Fine Art

Twin River was in full blast when Dave rode in, looking for Tex. He dropped off the pony and went into the Why-Not, but his man was not there; after a few unavoidable drinks-Dave could not have avoided one if it had invited from the middle of the Staked Plain-he looked in at Ike's and the I-Call. He sampled the liquor in both places but evidently Comin' Thirty was not in that part of the town and he jogged on up to the Sweet-Echo. He had not been in here since warned off by Slick, but fear of consequences had nothing to do with absenting himself; fear did not enter into his composition. Dave's fundamental fault lay in his hatred of being beaten. It had lead him to cheat at play; to outwit by foul means; to take the sure course to any desired end, deliberately regardless of what any one might think. The danger of such actions did not deter him in the least; he was always ready, usually overwhelmingly ready, to back them up in any manner his opponents demanded of him. The defeat, sure to be met when he opposed a superior intelligence, he confidently relied upon overcoming by sheer force of personality, mistaking violence for strength, deceit for ingenuity. The bad judgment of his failures ever wore the mantle of bad luck; and the thought and time he wasted in schemes for revenge might have been used more profitably in making success of his failure.

Since his employment by Schatz his mind had been fully occupied by the furtherance, as he considered it, of his employer's plan. Buck Peters, the Englishman, even Slick, at times pricked his memory, but he had resolutely put them aside until a more convenient season. Now, with whiskey spurring his Satanic temperament, he considered it obligatory to go into the Sweet-Echo. He wanted to find Comin' and no fancy bar-keep' nor roaring Scotchman should keep him from going wherever he wanted to go. He stepped from his stirrup onto the porch and went into the bar-room as if he owned it.

The expected trouble did not develop. Slick gave him a short nod and set up glass and bottle with praise-worthy promptitude. If Dave was without fear, so was Slick, who would have taken him on in any way whatever; preferably, as became his Irish ancestry, with his hands, but failing that, with anything from a pop-gun to a cannon. Dave, with his usual habit of ignoring the other man, imagined Slick to be overawed; this leavened his savagery with good nature. What was Slick Milligan, anyhow? Just a bar-keep'—Dave turned his back to the bar and surveyed the inmates of the room. Comin' was not there. Where in thunder was he?

Maybe bucking the tiger at Little Nell's. Dave had two or three drinks with men he knew and rode back to cross the ford. He was again out in his reckoning. He watched the cards flick from the box. Nell, herself, was dealing and Dave's fingers itched to get down, but he refrained. With the vague hints dropped by Schatz and his consequent hope of speedily winning Rose, he knew he must drop gambling-until he had won to the fulfilment of his desires, at least.

As he watched he suddenly realized he was hungry and strolled into the eating house, run by Nell as a paying adjunct to her other businesses. The whiskey, as it often does in healthy stomachs, was calling loudly for food and Dave answered the call with unstinted generosity. Being genuinely wishful to see Tex he did not linger but, as soon as finished, started to make the round again.

He got no farther than the Why-Not. His entry was met by a roar of laughter and shouts of encouragement: "Bully f' you, gran'pa!"—"Did he ever come back?"—"That's th' caper, Dirty!"—"*Let* him alone, *he* ain't chokin'."

Seated on a box on the top of a table (Dirty would be buried in a box; they would never have the heart to separate his attenuated figure from the object so long associated with it in life), old Pop Snow bent up and down, shrinking, shrinking, until his bony leanness threatened to vanish before their gaze; a wheezing gasp started him swelling again and his "he! he! he!" whistled above the uproar like a hiss in a machine shop.

He was astonishingly drunk-for Dirty. His pervious clay had developed innumerable channels for alcohol in the years of training he had given it; and he was seldom so joyously hilarious as this. For one reason it was seldom that any one would pay for it, and Dirty's means only went far enough to keep him everlastingly thirsty. The explanation appeared to Dave in the shape of a group of miners, whose voices, in their appreciation, were the loudest.

"He-he-he! He-he-he-he!" Pop Snow's shrill pipe continued, while the others demanded more. "Sawbones had n't been gone a week afore he was wanted. He-he-he! eh, dear! eh, dear! Lucky Jones come along-an' stopped. Ther' wearn't nothin' *to* do but stop. He comes to me an' he says: 'Wheer 's ther' a doctor?' 'Well,' I says, 'jedgin' from what I hears, if you jest foller th' river north fur about fifteen mile to Drigg's Worry,' I says, 'you 'll find a saw-bones as used to be yer-but when he left he swears as how he ain't never comin' back to th' P'int,' I says.

He-he-he! Send-I-may-live if he don't, though. Yep, an' Jones purty nigh goes into th' wet, too. 'Th' P'int?' roars th' Doc, 'No, siree, by G —d, no, sir! Twenty-eight mile th' last time to tend a stinkin' ole sow, on account o' a misbegotten son o' Beelzebub an th' North Pole they call Snow down there. This time I 'spose 't'ud be a skunk.' 'It's my wife,' says Jones, 'an' if yuh don't come right sudden I 'm a-goin' to blow off th' top o' yore devilish ole head,' says Jones; 'an' if she dies,' he sez, 'I blows her off, anyhow.' He-he-he! Saw-bones, he riz up an' come a-kitin'. I ain't much on Welshmen; they biles over too easy. But Saw-bones done a good job an' got away wi' his life. We hears all about it nex' day when Jones comes to me an' tells me it is two at once, boy an' a girl. Fust we knowed he 'd brung his wife. Not as she stays long. Winter 's one too many fur her an' she cashes in. Then Lucky Jones, he tries to cross th' river below th' P'int, 'stid o' th' ford, an' th' ice ain't strong enough, an' Jones, he was some drunk, I reckon. We calls th' river after him an' th' forks after th' kids. Lord, they was bad uns, both on 'em. Black Jack, he hez hisself hung for suthin' or other, an' Little Jill, she turns out just a plain —"

Every one jumped, it was so unexpected. The lead sung so close to Dirty's nose that the backward jerk almost took him off the table and he recovered his seat with a sideways wriggle and squirm that did credit to the elasticity of his aged muscles. Having managed to retain his seat, he continued to retain it. None of the others showed the least desire to move, though every last man of them yearned for absence-sudden, noiseless absence-of a kind so instantaneous as to preclude the possibility of notice: anything less were foolhardy in the face of those blazing eyes and that loosely held gun, its business end oscillating like the head of a snake and far more deadly.

"Don't be afeared, Dirty," purred Dave, in the kindliest tones. "I was jest a-puttin' in th' period. Yore eddication is shameful, Dirty, an' I grieves for you, account of it. You has a generous mixture o' commas an' semi-commas an' things like that, but yore periods is shore some scarce. You was a-sayin' as how Little Jill was a sweet, good gal, as never done wrong in her life, was n't you?"

Dirty swallowed hard and nodded. Speech was beyond him just then and perhaps he had spoken too much, already. He repeated his former contortion with equal skill and success, and every head in the crowd rose perceptibly and returned to its former level as the gun spoke again and another hole appeared in the wall, close to the first.

"A period comes after that, Dirty," said Dave. "Don't you never forget th' kind o' gal she was-an' then comes th' period. You 'll mebby hold yore liquor better." He shoved the gun back in the holster, eyed the crowd insolently for a moment, and turning his back on it, walked calmly from the room.

Pop Snow climbed down from the table in haste and pushed his way through the detaining arms and the medley of questions that assailed him on his way to the door, which opened and closed like a stage trap as he stepped out and sprang to one side; his anger was that of a sober and far younger man and he peered about with keen eyes. His caution was uncalled for: Dave was splashing through the ford and Dirty watched him set out in a swift lope along the Big Moose trail. Dave had no stomach for further company that night.

Dirty rubbed a pair of trembling lips as he gazed. "Black Jack!" he muttered, "Black Jack! He *warn't* hung, then. No, an' he won't never be 'less it's fur killin' pore ole Pop Snow. Pore ole Pop Snow," he repeated, whimpering as he hurried across the bridge toward shelter; "Jest like Dutch Onion. Dead an' gone, pore ole Dutch. Pore ole Pop." He stopped in the middle of the trail and with a flash of his former spirit, shook his fist after the distant Dave: "Shell I?" he jeered: "shell I, then? I been yer afore you, Jack, an' I 'll be a-livin' when you rot."

Hoofbeats coming out of the darkness where Dave had disappeared, startled him and he scuttled away like a rabbit.

Chapter XIV

Fighting the Itch

Monroe and the three men left to him after Bow-Wow had departed for Twin River and Way-back, in the company of Whitby, were too small a force to attempt the round-up, so they put in the day riding over those sections of the range farthest removed from the Hog Back, examining every cow they found. At nightfall they had the pleasure of reporting to Buck that the entire portion of the range along the Little Jill, extending from the river to the middle of the ranch, was free from infection; as a matter of fact the conclusion reached in council was that only that portion of range bounded by the Black Jack, the south line, and Blackfoot Creek needed to be cleaned up. This meant that two-thirds of the ranch was free from the itch, and the infected third contained less than a fourth of the Double Y cows.

Plans for the round-up were considered and soon arrived at. All the men with the exception of three, were to be actively engaged in the round-up. They were to start from the south line and drive northwest towards the Hog Back. The Black Jack made a natural barrier on the west and would hold the herd safely on that side. The three other punchers were to ride even with the drive line, but on the other side of Blackfoot Creek, and keep ambitious cows from crossing onto the non-infected portions of the range. This arrangement would constantly force the cattle onto the wedge-shaped range at the juncture of the two waters. Here the herd could be dipped and driven across the shallow Blackfoot onto a clean territory, where they would be held for further observation. Then if the rest of the range showed signs of infection the round-up and dipping could be carried on again at other points. If a strict line could be maintained along the Blackfoot the Hog Back range would be fenced off effectually from the non-infected cattle on the other parts of the ranch. The question of building an actual fence to separate the Hog Back range from the rest was gone into thoroughly and the decision was unanimous that twelve miles of fence was too big a proposition to be attempted at that moment; if necessary it could be put up later when it was found that patrolling the creek was inadvisable. But perhaps a side light can be thrown on this quiet decision when it is remembered how fervently a cowman hated fences. These men were all of the old school and preferred to keep barb-wire as a theory and not a fact.

That evening Bow-Wow returned with a crowd of cow-punchers of varying degrees of fitness, all eager to take cards in any game at fifty dollars a month. The majority of them were not up to the standards Buck cherished; if they had been, they would not have been waiting for a job. But it was certain they knew how to punch cows, enough for the demands of the moment-and Jake waxed eloquent and sarcastic when he hazarded a guess as to when they had eaten their last square meal. Perhaps, after all, digging huge ditches would not be so bad, for cooking three meals a day for twenty-odd hungry men was more of a task than he cared to tackle. But Bow-Wow had exercised some intelligence of his own, as after events showed. Two of his squad were ex-cooks. The "ex" is used advisedly, for if ever cooks were "ex" it was these two; this was the decision voiced simultaneously by twenty hungry men at the first meal prepared by the two. Sam Hawkins suggested that they had quit cooking to save their lives, and regretted that they had so made their choice.

The drive went ahead without more than the usual bluster and confusion, and the end of the first day found the round-up well under way. Outlying free range had been thoroughly combed, in which assistance had been given by neighboring ranches; Buck, in carrying out his policy of supplying his own help, had not failed to notify other owners and foremen that they could rely on the Double Y for its contingent of men when the general round-up should take place. The drivers were divided into two squads for day work and three for night riding around the herd; the two-squad arrangement was made for meal times, one squad eating while the other worked. There was no time lost at meals because each of the ex-cooks, in a chuck wagon alloted to him, preceded the drive and was never very far from the field of operations. Thus were system and order gained the first day, which meant time saved in the end.

Buck intended to spend his nights in the ranch house as usual, and when he gained it the first night he found two things of interest. The first announced itself by sending him to his hands and knees within three feet of his front door; the second was a telegram from McAllister saying that a special had the right of way, and from the wording Buck could see it pounding into the Northwest, over crossings and past switch towers, its careening red tail lights bearing a warning to would-be range-jumpers if they did but know it. The message further stated that the consignment was under the personal attention of a puncher who, having grown sick of the stock yards, was cheerfully availing himself of the opportunity of getting back to the open range at no expense. Buck sighed with relief as he realized that the ingredients of the dip were already on the way, and could not be sidetracked or lost without the subduing of a very irritable cow-puncher. As he put the message away he remembered the first thing that had impressed itself on him, and went out to take a look at it.

The light in his hand revealed the sodless strip fifty feet long and four feet wide. Its depth was to the under side of the grass, a matter of two or three inches. There was a stake at each corner of the bare rectangle and these supported a one-strand fence made of lariats.

Buck scratched his head and then growled a profane request to feel the head of the man who was responsible. He strode into the house and stopped in the kitchen door; and Jake very wearily turned around on his chair and looked at him with intent curiosity.

"What 'n h —l is that scalped grass for?" demanded Buck, evenly.

"That's th' beginnin' of ditch number one," replied Jake. "How 'd you like them lines, eh? Straight as a die. Took me all mornin' to lay 'em out like that."

"Did it? I congratulate you, Jake-likewise I sympathize with you. I reckon you 'll get it down a foot in a couple o' weeks, eh?"

"Oh, quicker'n that," modestly rejoined Jake.

"Did n't I tell you to dig them ditches close to where th' Blackfoot empties into th' Jack?" demanded Buck. "Are you figgerin' on extendin' it from here to there? I don't want a trench no fifteen miles long. To-morrow mornin' you ride with me an' I 'll show you where to dig. An' don't you bother stakin' it off exact, neither. I want them ditches all finished in *three* days. Did you reckon I was goin' to drive two thousand head of itch cows fifteen miles so I could dip 'em bang up agin my own front door!"

Pickles bounced in, his rifle under his arm. "Hullo, Buck!" he cried. "Shot a coyote to-day!"

"Good, Pickles," smiled Buck. "Want a job shootin' a *man* to-morrow?"

"Betcher life! Is it Dave?"

"No, it's Jake, here," replied Buck. "You take yore rifle an' come with me an' Jake to-morrow. If he don't dig fast enough to suit you, you shoot him in th' laig."

"Betcher life! Which leg?" asked Pickles, agog with anticipation.

"I 'm leavin' that to you, Pickles. You 're gettin' big enough to figger things out for yoreself."

"Will he limp like Hopalong?"

"Worse, mebby."

Jake, grinning, feared Pickles might be carried away with his zeal, and he put in a laughing objection; but he sobered instantly at Buck's sharp reply.

"I mean it. He 'll shoot if he 's a friend o' mine. I ain't goin' to lose a lot of cows 'cause I 've got a man too lazy to dig. You 've got yore orders, Pickles: obey 'em like a real Bar-20 puncher."

"Betcher life I will. Just like Hopalong Cassidy!"

Jake groaned at the intense earnestness in Pickles' declaration; to emulate the great Hopalong Cassidy was enduring honor in Pickles' eyes, and from past performances and several duels with the boy, Jake reached the conclusion that he was slated to do some very rapid digging on the morrow.

"Lemme use *yore* rifle, Buck!" asked Pickles, his eyes shining with the joy of living. He knew he could do a great deal better with Buck's repeater, and the thought of exploding .45-70 cartridges was a delight beyond his wildest dreams.

Jake's heart stopped for the reply and he sighed with relief as Pickles' face fell; but the boy's spirits rose like a balloon. "All right, Buck; I can get him with my gun, though I ought to have a repeater."

The round-up went forward swiftly and the day that McAllister's special puffed into Wayback and snorted onto the siding, found the Hog Back country swept clean of cattle, the herd being held close to Jake's two big ditches. Buck had known the magnitude of the task he set for Jake and when the cook showed he was anxious to do his share of the work, Buck had told off men enough to help him get through in time. The digging was hard and unaccustomed work and the men were changed frequently, all but Jake; he seemed to consider it a matter of pride to stick to the job and made a point of throwing the last shovelful of dirt as well as the first; as a consequence his altitude was below normal for a week afterwards, and it was a month before he forgot to grunt with every breath.

The hauling of the lumber exercised the ingenuity and strained the resources of Jean LaFrance, the only man in the locality who possessed anything on wheels capable of carrying it. Inasmuch as he could ill spare the time, although sorely needing the money, it exhausted Jean's stock of oaths to the point where his own language failed him; even English, which he understood, seemed singularly tame and unworthy the occasion; so that he fell back on his carefully reserved specimens of German expletives, which he did not in the least understand, and these with constant repetitions carried him through. Two men, driving the two borrowed chuck wagons, succeeded in transporting the rest of the shipment, and Whitby, to his great satisfaction, found that McAllister had not forgotten his fee.

The junction of the Blackfoot with the Jack presented a busy scene. The close-packed blue-clay, which had made hard work for the diggers, now proved a help, the timbers fitting snug without backing. Meanwhile the more important part, the preparing of the solution, went on under the direction of Whitby; his calm handling and frequent active coöperation without becoming warm or soiled was a wonder to see. Under the huge caldrons, which had been the first of the consignment to arrive, wood had been piled ready for the match; on bases made of logs stood rows of whiskey barrels; shallow troughs were filled and re-filled with water until the swelling wood took up and became water-tight. Far into the night they worked, and now the crackling fires were giving the night shift trouble with the snorting cattle. Weird shadows darted out over the ground, lengthened and vanished as the men moved about the fires, worked over the lime-slaking troughs or poured off the compound paste into the steaming caldrons. When the barrels were filled with the first lot of the mixture, Whitby relented and the men stumbled off to rest.

With the dawn they were at work again; and now the dipping troughs came into use as the saturated solution was drawn off from the barrels, leaving the sediment at the bottom, and dumped into the troughs, where water was added to reduce it to the required strength. Night was approaching again before the water arose to nearly the required level; the men were thoroughly tired and Whitby, reluctantly and as a result of a direct order from Buck, called a halt. Buck knew the temper of his men better than Whitby: at anything directly connected with range duties, provided they were familiar with it, they would work until they dropped; but this was something whose usefulness remained to be proven. Buck was too wise to push them in such a case, but he grinned cheerfully as he turned away from the reluctance on Whitby's face. The Britisher was surely a glutton for work.

The prudence of Buck's reasoning was shown by the eagerness with which the men responded to the call next morning. In less than an hour Whitby announced all ready and the men entered upon a scene which they individually and collectively swore repaid them for their trouble. At Whitby's shout, two of the men riding herd cut out the first bunch of cattle and drove them toward the dipping trough; the flimsily constructed horse corral swarmed with laughing, joking punchers who roped their mounts with more or less success in the first attempt, while outside the wranglers darted forward and back, wheeling on a pie dish, checking the more ambitious of the ponies that resented a confinement limited to a single line of lariats; saddles dropped onto recalcitrant backs and were cinched with a speed nothing short of marvellous to a layman, and the whooping punchers were jerked away to the herd.

The first lot of cows, some twenty in number, flirting their tails and snorting in angry impotence, entered the wide opening between a wedge-shaped pair of fences and galloped toward the narrow vent which led to the trough. And now was seen Buck's wisdom in continuing the fence along the edge of the troughs a few feet, both at entrance and exit: the first brute, a magnificent three-year-old, appeared to realize the crush that would come and spurted for the opening; the significance of the situation did not appeal to him until he was close to the edge; he slid to the very brink and gathered himself for a leap, but the fence was too high; the next instant the cattle behind, urged on by Cock Murray, whooping like an Indian, bumped into the hesitating brute and he fell forward into the trough with a bellow of rage and started on his swim to the other end.

When Cock Murray, with Slow Jack close behind, had followed the bunch between the fences, they were assailed by a chorus of shouts to which they paid no heed whatever. Slow Jack, being in the rear, caught a glimpse out of the tail of his eye of Whitby running and waving his arms; he looked around for the cause of so much excitement and was in time to see the second bunch, instead of being driven over to the other trough as they should have been, come thundering into the wedge and drive down upon him. Slow Jack shot up to the fence, threw one leg along the neck of his pony and skimmed through the opening he made for, with nothing to spare and a scratched saddle; after which he spent several profane seconds in telling the chaffing drivers what he thought of them. His annoyance was forgotten when they suddenly doubled up, shrieking with laughter, and pointed toward the shoot.

Slow Jack looked and then looked at them. The second bunch had gone galloping madly on to the narrow opening, against which they were wedged and dropping one by one as a third bunch pressed in after them. They were coming too rapidly and Ned Monroe, riding past from the other trough, was sending the next bunch in the proper direction and going on to the herd to put some sense of order into the heads of the rollicking punchers. Slow Jack quite failed to see anything funny in all this and said so with force and directness; he added, moreover, a prophecy regarding idiots, the fulfilment of which was due to take place in the near, in fact immediate, future, which threatened complete derangement of the internal economy of said idiots. The idiots were entirely oblivious. Jack was puzzled. He glanced ahead and noticed a lot more idiots. Disgusted with his vain attempt to get an explanation, he rode forward to see for himself.

Cock Murray, having quirted the last of the first bunch into the trough, became aware of the shouting, gesticulating men who had left their duties to run toward the fence to attract his attention. In the cross-fire of warnings he failed to understand any of them, but the rumbling rush behind brought him suddenly to a realization of his position. One glance and he saw it was too late to retreat. There was just one thing to do. "Holy mackerel!" gasped Cock. He put the quirt to his pony in a frenzy of blows and landed in the dipping mixture with a jump that carried his pony's feet to the bottom of the trough. Sputtering and swearing Cock went through to the end; it was useless, as he knew, to try to climb out over those smooth abrupt walls, and he was too obstinate to leave his saddle. Which was madder, Cock or the pony, it would be hard to say. It was when he went climbing up the cleated incline at the farther end that Slow Jack got his first inkling of the cause of mirth. He gave one astonished stare, made two or three odd noises in his throat, and then, gravely and in silence, dropped from his saddle to the ground. It was not until he lay at full length, the long reins of the bridle drooping from the bit and his pony gazing at him inquiringly, that he exploded-but then he laughed steadily for half an hour.

The cattle, which had not awaited these developments, were dropping into the trough with praise-worthy regularity and making their way to the other end; when about half way there and swimming resignedly, a kind-hearted puncher, wearing a delighted grin in addition to his regular equipment, and armed with a strong pole, forked at the business end, leaned forward swiftly, jammed the fork over the unsuspecting cow's head, and pushed zealously. The result was gratifying to the few on-lookers, and disconcerting to the cow so rudely ducked; just before the unfortunate bovine touched the sloping runway to dry earth, another grinning puncher repeated the dose. The cows, reluctant to enter the bath, showed no reluctance to leave it and the scene of their humiliation, and they lumbered away with a speed surprising to those whose ideas of cows are based upon observation of domesticated "bossies" in pasture in the East. But they were not allowed to run free, being driven slowly across a roughly constructed bridge to the farther side of the Blackfoot, onto the non-infected range, and held there.

"This yere trough is shore makin' some plenty of Baptists," grinned Chesty Sutton.

"Yep; but with Mormon inclinations," amended Bow-Wow.

"Bow to th' gents," reprimanded Chesty, ducking a cow. "You look like a drowned rat," he criticised.

"Bow agin," requested Bow-Wow, and the cow obeyed, with a show of fight when its head came up.

"Some high-falutin' picklin' factory," chuckled Chesty. "Messrs. Bow-Wow Baker an' Chesty Sutton, world's greatest mite picklers. Blue-noses, red-noses an' other kinds o' cow inhabitants a specialty. Give you a whole dollar, Bow-Wow, if you fall in."

"Is that just a plain hope, or a insinooation?" demanded the cheerful Bow-Wow. "I sleep next to you, so don't get too blamed personal. But we might put Jake in-though mebby his ain't th' right kind. Hey, Jake; come here."

"If you wants to see me, you come here," retorted the cook. "I 've seen all of them ditches I wants to. An' I ain't takin' no chances with a couple o' fools, neither."

"Hey, Chesty!" called Bow-Wow, delighted. "Here comes that LX steer we had such a h —l of a time with in th' railroad pens. Soak him good! Ah, ha, my long-horned friend; you was some touchy an' peevish down there in Wayback. Take *that* —don't worry, Chesty 's been savin' some for you, too. *Hard*, Chesty! That's th' boy-bet he 's mad as a rattler."

"Look at that moth-eaten scab of a yearlin'," laughed Chesty, pointing. "Th' firm could declare dividends on th' mites we 'll pickle on her. *Souse* she goes! Once more for luck-look at her steam up! H —l, *this* ain't work-it's fun. Under you go, Alice dear. Next!"

"Here comes Kinkaid o' th' Cyclone," announced Cock Murray, riding up to take a hasty look at the operations before he returned to the herd for another bunch of cows.

Chesty handed his pole to Murray, grabbed up a lariat, and started for the newcomer, shouting: "Here comes some itch! Dip him, fellers! Quick!"

Kinkaid manoeuvred swiftly, grinning broadly. "If that stuff is warmer 'n th' water in th' Jack, why, I might be coaxed into it. Howd'y, boys; thought I 'd come over an' pick up some points."

"How you makin' out on th' Cyclone?" asked Buck.

"Bad —*very* bad. We tried isolatin' th' mangy ones, but they 're dyin' like flies in frost time. Lost forty million so far an' I reckon th' other two 'll die to-morrow. We thought our north range was free, but they 're on that, too. We drove clean cows up in th' Rockin' Horse territory an' now they 're showin' signs o' havin' th' itch. Beats all how it travels."

Cock Murray listened intently, but held his peace. He thought he might explain how it had travelled toward the Rocking Horse.

"That's where we noticed it first," said Buck. "We found some o' yore cows on th' Hog Back, an' their trail left th' river just below th' Rockin' Horse."

Kinkaid looked surprised and asked questions. He sat very quietly for a few moments and then looked at Buck with a peculiar expression on his face. "Sick cows don't swim th' Jack, cold as it is now. I wonder who in h —l—?" he muttered, softly.

"We 're wonderin', too, Kinkaid," replied Buck, slowly. "It's lead or rope for anybody we ketch at it." Kinkaid nodded his emphatic endorsement of this.

Whitby was keeping a close watch on the tally of cattle as they emerged, comparing it with the amount of fresh mixture constantly being added to that already in the troughs, and he found reason to be thankful that he had ordered more than he expected to use. Any left over would make all the less needed at the fall shipment when, as he knew, the dipping would have to be repeated; not until then could they be assured that the disease was stamped out.

The first day's work finished less than half the herd, but they continued, the following day, until the last cow scrambled out. After which, as a matter of precaution, Buck gave the boys the fun of driving every pony through the mixture. What had been entertaining before now became side-splitting, for tired as they were, the savage natures of the furious victims drew energy from unexpected sources and made a scene well worth watching, and a little risky for those men waiting with ropes at the end of the dripping board. The cows were angry, but had neither the intelligence nor the fighting ability of the maddened animals who had only a short time before seemed to enjoy the discomfiture of the animals they were accustomed to drive and bully; and it was only agility and good luck that the flying hoofs landed on nothing more substantial than air.

While this did not take long it was too late when finished, and the men too weary, to break camp; but the next morning saw the chuck wagon piled high with barrels and caldrons on the way to the ranch house. Some of the extra men, having in mind the wording of the guarantee of a full month's pay, cherished the hope that there was no further use for their services and that they would be paid off and told to leave. They were disappointed, for instead of loafing or leaving, half of them were set to planting posts for the fence which it was found necessary to erect along the creek, while the others rode over the range on the look-out for cows with signs of itch. A small herd of about a hundred, found scattered along and near the creek, were dipped as a precautionary measure, and after a week had elapsed without finding further signs of the disease, Buck ordered the second squad to begin the Spring or calf round-up; the fence division patrolled the creek to effect a quarantine until the wire arrived. They had a two-strand fence extending along Blackfoot Creek from its source to the river, when the round-up was half over, and were immediately put to work with the others. When the last calf was branded, the extra force was let go and Buck waited for some new deviltry. It came, and turned his hair grayer and deepened the lines of care on his face. Calves had totalled up well and proved to him that there was lots of money to be taken out of the Double Y under fair conditions, but the next blow cut into his resources with crushing effect and made him waver for a moment.

Chapter XV
The Slaughter of the Innocents

The round-up was still under way when Cock Murray was taken off and sent to Twin River in a chuck wagon to get provisions for the ranch. He had loaded his wagon and left town behind him when he saw Dave riding hard to overtake him. He drew rein and nodded when the horseman pulled up beside him.

"Howd'y, Dave."

"Howd'y, Murray," replied Dave. "Spring round-up over yet?"

"Nope; 'bout half."

"Itch all cured good?"

"Can't find no more signs of it. That dippin' play was a winner an' it's a good thing to remember."

"I 've got a little job for you an' Slow Jack," Dave remarked, after a moment's thought.

"Yeh? Hope it's better'n some o' yore schemes."

"What do you mean? I never had no schemes."

"All right—my mistake," drawled Murray. "What's th' new one?"

"New nothin'. I just want you an' Slow Jack to drive a couple o' thousand head up in th' Hog Back country some 'rs an' hold 'em hid till I can take care o' 'em."

"If yo 're goin' to start up in business for yoreself, I 'd keep away from th' Hog Back," replied Murray gravely. "Better try down on th' southeast corner. There ain't no itch hangin' 'round there."

"Business nothin'!" snapped Dave, not liking his companion's levity. "I 've got somethin' in my head that 'll make a fortune for you an' Slow Jack. I don't want no profits-just th' joy o' takin' a good punch at Peters 'll do for me. But you two ought to split 'bout twenty thousand dollars a-tween you."

"Music to my ears!" chuckled Murray. "Slow Jack's goin' to work on a salary basis on *this* job-th' profits 'll be mine. Whereabouts is this gold mine located, did you say?"

Dave did not heed him but continued hurriedly: "There 's a good pasture atween th' Hog Back an' th' river, an' th' only way to it or out of it is up that ravine. You an' Slow Jack can drive cows to it whenever you gets a chanct, an' a couple o' ropes acrost th' ravine 'll hold 'em in. When you get a couple o' thousand there we 'll drive 'em north o' th' Cyclone's line to Rankin, put 'em on th' cars there an' get 'em south into Wyoming. There 's good money in it, Murray."

The driver was staring at his companion, blank amazement on his face. "Gosh! That sounds easy! 'Bout as easy as me an' you capturin' th' Fort an' makin' th' Government pay us a big war indemnity. Slow Jack 's goin' to get th' wages an' profits, too. I 'm too generous to cut in an' spoil his chance to make a fortune. I suppose we 're goin' to tie th' herd to balloons an' get 'em to Rankin that way?"

"You collect th' herd an' I 'll attend to all th' rest o' it," declared Dave. "I 've got this thing all worked out an' it's goin' through."

"Can't be did, Dave," emphatically replied the driver, dazed by the signs of insanity manifested by his companion.

"You say that because it ain't never been done," retorted Dave, angrily. "It *can* be done, an' I 'm goin' to do it. Put that in yore pipe."

"All right-you ought to know," responded Murray, tactfully. "Who are th' miracle-men that are goin' to get th' herd off that table-land an' to Rankin without bein' seen or leavin' a trail?"

"Big Saxe, th' hunchback, is one," Dave explained. "Th' trail we 'll leave ain't botherin' us any. They won't be missed till it's too late to look for tracks-an' by that time th' cows 'll be sold."

Murray thought of one objection that would kill the plan without mercy: the railroad was not in the habit of accepting unaccredited cows for shipment; curiosity would be shown as to the brand, where it came from, who owned it, and other pertinent facts. But Dave was so hopeful, so earnest, that Murray decided to talk the matter over with Schatz before dispelling Dave's dream.

"Well, that's true, Dave," he soberly replied. "When you think it over ca'm like, it ain't so plumb foolish. Me an' Slow Jack 'll see what we can do-let you know as soon as we can. I got to poke along. But say, Dave; it's shore death to anybody tryin' to fool with *Cyclone* cows along th' river-tell th' boys so they won't try to throw over any more scabby cattle on us. Kinkaid is some peevish 'bout his north range gettin' th' itch. Got any more plans you want to tell about? All right-don't get mad at *me*, Dave; I 'm only foolin'. So long."

Murray had crossed the north line of his ranch before he emerged from his trance. Then he shook himself, laughed and looked around, urging the team to livelier efforts. He nursed his secret until after dark and then slipped away from the ranch and struck out toward Twin River. When he had gone a mile in this direction he wheeled sharply and urged his pony toward the trail along the Little Jill. Arriving at the Schatz domicile he reconnoitred a little and then slipped up to the kitchen door and drummed lightly on it. Schatz opened it and dragged the visitor inside.

"You must nod come to see me more as iss necessary," began the German. "It iss such carelessness as puts peoples in chails. Vat iss it dis time?"

Murray, grinning, unfolded Dave's plans to the astonished German, who could only grunt his surprise and disgust. Suddenly Schatz brightened and a faint twinkle came into his eye. "Dot iss a goot plan, Murray. A very goot plan. *Aber* it goes too far. Dose railroad peoples vould spoil it quick. You get der herd like Dave says, more if you can; und hold it till *I* say somet'ing. Neffer mind vat Dave say-he iss *ein verruchter Mensch.* But ven *I* say somet'ing, den you do it. *Verstanden?*"

"All right, Schatz," agreed Murray, smiling. "I 'll back yore play to th' limit, every time. But what 'll I say to Dave when he gets anxious?"

"He von't ged anxious. I vill speak der vord before he haf time to ged anxious. I vill tell vat to do mit dot herd, und it von't be vat Dave vants."

"Then I 'll tell Slow Jack that th' collection takes place. Anything else?"

"*Nein* —careful you go. Alvays you must be careful. *Goot nacht!*" and the door closed quickly.

"Ach! Dot Dave!" ejaculated Schatz, his hands upraised.

* * * * *

Slow Jack must have been told of Schatz's wishes, because during the week following Murray's visit to the German's house, cattle had been disappearing from the southwestern part of the range; this was not strange enough to cause worry even if it had been observed, because cows go where they please; and it was not observed by any one but Cock Murray and Slow Jack. The fence, extending to within a short distance of the south line, was regarded as barrier enough to keep the cattle off the infected range, and Buck gave no particular thought to it. Slow Jack rode along the fence every few days to see that there were no breaks in it and as Cock Murray had the south line under his care, it was an easy matter to round up small herds and drive them over the Hog Back, down the ravine on the river side, and hold them on the plateau pasture by the means Dave had suggested. The grass was heavy and the water plentiful along the line patrolled by Murray and there were always large numbers of cows grazing there-so many, in fact, that those driven off could not be missed under ordinary circumstances. Thus the hidden herd grew rapidly and it was not long before a large herd grazed close to the edge of the precipitous cliffs frowning down on the cold, hard-looking Black Jack.

Murray, fussing around the horse corral, had put in a hard day's riding and had no desire to stray far from the bunk-house that chilly, windy night. He had been engaged in driving cattle onto the range he had been thinning, so as to cover the missing cows, and over five hundred extra head grazed near the springs that made the swampy headquarters of the creek.

Slow Jack was getting nervous because Schatz had not been heard from and he was grouchy and touchy even to his partner in the business on hand. He and Murray would be likely to have unpleasant questions asked of them if the herd should be discovered. They were in charge of that part of the range and it would not be easy to excuse the presence of so many cows on the infected section. The fence was intact and if it were not, then it would be squarely up to them; Buck would be profanely curious how it was that a respectable herd had managed to get past Murray and go around the end of the fence. And it would be hard to explain how the cattle willingly left the best grass on the ranch and wandered up the Hog Back, all finding the ravine and herding on the cliff-top pasture. And if the rope or the tracks of the two punchers' horses should be seen, gun-play would follow with deadly certainly.

"D —n that Dutchman!" growled Slow Jack to Murray, as they met and strolled away a short distance; "Seems like we ain't got enough cows up there to suit th' hog. He wants that pasture covered with 'em, I reckon. Word or no word, them cows has got to get back on th' range. An' th' itch is among 'em, too, Murray."

Murray smoked in silence for a while and then looked up, a frown on his face. "Smiler has got to be quick. Dave, th' fool, was out to see me again to-day. I asked him when he was goin' to rustle that bunch an' he says he 's got it all fixed-mebby th' first black night. Is it black to-night?" he asked, ironically.

"Black as h —l!" growled Slow Jack. "If Dave beats th' ol' man to it, an' gets away with that herd, I 'll be plumb tickled to death. An' if he gets away with it good an' clean, without bein' caught, it 'll go down in th' history o' cattle-stealin' as th' greatest miracle since th' Dead Sea was walked on. Holy Gripes! Would n't it be a sensation?"

"Th' laurels will remain with th' Dead Sea," grunted Murray. "Dave 's shore goin' to be fertilizer for th' daisies some o' these days if he don't get sane." After a moment he growled: "An' if he don't stop comin' to see me like he has, Smiler 'll have to dig up another ass to be father to."

"He was lookin' for me, yesterday," grinned Slow Jack, "but I seen him first. He ain't goin' to *sic* no lead *my* way if I can help it."

"Jack, did you ever figger out why Smiler lets Dave mess around like he does?" suddenly asked Murray. "Th' Dutchman is one clever individual, but every clever crook makes one mistake that ropes him. I hereby prophesy that Dave is Smiler's mistake an' will make th' Dutchman lose. Want to bet on it?"

"What you allus lookin' for shore things for?" jeered Jack. "You ain't got no sportin' blood in you! In course I know it-an' that's just th' reason I've got my stuff ready to move quick an' my trail all mapped out. I might want to leave before breakfast some day. Tell you one thing —*you* can drive cows over th' Hog Back but I 'm *all through*! D —n if I drive another one!"

"I 'm th' good little boy, too, from now on," replied Murray. "An' I 'm goin' to be awful busy farther east on that line. Savvy? I ain't goin' to be able to even guess how they got over th' Hog Back, an' I 'll take th' blame for bein' careless. I 'd ruther lose my job than house any lead under my skin. Aw! I 'm goin' in an' get some sleep."

"Me, too; I 'll come right soon," and Slow Jack drifted off into the darkness as his companion started for the bunk-house.

When Slow Jack entered the bunk-house half an hour after Murray, he paused in the door and looked at the western sky, where lightning zigzagged occasionally. The barely audible roll of thunder told him how far off the storm was and he noticed that the wind was blowing less steadily, coming in gusts from varying points. Even while he stood, the sound of the thunder increased in volume and the long, thin lightning reached out nearer to him, a livid whip that lashed the heavens into roaring anger.

"Huh! Reckon Spring is shore nuff here now," he muttered. "Fust real lightnin' I seen this year." Five minutes later he was asleep.

* * * * *

The Hog Back loomed up like a condensation of the surrounding night, its huge bulk magnified and made soft in its rugged outlines. A restless wind scurried like a panic-stricken animal, sighing through the brush and whispering through the rocks. At intervals the silence was so intense that the scraping of a twig, yards away, could be plainly heard; and at other times the bellow of a steer would have been lost in a few rods.

Something moved across the plain, slowly and carefully as if feeling its way, and toiled up the precarious trail, rolling pebbles clattering down; in the noise of their fall was lost the soft thudding that marked the course of the moving smudge. The lightning in the western sky flashed nearer and gave brief illumination of the scene. Four men rode single file up the dark trail, silent, intent, wary, the leader picking his way as though he knew it well; in reply to a low-voiced question from his nearest companion, he stretched out an abnormally long arm in a sharp gesture. He did not like to have his ability doubted.

Reaching the top, the procession strung along and finally dipped into a ravine, following the steeply slanting water-course until stopped by a lariat stretched across the way. Tossing aside the rope, the leader led the force onto the walled-in pasture where each man went swiftly to work without instructions. The fire at the leader's feet, fanned by the high wind, leaped from him through the sun-cured bunches of grass in a rapidly widening circle, the heavy smoke rolling down upon the restless cattle in pungent clouds, sparks streaming through them. Every cow on the pasture was on its feet, pawing and snorting with fear at this most dreaded of all enemies. While they stood, seemingly hypnotized for a moment by the low flames, the darkness to the east of them was streaked with spurts of fire and the cracks of revolvers on their flank sent them thundering toward the river. The confusion of the stampede was indescribable as the front ranks, sensing the edge of the cliff, tried in vain to check itself and hold back against the press of the avalanche of terror-stricken animals behind. The change was magical-one moment a frenzied mass of struggling cows lighted grotesquely by the burning grass, and then only the edge of the cliff and the swishing grayness of the river below. The wind was blowing the flames toward the edge of the cliff and they would die from lack of material upon which to feed, though the four cared little about that. Their horses stumbled with them along the ravine, leaving behind a blackened plain across which sparks were driven by each gust of wind, to glow brilliantly and die. Below, once more wrapped in impenetrable darkness, swished the Black Jack, cold, cruel, deep, and fugitive, its scurrying, frightened cross currents whispering mysteriously as they discussed the tragedy. Suddenly the rain deluged everything as if wrathful at the pitiable slaughter and eager to wash out the stain of it.

* * * * *

In the middle of the forenoon of the following day Slow Jack loomed up in the fog of the driving rain and the vapors arising from the earth and slid from his saddle in front of the ranch house, his hideous yellow slicker shining as though polished. Buck opened the door and instinctively stepped back to avoid the wet gust that assailed him. "There 's a lot o' cows floating in the backwater o' th' Jack where th' creek empties in —I roped one an' drug it ashore. Just plain drowned, I reckon. There was signs of itch, too," Slow Jack reported.

Buck hastened into his storm clothes, got Monroe from the corral, and started through the storm to see for himself. When he reached the river he saw a score of Double Y cows drifting in circles in the backwater, and at intervals one would swing into the outer current and be caught in the pull of the rushing river to go sailing toward Twin. The stream was rising rapidly now, its gray waters turning brown and roiled. Sending Monroe to follow the stream to town, he and Slow Jack rode close to the water toward the hazy Hog Back. When he met Monroe at the ranch house that afternoon he learned that most of the inhabitants of Twin River were swarming upon the point behind Ike's saloon, busily engaged in roping and skinning the cattle as fast as they drifted by; the count varied from one hundred to five hundred, and he knew that the fight was on again.

There had been no clues found upon which to base action against the perpetrators. True, the pasture behind the Hog Back had been burned since he last saw it, but Slow Jack's tardy memory recalled that one morning, several days before, he had detected the smell of grass smoke in the air. He was going to investigate it but hesitated to go through the quarantined range for fear of bringing back the itch. During the day the smell had disappeared and he had seen no signs of smoke at any time. He had meant to speak of it when he returned to the bunk-house but had forgotten, as usual.

When left alone Buck stared out of the window, not noticing that the storm had ceased, burning with rage at his absolute helplessness. The loss of the cows was not great enough to cripple him seriously but this blow, following hard upon the other, showed him what little chance he had of making the Double Y a success without a large outfit of tried and trusted men. Even while he looked at the plain with unseeing eyes his cattle might be stolen or driven to death in the swollen waters of either river-and he was powerless to stop it.

To his mind again leaped the recollection of Ned's warning regarding Schatz: he was a "hard nut," Ned had said. Buck was beginning to think he would have to crack him on suspicion. He looked in the direction of the German's cabin and a curse rumbled in his throat.

Whitby opened the door and reported that everything was all right on his part of the range and asked for orders for the next day. After a few minutes' conversation he moved on to the bunk-house, troubled and ill at ease at the appearance of his employer. In a way Whitby had certain small privileges that were denied to the other members of the outfit. He was a gentleman, as Buck had instantly realized, and he could make time pass very rapidly under most conditions. He paused now and finally decided to thrust his company upon Buck for the evening; in his opinion Buck would be all the better for company. He had almost reached the ranch house door when behind him there was a sound of furious galloping and Bow-Wow flung himself from his horse and burst into the room excited and fuming, Whitby close upon his heels.

"They 've shot a lot of cows on th' southeast corner, close to th' Jill. I 'd 'a' been in sooner only I went huntin' for 'em. Lost their tracks when they swum th' river. Three of 'em did it, an' they dropped nigh onto fifty head." Winded as he was, Bow-Wow yet found breath for a string of curses that appeared to afford him little relief.

A look came into Buck's face that told of a man with his back to the wall. The piling on of the last straw was dangerously near at hand. His fingers closed convulsively around the butt of his Colt and he swayed in his tracks. No one ever knew how close to death Whitby and Bow-Wow were at that moment, by what a narrow margin the range was spared ruthless murder at the hands of a man gone fighting mad. The Texan was cut to the heart by this last news, and only a swift reaction in the form of the habitual self-restraint of thirty years saved him from running amuck. The grayness of his face gave way to its usual color, only the whipcord veins and the deep lines telling of the savage battle raging in the soul of the man. He waved the two men away and paced to and fro across the room, fighting the greatest battle of his eventful life. One man against unknown enemies who shot in the dark; his outfit was an unknown quantity and practically worse than none at all, since he had to trust it to a certain extent. He thought that Ned Monroe was loyal, but his judgment might have become poor because of the strain he had undergone; and was not Monroe one who had lost when the ranch was turned over to its rightful owners? Bow-Wow was more likely to be honest than otherwise, but he had no proof in the puncher's favor. Chesty Sutton had no cause to be a traitor, but the workings of the human mind cause queer actions at times. Cock Murray and Slow Jack could be regarded as enemies, but there was not enough proof to convict them: they had been in charge of the western part of the ranch when the herd had been stampeded into the Black Jack-yet Buck realized that two men could hardly handle so large a tract of land; and again, the stampede had occurred at night while they were asleep in the bunkhouse. If he got rid of every man he could find reason to doubt, he would have no outfit to handle the routine work of the ranch. There remained Jake and Whitby. The cook could be dismissed as of no account one way or the other, since he was a fool at best and never left the ranch house for more than a few minutes at a time. The Englishman seemed to be loyal but there was no positive assurance of it; while he had undoubtedly killed the itch, it was so dangerous a plague that every man's hand should be turned against it.

When he tried to reason the matter out he came to the conclusion he had reached so often before: the only man in Montana whom he trusted absolutely was Buck Peters. If he had some of his old outfit, or even Hopalong, Red, or Lanky, one man in whom he could place absolute trust, he felt he could win out in the end-and he would have them. He ceased his pacing to and fro and squared his shoulders: He would give his outfit one last tryout and if still in doubt of its loyalty, he would send a message to Hopalong and have him pick out a dozen men from the Bar-20 and near-by ranches and send them up to the Double Y. Lucas, Bartlett, and Meeker could spare him a few men each, men friendly to him. It would be admitting preliminary defeat to do this but the results would justify the means.

When he thought he had mastered himself and was becoming calm and self-possessed, Chesty Sutton and the foreman entered with troubled looks on their faces. Monroe spoke: "Chesty reports he found a dozen cows lyin' in a heap at th' bottom of Crow Canyon, and Murray says th' fence has been cut an' stripped o' wire for a mile on th' north end."

Buck lost himself in the fury of rage that swept over him at this news. The fence had been intact that noon when he rode out to look over the floating cows in the Jack; this blow in daylight told him that the battle was being forced from several points at once; and again he realized how absolutely helpless he was-there was no hope now. When Ned and Chesty returned to the bunk-house, drawing meagre satisfaction from the clearing weather, they left behind them a man broken in spirit, weak from fruitless anger, who shook his upraised arms at Providence and cursed every man in Montana. A desperate idea entered his head: he would force the fighting.

He slipped out of the corral, roped his horse and led it around back of the ranch house, where he tethered it and returned to the house to wait for night. Night would see him at Schatz's cabin, there to choke out the truth and strike his first blow.

Jake came in, muttering something about lights and supper, to retreat silently at the curt dismissal. The long shadows stole into the room, enveloping the brooding figure, and deepened into dark. The time was come and Buck arose and went out to his horse. With his hand on the picket he paused and listened. Across the Jill a broad moon was beginning to cast its light and from the same direction, a long way off, came the sound of singing. The singer was coming toward him and Buck stepped into the house again to await his arrival. He might be the bearer of some message.

While he paced restlessly the singing died down and in a few minutes the squeaking of a vehicle caught his ear. He wondered who cared to drive over that trail when there were so many good saddle horses to be had for the asking and he started toward the door to see. Suddenly he stopped as if shot and gripped his hat with all his strength as another song came to his ears. He doubted his senses and feared he was going crazy, hoping against hope that he heard aright. Who in Montana could know that song!

>"Th' cows go grazin' o'er th' lea —
Pore Whiskey Bill, pore Whiskey Bill.
An' achin' thoughts pour in on me
Of Whiskey Bill.

Th' sheriff up an' found his stride,
Bill's soul went shootin' down th' slide —
How are things o'er th' Great Divide,
Oh, Whiskey Bill?'

"Hello th' house! Hey, Buck! Buck! *O*, Buck! Whoa, blame you-think I'm a fool tenderfoot? Hey, Buck! BUCK!"

Buck leaped to the door in one great bound and ran toward the creeping buckboard, yelling like an Indian. The bunk-house door flew open and the men tumbled through it, guns in hand, and sprinted toward the point of trouble. Bow-Wow led and close upon his heels ran Whitby, with Murray a close third. When the leader got near enough he saw two men wrestling near a buckboard and he manoeuvred so as to insert himself into the fracas at the first opportunity. Then he snorted and backed off in profound astonishment, colliding with the eager Englishman, to the pain of both. The wrestlers were not wrestling but hugging; and a woman in the buckboard was laughing with delight. Bow-Wow shook his head as if to clear it and began to slip back toward the bunk-house. This was against all his teachings and he would have no part in it. The idea of two cowmen hugging each other!

Whitby strolled after and overtook the muttering puncher. "I fancy that's one of those Texans he 's been talking about; or, rather, two of them. Perhaps we shall see some frontier law up here now-and God knows it is time."

Slow Jack veered off and swore in his throat. "*Texas* law, huh? We 'll send him back where he come from, in a box!" he growled.

He stopped when he heard Buck's laughing words, and sneered: "Hopalong Cassidy an' his wife, eh? She 'll be his widder if he cuts in *this* game. But I wonder if any more o' them terrible Texas killers is comin' up? Huh! Let 'em come-that's all."

Chapter XVI

The Master Mind

For a while, at least, Buck seemed to cast his troubles to the four winds and was a picture of delight; his happiness, bubbling up in every word, kept his face wreathed in one vast smile. At last he had a man whom he could trust. Jake was summoned and prepared the best meal he could and the three sat down to a very good supper, Buck surprised to find how hungry he had become. His visit to Schatz was forgotten as he listened to Hopalong and Mary chatter about old times and people he wished he could see again.

After a little, Hopalong noticed how tired his wife was and sent her to get a good night's rest. The long railroad journey and the ride in the buckboard had been a great strain on her.

When left alone, Buck demanded to know all about the Bar-20 and its outfit and laughed until the tears came as he listened to some of the tales. "What deviltry has Johnny been up to since I left?" asked Buck.

"Well, it's only been six months," replied Hopalong, "so you see he ain't really had much time; but he 's made good use o' what he did have. He fell in love again, had th' prospectin' fever, wanted to go down to th' Mexican line an' help Martin. I had th' very devil of a time stoppin' him. Him an' Lucas had their third fight an' Lucas got licked this time; then they went off to Cowan's an' blew th' crowd, near havin' another scrap 'cause each wanted to pay. He dosed Pete's cayuse with whiskey an' ginger, chased Lee Hop clean to Buckskin, so we ain't got no cook. Red licked him for that, so Johnny tied all th' boys together one night, tied chairs an' things to 'em an' then stepped outside an' began shootin' at th' stars. It was some lively, that mess in th' dark, judgin' from th' hair-raisin' noises; it scared th' Kid all th' way to Perry's Bend-leastways, we has no news for a week, when we hears he 'd pulled stakes there, leavin' th' town fightin' an' th' sheriff locked up in his own jail. Th' Bend has sent numerous invitations for him to call again. From there he drifts over to th' C80, wins all their money an' then rides home loaded down with presents to square hisself with th' boys. He wanted to fight when I made Red foreman while I was away-it's Red's first good chance to get square."

"That's th' Kid, all right," laughed Buck. "Lord, how I wish he was up here!"

"Red, he's th' same grouch as ever but he's all right if Johnny 'd let him get set. As soon as Red calms down th' Kid calls his attention to somethin' excitin' an' th' trouble begins again. They all wanted to come up here an' give you a hand till you got things runnin' right. I told 'em I could get a better crowd in two days, so they stayed home to spite me. From what I 've heard I wish I 'd told 'em they could come-things 'd run smoother for you with them wild men buckjumpin' 'round lookin' for trouble. Like to turn Red an' Johnny loose up here with a good grudge to work off. Th' railroad would report that Montana was jumpin' east fast."

"What was that your wife called you?" asked Buck, curiously.

"Billy-Red," laughed Hopalong. "That 's her own name for me."

"Billy-h —l!" snorted Buck. "Billy-goat would suit you better."

"Say, Buck, Pete saw som'ers there was lots o' money in raisin' chickens, so he borrows all our money, gets about a hundred head from th' East, an' starts in. For a week there was lots of excitement 'round our place-coyotes got so they 'd get under our feet an' th' nights was plumb full o' hungry animals with a taste for chicken. We put up a bomb-proof coop but they tunnelled it th' first night an' got all that was left o' th' herd 'cept about a dozen what was roostin' high. Pete, he was broken-hearted an' give up. He makes Mary a present o' what was left of his stock, an' what do you think she give him for 'em? Two day's work diggin'. He dug a ditch, four-sided, for th' foundations of a new coop. Then he has to sink posts in it in th' ground an' fill th' ditch with stones. Johnny got th' stones in th' chuck wagon from th' creek, so as to square hisself with Mary, an' she give him a whole apricot pie for it. He 's been a nuisance ever since. Well, th' posts rose four feet above th' ground an' when that hen-corral was roofed over, you could see, any moonlight night, plenty o' coyotes trottin' 'round it, prayin' for somethin' to happen. We got some fine shootin' for a while. But I got other things to talk about, Buck-Texas can wait."

"Kind of a dry job, Hoppy," replied Buck, going to a cupboard and returning with a bottle.

"Better stuff than Cowan ever sold," smiled the visitor, and then plunged into what he considered real news.

"When we got off th' train at Wayback, I went huntin' for a wagon an' purty soon we was on our way to Twin River. I knowed we 'd have to spend th' night there: Mary could n't stand forty miles in a buckboard after that train ride. We had n't got very far from town when I hears a hail an' looks around to see Tex Ewalt comin' up. He spotted me when I left th' train but he did n't want to show he knows me there."

"What!" exclaimed Buck, in great surprise. "Tex Ewalt! Why, I thought he went East for good."

"He thought so, too, at th' time," and Hoppy gave a brief history of their friend's movements. "When he got back to th' ranch he was restless an' decided to come up here an' help you. He 's been very busy up here in a quiet way. He tells me he knows th' man that put th' itch on yore range. Tex says he could 'a' stopped it if he knew enough to add two an' two. But he says there 's another man behind him, slicker 'n a coyote. Tex 's been hopin' every day to rope an' tie him but he ain't got him yet."

"Who is it?" asked Buck, with grim simplicity.

"Tex won't tell me. He says you can't do no good shootin' on suspicion. He's tried watchin' him but he might as well be goin' to church when he does leave home, his travels is that innocent."

"Why didn't Tex come here? I been wantin' one man I could trust, an' me an' Tex could 'a' wiped out th' gang."

"He says different-an' he was afraid o' bein' seen. You see, that would kill his usefulness. Just as soon as he could get to th' bottom o' th' game an' lay his fingers on th' real boss, *then* he 'd 'a' come out for you in th' open, put th' boss in th' scrap-pile for burial, an' burned powder till you had things where you wanted 'em. We about concluded you ain't makin' good use o' th' punchers you got, Buck, though I shore hates to say it."

"How can I make use o' men I don't trust? You don't know th' worst, Hopalong —"

"About th' couple o' thousand head went swimmin'? I ain't heard much else in Twin River. How 'd it happen?"

Buck ran over the day's occurrences graphically and without missing a single point. Hopalong's thoughtful comment was characteristic of the man upon whom Buck had unconsciously leaned in crises not a few.

"The two men on yore south pasture is liars," he declared. "Yore foreman is some doubtful: 'pears like to me if he 's honest an' attendin' to business, no point o' yore range ought to go shy o' him for long. Th' Britisher 's white: it's no part o' his business to help you, th' way Tex tells me; if he ain't square he just does his work an' don't offer no suggestions. Th' other two is all right if they ain't just fools what 'll do as th' foreman says 'cause he 's th' foreman, right or wrong. That's how I reckons you stand. Now we got to prove it."

"Fire away," said Buck, earnestly. "I agrees to every word. Provin' it's th' horse I ain't been able to rope."

"Th' outlyin' free range don't count. You ain't missed no cows in th' round-up, has you?"

"No, they tallied high."

"Goes to show there 's a head to th' deviltry. You don't get no losses on'y right on yore home range. Now, we divide th' range in sections, a man to each section, an' work 'em that way a few days. There won't be no night ridin' at first. Then we set 'em night ridin' when they ain't expectin' it an' shift th' men every night. We soon know who to trust, don't we?"

"Yo 're right-plumb right-an' it 's so simple I ought to be fed hay, for a cow. I got a map som'ers-or I 'll make one. We 'll lay out them sections right now."

"That's th' talk! There ain't no time like right now for doin' most things, Buck."

They were not long in laying out and perfecting their plans and had said good-night when Buck suddenly remembered the picketed pony. He turned it into the corral and went to bed.

Smiler Schatz, sleeping the sleep of the very wicked and the very innocent, did not dream how near he had come to an incident more exciting than any he had ever passed through.

Chapter XVII
Hopalong's Night Ride

Hopalong, passing the bunk-house on his way to the stable, paused to listen. Through the open window Pickles' voice had reached him quite clearly: "I don't guess I 'll ever get him, Whit, but if I do, it 'll be for keeps, you betcher."

Hopalong was interested. The death of Gottleib Gerken was an old story and so many things of pressing moment having occurred about the time of Hopalong's arrival, he had not been told of this. The finality of decision in Pickles' murderous intention was so evident that Hopalong wondered how the boy came to conceive so deadly a hatred. He stepped to the window and stood looking at the two figures within. They neither saw nor heard him.

Both were deep in thought. Whitby's inherent regard for due process of law had received numerous shocks since he left Chicago. Like many another square man finding his niche in a raw country, he was beginning to see that right must be enforced by might, until such time as wrong became subdued by the steady march of the older civilization. And this face-about in opinion is not accomplished in a day, even when on the spot and a personal sufferer. It was this new feeling that led him to listen with respect to Pickles' confidences, boy though he was. Boys imbibed men's ideas early in this country; too early, thought Whitby, recalling his own play-time at this lad's age. He stole a look at the glum face beside him and began to draw circles with the point of the switch he held in his hand-he was never without one. "It's a pity," he said, "a pity."

"What's a pity?" asked Pickles, a note of indignation in his voice at the implied suggestion.

Whitby ignored the tone. "It's a pity you never heard of the Witch's Spell," he explained, reminiscently.

"What's that?"

"But then, of course," reasoned Whitby, "if you can't find a Witch's Ring, you can't work the Spell; and I rather fancy there is n't a Witch's Ring in all the world outside of Yorkshire."

"What's it like?" demanded Pickles, with the practical insistence of Young America.

"Why, the Old Witch makes it, you know. She runs around in a ring and blows on the grass and it never grows any more. Inside the Ring and outside, the grass is just the same, but the Ring is always bare."

Pickles was silent. He was picturing to himself the process of the Ring in the making. So was Hopalong. It seemed very matter-of-fact as Whitby told it; still, there was something —

"What's she do that for?" asked Pickles-the very question Hopalong was asking himself.

"It's the bad fairies, you know, and Wizards, and that sort of thing; she 's afraid of them. But they can't pass the Ring, no matter how deep they dig, so the Witch is quite safe, you know. They 're a bad lot, those others, no end. But the Old Witch is quite a decent sort. She lives inside the Ring, under the ground, and that's where you go to get your wish."

Pickles pondered. His eyes began to glow. "Any wish?" he questioned, in subdued excitement.

"All sorts," declared Whitby. "There was Jimmie Pickering: he always got his wish; he told me so, himself; and Arthur Cooper: he wished to be a minister and he got his wish; and George Hick: he wished to see the world and he 's always travelling up and down the earth; and Allen Ramsey, who wished to be an athlete, strong, you know: he got his wish; then there was Maggie Sheffield, who wished to marry a soldier: she married a soldier; and Vi Glades, who wished to be a singer: she can sing tears into your heart, lad, so sweet you 're glad to have them there; so she got her wish. And ever so many more: they all got their wishes. She was a rare good one, that Witch."

"Did you get yore wish, Whit?"

"I could only count to seven," explained Whitby.

Pickles' lips moved silently. "How many do you have to count?" he asked, dubiously.

"Nine," said Whitby, with a regretful sigh. "You run around the Ring nine times, holding your breath and saying your wish to yourself over and over again. Then you run into the middle and lie down. You must n't breathe until you lie down. When you put your ear to the ground you can hear the Old Witch churning out your wish. 'Ka-Chug! Ka-Chug! Ka-Chug!' goes the churn, away down in the earth. Then you know you will get your wish."

Pickles straightened up and looked fixedly at Whitby. His voice was very solemn: "Whit, I take my oath there's a Witch's Ring right here on the range!"

"Nonsense!"

"Hope I may die! I 'll show you, to-morrow. An' I 'm a-goin' to wish —"

"I say! You must n't tell your wish, you know. That breaks the Spell. If ever you tell your wish, it does n't come true."

"Jiggers! —I won't tell. Nine times 'round the Ring an' hol' yore breath an' say yore wish fast an' then to th' middle —"

Hopalong lost the rest as he continued on his way to the stable. Pickles' Ring puzzled him only for a moment, for as he turned away from the window, he was chuckling. "Means some place where th' Injuns used to war-dance, I reckon," was his conclusion. "But that Britisher seems like he believed it himself."

Two minutes later and he was in the saddle and riding south, edging over toward Big Moose trail. He melted into the surrounding darkness like a shadow, silence having been the evident aim of his unusual preparations earlier in the evening. Not a leather creaked; an impatient toss of his pony's head betrayed no clink of metal on teeth; the velvety padding of the hoofs made as little noise as the passing of one of the larger cats, in a hurry. Hopalong meant to quarter the section of range allotted him like a restless ghost and, if the others did as well, he had a strong conviction that night-deviltry would lose its attractions in this particular part of the country.

It was not long before he began to test his memory. To a man of his experience this guard duty would have presented but little difficulty in any case, but Hopalong had been careful to make a very complete mental map of this section when riding it by daylight. He went on now like a man in his own house.

He turned abruptly to the left, heading for the Jill and taking the low ground between two huge buttes. Just short of the Big Moose trail he halted, listening intently for five minutes, and then, turning west again, began to quarter the ground like a hound, gradually working south. With the plainsman's certainty of direction his course followed a series of obliques, fairly regular, though he chose the low ground, winding about the buttes, to the top of which he lent a keen scrutiny. He stopped for minutes at a time to listen and then went on again.

It was during one of these pauses that he espied a dark shape at rest not far from him. He eyed it with suspicion. It should be a cow but there was something not quite normal in its attitude. He rode forward cautiously, being in no way desirous of disturbing the brute. Circling it at a walk a similar object loomed up, some little distance from the other. "Calf!" he decided. A few steps nearer and he changed his mind. "No, another cow. I don't know as I ever see cattle look like that. 'Pears like they was shore enough tuckered out-an' I bet they ain't drifted a mile in twenty-four hours." They were very still. There was no reason why they should not be and yet-the wind being right, he hazarded a few steps nearer.

And then there came to his ears a sound that stiffened him in his saddle. His pony turned its head and gazed inquiringly into the darkness. "Injuns!" breathed Hopalong, doubt struggling with conviction. He slipped to earth and ran noiselessly to the nearest recumbent figure. A single touch told him: it was a dead cow; warm, but unquestionably dead.

With his horse under him once more, Hoppy crept forward. Careful before, his progress now had all the stealth of a stalking tiger. There it came again: the unmistakable twang of a bow-string. The pony veered to the left in response to the pressure of Hoppy's knee, when there sounded a movement to the right and he straightened his course to ride between the two. His spirits began to rise with the old-time zest at the imminence of a fight to the death. Mary, back yonder in the ranch house, with her new proud hope, Buck and his anxieties, Tex in his indefatigable hunt for evidence, the far-distant Bar-20 with its duties and its band of loyal friends, all were forgotten in the complete absorption of the coming duel. Indians! Rebellious and treacherous punchers were foemen to beware of, but these red wolves, savage from the curb of the reservation and hungry with a blood lust long denied —a grin of pure delight spread over his features as he foresaw the instant transformation from cattle-killing thieves to strategic assassins at the first crack of his Colt.

The odds could not be great and he expected to reduce them at the opening of hostilities. Warily he glanced about him as he moved slowly forward, casting, at the last, a searching look off to the right. He saw that which brought him up standing, his breath caught in his distended lungs; it escaped in a long sigh of pleased wonder: "Great Land of Freedom! Please look at that," he pleaded to his unresponsive country.

Broadside on, head up and facing him with ears pricked forward, alert yet waiting, stood a horse that filled Hopalong's soul with the sin of covetousness. So near that the obscurity failed to hide a line, the powerful quarters and grand forehand betrayed to Hopalong's discerning eyes a latent force a little superior to the best he had ever looked on. "An' a' Injun's!" sighed Hoppy, in measureless disgust. "But not if I sees th' Injun," he added hopefully. Wishing that he might, his thought back-somersaulted to Pickles and Whitby and the Witch's Spell. A whimsical smile wrinkled the corners of his mouth and at this very moment the thing happened.

A nerve-racking screech, the like of which no Indian ever made, lifted the hair on Hoppy's head, and his pony immediately entered upon a series of amazing calisthenics, an enthusiastic rendering no doubt enhanced by the inch or two of arrow-head in his rump. Hopalong caught one glimpse of a squat, mis-shapen figure that went past him with a rush and let go at it, more from habit than with the expectation of hitting. When he had subdued his horse to the exercise of some little equine sense, the rapidly decreasing sound of the fleeing marauder told him that only one had been at work and with grim hopelessness he set after him. "Might as well try to catch a comet," he growled, sinking his spurs into the pony's side and momentarily distracting its attention from the biting anguish of the lengthier spur behind.

The pony was running less silently than when he left the ranch. Portions of unaccustomed equipment, loosened in his mad flurry, were dropping from him at every jump. This, and the straining of Hopalong's hearing after the chase, allowed to pass unnoticed the coming up of a third horseman, riding at an angle to intercept the pursuit. The first intimation of his presence Hopalong received was the whine of a bullet, too close for comfort, and Hopalong was off and behind his pony to welcome the crack of the rifle when it reached him. "Shootin' at random, d —n his fool hide!" snorted Hoppy; "an' shootin' good too," he conceded, as a second bullet sped eagerly after the first. Hoppy released a bellow of angry protest: "Hey! What 'n h—l do you reckon yo 're doin'?"

There was an interval of silence and then a voice from the darkness: "Show a laig, there: who is it?"

"Show you a boot, you locoed bummer! It's Cassidy." He mounted resignedly and waited for the other to ride up. "Could n't 'a' caught him, nohow," he reflected. "Never see such a horse in my life, never. Hope to th' Lord it don't rain. Be just like it."

The unknown rode up full of apologies. Hopalong cut him short. "What d' they call you?" he asked, curtly.

"Slow Jack," was the answer.

Hoppy grunted. "Well, you camp down right here," he ordered, "an' don't let nobody blot that sign. I 'm a-goin' to be here at daylight an' foller that screech-owl th' limit. Good-night."

He headed for the ranch house, satisfied that his section of range would remain undisturbed during the next few hours, at the least.

* * * * *

"Sweet birds-o'-paradise! Would you-would you oblige me by squintin' at that!"

Straight north, from the few dead carcasses where the trail started it led to the creek bank, east of the ranch house; and like hounds with nose to scent, Hopalong, Buck, and Ned had followed it from the point where Slow Jack had been found doing sentry-go and sent, in profane relief, to breakfast and sleep. Hoppy was in the lead and as he came to the creek he raised his eyes to look across at the other bank for signs of the quarry's exit from the water. It was the sign on the north bank, coupled with that on the somewhat higher bank where they stood, that had made him exclaim.

Ned Monroe's face cleared of the frowning perplexity that had darkened it at first sight of the hoof prints they tracked. "Must be a stranger," he affirmed. "Dunno th' country or he 'd never jump when he could ride through."

"Jump!" exclaimed Buck, startled. "Why, of course," he conceded. "Hoppy, that's shore one scrumptious jump"; and the dawning admiration grew to wonder as he mentally measured the distance.

Hoppy nodded his head. "*I* never see th' horse could do it right now; an' that bird flew over there last night. He was right on it afore he knew an' he did n't stop to remember how deep it was; he just dug in a spur an' lifted him at sight of th' breakin' bubbles: they 'd show purty nigh white last night-an' th' horse, he does n't know how much he has to jump, so he jumps a good one —a d —n good one, though Ned, here, don't think it so much. Mebby you know a horse as could do it right easy, eh, Ned?"

With Hopalong's sharp eyes on his face, Ned shook his head in denial, gazing stolidly at the sign. "Too good for any in these parts; would n't be no disgrace for a thoroughbred."

Buck glanced quickly at Ned and then, pulling his hat low over his eyes, struck up the brim with two snappy blows of the back of his hand.

"Well, Buck, I reckon I 'll leave you an' Ned to foller this. I got a feelin' I 'm wanted at th' ranch. So long." Hopalong rode off in obedience to one of the signals that had helped to simplify affairs among the Bar-20 punchers.

Buck had signified his desire for Hoppy's absence. He pushed Allday to the creek and set off at a lope. "Easy as follerin' a wagon, Ned," he remarked.

"Yep," agreed Ned.

"Stopped here," observed Buck. "Listenin', I reckon. Goin' slower, now."

"Some," replied Ned.

"Right smart jump acrost that creek," said Buck, questioningly.

"Uh-huh!" consented Ned, with non-committal brevity.

They rode a couple of miles before Buck hazarded another remark. "Seems like I oughta know that hoof," he complained. "Keeps a-lookin' more 'n more like I knowed it. Durn thing purty nigh talks."

Ned threw him a startled glance and then gazed steadily ahead. "Be at th' Jill in a minute," he announced.

"Yeah. Thought he was driftin' that-away. Lay you ten to two he don't *jump* th' Jill, Ned."

"Here 's Charley," was the irrelevant response. The Indian was a welcome diversion. Buck slowed to a walk, raised his eyes and waved Charley an amiable salute. The Cheyenne promptly left the trail and rode to join them.

"Hey, Charley, whose horse is that?" asked Buck, pointing to the hoof prints.

The Indian barely glanced at them. "French Rose," he declared. "Cross trail, swim river before sun. Heap good horse."

"Where goin', Charley-ranch?" asked Buck, evenly. He did not question the Cheyenne's conclusions. *He knew.* Buck was satisfied of that.

Charley grinned sheepishly and shifted uneasily under Buck's stare. "That's all right," assured Buck, "tell Jake to give you-no, wait for me. I 'll be there as soon as you are." He turned away and Charley accepted his dismissal in high good humor, riding off with cheering visions of a cupful of the "old man's" whiskey, which was very different from that dispensed over the bar in Twin River.

"Well, Ned," said Buck.

"Well, Buck," returned Ned.

"You knew it was Rose's horse."

"I was a-feared."

"You knew it, you durn ol' grizzly."

"Look a-here, Buck. You ain't goin' to tell me as how Rose —"

"Not by a jugful! That's a flower without a stain, Ned, an' I backs her with my whole pile."

"Here, too," coincided Ned, in hearty accord.

"We lost th' trail, Ned."

"You bet!"

"In th' Jill."

"Took a boat," suggested Ned, solemnly.

Buck concealed his amusement. "Or a balloon," he offered.

"Mebby," assented Ned. "Could n't pick her up agin, nohow."

"Not if we 'd had a dog," declared Buck.

"Or a' Injun," supplemented Ned. They gazed at one another for a second and, of one mind, spun their horses around and off for the ranch like thoroughbreds at the drop of the flag.

"I just thought o' Charley," explained Buck.

"Here, too," grunted Ned.

"Might talk," said Buck.

"You bet."

Charley heard them coming. When he saw them, the explanation to his untutored mind was a race. Determined to be in at the finish, he laid the quirt to his pony with enthusiastic zeal, casting a rapid glance over his shoulder, now and then, to see if he were holding his own. It was a sight to see the tireless little pony wake up under punishment. He had covered twenty miles that day and over forty the day before, but he shot forward on his wiry legs like a startled jack-rabbit and in one-two-three order they thundered up to the ranch house with a noise that brought Mary to the door.

"Well, Buck Peters!" she exclaimed, "ain't you *never* goin' to grow up? Yo're worse'n that loco husband o' mine, right now."

Buck grinned at the abashed Ned and winked knowingly at Mary. He and Mary were very good friends, Buck long ago having gauged her sterling worth and become aware of her mischievous propensity for teasing. As he led Charley indoors he asked for Hopalong and learned that he had set off for Twin River soon after his arrival at the ranch house.

* * * * *

Hopalong had taken his cue from Buck without question but not without curiosity. On his way to the house he decided, not without a longing thought in the direction of Red Connors, foreman *pro tem* of the Bar-20, that Tex Ewalt would be all the better for a knowledge of recent events. Therefore he paused only long enough to inform Mary of his intention before starting in search of him. At Twin River he pulled up at the Why-Not and went in for a drink. Tex was standing at the bar and ten minutes after Hopalong left, Tex had overtaken him on the Wayback trail. They struck off through the undergrowth until secure from observation, and Tex was soon acquainted with the latest attempt at stock reduction.

He listened silently until Hopalong mentioned the kind of man who had done the killing. "Big Saxe," he exclaimed. "So, that's his game. Well, we got 'em now, Hopalong. I can lay my hands on that cow-killer right soon, an' he 'll squeal, you bet. An' I got a long way to go. *Adios.*"

"Blamed grasshopper!" grumbled Hopalong. "Never even guessed where that horse come from. If Big Saxe is on him yet, you shore got a long journey, Tex."

Chapter XVIII
Karl to the Rescue

Dave, harboring a fermenting acerbity beside which the Spartan boy's wolf was a tickling parasite, lay hidden behind a stunted pine, his glasses trained on the Schatz cabin. Sourly he reviewed his several plans, each coming to nought as surely as if Peters had been made aware of it in its inception. The last grand coup, from which he had expected to derive immediate benefit, had arrived prematurely and mysteriously at its unexpected denouement; and that fool Saxe, upon whom he had relied to create a diversion, must needs keep himself hidden, to turn up when his efforts would be worse than useless. And then to come to Dave to be paid for making a fool of himself! He cursed aloud at the recollection. "It was a good scheme, too," he asserted savagely. No use telling him all those cows had stampeded and hurled themselves to destruction —"When the money for 'em was as good as mine." It had never been his real intention to allow Murray and Jack to divide the profits and by a curious mental strabismus he readily saw how he had been robbed. But losing the money was not the only nor the greatest blow. The injury to his sorely tried vanity hurt the most. He had been beaten, not so much by the enemy as by one of his friends.

Clouded by that same vanity his reason had acquitted all those who might have betrayed him, excepting Schatz. Rose, a woman who loved him-he had dismissed the thought with scorn; Comin', Cock Murray; they had all to lose and nothing to gain by treachery: and all the others were bound to him by ties, the weakest of which was stronger than any Buck could have formed in the time. Schatz alone might prove a gainer. He did not know in what way, but purposed to discover. That was why he was watching now. He knew Schatz was at home: he had seen the smoke of his breakfast fire. "Allus *is* home," he grated. He anticipated the calling of Schatz' agents at the cabin and when Schatz came out and finally rode off on the Twin River trail, Dave was disconcerted. He followed with much care, making good use of his glasses. The sight of Schatz turning off the trail and riding toward the Double Y ranch house filled him with a cold fury. —He determined to intercept him on his return and have it out on the spot.

But Dave, intent upon the unconscious back of Karl, had been careless of the surrounding country; and only his luck in choosing to wait in a place remote from cover, saved him just then from a rude awakening. Dodging about in the vain effort to approach to a point of vantage, was Pickles; he had finished certain mystic incantations involving the running at speed in circles, and was returning to await the fulfilment of his wish. Filled with awe as he was at this swift response, it did not prevent him from acting upon it.

His arrival at the nearest possible point showed him that Dave was still out of range. For the first time a doubt of Buck's omniscience assailed him: it was no part of wisdom to arm a man with a rifle of that sort. With cautious speed he retraced his steps, mounted the Goat, and scurried for the ranch by a roundabout route. There was nothing haphazard about this; his ideas were clearly defined: did n't Red Connors always borrow Hopalong's Sharps for long range? That showed. Pickles had implicit faith in the rifle. All that worried him was that Dave might not wait long enough.

Karl rode leisurely up to the ranch house and called. Mary came to the door and behind her Buck, whose brow was wrinkled in the effort of composing a letter to McAllister. It was not an easy letter to write and Buck had enlisted Whitby's services. He asked Karl to climb down and come inside. Mary had disappeared with a promptitude due to instinctive dislike. Karl was not a man to invite the admiration of any woman at the best of times and now his appearance gave abundant proof of its being long past "chipping-time."

Karl entered with the unexpected lightness of step so often a compensating grace in fat men, shook hands with Whitby, accepted the proffered chair, and plunged into the reason of his visit with but little preamble. Whitby sat making idle marks with his pen; soon he began to write swiftly.

"Big lot of cows you loose, ain'd it?" he asked.

"A few," replied Buck.

"Vat you t'ink: stampede?"

"Looks like it."

"*Look* like it? *Donnerwetter*! Look like a drive."

"You seen it?"

Karl nodded. "Look like a drive," he repeated.

"Would n't surprise me none," admitted Buck. "We had Injuns shootin' 'em on th' range last night."

"*Himmel*! Vat fools!"

"Looks like they 're tryin' to drive me off 'n th' range."

"*Yah, aber* not me. Ten years und no trouble come."

"Huh! Well, what would *you* do?"

"Fight," advised Karl. "I vill fight if you let me in. I haf a plan."

"In where?" asked Buck, in some wonder.

"In der ranch —a partner. Look! Cows you must haf, money you must haf, brains you must haf: I bring dem. I bring shust so much money as you und your partner togedder. Der money in der bank *geht*. You buy der cows, goot stock, besser as before. Goot cows, goot prices, ain'd it? You pay for everyt'ing mit der money in der bank. I stay here und stop dot foolishness mit precipices und parasites und shooting. Vat you dink?"

"Let me get you. You want to buy in on the Double Y, equal partners. I put in so much, McAllister puts in so much, and you put in as much as both of us. Th' money goes in th' bank an' I have th' spendin' of it. You do yore share o' th' work an' yo 're dead certain you can stop th' deviltry on th' range. Is that it?"

"*Yah!*" assented Karl, emphatically.

Buck was astounded at the audacity of the proposal. His gaze wandered to Whitby, whose pen was moving over the paper with a speed that impressed Buck, busy as his mind was. Outside, a horseman clattered up to the house and Mary, from the kitchen door, motioned Hopalong to come in that way. The door had no sooner closed behind him than Pickles sped from the security of the stable, slipped Hoppy's rifle from the saddle holster, and half a minute later the Goat went tearing away, bearing the triumphant boy and the coveted rifle to another scene of operations. For tenacity of purpose and facility of execution, Pickles was already superior to most men.

Buck recovered his wits and faced the expectant Schatz. "I just been a-writin' to McAllister," he informed him. "You 'll have to give me time to see what he says. Let's liquor."

* * * * *

Buck stood in the door watching Karl ride away; the expressionless face gave no hint of his feelings unless it were found in a certain cold hardness of the gray eyes in their steady stare, fixed upon the broad back of the receding German. Leaving this mark, his glance fell on the horse, waiting patiently for its late rider, and he turned back into the room and called: "Hoppy!" Hopalong came in from the kitchen and Buck met his entry with the question: "What do you think that Dutch hog come for?"

Hopalong glanced meaningly at Whitby, who still appeared to be writing against time. "That's all right," asserted Buck, "I 'm a-copperin' my bets from now on. Schatz wants to buy in as a partner an' reckons he can stop th' Double Y from losin' any more stock, long 's he 's in on th' deal."

"What 'd *you* say?" asked Hopalong.

"Nothin'. I wanted a chance to get my breath."

"Well, I would n't flirt with that proposition, not any."

"Why, curse his fool hide, what do I want with him or his money? If he can stop th' deviltry mebby he 's at th' bottom of it; an' if he is, it won't be long afore we know it. Next time he comes I 'll tell him to go plumb to h —l."

"I would n't, Buck."

"What's that?" asked Buck, staring hard at Whitby.

"I would n't," repeated Whitby. "I fancy it's time you learned what I know. This German chap, now. You can't fight him yet, Buck; you can't, really."

"Oh, can't I!" exclaimed Buck. "What do you know about it?"

"I know all about it, I should say all that can be found out. Do you mind if we have in Mrs. Cassidy? Clever woman, Mrs. Cassidy."

He left the room while Buck and Hopalong eyed each other helplessly. "D —d if he ain't tellin' me what kind of a wife I 've got," complained Hopalong. Mary came in, followed by Whitby.

"Now if you two boys 'll only listen to Whitby, you 'll learn somethin',", promised Mary.

"It began in Chicago," said Whitby. "Beastly hole, Chicago. I was n't at all sorry to leave it, except-but that's neither here nor there. McAllister is a friend of mine and he rather thought Buck under-rated the difficulties here; so he asked me to run out and look it over. I soon found it was jolly well too big for me so I wrote to the Governor-my father, at home you know-and he said he 'd foot the bills. So I put it in the hands of a detective agency; very thorough people, 'pon my word. They tell me this German chap is at the bottom of the mischief but they can't prove it. He is always behind somebody else. If Ned Monroe had not been honest and given up, McAllister would never have won his case in that court: Schatz owns the judge, so they tell me. Amazin' country, is n't it? And then he is far too clever to wage a losing fight: you would have won at the last, despite his efforts. Now he 's come with his offer of partnership. Clever idea, really. He 'll jolly well use you if he can't beat you; and no doubt he expects to trick you, Buck, in some way, perhaps lending you money-then, you out of it, he has McAllister at a disadvantage.

"My idea is this: take Schatz in as a partner and he 'll grow less careful. We shall be able to trip him up. Remarkable man, really. Not one of those he employs can be made to talk; they 're entirely loyal. But sooner or later he will make a mistake: rogues all do, even the cleverest of them; and if they continue to escape, it is merely because no one happened to be watching and catch them at it. I 'll lend you the money, Buck —"

"But what in-what do I need money for, Whit? Ain't th' range an' th' cattle enough?"

"Of course they are. But the German wants to see some cash capital and it will do no harm to give him plenty of rope, will it now?"

"But, Whit," objected Hopalong, "if yo 're shore it's th' Dutchman, we can drive him out of th' country so quick he 'll burn his feet. Men 's been shot for less 'n he 's done."

"You can't do it, Cassidy. The agency has n't been able to get a bit of proof. And McAllister is set against anything rash. I thought at one time he had put on another man. There 's a chap who makes his headquarters at Twin River who 's busy, no end. The agency rather suspected he was one of Schatz's men. Sharp chap, that. And he can't be working on his own hook, can he?"

He glanced at Buck as if expecting a reply.

"That's Tex Ewalt, Whit," informed Mary. "He 's on our side."

"Ah! do you know, I thought as much. My word, I 'm thirsty; wish I had a brandy and soda here." He paused to take a drink of water, shaking his head when Buck motioned to the whiskey. "I 'm afraid I shall never get used to that rye of yours," he declared, mournfully.

Buck turned to Hopalong. "What do you make of it?" he asked.

"If it depended on you alone, Buck, it would be easier to answer. But McAllister is in th' game an' it shore ain't Frenchy: we both know what he 'd 'a' done. What does McAllister think o' this partnership deal?" he asked Whitby.

"He has n't heard of it, but I 'm sure he would agree with me."

"All right!" exclaimed Buck. "We'll let Mac make th' runnin'. If it looks like he 's goin' to lose th' race it will be all th' easier to drop th' winner if we got him in gun range. But I shore hates to pay big interest, like I must, a-puttin' up money that way."

"Let me lend it you, Buck," advised Whitby. "The Governor will cable it fast enough when I ask for it. You won't have to pay me a penny interest. And when things settle down a bit you can turn it over to McAllister. I shall stop in this country. I like it, by Jove! And I 'm jolly well sure McAllister will sell out to me, particularly if—I say, Buck, have I made good out here in the West?"

Buck laughed as he grasped Whitby's hand. "Made good!" he repeated. "Yo 're th' best Britisher I ever knew an' I 've met some good ones in my time." With Hopalong's slap on his shoulder and Mary smiling at him from her chair by the window, Whitby felt that it was likely to prove a very pleasant country "when things settled down a bit."

"Let's get at that letter to Mac," suggested Buck. "Th' sooner I hear from him th' easier I 'll be in mind."

"I 've written it," answered Whitby. "If you like I 'll get it to Wayback to-night and stop over until morning."

"Go ahead," agreed Buck.

When he had left, Hopalong turned to his wife with the query: "How did he find out yo 're a clever woman, Mary?"

"Because he 's a clever man, only he hides it," replied Mary. "He was a-gassin' 'bout you an' Buck an' I naturally found out a thing or two myself. That's how he came to tell you. He regular confided in me an' I advised him to tell you-all."

"It was a safe bet you 'd find out more 'n you 'd let go," complimented Hopalong.

"Oh, you Billy-Red!"

* * * * *

When Pickles, mounted on the Goat, had left the ranch by a roundabout way he headed for the bottom of one of the range's many depressions and followed it until close to the Jill, where he turned south and began edging nearer and nearer to the place he had seen Dave. Pickles had listened to many tales of hunting and as his associates had been grown men, experienced in stalking, the boy had absorbed a great deal of healthy knowledge which he made use of in his playing, in the great outdoors. With a grave thoughtfulness beyond his years he now proceeded to put his knowledge to a sterner use and worked cautiously toward his objective without loss of time. When he rode up the bank of a draw, alert and wary, and saw the solitary horseman still keeping his patient vigil, he swiftly dismounted, picketed the Goat and, taking the heavy rifle, crept forward, crouching as he went.

He had come to the edge of the cover and saw Dave still very far away; and after vainly trying to find some way to get closer to the man he was after, he carefully opened the breech of the heavy Sharps to be again assured it was loaded. A bigger cartridge than he had ever used confronted him: four inches of brass and lead, throwing a 600-grain bullet by the terrific force of one hundred and twenty grains of powder. The forty-five Sharps Special raised Hopalong another notch in Pickles' estimation-truly it was a man's weapon.

"Gosh!" he gloated, and then glanced thoughtfully across the open plain towards the horseman. "Twelve hundred, all right," he muttered, regretfully, for one hundred would have suited him better. But a swift smile chased away the scowl. The rifle belonging to Hopalong never missed-he had Buck's word for that-and besides, he had made his wish. One last look around for a cover nearer to Dave, and the big sight was raised and set. The gun went to his shoulder and the heavy report crashed out of a huge cloud of gray smoke as the Sharps spoke.

The rifle belonging to Hopalong never missed — and besides, he had
made his wish

Dave's sullen temper was rudely jogged into fierce and righteous anger. Something hit his face. Something else screamed past him, struck a rock and whirred into the sky with a sharp, venomous burr. The pony, resenting Dave's painful appropriation of part of his ear, went up into the air and came down on stiff legs, its back arching once as it landed. The instant the hoofs were firmly on the ground it stretched out and ran as it never had before, Dave helpless to check it. The heavy, sharp report of the huge rifle in Pickles' hand had no sooner reached him than he had all he could do to hold his seat. But the sound of that bullet passing him, lingered in his mind long after he had regained control of his terrified mount.

Pickles, swallowing hard and holding one shoulder with a timidly investigating hand, blinked his dazed eyes as he looked about, inquiringly. He remembered pulling the trigger-and then the Goat had reached out thirty feet and kicked him in the neck-and if it wasn't the Goat, who threw the rock? Dave! He sat up and then struggled to his feet, looking eagerly out to see the remains of Dave scattered carelessly over the landscape. Dave was fast getting smaller, a cloud of dust drifting to the south along his trail.

"D —n it!" cried the boy, tears of vexation in his eyes. "He got away! I missed! I missed!" he shouted. "Buck lied to me! Th' old gun ain't no good!" and in the ecstasy of his rage he danced up and down on the discredited weapon. "Whitby's witches ain't no good! Nothin's no good; an' I missed him!"

Meanwhile his injuries were not becoming easier: his head displayed a large, angry lump, and ached fit to burst; his shoulder was n't broken, he decided, as he exercised it tentatively, but not far from it; and a piece of skin was missing from his bleeding cheek.

"I ought to 'a' got him," he muttered sullenly, picking up the rifle and moving slowly back to where his horse was picketed. "Well, anyhow, he was awful scared —I *knowed* he was a coward! I knowed it! If this old gun was as good as its kick I *would* 'a' got him, too." Pickles had gauged the distance perfectly and his hand had not even quivered when he pulled the trigger-but he had yet to learn of windage and how to figure it. Dave owed his life to the wind that swept the dust of his pony's feet southward.

When Pickles had turned the horse into the pasture he reloaded the rifle before slipping it back into its long leather scabbard. It must be found as he had found it and, besides, he was plainsman enough to realize how serious it might be for Hopalong if he believed the weapon was loaded and found it empty in a crisis.

"Never missed, hey?" he growled savagely as he moved away. "Huh! *Next* time, I 'll use *Buck's* gun!"

Chapter XIX
The Weak Link

The little buckskin pony stood with wide-planted feet and hanging head; his splendid bellows of lungs and powerful abdominal muscles sent the wind in and out of the distended nostrils in the effort to overcome the effect of that last mad burst of speed demanded of him; in his eyes alone, battling against the haze, shone his unconquerable spirit. Bearing saddle and bridle Dave strode away from him to the cabin.

Straight in from Wayback, without a stop, the game little buckskin had carried Dave. Jealousy consumed him. Rumors of Smiler's defection were floating about the town and, though no one but those intimately concerned, knew the actual agreement made, the presence of the principals and their several places of call had been noted and fully commented upon. From such premises the town's deductions came near the truth.

The facts as known were enough for Dave. Whatever Schatz might be planning, Dave was satisfied that he had no part in it. That Schatz intended to treat him fairly was beyond the angle of his narrow mind. He was very calm over it, his face smooth of wrinkles, his movements slow and assured. He had passed through all the stages from irritation to rage-and beyond: Calm is always beyond.

"Mein gracious, Dave, you vas in a hurry?" asked Schatz, as Dave entered.

He hung saddle and bridle on a peg in the kitchen and strode through into the other room before replying. "No," he drawled, dropping into a chair and stretching his legs full length.

"No? Schust try to kill a horse, *vas?*"

"Yes. Played a trick on me this mornin' an' I 'm showin' him who 's boss."

"*Dummer Esel*! Und vor a trick you kill him! Den no more tricks, *vas*?"

"Oh, to h —l with th' cayuse! What's all this I hear o' you an' Peters in a lovin' match?"

"*Ach*! '*Nun kommt die Wahrheit*'! If you not come to-day, I send for you. Vy you stay avay like dot?"

"I 'm busy tryin' to make Peters good an' sick o' th' range, tryin' to drive him back to Texas, where he come from. What are you doin': payin' his passage or backin' him to win?"

"Paying his passage, Dave; vere, I am not sure. Look: here iss Herr Peters," stabbing a finger into the palm of his extended right hand, "und here iss McAllister," duplicating with his left; "und ven I do so," closing both hands tightly, "nobody iss left but Schatz."

"Easy as that, eh?" said Dave, sceptically.

"Schust so easy like dot. Look! I make me a pardner by der Double Y."

"Fine," drawled Dave, with hidden sarcasm.

"Vine as gold. Peters, he get all der money vat he can. McAllister, he send der same as Peters. Me, I got dot money, already. Der money vas in der bank. Der range iss my property schust so much as Peters und McAllister."

"Fine," repeated Dave.

"Peters, he dink he spend der money. Soon he go to buy cows. Now iss de point: to-morrow I go by der bank, I dake oud all der money. Four men iss guard. I say I go over by der Bitter Root vere der Deuce Arrow herd for sale iss; und I take all der money. Because dot bank in Vayback too small. I leave der bank und stop by der Miner's Pick saloon. Ve drink. A man vot vears a mask comes in. He cover us mit a gun. He take der money, ride away to Coon River by der Red Bluff. Dere iss man und boat. Der man mit der boat take horse und ride to first relay und pretty soon he iss in Rankin. A relay every ten miles. Der man mit der money go down river in der boat five mile und dere iss man mit two horses; he ride to Vayback und den here mit der money. Vat you tink?"

"Fine," said Dave, for the third time. "An' who 's goin' to do all that ground an' lofty tumblin' with th' money?"

"Dave Owens," replied Schatz, with an air of conferring a great favor.

"Me!" exclaimed Dave. He laughed cynically. "Why, Karl, if I had somebody to do all th' hard work, I can make plans like that, myself. Talk sense."

"Hard vork! It iss easy, like a squirrel up a tree. Everybody iss by der station ven der train comes. You take all der guns und ve not make noise, *aber* some thief know you got all der money und catch you first und rob you. Ve got no horses ven ve go by train, und must run, get horses to run after you. So you get avay. You come here mit der money und who know it?"

"Who's makin' th' blind trail?"

"Denver Gus."

"I don't envy Gus none."

"Vy? I pay him goot. He vas go to Texas, anyvay, pretty quick."

"How you goin' to get out of it?"

"I don't get out of it. Peters, he gets sick und I say: 'Vell, some money I got yet, I buy you out'; *aber* he tink it iss a trick und get mad. Four men I got, gun-men, all. Dey shoot him so soon he get mad."

"An' then McAllister jumps on you with both feet for takin' that money out o' th' bank in th' first place."

"*Ach*! Vat you dink? Am I a fool? Ain'd I a pardner already?'

"What's that got to do with it?"

"I have schust so much right to take der money as Peters. I don't steal der money-it iss steal avay from me. Can I help it?"

"Is that th' law?"

"Der law iss my part. For der law, brains you must haf. Brains I got. To ride, you know. Vat you dink?"

"I go you," declared Dave. "But you shore take a big chance with th' money. I *might* get plugged an' have to drop it."

"*Mein lieber Gott!*" moaned Schatz, in despair. "Brains! Brains!" he roared. "*Ach*! Vat use? Alvays it iss der same. Von day Canada iss der United States; so England iss *gebunden*; South America iss Deutchland; soon all der continent iss Deutchland. Vat fools! No *Verstand-blos* for money. Und to make money iss der little part. Vat fools!"

"Wake up! Who 's th' fool if I drop that bundle an' somebody on a good horse gets away with it? Because you can bet yore whole pile I ain't aimin' to stop an' stand off th' beginnin' of a Judge Lynch party, not any."

"Dave, if a veek you sit und a veek you tink, und schust about von ting, you know somethings about it, *vas?*"

"Shore would."

"Und mit *your* head you must tink. Many days mit *my* head I tink und tink, everythings, possible und not possible. Den ven der plans iss made, *you* mit *your* head mistakes find. Der money vat you steal, it iss no matter, *aber* don't lose it-besser you burn it, as lose it."

"*Burn* it?"

"Yah! Paper it iss, schust paper."

"Paper!" Dave stared in doubt. "Paper," he repeated, struggling to grasp the idea. He gave it up and quite humbly asked for light. "What th' blazes am I a-goin' to run away with paper for?"

"Maybe somebody smarter as I tink. Two men, already, much questions ask. Maybe Peters take all der money before me. So I go by der bank und get der money first. Dey can't help it. It iss my bank anyvay und der check iss dere."

"You 've *got* th' money!"

"Yah, here in der house I got it. Everythings iss *vollkommen*. All der mistakes vat come I know, possible und not possible. Noding can slip, noding can break."

"Yo 're a wonder!" congratulated Dave, "th' one an' only original, sure-fire, bull's-eye wonder." He leaned forward suddenly, head bent in listening. "Somebody outside," he warned, softly. Gun in hand, he sprang to the door and passed out. The gloom of the coming night lay in wait in the valleys but it was light enough to detect any skulker. Dave made a systematic search, satisfying himself that no one was within a mile of the cabin, before returning. "It's all right," he assured, as he entered the room again. A deafening roar followed his words. Schatz gave a convulsive start and slid slowly from his chair to the floor; on his face was an overwhelming surprise.

"Huh-Huh! Huh! —" the grunting laugh spoke immeasureable contempt. "Brains!"

* * * * *

The half-open drawer of the sideboard revealed in the lamplight a number of packages, the wrappings of several being torn open. Dave sat thoughtfully contemplating them. He had removed them from their hiding place and put them in the drawer before lighting the lamp, both acts due to precaution: spying upon Karl had discovered to Dave the hiding place; he was distinctly opposed to finding himself in the same predicament regarding his suddenly acquired wealth. The still figure, resting under two feet of earth, close to the river bank, gave him no concern whatever. His mind was busy with the best way to pack the money; small bills were difficult to trace but bulky to carry. He shoved the drawer to with his foot and re-lit his pipe. His plans were already made. He had reasoned them out swiftly while hunting the supposed skulker. The disappearance of Karl would be associated with the disappearance of the money. The bank would maintain that the money had been drawn on the day the check was dated, which necessarily must be to-morrow. The four men who were to act as guards would conclude some difficulty had arisen and await further orders; it would be the same with all the others involved. The way was clear for him. There remained only Rose. He knocked the ashes from his pipe and went to bed.

Chapter XX
Misplaced Confidence

Pickles was hungry. He cocked his eye anxiously at the sun and sighed. He gazed in discouragement over the widespread furrowed earth where his best efforts left so small a trace and dropping the hoe, sighed again. With all his soul he wished he had not fled from the Double Y. Sudden resolution armed him. He shoved his hands in his pockets and marched manfully in the direction of the house. He refused to go hungry for anybody.

Topping a rise, his head barely showed against the sky-line when he dropped as if shot. The horseman making for the house might be Jean; his glance had been too hasty for recognition. Flat against the earth, Pickles pushed himself backward until he felt it safe to turn and gallop clumsily down grade on hands and feet. Far enough, he sat and thought. He could gain the barn unseen and if he ran, would have time to dash into the house, grab some chuck, and get away again before the horseman got there. He sprang to his feet and ran like a long-horn steer, gazed upon by the stock in pasture with interest: they were not accustomed to this style of locomotion in trousers.

Pickles made excellent time on the level but when he turned to breast the slope it was harder going; and Pickles was tired; he had been at work since sun-up with a short rest at breakfast. He gained the barn winded but went through and crossed to the house without pausing. Back of the house he stopped to listen. He had cut it too fine. The horse was coming up to the door. "Darn it!" said Pickles, with bitter emphasis.

The snap of the catch on the front door and Rose's voice told him she had gone outside. Maybe the rider was n't coming in; they could n't see the end window if they did and if he were quick-he squirmed over the ledge, dropped noiselessly to the floor, sped through the doorway-and almost dislocated his spine with the ferret-like turn he made in trying to get back into the room the same instant he left it: he had barely escaped the other's entry; if Rose came to the bedroom she would be certain to exclaim at sight of him. Pickles breathed a short —a very short-prayer. He put his hands to the window ledge-and stiffened.

"No, I can't stay. Rose, I 'm pullin' my freight. How soon can you come along?"

It was Dave-he was going away-and he wanted Rose to go, too. Pickles knelt silently by the bunk and muffled his rapid breathing in the blankets, while he listened.

"Where?" asked Rose.

"Anywhere you say. I 'm a-goin' to clean up a gold mine in a few hours an' yo 're goin' to help me spend it. We 'll get married first stop."

"A gold mine?"

"More money than you ever saw."

"And you want-me-to go with you?"

"Not with me. I got to get th' money first. I 'll get th' train to Helena to-night. You get on at Jackson. You can make it easy on Swaller."

"I must know more. Perhaps you tell true. Perhaps you run away. Tell me."

"Got a good opinion o' yore future husband, ain't you? Quit foolin', Rose. Have I got to show you the cards afore you take a hand?"

"Yes," was the decisive answer.

"All right. It's this way: Schatz deals to Peters from a cold deck. He gets all th' money out o' the bank, Peters', McAllister's, an' his. Then he lets me lift it, him not knowin' who I am, o' course. I do th' mysterious disappearance act an' Schatz makes foolish noises too late. A posse takes after me an' runs into a blind trail. I circle back to town. Right there is where I fool Schatz. He thinks I 'm driftin' along the Big Moose trail to hand th' money over to him graceful. 'Stead o' that I 'm snortin' along the track to Helena with you. Schatz dassent make no holler an' we leave him an' Peters to fight it out. Do you get me?"

"They will kill you."

"Oh, not a whole lot, I reckon. I 'm gettin' so used to bein' killed thataway, I sorter like it. Talk sense. Where's th' ole man?"

"I will leave a letter for him."

"Hip hooray! Mighty nigh kissin'-time, Rose. *Would* be, on'y I can't leave this blasted cayuse: 'fraid to trust him. Which way you goin'? Don't show in Wayback. Hit th' river farther west."

Pickles had heard enough. His exit through the window was rapid and silent. His retreat from the house, made along two sides of a triangle, was prompted by his knowledge of the positions of Rose and Dave and he manoeuvred so they should not be able to see him. Nevertheless the security of the barn was very welcome, although he gained it only to recall that the Goat was at pasture. Then Swallow must be in the corral. He looked from the rear door. Yes, there he was, close to the fence, gazing across the grass at the field stock and no doubt wishing he were with them. Whimpering with suppressed delight the boy ran silently to his rope, hanging in long loops over two pegs in the wall; he coiled it ready to hand, crept out the door, and was at Swallow with the rush of a bob-cat. The great stallion made one mighty bound, lashed out one foot and stood with flattened ears; he knew the meaning of a rope in that position as well as any cow-pony in Montana and the indignity vexed while it subdued him. Pickles never bridled and saddled so rapidly in his short life. Keeping the barn between him and the house, he rode a mile or more out of his course before he dared to turn; then he took his bearings, set a straight line for the Double Y ranch, and gave Swallow his head. The good horse, scarcely feeling the boy's light weight, went forward with a rush, but responded to the light hand on the bridle and settled down, travelling mile after mile with the tireless stride and ease of movement that had won him his name.

Greatly as he wished for the journey's end, Pickles rode with judgment. The first doubt assailed him as he neared the Jill: would Swallow take the water? He was not kept long in doubt. Swallow knew better than to refuse. A master rider had put him through this stream, close to that very spot, in the dark of a not long distant night. The sight of the water sent the horse's ears pricking forward; he entered readily and swam for the opposite bank the moment the ground left his feet. Pickles shouted his delight; it would have broken his heart to have been compelled to go back to the ford. Swallow scrambled out onto the bank with little trouble and stretched out once more in his sweeping gallop; he knew now where he was bound and pulled impatiently against the restraining touch. The pace was a source of wonder to Pickles; seven miles and a swim at the end of it and here he was asking for a loose rein, demanding it, and going faster than ever. "Darned if I believe he *can* get tired," said Pickles; "go on then," and he gave him his head and smiled a tired smile to note how the powerful limbs quickened their action and the horse gathered pace until Pickles was travelling faster than ever before in his life. Only the smoothness of the motion gave him confidence in his own ability to hold out. "I could never 'a' made it on th' Goat," he reflected. "Go on, boy! Eat 'em up!" One slender black ear slanted toward him and away again. Swallow was eating 'em up the best he knew how.

* * * * *

Having made her decision, Rose listened carefully to Dave's advice. The more he talked the better she understood the situation; and Dave had scarcely mounted to ride away before she began her own preparations. They appeared to be very simple, merely the apparelling for a ride and keeping watch after Dave to see that he kept on his way.

Dave's disappearance sent her hurrying to the stable. She was surprised to find her bridle missing. On the next peg was Pickles' bridle, the only one ready for instant use. She hesitated a moment at sight of the heavy bit, but took it down and hastened to the edge of the pasture, sending a clear call for Swallow as she ran. There came no answering hoof-beats and she waited to reach the fence before calling again. A glance to right and left and she put her hands to her mouth and sent forth a ringing summons that carried to the far corner of the enclosure. The wait of a few seconds told her that Swallow was not in the pasture. Vexed and wondering she glanced from one to another of the animals near her: two draft horses, a brood mare, its long-legged colt close by, all watching her with that spell-bound intensity of gaze frequently accorded the sudden appearance of a human among domestic animals running free. Swallow would never be turned in the same field as these; then where was he? Jean was riding the only saddle pony-no, there was the Goat. Suspicion awoke in Rose: was it possible Pickles had dared to ride away on Swallow!

The Goat had ideas of his own; he had positively no use for a bridle just then, but Rose had ideas of a distinctly superior order of intelligence and but little time was lost before the Goat was plunging away to where Pickles should be, carrying Rose astride and bareback. Her suspicions were confirmed in part: Pickles was not where he should be. She swung the Goat through a half circle on his hind feet and started back for the barn with a rush. Ten minutes later, the Goat, properly saddled, turned short out of the farm road with a cat-like scramble onto the Twin River trail. He had not carried so much weight since his old master rode him and he did not like it, but knew better than to shirk; he had tried that, and the spurs, two of them, clanking loosely on Rose's small boots, had ripped his sides with quite an old-time fervor. Rose had found time to adjust them after saddling; the last hole barely held them but they served. How she longed for the free-striding gallop of Swallow! The tied-in gait of the Goat was irksome to her but she kept him to his work and Twin River drew rapidly nearer. With Dave's instructions in mind she knew there was plenty of time but it would be foolish to lessen the margin of safety by loitering.

A quarter of a mile from the ford she passed the stage from Wayback. The driver was just whipping up to enter Twin River in style and the stage occupants had opportunity to appraise Rose as she forged ahead. "My heavens, what a beauty!" exclaimed a young lady on the seat beside the driver, herself no mean specimen of God's handiwork. "Who is she?"

The driver shifted his whip and swept off his hat with a flourish. He gazed admiringly after the rider. "That, ma'am, is the French Rose; an' this is certainly my lucky day. I ain't seen two such pretty women before in one day, not in a dog's age. I ain't never seen 'em," he amended with enthusiastic conviction.

The coach cut through the ford to the hiss of the swirling water and turned into the straight in time for them to see a man run out from the Sweet-Echo to meet Rose, standing with his hand on the bridle while Rose leaned forward in what looked suspiciously like a warm greeting.

Another exclamation escaped the young lady on the stage: "Whitby!" and the blush called forth by the driver's frank admiration paled as she watched the two whom they rapidly approached.

"Know him, ma'am?" asked the driver politely; but his companion was oblivious to all but the scene before her.

Rose's imperious gesture and call had brought Whitby running. They had achieved a warm regard for each other during Rose's numerous visits to the Double Y, made at Dave's instigation; visits that had not ceased until the arrival ef Hopalong and Mary, when Dave had declared it was no use to try longer. Whitby grasped the significance of Rose's hurried words in very brief time. "By Jove!" he exclaimed, thinking rapidly. "By Jove! he will do it, too. They can't refuse to honor his check, you know. Buck is the only one can stop it. Lucky Pickles was gone and you came here instead of going to the Wayback bank. Buck has n't long left me. I can catch him." He ran around to the shed at the rear and was going fast when he turned into the trail, astride his pony. His reassuring wave of the hand to Rose stopped in mid-air as he caught sight of Margaret McAllister, standing on the footboard of the coach and looking at him with an expression he did not in the least understand. He made as if to pull up, thought better of it, and sweeping off his hat, dug the spurs into his pony and shot out over the Big Moose trail at a speed that promised to get him somewhere very soon.

* * * * *

Dave had not left the LaFrance cabin far behind when he pulled up with an oath and after a short period of consideration, turned back, riding at fair speed. He found cause to congratulate himself in starting early: it gave him time to go back to Rose and furnish her money in case of need. He saw her sooner than he expected. Turning a slight bend in the trail, he had full view of the Goat, not two hundred yards away, and saw him bound forward like a racer as the spurs ripped into him; Dave gripped a shout in his throat at sight of this act: why was Rose in such a hurry? Suspicion ebbed and flowed in his mind. If she were in such a hurry, why was n't she on Swallow? But the spurring had been for speed, not for punishment. Maybe she was saving Swallow for the longer journey. But if content to tell her father by letter of her going, who in Twin River needed a personal call? She could not be going farther than Twin River-to the Double Y, for example: there was not time for that. And why should she want to go there, either? Dave shook his head impatiently. Either she was square or she was n't. If she was n't, there would be a group of hard-riding boys pounding along the trail in time to cut off Schatz at the bank. He decided to ride to within a short distance of town, lay off the trail, and wait. If no one showed up, he would stick to the original plan. If Rose played crooked, he would take a train East. If too hard pressed, he could use the relays south in place of Denver Gus. Denver might put up an argument but he had one answer to all arguments that had always silenced opposition the moment he produced it. "Get on, bronc," he commanded, heading for Wayback.

* * * * *

Buck had got farther south than Whitby suspected; so far, that Whitby was beginning to hope he had not struck off from the trail, when he sighted him. Buck was riding head on shoulder, as if he had heard the coming of his pursuer, and he pulled up at the other's wild gesture. "What's eatin' him?" said Buck, smiling for the thousandth time at Whitby's manner of riding; it was a constant wonder to Buck that a man could sit a horse like that and stick to the worst of them as Whitby did. "He shore ain't meanin' to swim the Black Jack to get to the Fort." The smile faded as he suddenly realized the appeal in the Englishman's frantic waving; he rode forward rapidly and they were soon near enough together for Whitby to be sure his words would be heard and understood.

"Twin River, Buck! Twin River! And ride like h —l!"

Buck's quirt bit into his pony's flank. Never before had he known the Englishman profane; it must be serious. Whitby turned and raced ahead of him, rapidly over-taken by Buck who rode a fresher and speedier mount. As they ran side by side, Whitby rapidly repeated Rose's news.

"I can make it, Whit," declared Buck. "They won't try to work th' game till closin' time at th' bank. Train bound west is due at Wayback about then. Wish I had Allday under me. So long."

Whitby slowed to a lope and Buck drew away rapidly. His duty accomplished, the English-man's thoughts turned to the puzzling expression on Margaret McAllister's face, as he had last seen it. He tried in vain to analyze it and unconsciously pressed his tired horse into a faster pace in his anxiety for an explanation.

Buck did not spare his pony. He *must* be at the bank before the money was paid over. The stringing up of Schatz by Judge Lynch would not bring the money back; and Buck had grave doubts of his ability to accomplish this retribution. Schatz appeared to grow stronger the more he knew of him. Nobody but a man very sure of himself and his power would dare such deviltry. Well, it would come to a personal straightening of accounts. Buck's grim face was never sterner. But first he must get to the bank. Resolutely putting aside all other considerations he gave his whole mind to his horse. Presently he shook his head: "Never make it," he muttered; "have to relay at Twin." Even as he said it he saw ahead of him another rider approaching at an easy lope; an expression of gratified pleasure appeared on Buck's face as he saw the other dismount and begin to lengthen the stirrup leathers. It was Rose. "By G —d! What a woman!" exclaimed Buck. "She thinks as quick as Cassidy an' never overlooks a bet."

He urged his pony to its best speed. With a fresh mount in sight, his object was practically assured. As he drew near, Rose called out: "Horse wait for you at Two Fork Creek."

He pulled short beside her in two jumps. "Rose, I love you," he declared, his eyes sparkling with pleasure; "you 'd oughta been a man!" He sprang to the ground while speaking and was astride the Goat at a bound, turning in his saddle to call back to her: "But I 'm most mighty glad yo 're not." A wave of his hand and he faced about, settling in his seat for the run to Two Fork, five miles beyond Twin River.

The crimson flood that burned in her face at his first remark, to recede at his second, returned in full tide as she stood with lips apart and eyes wide, watching him ride away. A trembling seized her, so that she clung to the saddle for support. The moving figure became blurred as the tears gathered in her eyes; she brushed them away impatiently with the back of her hand. "He is not mean it that way," she murmured; "it is only that he is glad I think about the horse."

She mounted and rode soberly toward Twin River. The pony, awaiting the customary notice to attend to business and finding it long in coming, began to entertain a sneaking affection for skirts, which until then he had regarded with suspicious hostility.

Chapter XXI
Pickles Tries to Talk

Mary sat at the window sewing —a continuous performance with her these days. The sound of a horse approaching caused her to glance up just as a faint call for "Buck" reached her. One look and the sewing fell to the floor as she sprang to her feet, crying out for Jake as she ran. With Swallow nuzzling at her dress, she supported Pickles until Jake came to aid; he lifted the boy from the saddle and carried him into the house.

Mary hastily got out the whiskey and Pickles gulped down a mouthful before he realized what it was. He choked, and pushed away the cup. "Don't want it," he declared, weakly; "ain't never goin' to drink."

"Good boy," encouraged Mary, patting his head. "You stick to that."

"Where 's Buck?" asked Pickles.

"He ain't come back yet," answered Mary.

"Where is he?" insisted Pickles.

"I don't know," was the patient reply.

"I gotta find Buck," the boy declared, starting to rise.

Mary pushed him back. "How can you find him when you don't know where he is?"

"Ain't he som'er's on th' range?"

"No; him an' Whit rode off Twin River way this mornin' an' they ain't neither of 'em back yet."

"Well, I gotta find him, an' I gotta find him now," declared Pickles. "Lemme go."

"What's eatin' you?" demanded Jake. "*You* ain't fitten to ride *no* place an' I 'm mortally certain you can't walk."

"Shut yore trap, Woolly-face. What's a sheep like you know, anyhow? Nothin'! Can't even dig holes less 'n yo 're prodded with lead. Lemme go."

The whiskey was having an effect on Pickles or he never would have shown malice like this. Besides, it was not true and Pickles knew it. To all questions he had but one answer and Mary was in despair when Hopalong strode into the room. Hoppy wanted to know things —"Where'd you get that horse?" he asked, sharply.

"Huh?" queried Pickles.

"Where 'd you get that horse-that horse you was ridin'?"

"That's Rose's horse-where 's Buck?"

"Rose who?"

"Huh? French Rose. Say, where's Buck?"

"French Rose, hey? Say, Mary, that's th' horse got away from me with that cow-killin' screech-owl th' other night."

"That horse? Rose LaFrance's horse? Oh, Billy!"

It seemed that Mary was deeper in Buck's confidence than his old friend Hopalong, in this matter, at all events.

"Say you, blast you! Where's Buck? Lemme go! What's eatin' you? Ah, h —l!" Pickles relaxed under the grasp of Jake's hands and limply essayed to retrieve his reputation. "I asks yore pardon, ma'am. I promises Buck I won't never swear afore a lady an' here I goes an' does it, first time I 'm mad."

Hoppy eyed the penitent keenly. "Say, Bud; what's wrong?" he asked, quietly. "Buck ain't got no better friend than me and I 'll find him for you; but there ain't no good huntin', less 'n I got somethin' to say when I get there."

"Will you? Bully for you! Tell Buck th' Dutchman 's goin' to get all th' money-then Dave 's goin' to get it-it's in th' bank-on'y Schatz don't know who it is-nobody catches Dave runnin' into a blin' trail thataway-then Dave takes th' money to th' Dutchman-but right here 's where he fools him-he don't take it-he keeps it-an' he marries Rose on th' train to Helena-Rose rides Swaller to Jackson to get th' train-on'y she has got to get another horse 'cause I rode Swaller here. D 'you get me?" Pickles stared expectantly at Hopalong, who turned to Jake.

"Put that horse in th' barn. Saddle Allday. Rope a cayuse an' set that smoke a-rollin' —take a blanket an' ball th' smoke three times at th' end o' every minute-go through th' Gut an' up th' north side. *Pronto!*"

Jake went out of the door on the jump. He moved fast for Buck on occasion-rare, it is true-but there was a volcanic danger in Hopalong's eye that put springs in Jake's boot-heels.

"That's th' way to talk," sighed Pickles, happily. Hopalong went to the rack and took down his rifle. "Reckon yo 're goin' to want that?" asked Pickles.

"Reckon I might," admitted Hopalong, gravely. "You see, after I find Buck I 'm a-goin' to look for Dave an' th' Dutchman."

"Jiggers! I shore hopes you find 'em. I 'd sooner you get Dave than any man I know, 'ceptin' me."

"Well, I sorter count on gettin' Dave. So long, Pickles."

"So long," echoed the boy.

Mary followed her husband outside. "Don't get hurt, Billy-Red," she warned him.

"That sort o' vermin never hurt me yet, Mary. When th' boys get here send 'em after me to Wayback. Tell Ned, rifles. Let me have all th' money you got; if I miss Buck I might want it."

Mary watched him until he rode by on Allday, waving to him from the corner of the house. Then she went indoors to Pickles.

"That's a bully man, that Hopalong, ain't he?" was his enthusiastic greeting.

"He shore is; an' you 're a bully boy, Pickles," replied Mary. She took up her sewing again. The boy watched her curiously and was about to ask a question, when Sleep floated past and Pickles forgot to ask it.

Chapter XXII
"A Ministering Angel"

Mrs. Blake surveyed her surroundings with the surface calm which comes from seeing and disbelieving. These were depths to which she never had expected to descend. She allowed herself half a moment of speculation on the possibility of there existing, somewhere in the world, a real lack of accommodations as appalling as her imagination could now conceive. "I have often thought Mr. Blake somewhat careless in his choice of a hotel during our wanderings, but the worst of them never even suggested-Margie, did you ever in your life imagine such a room could exist?"

"It is only for an hour or so," returned Margaret, listlessly.

"Oh, I don't complain, my dear. You are an equal sufferer. And I am distinctly relieved at the thought of removing some of this terrible dust before we-before-we —"

Her voice trailed off into silence as she caught sight of a motto over the door; it was one of those affairs worked in colored worsted over perforated cloth; the colors had been chosen with less regard to harmony than is usually exhibited by an artist; perhaps it was contrast that was sought; as a study in contrasts it was a blasting success. Mrs. Blake glared at it with the fascinated interest of a spectator within the danger zone of a bursting bomb. "'God bless our home,'" she read, in awed undertone. "Perhaps He will, but it is more than it deserves." She mounted laboriously onto a chair and turned the motto to the wall, hastily facing it about again with a suppressed scream: if the front were chaos the back was a cataclysm. In a spasm of indignation she jerked it loose from its fastening and dropped it out of sight behind the evil-looking washstand. In this position her glance fell on the crude specimen of basin provided. She picked it up doubtfully and struck it against the side of the washstand. "Tin!" she exclaimed. "A dishpan!" and went off into peals of laughter, banging the pan and calling "Dinner!" in an unnaturally deep voice, when she could speak from laughing.

Margaret turned a sullen face from the window. She had seen the French Rose in animated conversation with a tall, good-looking man in flannel shirt and overalls, who had ridden away up the road, evidently in obedience to her orders; while Rose, herself, rode in the direction taken by Whitby. The soft, broad-brimmed hat, the waist but little different from the flannel shirt of the man, the ill-fitting skirt, the mannish gloves and clumsy boots-the superb health of the splendid figure proclaimed itself through all these disadvantages. The woman was a perfect counterfoil for Whitby, and Margaret hid the ache in her heart under a sullenness of demeanor that a less astute companion might have attributed to the annoyances and inconveniences of the journey.

"For heaven's sake, Aunt, don't make such a noise," she insisted; "my head aches as if it would split."

"Your head aches! I 'm sorry, my dear. Still, there are worse things than head-aches, now are n't there?"

Margaret stared. "No doubt," she admitted, tartly; "but it is the worst I have to submit, at present. When a greater evil befalls me I will tell you."

"Why, that's honest," said Mrs. Blake, cheerfully; "and as long as we are to be honest, you are sure it is not your conscience that is at fault?"

"My conscience?" asked Margaret. "What has my conscience to do with a head-ache?"

"First class in Physical Geography, rise. Jessie, what is the origin of the islands of head-aches that vex the pacific waters of the soul? They are due to volcanic action of bad conscience."

"Oh, Aunt! how can you be so absurd?"

"I would rather be absurd than unjust, Margaret."

"I don't understand you."

"You understood me very well. Because you see Whitby talking to a pretty woman, is that a reason to condemn him?"

"Talking! He kissed her before my very eyes, in the public street."

"You cannot say that, Margaret. I saw the meeting as plainly as you did."

"How could you? You were inside! Why has he never mentioned her in his letters?"

"Has he ever mentioned anything but business? He would scarcely mention her to George, and you know he has not written to you."

"No, he had something better to do. This is an unprofitable discussion. I am utterly indifferent to Mr. Booth's actions, past, present, and to come, as well as the reasons for them. If you intend to use that basin for something other than a dinner-call, do so. I 'm not hungry, but we might as well get it over with. We have a long drive before us."

"With all my heart, my dear; unless the water is on a par with the other-er-conveniences."

* * * * *

"Seems like Buck Peters might be in a hurry," observed Slick Milligan, sufficiently interested to come from behind the bar and walk out onto the porch. "Which it's th' first time I see him use a quirt."

"None o' thea punchers think aucht o' a horse," was Sandy's opinion, based on a wide experience.

If Margaret had chanced to overhear Slick's remark it would have explained much. Mrs. Blake was resting, preparatory to sallying forth on the last stretch of their journey, and Margaret was about to make inquiries regarding a conveyance, when the rapid drumming of a horse's feet drew her to the window as Buck went past. Margaret had never met Buck but she was far too good a horsewoman to fail to recognize the pony. She had noted every detail when she had first seen Rose and you may be sure no point, good or bad, of the Goat as a saddle pony, had escaped her critical judgment. Her first thought, as the Goat went past, was one of surprise that he should make so little of the weight of his rider, a full-grown man and no light-weight, either; lean and hard as Buck was, Margaret's estimate of the number of pounds the pony carried was very near the mark; and then, in a flash, she knew him: the very animal that the French Rose had ridden. Margaret knew it to be out of the question that he had travelled to the Double Y ranch and back; they must have exchanged horses on the road. But, why?

The consideration of this enigma and the many possibilities it offered as collateral questions, occupied her fully, to the very grateful content of Mrs. Blake, who was genuinely tired and ashamed to say so. It was a consideration so perplexing that Margaret was prepared to allow Whitby to explain, when he was so unfortunate as to appear in company with Rose. He had overtaken her, a half-mile down the trail, but Margaret could not, of course, know this. They remained in earnest conversation for two or three minutes, when Rose went on and Whitby went around to the shed to put up his pony. Margaret ran down stairs and went out onto the porch. She felt better able to face him in the open.

It was thus that Whitby, coming in at the back door, was directed out through the front one. Rapidly as Margaret moved, she was too great an attraction to escape instant notice. Whitby advanced with outstretched hand. "Ripping idea, taking us by surprise, Miss McAllister. Awful journey, you know, really."

"We wished to avoid giving trouble. You are looking very well, Mr. Booth."

"Fit as a fiddle, thank you. But —I say-you 'll excuse me, —but are n't you feeling a little-ah-seedy, now? I mean —"

"I quite understand what you mean. Am I looking a little-ah-seedy, Mr. Booth?"

"No, certainly not! Very stupid of me, I'm sure. I —ah-rather fancied-but of course I 'm wrong. This confounded dust gets in a chap's eyes so —"

"Do you mean that my eyes look dusty, Mr. Booth?"

"Oh, I say! Now you 're chaffing me. As if —"

"Not in the least. Chaffing is an art in which I fail to excel. But if you mean that I look a little pale and dragged with the journey, you must remember that I do not pretend to have the vitality of a cow-girl."

"Ah! Just so. And Mrs. Blake-she is with you, I presume."

"The presumption is justified. Aunt's vitality was even less equal to the journey than my own. She is resting and begs to be excused until she can say 'How do' at the ranch."

"Why-ah-how did Mrs. Blake know I called in?"

Margaret bit her lip. "I happened to be looking from the window as you rode up," she explained, carelessly.

"Ah! Just so. Miss McAllister, you don't know me very well, not really; perhaps no better than I know you. I 'm no good at this sort of thing, this fencing with words, you know; I discovered that long ago; and I long ago adopted the only other method: to smash right through the guard. My presumption does n't presume so far as to imagine you are jealous; I am not seeking causes; all I know is, you made me a promise when I came West, a conditional promise, I grant you: I was to make good. Well, I have n't done half bad, really. I fancy Mr. McAllister would admit as much. Buck Peters admits more; and one has to be something of a man, you know, to merit that from Peters. He 's the finest man I ever knew, myself, bar none. It is very good of you to hear me so patiently. I 'm coming to the kernel of the difficulty just now:

"Rose LaFrance, the cow-girl you mentioned, is the right sort. She brought word this morning that will save Peters a goodish bit of money; incidentally Mr. McAllister, also. Buck had to be in Wayback at the earliest possible moment and I was fortunate enough to overtake him. Miss LaFrance not only was thoughtful enough to ride to meet Buck and give him a fresh mount and to send a man ahead with whom Buck will change again, but she insists that we follow him, which is a jolly good idea; these fellows are very careless with their fire-arms and he might require help. If the blackguard he is after succeeds in withdrawing the entire deposit from the bank and it is given to him in cash, before Peters gets there, he will certainly require help. I leave you to reflect on these facts, Miss McAllister. Give my kindest regards to Mrs. Blake."

He stalked back the way he had come, in the characteristic wooden manner which precluded any appeal, if Margaret had felt like making one; but her mind was too fully occupied with what she had heard to understand that he was actually leaving. He was splashing through the ford before she realized the significance of this part of his defence. Thoughtful, and without resentment, she went to rejoin Mrs. Blake.

Whitby pushed his horse sufficiently to overtake Rose who, he knew, was riding slowly. Just outside the town he met Cock Murray, astride the Goat; the Goat was a very tired pony and showed it.

"My dear man! Why are n't you following Peters?" asked Whitby, in surprised remonstrance.

"My dear Brit! I sorta allowed it was n't healthy," answered Cock. "I tells you th' same as I tells th' French Rose: 'When Buck says "Scoot for th' ranch an' tell Cassidy to hit Wayback *pronto* an' he 'll get news o' me at th' bank,'" it 'pears like, to my soft-boiled head, that's what I oughta do."

"I beg your pardon. Of course. Rather odd Peters didn't tell me."

"He meant to. I 'm sorry he did n't. So long."

"So long," echoed Whitby, mechanically. He pulled up to shout after Cock: "You won't get far on that horse; he 's done, you know."

"I ain't goin' far on that 'oss," Cock shouted back; "an' they 're never done till they 're down, you know."

"Impudent beggar, but a good man. They grow 'em good out here. I fancy the bad-plucked ones don't last." And Whitby hastened on to overtake Rose.

He had left Two Fork Creek four miles behind him before sighting her; in her impatience she had gone faster than she knew. Whitby had almost caught up, when he saw Rose bend forward, wave to him, and then dash away, as if she were inviting him to a race.

"Buck!" exclaimed Whitby, with intuitive conviction. "It's Buck as sure as little apples Kesicks." Fifty yards' advance showed him that he was right. The figure lying huddled in the road was certainly Buck, and beside him was his dead pony. Rose flung herself from the saddle and ran to him; and Whitby, wearing the terribly savage expression of the man slow to anger, was not far behind. Together they laid the unconscious figure at full length.

Rose flung herself from the saddle and ran to him

"It is there," said Rose, dully, pointing to the right thigh.

"Ah," breathed Whitby, in a sigh of relief. He cut the cloth but forbore to tear it away, the coagulated blood having stopped the bleeding. "Drilled through!" he exclaimed. "Why, the swine must have been near enough to do better than that. How ever did he miss? We 'll bandage this as it is, Miss LaFrance, and do it properly at-now, should you say take him to the doctor at Wayback?"

"No. He is a drunken beast. I will nurse him."

"Very well. A good nurse is better than a drunken doctor. Just cut this sleeve from my shirt, will you?"

Rose took the knife and cut, instead, a three-inch strip from the bottom of her skirt, Whitby meanwhile producing a flask, from which he carefully fed Buck small quantities of whiskey. Rose tendered him the bandage. "Well rolled, Miss LaFrance! Have you been taught this sort of thing?" Rose silently nodded her head. "My word! Buck is in luck. You apply the bandage then, while I give him this. You 'll make a better job of it than I should."

Buck slowly opened his eyes to see Whitby's face bending over his. "Got away, Whit," he whispered, weakly; "ambushed me, by G —d," and relapsed into unconsciousness.

"Much blood! He have lose much blood," murmured Rose.

"Yes," assented Whitby. "How shall we carry him? He can never ride."

"Travois," said Rose. "I show you."

Buck again regained consciousness and his voice was distinctly stronger. "Get after him, Whit. He must n't get away."

"Oh, nonsense, Buck. They know the cat's out of the bag by this time and they will never be such asses as to try it on now. As for Dave, he can't get away. The agency will be jolly glad to do something for the money they have had by turning over Dave if I ask it of them. And McAllister will think you are worth a good bit more than the money, I lay. I know I do."

Buck was attempting feeble remonstrance when Rose returned from her survey of the timber available and swiftly placed her hands over his lips. "Do not talk," she commanded. "It is bad to talk, now."

"What price the nurse-eh, Buck? Oh, you lucky beggar!"

"Rose," murmured Buck. "Why, that's right kind."

Admonishing him with raised forefinger, Rose gave instructions to Whitby and he hastened away to gather material for the travois.

* * * * *

When Margaret returned to Mrs. Blake she was carrying a pair of driving gloves and a jaunty sailor hat which Mrs. Blake knew had been packed in one of the trunks. "Are we going to start, Margie?" she asked, with languid interest.

"*I* am going to start but I am going the other way. We shall not be able to leave for the ranch before morning, probably."

Mrs. Blake sat up with a suddenness that surprised even herself. "The morning!" she echoed. "If you think that I shall stay in this horror of a room until morning, Margaret, you are mistaken. I will go, if I walk."

"It's a long walk," commented Margaret, carelessly.

"And may I ask why you are going the other way and when you purpose to return?"

"I am going to Wayback to telegraph. Some thief has planned to get all of papa's money from the bank there, and of course he will try to escape on the train. We shall catch him by telegraphing to the officers at the next town."

"If you do he is a fool. And who are 'we'? How did you learn all this?"

"Whitby told me."

"When?"

"Just now."

"Was Whitby here?"

"Yes."

"And never asked for me?"

"I told him you begged to be excused."

"You told him I —now see here, Margaret. There is such a thing as going too far, and this is an example of it. 'Beg to be excused'! What will he think of me? Where is he now?"

"He has gone on to Wayback. But he never will have the sense to telegraph. That is why I am going."

"Did you quarrel?"

"Well-we were n't exactly friendly."

"Oh! —oh! —oh!" The three exclamations were long-drawn, with pauses between them and in three different keys.

"Aunty!" cried Margaret, furiously, stamping her foot. "How dare you insinuate —I said I was going to *telegraph*!"

"All right, my dear. Have it your own way. I 'll immolate myself on the altar of friendship: in this case, a particularly uncomfortable bed. Please remember, Margaret, as you speed away on your errand of avarice, I said a *particularly* uncomfortable bed."

Margaret went out and slammed the door. Mrs. Blake chuckled until she laughed, and laughed until she gasped for breath and was obliged to loosen her corsets. "I am as bad as Margie," she sighed; "I don't know when I am well off. Now I shall have to stay marooned in this pesky room until Margie returns. I never can fasten these outrageous things without help."

In her fetching gown of figured brown cloth, bordered with beaver fur, with slanting drapery of plain green, above which a cutaway jacket exposed a full vest, and topped by a high beaver toque-with flush due to the recent passage-at-arms still in her cheeks and the fire of indignation in her eyes-Margaret presented a *chic* daintiness that met with the entire approval of the burly Sandy, who hastened from the bar-room at the sound of her descent.

"I want a hitch of some kind," requested Margaret; "something with speed and bottom, and the sooner the better."

"A hitch?" queried Sandy. He had ominous visions of the dainty figure being whirled to destruction behind a pair of unruly bronchos.

"A horse, a team, a rig, something to drive, and at once," explained Margaret, impatiently.

"Oh, ay! I ken ye meanin' richt enough. I ken it fine; but I hae doots o' yer abeelity."

"Very well, then I will buy it, only let me have it immediately."

"It's no' th' horses, ye ken. What would I tell yer mither, gin ye 're kilt?"

"Bosh!" said Margaret, scornfully. "I can drive anything you can harness."

"Oh, ay! Nae doot, nae doot. But it willna be ane o' Sandy's, I telt ye that."

Here a voice was heard from out front, roaring for Slick and demanding a cayuse, in a hurry.

"Losh! yon 's anither. They must theenk I keepit a leevery," and Sandy hastened out to the porch to see who was desirous of further depleting his stock. When he saw the condition of the Goat his decision was quick and to the point: "Ma certes! Ye 'll no run th' legs of ony o' my cattle, Cock Murray, gin ye crack yer throat crawin'. Tut, tut! Look at yon!" He shook his head sorrowfully as he gazed at the dejected appearance of the Goat.

"Won't, hey!" shouted Cock, slapping back the saddle, "then I 'll borrer Dutch Fred's, an' Buck Peters 'll burn yore d —d ol' shack 'bout yore ears when he knows it." A man, watching interestedly from the bar-room, left by the hall exit, running.

"Buck Peters! Weel, in that case-Slick, ye can lend him yer ain."

"I was just a-goin' to," declared Slick, hurrying off; "which yore d —very generous when it don't cost you nothin'."

Cock loosened the cinch. "Generous as-Miss McAllister!" he exclaimed, aghast.

"Why, of all the people! How delightful! What on earth are *you* doing out here?" Margaret ran down to him, extending both hands in warm greeting.

Cock took them as if in a dream. "Miss McAllister-Chicago-Oh, what a fool I 've been!"

The man who had left the bar-room tore around the corner of the hotel on a wicked-looking pinto which lashed out viciously at the Goat when brought to a stop, a compliment the Goat promptly returned, though with less vigor. "Here y' are, Cock. He 'll think he 's headin' for th' Cyclone an' he 'll burn th' earth." The Cyclone puncher pushed the straps into Murray's hand and led away the Goat to a well-earned rest.

"I have to go, Miss McAllister. See you at the ranch. I 'm punching for the Double Y. They call me Cock Murray. It-it's a name I took."

"I 'll remember. Cock Murray: it fits you like a glove," and Murray mounted to her ripple of laughter. "We shall be out there to-morrow. Aunt is with me," she called to him, while the pinto worked off a little of its superfluous deviltry, before getting down to its work. She watched him admiringly, Cock sitting firm and waiting, until presently the pony straightened out and proceeded to prove his owner's boast. "Tip-top, Ralph," praised Margaret; "but you always could ride." She turned and faced the dour Sandy. "See here! Do you *ever* intend to get out that rig?"

"Weel-gin ye 're a relative o' Buck Peters, I jalouse ye 'll gang yer ain gait, onyway," and he went grumbling through the hall to do her bidding.

A roaring volley of curses, instantly checked and rolling forth a second time with all the sulphur retained to add rancor to the percolator, drew Margaret curiously to overlook the cause. Seeing, she thought she understood Sandy's reluctance to let his team to her: a pair of perfectly matched bays, snipped with white in a manner that gave to their antics an air of rollicking mischief, they were lacking the angularity of outline Margaret already had come to expect in Western ponies, and their wild plunging seemed more the result of overflowing vitality than inherent vice. Drawn by the uproar, Slick appeared beside her.

"No team for a lady to drive," he declared, shaking his head.

"Ridiculous!" asserted Margaret. "Go help them." A devitalized imprecation from Sandy hastened his steps. Margaret was in doubt which amused her most: the trickiness of the ponies or Sandy's heroic endeavor to swear without swearing. She understood him far better than either of the others, who worked silently and with well directed efforts.

With Slick's invaluable assistance their object was soon accomplished, the team being hitched to a new buckboard that was the pride of Sandy's heart. "'T is a puir thing," he protested, eying it sourly. "I hae naething better."

"Why, it is perfect," declared Margaret, "but I shall want a whip."

"Ye 'll want nae whup," denied Sandy, shaking his head ominously.

The Cyclone puncher at the head of the nigh horse called to her: "Take 'em out o' th' corral, miss? They 'll go like antelopes when they start."

Margaret laughed in gay excitement. "No, no! please don't," she entreated, drawing on her gloves. "I could drive that pair through the eye of a needle."

Sandy glanced from her to the team and back again.

"Havers! I 'll gie ye ma ain whup," he promised. He was back in half a minute with a lash whip whose holly stock never grew in America.

"What a beauty!'" exclaimed Margaret. She ran down the steps, gathered up the lines, and sprang into the buckboard, bracing herself for the inevitable jerk. "Ready," she warned. "Let go."

It was lucky for Mrs. Blake that she had loosened her corset strings and was confined to her room; had she seen the start-and she knew Margaret's skill as well as any one-she certainly would have burst them in her fright. With the three men it was otherwise; they vented their admiration in a ringing cheer. The ponies, gathering speed in the short stretch to the ford, were coaxed over so near the I-Call that Dirty Snow tumbled precipitately from his box and fled around the corner of the saloon; missing the box by a foot, the wheels began a wide arc toward the water through which the rig whirled in an avalanche of spray, to shave the front of the Why-Not as closely as it had the I-Call. To the delighted astonishment of Twin River-by this time the entire inhabitants, excepting only Mrs. Blake, were more or less interested in the proceedings-the team was no sooner going in the straight than Margaret cracked the lash to right and left and the startled ponies bellied to the ground in their efforts to escape an unknown danger. Sandy guffawed in pride of ownership; Slick gazed with his soul in his eyes; the puncher danced up and down in his joy, thumping first one and then the other.

"Did you see it?" he demanded, "Did you see it?" The others admitted eyesight equal to the occasion. "Say," asseverated the puncher, "if I owned all Montany, from here to th' line, I gives it to get that gal. That's th' kind of a hair-pin I am. You hear me!"

* * * * *

Margaret's sudden exclamation hastened the speed of the ponies but she drew them firmly in and approached the group on the trail at an easy lope. Whitby ran up from the river bank as she pulled the team to a stand.

"Who is it, Miss LaFrance? How did it happen?" asked Margaret, guessing the answer to her own questions.

"It is M'sieu Peters, ma'am'selle. He is wounded," replied Rose.

"Just in time, Miss McAllister," said Whitby, coming up at that moment. "We 'll commandeer that wagon as an ambulance."

"Miss McAllister!" exclaimed Buck, wonderingly. Then, energetically: "Whit, you get after that pole-cat. I can get to th' ranch, now. Get a-goin'."

"Buck, I 'm like Jake: 'sot in my ways.' There is no necessity to follow that pole-cat, as you so aptly call him. And you are not going to the ranch, you know. Miss LaFrance has kindly volunteered expert service in nursing and I intend that you shall get it. Miss McAllister, Miss LaFrance, whose services you already know; and Mr. Peters, your father's partner."

"You must not think of going on to the ranch, Mr. Peters," persuaded Margaret. "I only hope it is not too far to Miss LaFrance's home. If we could lift you—I 'm afraid these horses won't stand."

"Lift! I reckon I got one good laig, Miss McAllister—" he fell back with a grunt.

"Dash it all, Buck! Do you want to break open that wound? 'Pon my word, I don't envy you your patient, Miss LaFrance. You lie still, you restless beggar. I 've packed more than one man with a game leg and gone it alone. Do you think you can manage those dancing jackasses?" He looked doubtingly from them to Margaret.

Margaret dimpled. "Ask Sandy," she advised, demurely.

"Ou, ay!" quoth Whitby and Margaret broke into bubbling laughter that reflected from Rose's face in the faint shadow of a smile.

"Too bad of me to be laughing this way, Mr. Peters," apologized Margaret, correctly interpreting the expression of Rose, whose glance had turned to Buck; "but I have so much cause to be merry when I least expected it that I forgot for the moment you are wounded."

She resolutely avoided looking at Whitby who, thus unobserved, displayed a grin more fittingly adapted to the countenance of the famous Cat of Cheshire. Rose glanced swiftly from Whitby to Margaret and the two women were already aware of that which the men would never guess in each other.

"Shucks! I been shot up worse 'n this, Miss McAllister," assured Buck; "if that pig-headed Britisher would on'y take orders like he oughta. He 's obstinater nor a cow with a suckin' calf."

"Right-o!" assented Whitby, who had finished his preparations for the lift. "Now, Miss LaFrance."

He had managed to pass the blanket under Buck's middle, looping it over his own neck; while this arrangement eased but little weight from Rose, it had the advantage of keeping Buck comparatively straight. Whitby, backing up into the buckboard, his hands tightly grasping Buck beneath the arms, was ably assisted by Rose, who moved and steadied her load without apparent effort. Margaret was genuinely surprised. "How strong you are!" she exclaimed, admiringly.

"Gentle as rain," commended Buck. "If you got that flask handy, Whit, I 'd like to feel it."

Chapter XXIII
Hopalong's Move

Hopalong, nursing Allday with due regard to the miles yet to be travelled, was disagreeably surprised to recognize Cock Murray in the horseman approaching. The explanation offered did not improve his temper. He turned on Murray a hard stare that was less a probe than an exponent of destruction to a liar. There was that about Hopalong which spelled danger; no strong man is without it; and few men, honest or not, fail of the impression when in the presence of it. Cock Murray was no coward. He was distinctly not afraid to meet death at a moment's notice or with no notice at all, if it came that way; yet he was grateful to be able to face that stare with an honest purpose in his heart.

"Murray, down Texas way h —l-raisin' on a range means sudden death. It's a-goin' to stop on th' Double Y. Which side are you on?"

"If it depends on my say-so, th' Double Y is as peaceful as a' Eastern dairy from this out."

"Let 'er go at that. How 's that cayuse?"

"Good, an' fresh as paint. I on'y breathed him, comin' from Twin."

"Swap. This bay has come along right smart for twenty miles. I ain't goin' to lose you much, either. Th' boys is after us but they won't catch you."

Hopalong was well past the Sweet-Echo before the pinto was recognized. Slick let out a yell of surprise. The Cyclone puncher sauntered to the window, where Slick was pointing, glanced up the trail and laughed. "That's a friend o' Buck's," he explained, "an' he 's certainly aimin' to get there, wherever it is, as quick as he can."

"Ain't that yore pinto?" queried Slick.

"Less 'n I 'm blind," agreed the cow-punch.

"Seems to me there's a lot o' swappin' goin' on som'ers along th' Big Moose," hazarded Slick. "Which they can't *all* be backin' winners," he added, thoughtfully.

They were still seeking light in useless discussion when the long-striding Allday went past. Slick shouted to Murray for news but Cock waved his hand without speaking. Twin River was beginning to show a languid interest. Day-and-night *habitués* of the I-Call lounged out into the open and gazed after Cock inquiringly, irritated Pop Snow into a frantic change of base by their apparently earnest belief in his knowledge of these events and their demands for information, and lounged back again; Dutch Fred soothed the peevish old man by talking "like he had some sense"; having sense proved an asset once more as Dirty, no one being near, suddenly discovered a thirst. Ike, wise old wolf, though unable to solve the riddle, smelled a killing. "Stay around," he advised several of his own trustworthy satellites. Little Nell alone, who looked on and read as the others ran, came near to supplying the missing print: "The French Rose has shook Dave," she decided. "Dave has pulled his freight and the Double Y is on the prod after him. Smiler ought to show for place but the minute he looks like a winner the Texan 'll pump him full of lead. The Double Y will win out. Maybe Ned —" Little Nell's wild heart had regretted bluff, kindly Ned, these many days.

The passing of the Double Y punchers, strung out half a mile, confirmed Nell's guess. The Cyclone puncher, hurriedly throwing the leather on the Goat, loped along beside Slow Jack, the last in the string, obtaining from him such meagre information as only whetted his curiosity. He returned to the Sweet-Echo and Slick, disdaining to reply to the I-Call loungers. Ike was too wise to risk a rebuff; he already knew enough from what he had seen. "Pickin's, boys," was his laconic comment; and soon a company of five Autolycus-minded gentlemen took the Big Moose trail, openly. The break-up of this chance foray was largely due to the simple matter of direction.

Hopalong, knowing nothing of the wagging tongues at Twin River, drove the pinto for every ounce there was in him. A vague uneasiness, risen with the delivery of Buck's message by Cock Murray, rode with Hopalong; he could not shake it off. Ten minutes beyond Two Fork he saw the buckboard and the curse in his throat had its origin in a conviction as accurate as Whitby's had been. He turned and rode beside them. "Well, they got you, Buck," was his quiet comment.

"Shore did," admitted Buck. "Ambushed at four hundred-first shot-bad medicine. I lit a-runnin' an' caves in just as th' next ball drops th' bronc. I lays most mighty still. He thinks I kicked th' bucket but he 's afraid to find out. I was hopin' he 'd come to see. He gets away quiet an' I lay an' bleed a-waitin' for him. Rose an' Whit here wakes me out of a sweet dream." He smiled up at Rose whose anxiety was evident.

"Too much talk," she warned him.

"Dave?" asked Hopalong, looking at Whitby, who nodded.

"How far?"

"Two miles; possibly less," answered Whitby.

"I 'll get him," said Hopalong, with quiet certitude. "So long, Buck."

"So long, Hoppy. Go with him, Whit. Can't afford another ambush."

"Very well, Buck. You will find a medicine-chest in my kit, Miss McAllister."

Whitby turned and rode hard after Hopalong who, nevertheless, arrived at the dead pony considerably in advance, and after a searching look around, rode straight to the ambush. The signs of its recent occupancy were plain to be seen. Hopalong got down and squatted under cover as Dave must have done, from which position his shrewd mind deduced the cause of the poor shot: a swinging limb, which had deflected the bullet at the critical moment. The signs showed Dave had led his horse from the spot, finally mounting and riding off in a direction well to the east of Wayback. Minute after minute Hopalong tracked at a slow canter; suddenly his pony sprang forward with a rush: even to the Englishman's inexperienced eyes there was evidence of Dave having gone faster; very much faster, Whitby thought, as he rode his best to hold the pace, wondering meanwhile, how it was possible to track at such speed. It was n't possible: Dave had set a straight line for Wayback and gone off like a jack rabbit. Hopalong was simply backing his guess.

Exhaustive inquiries in Wayback seemed to show that Hoppy had guessed wrong. No one had seen Dave. No one had seen Schatz, either; the bank president had gone to Helena and his single clerk, single in a double sense, was an unknown number of miles distant on a journey in courtship. The station agent declared Dave had neither purchased a ticket nor taken any train from the Wayback station. Whitby became downcast but Hopalong, with each fruitless inquiry, gathered cheerfulness almost to loquacity. It was his way. "Cheer up, Whit," he encouraged: "I'd 'a' been punchin' cows an' dodgin' Injuns in th' Happy Hunting Grounds before I could rope a yearlin' if I 'd allus give up when I was beat."

Whitby looked at him gloomily. "I 'm fair stumped," he admitted. "D' you think, now, it would be wisdom to go back and follow his spoor?"

"Spoor is good. He came to Wayback, Whit, sure as yo 're a bloomin' Britisher. Keep a-lookin' at me, now: There 's a bum over by th' barber's has been watchin' us earnest ever since we hit town; he 's stuck to us like a shadow; see if you know him. Easy, now. Don't scare him off."

Whitby won his way into Hopalong's heart by the simplicity of his manoeuvre. Taking from his lips the cigar he was smoking, he waved it in the general direction of the station. "You said a bum near the barber-shop," he repeated. His pony suddenly leaped into the air and manifested an inexplicable and exuberant interest in life. When quieted, Whitby was facing the barber's and carefully examining the bum. Hopalong chuckled through serious lips. Whitby had allowed the hot end of his cigar to come in contact with the pony's hide. "No, can't say I do; but he evidently knows me. Dashed if he does n't want me to follow him," and Whitby looked his astonishment.

Hopalong's eyes sparkled. "Get a-goin', Whit. Here's where ye call th' turn. What'd I tell you?" He wheeled and rode back to the station. Whitby followed the shambling figure down the street and around the corner of a saloon, where he discovered him sunning himself on a heap of rubbish, in the rear.

"Well, my man; what is it?" asked Whitby.

The crisp, incisive tones brought him up standing; he saluted and came forward eagerly. "Youse lookin' f'r Dave?" he responded.

"What of it?"

"I seen him jump d' train down by d' pens. She wuz goin' hell-bent-f'r-election, too. Wen Dave jumps, I drops. Dave an' me don't pal."

"Why not?"

"Didn't he git me run out o' Twin? Youse was dere. Don'tcher 'member Pickles an' Dutch Onion-Pickles' old man-an' dat Come Seven guy w'at stopped d' row? Don'tcher?"

"Yes; I do. Are you the man who shied the bottle?"

"Ke-rect. I 'd done f'r him, too, but dey put d' ki-bosh on me."

"And are you sure it was Dave? Did the train stop?"

"Stop nothin'! 'T was a string o' empties. Dave jumped it, all right. An' I 'd hoof it all d' way to Sante Fe to see him swing."

"Deuced good sentiment, by Jove. Here, you need-well, a number of things, don't you know."

Boomerang gazed after the departing Englishman and blinked rapidly at the bill in his hand. Did he or did he not see a zero following that two? With a fervent prayer for sanity he carefully tucked it out of sight.

Whitby returned to Hopalong as much elated as previously he had been cast down. "We have the bally blackguard," was his glad assurance.

"Where?" asked Hopalong; "in yore pocket, or yore hat, or only in yore mind." Whitby explained and Hopalong promptly appealed to the station agent.

It was a weary wait. Whitby, a patient man himself, found occasion to admire the motionless relaxation of Hopalong, who appeared to be storing energy until such time as he would require it. To Whitby, who was well acquainted with the jungle of India, it was the inertia of the tiger, waiting for the dusk.

The station door opened again but this time with a snappier purpose that seemed promising. Whitby turned his head. The railroader nodded as one well satisfied with himself. "Got your man," he announced, with a grin of congratulation. "He dropped off at X — —. Don't seem a whole lot scared. Took a room at th' hotel. Goin' to turn him over to the sheriff?"

"No," answered Hopalong, "an' I don't want nothin' to get out here, *sabe*? If it does, yo 're th' huckleberry. When 's th' next train East?"

"It's past due, but it 'll be along in twenty minutes."

"I 'll take a ticket," and Hopalong rose to his feet and followed him into the station. He returned shortly, to apologize for leaving Whitby behind. "I know you 'd like to go, Whit, but you ought to find out about that money. Better stay here an' see them bank people in th' mornin'."

Whitby acknowledged the wisdom of this and agreed to call on Buck at Jean's on his way back to the ranch. "You tell Buck Dave is at X — —," said Hoppy. "An' that's where he stays," he added, grimly. "Here she comes."

Long before this, the usual crowd of idlers had gathered; and now the rest of Wayback began to ooze into the road and toward the station. As the train drew in it attracted even a half-shaved man from the barber's, hastily wiping the soap from his face as he ran; after him came the barber, closing the razor and sticking it in his pocket. The first man off the cars was a fox-faced little hunchback, whose deformity in no way detracted from his agile strength; after him, with studied carelessness, came Tex. Hopalong grunted, turned his head as the clatter of hoofs sounded through the turmoil, and signalled Chesty Sutton, first man of the rapidly arriving Double Y punchers.

"Don't you stray none, screech-owl, or I 'll drop you," he warned the captive, who shot one impish glance at the speaker and froze in his tracks. "Chesty, tell Ned to take this coyote to th' ranch, an' don't let him get away, not if you has to shoot him."

"Hold hard, stranger. He looks mighty like Big Saxe to me, an' if he is, I wants him. I got a warrant for him in my clo'es." The deputy sheriff started forward.

"Wait!" commanded Hopalong. The deputy waited. "Tex, hold that train. You an' me are goin' th' same way. Mr. Sheriff, I got a warrant ahead o' yourn an' I wants him. You 'll find him at th' Double Y ranch when I gets through with him."

Slow Jack, the last of the Double Y punchers, loped up to the station, swung from his saddle and joined the interested group surrounding the disputants.

"If that's Big Saxe I wants him now an' I 'm goin' to take him."

226

"Don't you, son." Kind as Hopalong's tone sounded, the deputy halted again. "Bow-Wow, hit th' trail an' have eyes in th' back of yore head. Straddle, boys." The crowd scattered as the mounted punchers moved their ponies about, to open a clear space. Hopalong met the eye of the hunchback, whose clear, shrewd glance recognized the master of the moment. "Screechy! that pinto 's a-waitin' for you an' if any son-of-a-gun gets there first, *you* won't need no bracelets. Git!"

Struggling between indecision and duty, the deputy saw the group of punchers, the pinto in advance, turn into the Twin River trail. "Looky here!" he began fiercely to Hopalong, "'pears to me —"

"Bah! Tell it to Schatz"; and Hopalong sprang up the steps, followed by Tex, to the outspoken regret of Wayback's citizens there assembled.

Chapter XXIV
The Rebellion of Cock Murray

The buckboard, wheeling off the trail, was lost to view almost as soon as Murray saw it. Rose and Margaret he had recognized at a glance but whose figure had been the second in the wagon? Suddenly misgiving assailed him. Forgetting Hopalong and his orders, he turned and followed them. Every step of his horse increased his anxiety and urged him forward; and twin-born with it smouldered a growing anger that held him back: he hesitated to have his fears confirmed in the presence of two women, one of whom-well, that was done with but it had left a scar that was beginning to throb again with the old pain. He rode slowly but gaining steadily on the trio ahead. When they reached the cabin, Rose called; receiving no answer she was about to go for help when she saw Murray and pointed to him. Margaret motioned and he hurried to obey the summons.

He recognized Buck while still some distance away and the smoulder burst into a blaze. This was the game then? Schatz had emphatically stated it was to be one of freeze-out; when they found it would n't work then the good old way was good enough. The jauntiness of carriage which had earned him his nickname (he was responsible for the surname only) was gone when he joined the others; the gay insolence of his speech was gone also, and some of his good looks. The successful concealment of his feelings had lost him much but it had gained him more: Margaret thrilled to a sense of power she had not expected in him. Rose's gesture of finger to lips was superfluous: Murray never felt less like talking.

"How'd you get here, Cock?" asked Buck, dully. The strain of the drive was telling even upon his iron frame.

"Orders," answered Cock, briefly; and Buck was not sufficiently interested to inquire further.

The team was effectually secured and they got Buck from the wagon and into the cabin with but little difficulty; Murray, though he did not look it, was a far stronger man than Whitby; and Buck was laid gently in the bunk, his head brushing the spot where Pickles had muffled his breathing a few hours before.

The removal of the bandage brought a gasp to the lips of Margaret, who pressed her hand to her heart and stared with horrified eyes. She touched Rose on the shoulder: "Can you-can you dress the wound without me?" she asked, breathlessly.

"But certainly," answered Rose, mildly surprised.

"Then I will go-back-and send on the medicine chest. I am sure you will need it."

"That is good," commended Rose, looking curiously after Margaret, who swayed as she went out of the room.

Murray hurried after her. "It is nothing, Miss McAllister, except for the pain and possible fever. Buck will tell you so himself. Drink this."

The cold water made her feel better. "I never realized before-what fighting means," she murmured. "It may be nothing but it looks-terrible."

"Nothing dangerous, I assure you, and perfect health will bring him through. Shall you go on out to the ranch?"

"Why, I must send the medicines."

"Then wait for me to join you at Twin River. I shall not be long."

He controlled the restive team until she was ready and watched her start. When he returned to Rose she had bared and was bathing the wound from which but little blood came, now. When a fresh bandage had been put in place she turned to him with expressive gesture: "Remove all," she commanded, indicating Buck's clothing. She left the room and Murray heard her moving about in the attic while he busied himself in obedience to her orders.

"Who was it, Buck?" he asked, sombrely.

"Did n't see him. Dave, I reckon."

"Was it Dave you was after?"

"That's him. Did n't you know?"

"No." Murray slit viciously through the waist band of the trousers and raised Buck with one powerful arm while he eased away the severed cloth. He said nothing more until Rose came with a garment such as Buck had not worn for more years than he liked to remember. When it was donned and Buck made comfortable, Murray spoke with decision. In his earnestness he unconsciously reverted from the slip-shod manner of speech to which he had habituated himself.

"I have a confession to make," he began; "and I want to make it now. I don't think it will harm you to hear it."

"Let 'er go," said Buck, with awakened interest.

"I am a hypocrite. I am indirectly responsible for the loss of your cattle. I have been taking your money and working for another man. I am not at all proud of it. In fact, as things have turned out, I 'm d —d sick of it. All that I can say for myself is that I honestly thought the other man was in the right; now I know better. If it will be any satisfaction to you I would give my life this minute rather than have it known by-by certain people who are bound to know of it if you talk. So it has not been easy to tell you. I have only one thing more to add: I can't be treacherous to the other man although he has been treacherous to me; but if you are not afraid to trust me, I guarantee to make the Double Y sound on the inside, at least-that is, if they don't kill me."

"By th' Lord!" breathed Buck. "I 'm right glad I got that pill. Trust you? You bet!" He reached out his hand to Murray and the grip he felt confirmed his belief that the canker was surely healed on the Double Y.

Softly as Buck spoke, the sound of his voice brought Rose to the door. She looked sternly at Murray: "You must go," she declared; "So much talk bring fever."

"All right, ma'am," assented Murray, carefully keeping from her his tell-tale face, "sure you won't need help?"

"No, my father come soon." She advanced to the bunk and improved comfort and appearance with a few deft touches.

"Good-day, then, ma'am. So long, Buck. I 'm ridin' to th' ranch with Miss McAllister."

"So long, Cock. Get at it, son. Th' Double Y needs you, you bet," and the smile on the stern face was so winning that Murray left hastily, with long strides.

Chapter XXV
Mary Receives Company

Mary's heart skipped a beat and then pulsed ninety to the minute as her first suspicion became a certainty: a wagon was coming through the dark to the ranch. With a prayer for her husband on her lips she went slowly to the door. She recognized Murray's voice and Jake's in conversation and stood with her hand on the door until Jake's rough command was followed by the sound of the wagon going to the stable. No one wounded! Her relief was so great that she walked unsteadily in crossing back to her chair. Mary was nervous and easily upset, these days.

Surprise acted as a tonic when the two ladies entered, followed by Murray. A glance at Margaret's face stirred memories in Mary. She stammered: "Why-why—I know-who—"

Murray supplied the name: "It is Miss McAllister, Mrs. Cassidy."

"Why, of co'se," said Mary; "I 'd know Miss McAllister anywhere; she favors Frenchy like she was his own daughter."

"Did you know Uncle John?" asked Margaret, breathlessly.

"Yes, indeedy. I took to him first sight," and Mary smiled at the girl's eagerness.

"Aunt Jessie! Isn't that just glorious? Mrs. Cassidy, this is my aunt, Mrs. Blake-and I want you to tell me everything you can remember about Uncle John."

"Now you have done it," declared Mrs. Blake. "You will get no peace from Margaret while she thinks there is a wag of your tongue left about her Uncle John."

"Margaret-that's a right sweet name. But I 'm afraid Billy would insist —" she flushed a dull red as Mrs. Blake sharply addressed Murray: "Ralph, see that some one gets those trunks in, will you? That is, if they did not drop off into the bosom of this blessed wilderness, somewhere *en route.*"

"They did n't. But it's all Montana to an incubator Jake took them to the stable," and Murray promptly vanished.

"Certainly he would insist," agreed Mrs. Blake, resuming the thread of Mary's unconscious soliloquy. "And quite right, too. It would have to be-what did you say your name is, my dear?"

"Mary "—the shy smile made her seem very unlike the self-reliant H2 girl.

Mrs. Blake took her in her arms and mothered her. "Mary is every bit as sweet as Margaret," she declared. "And now you must came over here and sit down. That is six for me and a half dozen for myself. *How* I shall rejoice to land in a seat that neither shakes nor bumps!"

"I shore begs you-all 's pardon; but I ain't got over my surprise yet."

"Shall we put you to very much trouble, Mrs. Cassidy?" asked Margaret. "Perhaps if you get that lazy Murray to help —"

"Why, Murray ain't lazy. There ain't none of the boys lazy, 'cept maybe Jake. An' it's shore a pleasure to have you here."

"May heaven forgive my vegatative emotion in the cessation of motion," and Mrs. Blake carefully refrained from moving her foot forward one enticing inch: it was good enough as it was.

"You ain't use' to travelling, Mrs. Blake," suggested Mary.

"On the contrary, my dear," that lady assured her. "Mr. Blake hauled me over the entire country from the Mississippi to the Atlantic; but he never subjected me to the churning discomfort of a devil-drawn buckboard driven by a heartless madcap in petticoats." Mrs. Blake shifted the faintest imaginable distance to the left and back again immediately: the first position was the more comfortable, as she might have known.

The two younger women exchanged a smile, Margaret's a merry one, Mary's more sober as she thought how easily the buckboard might have carried a load indifferent for all time, to jolts. "Did you see anything o' th' boys?" she asked.

"I saw them all, I believe," answered Margaret. "They went through Twin River just before we started."

"Cock Murray came back with you. Did you see my husband? He started out to find Mr. Peters."

"Mr. Cassidy and Mr. Booth went after that Dave brute."

"Where was Buck?"

"He was wounded, Mrs. Cassidy. Not badly, they say. Dave shot him from ambush. We found him lying in the road."

"Oh! I ought to go to him," and Mary started from her seat.

"Certainly not," declared Mrs. Blake. "It is quite evident that you do not appreciate the comforts of inertia. Besides, from what Margaret tells me, he is well taken care of."

"Oh! and I forgot the medicine chest," exclaimed Margaret. "Yes, he has an attentive nurse, Mrs. Cassidy. We took him to the LaFrance place. And I must get that medicine chest from Whitby's kit and send it over. Where are Whitby's things, Mrs. Cassidy?"

"They 're in th' bunk-house. Murray will get them for you. So Buck is there? Did you see the French Rose, Miss McAllister?"

"Yes, haven't you? She is lovely; so serious and calm and strong. In some way she makes you feel that she is sure to do the right thing at the right time. Oh, I like her, immensely."

"Liking goes by contrasts," sleepily reminded Mrs. Blake. Mary smiled no less at Margaret's grimace than at Mrs. Blake's pointed sarcasm.

"She has n't been to the ranch since we-all came," said Mary. "Buck says she rid over quite often afore that. I 'm glad Rose is 'tendin' him; from what I hear of her he could n't be in better hands."

"Mr. Peters seemed glad, too," said Margaret, suggestively; "and Miss LaFrance did not seem at all sorry."

Before Mary could respond to Margaret's unspoken question, the door opened with a bang and Pickles rushed in. "Been a-helpin' them sheep with th' trunks," he informed them. "Where's Hopalong? Did he find Buck? That cacklin' Murray has forgot how to crow; he on'y grunts."

"Hopalong has gone after Dave. He shot Buck," answered Mary.

"Not dead!" Pickles was aghast.

"No, only wounded."

"I just *got* to kill that Dave. Rose has got to lemme off on that promise. I bet she will now he 's gone an' shot up Buck."

Mrs. Blake stirred in her chair and opened one eye. "Out of the mouths of babes and sucklings —"

"Sucker yoreself!" retorted Pickles. "Reckon you think I don't know nothin'. You wait." He slammed the door behind him and stamped off, greatly incensed. His advice to Jake, who told him to open the other door while he carried in a trunk, was impossible to follow, involving a journey from which no one, not even Jake, would ever be likely to return.

When Margaret, insisting that Mary direct operations from her chair, was satisfied with domestic arrangements, she asked Murray's advice about sending the medicine chest to Rose. Obeying Whitby's wishes seemed the most important thing in life at present. Cock demurred to her plan of sending him before morning; and he was opposed to leaving the ranch at all before Buck himself took charge again. Margaret was vexed at his stupidity. They had gone together to the bunk-house and argued the matter with the object of dispute on the floor between them. Glancing at them from his own especial bunk was Pickles, trying in vain to make sense from a jumble of sounds unlike any he had ever heard. Pickles' vocabulary was very limited. His snort of disgust as he gave it up and turned his back on the disputants, gave Cock an idea. "Pickles," he said, "Buck's sick and he needs this box. Buck told me to stay at the ranch. Will you take it if I saddle Swallow?"

"Shore will," and Pickles shoved one entirely nude leg from the bunk; before he could follow it with the other, he was much surprised and more embarrassed to find himself swooped upon, seized and swiftly kissed by Margaret, whose brown-clad form fled through the door like the flirt of a wood-thrush, vanishing into the dim recesses of the forest.

* * * * *

Ned Monroe and the boys, Big Saxe with them, came straggling up to the bunk-house in the early hours of the morning, Ned having acquired a change of mounts at Twin River. They secured their prisoner by the simple expedient of tying him in a lump-and a cow-punch makes knots that are exceedingly hard to struggle out of. Big Saxe did n't try.

Cock Murray was first out and he awoke Ned. In the open, safe from being overheard, they held conference, Monroe nodding his head understandingly as Cock made his points. After breakfast, Monroe delivered a speech, short and to the point, and when they separated to their duties, Cock and Slow Jack rode away together. Big Saxe, very effectually hobbled at the ankles, was put in charge of Chesty Sutton who tersely informed him that the first false move he made he would find himself humpbacked all the way to his feet.

Cock bent his powers of persuasion to the converting of Slow Jack. It proved an easy task. Secretly admiring Cock and his ways, Slow Jack also perceived the trend of events to be putting Schatz out of the running. The unbending will of Hopalong was over them all and Slow Jack was not averse to throwing his services to the winning side.

It was the middle of the afternoon when Whitby appeared. The women listened to his news with varying degrees of interest. Buck was doing well and had declared it would not be long before he was at the ranch; in the meantime, as he was obliged to be quiet, he seemed well contented where he was. Pickles had arrived safe and had constituted himself body-guard and messenger-at-need for Rose. As for Hopalong he could tell them no more than they had already learned from Monroe. Mary was not worried. She had supreme confidence in Hopalong's ability to take care of himself and would have smiled if any one had suggested danger.

The end of Whitby's budget was punctuated with a huge sigh from Jake, whose ear had never been far from the kitchen door. He now entered diffidently and addressed himself to the Englishman: "I wrastled some chuck for you, Whit; reckoned you might want some." His lumbering exit was closely followed by Whitby's, whose strangled appetite slipped the noose at Jake's invitation.

In the lively conversation of the three women, Margaret's voice groped about in Whitby's consciousness like a hand searching in the dark for a hidden spring; her sudden ringing laugh awoke him to his purpose and hastily finishing his meal he made his way to the barn. After an hour's delay, spent in selecting a pony for Margaret and taking the edge off the temper of the quietest —a favor that Margaret would have repudiated with scorn-he appeared at the house again with the offer to show her over the range if she cared to go.

It was the very thing Margaret most wanted to do and they set out with but little time lost. When she become accustomed to the saddle she suggested a race but Whitby had no intention of running any such risk. He easily held her interest in another way.

"I say, Miss McAllister, there 's one thing I did n't mention just now," he began.

"Not bad news?" questioned Margaret.

"Can't say it's good. That beastly German had the cheek to get away with the money after all. He checked against the blessed lot yesterday forenoon. I was at the bank this morning. It's right enough. They produced the check. Seems a bit odd, you know, they should be carrying that amount and pass it over in cash. I said as much; but the president-rummy chap, by the way-he explained it; something about big shipments of cattle. However, it's gone."

"Dear me! it seems very careless of somebody. Papa ought to know. What shall you do?"

"Oh, I notified the agency at once; they 've taken it in hand. But it won't do any good, you know. That bounder Schatz has it all planned out and if he loses it, why, there you are, you know."

"Yes, so it seems; but, to all intents and purposes, he steals it. Do you intend to let him triumph in such brazen robbery?"

"I rather fancy I shall have very little to say in the matter. That Cassidy chap who is trying to catch Dave, went off without knowing the money was gone. My word! I should n't care to be Schatz when Cassidy hears of it. Deuced odd no one saw him in Wayback but the banking people. However, the German will have to go. I wrote the Governor and Mr. McAllister this morning. Between them they can come to an agreement with Peters and we can buy the German out-or perhaps I should say his heirs. It's a good sporting chance that it will be his heirs. Cassidy has a proper amount of suspicion in his character and no one will ambush him, I 'll lay."

"Good gracious! But you can't afford to lose all that money, can you?"

"It is a bit of a facer. But what of it? The range can stand it. In twenty years it will bring ten times the money for farm land, or I 'm much mistaken. I 'm sure the Governor will chance it and Buck will be glad to have me an active partner. He said as much."

"Mr. Booth, did n't you advance the money to Peters in the last partnership agreement?"

"Oh, I say! Did they tell you that? Then you should know it was my advice that brought on his loss. But Buck is n't obliged to put up any money with us; his experience and services are quite equal to the money I shall put up. I fancy Mr. McAllister will agree with me in that. All Buck wants is fair play, don't you know."

Margaret pulled her pony so that she had the advantage of a few feet nearer the house when she spoke. "Whitby," she said, very clearly, "you are a dear."

Both ponies swung their noses towards home in the same moment. The burning blush on Margaret's face streamed from it on the air-currents and settled on Whitby's determined countenance, to leave him and float away to the rose clouds in the western sky. Whitby had the faster mount but Margaret rode a far lighter weight and the chase might have been a long one had she been very anxious to keep away. As it was a short half mile found them on even terms. Whitby's arm went about the girl's waist as the ponies ran stride for stride and she felt herself leaving the saddle. With reckless abandonment to the law of might she yielded and lay in his arms; their pace slowed to a walk, Whitby looking solemnly into the brilliant eyes that mockingly regarded him.

"The good old rule, the simpler plan, that he shall take who hath the power," quoted Margaret.

"And he shall keep who can," capped Whitby. "I can, Margaret, and I will," he declared, a deep note of earnestness in his voice.

Margaret reached up and covered the steady eyes whose searching threatened the unconscious secrets of her heart. But her voice reached him, fainter, fraught with the vibration of sureness: "Whitby, you are a dear."

Chapter XXVI
Hunters and Hunted

A string of empty cars backed onto the siding at X — —, bumping and grinding and squealing as the engine puffed softly; a running rattle and crash told of the shivering line coming to rest and the sibilant sighs of the engine seemed to voice its protest at being side-tracked for the passing of an engine of a higher caste. While it panted and wheezed, its crew taking advantage of the opportunity to look to and oil journals and rods, a man made his way through the brush several hundred yards down the track, swearing mildly as he brushed cinders and dust from his clothes. His only possessions besides his clothes were a revolver swinging in its buttoned holster, and a tightly rolled and securely tied gunny sack, to which he clung in grim determination.

"H —l of a ride," he growled as he headed in a circuitous course for the town a short distance away. "But it breaks th' trail. They 'll figger I went north to cross th' line, or up to Helena. Lucky they told me Denver Gus's relay was relieved. Brains, says Smiler-huh, devil a lot of good his brains done him. He is out of it, an' so is Peters, d —n 'em. Brains!"

He entered the town, looking for a place to put up. The Come-Again looked good and he entered it, securing a room on the second floor, which was under the roof. He was explicit to the proprietor: "It's got to be a back room, an' I want it for a couple of days, an' I don't want no noise, —I'm out here for my cussed nerves an' as soon as I can get a good job we 'll see about terms. Oh, I expect to pay in advance-will two days' pay keep you from layin' awake nights?"

"Reckon somebody made a mistake," replied the proprietor. "Yore nerves is purty strong."

"Have a drink and forget it," Dave smiled. When he had paid for the drinks he asked a question: "Who's got th' best horse in town? I'm a-goin' to buy it if it's good enough."

The proprietor looked him over and nodded toward a table in the farther corner: "That's him."

Dave sauntered over to the lone drinker: "Just been told you got th' best horse in town. That right?"

The other looked up slowly: "I might," he replied.

"I want to buy him. I don't give a d —n about th' price if he's good. Interested? Thought you'd be."

The other also looked the cocky stranger over: "Yes —I 'm interested —a little. I ain't h — l-bent for to sell that horse. He 's th' best ever came to these parts-that's why he 's good-he *came* here."

Dave was impatient: "Is he where I can see him?"

"Shore," drawled the horseman, arising languidly. "Come along an' you can see him if yore eyes is good."

The owner of the "best horse in town" studied Dave as they walked along and his mental comment was not flattering to the *protégé* of the late Herr Schatz. "Fake cow-puncher," was his summing up. "He don't know a *hoss* from a hoss-but he thinks he does."

When they came to the corral the owner pointed to a big gray in the corner: "That's him, stranger. He 's part cow-horse an' part Kaintuk, an' too good to be out here in this part of the country. *That's* th' hoss Bad Hawkins rid from Juniper Creek to Halfway in ten hours-one hundred an' forty miles, says th' map, an' Hawkins weighed a hundred an' seventy afore they got him. He weighed so much he broke off th' limb of th' best tree they could find. Why, *he 's* th' cuss what held up th' Montana Express down at Juniper Creek bridge-reckon you *are* a stranger to these parts."

"He don't look like no miracle to *me*," asserted Dave, closely scrutinizing the horse.

"No? Mebby you ain't up on miracles. If you want a purty hoss why did n't you say so? Dolly 's slick as silk an' fat as butter-you can have her if you wants her. Cost you about twenty-five dollars less. But you won't save nothin' on her if you wants a hoss for hard ridin', one that gets there quick, an' gets back quick."

"I ain't said nothin' 'bout savin' no money," retorted Dave. "An' it seems to me yo 're purty d —n high in yore prices, anyhow."

"Well, I sees you wants a hoss right bad; an' when a man wants a hoss bad he wants a *good* hoss-an' good hosses come high. Dolly 's gentle as a kitten," shrewdly explained the owner. "Big Gray, there, he 's some hard to ride, onless you can sit a saddle good as th' next."

"How much for Big Gray?" snapped Dave.

"One hundred dollars."

"I ain't buyin' a herd," remonstrated Dave.

"I ain't sellin' a herd," smiled the owner. "I told you good hosses come high. Mebby Dolly 'd suit you better. She 's my daughter's hoss."

"Here 's th' hundred," replied Dave, nettled. "Got a bridle or halter or piece of rope? An' I want to buy a saddle-one that's been broke in."

"There's a halter on him-good enough? All right; I got a saddle that's in purty fair shape-don't need it, so you can have it for twenty."

When Dave rode from the corral he was headed for the general store and bought a rifle, a rope, and sundry other necessaries, including food. Returning to the hotel he put his horse in the corral, had a drink, and went to his room carrying the saddle, the gunny sack, and his other purchases with him. The gunny sack had not been from under his arm an instant while he had been in town. The erstwhile owner of Big Gray drifted back to his table shortly after Dave's return and settled himself for another drink.

"Did you sell him one?" asked the proprietor, digging down for change.

"Yep," was the reply.

"Fifty, sixty, seventy-five —there 's yore change. I wonder who he is an' where he's goin'?" remarked the proprietor, in lieu of something better.

"Dunno; but he ain't no cow-punch, an' likewise he ain't no tenderfoot. Looks like a tin-horn to me. His fingers was purty slick gettin' th' bills off his roll. They was so slick I counted 'em to be sure he was n't robbin' hisself. But there was n't no folded bill there. Here, have a drink with me-business is pickin' up."

* * * * *

When the east-bound accommodation pulled into X — — at dusk two men jumped off and started toward the nearest hotel. The proprietor of the Come-Again assigned them a room and spoke of supper, to which they intimated their ability to do justice to "anythin' you got." As they turned away carelessly toward the "washroom" one of them halted: "We're expectin' a friend," and he gave a concise description of the third man.

"Why, he 's upstairs now-first door to th' left at th' top of th' flight-got in this afternoon. But he said he did n't want to be bothered none," hastily warned the proprietor.

"That's right-you can let that go for th' three of us," replied Hopalong, smiling.

"Said his nerves was all stampeded," commented the host, dubiously.

Hopalong winked, grinning: "Did n't act none that-a-way, did he?"

"Oh, I *told* him somebody was stringin' him," laughed the proprietor.

"Reckon we 'll go up an' hustle him down to his feed," Tex remarked, leading the way, with Hopalong stepping on his heels.

The proprietor studied the three names on his register, and spoke to the horseman, who now was playing solitaire in a negligent way. "Wonder what's up, Dick?"

"Dunno," replied Dick, holding aloft a queen of hearts and studying the layout. "Reckon you better let this deal go by. Keep yore chips out, Joe; don't like th' looks of th' pair of 'em. That red-head looks like a bad customer, if his corn 's stepped on. Mebby their nervous friend has did somethin' they don't like."

The knocking upstairs now reverberated through the house and a peevish voice threatened destruction to the door unless it opened speedily.

"That's th' red-head," remarked Dick. "What did I tell you?"

The proprietor hastened from behind the bar and went up the steep, narrow stairs with undignified haste. "Don't bust that door!" he cried. "Don't you bust it!"

"Aw, close yore face!" growled a voice, and Dick nodded his head wisely. "Both of 'em bad customers," he mumbled.

There was a crash and the sound of splintering wood, followed by disgusted exclamations. Dick arose and sauntered up to see the show: the host was nervously clutching a bill large enough to pay for several broken doors. The red-head was looking out of the open window while the other man rapidly searched the room.

"He dropped his belongings first," audibly commented the man at the window. "Then *he* dropped." He turned quickly to the proprietor: "Did he have a horse?"

"Yes; bought one first thing after he registered."

"We want one apiece," crisply demanded Hopalong, "with speed, bottom, an' sand. Got 'em? No? Then where can we get 'em to-night?"

"What'd he do?" blundered the host, rubbing the bill with tender fingers and looking for information instead of giving it.

"He dropped out th' winder," sharply replied Tex. "We never stand for that."

"Never, not under no circumstances," endorsed his friend. "It allus riles us. How 'bout them horses?"

"I reckon I can fix you up," offered Dick. "I sold him th' hoss he 's got. He wanted th' best in town, which he didn't get for bein' too blamed flip. But he paid for it, just th' same. I got a roan an' a bay that 'll run Big Gray off 'n his feed an' his feet. If yo 're comin' back this way I 'll buy 'em back again at a reduction —I 'd like to keep them two. I don't reckon I 'll get no chance to buy back th' other."

The horseman fell in behind the descending procession and lined up with it against the bar on Hopalong's treat. Then they left the proprietor to swear at the cook while they departed for the corral.

Dick chuckled. "Th' gray I sold yore missin' friend carried Bad Hawkins from Juniper Creek to Halfway in fourteen hours-ten miles an hour. Th' roan an' th' bay did it in ten hours even-which puts a period after th' last words of Hawkins. Bad Hawkins weighed less 'n you," he said to Tex, "an' th' gray shore sprains a laig a-doin' it. It don't show-that is, not when he was sold it did n't. That feller was too d —d flip-one of them Smart Alecks that stirs my bile somethin' awful."

Tex wearied of his voice: "Yore discernment is very creditable," he replied, with becoming gravity.

The horseman glanced at him out of the corner of his eye: "Yes —I reckon so," he hazarded.

When they reached the corral the two strangers looked in critically. Nearly a score of horses were impounded, among them several bays and roans. Hopalong pointed to one of the roans. "That looks like th' horse," he remarked, quietly, at the instant his friend singled out the bay.

"Them 's th' hosses-they 'll run th' liver out of Big Gray even if his laig does hold out," smiled their owner, glad that his first customer had not been as wise as either of these two men. The horses were cut out and accepted on the spot.

"How much?" demanded Hopalong, brusquely.

"Eighty apiece."

"That's a lot of money. But we got to have 'em. How 'bout saddles? We can do without 'em if we has to, but we ain't hankerin' very strong to do it."

"I got a couple of good ones," responded the horseman. Then he yielded to a sudden burst of generosity. "Tell you what I 'll do —I 'll sell you them saddles for forty apiece an' when I gets 'em back, you gets yore money back. An' if you don't kill th' hosses, we 'll have a little dicker over them, too. I would n't sell 'em only for a good price an' you won't have nothin' to complain about if I buys 'em back again."

"Yo 're a white man," responded Hopalong. "Now we all oughta have a drink to bind th' deal. An' I reckon supper 'll go good, too. We 'll be right glad to have you join us." The invitation was accepted with becoming alacrity.

After the meal, and a game of cards, during which both punchers had learned much about the surrounding country, they went on a tour of investigation. They had discovered that the only way south likely to be taken by a man not perfectly familiar with the several little-known mountain trails, was through Lone Tree Pass. A walk about the town, before turning in, disclosed to them the kind and amount of Dave's purchases: these showed that he expected to be in the saddle more than a few hours. Returning to the hotel they went at once to their room. Sitting on the edge of the bed Hopalong asked a question: "You 've got me on t' lay of th' land in this part of the country, Tex. Why do you figger he 'll head south?"

Tex blew out the light and settled himself snugly in his bed before replying. "Because anybody else would figger he 'd strike north for th' Canadian line, or up to Helena an' West, where a man can get lost easy. I 've sort of palled with Dave, an' I know th' skunk like a ABC book. His trail will show us th' way, but it won't tell us about th' country ahead of us. I allus like to know what I 'm goin' up against when I can."

"Shore; good-night," muttered Hopalong, and in a moment more soft snores vibrated out through the open window, to be mildly criticised by the cook in the cook shack below.

Down in the bar-room the proprietor, having said good-night to his last customer, pushed the column of figures away with a sigh of satisfaction and rested his chin on his hand while he reviewed the events of the day. "Why," he muttered, pugnaciously, coming out of his reveries and pouring himself a liberal drink on the strength of the day's profits; "why, now I know what that coyote wanted his room at the back of the house for-good thing I got th' money ahead of time! Well, he 's got a h —l of a lot of trouble chasin' him, anyhow, th' beat."

* * * * *

With three days' rations fastened to their saddles Hopalong and Tex whirled away from the Come-Again as the first streak of gray appeared in the eastern sky and after a short distance at full speed to take the devilishness out of their mounts, they slowed to a lope. Heading straight for the Pass, they picked up Dave's trail less than two miles from town and then settled into a steady gait that ate up the miles without punishing their horses. They had not made any mistake in their mounts for they were powerful and tough, spirited enough to possess temper and courage without any undue nervous waste, and the way they covered ground, with apparently no effort, brought a grim smile to Hopalong's face.

"I don't reckon I 'll do no swappin' back, Tex," he chuckled. "I 've allus wanted a cayuse like this 'n, an' I reckon he 'll stay bought, even at th' price."

"They look good-but I 'll tell you more about 'em by night," Tex replied. He glanced ahead with calm assurance: "I don't figger he's so very far, Hoppy?"

"Why no, Tex; he could n't ride hard last night, not over strange country-it was darker'n blazes. We did n't leave very long after him when you figger it in miles, an' he ain't reckonin' *shore* on bein' chased. He drops out th' winder an' sneaks that way 'cause he ain't takin' no chances.

"We 've got th' best cayuses, we 've had more sleep than him, we know this game better, we 're tougher, an' we can get more out of a cayuse than he can. I reckon we ought to get sight of him afore sundown, an' I would n't be surprised if we saw him shortly after noon. We 'll shore get him 'bout noon, if he 's had any sleep."

"I 'd ruther get him this side of Lone Tree Pass —I ain't hankerin' for no close chase through th' mountains after a cuss like Dave," Tex replied. "What do you say 'bout lettin' out another link?"

Hopalong watched his horse for a minute, glanced critically at his companion's, and tightened the grip of his knees. "That feller said a hundred an' forty in ten hours-how far is that pass? Well, might as well find out what this cayuse can do-come on, let 'em go!"

Pounding along at a gait which sent the wind whistling past their ears they dipped into hollows, shot over rises, and rounded turns side by side, stirrups touching and eyes roving as they searched the trail ahead. The turns they made were not as many as those in the trail they followed, for often they cut straight across from one turn to another. The ability to do this brought a shrewd smile to Hopalong's thin lips.

"Let his cayuse pick its way, Tex-told you he could n't go fast last night. Bet a dollar we come to where he slept afore long-an' say! luck 's with us, shore. Notice how he was bearin' —a little off th' course all th' time-that gray of his must a' come from som'ers up north. He had to correct that when he could see where th' Pass lay-come on, we 'll try another cut-off, an' a big one."

"Yo 're right-we 'll gain a hour, easy," Tex replied as they shot off at a tangent for the distant mountain range on a line for the Pass. The sun was two hours higher when Tex laughed aloud, stretching his hand across his friend's horse and pointing some distance ahead of him. "There's th' track again, Hoppy," he cried, "you was right-see it?"

Hopalong waited until they swept up along the fresh trail before he replied and the reply was characteristic of him. "Pushin' th' gray hard, Tex. Them toe prints are purty deep-an' d —d if th' gray ain't havin' trouble with his bad laig! See that off fore hoofmark? See how it ain't as deep as its mate? Th' gray's favorin' that laig, an' only for one reason: it hurts him more when he don't. Move away a little, Tex; don't do no good to be bunched so close where there 's so much cover. He ain't a long way off, judgin' from them tracks. We don't know that he ain't doubled back to pick us off as we near him."

Tex tightened his knee-grip and rowelled his spurs lightly along the side of his mount, darting ahead with Hopalong speeding up to catch him. It was a test to see how the horses were holding up and when the animals took up the new speed and held it with plenty of reserve strength, the two men let them go.

As they shot down a rough, sloping trail to a shallow creek, flowing noisily along the bottom of a wild arroyo, Hopalong looked ahead eagerly and called to Tex to slow down to a walk. Tex, surprised, obeyed and took the reins of the bay as Hopalong went ahead to cross the stream on foot. But Tex's surprise was only momentary; he quickly understood the reason for the play and he warmed to his sagacious friend while he admired his skill.

Hopalong waded the stream and looked carefully around on both side of the tracks where they left the water. Motioning Tex to come ahead, he grinned as the other obeyed. "Did n't want to splash no fresh water around here till I saw if th' water Dave splashed was all soaked up. It is; but th' spots is moist. An' another thing: see th' prints o' that hoof where he takes up an' sets down-where is he lame?"

"Shoulder," replied Tex with instant decision.

"Shore is. An' he 's been a-gettin' lamer every step. Bet he ain't an hour ahead, Tex."

"Won't take you-an' he 'll be above us all th' way till we cross th' top of th' range, so we better keep under cover as much as we can," Tex replied. "We 've trailed worse men than Dave, a whole lot worse, an' far better shots; but he ain't really due to miss twice in two days. Th' Pass ain't so far ahead now-there it is, with th' blasted pine stickin' up like a flag-pole. Half an hour more an' we 'll be in it."

Ahead of them, toiling up the Pass on a tired and limping horse rode Dave, not so fresh as he might have been with the four hours' sleep he had secured in the open at dawn. The night ride over strange, rough country had been hard and his rage at the shabby trick played upon him by the horse dealer had not helped him any. To win up to the point where success was almost his; and then to have a half-breed horse coper-one who had absolutely no connection with the game-threaten to defeat him! To fool all the players, to gain, as he thought, a big handicap and then to be delayed by a man who sought only to gain a little money and be well rid of a poor horse! Dave's temper was like that of a rattler hedged in by thorns and the rougher part of the mountain trail had been saturated with profanity. There was not much chance of meeting any one on that trail and by the time he reached a place where he could get another horse, the need for one would have gone. Let him see a horseman and he knew who would ride the horse. He struck the limping gray savagely as it flinched over a particularly rough part of the trail and he was growling and swearing as he rounded a turn in the Pass and came to a place where, by climbing a boulder just above him, he could get a good view of the way he had come. Dismounting, he made the climb and looked back over the trail. Miles of country were below him, the trail winding across it, hidden at times and then running on in plain view until some hill concealed it again. The sun was half down in the western sky and he swore again as he realized how much farther he should have been-how near the end of his ride.

"A hundred an' forty miles in ten hours!" he snarled, squirming back to descend to his horse. "No wonder Bad Hawkins got caught! Served th' d —n fool right; an' it 'd serve me right for being such a — —" the words ceased and the speaker flattened himself to the rock as he peered intently at a hill far down the trail, waiting to be sure his eyes had not deceived him.

The slanting sun had made a fairyland of the rugged scenery, bathing the rocks until they seemed to glow, finding cunningly hidden quartz and crystals and turning them into points of flame. The fresh, clean green coat that Spring had thrown over the crags as if to hide them, softened the harsher tones and would have thrilled even Dave, who was sated with scenery, if it had not been for his temper and the desperate straits in which he found himself. He lay like one dead but for the straining eyes. An eagle, drifting carelessly across the blue, missed him in its sharp scrutiny, so well did his clothes blend with the tones of the rock.

"H —l!" he muttered, for far below him something moved out into the trail again where it emerged from behind the hill, and two mounted men came into sight, riding rapidly to take advantage of the short run of level country.

Dave could not make them out-they were only two men at that distance, but he wasted no time nor gave heed to any optimism. He wriggled backwards, dropped to the trail, and looked around for a place to hide his horse. Not seeing one at hand he mounted again and forced the limping animal forward until he saw a narrow ravine cut into the mountain side by the freshets of countless years. Leading the gray into this and around a turn in the wall, he picketed the animal and then hastened back, scurrying to and fro in search of a hiding place that would give him a view of the trail for the greatest distance. His mind worked as rapidly as his feet. The coming horsemen might be innocent of all knowledge of him or of his need. If so, he preferred to ride behind them. If they were in pursuit-and he could not believe it to be a mere coincidence that any but an enemy would be following him so close through Lone Tree Pass-they had not started from the town he had just quitted-unless they had traced him by telegraph! Dave cursed softly and settled himself a little more at ease in his ambush.

Hopalong and Tex, enjoying that friendship that sets no embarrassment on silence, rode forward side by side when the trail permitted it, grim, relentless, dogged. They represented that class of men who can pursue one thing to the exclusion of all tempting side leads, needing nothing but what they themselves can supply; who approach all duties with cool, level-headed precision and gain their goal without a thought of reward and with small regard for danger. Danger they had both met in all the forms it took on the range and trail, dance-hall and saloon; both had mastered it by the speed and certainty of their hands and guns, and neither found anything exciting or fearful in this game of follow and take; on the other hand it was tiresome to have to follow, and one man, at that. If some bold, daring stroke of strategy or a reckless dash could have been hoped for, it would have made the game interesting. So they jogged on toward the opening of the pass, taciturn and sombre, but with the cold patience of Indians.

The trail narrowed again and Tex took the lead. "Closer now," he remarked, more to himself than to his companion, whose reply was a grunt, presumed to be affirmative. When they entered the pass itself it was Hopalong who led, and to see him as he sat slouching in his saddle, apparently half asleep, one would have wondered that a man whose wariness was the basis of so many famed exploits could ride thus carelessly, allowing his horse to pick the way. But in the shadow of his straight-brimmed hat, two hard, keen eyes squinted through the narrow lids, among the wrinkles, and missed nothing that could be seen; under the faded red shirt sleeve was an arm ready for the lightning draw that had never yet been beaten, and the hand-worn butt of the heavy Colt rubbed softly against the belt-strap of its holster.

Hopalong rolled a cigarette and took advantage of the movement to speak: "Goin' back to Texas, Tex?"

"Why," replied Tex, pausing to reflect. "Why, I said as how I would to all yore boys, but I reckon mebby Buck needs me worse'n you do. What think?"

"Stay up here an' run for sheriff," was the crisp reply. "This country 's sick with crooks."

"Reckon so."

"Good place for undertakers, while th' boom is on," continued Hopalong, smiling grimly at the truth in his jest. He knew Tex Ewalt.

"Th' boom 'll be busted flat afore you go home," Tex responded. "It's fallin' now. Dave was its high-water mark."

They were riding side by side now and Hopalong growled a suggestion: "Go slow, Tex; mebby he 's holin' up on us, like he did on Buck. He ain't more 'n a million miles ahead of us now."

"Uh-huh; an' if he is he ought to get us easy in this place. Got to take a chance, anyhow. Gimme a match —*Look out!*"

As he spoke he hurled his horse against Hopalong's and his left arm dropped to his side with a bullet through it, while his right hand flashed to his hip, where a pungent cloud of smoke burst out to envelop his horse's head. Off his balance from the unexpected shock, Hopalong's shot went wide, but the next five, directed at Dave's head-long rush as he came crashing down through the underbrush, gave promise of better aim.

As he spoke he hurled his horse against Hopalong's, while his right
hand flashed to his hip

"I owed him that, anyhow," muttered Tex, his ears ringing from the fusillade so close to him. "An' I owed you th' play, Hoppy, ever since that day in th' brush —"

"You don't owe me nothin' now, Tex; that's as close as any in ten years," returned Hopalong. "Well, he showed hisself a d —d ambushin' snake just as we thought he would. He could a' got us both if his nerves had n't got th' chills an' fever. We was some careless!"

"We was a pair of blasted kids," Tex remarked. "Now what 'll we do with him? We can't take him back, an' buryin' in solid rock ain't been in my schoolin'."

"We can cover him with rocks, I reckon, but we ain't got time-besides, how'd he leave Buck?" demanded Hopalong sharply. "Why, he got you, Tex! Here, you close-mouthed fool, lemme fix that hole."

Tex stood quietly thoughtful until Hopalong had finished his task. "We 'll just chuck him off th' trail, Hoppy; then we won't have to answer no question or shoot sense into no thick skulls. How 'bout it?"

"Uh-huh, go ahead," grunted Hopalong and the two walked over, picked up the unresisting bulk and placed it in a fissure in the rock wall.

"By th' Lord!" swore Tex: "Five shots out of five when you got yore balance —*that's* shootin'! *You* better run for sheriff."

"I had n't ought to 'a' done it when I knowed th' second got him-but he kept a-comin' an' I was a-thinkin' of Buck. Come on, let's get goin'." He mounted and waited impatiently for Tex, who was still standing beside his horse as if unwilling to leave the scene. "His pot-shootin' is over, so let's start back."

"Uh-huh," muttered Tex, still lost in thought. Hopalong waited, having acquired increased respect for his friend's brain capacity in the last few days.

"Hoppy, why did Dave ambush Buck an' have to run, just when he was goin' to skin Schatz for a pot of money?"

"Give it up," answered Hopalong.

"Well, why did n't Schatz turn up when everything was set for the play?"

"Got to pass again, Tex," was Hopalong's indulgent reply.

"Dave had plenty of chances to kill Buck-better chances than that one-an' no need to run, if he was careful. Th' Twin River trail is travelled some-it was shore risky-no time to waste in Wayback waitin' for Schatz after that, huh?"

"Mebby th' kid did n't get it right," suggested Hopalong.

Tex nodded his head convincingly. "Yes, he did. Told a straight story. Hoppy, Dave knew Schatz was n't comin'. Hoppy, I got —I got a feelin' —Hoppy, what 'll you bet Dave ain't got th' money right now?"

"By G —d!" exclaimed Hopalong, staring at his friend, his mind racing along the scent like a hound to the kill. "By G —d!" he repeated, softly, as he dropped from the saddle and became hidden in the crevice. "No money, Tex; only a few —"

"Where's his horse?" demanded Tex, eagerly.

"*Yo 're* goin' to run for sheriff," came the retort, and Hopalong followed the track of Dave's horse and turned into the ravine, out of sight of Tex, who waited impatiently.

Tex was surprised at the result of the quest when a crazy man came buck-jumping into sight, yelling like an Indian and frantically waving a tightly grasped saddle pad of sacking. He would have come out with more dignity if the money had been his, but belonging as it did to his old foreman, the big-hearted man who had been for so long a time on the verge of despair and defeat, allowed himself the luxury of free expression to the bubbling joy within him.

"Come on, Tex!" he cried. "Th' h —l with goin' back-we 'll take a chance of meetin' th' Dutchman as Dave Owens' personal executors an' ambassadors. If Schatz has got a wad like this, he 's th' man I want to see. Come on! We 'll bust all Montana records for hold-ups —come on, you wise old devil!"

"Now who 's goin' to be sheriff?" grinned Tex, and then allowed himself the relief of working off his joy in a short jig, which informed him that Dave had made a hit; not a bull's eye, but a hit just the same.

"Here, you drunk Apache," Hopalong cried, "let's count up an' see what we got."

Had any one drifted along a minute later he would have been torn between duty and discretion: duty to provide a sane guardian in himself for that part of the Government treasury strayed to the wilds of these western mountains, and discretion in facing the two capable-looking highwaymen who sat crossed-legged on the trail with guns on the ground close to their hands.

"Um-m-m," murmured Tex, who knew of the size of the joint account. "Schatz is lucky if he 's got carfare-th' capital of th' Peters-McAllister-Schatz combine is spread reckless under our gloatin' eyes; all except th' few miserable bills that Dave spent. Come on, you greedy hog-we 'll let Schatz have his two-bits an' be glad to get rid of him. I 'd hate to shoot any man as fat as him-no tellin' what 'd happen. Stick yore roll where it won't jar loose, load that right-hand gun, an' see that nobody holds you up."

"I 've allus been plumb a-scared o' hold-ups," grinned Hopalong, facetiously. "We all was. Lead costs money, an' there ain't no use wastin' it." The grin disappeared and a hard look focussed in his clear eyes as he thought of what a lovely time any hold-up squad would have when Buck's money was at stake.

They mounted and rode away down the pass. As they came to the first bend, Tex glanced back and saw Big Gray peacefully cropping the scanty vegetation along the trail by the ravine. He was without bridle or saddle and Tex glanced covertly at the happy man at his side who could put five bullets in a falling enemy without a pang, and immediately after release a limping horse so that it could live and grow strong, to roam free among the mountains.

Hopalong rolled both guns at once to end the celebration, the bullets striking a rock down the trail as fast as one could count and at intervals as regular as the hammer-stroke of a striking clock. To a man who looked upon a gun only as a weapon to be pointed and discharged at an object, this would have been sufficiently wonderful, but to a real gun-man, one acquainted with the delicacy of manipulation and absolute precision required to effect this result, it was far more wonderful. There are many good gun-men who never have acquired this art, and the danger of practising it is enough to deter most men from attempting it. To hold a six-shooter by a finger slipped through the trigger guard and make it spin around like a pinwheel, firing it every time the muzzle swung out and away from the body, is risky; and when two guns are going at once, it is trebly risky, while accuracy is almost impossible. Hopalong was accurate, so was Johnny, but the latter could work only one gun. Tex, being something of a master of gun-play, was capable of appreciating the feat at its true worth and his eyes glowed at the exhibition. To him came the memory of a day far back in the years when this dexterity had worked to his dishonor, yet it brought with it no malice and it was with the deep affection that a man has for a man friend-and usually for only one-that he playfully advised his companion to "load 'em up again." "Hoppy, there 's only one hand I ever see that I 'm more afraid of than that 'n o' yourn," he remarked.

Hopalong looked at him in mild surprise: "Whose is that?" he asked.

"Yore other one," and Tex grinned at his jest.

Chapter XXVII
Points of the Compass

The long-slanting shadows found Hopalong and Tex far from Lone Tree Pass, riding straight for the Double Y ranch. Their chase after Dave had taken them well to the west of south and they had concluded to keep the horses and equipment and strike for the ranch. As Hopalong sagely remarked: "Eighty dollars is eighty dollars, Tex, but these here two bronchs 'pear to me purty good stock; besides, what's eighty dollars 'longside the money-bag I 'm a-sittin' on?" and he eyed, complacently, the bloated gunny-sack that hid its wealth under so innocent an exterior.

They went ahead with that unerring instinct of the plainsman whose sense of direction seems positively uncanny to a tenderfoot, especially if the tenderfoot has ever been lost. There was no sign of a trail nor did they expect to see one, until they struck the Big Moose, north of the Reservation. This in itself was a source of gratification to them; they were quite content to meet with no one and all they asked was to be let severely alone until such time as the money was turned over to Buck and they should cease to be responsible for it.

The stumbling of the tired horses led them reluctantly to make camp. Hopalong was loath to be away from Mary longer than was necessary; only the grim determination to get Buck's money to him with as little risk as possible had decided him to ride to the ranch instead of taking the train from X——, which would have been hours quicker. They had discussed this matter, even to the thinking of a possible train hold-up, and Hopalong expressed his very decided preference for the open. "I was in a train hold-up once," he told Tex, "an' seven of th' boys was n't none too many to break it up. Skinny got plugged-not bad-but it might be us this time, an' it might be a whole lot worse."

He entertained Tex with the story while they made their simple preparations for their supper. Tex listened with the ear of a good listener, giving voice to his amusement, or endorsement of an action, or profanely consigning the whole troupe of train robbers to that region where go the "many who are called but not chosen." But all the while, though interested in the tale which concerned so many of his old friends, his analytical mind was pondering over the reason of Dave's action: How had he got the money from Schatz? Why had no one seen Schatz in Wayback? Where had the transfer of the money been made from Schatz to Dave? What had happened to change the plans of the fake hold-up, when Dave was to relieve Schatz of the money? His busy mind approached the riddle from many angles, as in the dark of night, a man with a lantern might cover a big stretch of country, searching everywhere for the track which would lead him to the finding of a hidden treasure. Farther and farther afield went Tex, examining, comparing, and rejecting every possibility that presented itself to his inward vision. Disappointed at the failure of his efforts to discover the solution, he cast from his mind all his useless speculation and adopted the slower but surer method which he should have tried at first: He put himself in the place of Dave-little by little he cast off his own personality and changed to that of the other, picturing to himself the effect upon Dave's cupidity when told of the part he was to play in the stealing of the money. So sensitive was his intelligence, so receptive to the shadowy suggestions that beckoned to him, perhaps from that lonely, unmarked grave beside the upper waters of the Little Jill, that presently his eyes began to gleam, his lips parted, and he stretched out his hand to Hopalong in unconscious emphasis. "Th' gunny sack, Hoppy! Where did he get th' gunny sack?"

The ghost of Schatz smiled. Tex was a man after his own heart.

Tex's abstraction had not escaped Hopalong. The end of his tale reached, he had put away the balance of the food, seen to the secure picketing of the two horses, put out the fire by the simple expedient of kicking over it sufficient sand, and had arranged the saddles in such a way that they completely hid the sack and could not be disturbed without arousing both him and Tex. From time to time he glanced at his silent companion, smiling to himself at the sight of such complete absorption. He could see himself over again in Tex, who was almost as old a man, recalling how he had been wont to ponder on the probable movements of an enemy and the pleasure he took, after a victory, in reviewing what had gone before and checking the mistakes and the successes in his reasoning. He wondered idly why it had lost its attraction for him and he concluded, with a whimsical grin, that marriage gave a man other things to think about.

But however lost Hopalong might be to inward speculation, no outward manifestation of the unusual or unlooked-for failed to appeal to his always active and alert senses. The pipe he had been smoking contentedly was held between his fingers, out and almost cold, his head was bent to one side and he was listening intently. He put his head to the ground and then arose to his feet, his ear turned to the stray breeze that was bringing to him faint and disagreeable sounds. When Tex's hand went out to him and Tex's voice broke in upon those barely audible sounds, he grasped the hand and gripped it hard to enjoin silence. Tex listened with all his ears but the ground noises had ceased and he was not high enough to have the advantage of the wind that was vexing Hopalong's hearing. Hopalong silently dragged him to his feet; they stood thus for a few seconds and then the look they turned upon each other was pregnant with significance.

"Makin' quite a noise," said Hopalong. "An' we ain't near th' trail yet. What do you make of it?"

"Dunno," answered Tex. "Had n't ought to be a man within twenty miles of us, Hoppy, 'less it's a Injun-an' them's no Injuns. Sounds to me like singin'."

"Same here," agreed Hopalong. "Can't be a drive herd, can it?"

"Not as I knows of. No herd ever come this way since th' railroad put through, an' then they stuck to th' trail."

"We got to find out, Tex," declared Hopalong, decisively. "Can't roost with a noisy bunch of coyotes like them runnin' 'round an' howlin' for gore."

"I 'll go, Hoppy," said Tex, "an' if I ain't back in an hour, you take both cayuses an' hike out for th' ranch."

"An' leave you afoot?" asked Hopalong. "Not by a d —n sight."

"You must, Hoppy. I got a reputation that 'll serve me with either honest men or thieves. I can't come to no harm. 'Tother way, you might get hurt. Two of us can't get away on them bronchs, they did too much to-day already. You 'll have to go at a walk, if you do go. 'Course I don't stop with that bunch 'less I has to. It's that bag I 'm thinkin' about, Hoppy. If I has to stop, you want to put as much ground as you can between them an' you. I 'm d —d glad they did n't see our fire."

"All right, Tex. I gives you an hour. 'Tain't more 'n a mile. Get a-goin'."

Tex started away and Hopalong began to get ready for a possible flight. Even if Tex did return they might decide that another location for their camp would be healthier. As he fastened the saddles to the two animals they each turned and looked at him with a disgust as expressive as if spoken.

Tex made for the spot from which the sounds had come, walking easily but silently, his form a mere shadow in the star-lit night and invisible on the lower levels, to which he carefully kept, at a distance of two hundred yards. At the end of ten minutes he was able to distinguish words and knew that Hoppy's and his surmise had been correct: they had heard the singing of night riders around a herd. It was the un-called-for presence of a herd in this vicinity which, more than all else, had led Tex to insist upon the reconnoitre being left to him. "Honest men or thieves," he had said. He was very doubtful of finding honest men. Only the condition of the horses had checked him from advising a departure on suspicion.

He was skulking along now, bent double; in his hand, the blade lying along his arm, was a knife such as few men in the West carried at that day and in the use of which Tex was unusually expert. It was entirely characteristic of him that he should possess such a weapon: silence in action is desired by the worst class of man, and Tex had been of that class before the enforced association of better men and the heroically magnanimous action of an opponent had changed him to the man he was. He slunk forward with the stealthy prowl of a wolf, glancing to right and left as he went, hoping to sight the camp of the cattlemen and get near enough without being seen, to learn what he had come to find out. He dropped flat to earth as a sudden snort startled him: he had come upon the herd without knowing it. A disquieted animal sprang to its feet and did not lie down again until the soothing voice of the herder was raised. The song floated down the wind and Tex listened as well as the cow:

> "'Now then, young men, don't be melancholy;
> Just see, like me, if you can't be jolly;
> If anything goes wrong with me
> I never sulk nor pout;
> In fact I am and always was
> The merriest girl that's out.'"

If the cow were soothed it was quite otherwise with Tex: his hair almost bristled as the rider went past, near enough for the heavy knife to have sped through the air and sunk haft-deep between his shoulders. "Chatter Spence!" sprang to Tex's lips. "Who's he driving for?" a question that he was still asking himself when another herder neared him, whose choice of lullaby was probably influenced by that of his companion, for he was calling out in most lugubrious voice:

'Buffalo gals, are you comin' out to-night,
Comin' out to-night, comin' out to-night?
Buffalo gals, are you comin' out to-night
To dance by th' light of th' moon?'

"It's all wrong," the singer broke off to say in a sing-song voice, that, as far as the cattle were concerned, had all the effect of a melody. "It's all wrong," he repeated. "There ain't no moon. 'To dance by th' light of th' stars,'" he corrected, and then: "Gentlemen, I rises to a question of order. I don't want to dance. I 'm too blasted sore to dance —I 'm too sore to be a-sittin' on this cross-eyed, rat-tailed, flea-bitten son-of-a-dog, too; an' if I ain't relieved pretty soon, Shanghai is a-goin' to hear —" his voice trailed away and the words were no longer distinguishable.

Tex cautiously sat up. "That's Argue Bennett. And Shanghai is with them. Why, d —n it! There must be a whole brood of Ike's chickens roosting around here. I 'm going to find them, even if I miss Hoppy in doing it."

He started to arise and back away before the first singer should approach again, only to drop back into his former prone position at the sound of a third singer, coming from his right. Bennett and Spence heard him too and were more than ready to resign the herd by the time he and his companion arrived. Bennett did not hesitate to announce his bitter condemnation of the way things were being done.

"That you, Ship?" he called.

"That's me," came the answer.

"Shore it's you," agreed Bennett, in sarcastic acknowledgment. "I 'd a' bet every cow I own it's you. An' I goes on record as bettin' every cow *you* own that Cracker is a-ridin' 'longside you. Do I win?"

"You win with yore own stock but I objects to you winnin' with mine. It *might* a' been Shanghai."

"Yes, it *might*; but if it was I 'd a' dropped dead from surprise. What I want to know is: what call has Shanghai got to hold down all th' soft snaps? Is he any better'n we are? Echo answers no-Echo bein' Chatter Spence, who has n't got pride enough to disagree with a hen."

"Aw, what's eatin' you! This ain't no regular drive. An' did you ever know Shanghai to get left on a deal? How'd we ever got through th' Cyclone if it hadn't been for Shanghai? You make me tired. Did you ever know a herd to get over th' ground so fast? Been you, we 'd be some're near Big Moose right now. You leave Shanghai alone an' we 'll have th' herd in our pockets afore Peters knows they 're gone. Nice little bunch, too. Go an' get yore chuck an' you 'll feel better. 'Jennie, my own true loved one, Wait till th' clouds roll by'" —he rode on to circle the herd.

"Did you ever hear such a pill? He thinks nobody knows nothin' but Shanghai. What do you say, Cracker?"

"Well, I kind o' sides with Ship. We ain't done as much as Shanghai, if it comes to that, 'ceptin' night herd."

"H —l! I 'm wastin' my breath talkin' to you. Come on, Chatter, we-why, th' greedy hog 's gone a'ready." Bennett made haste to get back to camp. He knew the supplies to be none too plentiful. So did Chatter Spence.

Tex stole away as silently as he had come, leaving the cattle-thieves happy in their ignorance of his discovery. He pushed himself hard on his return, fearful of having overstayed the time. Hopalong was waiting for him, however, and listened to his news with quiet interest.

"Buck's cows, Hoppy," was Tex's greeting, as he arrived on the run. "We got to get 'em but it's one sweet little job. Old Ship o' State is a holy terror in a row; Chatter Spence ain't bad, an' Argue Bennett an' Cracker impressed me as bein' good men to have around. But th' one we got to watch out for is Shanghai. He never falls down an' it would n't surprise me none to know he was watchin' them four same as I was. There's two of 'em ridin' herd an' three in camp. How do we go at it?"

"Got to get th' two night-ridin'. Tie 'em up an' th' other three is easy. Hol' on a minute till I get th' bank."

Ship o' State was beginning the twenty-seventh stanza in the melodious history of an incorrigible reprobate who deserved death in every one of them, when he was utterly confounded to hear a voice, almost at his ear, command him to "throw up his hands an' climb down of'n that cayuse, *pronto*." Contrary to what all his friends would have expected him to do, he obeyed the command instantly and to the letter. He was relieved of his gun and was being very effectually secured when the strangely quavering voice of Cracker was heard and came near. Ship eyed his captor in wonder. If Cracker were to be captured in the same manner, then this was the coolest man in the country. Nearer and nearer came the voice until Ship actually found himself worrying over the narrowness of the margin of safety. It was not until Cracker went by that he understood. The grotesque shape could only be accounted for in one way: Cracker's captor was straddling the same pony.

It was just when Ship had reached this conclusion that a very unpleasant bunch of rags was thrust into his mouth and he was lifted and thrown face down across the back of his horse. Hopalong got into the saddle and they rode away from the herd. They had not gone far before another horseman joined them and Ship could hear the singing Cracker as he circled the herd. "There's three of'em anyway," was his thought, wherein he was wrong. Cracker, with his hands trussed high behind his back and his feet hobbled, was stumbling slowly along with the threat in his memory that if he stopped singing until he was told, his head stood a good chance of being separated from the rest of his carcass, when he would never be able to sing again; and the further information that, if the herd should stampede, he was in a fair way to be crushed to a pulp. The latter he knew to be true and he was equally convinced that the other would be quite likely to take place.

Fifty yards from the herd, Ship was quietly dumped to the ground. Far enough away from him the horses were picketed and two forms crept carefully upon the three men in camp.

Dark as it was, there was no difficulty in finding two of the three. Spence and Bennett, the latter agreeably surprised to find that Shanghai had depleted the general treasury to the extent of one cow, had both eaten a large and satisfying meal; their hunger appeased, weariness had asserted itself in double force and nothing less than a determined kick would have awakened either of them. But Hopalong and Tex prowled around looking for Shanghai without success.

Shanghai was living up to his reputation. Having made his plans and given orders to insure their carrying out, he then stayed around and saw it done. Argue Bennett might grumble to the others but he knew the futility, as also the danger, of grumbling to Shanghai. When his two subordinates had eaten their fill and gone to sleep, Shanghai still sat hunched before the dying embers of the fire, smoking a meditative pipe. When the smoke ceased to float lazily from his nostrils he knocked the warm ashes onto the palm of his hand, got to his feet and slipped quietly away from the camp.

Any one who knew Shanghai well would have reasoned that he was probably going to look over the herd because he started away in the opposite direction. Going straight to his objective point was entirely too elemental for Shanghai. He fetched a wide circle before drawing near the herd, his approach being unheralded and made with the suspicious caution which marked all his movements. He listened inattentively to the husky voice of Cracker who was mourning the demise of somebody named Brown, and moved a little nearer. Presently he became vaguely uneasy at the silence of old Ship-o'-State. It was not the lack of song on Ship's part that troubled Shanghai-the cattle were resting easy enough-but where was he? When Cracker came around again Shanghai was near enough to see him and he craned his neck in wonder at the sight: Cracker on his two feet, staggering along like a man about three whiskeys from oblivion, and Ship off post. Here was something very wrong and Shanghai cursed softly to think how far away his horse was. What in blazes made him come afoot, anyway? He started back to camp to repair the oversight and to have Chatter and Argue behind him before making an investigation of Cracker's astonishing preference for night-herding on foot.

His descent upon the camp would have been creditable to an Apache. First making sure of his horse and leaving him in shape for instant departure, he circled the two sleeping forms, viewing them from all sides. There was something wrong. Shanghai did not know what it was but the figures of his two companions seemed actually to exhale menace and the longer he hesitated the stronger the feeling became. Shanghai stole quietly back to his horse, mounted and rode off with the settled conviction that sun-up was the proper time for investigating these unusual circumstances and that the proper spot was several miles distant from below the sky-line of some convenient knoll.

At the unmistakable sound of retreating hoofbeats the figures in camp came to life. They sat up and listened and then Tex looked at Hoppy with frank disapprobation. "Hoppy, my way was best," he declared. Hopalong nodded, in silent agreement, and Tex continued: "I been a-hearin' considerable talk about this here Shanghai an' I 'm bound to say I believe all I hears. D —n if he ain't got second sight."

Hopalong nodded again. "Let's round up th' rest of th' roosters, anyhow. We got four, an' four's a plenty to take care of."

"Shore is," admitted Tex. "Let's bring 'em in an' hog-tie 'em. Them cows would n't move for anythin' 'less 'n a Norther after th' way they 've come across country."

A half hour later Ike's four pets were lying side by side in camp, trussed to the point of immovability and all apparently, in spite of their discomfort, taking advantage of the opportunity to secure the sleep they so much needed after their unsuccessful exertions.

"Hoppy," said Tex, "I think that with that Shanghai party still runnin' at large, it 'd be some wise to split up that wealth. Better take a chance of losin' half of it than all of it. What you think?"

"Same here," agreed Hopalong. He opened the sack and dumped out the packages, dividing them roughly into two parts with a sweep of his hand, and proceeded to rip up the sack, preparatory to making two parcels of the money.

"'With milk an' honey blest,'" faltered a voice and they turned to find Argue Bennett's eyes almost starting from his head at the sight he beheld.

"Playin' 'possum, eh? It'd do you no harm to stretch hemp right now," and Tex's meditative air was fringed with ferocity.

"No offence, Comin', no offence. You woke me movin'. Is that what Dave got away with?"

"Yes-an' there won't no more Daves get away with it, you can bet all th' cows you own on that."

"An' me a-riskin' my neck rustlin' that bunch when all that beautiful wealth was a-leavin' th' country easy an' graceful an' just a-shoutin' to be brought back. Excuse me, Comin'. I ain't got no call to talk. I reckon I never did talk. Th' best I ever done since I was born is bray."

Thus it came about that Shanghai suffered the acute misery of seeing his four-footed fortune headed back the way it had come. Not that he lost heart all at once. After some hours of following he had decided that a bold stroke might put him again in possession and was perfecting the details of the stratagem his ready mind conceived, when a sudden check was given by a rapidly approaching cloud of dust from the northwest. The check became check-mate when the useful field-glasses disclosed to his pained vision the hilarious meeting that took place. A certain jaunty carriage, a characteristic swagger that did not forsake him even in the saddle, made Shanghai look hard at the leader of the new-comers and suspect Cock Murray. And his suspicion was well founded. Cock Murray had already redeemed his promise to Buck and it may be pardoned him if in the joy of his heart, his swagger became so pronounced as to disclose his personality across some miles of country.

Shanghai closed his glasses and moved slowly to his horse. "Well, it had to be," he conceded, philosophically. "An' I reckon it's about time I pulled my freight."

Chapter XXVIII

The Heart of a Rose

And the evening and the morning were the second day. At a time when, through the diffused and fading light of the sun-vacant sky, the silver-pale stars blinked one by one in their awakening; when the protesting twitter of disturbed birds seeking their rest sounded sweetly clear above the steady rumble of the marshland frogs; when the velvet-footed killers stretched and yawned and gazed with dilated pupils at the near approach of night; when the men who persuaded luck to their advantage, in various ways, began to gather about the tables in cow-town and mining-camp, and there was a lighting of lamps by the foresighted and a trimming of wicks by the procrastinators-the French Rose faced her father, Jean, and did battle for love and happiness, though she knew it not.

The easy-going Jean had known nothing of the manner in which their guest was wounded, nor by whom; and Rose had not thought it wise to tell him, even if it occurred to her in the stress of that first day. But Jean had heard many rumors in Twin River, many disquieting facts and equally disturbing inferences. He had hurried home beset with fears for the outcome, alarmed at the reckless step Rose had taken and vainly asking himself why. Immediately upon his entry he had set Pickles at a task which would occupy him away from the cabin. Standing moodily at the window he watched him go. Then he turned to his daughter for an explanation.

"Is Dave here yesterday?" he asked.

"Yes," replied Rose, non-committally.

Jean turned over in his mind this new fact and fitted it into the pattern. "For why you go so fast to Twin?" he questioned.

"No one is here but me. Fritz, he go to the Two Y's ranch."

"You tell him?"

"No. He hear Dave talk an' go to tell M'sieu Peters Dave have stole all his money."

"*Diable!* Steal?"

"Yes."

Jean knitted his brows in the effort to understand the reason for this; quite naturally he came back in a circle to his first inquiry and repeated it: "For why you go to Twin?"

"I go for men to catch Dave when he steal the money." This, while not strictly true, was the nearest to truth that Jean could understand.

The trend of his thoughts was shown by his next question. "Dave-he know?" he asked, and his anxiety was apparent.

"Yes," was the brief answer.

"*Mon Dieu!*" exclaimed Jean. He turned from her and stared with unseeing eyes over the land he had struggled hard to make his own. And now he must lose it. Rapidly calculating how long his slender resources would support him until Rose could dispose of his stock and follow, despair came upon him as he realized that the vengeance of Dave was not to be escaped. "For why," he asked, hoarsely, "for why you do this?"

"For why?" repeated Rose and the thrill in her voice caused him to turn and look at her in surprise. "Figure to yourself, then: That devil he come here and he sneer at you, and he insult me-yes. Many times he insult me that I have to hold myself, so! that I do not kill him. I endure. He send me ——-*Dieu!* that I should say it-he make dirt of me to walk on, to arrive at a man who is high, good, ah, a man! *mon père*, a man like you, one time when you have no fear. He send me. I say nothing. Many times he try, like a dog, to spring at his throat, but always, it is nothing but snap at his heels. Like a dog which he is. Then he come to me and say he is triumph. He get much money. And he tell me go with him. Me! me! he command like he is master and me slave. He steal money from M'sieu Peters and him and me, we go away together, like that, like man and his squaw. And I say nothing. Ah, *mon père!* it is too much-too much. If it be some other man-not M'sieu Peters-then I go. I save you, *mon père*, though it kill me. But-it is too much."

She bowed her head, filled with self-reproach, with a knowledge that her father could never see this thing as she did. Jean stared at her, motionless; but his dumb amaze slowly lifted. He came to her and rested his hand lightly on her bowed head. "*Ma Rose-ma belle Rose* —when you have for a good man so big love as that, I would die, with gladness, to know so big happiness is come to you." And he went swiftly from the cabin.

At the closing of the door she sprang to it and threw it wide again. "You will not go-now-to-night?" she called.

The answer, low, determined, in the tones of the father of that other time, reassured her: "No. We stay. Maybe-who knows? —God is good."

She went back and with steady hand lit the lamp and placed it on the table. The noble face was aglow with hopeful pride: he would face it at last, this thing that had embittered both their lives.

"Rose!"

She started and turned in dismay toward the inner room. He was awake-how long? —and calling her.

"Rose!" the call came again, gentle but insistent. "Rose, I —I want you."

She stood a moment longer, both hands pressed against her heart, her breath coming in great gasps and in her eyes the frightened look of a child. Then she caught up the lamp and with swift step went in and stood beside the bunk. "Is it then you rest ill, my friend?" she asked softly, and then bent to re-arrange the pillow. Buck's hand closed over hers.

"Rose," he whispered, "Rose —I heard."

She slipped to her knees, hiding her face in the pillow, her figure shaking with great tremors and sobs breaking from her so that she could scarcely speak. "Oh, I am ashamed," she said brokenly, "I am ashamed."

"Ashamed! And I——" he stopped, drawing in a deep breath at the wonder of it; then raising himself to rest on bent arm, he laid his cheek against her hair. "I 'm th' one as ought to be ashamed, Rose: a man o' my age, an' feelin' th' way I do-an' you a girl. But I 've got to have you, Rose. I just got to have you. An' if you don't say 'yes' I swear to God I 'll give up an' pull out o' this country. I don't want to stop another day if you say 'no.'"

She drew away from him and raised her head to look at him doubtfully, appealingly, believingly. A wonderful smile broke through her tears and stilled the trembling of her lips. "You mean it, Buck. Oh! You do! You do!" Her arms were about him and she lowered him gently back again. "Rest you, and get well quickly, wounded man," she murmured. "My man-my man until I die-and after."

Tex

At sight of a rattler his gun leaped into crashing life

[Page 314]

Chapter I
The Trail Calls

Memory's curtain rises and shows a scene softened by time and blurred by forgetfulness, yet the details slowly emerge like the stars at twilight. There appears a rain-washed, wind-swept

250

range in Montana, a great pasture level in the center, but rising on its sides like a vast, shallow saucer, with here and there a crack of more somber hue where a ravine, or sluggish stream, lead toward the distant river. Green underfoot, deep blue overhead, with a lavender and purple rim under a horizon made ragged and sharp by the not too distant mountains and foothills. An occasional deep blue gash in the rim's darker tones marks where some pass or canyon cuts through the encircling barriers. A closer inspection would reveal a half-dozen earthy hollows, the rutting holes of the once numerous buffalo which paused here on their periodic migrations. In the foreground a white ranchhouse and its flanking red buildings, framed by the gray of corral walls, nestles on the southern slope of a rise and basks in the sunlight. From it three faint trails grow more and more divergent, leading off to Everywhere. Scattered over the vast, green pastures are the grazing units of a great herd, placid and content, moving slowly and jerkily, like spilled water down a gentle, dusty slope. But in the total movement there is one thread with definite directness, even though it constantly turns from side to side in avoiding the grazing cattle. This, as being different and indicating purpose, takes our instant attention.

A rider slowly makes his way among the cattle, by force of habit observing everything without being fully conscious of it. His chaps of soft leather, worn more because of earlier associations than from any urgent need on this northern range, have the look of long service and the comfort coming from such. His hat is a dark gray sombrero, worn in a manner suggesting a cavalier of old. Over an open vest are the careless folds of a blue kerchief, and at his right hip rubs a holster with its waiting, deadly tenant. A nearer approach reveals him to be a man in middle life, lean, scrupulously neat, clean shaven, with lines of deep humor graven about his eyes and mouth, softening a habitual expression which otherwise would have been forbiddingly hard and cynical.

His roving glances reach the purple horizon and are arrested by the cerulean blue of a pass, and he checks his horse with a gesture hopelessly inadequate to express the restlessness, the annoying uncertainty of his mood, a mood fed unceasingly by an inborn yearning to wander, regardless of any aim or other condition. Here is a prospect about him which he knows cannot be improved upon; here are duties light enough practically to make him master of his time, yet heavy enough to be purposeful; his days are spent in the soothing solitudes of clean, refreshing surroundings; his evenings with men who give him perfect fellowship, wordless respect, and repressed friendship, speaking when the mood urges, or silent in that rare, all-explaining silence of strong men in perfect accord. His wants are few and automatically supplied: yet for weeks the longing to leave it all daily had grown stronger--to leave it for what? Certainly for worse; yet leave it he must.

He sat and pondered, retrospective, critical. The activities of his earlier days passed before him, with no hypocritical hiding or blunting of motives. They revealed few redeeming features, for he carelessly had followed the easy trails through the deceptive lowlands of morality, and among men and women worse even than himself in overt acts and shameless planning, yet better because they did not have his intelligence or moral standards. But he slowly rose above them as a diver rises above treacherous, lower currents, and the reason was plain to those who knew him well. First he had a courage sparkling like a jewel, unhesitant, forthright, precipitate; next he had a rare mixture of humor and cynicism which better revealed to him things in their right proportions and values; and last, but hardly least by any means, an intelligence of high order, buttressed by facts, clarified by systematic study, and edged by training. In his youth he had aimed at the practice of medicine, but gave too much attention to more imaginative targets and found, when too late, that he had hit nothing. His fondness for drinking, gambling at cards, and other weedy sowings resulted from, rather than caused, the poor aim. Certain unforgivable episodes, unforgivable because of their notoriety more than because of the things themselves, brewed a paternal tempest, upon which he had turned a scornful back, followed Horace Greeley's famous advice, and sought the healing and the sanctuary of the unasking West.

In his new surroundings he soon made a name for himself, in both meanings, and quickly dominated those whose companionship he either craved or needed. An inherent propensity for sleight of hand provided him an easy living at cards; and his deftness and certainty with a six-gun gave him a pleasing security. However, all things have an end. There came a time when he nearly had reached the lowest depths of moral submersion when he met and fought a character as strong as his own, but in few other ways resembling him; and from that time on he swam on the surface. It would be foolish to say that the depths ceased to lure him, for they did, and at times so powerfully that he scarcely could resist them. For this he had to thank to no small degree one of the bitterest experiences of his life: his disastrous marriage. Giving blind love and unquestioning loyalty, he had lost both by the unclean evidence unexpectedly presented to his eyes. In that crisis, after the first madness, his actions had been worthy of a nature softer than his own and he had gone, by devious ways, back to his West and started anew with a burning cynicism. But for the steadying influence of his one-time enemy, and the danger and the interest in the task which Hopalong Cassidy had set before him, the domestic tragedy certainly would have sent him plunging down to his former level or below it.

Time passed and finally brought him news of the tragic death of his faithless wife, and he found that it did not touch him. He had felt neither pity, sorrow, nor relief. It is doubtful if he ever had given a thought to the question of his freedom, for with his mental attitude it meant nothing at all to him. He had put among his belongings the letter from his former employer, who had known all about the affair and the names and addresses of several of his western friends, telling him that he was free; and hardly gave it a second thought.

Turning from his careless scrutiny of the distant pass he rode on again and soon became aware of the sound of hoofbeats rapidly nearing him. As he looked up a rider topped a rise, descried him, and waved a sombrero. The newcomer dashed recklessly down the slope and drew rein sharply at his side, a cheerful grin wreathing his homely, honest face. Pete was slow-witted, but his sterling qualities masked this defect even in the eyes of a man as sharp as his companion, who felt for him a strong, warm friendship.

"Hello, Tex!" said the newcomer. "What's eatin' you? You shore look glum."

Tex thought if it was plain enough for Pete Wilson to notice it, it must be plain, indeed. "Mental worms an' moral cancer, Pete," replied the cynic, smiling in spite of himself at the cogitation started in his friend by the words.

"Whatever that means," replied Pete, cautiously. "However, if it's what I reckon it is, there's just two cures." Pete was dogmatic by nature. "An' that's likker, or a new range."

"Somethin's th' matter with you today, Pete," rejoined Tex. "Yo're as quick as a reflex." He studied a moment, and added: "An' yo're dead right, too."

"There ain't no reflection needed," retorted Pete; "an' there ain't nothin' th' matter with me a-tall. I'm tellin' you common sense; but it's shore a devil of a choice. If it's likker, then you lose; if it's driftin' off som'ers, then we lose. Tell you what: Go down to Twin River an' clean 'em out at stud, if you can find anybody that ain't played you before," he suggested hopefully. "Mebby there's a stranger in town. You'll shore feel a whole lot better, then." He grinned suddenly. "You might find a travelin' man: they're so cussed smart they don't think anybody can learn 'em anythin'. Go ahead--try it!"

Tex laughed. "Where you goin'?" he abruptly demanded. He could not afford to have any temptations thrown in his way just then.

"Over Cyclone way, for Buck. Comin' along?"

Tex slowly shook his head. "I'm goin' th' other way. Wonder why we haven't got word from Hoppy or Red or Johnny?" he asked, and the question acted like alum in muddy water, clearing away his doubts and waverings, which swiftly precipitated and left the clear fluid of decision.

"Huh!" snorted Pete in frank disgust. "You wait till any of them fellers write an' there'll be a white stone over yore head with nice letterin' on it to tell lies forever. You know 'em. Comin' along with me?" he asked, wheeling, and was answered by an almost imperceptible shake of his friend's head.

"I'll shake hands with you, Pete," said Tex, holding out his deft but sinewy hand. "In case I don't see you again," he explained in answer to his friend's look of surprise. "I'm mebby driftin' before you get back."

"Cuss it!" exploded Pete. "I'm allus talkin' too blamed much. Now I've gone an' done it!"

"You've only hastened it a little," assured Tex, gripping the outstretched hand spasmodically. "Cheer up; I don't aim to stay away forever!" He spurred his mount and shot away up the incline, Pete looking after him and slowly shaking his head.

When the restless puncher stopped again it was at the kitchen door of the white ranchhouse. As he swung from the saddle something stung him where his trousers were tight and he stopped his own jump to grab the horse, which had been stung in turn. A snicker and a quick rustle sounded under the summer kitchen and Tex took the coiled rope from his saddle, deftly unfastening the restraining knot. The rustling sounded again, frantic and sustained, followed by a half-defiant, half-supplicating jeer.

"You can't do it, under here!" said Pickles, reloading the bean-shooter from a bulging cheek. "I can shoot yore liver out before you can whirl it!" Pickles was quite a big boy now, but threatened never to grow dignified; and besides, he had been badly spoiled by everybody on the ranch.

"Whirling livers never appealed to me," rejoined Tex, putting the rope back. "Never," he affirmed decidedly; "but I'm goin' to whirl yourn some of these days, an' you with it!"

"Those he loves, he annoys," said a low, sweet voice, its timbre stimulating the puncher like a draught of wine. His sombrero sweeping off as he turned, he bowed to the French Rose, wife of the big-hearted half-owner of the ranch. If only he had chosen a woman like this one!

"I seem to remember him annoyin' Dave Owens, at near half a mile, with Hoppy's Sharps," he slowly replied. "Nobody ever told me that he loved Dave a whole lot." At the momentary cloud the name brought to her face he shook his head and growled to himself. "I'm a fool, ma'am, these days," he apologized; "but it strikes me that you ought to smile at that name--it shore played its unwilling part in giving you a good husband; an' Buck a mighty fine wife. Where is Buck?"

"Inside the house, walking rings around the table--he seems so, so--" she shrugged her shoulders hopelessly and stepped aside to let Tex enter.

"I don't know what he seems," muttered Tex as he passed in; "but I know what he is--an' that's just a plain, ornery fool." He shook his head at such behavior by any man who was loved by the French Rose.

Buck stopped his pacing and regarded him curiously, motioning toward an easy chair.

"Standin's good enough for me, for I'm itchin' with th' same disease that you imagine is stalkin' you," said Tex, looking at his old friend with level, disapproving gaze. "It don't matter with me, but it's plain criminal with you. I'm free to go; yo're not. An' I'm tellin' you frank that if I had th' picket stake that's holdin' you, all h--l couldn't tempt me. Yo're a plain, d--d fool--an' you know it!"

Buck leaned back against the edge of the table and thoughtfully regarded his companion. "It ain't so much that, as it is Hoppy, an' Red, an' Johnny," he replied, spreading out his hands in an eloquent gesture. "They could write, anyhow, couldn't they?" he demanded.

"Shore," affirmed Tex, grinning. "How long ago was it that you answered their last letters?" He leaned back and laughed outright at the guilty expression on his friend's face. "I thought so! Strong on words, but cussed poor on example."

"I reckon yo're right," muttered Buck. "But that south range shore calls me strong, Tex."

" 'Whither thou goest, I go' was said by a woman," retorted Tex. " 'Yore people are my people; yore God, my God.' I'm sayin' it works both ways. You ought to go down on yore knees for what's come to you. An' you will, one of these days. Think of Hoppy's loss--an' you'll do it before mornin'. But I didn't come in to preach common sense to a lunatic--I come to get my time, an' to say good-bye."

Buck nodded. Vaguely disturbed by some unnamed, intermittent fever, he had been quick to read the symptoms of restlessness in another, especially in one who had been as close to him as Tex had been. He went over to an old desk, slowly opened a drawer and took out a roll of bills and a memorandum.

"Here," he said, holding both out. "Far as I know it's th' same as when you gave it to me. Ought to be seven hundred, even. Count it, to make shore." While Tex took it and shoved it into his pocket uncounted and crumpled the memorandum, Buck also was reaching into a pocket, and counted off several bills from the roll it gave up. These he gravely handed to his companion, smiling to hide the ache of losing another friend.

"I shore haven't earned it all," mused Tex, looking down at the wages in his hand. "I reckon I'm doin' this ranch a favor by leavin', for there ain't no real job up here no more for any man as expensive as I am. You got th' whole country eatin' out of yore hand, an' th' first thing you know th' cows will catch th' habit an' brand an' count 'emselves to save you th' trouble of doin' it."

"You'll be doin' us a bigger favor when you come back, one of these days," grinned Buck. "You shore did yore share in trainin' it to eat out of my hand. For a while it looked like it would eat th' hand--an' it would 'a', too. Aimin' to ride down?"

Tex's eyes twinkled. "How'd you come to figger I'm goin' down?"

Buck smiled.

"No, reckon not," said Tex. "Ridin' as far's th' railroad. I'll leave my cayuse with Smith. When one of th' boys goes down that way he can get it. I'll pay Smith for a month's care." Reading the unspoken question in his friend's eyes, he carelessly answered it. "Don't know where I'm goin'. Reckon I'll get down to th' SV before I stop. That'd be natural, with Red an' Hoppy stayin' with Johnny."

"They might need you, too," suggested Buck, hopefully. If he couldn't be with his distant friends himself, he at least wished as many of them to be together as was possible.

"I'm copperin' that," grunted Tex. His eyes shone momentarily. "Yo're forgettin' that our best three are together. Lord help any misguided fools that prod 'em sharp. Well, I'm dead shore to drift back ag'in some day; but as you say, those south ranges shore do pull a feller's heart." He looked shrewdly at his friend and his face beamed from a sudden thought. "We're a pair of fools," he laughed. "You ain't got th' wander itch! You don't want to go jack-rabbitin' all over th' country, like me! All you want is that southwest country, with yore wife an yore friends on th' same ranch; down in th' cactus country, where th' winters ain't what they are up here. I'm afraid my brain's atrophied, not havin' been used since Dave Owens rolled down from his ambush with Hoppy's slugs in him for ballast."

Buck looked at him with eager, hopeful intentness and his sigh was one of great relief and thankfulness. He need not be ashamed of that longing, now vague and nameless no longer. His head snapped back and he stood erect, and his voice thrilled with pride. Tex had put his finger on the trouble, as Tex always did. "I've been as blind as a rattler in August!" he exclaimed.

"Not takin' th' time to qualify that blind-rattler-in-August phrase, I admits yo're right," beamed Tex. He arose, shoved out his hand for the quick, tight grasp of his friend and wheeled to leave, stopping short as he found himself face to face with Rose Peters. "A happy omen!" he cried. "Th' first thing I see at th' beginnin' of my journey is a rose."

She smiled at both of them as she blocked the door, and the quick catch in her voice did not escape Tex Ewalt.

"I was but in the other room," she said, her face alight. "I could not but hear, for you both speak loud. I am so glad, M'sieu Tex--that now I know why my man is so--so restless. Ruth, she said what I think, always. We are sorry that you mus' go--but we know you will not forget your friends, and will come back again some day."

Buck put his arm around his wife's shoulders and smiled. "An' if he brings th' other boys back with him, we'll find room for 'em all, eh Rose?" He looked at his friend. "We're shore goin' to miss you, Tex. Good luck. We'll expect you when we see you."

Tex bowed to Rose and backed into the curious Pickles, whom he lightly spanked as a fitting farewell; and soon the noise of his departure drummed softer and softer into the south.

Chapter II

Refreshed Memories

The dusty, grimy, almost paintless accommodation train, composed of engine, combination smoking-baggage car, and one day coach, rumbled and rattled, jerked and swayed over the uneven roadbed, the clicking at the rail joints sensible both to tactual and auditory nerves, and calling attention to the disrepair into which the whole line had fallen. In the smoking compartment of the baggage car sat Tex Ewalt, sincerely wishing that he had followed his first promptings and chosen the saddle in preference to this swifter method of traveling.

All day he had suffered heat, dust, cinders, and smoke after a night of the same. It had been bad enough on the main line, but after leaving the junction conditions had grown steadily worse. All day he had crossed a yellow gray desolation, flat and unending, under a dirty blue sky and a dust-filled air shimmering with heat waves. He had peered at a drab, distant horizon which seemed hardly to change as it crept eastward past him, at all times barely more than a thin circle about as interesting and colorful as a bleached hoop from some old, weather-beaten barrel. Wherever he had looked, it had been to see sun-burned grass and clouds of imponderable dust, the latter sucked up by the train and sent whirling into every crack and crevice; occasional white spots darting rearward he knew to be the grim, limy skulls of herbiverous animals; arrow-like trails cut deep into the drought-cursed earth, and not too frequently a double line of straggling, dispirited willows, cottonwoods, and box elders, marked the course of some prairie creek, whose characteristic, steep earth banks, often undermined, now enclosed sun-dried mud, curling like heated scales, with here and there pools of noisome water hidden under scabs of scum. Mile after mile of this had dulled him, familiar as he had once been with the sight, and he sat apathetic, dispirited and glum, too miserable to accept the pressing invitation of a traveling cardsharp to sit into a game of draw poker. Gradually the mild, long swells of the prairie had grown shorter, sharper, and higher; gradually the soil had become rockier and the creek beds deeper below the rims of their banks. The track wound more and more as it twisted and turned among the hills, and for some hours he had noticed a constant rising, which now became more and more apparent as the top of the watershed drew nearer.

He dozed fitfully at times and once the sharper had roused him by touching his shoulder to ask him again to take cards in a game. To this invitation Tex had opened his eyes, looked up at the smiling poker devotee and made a slight motion, dozing off again as the surprised gambler moved away from one he now knew to be of the same calling as himself. Towns had followed each other at increasingly long intervals, insensibly changing in their aspect, and the horizon steadily had been narrowing. Here and there along the dried beds of the creeks were rude cabins and shacks, each not far from an abandoned sluice and cradle. Between the hills the pastures grew smaller and smaller, their sides more precipitous, but as they shrunk, the number of cattle on them seemed to increase. Rough buildings of wood or stone began to replace the low sod dugouts of a few hours ago, and he knew that he was rapidly nearing his destination.

Suddenly a ribbon-like scar on the horizon caught his eye. It ran obliquely from a north-eastern point of his vista southwesterly across the pastures, hills, and valleys, like a lone spoke in some great wheel, of which the horizon was both felloe and tire. At this he sat up with a show of interest. Judging from its direction, and from what he remembered of it at this section of its length, it would cross the track some miles farther on. He nodded swiftly at this old-time friend of his cattle-driving days--he had been a fool not to have remembered it and the cow-town not far ahead, but the names of all the mushroom towns he had been in during his career in the West had not remained in his memory. Years rolled backward in a flash. He could see the distant, plodding caravans of homesteaders, or the long, disciplined trains of the freighters, winding over the hills and across the flats, their white canvas wagon covers flashing against the sky, the old, dirty covers emphasizing the newness and whiteness of their numerous patches. But on this nearing trail, winding into the southwest there had been a different migration. He almost could see the spread-out herd moving deliberately forward, the idling riders, the point and swing men, and the plodding, bumping chuck wagon with its bumptious cook. This trail, a few hundred yards wide, beaten by countless hoofs, had deepened and deepened as the wind carried away the dust, and if left to itself would be discernible after the passing of many years.

The name of the town ahead and on this old trail brought a smile to his lips, a smile that was pleasantly reminiscent; but with the name of the town came nearly forgotten names of men, and the smile changed into one that was not pleasant to look upon. There was Williams, Gus Williams, often referred to as "Muttonhead." He had been a bully, a sure-thing gambler, herd trimmer, and cattle thief in a small way, but he had been only a petty pilferer of hoofed property, for his streak of caution was well developed. Tex had not seen him, or heard of him, for twenty years, never since he had shot a gun out of Williams' hand and beat him up in a corner of his own saloon.

The rapidly enlarging ribbon drew nearer and more distinct, and soon it crossed the track and ran into the south. He remembered the wide, curving bend it took here: there had been a stampede one rainy night when he was off trick and rolled up in his blanket under the chuck wagon. They had reason to suspect that the cattle were sent off in their mad flight through the dark by human agency. Two days had been spent in combing the rough plain and in rounding up the scattered herd, and there had been a sizable number lost.

A deeper tone leaped into the dull roar of the train and told of a gully passing under the track. It ran off at a slight angle, the dried bed showing more numerous signs of human labors and habitations, and when the train came to a bumping, screeching stop at a ramshackle one-room station he knew that he was at the end of his ride and within three stations from the end of the line, which here turned sharply toward the northwest, baffled by the treacherous sands of the river, whose bank it paralleled for sixty miles. Had he gone on in the train he would have come no closer to his objective and would have to face a harder country for man and horse. Gunsight, where his three friends were located, lay about a hundred miles southwest of the bend in the track; but because of the sharp bend it lay farther from the station beyond. From where he now was, the riding would not be unpleasant and the ford across the river was shallower, the greater width of the stream offset by a more sluggish current. This ford was treacherous in high water and not passable after sudden rises for a day or two, because the force of the swollen current stirred up the unstable sands of the bottom. As a veteran of the old cattle trails he knew what a disturbed river bottom often meant.

The wheezing exhaust and the complaining panting of the all but discarded engine added dismal sounds to a dismal view. He stiffly descended the steps, a bulging gunny sack over his shoulder and a rolled blanket and a sheathed rifle fully utilized his other arm and hand. Dropping his burdens to the ground he paused to look around him.

It was just a frontier town, ugly, patched, sprawling, barely existent, and an eyesore even to the uncritical; and cursed further by Kansas politics which at this time were not as stalwart as they once had been, reminding one of the mediocre sons of famous fathers. In place of the old daring there now were trickery and subtle meannesses; in place of hot hatreds were now smoldering grudges; where once old-time politicians "shot it out" in the middle of the street, there now were furtive crawlings and treacherous shots from the dark. Like all towns it had a name--it will suffice if we know it as Windsor. Being neither in the mining country nor on the cattle range, and being in an out-of-the-way position even on the merging strip between the two, it undoubtedly would have died a natural death except for the fortuitous chance which had led the branch-line railroad to reach its site. The shifting cattle drives and a short-lived townsite speculation had been the causes for the rails coming; then the drives stopped at nearer terminals and the speculation blew up--but the rails remained. This once flamboyantly heralded "artery of commerce" swiftly had atrophied and now was hardly more than a capillary, and its diurnal pulsation was just sufficient to keep the town about one degree above coma.

Tex sneered openly, luxuriously, aggressively, and for all the world to see. He promised himself that he would not remain here very long. Before him lay the squalid dirt street with its cans and rubbish, the bloated body of a dog near the platform, a dead cat farther along.

There were several two-story frame buildings, evidently built while the townsite game was on. The rest were one-story shacks, and he remembered most of them.

He picked up his belongings and sauntered into the station to wait until the agent had finished his business with the train crew, and that did not take long.

The agent stepped into the dusty, dirty room, coughed, nodded, and passed into his partitioned office. In a moment he was out again, looked closely at the puncher and decided to risk a smile and a word: "Is there anything I can do for you?" he hazarded.

Tex put his sombrero beside him on the bench and wiped his forehead with a sleeve. He saw that his companion was slight, not too healthy, and appeared to be friendly and intelligent; but in his eyes lay the shadow of fear.

"Mebby you can tell me th' best place to eat an' sleep; an' th' best place to buy a horse," he replied.

"Williams' hotel is the best in town, and I'd ask him about the horse. You might do better if you didn't say I recommended him to you."

"Not if you don't want me to," responded Tex, smiling sardonically for some inexplicable reason. "Reckon he'd eat you because yo're sendin' him trade? Don't worry; I won't say you told me."

"So far as I am concerned it don't matter. It's you I'm thinking about."

Tex stretched, crossed his legs, and smiled. "In that case I'll use my own judgment," he replied. "Been workin' for th' railroad very long?"

"Little too long, I'm afraid," answered the agent, coughing again, "but I've been out here only two months." He hesitated, looked a little self-conscious, and continued. "It's my lungs, you know. I got a transfer for my health. If I can stick it out here I have hopes of slowly improving, and perhaps of getting entirely well."

"If you can stick it out? Meanin' yo're findin' it too monotonous an' lonely?" queried Tex.

The agent laughed shortly, the look of fear again coming into his eyes. "Anything but the first; and so far as being lonely is concerned, I find that my sister is company enough."

Tex cogitated and recrossed his legs. "From what I have already seen of this town I'd gamble she is; but a man's allus a little better off if he can herd with his own sex once in a while. So it ain't monotonous? Have many trains a day?" he asked, knowing from his perusal of the time-table that there were but two.

"One in and one out. You passed the other on the siding at Willow, if you've come from beyond there."

"Reckon I remember it. Much business here to keep you busy?"

"Not enough to tire even a--lunger!" He said the word bitterly and defiantly.

"That's a word I never liked," said Tex. "It's too cussed brutal. Some people derive a great deal of satisfaction in calling a spade a spade, and that is quite proper so far as spades are concerned; but why go further? A man can't allus help a thing like tuberculosis--especially if he's makin' a livin' for two. Yo're not very high up here, but I reckon th' air's right. It's th' winter that's goin' to count ag'in' you. You got to watch that. You might do better across th' west boundary. Any doctor in town?"

"There's a man who calls himself a doctor. His favorite prescription is whiskey."

"Yeah? For his patients?"

"For his patients and himself, too."

"Huh," grunted the puncher. He cleared his throat. "I once read about yore trouble--in a dictionary," he explained, grinning. "It said milk an' aigs, among other things; open air, both capitalized, day an' night; plenty of sleep, no worryin', an' no excitement. Have many heavy boxes to rustle?"

"No," answered the agent, looking curiously at his companion. "I had plenty of milk and eggs, but the milk is getting scarce and the eggs are falling off. I--" he stopped abruptly, shrugging his shoulders. "D--n it, man! It isn't so much for myself!"

"No," said Tex, slowly arising. "A man usually feels that way about it. I'm goin' up to th' hotel. May drop around to see you tomorrow if I'm in town."

"I'll be mighty glad to see you; but there's no use for you to make enemies," replied the agent, leading the way outside. He stopped and took hold of a trunk, to roll it into the building.

"Han's off," said Tex, smiling and pushing him aside. "You forgot what th' dictionary said. Of course this wouldn't kill you, but I'm stiff from ridin' in yore palatial trains, mile after weary mile." Rolling the trunk through the door and against the wall, he picked up his belongings, gravely saluted and went on his way whistling cheerily.

The agent looked after him wistfully, shook his head and retired into his coop.

Tex rambled down the street and entered Williams' hotel, held a brief conversation with the clerk, took up his key, and followed instructions. The second door on the right-hand side, upstairs, let him into a small room which contained a chair, bed, and washstand. There was a rag rug before the bed, and this touch of high life and affluence received from him a grave and dignified bow. "Charmed, I'm sure," he said, and went over to the window to view the roofs of the shacks below it. He sniffed and decided that somewhere near there was a stable. Putting his belongings in a corner, he took out his shaving kit and went to work with it, after which he walked downstairs, bought a drink and treated its dispenser to a cigar, which he knew later would be replaced and the money taken instead.

"Hot," said Tex as though he had made a discovery. "An' close," he added in an effort not to overlook anything.

"Very," replied the bartender. This made the twenty-third time he had said that word in reply to this undoubted statement of fact since morning. He did not know that his companion had used it because it was colorless and would stamp him, sub-consciously, as being no different from the common human herd in town. "Hottest summer since last year," said the bartender, also for the twenty-third time. He grinned expectantly.

Tex turned the remark over in his mind and laughed suddenly, explosively. "That's a good un! Cussed if it didn't nearly get past me! 'Hottest summer since last year!' Ha-ha-ha! Cuss it, it is good!" He was on the proper track to make a friend of the second man he had met. "Have another cigar," he urged. Good-will and admiration shone on his face. "Gosh! Have to spring that un on th' boys! Ha-ha-ha!"

"Better spring it before fall--it might not last through th' winter, though some'r tougher'n others," rejoined the bartender, his grin threatening to inconvenience his ears.

Tex choked and coughed up some of the liquor, the tears starting from his eyes. He had meant it for an imitation choke, but misjudged. Coughing and laughing at once he hung onto the bar by his elbows and writhed from side to side. "Gosh! You oughter--warn a fel--ler!" he reproved. "How'd'y think of 'em like that?"

"Come easy, somehow," chuckled the pleased dispenser of liquor. "Stayin' in town long?" he asked.

"Cussed if I know," frankly answered Tex. He became candid and confidential. "Expectin' a letter, an' I can't leave till it comes. Where's th' post office? Yeah? Guess I can find it, then. Reckon I'll drift along an' see if there's anythin' come in for me. See you tonight."

Crossing the street he sauntered along it until he came to the building which sheltered the post office, and he stopped, regarded the sign over its door with open approval, and then gravely salaamed.

"'Williams's Mecca,'" he read. "Sign painters are usually generous with their esses. Wonder why? Must be a secret sign of th' guild. Why are monument works usually called 'monumental'? Huh: Wonder if it is th' same Williams? If it is, where did he ever hear of 'Mecca'?" It was a refreshing change from the names so common to stores in towns of this kind and size. "An' cussed if it ain't appropriate, too!" he muttered. "In a place like this what could more deserve that name than the general store and post office, unless it be the saloons, hotels, and gambling houses?" He started for the door, eager to see whom he would meet.

A burly, dark-visaged individual looked up at his entry. He would have been amazed had he known that a score of years had slipped from him and that he was a callow, furtive-eyed man in his early twenties, cringing in a corner with his present visitor standing contemptuously over him and daring him to get up again.

Tex's face remained unchanged, except for a foolish smile which crept over it as he gave greeting. "Though I ain't goin' to pray, I shore am turnin' my face to th' birthplace of th' Prophet," he said. "Yeah, I'm even enterin' its sacred portals." He watched closely for any signs of recognition in the other, but failed to detect any; and he was not surprised.

The heavy face stared at him and a tentative smile tried to change it. The attempt was abortive and the expression shifted to one of alert suspicion, shaded by one of pugnacity. He was not accustomed to levity at his expense. "What you talkin' about?" he slowly asked.

"Why, th' faith of all true believers: *There is but one God, and Mohammed is his Prophet* . May th' blessin's of Allah be on thee. Incidentally I'm askin' if there's a letter for th' pilgrim, Tex Jones?" He cast a careless glance at a cold-eyed individual who lounged in the shadow of a corner, and instantly classified him. Besides the low-slung holster, the man had the face of a cool, paid killer. Tex's interest in him was not to be correctly judged by the careless glance he gave him.

"Then why in h--l didn't you say so in th' first place, 'stead of wastin' my valuable time?" growled the proprietor, reluctantly shuffling toward the mail rack in a corner. He wet his thumb generously, not caring about the color given to it by the tobacco in his mouth, and clumsily ran through the modest packet of mail. Shaking his head he turned. "There ain't nothin'," he grunted.

"It is Allah's will," muttered Tex in pious resignation. He would have fallen over had there been anything for him.

"Look here, stranger," ominously remarked the proprietor, "if yo're aimin' to be smart at my expense, look out it don't become yourn. Just what's th' meanin' of all these fool remarks?"

"Why, yore emporium is named 'Mecca,' ain't it?" asked Tex innocently, but realizing that he somehow had got on the wrong trail.

"What's that got to do with it?" demanded Williams, who could talk as mean as he cared to while the quiet, cold man sat in the corner.

"Everythin'. Ain't you th' proprietor, like th' barkeep of th' hotel said? Ain't you Mr. Williams?"

"I am."

Tex scratched his head, frankly puzzled. "Well," he said, "Mohammed came out of Mecca to startle th' world, an'—-"

"He didn't do nothin' of th' kind!" interrupted the proprietor. "Mecca was out of Prophet, by Mohammed; an' a cussed good hoss she was, too. Though she didn't startle no world, she was my filly, an' plenty good enough for this part of th' country. Of course, mebby back from where you came from, mebby she wouldn't have amounted to much," he sneered. "Now, if you got any more smart-Aleck remarks to make, you'll be wise if you save 'em till you get outside."

Tex burst out laughing. "It's all my mistake, Mr. Williams. I thought you named yore store after a poem I read once, that's all. No offense on my part, sir. Are you th' Mr. Williams that keeps th' ho-tel?"

"I am: what about it?"

"I'm puttin' up there," answered Tex. "If a letter comes for me, would you mind puttin' it in yore pocket an' bringin' it over when you go there? It'll save me from botherin' you every day. Yore friend at th' station said I'd find you right obligin'. An' he knows a good ho-tel when he sees it. He sent me there."

"That scut!" bellowed Williams, his face growing red. "You'll come after yore own mail, my man; an' you'll do it polite. There ain't no mail here for you. Good day!"

"I'm patient an' I can wait. I didn't hardly expect to get any letter so quick, anyhow. After th' recent experience of reasonin' right from th' wrong premises, however, I'll not be a heap surprised if I get a letter on tomorrow's train. Thank you kindly, sir. I bid you good day."

"An' mind you don't call that cussed agent no friend of mine, th' job stealer!"

"Whatever you say; but, don't forget to bring over that letter when it comes," sweetly replied Tex, and he carefully slammed the door as he went out. Going down the street he grinned expansively and snapped his fingers because of a strange elation.

"Th' old thief!" he muttered. "Heavier, more ill tempered, and downright autocratic--an' how he has prospered! Regular, solid citizen, the bulwark of the commonwealth. An' cussed if he ain't got himself a bodyguard; a regular, no-mistake gunman with as mean an eye as any I ever saw. Of course, his brains have improved with the years, for they couldn't go the other way and keep him out of an asylum. 'Muttonhead' Williams! All right: once a sheep, always a sheep. I'm going to enjoy my stay in Windsor. Good Lord!" he exclaimed as a sudden fancy hit him. "Wouldn't it be funny if the old fool has been working hard and saving hard all these years for his old enemy, Tex Ewalt? He always was crazy to play poker, and I got a notion to make it come true. Gosh, if a man ever was tempted, I'm tempted now! Muttonhead Williams, allus stuck on his poker playing. Get behind me, Satan!"

Chapter III
Tempted Anew

A hand bell, ringing thin and clamorous somewhere below caused Tex to gather up the cards with which for two hours he had been assiduously practicing shuffling, cutting, and dealing. Putting them away he washed his face and hands in the tin basin, combed his hair without slicking it with water, and went down to supper.

He paused momentarily in the doorway to size up the dining-room. The long table was crowded by all sorts and conditions of men. Miners down on their luck and near the end of their resources because of the long drought which had dried up the streams and put an end to placer mining operations, rubbed elbows with more fortunate men of their own calling, who had longer purses. Two cowpunchers from a distant ranch sat next to two cavalrymen on a prized leave from the iron discipline of a remote frontier post, both types dangerous because free from the restraint which had held them down for so long a time. A local tin-horn gambler and the traveling card-sharp were elbow to elbow, and several other men, evidently belonging to the town, nearly filled both sides of the table.

At the head sat Gus Williams, most influential citizen and boss of the town, and he made no attempt to hide his importance. Next to him on the left was a lean, hard-looking, shifty-eyed man who seemed to shine in reflected light, and who showed a deference to the big man which he evidently expected to receive, in turn, from the others. If it was true that there was only one boss, it was also true that he had only one nephew. To the right of the boss was the cold-eyed person whose seat in the general store was well back in the corner. No one moved or spoke except under his critical observance. His cocksure confidence irritated Tex, who was strongly tempted to try the effect of a hot potato against a cold eye. He thought of his friend Johnny Nelson and grinned at how that young man's temper would steam up under such an insolent stare. Moving forward under the gunman's close scrutiny Tex dropped into the only vacant chair, one near the nephew, and fell to eating, his vocal chords idle, but his optic and auditory apparatus making up for it. The conversation, jerky and broken at first, grew more coherent and increased as the appetites of the hungry men yielded to the bolted food. The protracted drought was referred to in grunts, growls, monosyllables, sentences, and profane speeches. It was discussed, rediscussed, and popped up at odd moments for new discussion.

"Never saw it so bad since th' railroad came," said a miner.

"Never saw it so bad since th' first trail herd ended here," affirmed the nephew.

" *I* never saw it so dry, for so long a spell, since th' first trail herd *passed* here," said the uncle, his remark the strongest by coming last; but he was not to enjoy that advantage for long.

"Hum!" said a cattleman, apologetically clearing his throat. "I never saw it as dry as it is now since I located out here."

The miner frowned, the nephew scowled, and the uncle snorted. The last named looked around belligerently and smote the table with his fist. "I remember, howsomever, that I did see it near as dry, that year I strayed from th' Santa Fe Trail, huntin' buffalers for th' caravan. We passed right through this section an' circled back. I come to remember it because when we crossed th' Walnut I jumped right over it, dry-shod. Them was th' days when men was men, or soon wasn't nothin' a-tall."

"I reckon they wasn't th' kind that would play off sick so they could get another man's job away from him, anyhow," growled the nephew, introducing his pet grievance. "I run that station a cussed sight better than it's bein' run now; an' anybody's likely to make mistakes once in a while."

"A few dollars, one way or another, ain't bustin' no railroad," asserted the uncle. "It was only th' excuse they was a-waitin' for."

"Nobody can tell me no good about no railroad," said the freighter, his fond memory resurrecting a certain lucrative wagon haul which had vanished with the advent of the first train over the line.

"Hosses are good enough for me," said Tex, looking around. "Which remark reminds me that a rider afoot is a helpless hombre. Bein' a rider, without no cayuse, I'm a little anxious to get me a good one. Anybody know where I can do it reasonable?"

All eyes turned to the head of the table, where Williams was washing down his last mouthful of food with a gulp of hot, watery coffee. He cleared his throat and peered closely, but pleasantly, at the stranger. "Why, it's Mr. Jones," he said. "I reckon I have such a hoss, Mr. Jones. Mebby it ain't any too well broken, but that hadn't oughter bother a rider."

Tex grinned. "If that's all that's th' matter with it I reckon it'll suit me; but I can tell better after I ride it, an' learn th' price."

"Want it tonight?" frowned Williams.

"No; I ain't in no hurry. Tomorrow'll be plenty of time, when you ain't got nothin' else to do but show it. Speakin' of railroads like we was, I reckon they ain't done nothin' very much for this town. While I'm new to these parts, I'm betting Windsor was a whole lot better when th' drive trail was alive an' kickin'."

Williams nodded emphatically. "I've seen these plains an' valleys thick with cattle," he said, regretfully. "There was a time when I could see th' dust clouds rollin' up from th' south an' away in th' north, both at once, day after day. This town was a-hummin' every day an' night. Money come easy an' went th' same way. Men dropped in here, lookin' like tramps, almost, who could write good checks for thousands of dollars. Th' buyers bought whole herds on th' seller's say-so, without even seein' a hoof, an' sold 'em ag'in th' same way. Money flowed like water, an' fair-sized fortunes was won an' lost at a single sittin'. I've seen th' faro-bank busted three days hand-runnin'—but, of course, that was very unusual. Mostly it was th' other way 'round. All one summer an' fall it was like that. Then th' winter come, an' that was th' end of it so fur's Windsor was concerned. Th' Kiowa Arroyo branch line was pushed further an' further southwest until th' weather stopped it; but it went on ag'in as soon as spring let it. By th' time th' first herds crossed th' state line, headin' for here, that line of rails was ready for 'em, an' not another big herd went past this town. Of course, there was big herds drivin' north, just th' same, bound for th' Yellowstone region on government contract, an' some was bein' sent out to stock ranges in th' West, but they followed a new trail found by Chisholm, or old McCullough. I've heard lately that Mac is workin' for Twitchell an' Carpenter. But if you'd seen this town then you shore wouldn't know it now. D--n th' railroads, says I!"

Tex frowned honestly at the thought of the passing of this once great cattle trail, for the memories of those old trails lay snug and warm in the hearts of the men who have followed them in the saddle. He looked up at Williams, a congratulatory look on his face. "Well, that shore was hard; but not as hard, I reckon, as if you had been a cattleman, an' follered it. It sort of hurts an old-time cowman to think of them trails."

"That's where yo're wrong," spoke up the nephew. "He is a cattleman. Th' GW brand is known all over th' state, an' beyond. It was knowed by every puncher that followed that old trail."

"There wasn't no such brand in them days," corrected Williams. He did not think it necessary to say that the GW mark was just starting then, far back in the hills and well removed from the trail; that it grew much faster by the addition of fully grown cattle than it did by natural increase; or that a view of the original brands on the full-grown cattle would have been a matter of great and burning interest to almost every drive boss who followed a herd along the trail. Later on, when he threw his herd up for a count, the drive boss was likely to have re-added his tally sheet and asked heaven and earth what had happened to him. "Well, them days has gone; but when they went this town come blamed near goin' with 'em. It shore ain't what it once was."

Tex thought that it was just as well, since the town was mean enough and vicious enough as it was; he remembered vividly its high-water period; but he nodded his head.

"It ain't hardly fair to judge it after such a long dry spell," he said. "Th' whole country, south an' west of th' Missouri is fair burnin' up. Th' Big Muddy herself was a-showin' all her bars."

"That's th' curse of this part of Kansas," said the nephew. "That an' job jumpers."

"Yes?" asked Tex. "How's that?"

"Station agent a friend of yourn?"

It became evident to Tex that the uncle and the nephew had been discussing him. Gus Williams was the only man to whom he had mentioned the agent. He shook his head. "Never saw him before I stepped off th' train today," he answered, looking vexed about something. "We up an' had some words, an' I told him I reckoned he might find healthier towns further west, across th' line. I'm a mild man, gents: but I allus speak my mind."

"An' you gave him some cussed good advice," replied the nephew warmly. "This ain't no place for any man as plays off sick an' does low-down tricks to turn another man out of a job. If it wasn't for his sister I'd 'a' buffaloed him *pronto* . Which reminds me, stranger," he warned with an ugly leer. "She's a rip-snortin' fe-male--but I shore saw her first. I'm just tellin' you so you won't get any notions that way. I'm fencin' that range."

"Don't you worry, Hen," consoled a friend. "Yo're able to run herd on her, balky as she is, an' when th' time's ripe you'll put yore brand on her. So fur's th' job's concerned, yore uncle'll get it back for you when he gets ready to move. We ought to ride that Saunders feller out of town, *I* say!"

"There's plenty of time for that," said Williams, as he turned to address another diner. "John, show Mr. Jones that gray when he gits around tomorrow. Aimin' to stay in town long, Mr. Jones?"

Tex shrugged his shoulders. "Got to wait for a letter--don't know what to do; but I shore could be in worse places than this here hotel, so I ain't worryin' a lot. Bein' a stranger, though, I reckon time'll drag a little evenin's."

Various kinds of smiles replied to this, and Williams laughed outright. "I reckon you understand th' innercent game of draw?" he chuckled.

Tex froze: "Sometimes I think I do," he said, and laughed to hide his struggle against the pressure of the old temptation. He fairly burned to turn his poker craft against this blowhard's invitation, to wipe from that self-complacent face its look of omniscience. "An' then, sometimes I reckon I don't," he continued; "but I'm admittin' she's plumb fascinatin'. From th' pious expressions around me I reckon mebby I've shocked somebody."

Williams led in the laughter that followed, his bull voice roaring through the room. "You'd better buy that hoss before you assist in th' evenin's worship," he cried in boisterous good humor, "for I'm sayin' a puncher ain't nowhere near in th' prospector's class when it comes to walkin'; though I reckon th' boys will play you for th' hoss, at that, an' you'd be no better off in th' end.

My remarks as how this town has slid back didn't have nothin' to do with our poker playin', Mr. Jones. If you feel like settin' in ag'in' a Kansas cyclone, you can't say I didn't warn you."

Tex wondered what the crowd would say if he should lean over and pull a royal flush out of Williams' ear, or a full-house from the nephew's nose. They might be surprised if they found out that the cold-eyed gunman at Williams' elbow carried a handful of Colt cartridges in his tight-shut mouth. He had no rabbits to lift out of hats, but that trick was threadbare from being overworked, anyhow. He waved both hands, a smart-Aleck grin sweeping across his face. "I've rode cayuses, punched cows, an' played draw from Texas to Montanny, an' near back ag'in. So far I ain't throwed, rolled under, or cleaned out; an' I'm allus willin' to be agreeable. Where you gents lead I'll foller, like a hungry calf after its ma." His voice had grown loud and boastful and he joined the swiftly forming card group with a swagger as it settled around the table in the barroom, his bovine conceit hiding the silent struggle going on within him.

Tex of the old days was fighting Tex of the new. The smug complacency of the local boss stirred up the desire to break him to his last cent, to make a fool of him in the way others had been broken and made ridiculous; but the new Tex won: As usual he would play Hopalong's game--which was as his opponents played, straight or crooked, as they showed the way. He had no real wish for large winnings, for if he made his expenses as he went along he would be satisfied, and he could do that from his knowledge of psychology, a knowledge gained outside of classrooms. He now had no reputation to defend or maintain, for Tex Jones was not Tex Ewalt, famed throughout the cow-country. The new name meant nothing. But how pleasant it would be to repeat history in this town, so far as Williams was concerned!

He always had claimed that he could learn a man's real nature more quickly in a game of poker than in any other way in the same length of time, and he did not mean some one more prominent trait, but the man's nature as a whole; and now he set himself to study his new acquaintances against some future need. The game itself would not engross him to the exclusion of all else, for while he was Tex Jones externally, it would be Tex Ewalt who played the hands, the Tex Ewalt who as a youth had discovered an uncanny ability in sleight of hand and whose freshman and sophomore years had given so much time to developing and perfecting the eye-baffling art that every study had suffered heavily in consequence; the Tex Ewalt who had found that his ability was peculiarly adaptive to cards, and who had given all his attention to that connection when once he had started to travel along the line of least resistance. So well had he succeeded that seasoned gamblers from the Mexican line north to Canada had been forced to admit his mastery.

Before the end of the second deal he had learned the rest of the nephew's more prominent characteristics, but had not bothered to retaliate for the cheating. On the third deal he was forced to out-cheat a miner to keep even with the game. Before the evening's play was over he had renewed his knowledge of Gus Williams, and now knew him as well as that loud-voiced individual knew himself; and he had not incurred the enmity of the boss, because while Tex had won from the others he had lost to him. While not yielding to the temptations rampant in him, he had compromised and left Williams in a ripe condition for a future skinning. At the end of the play only he and Williams had won.

As the others pushed back their chairs to leave the table, Williams ignored them and looked at Tex. "You an' me seem to be th' best," he said loudly. "So there won't be no doubt about it, let's settle it between us."

Tex raised a belated hand too late to hide his yawn, blinked sleepily, and squinted at the clock. "I'm surprised it's so late," he said. "It takes a lot out of a man to play ag'in' this crowd. My head's fair achin'. What you say if we let it go till tomorrow night? I been travelin' for three days an' nights an' ain't slept much. You'd take it away from me before I could wake up."

Williams laughed sarcastically. "You shore been crossin' a lot of sand since you left th' Big Muddy, but I don't reckon none of it got inter yore system." He paused to let the words sink in, and for a reply, and none being forthcoming he laughed nastily as he arose. "Texas is a sandy state, too. Reckon you was named before anybody knowed very much about you."

Tex paled, fought himself to a standstill and shrugged his shoulders. Out of the corner of his eye he saw Bud Haines, the cold-eyed bodyguard, become suddenly more alert.

"Windsor's got a h--l of a way of welcomin' strangers," he said. "You'll have a different kind of a kick to make tomorrow night, for you'll be eatin' sand. I play poker when I feel like it: just now I don't feel like it. I'll say good night."

"Ha-ha-ha!" shouted Williams. "He don't feel like it, boys! Ha-ha-ha!"

Tex stopped, turned swiftly, pulled out a roll of bills that was a credit to his country and slammed it on the table, reaching for the scattered deck. "Mebby you feel like puttin' up seven hundred dollars ag'in' mine, one cut, th' highest card, to take both piles? Ha-ha-ha!" he mimicked. "Here's action if that's what yo're lookin' for!"

Williams' face turned a deep red and he cursed under his breath. "That's a baby game: I said poker!" he retorted, making no effort to get nearer to the table.

"That's mebby why I picked it," snapped Tex, stuffing the roll back into his pocked. "You can wait till tomorrow night for poker." Turning his back on the wrathful Williams and the open-mouthed audience, he yawned again, muttered something to express his adieus, and clomped heavily and slowly up the stairs, his body shaking with repressed laughter; and when he fell asleep a few minutes later there was a placid smile on his clean-shaven face.

Chapter IV
A Crowded Day

After a late breakfast about noon Tex got the gunny sack, threw it over his shoulder and went to the Mecca, nodding to the proprietor in a spirit of good-will and cheerfulness. Bud Haines did not appear to be about.

"I come in to see about that cayuse," he said. "Where'll I find it?"

"Go down to th' stable an' see John," growled Williams. "You'll find it next to Carney's saloon, across th' street. Got rested up yet?" The question was not pleasantly asked.

Tex threw the sack over the other shoulder, hunched it to a more comfortable position, and grinned sheepishly. "Purty near, I reckon; anyhow, I got over my grouch. I was shore peevish last night; but th' railroad's to blame for that. They say they are necessary, an' great blessin's; but I ain't so shore about it. Outside of my personal grudge ag'in' 'em, I'm sore because they've shore played th' devil with th' range. Cut it all up--an' there ain't no more pickin' along th' old trails no more, like there once was. I don't reckon punchers has got any reason to love 'em a whole lot."

Williams flashed him a keen look and slowly nodded. "Yo're right: look at what they've done to this town. We ain't seen no real money since they came."

Tex shifted the sack again. "Everybody had money in them days," he growled. "If a feller went busted along th' trails he allus could pick up a few dollars, if he had a good cayuse an' a little nerve. Why, among them hills--but that ain't concernin' us no more, I reckon." He shook his head sadly. "What's gone is gone. Reckon I'll go look at that cayuse. You ain't got no letter for me yet, have you?"

"Le's see--Johnson?" puzzled the storekeeper, scratching his unshaven chin.

"No; Jones," prompted Tex innocently, hiding his smile.

"Oh, shore!" said his companion, slowly shaking his head. "There ain't nothin' for you so far."

Tex did not think that remarkable not only because there never would be anything for him, but also because there had been no mail since he had asked the day before; but he grunted pessimistically, shifted the sack again, and turned to the door. "See you later," he said, going out.

He easily found the stable, grinned at the bleached, weather-beaten "Williams" painted over the door and going into the smelly, cigar-box office, dumped the sack against the wall and nodded to John Graves. "Come down to look at that cayuse Williams spoke about last night," he said, drawing a sleeve across his wet forehead.

"Shore; come along with me," said Graves, arising and passing out into the main part of the building, Tex at his heels. "Here he is, Mr. Jones--as fine a piece of hossflesh as a man ever straddled. Got brains, youth, an' ginger. Sound as a dollar. Cost you eighty, even. You'll go far before you'll find a better bargain."

Tex looked at the teeth, passed a hypnotic hand down each leg in turn as he talked to the gray in a soothing voice. Children, horses, and dogs liked him at first look. He frankly admired the animal from a distance, but sadly shook his head.

"Fine cayuse, an' a fair price," he admitted; "but I'm dead set ag'in' grays. Had two of 'em once, one right after th' other--an' come near to dyin' on 'em both. If I didn't get killed, they did, anyhow. It's sort of set me ag'in' grays. Now, there's a roan that strikes me as a hoss I'd consider ownin'. Of course, he ain't as good as th' gray, but he suits me better." He walked over to the magnificent animal, which was far and away superior to the gray, and talked to it in a low, caressing voice as he made a quick examination. "Yes, this cayuse suits me if th' price is right. If we can agree on that I'll lead him down th' street an' see how he steps out. Ain't got nothin' else to do, anyhow."

Graves frowned and slowly shook his head. "Rather not part with that one--an' he's a two-hundred-dollar animal, anyhow. It's a sort of pet of th' boss--he's rid it since it was near old enough to walk. That gray's th' best I've got for sale, unless, mebby, it might be that sorrel over there. Now, there's a mighty good hoss, come to think of it."

Tex glanced at the beautiful line of the roan's back and thought of the massive weight of Williams, and of the sway-back bay standing saddled in front of his store. He shook his head. "Two hundred's too high for me, friend," he replied. "As I said, I don't like grays, an' that sorrel has shore got a mean eye. It ain't spirit that's showin', but just plumb treachery. If you got off him out on th' range he'd head for home an' leave you to hoof it after him. I got an even hundred for th' roan. Say th' word an' we trade."

Graves waved his arms and enumerated the roan's good points as only a horse dealer can. The discussion was long and to no result. Tex added twenty-five dollars to the hundred he had offered and the whole thing was gone over again, but to no avail. He picked up the sack, slung it onto his back, and turned to leave.

"I'm shore surprised at th' prices for cayuses in this part of th' country," he said. "Mebby I can make a dicker with somebody else. Of course, I'm admittin' that th' roan ain't got a sand crack like th' sorrel, or a spavin like th' gray--but that's too much money for a saddle hoss for a puncher out of a job. See you tonight, mebby."

Graves waved his arms again. "I'm tellin' you that you won't find no hoss in town like that roan--why, th' color of that animal is worth half th' price. Just look at it!"

"All of which I admits," replied Tex; "but, you see, I'm buyin' me a hoss to ride, not to put on th' parlor table for to admire. Comin' right down to cases, any hoss but a gray, that's sound, an' not too old, is good enough for any puncher. You should 'a' seen some that I've rode, an' been proud of!"

"Seein' that yo're a lover of good hossflesh, I'll take a chance of Gus gettin' peeved, an' let you have th' roan for one-ninety. That's as low as I can drop. Can't shave off another dollar."

"It's too rich for Tex Jones," grumbled the puncher. "See you tonight," and the sack bobbed toward the door just as a sudden brawl sounded in the street. Tex took two quick steps and glanced.

A miner and a cowpuncher were rolling in the dust, biting, hitting, gouging, and wrestling and, as Tex looked he saw the puncher's gun slip out of its open-top sheath. The fighting pair rolled away from it and someone in the closely following crowd picked it up to save it for its owner. The puncher, pounds lighter than his brawny antagonist, rapidly was getting the worst of the rough-and-tumble in which the other's superior weight and strength had full opportunity to make itself felt. Suddenly the miner, thrown from his victim by a tremendous effort, leaped to his feet, snarling like a beast, and knicked at the puncher's head. The heavy, hob-nailed boot crashed sickeningly home and as the writhing man went suddenly limp, the victor aimed another kick at his unconscious enemy. His foot swung back, but it never reached its mark. A forty-pound saddle in a sack shot through the air with all of a strong man's strength behind it and, catching the miner balanced on one foot, it knocked him sprawling through ten feet of dust and débris. Following the sack came Tex, his eyes blazing.

The miner groped in the dust, slowly sat up, moving his head from side to side as he got his bearings. At once his eyes cleared and his hand streaked to the knife in his belt as he half arose. Tex leaped aside as the heavy weapon cut through the air to sink into a near-by wall, where it quivered. The thrower was on his feet now, his face working with rage, and he sprang forward, both arms circling before him. Tex swiftly gripped one outstretched wrist, turned sharply as he pushed his shoulder under the armpit and suddenly bent forward, facing away from his antagonist. The miner left the ground on the surging heave of the puncher's shoulder, shot up into the air, turned over once as Tex, not wishing him to break his neck, pulled down hard on the imprisoned arm, and landed feet first against the wall, squarely under the knife. Bouncing up with remarkable vitality, the miner wrenched at the wicked weapon above him and then cursed as the steel, leaving its point embedded in the wood, flew out of his hand.

Tex shoved the smoking Colt back into his holster and peered through the acrid, gray fog. "If you don't know when yo're licked, you better take my word for it," he warned. "Seein' as how yo're a rubber ball, I'll make shore th' third time!"

A snarl replied and the miner leaped for him, the hairy hands not so far extended this time. Tex broke ground with two swift steps and then, unexpectedly slipping to one side and forward in two perfectly timed motions, swung a rigid, bent arm as the charging miner went blunderingly past. The bony fist landed fair above the belt buckle and it was nearly half an hour later before the prospector knew where he was, and then he was too sick to care much.

Tex turned and faced the crowd with insolent slowness. His glance passed from face to face, finding some friendliness, much surprise, and a few frank scowls. He stepped up to the man who had retrieved the puncher's gun and, ignoring the crowd altogether, took the weapon from the reluctant fingers which held it and went back to the front of the stable, where Graves had succeeded in bringing the prostrate puncher back to consciousness. Tex ran his fingers over the wobbly man's head and face, grunted, nodded, and smiled.

"Bad bruise, but nothin' is busted. Why there ain't I'm shore *I* don't know. I figgered you was a goner. Here, take yore gun, an' let us help you into th' stable."

Once on his feet the puncher pushed free from the sustaining hands and staggered to a box just inside the door, where he carefully seated himself, drew the Colt, and rested it on his knees, his blurred, throbbing eyes watching the street.

Tex grinned. "You can put that up ag'in--he's had all he can digest for a little while. Punchin' for Williams?"

"I'm ridin' for Curtis: C Bar. Over northeast, a couple of hours out. I'm keepin' th' gun where it is: th' miners run this town. Where do you fit in? One of th' GW gang?"

"Nope; I'm all of th' Tex Jones outfit. Stranger here, but shore gettin' acquainted rapid. Got any good cayuses for sale out at yore place? Our mutual friend, here, wants th' Treasury for th' only good animal he's got. Bein' a stranger is a handicap."

Graves leaned forward. "That hoss is worth--" he began in great earnestness.

"--not one red cent to me, now," interrupted Tex, smiling. "Come to think of it, I ain't goin' to buy no hoss, a-tall. I've changed my mind."

"We got th' usual run out on th' ranch," said the injured man. "You know 'em, I reckon. Poor on looks, mean as all h--l, with hearts crowded with sand. I'll be leavin' in half an hour if th' miners don't interfere--borry a cayuse an' ride out with me."

"Nope," replied Tex. "I ain't goin' to buy, a-tall, as I just said." He turned. "Good luck to you, friend. Barrin' th' soreness, an' yore looks yo're all right," and he went out, picked up the bulging sack, and passed down the street. Leaving the sack with the bartender in the hotel he went on to the station and smiled at the agent, who was joking with a red-headed Irishman.

"Hello; here he is now," exclaimed the boss of the depot. "Friend, shake hands with Tim Murphy. Tim, this is Mr.–Mr.—-"

"Jones," supplied Tex. "Tex Jones, of Montanny, Texas, an' New York."

"Pleased to meet you, Mr. Geography," grinned Murphy. "Th' lad here was a-tellin' me ye gave him a friendly word an' some good advice. From that I was knowin' ye didn't belong around here. I'll shake yer hand if ye don't mind. Th' sack wint like an arrow, th' wrestlin' trick couldn't be bate, I never saw a nicer shot, an' th' finish does ye proud. Ye fair tickled me when ye wint for th' soft spot. 'Tis a rare sight in street fights, an' in th' ring, too, for that matter. Welcome to Windsor!"

Tex laughed heartily and gripped the hairy fist. He liked the feel of the great, calloused hand, and the look on the smiling, tanned face, from which twinkled a pair of blue eyes alight with humor, honesty, and courage. "But did you ever see a man come back as quick as he did?" he asked.

"'Twas surprisin' for a bully," admitted Murphy, grudgingly.

"That's where yo're wrong: he's no bully," contradicted Tex. "He's a brute, all right, savage as th' devil, an' foul in his fightin'–but he ain't any coward. It fair stuck out of his eyes."

"Trust me to miss anything like that," growled the agent; "and trust Tim not to," he added.

"Hist, now!" warned Murphy, motioning with his thumb held close to his vest. "Here comes th' lass. An' what do ye be thinkin' av th' town now, Mr. Jones?"

"Just what you do," laughed Tex, turning slowly.

"An' how are ye this day, miss?" asked Murphy, his hat in his hand and his red face beaming.

"Very well, indeed, Tim," replied the girl. She glanced at Tex as she turned to her brother, holding out the lunch basket. "Jerry, I couldn't get any decent eggs--and they had no milk for me." There was a poorly hidden note of distress in her voice, and a faint look of anxiety momentarily clouded her face. Neither was lost to the observant puncher.

Tex liked her instantly. Her voice was full and sweet, of resonant timbre--a voice one would not easily tire of. Her figure was slender, and yet full and rounded, promising a wiry strength and great vitality. The sunbonnet she wore hid most of the chestnut-brown hair, but set off the face within it with a bewitching art. Altogether she made a very pretty picture.

"It doesn't matter, Jane," smiled her brother, quick to sense her worry. He pinched the full lips with caressing playfulness. "I'm getting stronger every day, and food isn't as critical a subject as it once was. The credit is all yours--Jane, meet Mr. Jones. I was speaking about him last night."

Tex bowed gravely. "How do you do?" he murmured. "Conscientious care is more than half of the battle. The credit he gave you appears to be well deserved."

Jane Saunders, accustomed to embarrassed self-consciousness or stammering volubility, smiled faintly as she acknowledged the introduction. The man was as impersonal and as sure of himself as any she ever had met. She looked him fairly in the eyes.

"How did you come to advise my brother to go farther west?" she asked, but while her voice was casual, her look challenged him.

"It was given upon certain conditions of the weather this winter, Miss--I do not believe I caught the name."

"No fault of yours," she laughed. "Jerry always ignores it in his introductions. It is Jane Saunders. Then it was only in the nature of a physician's advice?" she persisted, her eyes searching his soul for the truth.

Tex nodded. "My knowledge of his complaint is very sketchy; but like all amateurs I paraded what little I had. I thought that perhaps the winters out here might not be as dry as they are farther west. No doubt it was entirely uncalled for. We will hope so, anyway."

"Are you a physician, Mr. Jones?"

"No, indeed; although I went part way through the course. What little time I had left from more interesting activities, I gave to study."

"Ye was speakin' about th' aigs an' milk, miss," said Murphy, his face alight with eager anticipation. He chuckled. "Ye needn't be askin' no more favors av Williams' black heart. I've a little somethin' to show ye all, if ye'll step down th' track a bit. An' Costigan is goin' to get him a cow. Th' missus said th' word, an' divvil a bit Mike can wiggle out av it. Ye'll have first call on th' milk, so I hear. Mr. Jones, if ye'll be kind enough to escort Jerry, I'll lead th' march with th' lass."

"Oh, well," sighed Tex, gravely offering his arm to the station agent, "I suppose it *is* yore party; but I'm admittin' yo're not overlookin' Number One. Lead on, MacDuff." He caught her quick glance at the abrupt change in his language, and smiled to himself. It never paid to be too well understood by a woman.

"Th' Irish are noted for bein' judges av good whiskey, fine hosses, an' fair wimmin," retorted Murphy. "I'll take no chances of any pearls bein' cast careless."

"I notice you put th' wimmin last," countered Tex. "Grunt, Jerry! Quick, man! Before Miss Saunders looks around!"

"He said pearly, Mr. Jones," said Jane, laughingly. "I'm afraid he intended it all to be plural."

"It was wrongly written in th' first place," complained Tex. "Tim has an uncanny instinct; he only met me about ten minutes ago."

"Ten is a-plenty, sometimes," chuckled Murphy. "But I'll own to havin' a previous sight av ye. Wait now: here we are."

They stopped in front of the toolhouse and watched Murphy walk along one of the two ties spanning the drainage ditch at the edge of the roadbed. He unlocked the doors and flung them wide open as a clamorous cackling broke out in the building. On one end of a hand car was a crate of chickens and leaning against it were several bundles of long stakes. A pile of new lumber could be seen in the back of the shed, while a fat spool of wire rested near the stakes.

Murphy turned, his face red with delight at his surprise. "There ye are, miss," he cried proudly. "A round dozen av them, with their lord an' master. I couldn't let that Mike Costigan go puttin' on his airs over his boss, so now there'll be aigs for aignoggs that I'll have a claim to. For safe-keepin' we'll build th' coop in yore back yard where it will be right handy for ye. Ye can now tell Williams to kape his aigs. If he don't understand yer soft language, I'll be tellin' him in a way he can't mistook."

"You angel!" whispered Jane, tears in her eyes. She was not misled by his remarks about eggnoggs. "Oh, Tim--you shouldn't have done it! Why didn't *I* think of it? And how is it that Mrs. Costigan suddenly needs a cow? If I've heard her aright, she has stalwart, old-fashioned ideas, bless her, about nursing children. And I never knew she was partial to eggnoggs. Jerry, what shall we do to them?"

Jerry blew his nose with energy. "For a cent I'd lick Murphy right now, and Mike immediately afterward," he laughed, sizing up the huge bulk of bone, sinew, and toil-hardened muscle of the section-boss. "Tim, you and your boys are the one redeeming feature of this country. And you redeem it fully. How long have you been plotting this?"

"G'wan with ye, th' pair av ye!" chuckled the section-boss, his face flaming. "If Casey hadn't stopped th' train down by this shed yesterday we couldn't 'a' surprised ye. Ye never saw a consignment handled quicker or more gintly."

"And I was wondering why he did it," confessed Jerry. "The brakeman said he was trying his brakes. Tim, you should be ashamed of yourself!"

"An' I've been that, many a time," retorted Murphy. He turned to Tex. "I'll be leavin' it to ye, Mr. Jones, if a man hasn't certain rights after bein' nursed for three weeks by a brown-haired angel, an' knowin' that th' same angel nursed Mrs. Costigan an' th' twins whin they was all down with th' measles. Patient an' unselfish, she was, with never a cross word, day or night--an' always with a smile on her pretty face, like th' sun on Lake Killarney."

Tex looked gravely and judicially at Jane Saunders. "You haven't a word to say, Miss Saunders. The verdict of the court is for the defendant. Case dismissed, without costs of either party against the other." He turned to the section-boss. "When are we buildin' that coop, Murphy?" he asked.

"Tomorrow, Tex," answered the Irishman. "We'll be after runnin' th' darlin's up there right away, an' come back for th' lumber an' wire. That'll give us an early start. Th' sidin' will let us ride 'em near halfway an' save a lot of flounderin' in th' sand."

"We'd better come back for th' darlin's after th' coop is ready for 'em," said Tex, grinning. "If I know coyotes as well as I reckon I do, th' harem will be a lot safer in this here shed; an' I'm glad it's got a board floor, too. Lend a hand here an' we'll change th' cargo on this meek steed. *Gently, brother, gently pray* . Now for th' lumber." He burst into a chant: " *I once was a bloody pirate bold, an' I sailed on th' Spanish Main, yo-ho! Th' treasure chests were full of gold, which gave us all a pain you know.* " He glanced at one of his hands and grimaced. "Blast th' splinters. An' would you look at that corn? Blessed if th' man hasn't got enough to feed another Custer expedition! Murphy, you certainly do grow on one!"

Murphy paused with a huge armful of lumber, and looked suspicious. "On one what?" he demanded.

"Prickly pear plant, I reckon, in lieu of anything else; or on a mesquite tree, perhaps, for you shore do know beans when th' pod's open. *An' it stopped--short--never to go again, when th' old--man--died,* " hummed Tex. "All aboard. Clang-clang! Clang-clang! I can still hear that bell in my sleep. Yo're th' engineer, Murphy; I'll act in an advisory capacity, at th' same time pushing hard on my very own handle. Ladies first! Miss Saunders, if you please! That's right, for you might as well ride in state. Up you go. From your elevated position you may scan the country roundabout and give us warning of the approach of redskins. *A Book of Verses underneath the Bough, a Jug of Wine, a Loaf of Bread* —and fried eggs-- *Oh, Wilderness were Paradise enow!* "

"I see no redskins, Advisory Capacity," called Jane, who thoroughly was enjoying herself; "but hither rides a horseman on a horse."

Tex looked up and saw a recklessly riding puncher coming toward them. He slyly exchanged grins with Murphy and kept on pushing.

The rider, smiling as well as a swollen face and throbbing temples would permit, slid to a stand, removed his sombrero and bowed.

"My name's Tom Watkins," he said. "I just come down to tell you, friend, that I've learned what you done for me, awhile back. I'm-—"

Tex interrupted him. "You just came down in time, Thomas, to drop yore useful rope over that bobbin' handle an' head west at a plain, unornamental walk. High-heeled boots was never made for pushin' han' cars over ties an' rocks. An' I suspect Murphy of stealin' a ride every time my head goes down."

"Then I'd be cheatin' myself," retorted Murphy, looking upon the newcomer with strong favor. "Th' car would be after stoppin' every time I rode, like th' little boat with th' big whistle." He turned to the agent. "Jerry, there's no tellin' how fast this car will be goin', for I misdoubt that animal's intentions. Suppose ye run along an' throw th' switch for us. Hadn't ye better get down, miss?"

"Not for the world, Tim!"

The disfigured puncher grinned even wider, dropped his rope over the handle with practiced art and wheeled his horse. "What'll I do when I git to th' end of th' rails?" he asked, mischievous deviltry, unabashed by what had befallen him, shining in his eyes, and there was an eager curiosity revealed by his voice.

"What'll he do, Murphy?" demanded Tex.

"He'll stop, blast him!" emphatically answered the section-boss.

"You'll stop, Thomas," said Tex. "As Hamlet said: 'Go on, I'll follow thee!'"

"But he's not nearly a ghost yet," objected Jane. Her cheeks were flushed, her eyes sparkling from the fun she was having. Many days had passed since she had had so good a time. It was a treat to get away from the ever-lasting "Yes, ma'am" and "No, ma'am" which had been the formula for conversation with everyone to whom she had talked except her brother and Murphy.

"No, ma'am," said the puncher. "Not yet."

Jane shuddered and grimaced at Tex as the rider turned away. "That's all I've heard since I've been out here," she softly called down to him.

"Yes, ma'am," he replied, not daring to look up. The procession wended onward to the edification of sundry stray dogs, and Costigan's goats, tethered near the toolshed, promptly went into consultation as to what measures to pursue, apparently deciding upon a defensive course of action if the worst came to pass.

The end of the rails reached, the engineer of the motive power stopped, sized up the ground roundabout and then looked hopefully at his companions. "Reckon we can manage th' haul. Totin' them boards afoot shore will be tirin'. Where we drivin' to?"

Jerry pointed out the little house, but shook his head. "We can't make it."

"Cowboy," said Tex, "that ain't no plowhorse. When she feels th' drag of this vehicle in th' sand she'll display her frank an' candid thoughts about it."

"Then blindfold her," suggested Tom Watkins. "She won't know it ain't a steer she's fastened to. You fellers can git behind an' push, too."

"' *Sic transit gloria mundi,* '" murmured Jane, preparing to descend to earth.

"' *Sic transit* ' glorious Monday," repeated Tex, stepping to assist her. "Only it ain't Monday. Take my honest hand, lady, and jump." He turned and looked at the grinning engineer. "Now, you cactus-eatin' burro, try yore handkerchief. If *our* idea works, all right; if yore idea don't work, it's Murphy's fault. Commence!"

"I'm thinkin' it would work better if th' car was off th' track," caustically commented Murphy. "I misdoubt if we can climb that buffer; th' flanges on these wheels are deep an' strong an' I'm shore we can't pull th' rails over. If th' engineer will lend a hand here we mebby can clear th' track without unloadin'. I'll take th' off side; ye byes take th' other, which makes it even, for it is a well-known fact that one Irish section-boss is worth two punchers. Are ye ready, now?"

"I've heard they can run faster than two cowpunchers," retorted Tex. "For the ashes of your fathers, *lift* ! Try it again--now. Inch her over--that's the way. Now then, *lift* ! Once more-- *lift* ! Phew! All right: proceed, cowboy," he grunted.

"Hold yer horses!" shouted Murphy. "What's th' good av a section-boss that can't lay a track?" he demanded, taking up a two-by-four, Tex following his lead. The car was lifted onto the timbers and the procession went on again. "Will they spread, now?" queried Murphy doubtfully, watching them closely. He had just decided they would not when they did. After numerous troubles the little house was reached, the lumber unloaded, and the car sent back without rails.

"Goin' to make any more hauls?" asked the horseman.

"We are not," said Tex with emphasis. "We could 'a' toted this stuff over in half th' time. *Tempus* fidgets, an' I'm catchin' it. Yore ideas are plumb fine till they're put in practice."

" *My* ideas?" queried the disfigured rider, his rising eyebrows pushing wrinkles onto his forehead. "Didn't you tell me to chuck my rope over that bobbin' handle?"

"Do you allus have to do what yo're told?" retorted Tex. "Answer me that! Do you?"

The rider looked down at Jane, who was nearly convulsed, and sighed with deep regret, and because her presence forbade the only appropriate retort, he shook his head sorrowfully and turned to haul the car back to the track.

"Hey!" called Tex. "Sling them spools of barb wire across yore saddle. We might as well get more of that stuff while we have yore good-natured assistance. Just chuck it on any place an' bring it here."

"You just can't chuck a spool of wire on a saddle any place," retorted the puncher. "Was you speakin' about ideas?"

"An' while yer about it," said Murphy, "ye might bring back a spade, th' saws, three hammers, that box av nails, an' them staples. Th' staples are in a little keg--th' one without th' handle.

I've a mind to start buildin' today. What do ye say, Tex? Good for ye: yer a man after me own heart."

Despite his aches and bruises the puncher's feet left the stirrups and slowly went up until he stood with his shoulder on the saddle. He waved his legs three times and resumed the correct posture for riding. Words were hopelessly inadequate. He looked at Jane, who was shrieking and pointing at the ground under the horse. Thomas craned his neck and looked down. He thereupon dismounted and picked up one Colt's .45, one pocket-knife, one watch which now needed expert attention, various coins, a plug of tobacco, and three horseshoe nails. Murphy stared at him, spat disgustedly, and attacked the pile of lumber.

After the puncher's return the work went on rapidly, and when the roof of the coop was finished, the three perspiring workmen stepped back to admire it.

"We've got to slat them windows," said Tex, thinking of coyotes.

"An' we got thirteen nests to build," said Thomas Watkins.

"Th' saints be praised!" ejaculated Murphy, staring incredulously at the battle-scarred recruit. "Mebby there'll be a coincidence about twelve layin' all at once, but there won't be no thirteenth on th' job. Mebby yer thinkin' th' Sultan will nest down alongside them to set them a good example? Six boxes will be a-plenty, Tommy, my lad."

Tommy tilted his sombrero to scratch his head. "Well, if you reckon there won't be no stampedin', mebby six will be enough, 'though I'd hate to think of 'em milling frantic for their turn on th' nests. An' while we're speakin' of calamities, I'm sayin' good chickens will fly over th' fence you fellers aim to build. Six feet ain't high enough, nohow."

"We clip their wings, Tommy," enlightened Tex.

"We clip one wing close up," corrected Murphy. "That lifts 'em on one side an' flops 'em around in a circle. I can easy see you ain't no *hen puncher* ."

"Th' principle is sound in theory an' proved by practice," said Tex. "Just like when you saw off th' laigs on one side of a steer. That allus keeps 'em from jumpin' fences."

"Too cussed bad you stopped that miner," growled Watkins. "I'd 'a' been a whole lot better off dead."

"We're sorry, too," retorted Murphy. "Now, then; we got a four-sided fence to build, three posts to a side. That's a dozen holes to dig."

"Tell you what," suggested Tommy, winking at Tex. "You can handle a spade all around us, one Irish section-boss bein' worth two punchers. Besides we only got one spade for th' three of us. You dig th' north an' south sides while me an' Tex start on nests an' put up th' roosts. Then we'll dig th' east an' west sides while yo're settin' yore posts an' tampin' 'em."

"An I'll have mine set while you fellers git ready to start on yer roosts," boasted Murphy, grabbing the spade and starting to work. Jane Saunders, who had come up unobserved, suddenly stuffed her handkerchief in her mouth and fled back to the house.

There ensued great hammering and frantic dirt throwing. Tex and his companion were hampered by mirth and were only building the last nest when Murphy stuck his head in the door.

"Ye wouldn't last in no gang av mine!" he jeered. "I got me holes dug an' th' posts set. Set 'em single-handed an' they're true as a plumb line."

"All right, Murphy," said Tommy without looking up. "Run along an' do th' other two while we're finishin' up. It's gettin' late."

"Tryin' to lay it onto me, eh?" demanded Murphy. "You an' yer two post holes! Ye must think--" he stopped short, thought a moment, and then slyly glanced out at the unfinished sides of the enclosure. "Hivin save us!" he muttered and slipped out without another word.

Tommy wiped his eyes and leaned against the wall for support. "Four sides," he babbled. "Three to a side: that's a dozen holes to dig! He will make smart remarks about my thirteen nests, will he?"

"Figures don't lie, an' logic is logic," laughed Tex. "Reckon we can't finish th' fence today; but it don't make no difference, anyhow. Them chickens are as safe in th' toolshed as they'd be up here. Did you close th' doors when you left?" he demanded anxiously.

"Yes; too many hungry, stray dogs around. I'd liked to 'a' gone to th' finish with you boys, but I got to get back to th' ranch. Climb up behind me an' I'll let you off at th' hotel."

"I'll wait for Murphy," replied Tex. "He'll mebby need help about somethin'. I'm cussed glad to know you, Watkins; an' I've shore had a circus today."

"You pulled me out of a bad hole, Tex; an' you shore as shootin' dug one for yoreself. This town's run by th' miners, a lot of hoof-poundin' grubs, with pack mules for pardners. There's been feelin's between us an' them walkin' fools," here he voiced the riders' contempt for men who walked, "for a long time. Yo're a puncher, an' you shore come out flat an' took sides today. Tell you what--either you come out to th' ranch with me, or I'll stay here in town with you. Come along: we'll find you a good cayuse, an' not rob you, neither."

"Can't do it, Tommy," replied Tex, warming to his new acquaintance. "I got my eye on a roan beauty an' I'm goin' to own him by tomorrow. He won't cost me a red cent. So far's danger is concerned, I ain't in none that my tongue or my six-gun can't get me out of. But I'll ride out an' pay yore outfit a visit after I get th' roan."

"That's th' third best cayuse in this section," replied Tommy. "Williams owns all three of 'em, too. There ain't nothin' on th' ranch that can touch any of 'em." He paused and looked closely at his companion. "You heard any war-talk ag'in' th' agent?"

"Only a rumblin', far off," answered Tex. "Th' dust ain't plain yet, so I can't tell how it's headin'. What do you know about it?"

"Not half as much as Murphy, I bet," replied Watkins. "You ask him. It's a cussed shame for a man to be hounded by a pack of dogs. Well, I'm off. Remember that you got friends on th' C Bar when you need 'em, which you shore as shootin' will. We'll come a-runnin'." He shook hands and went out, Tex loafing after him as far as the door. "Tim, I reckon you an' Tex can manage to get along without me now, so I'll drift along. I'm due at th' ranch."

"Whose?" asked Murphy carelessly, trying a post to see if it was well set.

"Julius Caesar Curtis: Judy, for short," answered Watkins, holding out his hand. "You can leave th' other four posts for me to set when I come in again," he grinned.

"For a bye's-sized chew av tobaccy I'd skin ye," chuckled Tim, shaking the hand heartily. "Much obliged, Thomas, me son. Come in an' see us when ye can. There's so few decent men in this part av th' country that ye'll be welcome as th' flowers av spring."

Tommy swung into the saddle, raised his hat to the woman who appeared in the kitchen door, and whirled around to leave.

"Mr. Watkins!" called Jane, running toward the little group. "You are not going to leave without your supper? Your place is set and Jerry is pouring the coffee."

Tommy Watkins flushed, swallowed his Adam's apple, looked blankly at Tex and Tim, stammered gibberish, and managed to convey the impression that the salvation of the ranch and its outfit depended on his immediate departure. His mute appeal for moral support was coldly received by his fellow-builders.

"I do not wish to be rude, Mr. Watkins," smiled Jane, "and I would not wish to turn you from your duty: but I shall be a little disappointed if you won't allow me to show my poor appreciation of what you have done for us. But I will not press you: if not tonight, then some other time?"

The savior of the C Bar flushed deeper, received scowling looks from his late bosom companions, who knew a liar when they heard one, and he ducked his head quickly. "Yes, ma'am," he blurted eagerly. "I'd admire to stay, but Curtis shore is dependin' on me to git back. If you'll excuse me, ma'am--I--so--by," and he was whirling away in a cloud of dust, his sombrero held out at arm's length.

Murphy looked gravely at Tex and flushed slightly. "He has an important job, miss," he said.

Tex looked gravely at Murphy and did not flush. "A great weight for shoulders so young," he lied, suspecting, however, that Tommy might have acquired, during the course of the day, a very great weight, indeed. He had observed his glances at Jane.

She smiled inscrutably and turned to look at the coop, clapping her hands in delight. "Isn't it fine, and new, and piney!" she exclaimed, sniffing the tangy odor. "And it looks so strong--I must peek in for a moment."

There was not much room to spare when they all had entered, a fact which Tex easily explained.

"You see, Miss Saunders," he said, waving his hands, "it is to serve only as a nesting place and a shelter from predatory animals. During the day your flock will roam about the enclosure outside; but at twilight, without fail, it must be confined securely in this coop. No self-respecting coyote will be restrained for five minutes by the wire--he either will force himself between the strands, or dig under; and there are any number of those thieves around this town. They cannot be trapped or baffled--they will outwait or outwit any watcher. The only thing that will stop them is something physically impregnable.

"Tim and I intend to weave slats and laths between the lower strands of wire, running them vertically up from the ground, in which their lower ends will be driven. They will offer some protection, but their chief value will be to keep the chickens from getting outside. No coyote will be bothered by them for very long, and in order to save yourself the labor of filling up the tunnels they surely will dig if they can get in in no other way, I'd advise you to leave the fence gate wide open every night.

"We lay this floor for that reason. No matter what they are able to do, they can't get into the coop. I'll wager that you will find tunnels running under it before long. Don't fail to close this building before nightfall, and your flock will be safe."

"Amen," said Murphy. "They're cunnin' divvils, coyotes are!"

"I don't know how to thank you," said Jane, impulsively putting her hands on the arms of her companions. "Think what it will mean to Jerry--a dozen fresh eggs a day!"

Murphy chuckled. "Four a day will be doin' good, an' not that many for awhile. I'll get ye some grit, an' make a batch av whitewash."

"Hey!" called a voice. "Everything's getting cold!"

"There's Jerry, playing domestic tyrant," laughed Jane. "Isn't it remarkable what a difference it makes to the cook? He thinks nothing of making me wait. Come on--you can tell me all about chicken raising after supper." She cast a furtive glance at Tex, and past him at the twilight-softened range beyond, where Tommy Watkins somewhere rode to save his ranch and outfit.

Chapter V
A Trimmer Trimmed

About ten o'clock that night Murphy and Tex neared the station and stopped short at the former's sudden ejaculation.

"Th' switch is open," he said. "Not that anythin' serious might happen, unless th' engineer went blind; but either av them would have plenty to say about it. Trust 'em for that. An' tomorrow is Overton's trick east-bound. He's worse than Casey. Wait here a bit," and the section-boss went over, threw the switch, and returned.

Soon they stopped again at the station to say good night to each other. Murphy seemed a little constrained and worried and soon gave the reason for it.

"Tex," he said in a low voice, "yer takin' sides with th' weakest party, an' yer takin' 'em fast an' open. Right now yer bein' weighed an' discussed, an' to no profit to yerself. I can see that yer a man that will go his own way--but if th' hotel gets unpleasant an' tirin', yer more than welcome in my shanty. 'Tis only an old box car off its wheels, but there's a bunk in it for ye any time ye want to use it. Tread easy now, an' keep yer two eyes open; an' while I'm willin' to back ye up, I daren't do it unless it's a matter av life an' death. I'm Irish, an' so is Costigan. There's a strong feelin' out here ag'in' us--an' when a mob starts not even wimmin an' childer are safe. Costigan has both, an' there's th' lass, as well. I've urged Mike to send his family back along th' line somewhere, but his wife says *no* . She's foolish, no doubt, but I say, God bless such wimmin."

"She's not foolish," replied Tex with conviction. "She's wise, riskin' herself mebby, on a long chance. While she stays here Costigan will use a lot of discretion--if she goes, he might air his opinions too much, or get drunk and leave her a widow. I'll do what I can to stave off trouble, even to eatin' a little dirt; but, Tim, I'd like nothing better than to send for a few friends an' let things take their natural course. Every time I look at that nephew I fair itch to strangle him. It can't be possible that Miss Saunders gives him any encouragement? I'm much obliged about yore offer. I'd take it up right now except that it would cause a lot of talk an' thinkin'. Here, you better hand me two dollars for my day's work--there ain't no use lyin' about anythin' if th' truth will serve. I'll return it th' next time I see you."

"Th' lass won't look at that scut. He follers her around like a dog," Murphy growled, and then a grin came to his face as he dug into his pocket. "Here. Yer overpaid, but I should 'a' dickered with ye before I let ye go to work."

"Thanks, boss," chuckled Tex. "You'll need me tomorrow, for th' wire stringin'?"

"Yer fired!" answered Murphy, his voice rising and changing in timbre. "Yer a loafin', windy, clumsy, bunglin' no-account. By rights that ought to make ye mad. Does it?"

Tex could not fail to read the answer he was expected to make, for it lay in the section-boss' tones; and he thought that he had seen something move around the corner of the station. He stepped on the toe of one of his companion's boots to acknowledge the warning.

"Am I?" he demanded, angrily. "Yo're so d--d used to bossin' Irish loafers that you don't know a good man when you see one. You don't have to fire me, you Mick! I'm quittin', an' you can go to h--l!"

Murphy's arm stopped in mid-air as Tex's gun leaped from its sheath.

"You checked it just in time," snapped Tex. "Any more of that an' I'll blow you wide open. Turn around an' hoof it to yore sty!"

Murphy, strangling a chuckle, backed warily away. "If ye was as handy with tools as ye are with that d--d gun--" he growled. "'Tis lucky for ye that ye have it!"

"This is my tool," retorted Tex. "Shut up an' get out before you make me use it. Fire me, hey? You got one —- —- gall!"

He stood staring after the shuffling Irishman, muttering savagely to himself, until the section-boss had been swallowed up by the darkness. Then he turned, slammed the gun back into its holster and stamped toward the hotel; but he stopped in the nearest saloon to give the eavesdropper, if there had been one, a chance to get to the hotel before him.

The bar was deserted, but half a dozen prospectors were seated at the tables, and they greeted his entrance with scowls. The two cavalrymen present glanced at him in disinterested, momentary curiosity and resumed their maudlin conversation. Some shavetail's ears must have been burning out at their post.

Tex stormed up to the bar and slammed two silver dollars on it. "Take this dirty money an' give th' boys cigars for it," he growled. "Me, I'm not smokin' any of 'em. Fire me, huh? I'd like to see th' section-boss that fires me! 'Overpaid,' he says, an' me workin' like a dog! 'I don't need ye tomorry,' he says: I cussed soon told him what he needed, but he didn't wait for it. Fire me?" he sneered. "Like h--l!"

The cavalrymen grinned sympathetically and nodded their thanks for the cigars, which they had no little difficulty in lighting. The other men in the room took their gifts silently, two of them abruptly pushing them across the table, away from them.

"There'll be others that'll mebby git what they're needin'," said a rasping, unsteady voice from a corner table. "Specially if he sticks his nose in where it ain't wanted."

Tex casually turned and nodded innocently. "My sentiments exactly," he agreed, waiting to receive unequivocal notification that it was he for whom the warning was meant. A little stupidity was often a useful thing.

"Nobody asked you for yore sentiments," retorted the prospector. "Strangers can't come into this town an' carry things with a high hand. Next time, Jake will kill you."

Tex looked surprised and then his eyes glinted. "That bein' a little job he can start 'most any time," he retorted. "When a man fights worse'n a dog he makes me mad; an' he fought like a cur. I'd do it ag'in. He got what he was needin', that's all."

The miner glowered at him. "An' he's got friends, Jake has," he asserted.

"Tell him that he'll need 'em--all of 'em," sneered Tex. "Our little session was plumb personal, but I'll let in his friends. Th' gate's wide open. They don't have to dig in under th' fence, or sit on their haunches outside an' howl. An' let me tell you somethin' for yore personal benefit--I've swallered all I aim to swaller tonight. I'm peaceable an' not lookin' for no trouble--you hold yore yap till I get through talkin'--but I ain't dodgin' none. Somehow I seem to be out of step in this town; but I'm whistlin' that I'm cussed particular about who sets me right. I ain't got no grudges ag'in' nobody; I'm tryin' to act accordin' to my lights, but I ain't apologizin' to nobody for them lights. Anybody objectin'?"

"Fair enough," said one of the cavalrymen. "I like his frank ways."

"That rides for me, too," endorsed his companion, aggressively.

"Shut up, you!" cried the bartender.

"For two bits--" pugnaciously began a miner, but he was cut short.

"An' you, too!" barked the man behind the counter, a gun magically appearing over the edge of the bar. "This has gone far enough! Stranger, you spoke yore piece fair. Tom," he said, looking at the angry miner, "you got nothin' more to say: yo're all through. If you think you has, then go outside an' shout it there. Th' subject is closed. What'll you-all have?"

Tex tarried after the round had been drunk but he did not order one on his own account, feeling that it would be a mistake under the circumstances. It might be regarded as a sign of weakness, and was almost certain to cause trouble. Turning his back on the sullen miner he talked casually with the bartender and the cavalrymen, and then one of the miners cleared his throat and spoke.

"Did you have a run-in with th' big Irishman?" he asked.

Tex leaned carelessly against the bar, grinned and frankly recounted the affair, and before he had finished the narrative, answering grins appeared here and there among his audience. The sputter of a sulphur match caught his eye as his late adversary slowly reached for and lit the cigar he had pushed from him a few minutes earlier, but Tex did not immediately glance that way. When he had finished the story he looked around the room, noticed that all were smoking and he nodded slightly in friendly understanding. A little later he said good night, smiled pleasantly at the once sullen prospector, and went carelessly out into the night. The buzz of comment following his departure was not unfavorable to him.

When he entered the hotel barroom all eyes turned to him, and he noticed a grim smile on Williams' face and that the evil countenance of the nephew was aquiver with suspicion. Walking over, he stepped close to the table, watching the play, and from where he could keep tabs on Bud Haines' every move. During the new deal Williams leaned back, stretched, and glanced up.

"Had yore supper?" he carelessly asked.

Tex nodded. "Shore: reg'lar home-cooked feed. It went good for a change. I reckon I shore earned it, too." He drew out a sack of tobacco, filled a cigarette paper and held the sack in his teeth while he rolled himself a smoke. "What's paid around here for a good, half-day's work?" he mumbled between his teeth.

"What kind of work?" judicially asked Williams.

Tex removed the sack, moistened the cigarette and held it unlighted while he answered. "Freightin' on foot, carpenterin', diggin', an' doin' what I was told to do."

"Dollar to a dollar four bits," replied Williams. "What you doin'? Hirin' out?"

"I was; but I ain't no more," replied Tex, lighting up. He exhaled a lungful of smoke and dragged up a chair. "I asked two dollars, an' there was an argument. That's all."

The hands lay where they had been dealt, Williams having let his own lay, and the players were idly listening until he should pick it up.

"What's it all about?" asked Williams. "You talk like a dish of hash."

The eager nephew squirmed closer to the table and his assumed look of indifference was a heavy failure.

Tex laughed, leaned back, and with humorous verbal pigments painted a rapidly changing picture to the best of his by no means poor ability. He took them up to the digging of the post holes, and then leaned forward. "Murphy said we'd build a four-sided fence, three posts to th' side, makin twelve in all. That suited us, an' as there was only one spade, we told him to go ahead an' dig his holes while we worked on th' nest boxes. He was to do th' north an' th' south sides, which he said was fair." The speaker paused a moment, leaning back in his chair, his eyelids nearly closed. Between their narrowed openings he looked swiftly around. The card players grinned in expectation of some joke about to appear, Williams looked suspicious and puzzled, but the bartender's eyes popped open and he choked back a sudden burst of laughter. Tex drew in a long breath, pushed back into his chair and glanced around at the players. "I was honest an' fair enough to say th' diggin' wasn't evenly divided, us bein' two an' him only one. What do you boys say?"

"What's it all amount to anyhow?" snarled the nephew. "Who cares if it was or not? What did you think of th' gal?" he demanded.

Tex breathed deeply, relaxed, and gravely considered his boots. "Well, if I was aimin' to start a kindergarten I might have took more notice cf her--an' you, too, bub. Can't you do yore own lookin'?" he plaintively demanded. "Anyhow, I was warned fair, wasn't I? Huh! When you get to be my age an' have had my experience with this fool world you won't be takin' no more interest in 'em than I do. Beggin' yore pardon for interruptin' th' previous conversation we was holdin'. I'll perceed from where I was." He looked back at the card players. "We was debatin' th' fairness of th' offer to dig them holes. What you boys say?"

The man nearest to him pursed his lips and cogitated. The subject was no more frivolous than the majority of subjects which had furnished bones of contention many a night. Most barroom arguments start on even less. "I reckon it was, him bein' more used to diggin'."

His partner leaned forward. "What did he say about it, at first?"

"He was shore satisfied," answered Tex as the bartender, turning his back on the room, shook with the ague.

The last questioner bobbed his head decisively. "Then it shore was fair."

Williams nodded slowly, for his opinions were not lightly given. "I'd say it was. What about it?"

"Oh, nothin' much," growled Tex. "I reckon he changed his mind later on." He looked over at the gambler leaning against the wall, the same gambler he had seen on the train. At this notice Denver Jim, sensing possible bets, straightened up, winked, and made a sign which among his class was a notification that he had declared himself in for half the winnings of a game. Tex shook his head slightly and frowned, as if deeply puzzled over Murphy's conduct. The gambler repeated the sign and moved forward.

Tex did some quick thinking. He could not afford to be linked to a tin-horn and he did not intend to make any money out of his joke. Whatever he won in this town he would win at cards, and win it alone. His second signal of refusal was backed up by his hand dropping carelessly and resting on the butt of his gun. The gambler scowled, barely nodded his acquiescence and went to the bar for a drink. Bud Haines glanced up from the weekly paper he was reading, saw nothing to hold his interest, and returned to his reading.

Tex went on with his story, telling about the supper and his scene with Murphy at the station, repeating the latter word for word as nearly as he could from the time when he had detected the approach of the eavesdropper. From the constantly repeated looks of satisfaction on Williams' face he knew that the local boss had been given a detailed account of the incident, and that he was checking it up, step by step. Briefly sketching his trouble in the saloon, Tex threw the cigarette butt at a distant box cuspidor and stretched. "An' here I am," he finished.

Williams picked up his hand, glancing absent-mindedly at the cards. "Yes," he grunted, "here you are." Putting the cards back on the table he carelessly pushed them from him, squaring the edges with zealous care. "You come near not bein' here, though," he said, his level look steady and accusing. "Whatever made you jump on Jake that way?" he demanded coldly.

"Shucks! Here it comes again!" said Tex. He looked suspicious and defiant. "I did it to stop a murder, an' a lynchin'," he answered shortly.

"Very fine!" muttered Williams. "You was a little mite overanxious--there wouldn't 'a' been no lynchin' of Jake; but there might 'a' been one, just th' same. I had to do some real talkin' to stop it. It ain't wise for strangers to act sudden in a frontier town--'specially in this town. That's somethin' you hadn't ought to forget, Mr. Jones."

"If I get yore meanin' plain, yo're intendin' me to think I was in danger of bein' lynched?"

"You shore was."

"Then yo're admittin' that this town of Windsor will lynch a man because he keeps a murder from bein' committed, by lickin' th' man who tried to do it?"

"Exactly. Jake has lots of friends."

"He's plumb welcome to 'em, an' I reckon, if he's that kind of a man, he shore needs 'em bad. But from what I saw of Jake he ain't that kind of a man. I'm a friend of his'n, too. I'm so much a friend of Jake's that if he treads on my toes I'll save him from facin' th' trials an' hardships that come with old age. His existence is precarious, anyhow. He's allus just one step ahead of poverty an' grub stakes. Life for Jake is just one placer disappointment after another. He allus has to figger on a hard winter. Then he has to dodge sickness an' saddles, wrestlin' tricks, boxin' tricks, an' fast gunplay. But Jake is th' kind of a man that does his own fightin' for hisself. Yo're plumb mistaken about him."

"Mebby I am," admitted Williams. "I didn't know you was acquainted with anybody around here, 'specially th' C Bar outfit."

"I wasn't," replied Tex. "It ain't my nature to be distant an' disdainful, however." He grinned. "I get acquainted fast."

"You acted prompt in helpin' that Watkins," accused Williams.

"I shore had to, or he'd 'a' quit bein' Watkins," retorted Tex. "You look here: We'll be savin' a lot of time if we come right down to cases. I saw a big man tryin' to kick th' head off another man, a smaller one, that was down. I stopped him from doin' it without hurtin' him serious. If it'd been th' other way 'round I'd done th' same thing. As it stands, it's between Jake an' me. We'll let it stay that way until th' lynchin' party starts out. Then anybody will be plumb welcome to cut in an' stop it. Excuse me for interferin' with yore game--but th' fault ain't mine. Talkin' is dry work--bartender, set 'em up for all hands. Who's winnin'?"

Williams picked up his cards again, looked at them, puckered his lips and glanced around at his companions. He cleared his throat and looked back at Tex. "I reckon I was, a little. Want to sit in? After all, Jake's troubles are his own: we got enough without 'em."

Tex looked at the table and the players, shrugged his shoulders and answered carelessly. "Don't feel like playin' very much--ate too much supper, I reckon. Later on, when I ain't so heavy with grub, mebby I'll take cards. I'd rather play ag'in' fewer hands, tonight, anyhow."

Williams looked up and sneered. "Think you got a better chance, that way?"

"I get sort of confused when there's so many playin'," confessed Tex; "but I shore can beat th' man that invented th' game, playin' it two-handed. I used to play for hosses, two-hand. Allus had luck, somehow, playin' for them. Why, once I owned six cayuses at one time, that I'd won."

"That so? You like that gray: how much will you put up ag'in' him?"

"I wouldn't play for no gray hoss--they're plumb unlucky with me. I ain't superstitious, but I shore don't like gray hosses."

"Got anythin' ag'in' sorrels?" Williams asked with deep sarcasm.

"Nothin' much; but I'm shore stuck on blacks an roans. I call them hosses!" Tex grinned at the crowd and looked back at Williams. "Yes, sir; I shore do."

"How much will you put up ag'in' a good roan, then?"

"Ain't got much money," evaded Tex, backing away.

"Got two hundred dollars?"

"Not for no cayuse. Besides, I don't know th' hoss yo're meanin'."

"That roan you saw today," replied Williams. "John said you liked him a lot. I'll play you one hand, th' roan, ag'in' two hundred."

Tex glanced furtively at the front door and then at the stairway. "Let it go till tomorrow night," he mumbled.

"Yo're a great talker, ain't you?" sneered Williams. "I'll put up th' roan ag'in' a hundred an' fifty. One hand, just me an' you."

"Well, mebby," replied Tex. "Better make her th' best two out of three. I might have bad luck th' first hand."

Williams' disgust was obvious and a snicker ran through the room. "I wouldn't play that long for a miserable sum like that ag'in' a stranger. One hand, draw poker, my roan ag'in' yore one-fifty. Put up, or shut up!"

"All right," reluctantly acquiesced Tex. "We allus used to make it two out of three up my way; but I may be lucky. After you get through--I ain't in no hurry."

Williams laughed contemptuously: "You shore don't have to say so!" He smiled at his grinning companions and resumed his play.

Tex dropped into the seat next to the sneering nephew, from where he could watch the gun-fighter. Bud's expression duplicated that of his boss and he paid but little attention to the wordy fool who was timid about playing poker for a horse.

"Hot, ain't it?" said Tex pleasantly. "Hot, an' close."

"Some folks find it so; reckon mebby it is," answered the nephew. "What did you people talk about at supper?" he asked.

"Hens," answered Tex, grinning. "She's got a dozen. You'd think they was rubies, she's that stuck up about 'em. Kind of high-toned, ain't she?"

The nephew laughed sneeringly. "She'll lose that," he promised. "I don't aim to be put off much longer."

"Mebby yo're callin' too steady," suggested Tex. "Sometimes that gives 'em th' idea they own a man. You don't want to let 'em feel too shore of you."

Henry Williams shifted a little. "No," he replied; "I ain't callin' too often. In fact, I ain't done no callin' at all, yet. I've sort of run acrost her on th' right-of-way, an' watched her a little. I get a little bit scary, somehow--just can't explain it. But I aim to call at th' house, for I'm shore gettin' tired of ridin' wide."

"Ain't they smart, though?" chuckled Tex; "holdin' back an' actin' skittish. I cured a gal of that, once; but I don't reckon you can do it. It takes a lot of nerve an' will-power. You feel like playin' show-downs, two-bits a game?"

"Make it a dollar, an' I will. How'd you cure that one of yourn?"

"Dollar's purty steep," objected Tex. "Make it a half." He leaned back and laughed reminiscently. "I worked a system on her. Lemme deal first?"

"Suit yourself. Turn 'em face up--it'll save time. What did you do?"

"Made her think I didn't care a snap about her. Want to cut? Well, I didn't know--some don't want to," he explained. "Saves time, that's all. Reckon it's yore pot on that queen. Deal 'em up."

"How'd you do it? snub her?"

"Gosh, no! Don't you ever do that: it makes 'em mad. Just let 'em alone--sort of look at 'em without seein' 'em real well. You dassn't make 'em mad! You win ag'in. Yo're lucky at this game: want to quit?"

"Give you a chance to get it back," sneered the nephew. "Think it would work with her?"

"Don't know: she got any other beaux?"

"I've seen to that. She ain't. Take th' money an' push over yore cards. Do you think it will work with her?" Henry persisted.

"Gosh, sonny: don't you ask me that! No man knows very much about wimmin', an' me less than most men. It's a gamble. She's got to jump one way or th' other, ain't she? How was you figgerin' to win?"

"Just go get her, that's all. She'll tame down after awhile."

"But you allus can do that, can't you? Now, if it was me I'd try to get her to come of her own accord, for things would be sweeter right at th' very start. But, then, I'm a gambler, allus willin' to run a risk. A man's got to foller his own nature. I got you beat ag'in: this shore is a nice game."

"Too weak," objected the nephew. "Dollar a hand would suit me better. My eights win this. Want to boost her?"

Tex reflected covetously. "Well, I might go high as a dollar, but not no more."

"Dollar it is, then. What's yore opinion of that gal?"

"Shucks," laughed Tex. "She's nice enough, I reckon; but she ain't my style. Yore uncle's game is bustin' up an' he's lookin' at me. See you later. You win ag'in, but I allus have bad luck doublin' th' stakes, 'though I ain't what you might call superstitious. See you later."

Tex arose and went over to the other table, raked in the cards, squared them to feel if they had been trimmed, thought they had been, and pushed them out for the cut, watching closely to see how the face cards had been shaved. Williams turned the pack, announced that high dealt, grasped the sides of the pack and turned a queen. Tex also grasped the sides of the pack remaining and also turned a queen. He clumsily dropped the deck, growled something and bunched it again, shoving it toward his companion in such a way that Williams would have to show a deliberate preference for the side grip. This he did and Tex followed his lead. The ends of the face cards and aces had been trimmed and the sides of the rest of the deck had been treated the same way. Because of this the sides of the face cards stuck out from the deck and the ends of the spot cards projected. Yet so carefully had it been done that it was not noticeable. Williams cut again, turning another queen. Tex cut a king and picked up the pack. As he shuffled he was careful not to show any of his characteristic motions, for although his opponent had forgotten his face in the score of years behind their former meeting, it might take but very little to start his memory backtracking.

"My money ag'in' th' roan," said the dealer, pushing out the cards for the cut. "Hundred an' fifty," he explained.

Williams cut deep and nodded. "This one game decides it: a discard, a draw, an' a showdown. Right?"

"Right," grunted Tex, swiftly dropping the cards before them. Williams picked up his hand, but gave no sign of his disappointment. There was not a face card in it. He made his selection, discarded, and called for three cards. Tex had discarded two. Williams wanted no face cards on the draw, since he held a pair of nines. One more nine would give him a fair hand, and another would just about win for him. He drew a black queen and a pair of red jacks.

"Well," he said, "ready to show?"

Tex grunted again, glanced at Bud Haines, and lay down three queens, a nine, and a jack. "What you got?" he anxiously asked.

"An empty box stall, I reckon," growled his adversary, spreading his hand. He pushed back without another word to Tex, looked at his stableman and spoke gruffly. "John, give that roan to Mr. Jones when he calls for it. He's to keep it somewhere else. I'm turnin' in. Good night, all."

Chapter VI

Friendly Interest

Freshly shaven, his boots well rubbed, and his clothes as free from dust as possible, Tex sauntered down the street after breakfast the next morning and stepped into the stable. John Graves met him, nodded, and led the way to the roan's stall.

"You got a fine hoss, Mr. Jones," he said, opening the gate.

"Yes, I have; an' you've taken good care of him. His coat couldn't be better. I like a man that looks after a hoss."

"I ain't sayin' nothin' about nobody, but I'm glad to see him change owners," said Graves, glancing around. "Rub yore hand on his flank. I got th' coat so it hides 'em real well."

Tex stroked the white nose, rubbed the neck and shoulders, and slowly passed his hand over the flank. The scars were easily found. He wheeled and looked at the stableman. "Who in h--l did that, an' why?" he demanded.

"That ain't for me to say, an' sayin' wouldn't do no good; but I'm plumb glad he's in other hands. Just because a hoss fights back when he's bein' abused ain't no reason to cut him to pieces. An' a big man can kick hard when he's mad."

Tex held a lump of sugar to the sensitive, velvety lips before replying. "Yes, he can," he admitted. "Anybody in town that'll treat this hoss right, an' give him a stall?"

"Better see Jim Carney in his saloon. He's a good, reliable man an' likes hosses. He'll take good care of Oh My."

Tex stared at him. "Of what?"

"Oh My," replied the stableman. "Th' rest of th' name is Cayenne."

"'Suffer little children!'" exclaimed Tex. "Who named him that, an why?"

"I reckon Williams did, because he's peppery an' red."

"Good heavens!" ejaculated Tex. He thought a moment. "Huh! Prophet! Mecca! Mohammed!" he muttered. Suddenly seeing a great light, he flipped his sombrero into the air, caught and balanced it on his nose when it came down, sidestepped, and as it fell, punched it across the stable. Turning gravely he shook hands with the surprised stableman, slapped him on the shoulder and burst out laughing. "Where'n blazes did he dig 'em up? He don't know what one of them names means; *There was the Veil through which I might not see* . Come, John: *Oh, many a Cup of this forbidden Wine must drown the memory of that insolence!* Wait till I get my hat: *Better be jocund with the fruitful Grape than sadden after none, or bitter, Fruit.* "

Carney gave them a nonchalant welcome and displayed little interest in them until Graves told him about the horse.

"Th' roan, eh?" exclaimed the saloonkeeper. "I'll shore find a place for it, but I'm afraid it'll miss th' beatin's. There's a closet built across one corner of th' stable: I'll give you a key to it, Mr. Jones. It'll be handy for yore trappin's."

After a few rounds Tex went out, mounted bareback and, leaving Graves in front of the stable, rode to the hotel to get his saddle. Soon thereafter he dismounted at the station and smiled at the agent.

"'Richard is himself again,'" he chuckled, affectionately patting Omar. "An' I still have my kingdom."

"He looks fit for a king to ride," replied Jerry.

"He'd honor a king. How's th' hen ranch comin' along? Got th' fence up yet?"

"Yes; Murphy just finished it. That looks like Williams' roan."

"It was. I won it at poker. I could feel in my fingers that I was goin' to be lucky. Hello!" he exclaimed, looking at a box across the track. On it were painted irregular, concentric circles. "Looks like it might be a target."

Jerry laughed. "It is; and so far, unhit."

Tex glanced at the other's low-hung belt and gun. "Have you shot at it yet?"

Jerry nodded.

"From where?"

"Right here."

"Great mavericks!" said Tex. "Here: let's see how fast you can get that gun out, an' empty it at that box. I got a reason for it."

At the succession of reports the toolshed door flew open and a huge Irishman, rifle in hand, popped into sight. Seeing Tex he grunted and slowly went back again.

Tex looked from the box to the marksman, shook his head, silently unbuckled the belt from its owner's waist, took the empty gun from the agent's hand, and tossed the outfit on a near-by box.

"Don't you carry it, Jerry," he said. "Load it up an' leave it home. Popular feelin', even in this town, frowns at th' shootin' of an unarmed man. It's somethin' that's hard to explain away."

"But then I'll be defenseless!" expostulated Jerry, "It's some protection."

"You were defenseless before I took it from you," said Tex.

"But it is some protection," Jerry reiterated.

Tex shook his head. "It's a screaming invitation for a killin', that's what it is. Here: That's you," pointing to the target. "You got somethin' I want plumb bad. You try to stop me from gettin' it, an' I won't listen to you. I force th' hand an' you make a move that I can claim was hostile. Yo're armed, ain't you? I might even slap yore face. Then this happens."

The spurting smoke enveloped them both, the stabs of flame and the sharp reports coming with unbelievable rapidity. Stepping from the gray fog, Tex pointed. The box was split and turned part way around. The inner two circles showed six holes.

"I did it in self-defense. What chance did you have?" demanded the puncher.

"Great guns! What shooting!" marveled Jerry, his mouth open.

"That's good shootin'," admitted Tex. "Better, mebby, than most men in this town can do, quite a lot better than th' average. There's plenty of men who can't do as good. Th' draw was more'n fair, too; better than most gun-toters; but I know two men that would 'a' killed me before I jerked loose from th' leather. I wasn't showin' off: I was answerin' yore remark about a gun bein' some protection to you. While we're speakin' about guns, can Miss Saunders use one? Bein' a woman I hardly thought so, unless Hennery has taught her."

"Henry!" growled Jerry. "Why would he teach her?"

"Why a young woman like her would be right popular, out here, or anywhere else," replied Tex. "House full of admirers, an' others taggin' along. I reckoned Hennery might have showed her how to shoot."

"The devil had a better chance," retorted Jerry. "If Henry ever calls at our house she'll scald him. She thinks about as little of Henry as she does of a snake."

"I'm admirin' Miss Saunders more every day," said Tex. "Havin' disposed of th' interpolation, we'll get at th' main subject. As I was sayin', bein' a woman, she's not likely to be shot at. But I'm sorry yore Colt is so big: she couldn't drag a gun like that around with her. Besides, th' caliber needn't be so big."

"I got a short-barreled .38 home," said Jerry. He looked a little worried. "What makes you talk like that?"

"Bein' a gunman, I reckon; an' my ornery, suspicious nature," answered Tex. "Bein' a poker player for years, readin' faces is a hobby with me. I've read some in this town that I don't like. 'Taint nothin' to put a finger on, but I'm so cussed suspicious of every male biped of th' genus homo that I allus look for th' worst. Anyhow, it wouldn't be no crime if Miss Saunders knew how to use that snub-nosed .38, would it? Sort of give her a sense of security. Then, if Murphy or our adolescent Watkins took her out ridin' an showed her how to get th' most out of its limited possibilities, it ought to relieve yore mind."

"I don't know of anyone better qualified to get the most out of a gun than yourself," replied Jerry. "If it ain't asking too much," he hastily added.

"Havin' a brand-new, Cayenne pepper cayuse to learn about, an' show off," laughed Tex, "it wouldn't set on me like a calamity. Shall I bring a horse for Miss Saunders, or saddle up her own?"

"She hasn't any; but——"

"—me no buts," interrupted Tex. "I'll now pay my respects to yore sister, with yore permission, an' invite her to ride out with me, tomorrow, an' view th' lovely brown hills an' dusty flats, where every prospect pleases, an' only man is vile. Procrastination never was a sin of mine: it's th' one I overlooked. We'll likely go far enough from town so there won't be no panicky fears of a hostile raid. Does Miss Saunders favor any particular hoss?"

"No, and she can ride, so you won't have to get one that's nearly dead."

Tex laughed. "All right; but when she gets it, it won't be as ornery as it might be. How is it that nobody but Murphy paid any attention to our shootin'?"

"They're used to it by this time."

"Well, so-long," and Tex swung into the saddle and rode off.

Jane showed her pleasure at his visit and smilingly accepted his invitation to go riding. They examined the coop and yard, talked of numerous things and after awhile Tex turned to leave, but stopped and grinned.

"Bring your six-gun, Miss Saunders, and we'll have a match," he said. "The great western target, the ubiquitous tin can, is sure to be plentiful, despite the killing drought."

"My gun?" she laughed. "I have no gun. Do you think that I go around with a gun?"

He tapped his forehead significantly. "I'm so used to carrying one that I forgot. Shucks, that's too bad. Well, if we overtake any wild cans you can use mine, although a smaller gun would be more pleasant for you. Too bad you haven't a short-barreled gun--a .32, for instance. Shooting is really great sport. Then I'm to call at two o'clock?"

"If there was some place where we could enjoy a lunch," she murmured. "We could leave earlier and get back earlier."

"There is sure to be," assured Tex, smiling. "Say ten o'clock, then?"

"That will be much better. I'll have everything ready when you come. Is there anything in the eating line which you particularly fancy?"

Tex fanned himself with the sombrero, a happy expression on his face. "Yes, there is," he admitted. "Mallard duck stuffed with Chesapeake oysters. Plenty of cold, crisp, tender celery, and any really good brand of dry champagne. I'll enjoy anything you prepare, and I'll have a round-up appetite."

"I'll try to give you a change from hotel food," she laughed as he swung into the saddle.

She watched him ride away and walked slowly back to the house. Then her face brightened a little as she thought of the revolver in Jerry's room. Jerry had said it was a .38.

The station agent answered the hail and went out to the edge of the platform.

"All fixed?" he asked.

Tex nodded. "You get her to bring that gun. I paved the way for it, but you know her better than I do, and how to persuade her without making her frightened. What's it shoot: longs, or shorts? That's good; shorts are O.K. Is Murphy in th' toolshed?"

"He's married to it," smiled Jerry.

"If you see him, tell him I'm goin' to call on him late tonight. If his light's *out* I'll know he's home. Any fool would know it if it was lit. Well, so-long."

Jerry looked after him and shook his head, a peculiar, baffled, friendly light in his eyes. "I don't know when you are most serious: when you are serious, or when, you are joking. Was your warning about my gun just a general one, or did it have a special meaning? And about Jane learning to shoot? What do you know, how much do you know, and why are you bothering about us? The Heathen Chinee was simple beside you, Tex Jones."

He coughed and turned to enter the station, but stopped in his tracks as a possible solution came to him. "I wonder, now," he cogitated, and fell into the vernacular. "She's a fine girl, sis is; but headstrong. Cuss it, if it ain't one thing it's another. I don't even know his name is Jones, or how many wives he may have. Oh, well: I'll have to wait and see how it heads."

Tex rode slowly down the street, very well satisfied with himself. He had warned the agent, owned a fine horse that cost him nothing, and was going riding on the morrow with a very interesting and pretty young woman. Suddenly he took cognizance of a thought which had been trying to get his attention for quite some time: Where was Jake and what was he doing?

"I'm gettin' careless," he reproved himself. "I ain't seen my little playmate since I paralyzed his nerve system. He didn't act like a man who would go into retirement with a thing like that tagged to him. I reckon he's plannin' a comeback: but a man like him usually acts quicker. All right, Jake: you take plenty of time an' work it out well. An' that's shore good advice."

There came a sudden yelping from the other side of a near-by building, so high-pitched, continuous, and full of agony that something moved along his spine. He reacted to the misery in the sound without giving it any thought, and when he turned the corner of the store and saw a chained dog being beaten by one of the town's ne'er-do-wells his hand of its own volition loosened the coiled rope at the saddle and swung it twice around his head. The soft lariat leaped through the air like a striking snake, and as it dropped over its victim, the roan instantly obeyed its training.

Jerked off his feet, his arms imprisoned at his sides, the dog beater slid, rolled, and bumped along the ground, at first too startled to protest. Then his voice arose in a stream of blasphemous inquiry, finishing with a petition. Tex rode along without a backward glance, deeply engrossed by some interesting problem and nearly had reached Carney's saloon before he became conscious of his surroundings. A miner, cursing, leaped to the roan's head and checked her, shouting profanely at the rider.

Tex checked the horse, looked curiously down at the protestor and then, sensing the burden of the other's remarks and becoming aware of the maledictions behind him, turned languidly in the saddle and looked back in time to see a dust-covered figure stagger to its feet and throw off the slackened rope.

"Hey!" shouted Tex indignantly. "What you doin' with my rope? Think it's worth th' price of a few drinks, eh? You drop it, *pronto* ! An' as for you, my Christian friend," he said to the man at the roan's head, "if you ever grab my cayuse like that again me an' you are shore goin' to have an impolite little party all to ourselves. Drop that hackamore."

"You was killin' that man!" yelled the miner, loosening his hold and showing fight.

"Well, what of it?" demanded Tex. "Any man that chains up a dog an' then beats it like he was, ain't got no right to live. If I don't kill him, somebody else will. What you raisin' all th' hellabaloo about?"

"I reckon you ain't far from wrong," said the other, by this time fully aware of the identity of the dog beater. "I'm nat'rally for law an' order. Whiskey Jim ain't no good, I'm admittin'!"

"If yo're for law an' order you must be lonesome associatin' all by yoreself in this squaw town," replied Tex, grinning, but not for one moment losing sight of Whiskey Jim, who at that moment was stooping to pick up a stone lying against the corner of a building. Tex sent a shot over his head and the incident was closed. "What do you do for company?"

"I ain't hankerin' for none," answered the miner, smiling grimly. "I only come in for supplies, an' don't stay long. You a stranger here?"

"That's unkind; but, seein' as how I ain't as much a stranger now as I was when I come, I won't hold it ag'in' you. Mebby I am gettin' to look like I belonged here." He laughed. "I don't know very many, but everybody knows me. They point with pride when they see me comin'; an' cock their guns behind their backs with their other hand. Where you located, friend?"

"Second fork on Buffaler Crick, th' first crick west of town. Quickest way is to foller th' track. Be glad to see you any time. Mine's th' shack above Jake's."

"I envy you," replied Tex. "See much of our mutual friend?"

"Only when he wants to borry somethin'," grinned the other. "I see you got th' pick of Williams' animals under yore saddle."

"I was lucky pickin', I admits," beamed Tex. "Nice feller, Williams."

"For them as likes him. Well, friend, I'm mushin' on. Name's Blascom."

"Tex Jones is my *nom du guerre* ," replied Tex. "Th' north is a better country than this for minin'. How'd you ever come to leave it?"

Blascom looked at him questioningly. "Yes, reckon it is; but how'd you know I come from there?"

"They don't mush nowhere else that I know of," chuckled Tex. He coiled the dusty lariat, shook it, and brushed his chaps where it had touched, waved his farewell; and went on to Carney's, where he dismounted and went in.

"Just met Whiskey Jim," he said across the bar.

"I congratulate you."

"Who's he livin' on?"

"Th' whole town," answered Carney. "He used to hang around here, seein' what he could steal, but I kicked his pants around his neckband an' he ain't favorin' me no more. Reckon he belongs to Williams."

"Then he must do somethin' for his keep," suggested Tex. "Our friend Gustavus Adolphus ain't no philanthropist, I'm bettin'."

"No; Gus is a Republican," replied Carney. "Whiskey Jim used to ride for him, an' mebby Gus is scared not to look after him a little."

Tex nodded. "Good reason; good, plain, practical, common-sense reason. Now, Carney--I want a good hoss for a lady, an' I'll have a little ride on it before I turn it over. Want it tomorrow mornin' at eight o'clock."

"Miss Saunders won't thank you much for tirin' it out."

"You couldn't help guessin' right th' first time," accused Tex. "There ain't no other ladies that I've seen or heard about. What th' lady don't know won't hurt her pride or spoil her appetite. Cuss it, man; I ain't aimin' to kill th' beast!"

"I reckon you know what yo're goin' to do with th' hoss," replied Carney, thoughtfully; "but I wonder do you know what yo're doin', goin' ridin' with that little lady?"

Tex regarded him with level gaze. "Meanin'?" he coldly demanded.

"Meanin' that claim is staked, th' notices posted, an' trespassers warned off; which is a d--d shame!"

"Hearsay ain't no good. I ain't been formally notified in writin'," replied Tex. "Until I am, I act natural; an' after I am, twice as natural, bein' mean by nature an' disposition. All of which reminds me that this is a remarkable town, an' that there's a re-markable man in it."

His companion studied him for a moment. "You should keep yore hat on when yo're ridin' around in th' sun. Th' only remarkable thing about this town is that it's still alive. Th' only remarkable man in it has been buried these last twenty years, up yonder on Boot Hill."

"I'm joinin' issue with you on that," replied Tex. "Th' sense of loyalty an' affection of this town for its leadin' citizen is a great an' beautiful thing for these degenerate, money-mad days. Parenthetically, I wonder if there was ever a time when th' days were anythin' else? Why, everybody is his friend! There's Jake, an' th' nephew, Whiskey Jim, Tim Murphy, Jerry Saunders, John Graves, Blascom, you, an' me. I don't know any more at this writin'. An' that leadin' citizen, a man of culture, wealth, and discernment, is our most esteemed Mr. Gus Williams. Hear! Hear!"

"There's some names you can scratch, Carney among 'em," growled the saloonkeeper, spitting in violent disgust. "Yore touchin' paregoric near makes me weep. an' I'm hard-shelled, like a clam. Two-thirds of th' people here do what he says, because he either scares or fools 'em. Th' rest dassn't lynch him because they ain't strong enough. Wealth? Shore. He got most of it when th' trail was in full swing. His brands, an' he had a-plenty, were copied from some on th' south ranges near th' old trail. A herd comin' up, grazin' wide, or passin' through that scrub an' hill country would near certain pick up a few local head on th' way, cattle bein' gregarious. Whiskey Jim was th' local herd trimmer. He'd throw up a herd, claim any of th' stray brands as belongin' around here. He had th' authority an' th' drawin's of them brands. If it was a herd of Horseshoe an' Circle Dots he claimed every other brand with them that was found this side of th' Cimarron. You know th' rules. He got 'em. Then there was stampedes, an' cattle run off at night. One time it got so bad that there was talk of a third Texan Expedition to clean it up. Only this one would 'a' been for a different purpose than th' other two."

"You better keep off th' Texas Expedition," said Tex. "That was a covered invasion for th' freedom of th' pore, robbed, browbeaten New Mexicans; an' it come to a terrible end."

"Not th' one I'm referrin' to," retorted Carney, his face set and determined. "Th' second one--that plundered caravans on th' old Santa Fe. I called this other one th' third only because of th' number of men who would have been in it, an' because it was a Texas idea. But we'll not quarrel. I had a good friend in th' second, avengin' th' first."

"I won't quarrel about Texas," said Tex. "Not bein' a Texan, my withers are unwrung. What did Williams do in th' face of that threat?"

"Drifted his herds off before snow flew, to a distant winter range an' let th' trail herds alone."

"That story ain't unusual," observed Tex. "He's a strange man. Picks queer names for his hosses. I never heard such names. Take my roan, now: his name is Oh My Cayenne. That's a devil of a name for anythin', let alone a hoss. Where'd he ever git it?"

Carney laughed. "I'm agreein' with you, but he didn't name th' roan. That hoss was named by Windy Barrett, when he was blind drunk. Windy was a peculiar cuss; allus spoutin' poetry an' such nonsense. Read books while he was line ridin'. Well, he woke up one mornin' after a spree in Williams' stable. As he turned his head to see where he was, th' roan, then a colt, poked its nose over th' stall an' nuzzled him. One of th' boys was just goin' in th' stable an' saw th' whole thing. Windy pushes th' hoss away an' says, sadlike: 'Yo're dead wrong, Oh My Cayenne; it don't banish th' sorrers with its whirlwind sword.' Th' boys thought it was such a good joke they let th' name stick."

Tex looked dubious. "Mebby they thought so, but I'm not admittin' that I do; an' it's no joke for any cayuse to have a name like that. There goes Bud Haines, ridin' out of town: he ain't earnin' his pay. Well, reckon I'll drift up an' see Williams. I allus like to be sociable. So-long."

Chapter VII
Weights and Measures

The proprietor of the general store glanced out of the window as the roan stopped before his door, and he frankly frowned at Tex's entry.

"Ain't no letters come for no Joneses," he said brusquely.

"Hope springs eternal," replied Tex. He sauntered up to the counter and was about to turn and lean against it when his roving glance passed along a line of wide-necked bottles. They looked strangely familiar and he glanced at them again. A label caught his eye. "Chloral Hydrate" he read silently. He looked at Williams and chuckled. "I don't claim to be no Injun, but just th' same I got a lot of patience when it comes to waitin'. Looks like I'm goin' to need it, far as that letter is concerned." He looked along the walls of the store. "You shore carry a big stock for a town like this, Mr. Williams," he complimented, his eyes again viewing the line of bottles with a sweeping glance. "Strychnine," he read to himself, nodding with understanding. "Shore, for wolves an' coyotes. Quinine, Aloes, Capsicum, Laudanum--quite a collection for a general store. Takes me back a good many years." Aloud he said. "I was admirin' that there pipe, an' I've got to have it; but that ain't what I'm lookin' so hard for." Again he searched shelves, up and down, left and right, and shook his head. "Don't see 'em," he complained. His mind flashed back to one word, and his medical training prompted him. "Chloral hydrate--safe in the right hands and very efficient. Ought to be tasteless in the vile whiskey they sell out here. You never can tell, an' I might need every aid." He shook his head again, and again spoke aloud. "Too bad, cuss it."

"If you wasn't so cussed secret about it I might be able to help you find what yo're lookin' for," growled Williams. "Bein' th' proprietor I know a couple of things that are in this store. Yore article might be among 'em."

"I'm loco," admitted Tex. "What I want is some center-fire .38 shorts. Couple of boxes will be enough."

Williams flashed a look at the walnut handle of the heavy Colt at his customer's thigh. He could see that it was no .38. Suspicion prompted him and he wondered if his companion was a two-gun man, with only one of them being openly worn. Such a combination was not a rarity. A gun in a shoulder holster or a derringer on an elastic up a sleeve might well use such a cartridge. This would be well to speak to Bud Haines about.

"You would 'a' saved yore valuable time, an' mine, if you'd said so when you first come in," ironically replied Williams. "Got plenty of .45's, quite some .44's, less .41's, and a few .38's in th' long cat'ridges. I ain't got no .38 shorts, nor .32's, nor .22's, nor no putty for putty blowers. Folks around these diggin's as totes guns mostly wants 'em man-size."

"I reckon so," agreed Tex pleasantly. "Don't blame 'em. Failin' in th' other qualifications they'd naturally do th' best they could to make up for them they lacked. I'm shore sorry you ain't got 'em because my rifle cat'ridges are runnin' low. That's what comes of havin' to buy a gun that don't eat regulation food. It was th' only one he had, an' I had to take it quick, bein' pressed hard at th' time. Time, tide, an' posses wait for no man. Yo're dead shore you ain't got 'em, huh?"

"Well, lemme see," cogitated the proprietor, scratching his head. "I did have some--they sent me some shorts by mistake an' I never took th' time to send 'em back. You wait till I look."

"Then you've got 'em now," said Tex. "You never could sell 'em in these diggin's, where folks as totes guns mostly wants 'em man-size. I'll wait till you see." He idly watched the scowling proprietor as he went behind the counter and dropped to one knee, his back to his customer. As he started to pull boxes from against the wall Tex silently sat on the counter as if better to watch him.

Williams was talking more to himself than to Tex, intent on trying to remember what he had done with the shorts, and save himself a protracted search. "Kept 'em with th' rest of th' cat'ridges till I got mad from nearly allus takin' 'em down for longs. I think mebby I put 'em about here."

Tex leaned swiftly backward, his hand leaping to one of the wide-mouthed bottles on the shelf. "They shore are a nuisance," he said in deep sympathy.

"I allus have more or less trouble gettin' 'em," he admitted, his hands working silently and swiftly with the cork. "Didn't hardly hope to get 'em here," he confessed as he swung back and replaced the depleted bottle. He assumed an erect position again, one hand resting in a coat pocket. "Shore sorry to put you to all this trouble," he apologized; "but if you got 'em you are lucky to git rid of 'em, in this town."

Williams turned his head, saw his customer perilously balanced on the edge of the counter, and watching him with great interest. "I can find 'em if they're here, Mr. Jones," he growled. "You might strain yore back, leanin' that way--yep, here they are, four boxes of 'em. Only want two?"

"Reckon I better take all I can git my han's on," answered Tex. "No tellin' where I can git any more, they're that scarce."

"Yore rifle looks purty big an' heavy for these," observed Williams, craning his neck in vain to catch a glimpse of it. It lay on the other side of the horse. "Yes, it's one of them *sängerbund* , or shootin'-fest guns," replied Tex. "Made for German target clubs, back in th' East. Got fine sights, an' is heavy so it won't tremble none. Two triggers, one settin' th' other for hair-trigger pullin'. Cost me fifty-odd. Don't bother to tie 'em up; they carry easier if they ain't all in one pocket. Don't forget that pipe."

Williams did some laborious figuring. "I see yo're gettin' acquainted fast," he remarked, pushing the change across the counter. "Them Saunders are real interestin'."

"Oh, so-so," grunted Tex. "Tenderfeet allus are. But I reckon she'll make yore nepphey a good wife. Seems to be real sensible, an' she shore can cook!"

"Hennery is a fortunate boy," replied Williams complacently, so complacently that Tex itched to punch him. "He'll make her a good husban', bein' nat'rally domestic an' affectionate. An' he's so sot on it that I'm near as much interested in their courtship as they are. I shore would send anybody to dance in h--l as interfered with it. Gettin' cooler out?"

"Warmer out, an' in," answered Tex. "Well, they ought to be real happy, bein' young an' both near th' same age. I'm sayin' age is more important than most folks admit. Me an' you, now, would be makin' a terrible mistake if *we* married a woman as young as she is. We got too much sense. An' I'm free to admit that I'm rope shy--don't like hobbles of any kind, a-tall. I'm a maverick, an' aim to stay so. When is th' weddin' comin' off?"

"Purty soon, I reckon," replied Williams, his voice pleasanter than it had been since Tex had appeared in town. "She's nat'rally a little skittish, an' Hennery is sort of shy. Young folks usually are. He was tellin' me you gave him some good advice."

Tex laughed and shrugged his shoulders. "Don't know how good it is," he replied. "An' it wasn't no advice. I just sort of mentioned to him somethin' I found worked real well; but what works with one woman ain't got no call to get stuck on itself--th' odds ain't in favor of its repeatin'. If it was me, howsomever, I'd shore try it a whirl. It can't do no harm that I can see."

"He's goin' to back it a little," responded Williams, "till he sees how it goes."

"A little ain't no good, a-tall," replied Tex. "It might not show any results for awhile, an' then work fast an' sudden. Well, see you later mebby. This cayuse of mine needs some exercise. So-long."

Williams followed him to the door, hoping for a glimpse of the German shooting-club rifle, but Tex mounted and rode away without turning that side of the horse toward the store.

His next stop was the hotel, where he had a few sandwiches put up for him and then he left town, heading for Buffalo Creek. He had no particular object in choosing that direction, the main thing being to get out of town and to stay out of sight until after dark. As he rode he cogitated:

"Chloral hydrate. Twenty to thirty grains is the dose soporific. Yes; that's right. In a hydrous crystal of this nature that would just about fill--what?" He rode on, oblivious to his surroundings, trying to picture the size of a container that would hold the required weight of crystals. "In our rough-and-ready weights a silver half-dime was twenty grains; a three-cent piece was forty grains, and I think my three-cent silver piece of '51 weighed ten grains. But not havin' any of 'em now, all that does me no good. Shucks--there's plenty of miners' scales in this country. Bet Blascom has one that'll help me out: an' a grain is a grain, all th' way through." He hitched up his heavily loaded belt and as his hand came into contact with the ends of the cartridges he chuckled and slapped the horse in congratulation.

"Omar, we're gettin' close. Bet a .45 shell will hold the dose. However, not wantin' to kill nobody, we'd better make shore. Yo're a willin' cayuse, an' I like yore gait: suppose you let it out a little? We got business ahead."

When he came to the dried bed of a creek he followed it at a distance and had not gone far before he espied the first fork. On the north side of the gully was a miserable hut. "That must be Jake's: we'll detour so he won't see us." Twenty minutes later he came to the second fork and a second hut, not much better than the first. A familiar figure was just emerging from it, and soon Tex rode down the steep bank and hailed.

The prospector looked up and waved, turning to face his visitor. "Glad to see you," he called. "Hope Whiskey Jim ain't run you out of town."

"He might if he kept close to me, up wind," laughed Tex. "Busy doin' nothin'?"

"Busy as a hibernatin' bear. Git off an' come in th' house, where th' sun ain't so hot. An' I reckon yo're thirsty."

Tex accepted the invitation and found a box to sit on. The interior of the shack was not out of keeping with the exterior, and it was none too clean. His roving glances saw and passed the gold scales, two metal cups hanging by three threads each from a slender, double-taper bar. Beside it was a tin box which he guessed contained weights.

"Washin' out lots of gold, Blascom?" asked Tex, smiling.

"Can't even wash my face without totin' water, or goin' up to th' sump. Th' crick's like it is out there for as far up as I've been. If it wasn't for a sump I've dug in a sandy place in its bed I'd had no water at all." He reached into his pocket and produced several bits of gold, none of them much larger than a grain of wheat. "Found these when I was gettin' water just now. That sump's goin' to go deeper right quick, 'though I'm scared I'll lose my water."

"What'll they weigh?" asked Tex curiously, handing them back.

"About a pennyweight, I reckon," replied Blascom.

Tex shook his head. "Not them. You've got too trustin' a nature. Yo're too hopeful: but I reckon that's what makes miners."

Blascom arose, dropped the flecks into a scale pan and dug around in the tin box. There was a metallic clink and the two pans slowly sought the same level. "Couple of grains under," he announced. "About twenty-two, I'd say. That's close figgerin', close enough for a guess."

"Cussed good," complimented Tex as the prospector put back the weights and dumped the gold out into his hand. "I ain't never dug out no hunks of gold an' I'm curious. If you aim to put that sump down farther I'm just itchin' to give you a hand. Come on--what you say?"

"You'd be a mess, sloppin' around with me," laughed Blascom. He shook his head. "Better set down an' watch me, lendin' yore valuable advice; or stay here an' keep out of th' sun."

"I can do that in town."

Blascom considered, looking dubiously at his guest's clothes. "Here," he said, finally. "You can help me more by carryin' water an' fillin' up everythin' in here that'll hold it. After I get through wrastlin' with a pan in that sump th' water won't be fit to drink before mornin'. That suit you?"

"Good enough," declared Tex, arising and picking up the buckets. "Come on: reveal yore gold mine. I'm a first-class claim jumper. You had yore dinner yet?"

Blascom shook his head, picked up a shovel and his gold pan and led the way. "That can wait. It ain't often I have any free help forced on me an' I'd be a sucker to let an empty belly cut in."

"I can cook, too," said Tex. "After I fill th' hut with water I'll get you a meal that'll make you glad yo're livin'; but you got to come after it to eat it; an' when I yell, you come a-runnin'. If you don't I'll eat it myself."

The sump lay about a hundred yards up the creek bed, around a bend which was covered with a thin growth of sickly willows and box elders. It was a hole about two feet square, the sandy sides held up by a cribwork of sticks, pieces of boxes, and barrel staves. Blascom dipped both pails in and started back with them.

"Wait a minute," objected Tex, reaching for them. "Thought you was goin' after nuggets while I toted th' water?"

"I thought so, too," answered Blascom, "till I had sense enough to think that I couldn't go rammin' around in there with my shovel until after th' water was saved. You can carry 'em th' next trip. Sit down an' do th' gruntin' for me, this time. A dozen buckets will empty her, almost."

Tex shrugged his shoulders and obeyed, rolled a cigarette, and then plucked a .45 from its belt loop. Wiping off the grease, he placed his thumb against the lead and pushed, turning the cartridge slowly as he worked. When he heard Blascom's heavy, careless tread nearing the bend he slipped the loosened cartridge into his vest pocket and lazily arose.

"There ain't nothin' else to fill but these here buckets," said the prospector as he appeared. Filling them again he passed them to Tex and reached for the shovel and the gold pan. "There's beans you can warm up, an' some bacon. There's also some sour-doughs. Make a good pot of coffee an' yell when yo're ready. I'm surprised at th' way this hole's fillin' up, but I ain't mindin' that. As long as I dump it close by it's bound to get back again."

Tex picked up the buckets and departed clumsily, his high-heeled boots not aiding his progress. Reaching the house he set down his load and wheeled swiftly toward the swaying balance. The pennyweight disk slid into one pan as his other hand brought from his pocket a generous quantity of the whitish, translucent crystals. Sniffing them, he smiled grimly and then nodded as the biting odor gripped his nostrils. He let them drop slowly into the other pan and when the balance was struck he added one more crystal and put the rest back into his pocket. Glancing around the hut he saw a torn, discarded pamphlet in a corner and he removed some of the inner sheets. When he had finished weighing and wrapping he had a dozen little packages of more than twenty-four, and less than thirty, grains. Wiping out the little tray he replaced the weight, drank deeply from a bucket and then started a fire in the home-made rock-and-clay stove. While it caught he went out, picked up some clean pebbles and returned to the scales, soon selecting the pebble that weighed the same as his powders. He might have use for it sometime in the future. Taking another piece of paper he emptied into it the rest of the crystals from his pocket and, sorting out pieces of thickened lint and bits of tobacco, wrapped the chloral up securely. Then he got busy with the meal and when the coffee was ready he went to the door and shouted the old bunkhouse classic: "Come an' get it!"

Blascom soon appeared, his clothing wet and sandy, and in his hand were several rice grains of gold with quite some dust. "Looks fair to me," he said. "I can't hardly tell what I'm doin', th' sump fills up so fast, an' th' sand is washed in with th' water, fillin' it up from th' bottom as fast as I can dig it out an' pan it. I can't understand where all that water comes from. I know there's cussed little of it further down th' crick bed. When she dried up I nat'rally wanted a sump nearer th' hut, but I couldn't get one nearer than I have. Must be a spring somewhere under it." He sniffed cheerfully. "That coffee shore smells good," he declared, going out to wash his hands.

The meal was eaten rapidly, without much talking, but when it was finished Blascom packed his pipe and passed the pouch to his companion. "New pipe?" he asked. "Then wet yore finger an' rub it around in th' bowl before you light her. You don't want a job cookin', do you? I never drunk better coffee."

The new pipe going well, Tex leaned back and smiled. "I'll cook th' supper if you want. I ain't anxious to get back to town before dark. An' I'll put on them old clothes over there an' help you at th' sump th' rest of th' day. Let's get goin'."

"All right; it's a two-man job with that water comin' in so fast," answered the prospector. "We'll not do any pannin'—just get th' sand out an' dump it up on th' bank, out of th' way of high water. I can pan it any time. You see, this dry spell is due to end 'most any time, an' when it does it'll be a reg'lar cloud-burst. That'll mean no more placerin' near th' sump. Ever see these creek beds after a cloud-burst? They're full from bank to bank an' runnin' like bullets."

Tex nodded and looked steadily out of the door, his mind going back some years and vividly presenting an arroyo and the great, sheer wall of water which swept down it on the day when he and his then enemy, Hopalong Cassidy, were fighting it out in the brush. His eyes glowed as the details returned to him and went past in orderly array. From that sudden and unexpected danger, and the impulsive chivalry of the man who had had him at the mercy of an inspired six-gun, had come his redemption.

"Yes," he said slowly. "I've seen 'em. They're deadly when they catch a man unawares." He drew a deep breath and returned to the main subject. "Why don't you hire somebody, Jake for instance, an' clean up that sump as quick as you can?"

"An' have a knife in my back?" exclaimed Blascom, "or be killed in my sleep? I don't know much about Jake, but what little I do know about him, th' less he, or any of th' fellers in town know about that sump, th' better I'll like it. There ain't one I'd trust, an' most of 'em are busted an' plumb desperate. I've been pannin' a lot better than fair day's wages out here, but I'm doin' without everythin' that I can because I dassn't look so prosperous. Let me show much dust in town an' I'd be raided an' jumped th' same night. They're like a pack of starvin' coyotes. I don't even keep my dust in this shack. I cache it outside at night."

"Suppose you was to buy things in town with coin or bills, lettin' on that it is yore bedrock reserve that yo're livin' on," suggested Tex. "That ought to help some."

"But I ain't got 'em," objected Blascom. "Got nothin' but raw gold."

Tex laughed and dug down into his pocket. "That's easy solved. Here," he said, bringing up a handful of double eagles. "Gold weighs as much in one shape as it does in another--even less, bulk for bulk, without th' alloy. I'll change with you if you want." Then he drew back his hand and grinned quizzically. "It's allus well to think of th' little things. It might be better if we didn't swap. You fellers ain't likely to have a currency reserve: more likely to have it just as you dug it out. That right?"

Blascom nodded. "Yes; 'though I knowed a feller that allus carried big bills in place of gold when he could get 'em, an' when he wasn't broke. They weighed a lot less. Raw gold would be better, out here."

"All right; how'd you like to drop into th' hotel about eleven tonight an' win heavy from me in a two-hand game of draw? Say as much as we can fix up? How much you want to change? Couple of hundred?" He chuckled. "We can fix it either way: raw gold or currency."

"Make it raw gold, then; better yet, mix it," said Blascom, arising, his face wrinkled with pleasure. He nodded swiftly. "Be back in a minute," and he went out. When he returned he went into a corner where he could not be seen by anyone passing the hut and took several sacks from his pocket. It did not take him long to weigh their contents and, calling his visitor over to verify the weights and the cleanness of the gold, he put the odd gold back into a sack and handed the other to his companion.

"Two hundred even," he said. "Keep yore money till I take it away from you tonight. Much obliged to you, Jones."

"How do you know I'll be there?" asked Tex, smiling. "I got th' gold an' a cussed good cayuse. With such a good start it'll be easy."

Blascom chuckled and shrugged his shoulders. "Yore little game with Whiskey Jim an' your soiree with Jake tell me different," he answered. "I've rubbed elbows with all sorts of men for forty-odd years--ever since I was a boy of sixteen. A man's got to back his best judgment: an' I'm backin' mine. If I wasn't shore about you do you reckon I'd be tellin' you anythin' about that sump? Now then: what you say about settin' here an' takin' things easy for th' rest of th' day? I don't want you to get all mucked up."

Tex arose, took the boxes of .38 shorts out of his pockets and lay them on a shelf. He put the heavy little sacks in their places and turned. "It'll do me good; an' I might learn somethin' useful," he said. "A man can't never learn too much. Come on; we'll tackle that sump." As he changed his clothes for those of his host the latter's words of confidence in him set him thinking. To his mind came scenes of long ago. "Deacon" Rankin, "Slippery" Trendley, "Slim" Travennes, and others of that savage, murderous, vulture class returned on his mental canvas. Of the worst class in the great West they had stood in the first rank; and at one time he had stood with them, shoulder to shoulder, had deliberately chosen them for his friends and companions, and in many of their villainies he had played his minor parts. He stirred into renewed activity and dressed rapidly. Changing the gold sacks into the clothes he now wore and putting on his host's extra pair of boots, he stepped toward the door and then thought of Jake, who reminded him somewhat of his former friends, lacking only their intelligence. He turned and swept up his gun and belt, buckling it around him as he left the shack to help his new friend.

Chapter VIII
After Dark

Murphy's blocked-up box car was dark and showed no signs of life, making only a blacker spot in the night. To any prowler who might have investigated its externals, the raised shades and the closed door would have left him undecided as to whether or not its tenant was within; but the closed windows on such a night as this would have suggested that he was not, for the baked earth radiated heat and the walls of the modest habitation were still warm to the touch. Inside the closed car the heat must have been well-nigh intolerable.

The silence was natural and unbroken. The brilliant stars seemed rather to accentuate the darkness than to relieve it. An occasional breath of heated air furtively rustled the tufts of drought-killed grass, but brought no relief to man or beast; but somewhere along the branch line a stronger wind was blowing, if the humming of the telegraph wires meant anything. In the west gleamed a single glowing eye of yellow-white, where the switch light told that the line was open. To the right of it blotches of more diffused and weaker radiance outlined the windows and doors of the straggling buildings facing the right-of-way. An occasional burst of laughter or a snatch of riotous song came from them, mercifully tempered and mellowed by the distance. From the east arose the long-drawn vocal atrocity of some mournful coyote who could not wait for the rising of the crescent moon to give him his cue. Infrequent metallic complaints told of the contraction of the heat-stretched rails.

In the south appeared a swaying thickening of the darkness, an elongated concentration of black opacity. Gradually it took on a more definite outline as its upper parts more and more became silhouetted against a sky of slightly different tone and intensity. First a moving cone, then a saucer-like rim, followed slowly by a sudden contraction and a further widening. Hat, head, and shoulders loomed up vaguely, followed by the longer bulkiness of the body.

This apparition moved slowly and silently toward the rectangular blot at the edge of the right-of-way, advancing in a manner suggesting questionable motives, and it paused frequently to peer into the surrounding void, and to listen. After several of these cautious waits it reached the old car, against whose side it stood out a little more distinctly by contrast. The gently rolling tattoo of finger nails on wood could scarcely be heard a dozen feet away and ceased before critical analysis would be able to classify it. Half a minute passed and it rolled out again, a little louder and more imperative. Another wait, and then came a flat clack as a tossed pebble bounced from the wall at the waiter's side. Its effect was magical. The figure wheeled, crouched, and a hand spasmodically leaped hip high, a soft, dull gleam tipping it. While one might slowly count ten its rigid posture was maintained and then a rustling not far from the door drew its instant attention.

"What ye want?" demanded a low, curious voice. "If it's Murphy, he's sleepin' out, this night av h--l."

The figure at the door relaxed, grew instantly taller and thinner and a chuckle answered the query of the section-boss. "Don't blame you," it softly said, and moved quietly toward the owner of the car.

"To yer left," corrected the Irishman. "Who's wantin' Murphy at this time av night, an' for what?"

"Yore fellow-conspirator," answered Tex, sinking down on the blanket of his companion. "Didn't Jerry tell you to expect me?"

"Yes, he did; but I wasn't shore it was you," replied Murphy. "So I acted natural. Th' house is past endurin' with th' winders an' door closed; an' not knowin' what ye might have to talk about I naturally distrusted th' walls. This whole town has ears. Out here in th' open a man will have more trouble fillin' his ear with other people's business. How are ye?"

"Hot, an' close," chuckled Tex. "Also curious an' lonesome." He crossed his legs tailor fashion, and then seemed to weigh something in his mind, for after a moment he changed and lay on his stomach and elbows. "I don't stick up so plain, this way," he explained.

"I hear ye trimmed old Frowsyhead at poker," said Murphy, "an' won a good hoss. Beats all how a man wants to smoke when he shouldn't. Have a chew?"

"I'll own to that vice in a limited degree and under certain conditions," admitted Tex, taking the huge plug. "An' I'll confess that to my way of thinkin' it's th' only way to get th' full flavor of th' leaf; but I ain't sayin' it's th' neatest."

"'Tis fine trainin' for th' eye," replied Murphy, the twinkle in his own hidden by the night.

"An' develops amazin' judgment of distance," supplemented Tex, chuckling. "There's some I'd like to try it on--Hennery Williams, for instance."

"Aye," growled Murphy in hearty accord. "He'll be lucky if he ain't hit by somethin' solider than tobaccy juice. I fair itch to twist his skinny neck."

"A most praiseworthy longing," rejoined Tex, a sudden sharpness in his voice. "How long has he been deservin' such a reward?"

"Since *she* first came here," growled his companion. "That was why I wanted Mike Costigan to get his family out av th' way, for I'm tellin' ye flat, Costigans or no Costigans, that little miss will be a widder on her weddin' day, if it gets that far. Th' d--d blackguard! I've kept me hand hid, for 'tis a true sayin' that forewarned is forearmed. They'll have no reason to watch me close, an' then it'll be too late. Call it murder if ye will, but I'll be proud av it."

"Hardly murder," murmured Tex. "Not even homicide, which is a combination of Latin words meanin' th' killin' of a human bein'. To flatter th' noble Hennery a little, I'd go so far as to admit it might reach th' dignity of vermicide. An' no honest man should find fault with th' killin' of a worm. Th' Costigans should be persuaded to move."

"Ye try it," grunted Murphy sententiously. "Can ye dodge quick?"

"Nobody ever justly accused me of tryin' to dodge a woman," said Tex. "There must be a way to get around her determination."

"Yes?" queried Murphy, the inflection of the monosyllable leaving nothing to be learned but the harrowing details.

"Coax her to go to Willow," persisted Tex.

"She don't like th' town."

"Yore inference is shore misleadin'," commented Tex. "I'd take it from that that she does like Windsor."

"Divvil a bit; but she stays where Mike is."

"Then you've got to shift Mike. There's not enough work here for a good man like Costigan," suggested Tex.

"Yer like a dog chasin' his tail. Costigan stays where th' lass an' her brother are."

"Huh! Damon an' Pythias was only a dual combination," muttered the puncher. "Cussed if there ain't somethin' in th' world, after all, that justifies Nature's labors."

"An'," went on Murphy as though he had not been interrupted, "th' lass sticks to her brother, an' he stays where he's put. He's not strong an' he has a livin' to make for two. Ye can take yer change out av that, Mr. Tex Jones."

Tex grunted pessimistically. "Well, anyhow," he said, brightening a little, "mebby Miss Saunders won't be pestered for a little while by Hennery--an' then we'll see what we see. I'm unlucky these days: I'm allus with th' under dog," and he went on to tell his companion of his suggestions to the nephew.

"'Tis proud av ye I am," responded Murphy. "May th' saints be praised for th' rest she'll be gettin'. We can all av us breathe deep for a little while; an' meanwhile I'll be tryin' my strength with Lefferts, th' boss at th' Junction. I've hated to leave town even that long, but now I can make th' run; 'though I know it will do no good. Ye'll be stayin' in town tomorry?"

"Why, no; I'm goin' ridin' with Miss Saunders," and Tex explained that, to his companion's admiration and delight.

"It'll be a pleasure for her to be able to leave th' house without bein' tagged after by that scut," said the section-boss. "Yer a bye with a head. An' I see where ye not only get th' suspicions av that Tommy lad, but run afoul of that Henry an' his precious uncle. Haven't ye been warned yet?" The gleam of hope in his eyes was hidden by the darkness. "Ye'll mebby have trouble with th' last two--an' if ye do, keep an eye on Bud Haines. Ye'll do well to watch him, anyhow. Why don't ye slip out quiet-like, straight southwest from her house? Less chance av bein' seen; but a mighty slim one. They've eyes all over town."

"We are shore to be seen," quietly responded Tex. "If we sneak out it will justify their suspicions. I don't want to do that. I'm aimin' to ride plumb down th' main street, through th' middle of town, an' pay Tommy a little visit out at his ranch. *There is no shuffling, there th' action lies in his true nature* . Like Caesar's wife, you know. An', by th' way, Tim: we have some friends in town, an' I'm addin' an ally from Buffalo Crick. Time works for us." He paused and then asked, curiously: "Who is our friend Bud Haines, an' what does he do for a livin'? I've my suspicions, but I'd rather be shore."

Murphy swore softly under his breath. "He used to ride for Williams till he earned a reputation as a first-class gunman; but now he follows old Frowsyhead around like a shadder. Cold blooded, like th' rattlesnake he is; a natural-born killer. They say he's chain lightnin' on th' draw."

"I've heard that said of better men than him; some of them now dead," said Tex. "Must be a pleasant sort of a chap." He cogitated a bit. "An' how long has he been playin' shadow to friend Williams? Since I come to town, or before?" he asked as casually as he could, but tensely awaited the answer.

"Couple av years," answered Murphy; "an' mebby longer." He tried to peer through the darkness. "Was ye thinkin' ye made th' job for him?"

"Well, hardly," replied Tex. "I'm naturally conceited, suspicious, and allus lookin' out for myself. Th' thought just happened to hit me."

Their conversation began to ramble to subjects foreign to Windsor and its inhabitants, and after a little while Tex arose to leave. He melted out of sight into the night and half an hour later rode into town from the west, along the railroad, and soon stopped before the hotel.

The customary poker game was in full swing and he nodded to the players, received a civil greeting from Gus Williams, and after a short, polite pause at the table, wandered over to the bar, where Blascom leaned in black despondency.

"How'd'y," said Tex affably. "Fine night, but hot, an' close."

"Fine, h--l!" growled Blascom, sullenly looking up. "Not meanin' you no offense, stranger," he hastily added. "I'm grouchy tonight," he explained.

"Why, what's th' trouble?" asked Tex after swift scrutiny of the other's countenance. "Barkeep, give us two drinks, over yonder," and he led his companion to the table. "No luck?"

Blascom growled an oath. "None at all. My stake's run out, all but this last bag," and he slammed it viciously onto the table. "Th' claim's showin' nothin'." He scowled at the bag and then, avarice in his eyes and desperation in his voice, he looked up into the face opposite him. "This is next to no good: I'll double it, or lose it. What you say to a two-hand game?"

Tex looked a little suspicious. "I don't usually play for that much, rightaway, ag'in' strangers." He looked around the room and flushed slightly at the knowing smiles and sarcastic grins. "Oh, I don't care," he asserted, swaggering a little. "Come on; I'll go you. Deck of cards, friend," he called to the dispenser of drinks, and almost at the words they were sailing through the air toward his hands. "You've got as much chance as I have; an' if I don't win it, somebody else will. Draw, I reckon?" he asked nervously. "All right; low deals," and the game was on.

Blascom won the first hand, Tex the second. For the better part of an hour it was an up-and-down affair, the ups for Tex not enough to offset the downs. Finally, with a big pot at stake he pressed the betting on the theory that his opponent was bluffing. Suddenly becoming doubtful, he let a palpable fear master him, refused to see the raise, and slammed his hand down on the table with a curse. Blascom laughed, grandiloquently spread a four-card flush under his adversary's nose, and raked in his winnings.

"Shuffle 'em up." chuckled the prospector. "Things are lookin' better."

Glancing from the worthless hand into Blascom's exultant face Tex kicked the chair from in under him, arose and went to the bar where he gulped his drink, glanced sullenly around the room, and strode angrily to the stairs to go to his room. Wide and mocking grins followed him until he was hidden from sight, the expressions on the faces of Williams and his nephew transcending the others.

The prospector gleefully pocketed the money and dust, sighed with relief and swaggered over to the other table, one thumb hooked in an armhole of his vest. He stopped near Williams and beamed at the players, patting his pocket, but saying nothing until the hand had been played and the cards were being scooped up for a new deal.

"Williams," he said, laughing, "my supplies are cussed low, but now that I can pay for what I want I'm comin' in tomorrow mornin' an' carry off 'most all yore grub."

The storekeeper had glanced meaningly at one of the players and now he lazily looked up, his face trying to express pleasure and congratulation. The man he had glanced at arose, yawned and stretched, mumbled something about being tired and out of luck and pushed back his chair. As he slouched away from the table he turned the chair invitingly and nodded to Blascom.

"Take my place; I'm goin' to turn in soon," he said.

"Why, shore," endorsed Williams. "Set in for a hand or two, Blascom. It's early yet, too early to head for yore cabin. This game's been draggin' all evenin'; mebby it'll move faster if a new man sets in." Waiting a moment for an answer and none being forthcoming, he leaned back and stretched his arms. "How you makin' out on th' crick--bad?"

"Couldn't be much worse," answered the prospector, his face becoming grave. "I can't do much without water, an' th' only water I got is a sump for drinkin' an' cookin' purposes. You know that I ain't th' one to put up no holler as long as I'm gettin' day wages out of it; but when I can't make enough to pay my way, then I can't help gettin' a little mite blue."

"We all have our trials," replied Williams. He waved his hand toward the vacant chair. "Better set in for a little while. You've had good luck tonight: give it its head while it's runnin' yore way. Besides, a little fun an' company will shore cheer you up. You ain't got no reason to be hot-footin' off to yore cabin so early in th' evenin'."

The prospector smilingly shook his head. "I ain't needin' no cheerin' now," he asserted, again slapping the pocket. "I got a little stake that'll let me stick it out till we get rain. I got too much faith in that claim to clear out an' leave it; but now I got still more faith in my luck. It broke for me tonight an' I'm bettin' it's th' turnin' point; an' if a man ain't willin' to meet a turn of good luck at sunrise, with a smile, he shore don't deserve it. At sunup I'll be in that crick bed with a shovel in my hand, ready to go to work. I've been busted before; more'n once; but I don't seem to get used to it, at all. Well, good luck, everybody, an' good night," and he turned and strode briskly toward the door and disappeared into the darkness.

Williams looked disappointed and cautiously pushed the substitute deck farther back in its little slot under the table. Looking around, he beckoned to the unselfish player and motioned for him to resume his seat. The lamb having departed, the regular friendly game for small stakes would now go on again.

"You fellers heard what I said about sand, th' very first night that Jones feller showed up," remarked Williams, chuckling. "I'm sayin' it ag'in: he figgered Blascom was bluffin', played that way until th' stakes got high an' then got scared out an' quit. Quit cold without even feedin' in a few more dollars to see th' hand. Left th' table in a rage just because he lost a hundred or two. I was watchin' him as much as I could, an' I could see he was gettin' madder an' madder, nervouser an' nervouser all th' time; an' when a man gets like that he can't play poker good enough to keep warm in h--l. He ain't no poker player; an' as soon as I can buffalo him into a good, stiff game, I'll show you he ain't!"

He paused and looked around knowingly. "He didn't win that roan. I just sorta loaned it to him. Might have to bait him ag'in, too; but before he leaves this town I'll git it back, with all he's got to-boot. There ain't no call for nobody to start yappin' around about what I'm sayin'," he warned.

"I was a-wonderin' about him winnin' that hoss," said the unselfish player as he resumed his seat and drew up to the table. A broad grin spread itself across his face. "Prod him sharp, Gus: we'll get him playin' ag'in' th' gang, some night, an' win him naked."

The subject of their conversation was upstairs behind his closed door. He had taken off his coat and vest and was seated facing the washstand, from which he had removed the basin and pitcher. On the bench was a pile of 45's, their bullets greaseless, and he was working assiduously at the slug of another cartridge, his thumb pressing this way and that, and from time to time he turned the shell for assaults on the other side. It was hard on the thumb, but no other way would do, for no other way that he could take advantage of would leave the soft lead entirely free from telltale marks.

Time passed, but still he labored, changing thumbs at intervals. At last, all the leads removed and each one standing against its own shell, he emptied the powder from the brass containers and made a little paper package of it. Going to his coat and taking out the packets of chloral, he put the powder package in their place and returned with them to the bench.

The translucent crystals were of all sizes, some of them too large to be economically contained by the shells, which he had cleaned of powder marks. These crystals were larger only in two dimensions, for in thickness they were practically the same as the others. Doubtful whether the shells would hold a full dose and permit the leads to be replaced, he felt some anxiety as he placed the chloral in the folds of a clean kerchief and began crushing them by the steady pressure of the butt of his Colt. This was slower than pounding, but the latter was too noisy a process under present conditions. Dumping the reduced crystals into a shell lined with paper against possible chemical action on the brass, he gently tapped the outside of the container and watched the granules settle until there was room for the lead. He did not dare tamp it for fear it would not easily empty when inverted. Pushing home the bullet he up-ended the cartridge and tapped it again to loosen the contents. Shaking it close to his ear, he smiled grimly. The dose was loose enough to fall out readily, large enough to insure its proper effect, and the granules of a size small enough to dissolve quickly. When he had filled and reloaded the last shell he chuckled as he made a slight notch on the rim of each, for they would bear close inspection by weight, sight, and sound, and it was necessary that he mark them to keep from fooling himself.

He put them back into the pocket of the coat and grinned. "As I remember the action of chloral hydrate somebody may lose consciousness and muscular power and sensibility. Their expanding pupils as they wake up will expand under sore and inflamed eyelids. They'll sleep tight and not be worth very much for an hour or two after they do awaken. And these men gulp their whiskey without waiting to taste it, and it is so vile that they'll never suspect an alien flavor, 'specially if it's not too strong. Gentlemen, I bid you all good night: and may you sleep well and soundly."

Chapter IX
A Pleasant Excursion

After an early breakfast, early for him these days, Tex went down the street toward Carney's. As he passed Williams' stable he heard hammering, and paused to glance in at the door to see what his friend, Graves, was doing.

The stableman looked up and turned halfway around at the hail. "Hello!" he mumbled through a mouthful of nails. Removing them he nodded at the door. "Tryin' to fasten that lock so it'll do some good. It must 'a' been forced off more'n once, judgin' by th' split wood, which is so old that it ain't much good, anyhow. Th' nails sink into it like it was putty."

Tex was about to suggest the sawing out of the poorest part of the plank and the in-letting of a new piece in its place, but some subconscious warning bade him hold his peace.

"Much ado about nothin', Graves," he said, smiling ironically. "Hoss stealin' is a bigger risk in these parts than it is a profit; an' anyhow, th' slightest noise will wake you up, sleepin' like you do right next to th' door." He examined the wood. "Huh; them splits were made when th' wood was tough--it wouldn't split as dead as it is now: th' nails would just pull out. So you see it was done years ago. Hoss stealin' has gone out of style since then. All you want is a catch to hold it shut ag'in' th' wind." He winced suddenly and held a hand gently against his jaw. "That's all it wants."

"Reckon yo're right," agreed the stableman, glancing curiously at his companion's hand. "What's th' matter? Toothache?"

Tex growled a profane malediction and nodded. "Reckon I'll have to go around an' see th' doc, an' get some laudanum."

"An' pay that thief three prices!" expostulated Graves indignantly. "Chances are he's so drunk he'll give you strychnine instead. Why don't you go up to Williams' store? He's got th' laudanum, an' knows how to fix it up for toothaches an' earaches, I reckon."

"Williams?" queried Tex in moderate surprise. "What you talkin' about? He ain't runnin' no drug-store! What's he doin' with drugs an' such stuff?"

Graves laughed and contemplated the lock with strong disapproval. "No, it ain't no drug-store," he replied. "But th' doc drinks so hard he ain't got no money left to carry a full line of drugs, so Williams carries 'em for him, an' sells him stuff as he needs it. Besides, he allus did sell strychnine to th' ranchers, for coyotes an' wolves--though I ain't never heard it said that any wolves was ever poisoned. Sometimes they do get a coyote--but not no wolves. They've been hunted so hard they just about know as much as th' hunters." He stepped forward and felt of the wood around the lock. "I reckon yo're right," he admitted; "though while I ain't nat'rally a sound sleeper, it would take quite some racket to wake me up if I'd had a couple of drinks before goin' to bed, which I generally do have. I'll just let her stay like she is."

Tex looked at the lock and at the bolt receptacle on the door jamb. The lock was fastened securely for most people, seeing that the pressure from being pushed inward would not work against it very much; but the receptacle, the keystone of the door's defense, was nailed to even poorer wood than the lock itself and he saw at once that any real strain would force it loose.

"Shore; good enough," he said. "Have an eye-opener?"

Graves accepted with alacrity and in a moment they were smiling across Carney's bar at the good-natured proprietor.

"That hoss ready?" asked Tex when the conversation lulled.

"In th' stall next to th' roan," answered Carney. "Th' stable boys went to Europe last night an' won't be back till tomorrow; but I reckon you can saddle her yoreself."

"I'd rather do it myself," replied Tex.

"Labor of love?" queried Carney, grinning.

"Measure of precaution," retorted Tex, a slight frown on his face.

Carney nodded endorsement. "Can't take too much," he rejoined. "That goes for every kind, too. Nice gal, she is--though a little mite stuck up. I reckon she---"

"Nice day," interrupted Tex, looking straight into the eyes of the proprietor; "though it's hot, an' close," he added slowly.

"It is that," muttered Carney. "As I was sayin', you'll find both hosses ready for saddles," he vouchsafed with slight confusion.

"Much obliged," answered Tex with a smile, turning toward the rear door. "See you boys later," he said, going out. In a few minutes they saw him ride past on a nettlesome black which put down its white feet as though spurning contact with the earth.

"Whitefoot shore glistens," observed Graves.

"She ought to," replied Carney. He mopped off the bar and looked up. "Beats all how them fellers ride," he observed. "They sit a saddle like they'd growed there. An'," he cogitated, "beats all how touchy some of 'em are. I can't figger him, a-tall," whereupon ensued an exhaustive critique of cowpunchers, their manners, and dispositions.

Meanwhile the particular cowpuncher who had started the discussion was riding briskly northeastward along the trail which he knew led to the C Bar, and after he had put a few miles behind him he took a package from his pocket and sowed black powder along the edge of the trail. After a short while he turned and rode back again.

Jane Saunders answered the knock and smiled at the self-possessed puncher who faced her, hat in hand. "Come in a moment," she invited, stepping aside. "This coffee is hardly cool enough to be put into the bottles, but it won't be long before it is. I am so glad you have brought Whitefoot. I have ridden her before."

"She's quite a horse," he replied. "Gaited as easy as any I ever rode."

She flashed him a suspicious glance. "Then you've ridden her? When, and what for?"

"I thought it would do no harm to learn her disposition," he answered carelessly. "She hasn't been out of the stable for two weeks. We had a nice five-mile ride, and she took it with plenty of spirit. She's a good hoss."

After awhile Jane filled two bottles with coffee and placed them with the lunch on the table. Tex took down a blackened tin pail from a hook over the stove and, picking up the bottles and the lunch, went out to his horse, followed by Jane, who had at the last moment buckled on a cartridge belt and the .38 Colt.

Tex looked at them and cogitated. "That'll be quite heavy and annoying, bobbing up and down at every step," he observed. "Why not leave the belt behind and let me slip the gun into my pocket?"

"But I should get accustomed to it," she protested.

"Intend to wear it steadily?"

"No; hardly that," she laughed.

"Then there's no reason to get accustomed to it," he replied. "Surprise is a great factor, because what is known can be guarded against. Will you allow me to advise you in a matter of this kind?"

"Jerry says I couldn't have a better adviser," she replied. She regarded him with level gaze. "Of course, Mr. Jones; but I want to carry it: you have too much without taking it. Frankly, I'm amused by your suggestion that I learn to use it, by Jerry's earnestness that I do learn, and by Tim's fear that I will not. Let us start out by being frank: Why do you think it necessary that I do?"

"Necessary?" asked Tex. "Why, I am not claiming that it is necessary; but I do know that it is a very pleasant diversion. Miss Saunders, there is a great deal said and written about the chivalry of western men. I won't say that most of it, or even nearly all of it is not deserved, for I believe that it is; but I will say that there are men who have no idea of chivalry, honesty, or even decency. You find them wherever men are, be it any point of the compass, or in any stratum of society. The West has some of them, even if less than its proportionate share; and this town of Windsor was not overlooked in their distribution. I know of no particular reason why you should learn the use of a revolver; but we are dealing with generalities. They suffice. With the odds a hundred to one that you never will have need to call upon knowledge of firearms, why refuse that knowledge when it is so easily acquired; and when the acquirement not only will be a pleasure but will lead to further pleasures? Shooting calls for that coordination of nerves and muscles which make all sports sport. And let me say, further, that the feeling of confidence, of security, which comes from the proper handling of a six-shooter is well worth what little effort has been expended to learn its use. Later I hope you will make use of my rifle--after I reduce the powder charges a little--but the short gun should come first. And I would much prefer that you carry it yourself, and make its carrying a habit rather than an exception."

"You are a very difficult man to argue against successfully, Mr. Jones," she said smiling. "I believe, quite the hardest I ever have met."

She took off the belt, slipped the gun inside her waist and hung the belt on a branch of a small tree beside her.

Tex dismounted, took the belt and carried it into the house and, returning, lifted her into the saddle, which she wisely sat astride. Swinging onto the roan he led the way toward town. She was about to speak of the direction when she decided to keep silent, and, glancing sidewise at him, smiled to herself at his easy assurance and rather liked his open defiance of the townspeople. She had no illusions as to what effect their ride together might have in certain minds, and she allowed her feelings, if not her thoughts, to choose her words.

"What a relief it is to have a day's freedom," she exulted, patting the black.

Tex nodded understandingly. "Yes," he said. "Being cooped up and hedged around does get tiresome, I suspect. Well," he laughed, "the fences are all down today. We ride where we listeth and let no man say us nay."

She looked at him smilingly. "Do you know that you are something of an enigma? I'm curious to know what's going on in your head," she daringly declared. "You just said the fences are all down, you know."

He laughed and glanced down the main street, into which they at that moment turned, and a certain grimness came to his face, which she did not miss. "Why allow yourself to be disappointed?" he asked. "Illusions have their worth; and a mystery solved loses its interest. As a matter of fact, the less that is known of what goes on in my head, the better for my reputation for wisdom and common sense. It reminds me of the mouse in the cave."

"Yes?"

"Yes. It was such a big cave and such a little mouse," he explained. "And except for the little mouse the cave was empty."

"I admire your humility; it is refreshing, especially in this country; but I fear it is a very great illusion. Like the other illusions to which you just referred, has it its worth?"

"Confession is good for the soul, and always has worth."

While he spoke he saw a lounger before the hotel come to startled life and hurry inside. Down the street three conversing miners stopped their words to stare open-mouthed at the two riders nonchalantly jogging their way. The door of the hotel became jammed and curious, surprised faces peered from its dirty windows, among them the angry countenance of Henry Williams.

The ordeal of proceeding naturally and carelessly down that street under such frank scrutiny would have tried the balance of any poise, and Jane, flushing and trying to ignore the stares, flashed a searching glance at her companion and felt a quick admiration for him. She could imagine Tommy under these conditions. For all she could detect, her companion might have been riding across the uninhabited plains with no observing eyes within a day's ride of him. Swaying rhythmically to the motion of his horse, relaxed, unconcerned, and natural, he talked with ease and smoothness; and unknowingly made an impression on her which time never would efface.

"That simile of the mouse in the cave," he was saying, "naturally sets up a train of thought--all thought being an unbroken, closely connected, although not necessarily manifest to us, concatenation--and leads to the ass in the lion's skin, being helped materially by the great number of asses in sight, despite the scarcity of even the skins of the nobler beasts. The dual combination does not end there, however; there are jackals in lobos' hides, and vultures posing as eagles. Even the lowly skunk has found a braver skin and bids for a reputation sweeter to bear than the one earned by his own striking peculiarity. For such a one there is nothing so disconcerting as a six-gun appearing from a place where no six-gun should be--and it loses none of its potency even if the bore be small and the charge light. Have you ever had the opportunity to study animals at close range, Miss Saunders?"

His companion, bent over the saddle horn in her mirth, gasped that she never had enjoyed such an opportunity, especially before today, whereupon he continued.

"The ass in the lion's skin was all right and got along famously until he brayed," he explained; "but the skunk fools no one for one instant, not even himself. He can't even fool Oh My, here," and he slapped the glossy neck of the roan.

"Who?" demanded Jane, her face red from laughter.

"Oh My; my horse," he answered. "He was named by one Windy Barrett, when that person awakened from a stupor acquired by pouring libations to Bacchus. The rest of the name is Cayenne."

"Why, that's an exclamation, not a name--Oh!" Jane went off into another fit of laughter. " *Omar Khayyam* ! Isn't that rich! Whatever did you do when you heard it?

"I led Graves to the tavern door agape," answered Tex, grinning.

By this time they had swung into the trail leading to the C Bar and the miles rolled swiftly behind them. Suddenly Tex touched his companion's arm, both reining in abruptly. Squarely in the middle of the trail was a rattlesnake, huge for the prairie, and it coiled swiftly, the triangular head erect and the tail whirring.

"Ugh!" exclaimed Jane, a wave of revulsion sweeping over her. "What a monster! Can you shoot it from here?"

Tex nodded. "Yes, but while I usually do, I rather dislike the job. He's a snake all right, man's hereditary enemy since the world was young, and the hatred for him comes to us naturally. Sinister, repellant, and all that, that chap is as square as any enemy in the wild, and he is coolly business-like. He hasn't a friend outside his own species, and even in that is to be found one of his chief enemies. There he lies, for all to see, his gauntlet thrown, whirring his determination to defend himself, and to depart if given a chance. Look at those coils, their grace and power, not an ungainly movement the whole length of him. Look at his markings--from the freshness of his skin and its vivid coloration I'd say he has very recently parted with his old skin, and the parasites which infected it. You shed your skin in vain, Old-Timer--you'll not enjoy it long," and his hand dropped to the holster. A flash and a roar, a rolling burst of smoke, and the defiant head jerked sidewise, hanging by a few shreds of muscle to the writhing coils. "'Dead for a ducat, dead!'" quoted Tex, leading the way past his victim.

A little farther on he pointed to a track along the side of the trail.

"Dog or wolf," he said. "They're identical except for directness. A dog's track wavers, a wolf's does not. From the fact that it follows the trail I'd say that was a dog; but it may puzzle us before we lose it. He was a big animal, though, and if a wolf he's a lobo, the gray buffalo wolf, cunning as Satan and brave as Hector. And what a killer! No carrion for him, no meat killed by anyone but himself, and usually he's shy about returning to that. He creates havoc on a cattle range. Poison he sneers at, and it takes mighty shrewd trapping to catch him. To avoid the scent of man is his leading maxim. Before the snow comes he is safe--afterwards his troubles begin if a tracer crosses his trail."

"Why I thought he was a big coyote," said Jane. "You make him out to be quite a remarkable animal."

"And justly," responded her companion. "Coyote? They shouldn't be mentioned together in the same breath. The buffalo gray is a king--the coyote a crawling scavenger, with wits in place of courage. The difference in the natures is indicated graphically by the way they hold their tails. The coyote's droops at a sharp angle, but the lobo's is held straight out. A single wolf is more expensive to ranchers now than he once was, because he has been hunted so hard with traps and poison that he now has learned not to eat dead animals, and in some cases even to ignore his own kill after once he has left it. I've heard of several wolves, each of which have been blamed for the killing of sixty cows in a year, and their score might have run quite some higher. Have you been watching this track? I'd say it's wolf--and as direct as an arrow. And there is the great western target--tomato, from the color of it. Suppose you try your hand at it?"

Jane produced the pistol and listened intelligently (and how rare a gift that is!) to all her companion had to tell her. When the pistol was emptied the can was still untouched. Laughing, Tex dismounted, and drew a long rectangle in the sand, with the can in the median line and to one end.

"The ground laying flat instead of standing up like a man," he explained, "I had to figure on your line of vision. If the upper half of a man's body were placed on the line nearer you, his head would just about intercept your view of the farther line. Now your third and sixth shots, having struck inside the four lines, would have hit a man at that distance. I'd say you hit his stomach with the third shot, and his right shoulder with the other. The can is of no moment, for cans are not dangerous; but when I show you how to reload, I want you to aim at the can, as if it were the buckle of a belt. You take to that Colt like a duck takes to water--and before you get home today you'll surprise yourself. Now, to eject the empties and to reload--and by the way, Miss Saunders, if I were you, carrying that gun as you must carry it, I'd leave one cartridge out, and let the hammer rest on the empty chamber."

The lesson went on, his pupil slowly becoming enthused and finding that it truly was a sport. When she had made four out of five in the marked-off space she was greatly elated and would have continued shooting after she was tired, but her tutor refused to let her.

"That is enough for now," he laughed. "On our way back you may try a few more rounds if you wish. No use to tire yourself, especially after such a creditable showing. In these few minutes you graduated out of the defenseless-woman class, and may God help anybody who discounts your defense. You see, the main thing is not the shooting, but the freedom from fear of weapons and knowing how to use them. There is nothing mysterious about a Colt--it won't blow up, or shoot behind. Whatever timidity you may have had about handling one has been overcome, and in a few minutes you have learned to hold it right and to shoot it. The bare threat of a gun held in capable hands is in most cases enough. Now, if you please, I'll try my left hand at the can. I wear only one gun, but it may be necessary to wear two--and while my left hand has been trained to shoot well, this is a good opportunity to exercise it."

Filling the can with sand and dirt to weigh it against rolling, he stepped back twenty paces, tossed his own Colt into his left hand, dropped the butt to his hip and sent six shots at the crimson target. Stepping from the smoke cloud he advanced and examined the can. One bullet had clipped its upper edge, another had grazed one side, while the other four were grouped in the sand within a radius only; a little larger than that of the target.

"That wouldn't do for two of my friends," he laughed, "but it's good enough for me. Not a shot would have missed the target I had in mind. Had I shot as quickly as I could, I might have missed the target altogether, but close enough for practical purposes. On the other hand, had I taken a little more time, the score would be better."

Jane's mouth still was open in delighted surprise. "Do you mean to tell me that anyone can do better than that, from the hip, without sighting at all?" she demanded incredulously.

"Oh, yes," he replied, reloading the weapon. "Quite some few, notably those two friends of whom I spoke. You see I am satisfied in attaining practical perfection in my left hand, knowing that my other is skilled to a higher degree; but my friends must spend their time and cartridges painting the lily. Either Johnny or Hopalong would feel quite chagrined if at least five hadn't cut into the can. You should see them shooting against each other, breaking matches to get the exact measurements and arguing as if a fortune depended on it. Why, Miss Saunders, either of them could walk into Williams' hotel on a busy night, give warning, and empty two guns in less than ten seconds, every shot hitting a man. They have faced greater odds than that, both of them."

"You mean that one man could defeat a crowd like that?"

"Exactly; but they would not have to fire a shot," he said, smiling. "You see, such a man would only have to throw down on the crowd to hold them in check, if they know he will go through with his play. It isn't unlike an arch. The keystone in this case is the fear of certain death to the man who leads. The first man in the crowd to make a play would die. To some people martyrdom has a morbidly pleasant appeal as an abstract proposition; but in a concrete state, where the suffering is not vicarious, it really has few devotees. And here is a psychological fact: every man in the front rank of such a crowd is fully convinced that he has been selected for the target if the rush starts. Hopalong and Johnny would go through with their play if their hand was forced, and they are the kind of men whose expressions assure that they will. It is a great comfort to have them with you if you must enter a hostile town. It's a gift, like the gift of keener, swifter reflexes."

"It seems so impossible," commented Jane. "Won't you please try your other hand at a can? Somehow I felt that the snake was killed by accident more than skill. It seemed absurd, the offhand way you did it."

"This really is no test," he responded, filling another can and stepping back as he shifted the weapon to the right hand. "There is not the tenseness which a great stake causes; but, on the other hand, there is not the high-tension signals to the muscles. Watch closely," and the jarring crashes sounded like a loud ripping. One hole through the picture of a perfect tomato, two just above it, two lower down, and the sixth on the upper edge of the can gave mute testimony that he shot well.

She fairly squealed with delight and clapped her hands in spontaneous enthusiasm. "Wonderful! Wonderful! Oh, if I ever could shoot like that! I don't believe those friends can even equal it, and I don't care how good they are." Her face beamed. "But that must have taken a great deal of practice."

"Years of it," he replied, "coupled to a natural aptitude. While the accuracy is good enough, that is of secondary consideration. Had only one bullet struck the target, or grazed it, the other five would not have been necessary. The speed of the draw is the great thing. Any man used to shooting a revolver can hit that mark once in six--but he is far from a real gunman if he can't beat ninety-nine men out of a hundred in firing the first shot. That is what counts with a gun-fighter. His target is almost any place between the belt and the shoulders. If he strikes there and does not kill his man he will have time for a second shot if it is needed. My left hand is as deadly as my right against a living target so far as accuracy is concerned; but pit it against my right and it would be hopelessly lost, dead before it could get the gun out of the holster. And Hopalong Cassidy twice gave me lessons in the fine art of drawing--once in an exhibition and the second time in what would have been mortal combat if he had not allowed his heart to guide his head. I did not in the least merit his mercy. I had lived a wild, careless life, Miss Saunders; but it changed from that day."

"Jerry told me why you made him give up wearing his revolver," she said, thoughtfully. "I did not fully appreciate his words; but the graphic exposition lacks nothing to be convincing. Was your interest in his welfare another of your generalities?"

Her companion laughed. "Jerry is a very likable chap, Miss Saunders. Knowing that some feeling against him existed, and not knowing into what it might develop, I only followed the promptings of caution. He is a gentleman and a man infinitely finer grained than the rest of the inhabitants of Windsor. He is honorable and he lacks insight into the common motives which impel many men to perform acts he would not countenance. I have knocked about the West for twenty years, seeing it at its best and at its worst--and you simply cannot conceive what that worst is. I have met many Gus Williamses and Jakes and Bud Haineses and Henry Williamses. They are almost a distinct variation of the human species; they are a recognized and classified type. I knew them all as soon as I saw them. Bud Haines is a natural killer. He'd kill a man at a nod from the man who hired him. Gus Williams hires him, knowing that. Henry, the nephew, is foul, a sneak, and a coward. I'd rather see a sister of mine in her grave than married to him. But he is Gus Williams' nephew, the second power in town and must not be overlooked; and he never will know how close to death he has been these last few days. It fairly has breathed in his face. But we've had enough of this: not far ahead is a fairly good place for our lunch, unless you would prefer to go on to the C Bar."

"Why have you mentioned the nephew to me?" demanded Jane, her cheeks flushed and a fear in her eyes.

"Did I single him out?" asked Tex in surprise. "Why, I only mentioned him, along with the others, while giving examples of a detestable type and to explain why Jerry should not go about armed. I hope I have not frightened you, Miss Saunders?"

"You have not frightened me," she answered. "I have been frightened for a long time. We are so helpless! Things which bother me, I dare not speak to him about them, for he only would get into trouble and to no avail. He cannot pick and choose; and I must stand by him, no matter where he goes, or what he does. Is there mercy in heaven, is there justice in God, that we should be so circumscribed, forced by ills hard enough in themselves to bear, into still greater ills? Jerry's lungs would be tragedy enough for us to bear; but when I look around at times and see--do you believe in God, Mr. Jones?"

"What I may or may not believe in is no aid to you, Miss Saunders," replied Tex, amazed at his reaction to her distress. It was all he could do to keep from taking her in his arms. It was a lucky thing for Henry Williams that he finally abandoned the idea of following them. "If you have been taught to believe in a Divine Power, then don't you turn away from it. To say there is no God is to be as dogmatic as to say there is; for every reasoning being must admit a First

Cause. It is only when we characterize it, and attempt to give It attributes that differences of opinions arise. I am not going to enter into any discussion with you on subjects of this nature, Miss Saunders. Nor am I going to tell you what my convictions are. They do not concern us. If you have any religious belief, cling to it: this is when it should begin paying dividends."

"Have you read Kant?"

"Yes; and Spencer tears him apart."

"You are familiar with Spencer?"

"As I am with my own name. To my way of thinking his is the greatest mind humanity ever produced--but, with your permission, we will change the subject."

"Not just yet, please," she said. "You admire his logical reasoning?"

"I refuse to answer," he smiled. "Here, let me give you an example of logical reasoning, Miss Saunders. Here are two coins," he said, digging two double eagles out of his pocket, "which, along with thousands of others, we will say, were struck from one die. You and I would say that they are identical, especially after the most thorough and minute examination failed to disclose any differences. I hardly believe that any man, no matter how much he may be aided by instruments of precision, can take two freshly minted coins from the same die and find any difference. But what does pure logic say?"

"Certainly not that there is any difference?" she challenged in frank surprise.

He chuckled. "That is just what it claims, and here is the reasoning: No one will deny that the die wears out with use, which is the same as saying that the impressions change it. To deny that they do is to say that it does not wear out, which is absurd. Therefore each impression, being a part of the total impressions, must have done its share in the changing. And each impression, having changed it, must be different from those preceding and following it. Now, if the die changes, as we have just proved that it does, so must the coins struck off from it, for to say otherwise is to claim that effects are not produced by causes, and that a changed die will not make changed coins. Therefore, there are no two coins absolutely alike, never have been, and never can be, even at the moment they leave the die. Put them into circulation and the hypothetical differences rapidly increase, since no two of the coins can possibly receive the same treatment in their travelings. There you have it, in pure logic: but does it get you any place? On the strength of it, would you persist in denying that these coins are dissimilar? Are they so practically? And it is from practical logic that we draw the deductions by which we think and move and live. So you take my word that it will be better for you to cling to whatever faith you may have. If it is not practical enough for you, I'll look after that end for you; and between your faith and the cunning of my gun-hand I'll warrant that your brother will come to no harm. Shall we lunch at the C Bar, or in that little clump of burned and sickly timber on the bank of that dried-up creek?"

"I'm really too hungry to postpone the lunch," she said, smiling; "besides I want to watch you in camp, and to listen to you. It seems to me that you have too keen a brain to be spending your life where it all is wasted."

"Your compliment is disposed of by the fact that I am what I am," he responded. "The return compliment of not being able to be in a better place, under present conditions, is so obvious that I'll not spoil its effect by saying it. Anyhow, a fair vocabulary and a veneer of knowledge are not the measures of wisdom, but rather a disguising coat. To come right down to elementals, I heartily agree with you about the lunch. I'll be better company after the inner man has been properly attended to, for food always leavens my cynicism. Did I hear you ask why I do not eat continually?"

The clump of browned trees reached, it took but little time to unpack the lunch and start a cunningly built fire of twigs and broken branches, over which the coffee quickly heated. Depressing as the surroundings were, barren and sun-baked as far as eye could see, the bed of the creek dried and cracked and curling, this scene was destined to live long in the memory of Tex Ewalt. The food, better cooked and far more daintily prepared than any he could recall, tasted doubly good in the presence of his intelligent, good-looking companion. The subjects of their interested discussions were wide in range and neither very long maintained a certain restraint which had characterized their earlier conversations. She led him to talk of the West as it was, as he had seen it, and as he hoped it would become; a skillful question starting him off anew, and her intelligent comments keeping him at his best. So absorbed were they that even he failed to hear the step of a horse and did not know of its presence until an eager, if timid, hail stopped him short.

"Gosh, you people look cheerful," called Tommy Watkins, gazing at Jane with his heart in his eyes.

"Sorry I can't say the same about your looks," chuckled Tex, his quick glance noting the boyishness of their visitor, his youthful freshness and the rebellious admiration in his unblinking eyes. Tex took himself in hand and crushed the feeling of jealousy which tingled in him and threatened to show itself in words, looks, and actions. He looked inquiringly at his companion and at her slight nod, he beckoned to the youth. "Come over here an' make it three-handed, cowboy," he called. "We'll salvage what we can of th' lunch an' feed it to you. Did you find the ranch there, when you got home th' other night?"

Tommy rode up and gravely dismounted. "Yes, it was there. They said you hadn't been around so far as they knew, so I had my hasty ride for nothin'. How'd'y do, ma'am?" he asked, his hat going under his arm.

"Very well, indeed," replied Jane, smiling and fixing a place for him at her other side. "I'm sorry you did not come while there was more to eat, although I'll confess that I am not apologizing for my share of the havoc. It has been a long time since I have enjoyed a meal as I have this lunch. Sit here, Mr. Watkins--I am glad that there is some coffee left."

"That's what I get for being thrifty and thinking of the future," laughed Tex. "It's like the men who work hard and save all their lives, so that someone else can spend for them. Here you go, Thomas: look out--it's still hot."

"Thank you, ma'am," said Tommy, flushing and embarrassed, as he dropped onto the spot indicated. "I ain't a bit hungry, though."

"You will be after the first bite," assured Tex. "The cups have been used, and there's no water for washing them. That's excuse enough for any man to drink out of the pail, and I envy you there, Tommy Watkins. Cattle gettin' along all right in spite of the drought? Expect to have a big gain this round-up? They ought to bring top-notch prices if they're in good shape."

Steered easily into familiar channels of conversation, Tommy got on well, so well that his embarrassment gradually disappeared and he was nearly his natural self; but he did envy his friend's ability to think coherently and to talk with fluent ease on any subject mentioned. Jane Saunders learned more about cows, cattle, steers, calves, cows, cattle, riding, roping, round-ups, branding, cows, calves, horses, cattle, and other ranch subjects than she thought existed to be learned. And she shot a glance of grateful appreciation at Tex Jones for the way in which he put their guest on his feet and kept him there through several vocal flounderings. It was so tactfully done that Tommy did not realize it.

Gradually Tex worked out of the conversation and studied his companions. He saw clean youth entertaining clean youth; a bubbling mirth free from suspicion or irony; an absence of cynicism, and an unbounding faith in the future. He hid his smile at how Tommy was led to talk of himself and of his ambitions. They looked to be about the same age, Tommy perhaps a few years her senior; and when she looked at Tommy there was friendliness in her eyes; and when Tommy looked at her there was a great deal more in his.

The keen, but apparently careless, observer silently and fairly reviewed the years that had passed since he had been at Tommy's age; the lack of illusions, the cold, cynical practicality of his thoughts and actions; the laws, both civil and moral, which he contemptuously had shattered. He could not remember the time when he had had Tommy's faith in men, nor his enthusiasm. Tommy was looking forward to a life of clean, hard work, and actually with a fierce eagerness. Never had such a thing been an impelling motive in the life of Tex Ewalt. Instead he had planned shrewdly and consistently how to avoid working for a living, and when it was solved, then how to live higher and higher with the least additional effort. And he now admitted that if he had the chance to live that period over again, under the same circumstances, he would repeat his course in the major things. He felt neither regret nor remorse at the contrast--he had lived as it pleased him, and the Tex Ewalt of today had no censure for the Tex Ewalt of yesterday. But he was fair, at all events; and to draw true deductions from accepted facts was an art not to be perverted because expediency might beckon. After all, he did not try to fool himself; and he was no hypocritical whiner. Being fair, he calmly realized that he was the unfitting unit of this triangle, that he did not belong there. But there would be time enough for such cogitation later on.

"Shore," Tommy was dogmatically asserting. "Th' rattler gets all cramped up an' tired, an' there is an instant when he can't turn fast enough to keep his nasty little eyes on th' other, that's racin' around him like a flash. That's th' end of th' rattler. Th' kingsnake darts in, grabs th' rattler behind th' head, an' after a great thrashin' around, kills him dead. *Ain't* that so, Mr. Jones?"

Tex lazily turned his head and looked at the doubting auditor and then at the anxious Tommy. He gravely nodded. "Yes that's th' end. That's the enemy within the snake's own species which I mentioned back on the trail, Miss Saunders."

The look of doubt faded from her face and a nebulous smile transformed it. She was certain of it now.

Tex flamed at what that change told him, tingling to his finger tips with a surging elation. He felt that he had but to speak three words to put her vague feelings into a coherent wonder of wonders; but to crystallize them into an everlasting passion by the alchemy of his avowal, or the touch of his lips. The lulled storm within him broke out anew and blazed fiercely. He arose, kicked an inoffensive tin can over the bed of the creek and spun it in mid-air by a vicious, eye-baffling shot from his Colt. Realizing how he had forgotten himself, and his resolutions, he, the cool, imperturbable Tex Ewalt, he recovered his poise and bowed, smilingly, to the surprised pair.

"That's shootin', Tex!" cried Tommy.

"It's more than that," smiled Tex. "It's notice that it's time to try that .38, Miss Saunders," he announced. "She is learning to use a gun, Tommy--I've been telling her how much fun it is. I'll call th' shots while you stand by her to answer questions. Suppose we have a more suitable target, this time. What can we use?"

Tommy grinned expansively. "Who's goin' to do th' shootin'?" he demanded.

"Miss Saunders," answered Tex. "Why?"

"Oh; all right then--here, prop up my hat," offered Tommy; "But not too all-fired close!" he warned.

"There's chivalry for you, Mr. Jones!" triumphantly exclaimed Jane, her eyes dancing.

"Think so?" queried Tex, grinning. "Huh!" He shook his head. "I'd say he is not paying you any compliment. Just for that I hope you shoot it to pieces."

He took the sombrero from Tommy's extended hand, went down and crossed the creek bed, and placed the hat against the opposite bank. Stepping off twenty paces he drew a line on the earth with the side of his boot sole and beckoned to the flushed markswoman.

"That hat is a pressing danger," he warned. "You've got to get it, or it'll get you. Don't be careless, and don't waste any sympathy on the grinning wretch who owns it."

"But I don't want to ruin it," she protested. "Surely something else will answer?"

"You go ahead an' ruin it, if you can," chuckled Tommy. "Don't *you* worry none-- *I* ain't!"

"I do believe it wasn't a compliment, or chivalry, at all," she laughed. "All right, Mr. Watkins: here goes for a new hat!" Slowly, deliberately, holding her arm as she had been instructed, she aimed and fired until the weapon was empty. The hat had a hole near one edge of the crown and another near the edge of the brim.

"Glory be!" exclaimed Tommy. "I'm votin' for a new target! Why that's plumb fine, Miss Saunders--if it ain't an accident!"

"Let's see if it was," suggested Tex, handing her another round of cartridges. "Here!" he exclaimed, glancing at Tommy. "Where you goin' so fast?"

"To collect th' ruins," retorted the puncher over his shoulder. " *You* got a hat, ain't you?"

"I have, and I'm keeping it right where it belongs," rejoined Tex. "I didn't suggest that it was any accident, did I?"

Chapter X
Speed and Guile

Tex and Tommy said their adieus, watched Jane enter the house, and then rode slowly toward the station where, after a few words with Jerry Saunders, Tommy went on alone, leaving Tex talking with the agent.

The C Bar puncher rode down the main street full of more kinds of emotion than he ever had known before, and among them was a strong feeling of his inability to gain Jane's attention while Tex Jones was around. Jealousy was working in the yeasty turbulence of his heart and mind. Taking off his perforated sombrero he gazed at it as though it were something sacred. There they were, two of them, made by her blessed bullets! Reverently pushing the ragged felt of their rims back into place, he patted the nearly closed holes and put the sombrero on his head again. There would be no new hat for Tommy Watkins, as she had laughingly said. No, sir! No, sir-e-e!

Opposite the hotel he became aware of his surroundings and suddenly decided that he needed a drink to steady himself, to shock himself into a more natural condition of mind. As he made the decision, he idly observed Bud Haines emerge from the door of the general store and start toward him on the peculiar, bow-legged, choppy stride he so much affected. And as Tommy swung off the horse and carelessly tossed the reins across the tie-rail he caught sight of Tex Jones waving to the agent and slowly wheeling the roan.

Tommy made his way through the card-table end of the room, noticing without giving any particular weight to the fact, that he was the cynosure of all eyes. Still strange to himself and very much occupied by his thoughts, he did not note whether there were six or two dozen men in the room; nor that their eager and low-voiced conversation abruptly ceased upon his entry, and that there was an air of expectancy which seemed to fill the room. He passed Henry Williams, who was seated at a small table, with a nod and rested his elbows on the bar. Silently a bottle and glass were placed before him, silently he poured out a drink and downed it mechanically. Then Henry spoke, his ratlike eyes for a moment not shifting.

"That's a fenced range," he said in a low, tense voice. "You keep off it!"

Tommy, not realizing that the words were intended for him, still rested his elbows on the bar, his back to the speaker and the rest of the room, buried in his abstractions. He neither saw nor heard the quiet, quick entry of Bud Haines through the front door, nor knew that the gunman stopped suddenly and leaned against the jamb. Neither he, nor anyone else, caught the quiet step nearing that same door from the street.

Henry Williams, finding his warning totally ignored, let his anger leap to rage.

"You!" he snarled. "I'm talking to you, Watkins!"

Tommy started and swung around, momentarily out of touch with his surroundings. The meanness in the voice, the deadly timbre of it, warned him subconsciously rather than acutely, and he stared at the speaker.

"What you say, Williams?" he asked, rapidly sensing the hostility in the air. "I was thinkin' of somethin'," he explained.

"I'm givin' you somethin' to think about!" retorted Henry, slowly arising and slowly leaning forward on the table. "You don't want to stop thinkin' about it, neither--unless you want to join th' dead uns on Boot Hill. I said that range is fenced-- *you keep off* !"

Tommy, alert as a coiled snake now, watched the angry man while he considered. A fenced range. He was to keep off. "I ain't gettin' th' drift of that," he said, slowly. "Any reason why you shouldn't talk so I'll know what yo're meanin'?"

"Yo're dumb as h--l, ain't you?" sneered Henry, his voice rising shrilly and the little, close-set eyes beginning to flame. "I wouldn't have nobody say you wasn't warned plain. I'm tellin' you for th' last time, to do yore courtin' somewhere else! I'm claimin' that Saunder gal. Keep away, that's all!"

Tommy went a little white around his stiffening lips. When his words came they sounded the spirit of the C Bar, but where they came from he did not know; perhaps he had heard them or read them somewhere. Certainly they did not by right belong to his direct method of conveying thought. He knew Henry Williams, his baseness, his petty villainies, his bestial nature. The picture of Jane, innocent and sweet, came to him and made a contrast which sickened him. Looking straight into Henry's eyes his voice rasped its insulting, deadly reply.

"It's bad enough for a coyote like me to admire a rose; but I'm d--d if any polecat's goin' to pluck it!"

Before the words were all spoken and before either of the disputants could move they heard the startling crash of a gun and instinctively glanced toward the sound. They saw Bud Haines, his smoking revolver forced slowly up behind his back, higher and higher, the gun wrist gripped in the sinewy fingers of Tex Jones, whose right hand held his own Colt at his hip, the deadly muzzle covering the two in front of the bar, without a tremble of its steely barrel. His gripping fingers kept on twisting, while one knee held the killer from writhing sidewise to escape the grip of the punishing bending of the imprisoned arm. Slowly the tortured muscles grew numb, slowly beads of perspiration stood out on the killer's forehead, and as his throbbing elbow neared the snapping point, he gasped, released his hold on the Colt and then went spinning across the room from the power of his captor's whirling shove. When he stopped he froze in his tracks, for Tex carelessly held two guns now, the captured weapon covering its owner.

"Phew!" sighed Tex, a grin slowly spreading across his red face. "That was close, that was! Reckon I done saved quite a mess in here." He glared at Tommy. "You get th' h--l out of here an' don't come back till you know how to act! Runnin' around like a mad dog, tryin' to kill men that never done you no harm! G'wan, or I'll let Hennery loose at you! I heard what you said, an' I wouldn't blame him if he blowed you wide open! G'wan! Shove that gun back where it belongs, an' git: *Pronto* ! You've gone an' got Bud an' me bad friends, I reckon, an' I can't hardly blame him, neither."

Henry's eyes were riveted on the menacing Colt, his hand frozen where it had stopped, a few inches above the butt of his own. Bud Haines leaned forward, balanced on the balls of his feet, but not daring to leap. The spectators were staring, open-mouthed, quite content to let things take their course without any impetus from them.

Tommy sullenly slid the gun back into its holster and walked toward the door, too angry to speak. Glaring at Tex he went out, mounted and rode toward the ranch; and it was half an hour later before he came to the realization that his life had been saved from a shot from the side, and by the time he had reached the ranchhouse he was grinning.

Tex flipped the captured gun into the air, caught it by the barrel, and tossed it, butt first, to the killer. "I shore am apologizin' to you, Bud," he said, "for cuttin' in that way--but I had to act sudden, an' rough."

As the weapon settled into its owner's hand it roared and leaped, the bullet cutting Tex's vest under the armpit. Before a second shot could follow from it Bud twisted sidewise and plunged face down on the floor.

Tensed like a panther about to spring, Tex peered through the thinning cloud of smoke rising from his hip, his attention on the others in the room. "Sorry," he said. "You saw it all. I gave him his gun, butt first, an' he shot at me with it. Clipped my vest under my left shoulder. I couldn't do nothin' else. I'm sayin' that doin' favors for strangers is risky business--but is anybody findin' any fault with this shootin'?" He glanced quickly from face to face and then nodded slightly. "It was plain self-defense. If I'd 'a' thought he was a-goin' to shoot I shore wouldn't 'a' chucked him his loaded gun. Reckon I'm a plain d--d fool!"

There were no replies to him. The tense faces stared at the man who had killed Bud Haines in a fight after the killer had shot first. While there were no accusations in their expressions, neither was there any friendliness. The killing had been justified. This seemed to be the collective opinion, for in no way could the facts be changed. Bud had been man-handled in a manner which to him had been an unbearable insult, the fight could be considered as of his adversary's starting, but the actual shooting was as the victor claimed; and it was the shooting which they were to judge.

Tex, feeling ruefully of the bullet-torn vest, shoved his gun into its sheath and went over to Henry's table. The nephew hardly had moved since the first shot.

"I got somethin' to talk to you about, Henry," said Tex in a low, confidential voice. "'Tain't for everybody's ears, neither; so sit down a minute. That fool Watkins came cuttin' in as we was ridin' back, or I might have more news."

Henry slowly followed his companion's movements and straddled his chair. He motioned to the bartender for drinks and then let his suspicious eyes wander over his companion's face. He had a vast respect for Tex Jones.

"I reckon he's been cured of cuttin' in," he growled, a momentary gleam showing. "That's a habit of yourn, too," he said. "An' it's a cussed bad one, here in Windsor."

Tex spread his hands in helpless resignation. "I know it. Ever since I've been in this town I been puttin' my worst foot forward. I'm allus bunglin' things; an' just when I was beginnin' to make a few friends, Bud had to go an' git blind mad an' spoil everythin'. I didn't have nothin' ag'in' Bud; but I reckon mebby I was a little mite rough."

"Oh, Bud be d--d!" coldly retorted Henry. "He had th' edge, an' lost. That's between him an' you. What I'm objectin' to, Jones, is th' way you spoiled my plans. Don't you never cut into my affairs like you did just now. I'm tellin' you fair. I'm admittin' yo're a prize-winnin' gun-thrower; but there's other ways in this town. Savvy?"

Tex shook his head apologetically and nodded. "You an' me ain't goin' to have no trouble, Hennery," he declared earnestly. "If you want that C Bar fool, go git him. It ain't none of my business. But I'm worryin' about what yore uncle's goin' to say about me shootin' Bud," he confessed with plain anxiety. "He's a big man, Williams is; an' me, shucks: I ain't nothin' a-tall."

"He'll take my say-so," assured Henry, "after he cools down. Now what you got to tell me?"

"It's about that Saunders gal," answered Tex. He hitched his chair a little nearer to the table. "You remember what I told you, couple of nights ago? Well, I got to thinkin' about it when I was near th' station yesterday, so I went in an' got friendly with her brother." He rubbed his chin and grinned reminiscently. "There was a box across th' track that he had been using for a target. I asked him what it was an' he told me, an' he said he couldn't hit it. I sort of egged him on, not believin' him; an' shore enough he couldn't--an', Hennery, it was near as big as a house! I cut loose an' made a sieve of it--you must 'a' heard th' shootin'? His eyes plumb stuck out, an' we got to talkin' shootin'. Finally he ups an' asks me can I show his sister how to throw a gun an', seein' my chance to learn somethin' about her, I said I shore could show anybody that wasn't scared to death of one, an' that had any sense. 'How much will you charge for th' lessons?' says he. I had a good chance to pick up some easy money, but that wasn't what I was playin' for. I just wanted to get sort of friendly with her, an' him, too. I says, 'Nothin'.' Well, we fixed it up, an' today we goes off practicin'--you should 'a' seen that lunch, Hennery! I'm cussed near envyin' you!" He laughed contentedly, leaned back, and rubbed his stomach.

"Well?" demanded Henry, grinning ruefully.

"Well," echoed Tex. "You know that sewin' an' crochetin' is a whole lot different from shootin' a .45; an' so does she, now. I reckon a .22 would 'most scare her to death. Did you ever shoot with yore eyes shut? You don't have to try: it can't be done, an' hit nothin'. Six-guns an' wimmin wasn't never made to mix; an' they shore don't. We ate up th' lunch an' started back ag'in, an' I was just gettin' set to swing th' conversation in yore direction, carelesslike, but real careful, an' see what I could find out for you, when cussed if that C Bar coyote didn't come dustin' up, an' I don't know any more than I did before. But I'm riskin' one thing, Hennery: I'm near shore she ain't got nothin' ag'in' you; an' on th' way out, when I refers to you she speaks up quicklike, with her nose turned up a little, an' says: 'Henry Williams? Why, he'll be a rich man some day, when his uncle dies. Ain't some folks born lucky, Mr. Jones?' Hennery, there ain't none of 'em that are overlookin' th' good old pesos, U.S. You keep right on like you are; an' save me a front seat at th' weddin'.'"

Henry sat back, buried in thought. He glanced at the huddled figure near the door and then looked quickly into his companion's bland eyes. "Her brother's dead set ag'in' it. He knows he done me a dirty trick, stealin' my job, an' like lots of folks, instead of hatin' hisself, he hates me. Human nature's funny that way. So he can't hit a box, hey?"

Tex chuckled and nodded. "He up an' says he's so plumb disgusted with hisself that he ain't never goin' to tote a gun again, not never. Seems to me yo're doin' a lot of foolish worryin' about losin' that job. That ain't no job to worry about. If I was Gus Williams' only relation, you wouldn't see me lookin' for no jobs! You shore got th' wrong idea, Hennery. What do you want to work for, anyhow?"

"Well," considered the nephew of the uncle who some day would die, "that is one way of lookin' at it; but, Tex, he did me out of it. That's what's rilin' me!"

Tex leaned back and laughed heartily. "Hennery, you make me laugh! If I got mad an' riled at every dog that barked at me I'd be plumb soured for life by this time. A man like you should be above holdin' grudges ag'in' fellers like Saunders. It ain't worth th' risk of spoilin' yore disposition. Let him have his dried-out bone: you would 'a' dropped it quick enough, anyhow. An' if it wasn't for him gettin' that two-by-nothin' old job you wouldn't never 'a' seen his sister, would you? Ever think about it like that? Well, what you think? Had I better try to go ridin' with her ag'in an' git her to talkin'? Or shall I set back an' only keep my eyes an' ears open?"

"What's interestin' you so much in this here affair?" questioned Henry, his glance resting for a moment on the face of his companion.

"Well, I ain't got that letter," confessed Tex, slyly; "an' what's more, I'm afraid I ain't goin' to get it, neither, th' coyote. He lets me come out here, near th' end of th' track, an' then lets me hold th' sack. Time's comin' when I'll be needin' a job; an' yo're aces-up with yore uncle." He grinned engagingly. "My cards is face up. I got to look out for myself."

Henry laughed softly. "You shore had me puzzled," he replied. "Well, we'll see what we see. I don't hardly know, yet, what kind of a job you ought to have. There's good jobs, an' poor jobs. An' while I think of it, Tex, you'd mebby better go ridin' with her ag'in. But don't you forget what I was sayin' about there bein' other ways than gun-throwin' in Windsor. I——"

The low hum of conversation about them ceased as abruptly as did Henry's words. He was looking at the door, and sensing danger, Tex pushed back quietly and followed his companion's gaze. Jake, under the influence of liquor, stood in the doorway, a gun in his upraised hand, staring with unbelieving eyes at the body of Bud Haines.

"Stop that fool!" whispered Tex. "I've done too much killin' today: an' he's drunk!"

Henry arose and walked quietly, swiftly toward the vengeful miner, who now turned and looked about the room. A spasm of rage shot through him and his hand chopped down, but Henry knocked it aside and the heavy bullet scored the wall. Two men near the door leaped forward at the nephew's call and after a short struggle, Jake was disarmed, pacified, and sent on his way again.

Tex dropped his gun back into the holster and went up to the nephew. "Much obliged, Hennery," he said. "I've been expectin' him most every minute an' I'm glad you handled it so good. Where's he been keepin' hisself, anyhow?"

"Out in his cabin, nursin' his grudge," answered Henry. "He's one of them kind. He's got it chalked up ag'in' you, Tex, an' it'll smolder an' smolder, no tellin' how long. Then it'll bust out ag'in, like it did just now. Keep out of his way--he's a good man, Jake is. He's a friend of mine."

"That's good enough for me," Tex assured him. "I ain't got no grudge ag'in' Jake. It's th' other way 'round. Reckon I'll put up my cayuse. See you later."

Chapter XI
Empty Honors

The dramatic death of Bud Haines created a ripple of excitement in Windsor which ran a notch higher than any killing of recent years. The late gunman posed as a gunman, swaggeringly, exultantly. Himself a contributor of victims to Boot Hill, his going there aroused a great deal more satisfaction than resentment. He was unmourned, but not unsung, and the question raised by his passing concerned the living more than the dead. How would his conqueror behave?

Bud was an out-and-out killer, cold, dispassionate, calculating; one whose gun was for hire and salary. He had no sympathy, no softer side to his nature, if his fellow-townsmen knew him right. The crooked mouth, grown into a lop-sided sneer, had been a danger signal to everyone who saw him, and through his up-to-then invincible gun Williams had passed his days in confidence, his nights in sleep. He had been taciturn, unsmiling, grim, and the few words he occasionally uttered were never cryptic. On the other hand Tex Jones was voluble, talked loosely and foolishly and had shown signs at poker that his courage was not what it should be to wrap the mantle of the fallen man about him and play his part; but had it been truly shown? Was his poker playing a true index to his whole nature? There was his brief, high-speed, complete mastery over Jake, himself a man bad enough to merit wholesome respect; there was the cool killing of Bud, and the nonchalant actions of the victor after the tragedy. He scarcely had given his victim a second look.

This question, as all questions do, provided argument. Gus Williams, sullen and morose at losing a valuable man in whose fidelity he could place full trust, and on whose prowess his own power largely rested, maintained that Tex Jones had pulled the trigger mechanically, and that it had been for him a lucky accident. His nephew took issue with him and paid his new companion full credit. The miners were about evenly divided, while Carney openly exulted and made the victory his principal topic of conversation. It helped him in another way, for there are some who blindly follow a champion, and the Windsor champion kept his horse and spent many of his spare hours at Carney's. John Graves sighed with relief at Bud's passing, due to an old score he had feared would be reopened, and he urged the appointment of Tex Jones for city marshal, a position hitherto unfilled in Windsor. Carney was for this heart and soul, and offered a marshal's office rent free. It was a lean-to adjoining his saloon.

The railroad element breathed easier now. Tim Murphy wanted to bet on the new man against anyone, at any style, and he glowed with pride as he realized that he, perhaps, was nearer to Tex Jones than any man in town. He had no trouble in persuading Costigan to look with warm favor on the successor to Bud Haines. Jerry Saunders, remembering a bit of gun practice, said he was not surprised and he exulted secretly. Tex Jones had been the first man outside of the railroad circle to give him a kind word and to show friendship; but he had little to say about it after the door of his home closed upon him.

Jerry's sister puzzled him. He saw traces of tears, strange moods came over her which swept her from gaiety to black despondency in the course of an hour or two, and no matter how he figured, he could not understand her. The story of how the affair had started and of Tommy Watkins' part in it made her moods more complex and unfathomable. Jane, he decided, was not only peculiar, but downright foolish. Bud Haines, being but a free member of Williams' own body, executing his wishes and the wishes of the detestable nephew, had been an evil whose potentiality could only be conjectured. He had been swept off the board and his conqueror was at heart very friendly to the Saunders family. They no longer were the most helpless people in town.

When Jerry had gone home on the day of the tragedy he had been full of the exploit, for Murphy and he had discussed it from every angle, and he had absorbed a great deal of the big Irishman's open delight.

Stunned at first, Jane flatly refused to talk about it, and had fled from the supper table to her room. Later on when he had cautiously broached the subject again, quoting the enthusiastic Murphy almost entirely, to show that his own opinions were well founded, she had listened to all he had to say, but had remained dumb. The evening was anything but pleasant and he had gone to bed in an unconcealed huff. She gave credit to Watkins but withheld it from Jones, who had earned it all. "D--n women, anyhow," had been his summing up.

The following morning he ate a silent breakfast and hurried to the station as he would flee to an oasis from the open desert. He found Tim waiting for him, eager to talk it all over again.

Hardly had the station been opened when Tex rode up, leaped from the magnificent roan, and sauntered to the door. His face was grave, his manner dignified and calm. "How'd'y, boys," he said in greeting.

"Proud I am this mornin'," beamed Murphy, his thick, huge hand closing over the lean, sinewy one of the gunman. "'Twas a fine job ye done, Tex, my boy; an' a fine way ye did it! Gave th' beast th' first shot! There's not another man could do it."

"There's plenty could," answered Tex. "I can name two, an' there's many more. I'm no gunman, understand: I'm just plain Tex Jones. But I didn't come here to hold any pow-pow- -I'm wonderin' if you'd let me look in th' toolhouse--I might 'a' left it there when we loaded th' hand car."

"An' what's 'it'?" asked Murphy.

"My knife."

"Come along then," said the section-boss, swinging his keys and leading the way. They found no knife, but Murphy was given some information which he considered worth while. As they reached the station door again Tex burst out laughing.

"I know where it is! Cuss me for a fool, I left it in Carney's stable, stickin' in th' side of th' harness closet. Oh, well; there's no harm done." He turned to Jerry. "I wonder if Miss Saunders would like another bit of practice today?"

Jerry's face clouded. No matter how much he might admire Bud Haines' master in the late Bud's profession of gun-throwing, and no matter how much he might admire him for sundry other matters, nevertheless none of them qualified the new-found friend as an aspirant for his sister's hand. He did not wish to offend Tex, and certainly he did not want his enmity. To him came Jane's inexplicable behavior and in coming it brought an inspiration. Jane, he thought, could handle this matter far better than he could.

"She didn't seem to be feeling well this morning," he answered. "Still, I never guess right about her. If you feel like riding again, go up and ask her."

"I hear there's some talk about them makin' you marshal of this town," said Tim. "Don't you shelve it. This town needs a fair man in that job. It's been quiet of late, but ye can't allus tell. Wait till th' rains come an' start th' placerin' a-goin'. They'll have money to spend, then, an' trouble is shore to follow that. You take that job, Tex."

Jerry nodded eagerly, pointed to some bullet holes in the frame of one of the windows of the office and, grasping Tex by the arm, led him closer to the window. "See that bullet hole in there, just over the table an' below the calendar? The first shot startled me and made me drop my pen--I stooped to pick it up. When I sat up again there was a hole in the glass and under the calendar. When I stooped I saved my life. Just a drunken joke, a miner feeling his oats. One dead man a week was under the average. This town, under normal conditions, is a little bit out of h--l. Take that job, Jones: the town needs you."

Tex laughed. "You better wait till it's offered to me, Jerry. There's quite some people in this town that don't want any marshal. Gus Williams is the man to start it."

"He will," declared Tim. "Bud was his bodyguard, but he was more. Williams has a lot of property to be protected, an' now Bud is gone, th' saints be praised. He'll start it."

While they spoke, a miner was seen striding toward the station and soon joined them. "How'd'y," he said, carelessly, glancing coldly at Tim and Jerry. His eyes rested on Tex and glowed a little. "Th' boss wants to talk with you, Jones. Come a-runnin'."

"Come a-runnin'," rang in Tex's ears and it did not please him. If he was going to be the city marshal it would be well to start off right.

"Th' boss?" he asked nonplused.

"Shore; Gus--Gus Williams," rejoined the messenger crisply and with a little irritation. "You know who I mean. Git a move on."

"Mr. Jones' compliments to Mr. Williams," replied Tex with exaggerated formality, "an' say that Mr. Jones will call on him at Mr. Jones' convenience. Just at present I'm very busy--good day to you, sir."

The miner stood stock-still while he reviewed the surprising words.

Tex ignored him. "No," he said, "I ain't lookin' for no change in th' weather till th' moon changes," he explained to the two railroad men. "But, of course, you know th' old sayin': 'In times of drought all signs fail.' An' there never was a truer one. I wouldn't be surprised if it rained any day; an' when it comes it's goin' to rain hard. Still, I ain't exactly lookin' for it, barrin' the sayin', till th' moon changes. That's my prophecy, gents; you wait an' see if I ain't right. Well, I reckon I'll be amblin'. Good day."

They watched him walk to the roan, throw the reins over an arm, and lead it slowly down the street, followed by the conjecturing messenger. Tex Jones evidently was in no hurry, for he stopped in two places before entering the hotel, and in there he remained for a quarter of an hour. When premature congratulations were offered him he accepted them with becoming modesty and explained that he was not yet appointed.

Gus Williams looked up with some irritation when the door opened and admitted Tex into the store. The newcomer leaned against the counter, nodded to Gus and grinned at Henry. "Hear you want to see me about somethin'," he said, flickering dust from his boots with a softly snapping handkerchief.

"What made you shoot Bud Haines?" growled the proprietor, turning on the stepladder against the shelves.

Tex shook his head in befitting sorrow. "I shore didn't want to shoot Bud," he answered slowly. "Bud hadn't never done nothin' to me; but," he explained, wearily, "he just made me do it. I dassn't let him shoot twice, dast I?"

Williams growled something and replaced several articles of merchandise.

"Hennery says you had to do it," he grudgingly admitted. "I reckon mebby you did-- *but* , I don't see why you went at Bud like that, in th' first place."

"I aimed to stop a killin'," muttered Tex, contritely; "an', instead of doin' it, I went an' made one. I ain't none surprised," he said, sighing resignedly, "for I generally play in bad luck. Ever since I shot that black cat, up at Laramie, I've had bad luck--not that I'm what you might call superstitious," he quickly and defiantly explained.

"Well, a man can't allus help things like that," admitted Williams. "I had streaks of luck that looked like they never would peter out." He shifted several articles, leaned back to study their arrangement, and slowly continued. "You see, Bud had a job that ain't very common; an' men like Bud ain't very common, neither. He allus was plumb grateful because I saved his life once in a--stampede," he naively finished. "I got a lot of valuable property in this here town, and Windsor gets quite lively when th' placerin' is going good. I shore feel sort of lost without Bud." He wiped his dusty hands on his trousers and slowly climbed down. "Now, I remembered that Scrub Oak an' Willow both has peace officers, an' Windsor shore ain't taking a back seat from towns like them. Hennery was sayin' that folks here sort of been talkin' about a city marshal, an' mentionin' you for th' office. We ought to have our valuable property pertected, an' me, bein' the owner of most of th' valuable property here an' hereabouts, nat'rally leans to that idea; but, bein' th' biggest owner of valuable property, I sort of got to look the man over purty well before I appoint him. I got to have a good man, a man that'll pertect th' most property first. What you think about it?"

Tex removed his sombrero, turned it over slowly in his hands and stared at its dents. Punching them out and pushing in new ones, he gravely considered them. "Well," he drawled, "you see, if that letter comes--I don't know how long I'm goin' to stay in town; but if I did stay, I'd shore do my damndest to pertect property, an' you havin' the most of it, you'd nat'rally be pertected more'n others that had less."

Williams glanced swiftly at his nephew. "You still expectin' that letter, Jones?" he slyly demanded.

Tex hesitated and turned the hat over again. "Can't hardly say I am," he admitted, frowning at Henry. "But there's a sayin' that hope springs infernal--an' I reckon that's th' h--l of it; a man never knows when to quit waitin' for it to spring. Meanwhile I got to eat--an' I like a game of poker once in awhile. Here, tell you what--I'll take the job as long as I can hold it, if the pay is right. What you reckon the job's worth, in a lawless, desperate town like this, where no man's life or property is worth very much?"

Williams scowled. "This here town ain't lawless an' desperate," he denied. "There ain't a more peaceable town in Kansas!"

"Which same ain't payin' no compliments to Kansas towns, once the rains come," chuckled Tex. "I'm admirin' your humor, Mr. Williams--I ain't never heard dryer," he beamed in frank admiration. "But, wet or dry, there's allus them mean low-down cow-wrastlers comin' to town to likker up--an' them an' miners are as friendly as a badger and a dog. Let's name over them as would want the pertection of a marshal, an' then figger how much they'd sweeten the pot. Take Carney, now--he ought to be willin' to ante up han'some, his business bein' so healthy."

"Carney," sneered Williams in open contempt. "Huh! Here, gimme that pencil an' that old envelope!" He worked laboriously, revised the figures several times and then looked up. "I reckon two hundred a month ought to be enough. Scrub Oak pays that--Willow does likewise. You got your outfit. We furnish th' office, ammernition, an' pay extra expenses. That's th' best Windsor can do. Yore office will be next door to this store."

Tex looked questioningly at Henry, who nodded decisively, and carefully put the hat back on his head. "All right," he said. "When do I start in?"

"Right now," answered Williams, fumbling under the counter. "We ain't got no marshal's badge, but I got a sheriff's star somewhere around. He was killed up on Buffaler Crick last spring. Yep--here it is: this'll do for awhile. Lean over here, Marshal," he chuckled. "There: It ain't every marshal that's a sheriff, too." Smiling at Henry he said, jokingly, "Now let her rain!"

Tex nodded. "Let it come," he said. "Everybody that deserves it will have a slicker ag'in' th' rain. As marshal I'm playin' no favorites--there's no strings to a city marshal. My job's to keep th' peace of Windsor, an' let th' devil whistle." He smiled enigmatically, hitched up his belt, and then looked at Henry. "You know where Bud's belt an' gun are?"

Henry nodded. "Baldy's got 'em, behind th' bar. Want 'em?"

"Yes," answered Tex, slowly turning. "When it starts rainin', two guns will keep me on an even keel. My left hand feels empty-like. Reckon I'll go git Bud's outfit an' have th' harness-maker turn th' holster so it'll set right for th' left side; or mebby he's got a cavalry sheath, which won't need so much changin'."

"But you ought to have a rifle heavier than a .38 short," suggested Gus Williams. "That ain't no gun for this country."

Tex smiled. "For town use that's plenty heavy enough. But we won't argue about that because I ain't got it no more. I swapped with that section-boss, paying him fifteen dollars to-boot. To a thick Mick like him there ain't much difference between a .38 short and a .45-90. He can't use either one worth a cuss, anyhow. I'd say I was lucky stumblin' on him." He turned and walked toward the door, glanced up at the cloudless sky, and chuckled. "No signs of rain, yet. Oh, well; it'll come when it gets here. *Adios* ," and the slow steps of the walking roan grew softer down the street.

The harness-maker looked from the belt and holster to an up-ended box and waved at the latter. "Set down, Mr. Jones. 'Twon't take a minute, but you might as well set. Many a one I've turned. A new cut here, a new strap, an' a scallop out of th' top on th' other side so yore fingers'll close on th' butt first thing. Let's see th' other. Yep; deep cut down to th' guard. Now, if I put it back on th' belt at th' same place, it'll throw th' buckle around back--all right, then. They won't match each other, but that don't make no difference, I reckon. Ain't there been some talk of appointin' you city marshal?"

Tex nodded. "This star was th' only one they had," he explained.

"Well, you may be workin' both jobs afore long if Gus Williams has th' say-so," commented the harness-maker. "Funny, but I never work on a gun sheath but I think of th' one I made to order for Jack Slade after he got around ag'in from Old Jules' shotgun. Jack blamed it on his holster, an' it shore made him particular. That was back in Old Julesburg when I was a harness-apprentice there. Soon after that he was sent up to take charge of th' Rocky Ridge division of th' stage line, which was th' worst division of th' whole line. Holdups was a reg'lar thing. They soon stopped after he took charge. He was th' best man with a short gun I ever saw. I heard that he wore that holster to th' day th' vigilantes got him, up in Virginia City, Montanny. Now, Mr. Marshal, strap this on you an' see if th' gun comes out right. Sometimes they got to be shaped a little mite--ah, that looks all right. Reckon it'll do?"

With the newly acquired belt hanging over the old one, sloping loosely from the right hip across his body to a point below the left, the marshal went out, mounted the roan, and rode carelessly down to the toolshed, where he told Murphy of his appointment and of the fictitious swapping of rifles, and then went up to the station. As he neared it Jerry came out of the door, caught the flash of the sun on the nickel-plated star and turned, grinning, to await the coming of the new marshal.

"That looks mighty good to the station agent," Jerry laughed. "An' so you're wearin two guns instead of one? Gosh, that looks business-like!"

Tex reined in and grinned down at him. "Any time you feel urged to shoot up th' town, Mr. Agent, you'll find out that it is business-like. Better start by gettin' th' marshal first: it'll be a lot safer, that way."

"That's good advice, and I won't forget it," replied Jerry. "I'll notify the company of your appointment. That ought to make it feel good, and it might want to pay its share of your salary. I'm certainly wishing you luck."

"I may be needin' it," responded the marshal. "Reckon I'll go on to th' house an' show off my new bright an' shinin' star." He glanced down at the badge and grinned. "Seein' how you reads 'Sheriff' instead of 'Marshal' she'll mebby wonder what you are. So-long, Jerry!"

Reaching the little house, Tex swung gravely off Omar and proceeded to the door in mock dignity. Knocking heavily, he assumed a stern demeanor and waited. When the door opened he removed his sombrero, bowed, and grinned. "Behold the Law, Miss Saunders, in the person of the marshal of Windsor."

"I congratulate you, Marshal," she coldly replied. "Doubtless you may now take life with legal authority. It is too bad it comes a little late."

"I did not need legal authority, Miss Saunders, if I rightly interpret your remark," he rejoined. "The authority of Nature ever precedes and transcends it. Self-preservation is the first law. He fired, and I did not dare let him fire again."

"You provoked his attack!" she flashed. "He could do nothing else."

"That was because I preferred to risk his life than the certainty of him taking that of Tommy Watkins, who was being deliberately baited. Bud lost his rights when he drew his gun against an unsuspecting man. I am sorry if you look upon the unfortunate incident in any other light; but I am so sure of my position that I would repeat it today under the same conditions. Besides I am naturally prejudiced against assassins."

"Why did you give him his gun before he had time to master his anger?" she demanded, her eyes flashing.

"Because I wanted to show him how impersonal my interference was, and to help smooth over a tense situation. It was one of those high-tension moments when a false move might easily precipitate a shambles. There were a dozen armed men in the room, a ratio of ten to two. I followed my best judgment. I am not apologizing, Miss Saunders, even to you; I am merely explaining the situation as it existed. When Bud Haines drew his gun from the side to shoot a man who did not know of his danger, he broke our rules. I would have been justified in shooting him down at the move. Instead I tried to stop his shot and give him a way out of it." While he spoke his right hand had risen to his belt and now hung there by a crooked thumb, a position he was in the habit of assuming when he spoke earnestly.

She glanced down at it involuntarily, shuddered, and slowly closed the door.

"I am very sorry, Mr. Jones, but--" the closing of the door ended the conversation for both.

He studied the warped, weather-beaten panel and the white, china knob for a full minute, and then slowly replaced his hat and slowly walked back to his horse. Patting the silky neck he shook his head. "Omar, it's been comin' to me for twenty years--but it might have waited till I really deserved it. Come on--we'll go back to th' herd, where we belong."

Thoughtfully he rode away, his face older and sterner, its lines seemingly a little deeper.

Chapter XII
Closer Friendships

In the selection of the marshal's office Williams was overruled and rather than make a contest of it, since he could not deny the economy in using a building already erected, and knowing that his store was nearly as well protected, he gave his slow assent to Carney's offer; and soon the lean-to was cleared out, a table, some chairs, and a rough bunk put in it, the latter at the marshal's insistence. Over the door were two words, newly painted: CITY MARSHAL. The question of a jail came next, and was quickly solved by the addition to the lean-to of a room constructed of two-inch planks, walls, floor, and roof. Two pairs of new, shining handcuffs and a new badge, appropriately labeled, completed the civic improvements in the way of law and order. All prisoners guilty of major offenses were to be taken down to Willow and there tried; while minor offenders could sit in the jail until a suitable time had elapsed.

From his chair in the door of his office, Tex could keep watch of nearly all of the main street, and the trail leading in from the C Bar for half a mile. The end of his first week as peace officer found him in his favorite place, contentedly puffing on his pipe, despite the heat of the day. A few miners straggled past, grinning and exchanging shafts of heavy wit with the smiling officer. Blascom drifted into town a little later, learned of the appointment, and hurried down from the hotel to congratulate his new friend.

Tex reached behind him and pulled a chair outside the door. "Sit down, Blascom," he invited. "How's th' sump comin' along?"

Blascom glanced around before replying. "I'm sorry you ain't sheriff, as well," he replied. "I reckon I'm out of bounds, out there on Buffalo, an' I'm shore to be rushed if I'm figgerin' right on that crick. Anybody in th' new jail?"

"Not yet," smiled Tex. "Talk low an' nobody'll hear you. Strike somethin'?"

"I'll gamble on it. I'm so shore of it, I'm filin' a new claim: th' old one didn't quite cover it. You know where th' sump's located, of course; an' you remember how rapid it filled up with water every time I tried to bail it out?"

Tex nodded and waved carelessly at the C Bar trail as though discussing something far from placering. "Send th' location papers off through Jerry Saunders--tell him they're from me. Ever follow a trail herd day after day?" he asked.

"No; why?"

"Ever do anythin', out here, except minin'?"

"Shore; why?"

"What was it?"

"Freightin' from Atchison to Denver an' back: why?"

"Then yo're tellin' me about it now," prompted Tex, handing him a cleaning rod. "Trace th' old trail in th' sand an' keep referrin' to it while you talk. You don't know me good enough to talk long an' steady an' earnest. Here, gimme that rod--" and the marshal took it and drew a line. "This end is Atchison--from there you went up th' Little Blue, like this. Then, crossin' that divide south of th' Platte, you rolled down to that river near Hook's Station, an' follered it past Ft. Kearney, Plumb Crick, an' O'Fallon's Bluffs, an' so on. Here's Hook's Station, th' Fort, Plumb Crick, an' O'Fallon's--now you go on with it."

Blascom took the rod and finished the great curve. "As I was sayin', th' water in that sump kept me guessin'. I couldn't figger where it all come from. I had tried for sumps nearer to th' shack, of course, but got nothin'. Then I found water a-plenty when I dug *this* one." He jabbed at Ft. Kearney and waved his other arm. "I kept gettin' curiouser all th' time, an' yesterday, when th' idea hit me all of a sudden, I went back down th' crick bed twenty paces an' started diggin'. No water; an' yet, sixty feet up stream was more'n I could handle. I just sat down an' wrastled it out."

Tex leaned over and drew another line, one starting on the great curve. "Th' Salt Lake branch run up here, didn't it, Blascom? Th' ones th' troops used, near Old Julesburg, goin' out to lick th' Mormons?"

"How'd you come to know so much about that old trail?" demanded the miner. "It shore did--an' it was a bad section for stages. Well, I cut me a pinted stick an' after it got dark I went out an' jabbed it inter th' crick bed between th' wet sump an' th' last one I put down. About five feet below th' wet one I hit rock, not more'n six inches under th' sand, an' it sloped sharp, both ways, I'm tellin' you. Sort of a sharp hog-back, it is. Humans are blasted fools, Marshal: we can set right on top of a thing that's fair yellin' to be seen, an' not know it's there till somethin' knocks it inter our fool heads. Do you know what I got up there at that sump?"

Tex shook his head and grabbed the stick, a trace of vexation on his face. "You got it all wrong, Blascom," he declared loudly, drawing another line. "Th' old, original Oregon Trail never went up th' Rocky Ridge a-tall. It followed th' North Fork of th' Platte, all th' way to Ft. Laramie. It crossed th' river at Forty Islands, about twelve miles south of th' Fort. I crossed it there with a herd, myself. If you don't believe me, ask Hawkins--he was apprenticed to th' harness-maker at Old Julesburg, on th' South Fork."

"I got you there," laughed Blascom. "Th' Oregon Trail didn't cross at Forty Islands; but a lot of trail herds did. There was a waggin ferry at th' Fort that th' chuck waggins often used."

"It crossed either at Forty Islands or between 'em an' th' Fort," asserted Tex.

"Well, mebby yo're right, Marshal," admitted Blascom. He took the rod again. "That sump of mine is located in a rocky basin that's full of sand. Th' downstream side is that hog-back. That means that there's a thunderin' big, natural riffle in th' bed of th' crick, an' it's stopped and held th' sand till th' basin was full. Every freshet that comes along riles that sand up, lots of it bein' washed over th' riffle, an' carried along. More sand settles there as th' water quits rushin'; but here's th' pint." He jabbed at Denver and drew a line into the Gilpin County country, stopping at Central City. "Gold is heavy, an' it don't wash over riffles if it can settle down in front of 'em. While th' sand is soft from bein' disturbed by a strong current, it can settle. Ever since that crick has been a crick, gold has been settlin' in front of that riffle, droppin' down through th' sand till it hit th' rock bottom. Great Jehovah, Marshal--can you figger what I got?"

Tex roughly took the cleaning rod, traced a line in sudden vexation, slammed the rod on the floor behind him, and fanned his face with his hat.

"An' how long you been settin' on that?" he asked in weary hopelessness.

Blascom waved his arms and slumped back against the chair. "Three years," he confessed, and went off into a profane description of his intelligence that left nothing to imagination.

Tex laughed heartily. "If you was as bad as you just said I'd shore have to take you in. Cheer up, man: it's there, ain't it? You only have to git it out."

Blascom looked at him reproachfully. "Shore: that's all," he retorted with sarcasm. "Git it out before th' rain starts again, an' do it without Jake catchin' me at it! If he learns what I got, I'm in for no sweet dreams; an' if this starvin' bunch of gold hunters learn about it, I'll be swamped in th' rush! Good Lord, man! It'll take me a week to git th' water out, an' then there's th' sand!"

Tex stretched, caught sight of a rider bobbing along the C Bar trail and looked reflectively at Williams' Mecca. "You got to get some dynamite or blastin' powder. Dynamite's better. Put some sticks on th' down-stream side of that rock riffle an' wait till Jake comes into town. You crack that riffle open an' th' water will move out for you. Then you can dig down th' other face of it an' get to th' pocket a lot quicker." He laughed suddenly. "Do that blastin'. Then when Jake gets back to his shack, saunter over with a jug of whiskey an' forget to take it home with you. That'll give you a solid week for yore diggin' without him botherin' you."

"Good idea," said Blascom, arising. "I'll go over an' see if Williams has got any sticks. That's th' way to handle it, Marshal. You ever do any prospectin'?"

Tex pushed him back again. "No, I ain't; but I've been doin' a lot of thinkin' these days. Sit still. What does a miner want explosives for? To get gold, of course. Bein' a placer worker don't make no difference: th' connection is there, just th' same. It'll only make 'em that much more curious. You go buyin' any dynamite an' th' parade will start for yore place before night. I'd get it for you, only me not havin' no reason to buy th' stuff, it would be near as big a mistake as you buyin' it. *I* ain't got no call to want any dynamite. Sit still: you ain't in no hurry!" He leaned over and put his finger on the map in the sand. "They hit Ft. Hall about here," he explained. "We got to get somebody that ain't connected with you, gold diggin', or Buffalo Crick, that won't make no troublesome connections. They usually left their waggins at Ft. Hall an' went up this way. If this feller comin' down th' trail is young Watkins, an' I'm sayin' he is, we got th' way. I reckon he can buy dynamite for th' ranch. That'll be all right, but suppose somebody else from that outfit comes ridin' in an' gets pumped dry? Lean back, stick yore feet on th' Overland, an' don't look so cussed tense. Here: I got it! Th' railroad uses dynamite! I shore got it, Blascom. Tim Murphy can buy it as innocent as you can buy chewin' tobacco!"

"But I don't know him well enough!" expostulated Blascom. "Anyhow, what excuse can I give him?"

"None at all," said Tex. "Wait till yore feet are in th' stirrups before you spur a hoss! You don't have to know him. *I* know him, an' that's a-plenty. Here, you listen close to every word I say, an' act careless-like while yo're doin' it." The explicit directions were rich in details, but Blascom soaked them into his memory like water in a sponge. "Th' whole thing is gettin' to him nat'ral, an' then gettin' th' stuff from him afterward," Tex wound up. Thoughtful for a moment, he nodded in sudden decision. "Got it ag'in! It's near train time. You, bein' restless an' lonesome, hanker to watch it come in. Th' Lord knows nobody in towns like this ever needs any excuse to see a train come in. That's one of th' idle man's inalienable rights--an' it seldom weakens. An' now I know how yo're goin' to git it from him afterwards: you listen ag'in," and further directions came in rapid-fire order.

The rider was near enough now to dispel all doubts as to his identity. Blascom arose, gripped the marshal's hand and faced the Mecca.

"I'm goin' over to git a jug: much obliged, Marshal." He crossed the street diagonally and disappeared in the store.

The rider came nearer and nearer, a great dust cloud rolling behind him not much unlike the smoke of a moving locomotive. When even with Carney's he drew rein suddenly and in another moment had dismounted in front of the lazy Tex.

"I'll be cussed!" he exclaimed, staring from Tex to the sign over the door and then back at the new peace officer, cocking his head as he read the badge.

"Good for you!" he cried. "It's about time this dog's town had a white man to run it; an' they couldn't 'a' picked a better, neither!" His enthusiasm ebbed a little and he looked curiously and thoughtfully into the marshal's eyes. "How'd you come to get th' job?" he demanded.

Tex stuck his thumbs in the armholes of his vest and grinned. He knew the thought that had sobered his companion's face. "Pop'lar clamor, Thomas; 'an' all that sort of a thing,' as Whitby used to say. My great popularity an' my pleasin' nature an' disposition, not to mention my good looks an' winnin' ways, seem to have turned th' balance in my favor. But, outside of that I don't know why I got it. Carney thought I'd mebby bring him more trade; Williams mourned th' lack of anybody to give him adequate police protection, an' th' harness-maker mentions Jack Slade. He admires Jack Slade, an' says I remind him of that person by th' way I let him fix up my left-hand holster. That suits me because Slade was lynched."

"Then Williams really made th' play stick?" Tommy asked with poorly concealed suspicion.

"Williams pinned on my nickel-plated authority," said Tex. "Nobody else had one. He reckons I'm wearin' his colors; but, my Christian friend, th' only colors th' new marshal wears are his own. I'm to keep order in 'this dog's town,' as you put it, an' I'm goin' to do it. Miners, railroaders, storekeepers, cattlemen, an' ornery punchers please listen an' be enlightened. Th' badge is only a nickel-plate affair; but there ain't no nickel, nor rust, neither, on my Cyclopean twins. They're my real authority. Now, then, don't walk all over Blascom's Overland Trail, but set down in th' chair he just vacated. Tell me all about yoreself."

"Marshal," began Tommy in some embarrassment, "I didn't get th' hang of that little mix-up in th' hotel till I got quite some distance out of town. My head was whirlin' a little, an' I'm nat'rally stupid, anyhow. I just want to say that yo're wrong about them Colts bein' some kind of twins. Mebby they are durin' these peaceful days; but if things get crowded they'll turn into triplets, th' missin' brother bein' right here on my laig. Besides that, you got a craggy lot of deputies out on th' C Bar any time you need 'em. Don't stop me while I'm runnin' free! I'm sayin' I never saw a squarer, cleaner piece of shootin' than you showed us all in th' hotel th' other day. An'--you keep off th' trail while I'm comin' strong!--an' I've been somethin' of a fool about us an' that little lady. From now on I'm afoot where she's concerned, an' you know what us punchers amount to, afoot."

"I'm glad you said you was stupid," replied Tex. "It saves me from sayin' it, an' comin' from me it might sound sorta official." He glanced up the street and back to his companion. "Yo're not afoot, cowboy; yo're ridin' strong. I'm th' one that's afoot, an' I'll agree with you about a cowpunch amountin' to nothin' off his cayuse. Did you ever have a door slammed plumb in yore face, Tommy?"

Tommy wiped out Denver, Central City, Old Julesburg, and Ft. Kearney with one swing of his foot. "You--I--you *mean* that?"

The marshal nodded. "Every word of it. Outlawed steers should keep to th' draws an' brakes, Tommy. Besides, I'm over forty-five years old, an' I never was any parson. Keep right on ridin', Adolescence; an' I'm hopin' it's a plain, fair trail. Tommy, did you ever shoot a man?"

"Not yet I ain't; but I've come cussed near it. Seein' what's goin' on in this town, I has hopes."

"Don't yield to no temptations, Tommy; an' let yore hopes die," warned the marshal. "If there's any of that to be done, I'll do it. I reckon you'll shore have a easy trail."

"I--will--be--tee-totally--d--d!" said Tommy. He shook his head and leaned back against the front of the office. "Does she know all about it?"

"Everythin'; I owed myself that much," answered Tex, and then he helped to maintain a reflective, introspective, and emotional silence.

Blascom emerged from the Mecca with a two-gallon jug, empty from the way it jerked and swung. He looked at the silent pair leaning against the marshal's office, abruptly made up his mind, and strode over to them.

"You shore look sorrerful," he said.

"We've just been to a funeral," said Tex. "Th' corpse looked nat'ral, too."

"Sufferin' wildcats!" ejaculated Tommy in pretended dismay, his chair dropping to all fours. "Whiskey by th' jug! I'm plain shocked, but mighty glad to see you, Mr. Blascom." He turned to the marshal. "Here, Officer! Shake han's with Mr. Blascom, of Buffaler Crick. Give th' gentleman a cordial welcome."

Tex regarded the newcomer and his jug with languid interest. "Huh! I reckoned th' drought would shore end some day, but I figgered on rain. However, facts are facts. Pleased to meet you, sir!" He waved at Tommy. "Pass it to our friend first. It's dry work, settin' here, listenin' to me."

"It's like workin' in pay-dirt," retorted Blascom. He tapped the jug and it rang out hollowly. "I ain't give Baldy a chance at it, yet. Anyhow, a man's got to have some protection ag'in' snakes," he defended.

"A protection ag'in' snakes!" repeated Tex, thoughtfully. "Yes; he has."

"I'll pertect you ag'in' 'em as far as th' hotel," offered Tommy, arising and whistling to his horse, "seein' as yo're temporary defenseless. Come on, Blascom. See you later, Marshal," and he grabbed at the jug, missed it, and led the way, Tex smiling after the grinning pair.

Tommy's stride was swift and long for a puncher, due to his agitated frame of mind, and he suddenly slowed it to make an observation to his companion.

"Blascom, th' new marshal is shore quick on th' gun--this town ought to be right proud of him. I'm admittin' that he's a reg'lar he-man."

"He's a cussed sight quicker with his head," replied the miner, "an' that's shore sayin' a large an' bounteous plenty. If he don't play no favorites he's shore as h--l goin' to need friends, one of these days. I'm admittin' myself to that cat-e-gory: but it'll be my hard luck to be out on th' Buffaler when it starts."

Tommy nodded and spat emphatically. "I'll be a cat, an' gory, too," he affirmed. "Wild as a wildcat, an' gory as all h--l. That's me!" He glanced up quickly. "Talkin' ceases, for here we are." He tossed the reins over his pony's head and followed his companion into the hotel, where half a dozen men lounged dispiritedly.

Baldy grinned and lost no time in filling the jug, his efforts creating pleasant, anticipatory smackings among the dry onlookers, who from their previous unobserving weariness suddenly snapped into Argus-eyed interest. The alluring gurgle of the wicker-covered demijohn, the *slap-slap, plop-plop* of the leaping, amber stream, ebbing and flooding spasmodically up and down and around the greenish copper funnel, truly was liquid music to their ears, and the powerful odor of the rye diffused itself throughout the room, penetrated the stale tobacco smoke, and wrought positive reactions upon the olfactory nerves of the staring audience. It was scarce enough by the glass, these days, yet here was a reckless Croesus who was buying it by the gallon!

Blascom, smiling with quiet reserve, leaned against the bar to the right of the jug; Tommy, grave and forbidding, leaned against the bar to the left of the jug, both making short and humorous replies to the gift-compelling remarks of the erect crowd. The jug at last filled, Blascom pushed the cork in and slammed it home with a quick, disconcertingly forbidding gesture, which was as cruel as it was final. He paid for the liquor with one of the bills he had won from Tex, nodded briskly, and went out, Tommy bringing up the rear.

Reproachful, accusing eyes followed their exit, hoping against hope. A lounger nearest the bar, thirsty as Tantalus, shook his head in sorrowful condemnation.

"A man can be mean an' pe-nurious up to a certain, limit," he observed; "but past that it's plumb shameful."

An old man, his greasy, gray beard streaked with tobacco stains, nodded emphatically. "There *is* limits; an' I say that stoppin' before ye begin is shore beyond 'em!"

"Yo're dead right," spoke up a one-eyed tramp who honored himself with the title of prospector. "As for me, I never *did* think much of any man as guzzles it secret. Show me th' man that swizzles in public, an *I'll* show you a man as can be trusted. Two whole gallons of it! A whole, bloomin' jugful, at onct! Where'd he git all that money? I'm askin' you, *where'd* he git it? On Buffaler Crick?" His voice rose and cracked with avarice and suspicion.

"Naw!" growled the man in the far corner, slumping back against his chair. "He won it from that Tex Jones feller--th' new marshal--two hundred or more-- playin' poker. Th' same Tex Jones as shot Bud Haines. There ain't more'n day wages on Buffaler Crick. I know, 'cause I been lookin' around out there, quiet-like." He stiffened suddenly and sat up, excitement transforming him. "Boys, this here marshal has got money--I saw his wad when he an' Blascom was a-playin'."

"Yo're shore welcome to it," pessimistically rejoined the man nearest the bar, his vivid imagination picturing the amazing death of Bud Haines. "Yes, sir; yo're welcome to *all* of it. I don't want none, a-tall!"

The discoverer of the marshal's roll regarded the objector with deep scorn.

"That's you!" he retorted. "Allus goin' off half-cocked, an' yowlin' calamity! This here marshal likes poker, don't he? An' he can't play it, can he? Didn't Blascom clean him? He's scared to bluff, or call one, no matter how brave he is with a gun. Who's got any dust? Dig down deep, an' we'll pool it, lettin' Hank an' Sinful do th' playin' for us. Where's Hennery?" he demanded of the bartender.

Baldy mopped the bar and glanced at the ceiling. "Upstairs, sleepin' off a stem-winder. He got drinkin' to th' mem'ry of th' dead deceased last night--an' his mem'ry is long an' steady. He's too senti-mental, Hennery is, for a man as can't handle his likker good. If you fellers are goin' after th' marshal's pile, I'm recommendin' stud-hoss. He's nat'rally scared of poker, an' stud's so fast he won't have no time to start worryin'. Draw will give him too much time to think. Better try stud-hoss," he reiterated, unwittingly naming the form of poker at which the marshal excelled.

"Stud-hoss she is, then," agreed Sinful, licking his lips. "I like stud-hoss. We'll bait him tonight; an' we'll all have jugs of our own by mornin', since Buffaler Crick's settin' th' style."

The meeting forthwith went into executive session, depleted gold sacks slowly appearing.

Outside, Blascom offered the jug to his companion, who pushed it away, and shook his head in sudden panic.

"Don't want to smell like no saloon where I'm goin'," he hastily explained. "Now that yo're safe from snakes I'll be driftin' to my cayuse."

"All right, Watkins; I'll treat next time," and the miner, jug in hand, strode toward the station as Tommy mounted and wheeled to ride in the direction of the Saunders' home.

Blascom had timed his arrival to a nicety, for Murphy was on his way from the toolshed to the station to await the coming of the train, the smoke from which could be seen on the eastern horizon.

Blascom held up the jug invitingly and grinned. The section-boss came to an abrupt stop, saluted, and stepped on again with the bearing of a well-trained English soldier. "Hah!" he called. "'Tis better from a jug; an' 'twould be better yet if it had a little breath av th' peat fire in it; but 'tis well to be content with what we have. Thank ye: I'll drink yer health!" Handing the jug back to its owner Murphy wiped his lips with the back of his hand and seated himself on the bench at the prospector's side. "Have ye seen th' new marshal?" he asked, glancing from the distant smudge of smoke to his watch. "I hear he's fixed up in style."

"Yes; an' he gave me a message for you, if you'll lean over a little closer," replied Blascom, and, as Murphy obeyed his suggestion, he said what he had come for.

"It sounds like Tex," grunted Murphy. "All thought out careful. Have ye ever used stick explosive? It's treacherous stuff at any time above freezin', an' more so after this spell av hot weather. Ye have? Then there's no use av me tellin' ye to handle it gintly. If I was knowin' th' job ye have, I might help ye in th' number av sticks. But if yo're used to it, ye'll know. I'll get it after Number Three pulls out; an' after dark tonight ye'll find it where he said--but deal gintly with it, Mr. Blascom. I've seen it exploded by impact--it was a rifle ball fired into it--this kind av weather. Ye might even do better to load th' shots, this kind av weather, after th' sun goes down. Carry it as ye find it, without unpackin' th' box."

Blascom nodded. "If I leave th' jug for you to put away when you go down for th' box, would you mind puttin' it out tonight with th' dynamite? No use of me makin' two trips to my cabin, an' I don't want to tote it around till dark."

"I will that, an' be glad to. There she comes now, leavin' Whiterock Cut. Casey's late ag'in; but that's regular, an' not his fault, as I've told them time an' time ag'in. Th' grades are ag'in' him comin' west, an' with his leaky packin's an' worn cylinders it's a wonder he does as well as he has. 'Economy,' says th' super. 'No money for repairs that are not needed on this jerk-water line.' I wonder does he ever figger th' fuel wasted through them steam leaks? An' poor Casey gets th' blame--though divvil a bit he cares."

Number Three wheezed in, panted a moment, and coughed on again. Murphy took a package consigned to him, picked up the jug and went down the track toward the toolshed, Blascom wandering idly over to the Railroad Saloon to pass some of the time he had on his hands. In a little while the big Irishman, a small wooden box under his arm, sauntered carelessly down the street, nodded politely from a distance to the sleepy marshal and went into the Mecca.

"Good day, Mr. Williams," he said with stiff formality. "I'll be havin' six dynamite sticks if ye have them, with th' same number av three-minute fuses. Handle it gintly, if ye don't mind. Th' weather is aggravatin' to th' stuff, an' it's timpermental enough at best."

Williams glowered at him. "Don't you worry about me handlin' it gentle, because I ain't goin' to handle it at all. If you want any I'll give you th' key to th' powder-house an' wish you good luck. Th' sun beatin' down on that house, day after day, has got me plumb nervous. I wish you'd come for it all!" He shook his head. "I wouldn't let you even open th' door if it wasn't for gettin' that much more of it out of th' way."

"Is it ventilated well?" demanded Murphy, smiling a little.

"As well as it can be," sighed Williams. "You'll never catch me carryin' anythin' but powder over th' summer any more. I'm afraid a thunderclap will set it off every storm. What you got in that to pack it in?"

"Sawdust. While yo're cuttin' th' fuses I'll be gettin' th' stuff."

"You'll not come back for any fuses! Wait an' take em' with you! An' when you are through with th' powder-house, throw th' key close to th' back door: I don't want no man with six sticks of dynamite hangin' around this store today. Want a bill?"

Murphy nodded. "Two av them is th' rule av th' company. You can mark 'em paid an' take it out av this."

The receipted bills in his pocket, he threw the fuses over his shoulder, their wickedly shining copper caps carefully wrapped in a handkerchief, took up the bunch of keys and the box, and grinned. "If ye hear an explosion out back, ye needn't come out to gimme any help. I'm cleanin' up some bad cracked rocks hangin' from a cut west av town, over near Buffalo Crick. I'm tellin' ye th' last so ye won't think it's thunderclaps on their disturbin' way to town. But ye'll sleep through it, no doubt, an' never hear th' shot."

"Blastin' at night?" exclaimed Williams in incredulous surprise.

"I don't like th' sun shinin' on th' darlin's while I'm pokin' 'em in th' hot rocks, so I may load her an' shoot her after dark," replied Murphy. "I've a lot av respect for th' stuff, much as I've handled it. Good day, sir," and he left behind him a man who was nervous and jumpy until after the keys had tinkled on the ground near the rear door; indeed, such an impression had been made on him that he mentioned it, with profane criticisms and observations, at the table that night in the hotel.

The marshal moved his chair farther around in the shade and on his tanned face there crept a warm, rare smile. "'Lo, I will stand at thy right hand, and keep the bridge with thee!' Well said, Herminius! Yonder you go in spirit: Tim Murphy, you'd make complete any 'dauntless three'!"

The shadows were growing long when Tommy came into sight again, buried in thought as he rode slowly down the street. He stopped and swung to the ground in front of the lazy marshal.

"They shore do beat th' devil," he growled, throwing himself into the vacant chair and lapsing into silence.

Tex nodded understandingly. "They do," he indolently agreed, a smile flickering across his face. "Black is white an' red is green--they're the worst I've ever seen," he extemporized. "They're intuitive critters, son; an' don't you let anybody tell you that intuition hasn't any warrant for existing. It has. It's got more warrant than reason. It was flowering long before reason poked its first shoot out of the ground. Reason only runs back a few thousand generations, but intuition goes back to the first cell of nervous tissue--I might qualify that a bit and say before nervous tissue was structurally apart from the rest. Reason starts anew in every life, usually upon a little better foundation--often a poorer one. It is nursed and trained and cultivated an' when its possessor dies, it dies with him. Not so our venerable friend, intuition. He, or rather she, is cumulative. She is th' sum of all previous individuals in the life chain of th' last. She picks up an' stores away, growing a little each time--an' while she is vague, an' can be classified as a 'because,' or 'I don't know why,' she operates steady. Don't ask me what I know about it, for it has been a long time since I gave any study to things like this. I might guess an' say that it's th' physical changes in th' thought channels due to experience, or in th' structure of th' brain cells or th' quality of their tissues. Anyway, so far as practicability is concerned, you've summed up th' whole thing: 'They shore do beat th' devil'."

Tommy was looking at him, puzzled and intent; but puzzled intelligently. There is a difference.

"With me an' you, two opposites in thought result in th' cancellation of one of them. We don't say of th' same object: 'This is white, this is black,' at th' same time an' believe 'em both. Th' words themselves are intelligible; but th' conception ain't. We can't do it. One is chosen an' th' other dies. But I won't bet you that a woman cancels. She may not get a dirty white or a slate gray, but she gets a combination, all right. That's where intuition's family tree comes in. No matter how absurd its contentions may be they have force because of th' impetus coming from age. What did she get out th' colors for you?"

"Yo're th' easiest man to talk to that I ever met," said Tommy, wonderingly. "I don't know how you do it. Why, she got a bright red with a dull green cast--said you was justified, 'but a life's a life': an' then she cried!"

Over Tex's face came a light which only can be compared to the rising sun seen from some lofty peak, for in the radiance there were shadows.

Chapter XIII
Outcheating Cheaters

Gus Williams left the supper table, where he had held forth volubly upon the subject of dynamite, in his almost lecture to the other diners, some of whom knew more about it than he did, and walked ponderously toward the poker table for his usual evening's game. Seating himself at the place which by tacit consent had become his own, he idly shuffled and reshuffled the cards and finally began a slow and laborious game of solitaire to while away the time until his cronies should join him. This game had become a fixture of the establishment, played for low stakes but with great seriousness, and often ran into the morning hours.

The rest of the diners tarried inexplicably at the plate-littered table, engaged in a discussion of stud poker and of their respective abilities in playing it, and of winnings they had made and seen made. It slowly but surely grew acrimonious, as any such discussion is prone to among idle men who are very much in each other's company.

The new marshal sat a little apart from the eager disputants, taking no share in the wrangling. Finally Sinful, scorning a shouted ruling on a hypothetical question concerning the law of averages, turned suddenly and appealed to the marshal, whose smiling reply was not a confirmation of the appellant's claim.

Sinful glared at his disappointing umpire. "A lot you know about stud!" he retorted. "Bet you can't even play mumbly-peg!"

"That takes a certain amount of skill," rejoined Tex without heat. "In stud it's how th' cards fall."

Hank laughed sarcastically. "Averages don't count? We'll just start a little game an' I'll show you how easy stud-hoss is. Come on, boys: we'll give th' marshal a lesson. Clear away them dishes."

All but Sinful held back, saying that they had no money for gambling, but they were re-markably eager to watch the game.

Sinful snorted. "Huh! Two-hand is no good. I'm honin' for a little stud-hoss for a change. It's been nothin' but draw in this town. Reckon stud's too lively to suit most folks: takes nerve to ride a fast game. A man can have a-plenty of nerve one way, an' none a-tall another way. Fine bunch of paupers!"

Hank's disgust was as great. "Fine bunch of paupers," he repeated. "An' them as ain't busted is scared. You called th' turn, Sinful: it shore does take nerve--more'n mumbly-peg, anyhow. A three-hand game would move fast-- *too* fast for these coyotes."

"Don't you let th' old mosshead git off with that, Marshal!" cried a miner, "Wish *I* had some dust: I'd cussed soon show 'em!"

Tex was amused by the baiting. Hardly an eye had left him while the whole discussion was going on, even the two principals looking at him when they spoke to each other. He looked from one old reprobate to the other, and let his smile become a laugh as he moved up to the table, a motion which was received by the entire group with sighs of relief and satisfaction.

"I reckon it's my luck ag'in' yore skill," he said; "but I can't set back an' be insulted this way. I'm a public character, now, an' has got to uphold th' dignity of th' law. Get a-goin', you fellers."

Sinful and Hank, simultaneously slamming their gold bags on the table, reached for the cards at the same time and a new wrangle threatened.

"Cut for it," drawled Tex, smiling at the expectant, hopeful faces around the table. Williams' irritable, protesting cough was unheeded and, Hank dealing, the game got under way. Tex honorably could have shot both of his opponents in the first five minutes of play, but simply cheated in turn and held his own. At the end of an hour's excitement he was neither winner nor loser, and he shoved back from the table in simulated disgust. He scorned to take money so tragically needed, and he had determined to lose none of his own.

"This game's so plumb fast," he ironically observed, "that I ain't won or lost a dollar. You got my sportin' blood up, an' I ain't goin' to insult it by playin' all night for nothin'. I told you stud was only luck: That skill you was talkin' about ain't showed a-tall. If there's anybody here as wants a *real* game I'm honin' to hear his voice."

"Can you hear mine?" called Williams, glaring at the disappointed stud players and their friends. "There's a real game right here," he declared, pounding the table, "with real money an' real nerve! Besides, I got a hoss to win back, an' I want my revenge."

Tex turned to the group and laughed, playfully poking Sinful in the ribs. "Hear th' cry of th' lobo? He's lookin' for meat. Our friend Williams has been savin' his money for Tex Jones, an' I ain't got th' heart to refuse it. Bring yore community wealth an' set in, you an' Hank. Though if you can't play draw no better'n you play stud you ought to go home."

"I cut my teeth on draw," boasted Sinful. He turned and slapped his partner on the shoulder. "Come on, Hank!" he cried. "Th' lone wolf is howlin' from th' timber line an' his pelt's worth money. Let's go git it!"

They swept down on the impatient Williams, their silent partners bringing up the rear, and clamored for action. Tex lighting a freshly rolled cigarette, faced the local boss, Hank on his right and Sinful on his left, the eager onlookers settling behind their champions. The thin, worried faces of the miners appealed to the marshal, their obvious need arousing a feeling of pity in him; and then began a game which was as much a credit to Tex as any he ever had played. He rubbed the saliva-soaked end of his cigarette between finger and thumb and gave all his attention to the game.

Williams won on his own deal, cutting down the gold of the two miners. On Hank's deal he won again and the faces of the old prospectors began to tense. Tex dealt in turn and after a few rounds of betting Williams dropped out and the game resolved itself into a simulated fiercely fought duel between the miners, who really cared but little which of them won. Hank finally raked in the stakes. Sinful shuffled and Tex cut. Williams forced the betting but had to drop out, followed by Tex, and the dealer gleefully hauled in his winnings. Again Williams shuffled, his expression vaguely denoting worry. He made a sharp remark about one of the onlookers behind Tex and all eyes turned instinctively. The miner retorted with spirit and Williams suddenly smiled apologetically.

"My mistake, Goldpan," he admitted. "Let's forget it, an' let th' game proceed."

Tex deliberately had allowed his attention to be called from the game and when he picked up his cards he was mildly suspicious, for Williams' remark had been entirely uncalled for. He looked quickly for the nine of clubs or the six of hearts, finding that he had neither. He passed and sat back, smiling at the facial contortions of Hank and the blank immobility of Sinful's leathery countenance. Hank dropped out on the next round and after a little cautious betting Sinful called and threw down his hand. Williams spread his own and smiled. That smile was to cost him heavily, for in his club flush lay the nine spot, guiltless of the tobacco smudge which Tex had rubbed on its face in the first hand he had been dealt.

Tex wiped the tips of his sensitive fingers on his trousers and became voluble and humorous. As he picked up his cards, one by one as they dropped from Hank's swiftly moving hand, he first let his gaze linger a little on their backs, and his fingers slipped across the corners of each. Williams had cheated before with a trimmed deck and now the marshal grimly determined to teach him a lesson, and at the same time not arouse the suspicions of the boss against the new marshal. With the switching of the decks Williams had set a pace which would grow too fast for him. Marked cards suited Tex, especially if they had been marked by an opponent, who would have all the more confidence in them. After a few deals if he wouldn't know each card as well as a man like Williams, whose marking could not be much out of the ordinary, and certainly not very original, then he felt that he deserved to get the worst of the play. He once had played against a deck which had been marked by the engraver who designed the backs, and he had learned it in less than an hour. So now he prepared to enjoy himself and thereafter bet lightly when Williams dealt, but on each set of hands dealt by himself one of the prospectors always won, and with worthy cards. Worthy as were their hands they were only a shade better than those held by the proprietor of the hotel and the general store. One hand alone cost Williams over eighty dollars, three others were above the seventy-dollar mark and he was losing his temper, not only because of his losses, but also because he did not dare to cheat too much on his own deal. Tex's eyes twinkled at him and Tex's rambling words hid any ulterior motive in the keen scrutiny. Finally, driven by desperation, Williams threw caution to the winds and risked detection. He was clever enough to avoid grounds for open accusation, but both of the miners suddenly looked thoughtful and a moment later they exchanged significant glances. Thereafter no one bet heavily when Williams dealt.

The finish came when Tex had dealt and picked up his hand. Sinful stolidly regarded the cheery faces of three kings--spades, clubs, and hearts. Williams liked the looks of his two pairs, jacks up. Hank rolled his huge cud into the other cheek and tried to appear mournful at the sight of the queen, ten, eight, and five of hearts. Tex laid down his four-card spade straight and picked up the pack.

"Call 'em, boys," he said.

Sinful's two cards, gingerly lifted one at a time from the table, pleased him very much, although from all outward signs they might have been anything in the card line. They were the aces of diamonds and clubs. He sighed, squared the hand, and placed it face down on the table before him. Williams gulped when he added a third jack to his two pairs, and Hank nearly swallowed his tobacco at sight of the prayed-for, but unexpected, appearance of another heart. All eyes were on the dealer. He put down the deck and picked up his hand for another look at it. After a moment he put it down again, sadly shaking his head.

"Good enough as it is," he murmured. "I ain't havin' much luck, one way or th' other; an' I'm gettin' tired! of th' cussed game."

"Dealer pat?" sharply inquired Williams, suspicion glinting in his eyes.

"Pat, an' cussed near flat," grunted Tex. "Go on with her. I'll trail along with what I got, an' quit after this hand."

Notwithstanding the dealer's pat hand and his expression of resignation, the betting was sharp and swift. On the first round, being forty-odd dollars ahead, Tex saw the accumulated raises and had enough left out of his winnings to raise five dollars. He tossed it in and leaned back, watching each face in turn. Sinful was not to be bluffed by any pat hand at this stage of the play, no matter how craftily it was bet. He reflected that straights, flushes, and full houses could be held pat, as well as threes or two pairs, all of which he had beat. A straight flush or fours were the only hands he could lose to, and Williams had not dealt the cards. Pat hands were sometimes pat bluffs, more terrifying to novices than to old players. He saw the raise and shoved out another, growling: "Takes about twenty more to see this circus."

Williams hesitated, looking at the dealer's neat little stack of cards. He was convinced from the way Tex had acted that the pat hand was a bluff, for its owner had not been caught bluffing since the game started, which indicated that he had labored to establish the reputation of playing only intrinsic hands, which would give a later bluff a strong and false value. He saw and raised a dollar, hoping that someone would drop out. Hank disappointed him by staying in and boosting another dollar. They both were feeling their way along. Hank also believed the pat hand to be worthless; and worthless it was, for Tex tossed it from him, face down, and rammed his hands into his pockets.

Sinful heaved a sigh of relief, which was echoed by the others, squinted from his hand to the faces of the two remaining players, and grinned sardonically. "Bluffs are like crows; they live together in flocks. I never quit when she's comin' my way. Grab a good holt for another raise! She's ten higher, now."

With the disturbing pat hand out of it, which was all the more disturbing because it had belonged to the dealer, Williams gave more thought to the players on his left and right. He decided that Hank was the real danger and that Sinful's words were a despairing effort to win by the default of the others. He saw the raise and let it go as it was. Hank rolled the cud nervously and with a sudden, muttered curse, threw down his hand. A flush had no business showing pride and fight in this game, he decided. Sinful grinned at him across the table.

"Terbaccer makin' you sick, Hank?" he jeered. "I'm raisin' ten more, jest to keep th' corpse alive. He-he-he!"

There was now too much in the pot to give it up for ten dollars and Williams met the raise, swore, and called, "What you got, you devil from h--l?"

"I got quite a fambly," chuckled Sinful, laying down a pair of aces. "There's twin brothers," he said, looking up.

Williams snorted at the old man's pleasure in not showing his whole hand at once, and he tossed three jacks on the table. "Triplets in mine," he replied.

Sinful raised his eyebrows and regarded them accusingly. "Three jacks can tote quite some load if it's packed right," he said. "Th' rest of my fambly is three more brothers, an' they bust th' mules' backs. Ain't got th' extry jack, have you?"

Slamming the rest of the cards on the table Williams arose and without a word walked to the bar. Sinful's. cackles of joy were added to by his friends and they surrounded the table to help in the division of the spoils, in plain sight of all.

"Win or lose, Marshal?" demanded Sinful shrilly above the hubbub of voices.

"Lost a couple of dollars," bellowed Tex.

"Much obliged for 'em," rejoined Sinful. He looked at Hank, winked and said: "Marshal's been real kind to us, Hank," and Tex never was quite certain of the old man's meaning.

Williams looked around as Tex leaned against the bar. "How'd *you* come out?" he asked, his face showing his anger.

"I lost," answered Tex carelessly. "Not anythin' to speak of: a few dollars, I reckon. I told 'em two dollars, for they're swelled up with pride as things are. They must 'a' got into you real heavy."

Williams sneered. "Heavy for them, I reckon. I ain't limpin'. They got too cussed much luck."

"Luck?" muttered the marshal, gazing inquiringly at the glass of whiskey he had raised from the bar, as though it might tell him what he wanted to know. "I ain't so shore of that, Williams," he slowly said. "Them old sour-doughs get snowed in near every winter, up in th' hills; an' then they ain't got nothin' to do but eat, sleep, swap lies, an' play cards. Somethin' tells me there wasn't a whole lot of luck in it. I know I had all I could do to stay in th' saddle without pullin' leather--an' I ain't exactly cuttin' my teeth where poker is concerned. Listen to 'em, will you? Squabblin' like a lot of kids. I reckon they had this cooked up in grand style. They're all sharin' in th' winnin's, you'll notice." He paused in surprise as a dull roar faintly shook the room. "What's that?" he demanded sharply. "It can't be thunder!"

His companion shook his head. "No, it ain't; it's that Murphy blowin' up rock, like I was sayin' at supper. Hope he went up with it!" He laughed at a man who was just coming in, and who stopped dead in the door and listened to the rumble. "Yore shack's safe, Jake," he called. "Th' Mick's blastin' over past yore way. You remember what I've told you!" he warned.

Jake looked from the speaker to the careless, but inwardly alert, city marshal, scowled, shuffled over to a table, and called for a drink, thereafter entirely ignoring the peace officer.

Henry came in soon after and joined the two at the bar. "Yes, I'll have th' same. You two goin' ridin' ag'in, Marshal?" he asked.

Tex shrugged his shoulders. "It shore don't look like it. She mebby figgered me out. Anyhow, she slammed th' door plumb in my face." He frowned. "Somehow I don't get used to things like that. She could 'a' treated me like I wasn't no tramp, anyhow, couldn't she?"

Henry smiled maliciously, and felt relieved. "They're shore puzzlin'. I hear that coyote Watkins was out there this afternoon. There wasn't no door slammed in *his* face." His little eyes glinted. "I see where he's goin' to learn a lesson, an' learn it for keeps!"

"Oh, he got throwed, too," chuckled Tex, as if finding some balm in another's woe. "He stopped off on his way home an' told me about it. Got a busted heart, an' belly-achin' like a sick calf. That's what he is; an' it's calf love, as well. Shucks! When I was his age I fell in love with a different gal about every moon. Besides, he ain't got money, nor prospects: an' she knows it."

Henry took him by the arm and led him to a table in a far corner. "I been thinkin' I mebby ought to send her a present, or somethin'," he said, watching his companion's face. "You, havin' more experience with 'em, I figgered mebby you would help me out. *I* don't know what to get her."

"Weakenin' already," muttered the marshal, trying to hide a knowing, irritating smile. "Pullin' leather, an' ain't hardly begun to ride yet!"

"I ain't pullin' no leather!" retorted Henry, coloring. "I reckon a man's got a right to give a present to his gal!"

"Shore!" endorsed Tex heartily. "There ain't no question about it--when she comes right out an' admits that she is his gal. This Saunders woman ain't admittin' it, yet; an' if she figgers that yo're weakenin' on yore play of ignorin' her, then she'll just set back an' hold you off so th' presents won't stop comin'. This is a woman's game, an' she can beat a man, hands down an' blindfolded: an' they know it. I tell you, Hennery, a wild cayuse that throws its first rider ain't no deader set on stayin' wild than a woman is set on makin' a man go through his tricks for her if she finds he's performin' for her private amusement, an' payin' for th' privilege, besides. It ain't no laughin' matter for you, Hennery; but I can't hardly keep *from* laughin' when I think of you stayin' away to get her anxious, an' then sendin' her presents! It's yore own private affair, an' yo're runnin' it yore own way--but them's *my* ideas."

Henry stared into space, gravely puffing on a cold cigarette. His low, furrowed brow denoted intense mental concentration, and the scowl which grew deeper did not suggest that his conclusions were pleasant. The simile regarding the wild horse sounded like good logic to him, for he prided himself that he knew horses. Finally he looked anxiously at his deeply thinking companion.

"It sounds right, Marshal," he grudgingly admitted; "but it shore is hard advice to foller. I'm plumb anxious to buy her somethin' nice, somethin' she can't get in this part of th' country, an' somethin' she can wear an' know come from me." He paused in some embarrassment and tried to speak carelessly. "If you was goin' to get a woman like her some present--mind, I'm sayin' *if* --what would you get?"

Tex reflected gravely. "Candy don't mean nothin'," he cogitated, in a low, far-away voice. "Anybody she knew at all could give her candy. It don't mean nothin' special, a-tall." He did not appear to notice how his companion's face fell at the words. "Books are like candy--just common presents. A stranger almost could give 'em. Ridin' gloves is a little nearer--but Tommy, or me, could give them to her. Stockin's? Hum: I don't know. They're sort of informal, at that. 'Tain't everybody, however, could give 'em. Only just one man: get my idea?"

"I shore do, Marshal," beamed Henry. "You see, livin' out here all my life an' not 'sociatin' with wimmin--like her, anyhow--I didn't know hardly what would be th' correct thing. Wonder what color?"

Tex was somewhat aghast at his joke being taken so seriously. "Now, you look here, Hennery!" he said in a warning voice. "You promise me not to send her no stockin's till I says th' word." He had wanted to give Jane more reason to dislike the nephew, but hardly cared to have it go that far. "Stayin' away, are you? You make me plumb sick, you do! Stayin' away, h--l!"

A roar of laughter came from the celebrating miners and all eyes turned their way. Sinful and Hank were dancing to the music of a jew's-harp and the time set by stamping, hob-nailed boots. They parted, bowed, joined again, parted, courtesied and went on, hand in hand, turning and ducking, backing and filing, the dust flying and the perspiration streaming down. It seemed impossible that in these men lurked a bitter race hatred, or that hearts as warm and happy could be incubating the germs of cowardly murder. Not one of them, alone, would be guilty of such a thing; but the spirit of a mob is a remarkable and terrible thing, tearing aside civilization's training and veneer, and in a moment hurling men back thousands of years, back to the days when killing often was its own reward.

Chapter XIV
Tact and Courage

Things were going along smoothly for the new marshal until two of the C Bar punchers, accompanied by two men from a ranch farther from town, rode in to make a night of it. It chanced that the C Bar men had been with a herd some forty miles north of the ranch, where water and grass conditions were much better, and they had become friendly with the outfit of another herd which grazed on the western fringe of the same range. A month of this, days spent in the saddle on the same rounds, and nights spent at the chuck wagon with nothing to vary the monotony of the cycle, had given the men an edge to be bunted at the first opportunity; and their ideas of working off high-pressure energies did not take into consideration any such things as safety valves. Action they craved, action they had ridden in for, and action they would have. The swifter it started, the faster it moved, the better it would suit them. So, with an accumulation of energy, thirst, and money they tore into Windsor one noon at a dead run, whooping like savages, and proclaiming their freedom from restraint and their pride of class by a heavenward bombardment which frightened no one and did no harm.

It so chanced that when they passed the new marshal's office they were going so fast, and were so fully occupied in waking up the town, that the lettering over the door of the lean-to escaped their attention. And they were past, bunched in a compact group, and nearly hidden in dust before the mildly curious officer could get to the door. He watched them whirl up to the hotel, the stronghold and stamping ground of Williams and the miners and, dismounting with shrill yells, pause a moment to reload their empty guns, and then surge toward the door.

Tex rubbed his chin thoughtfully as he considered them. Carney's was the cowman's favorite drinking place, yet these four cheerful riders had not given it a second glance, judging from the way they had gone past it. This was no matter for congratulation, but bespoke, rather, a determination to show off where their efforts would create more interest. Who they were, or what they came in for, he neither knew nor cared. They were celebrating punchers from somewhere out on the range and they were going to hold their jamboree in the miners' chosen place of entertainment. A less experienced marshal, filled with zeal and conceit, might forthwith have buckled on his guns, and started for the scene of the festivities, to be on hand as a preventive, rather than a corrective, or punitive, force; and very probably would have hastened the very thing he sought to avoid. Tex hoped to take the edge from the class feeling, and determined to be openly linked with neither one side nor the other. His place was to be that of a neutral buffer and his justice must be impartial and above criticism. So, after turning back to buckle on the left-hand gun, he did not sally forth to blaze the glory of the law and precipitate a riot; he sat down patiently to await the course of events.

Williams poked his head out of the door of his store and looked anxiously down the street at the dismounting four. As they went into the hotel he hurried across to the marshal's office and stopped, panting, in the doorway.

"See 'em?" he asked excitedly. "Hear 'em?"

"What or who?" asked Tex, throwing one leg over the other.

"Them rowdy punchers!" exclaimed the storekeeper. "Nobody's safe! Go up an' take 'em in, quick!"

"What they do?" interestedly asked the marshal.

"Didn't you *see* an' *hear* ?" demanded Williams incredulously.

"I saw 'em ride past, an' I heard 'em shootin' in th' air; but what did they do so I can arrest 'em?"

"Ain't that enough? That, an' th' yellin', an' everythin'?"

"Sinful and his friends made more noise th' other night when they left town," replied the marshal. "I didn't arrest them. Hank was of a mind to see if it was true that a bullet only punches a little, thin-edged hole in a pane of glass an' don't smash it all to pieces. Bein' wobbly, he picked out yore winder, seein' they was th' biggest in town; but Sinful held him back, an' they had a scufflin' match an' made more noise than sixteen mournful coyotes. There bein' no pane smashed I didn't cut in. A man is only a growed-up boy, anyhow."

Williams looked at him in frank amazement. "But these here fellers are punchers!" he exploded.

"I shore could see that, even with th' dust," confessed the marshal. "That ain't no crime as I knows of."

"It ain't th' four to one that's holdin' you back, is it?" demanded Williams insinuatingly. "They're punchers, too: bad as h--l."

Tex languidly arose and removed the pair of guns and the belts, laying them gently on the floor. He pitched his sombrero on the bunk and faced his caller.

"Mebby I didn't understand you," he coldly suggested. "What was it you said?"

Williams raised both hands in quick protest, one foot fishing desperately behind him for the ground below the sill. "Nothin' to make you go on th' prod," he hastily explained.

"Listen to me, Williams," said the cool peace officer, his voice level and unemotional. "Anybody callin' me a coward wants to go into action fast, an' keep on goin' fast. That includes everybody from King Solomon right down to date. I'm responsible for th' peace in this town, an' when *anybody* starts smashin' it I'll go 'em a whirl. Yellin', ridin' fast, an' shootin' in th' air, 'specially by sober men, ain't smashin' nothin' in a town like this. I don't aim to run no nursery, nor even a kindergarden. I ain't makin' a fool out of myself an' turnin' th' law into a joke. Once let ridicule start an' h--l's pleasant by contrast. They ain't shootin' now. Th' first shot fired inside any buildin', or dangerously low, an' I inject myself an' my two guns. I can't make no arrests on a blind guess, mine nor yourn. You better go back to th' store an' keep th' vinegar from sourin' on its mother."

Williams' jaw dropped. This was not Tex Jones at all, at least it didn't sound like him. "As th' owner of th' most valuable property in town I want them coyotes stopped from ruinin' it. I--—"

"When they show any signs of ruinin' *any* property I'll step in an' stop 'em," the marshal assured him. "I got my ears open, an' had my authority buckled on--which I'll now resume wearin'." He picked up a heavy belt and slung it around him, deftly catching the free end as it slapped against him. "We'll have law an' order, Williams--even if I have to fill some fool as full of holes as a prairie-dog town; but I ain't goin' out an' trample on a man's pride an' make him get killed defendin' it, unless I got good reason to. This is a long speech, but I'm goin' to make it longer so I can impress somethin' on yore mind. Bein' a busy merchant you've mebby never had time to think about it much; but me, bein' a marshal, I *got* to think of everythin' like that. This is one of 'em: When bad feelin's exist between two classes, helpin' one ag'in' th' other, without honest reasons, is only goin to make more bitterness. It can be held down only by impersonal justice. That's me. I don't give a d--n what a man is as long as he behaves hisself." Picking up the second belt he slung it around him the other way and buckled it behind him. As he shook them both to a more comfortable fit a yell rang out up near the hotel, followed by a shot. Grabbing his hat from the bunk he pushed Williams out of his way and dashed through the door, flinging over his shoulder: "I'm injectin' myself *now* ! You better go look to th' vinegar!"

He saw Whiskey Jim, the man whom he had caught beating the dog, in his blind terror run against the side of the harness-shop, recover from the impact and, stupefied by fear, frantically claw at the bleached boards. A spurt of dust almost under one of his feet made him claw more frantically. The hilarious puncher walked slowly toward him, raising the Colt for another shot. Behind him, laughing uproariously, stood his three friends, solidly blocking the hotel door.

"Hold that gun where it is!" shouted the marshal, dropping into a catlike stride. He was coming down the middle of the street, not more than forty paces, now, from the performing puncher.

The gun arm stiffened in air as the whiplike, authoritative phrase reached its possessor and, grinning exultantly, the puncher wheeled to get a good look at his next victim. He saw a grave-faced man of forty-odd years walking toward him, a bright star pinned to the open vest, two guns hanging low down on the swaying hips, the swinging hands brushing the walnut grips at every lithe, steady step.

"See what we got to play with!" exulted the surprised puncher, calling to his friends. "I want his badge: you can have th' rest!" His hand chopped down and a spurt of dust leaped from the ground at the marshal's side.

Disregarding it, the peace officer maintained his steady, swinging stride, his eyes fixed on those of the other, intently watching for a change in their playful expression. Another shot and the dust spurted close to his left foot. The hilarious laughter of the three in the doorway died out, and their friend in the street stood stock still, trying to figure out what he had better do next. The deliberate marshal was now only five paces away and at the puncher's indecision, plain to be seen in the eyes, he leaped forward, wrested the gun from the feebly resisting fingers, whirled the nonplussed man around and then kicked him his own length on the ground.

Ignoring the three men in the doorway, thereby tacitly admitting their squareness, the marshal calmly ejected the cartridges from the captured weapon and, as the angry and astonished puncher arose, handed it to him.

"It's empty," he said in a matter-of-fact voice. "Keep it that way till you leave town; an' when you come in again, intendin' to likker up an' raise h--l, either unload it or leave it with me, unless you promise to behave yoreself." He turned to Whiskey Jim, who appeared to be frozen into a statue. "Come over here, Jim," he commanded, and again turned to the puncher, who did not know whether to laugh or to curse. "I reckon Jim's th' only injured party. His feelin's has been trampled on to th' tune of about five dollars. Pay him before he takes it out of yore hide. He's a desperate bad man, Jim is!"

The three men in the door, who were nowhere near drunk yet, knew sparkling courage when they saw it, and they shouted with laughter at their crestfallen friend, who grudgingly was counting the fine into the eager hand of the aggrieved citizen.

"Hey, Walt!" burbled one of them, a beardless youth on one end of the line. "Still want to play with that badge?"

"If you do," jeered the man in the middle, laughing again, "better rustle, *pronto* , 'cause I'm buyin' its boss a drink."

Walt grinned expansively, shoved the money into Whiskey Jim's clutching fingers, took hold of the quiet marshal, and turned toward the hotel. "You come along with me, officer," he said. "I'll pertect you. That fool says he's buyin' you a drink--mebby he is, but I'm payin' for th' first one. Yo're about th' best he-man I've seen since I looked into a lookin'-glass. I'm obliged to you for not losin' yore valuable temper." He waved a hand at the unbelieving Jim, who doubted his reeling senses. Five whole dollars, all at once! Gosh, but the new marshal was a hummer. "Now don't you lay for me, Jim," laughed the puncher. "We're square, all 'round, ain't we?"

The cheerful three in the door grabbed the marshal of Windsor and hauled him in to the bar, where he pushed free and surveyed them.

"Four cheerful imbeciles," he murmured sadly. "Don't you reckon you better quit drinkin', or else empty them guns?"

"Now don't you be too hard on us, Marshal," chuckled the eldest. "We're so dry we rattles, an' th' dust, risin' out of our throats gets plumb into our eyes. Here," he said, dragging out his gun and gravely emptying it, "these are shore heavy. I'll carry 'em in my pocket for a change," and he made good his words. The others laughingly followed his. example, Tex's smile growing broader all the time.

"This ain't nothin' personal, boys," he said. "It's only that th' law has come to town. Knowin' you'll leave 'em empty till after you get out, I'll have one drink an' go about my business." He made no threats and his voice was friendly and pleasant; and it did not have to be otherwise. He had made four friends, and they knew that he would go through with any play he started. "Know Tommy Watkins?" he asked as he put down his glass.

"Shore!" answered Walt. "He's workin' with my outfit--C Bar. Ain't seen him for a month, him bein' off somewhere when we rode in for our pay. Marshal, shake hands with another C Bar rider--Wyatt Holmes. These two tramps is Double S punchers--Lefty Rowe, an' Luke Perkins. My name's Butler--Walt Butler. What's Tommy up an' done?" he finished somewhat anxiously.

"Glad to see you, boys," said Tex, heartily shaking hands all around. "My name's Tex Jones. Come in ag'in," he invited. "Oh," he said in answer to Walt's question, "Tommy ain't done nothin', yet. I was just wonderin'. Good boy, Tommy is. Sort of wild, I reckon, bein' young. Busy after th' gals. Most young fellers are hellers anyhow, or think they are. But he's a likable pup."

Walt laughed and the others grinned broadly. "You've shore figgered him wrong, Marshal. He's scairt of th' gals--won't have nothin' to do with 'em; an' I ain't never seen him nowhere near drunk; but" he hastily defended in loyalty to his absent friend, "he's all right, other ways. Yes, sir--barrin' them things, Tommy Watkins is a good man, an' I can lick any feller that says he ain't."

"Which won't be me," replied Tex, smiling. "I like him, first-rate. We been gettin' acquainted fast. Well, boys," he said, turning toward the door, "have a good time an' come in often. I like a little company from th' outside. It relieves th' monotony. So-long."

"You shore had th' monotony busted wide open today," chuckled Walt. "But Tommy's a good boy--whatever th' h--l he's been doin' since I saw him last." Watching the marshal until out of sight past the door he turned and regarded his companions. "I'm tellin' you calves there's a man who'd spit in th' devil's eye," he said. "We was playin' with giant powder like four fools. Here's to Tex Jones, Marshal of Windsor!"

Lefty, tenderly putting the glass on the bar, looked thoughtfully around the room and then at the partially stunned barkeep. "How's friend Bud takin' th' new marshal? Bud an' him shore will have an' interestin' Colt fandango some of these fine days."

Baldy sighed, wiped off the bar, and looked sorrowfully at the group. "Bud's planted on Boot Hill. They done had th' fandango, an' he did th' dancin'. My G--d, I can see it yet! It was like this--" and he left the bar, walked to the door, and painstakingly enacted the fight. When it was finished, he mopped his head and slowly returned to his accustomed place.

Wyatt Holmes reached out and gravely shook hands with his friends and finished by shaking his own. "You allus was a fool for luck, Walt," he said thoughtfully. "Giant powder?" he muttered piously. "Giant h--l! It was dynamite with th' fuse lit. Here," he demanded, wheeling on the startled Baldy. "I *need* this drink! Set 'em up!"

Walt shook his head. "Now, what th' devil has Tommy done?" he growled.

Baldy, remembering Tommy's share in the altercation, maintained a discreet silence.

Chapter XV
A Good Samaritan

Out on Buffalo Creek, Blascom, haggard, drawn, gaunt, and throbbing with an excitement which was slowly mastering him, scorning time to properly prepare and eat his food, drove himself like a madman. The creek bed at the old sump showed a huge, sloping-sided ditch from bank to bank, the upper side treacherous dry sand, the lower side a great, slanting ridge of rock, riven through in one place by the force of the dynamite, which had blown a great crater on the down-stream side of the natural riffle. In the bottom of the ditch a few inches of water lay, all that had saved him from fleeing from the claim because of thirst.

For year after weary year the miner had labored over the gold-bearing regions of the West, South, and North, beginning each period full of that abiding faith which clings so tenaciously to the gold-hunter and refuses to accept facts in any but an optimistic manner. A small stake here, day wages there, grubstakes, and hiring out, he had persistently, stubbornly pursued the will-o'-the-wisp and tracked down many a rainbow of hope, only to find the old disappointment. From laughing, hope-filled youth he had run the gauntlet of the years, through the sobered but still hopeful middle age, scorning thought of the twilight of life when he should be broken in strength and bitter in mind. Teeming, mushroom mining camps, frantic gold rushes, the majestic calm of cool canyons, and the punishing silences of almost unbearable desert wastes had found him an unquestioning worshiper, a trusting devotee of his goddess of gold. It was in his blood, it was woven into every fiber of his body, and he could no more cease his pursuit than he could stop the beating of his heart, or at least he could not cease while the goal remained unattained. Now, after all these years, he had won. He had proved that his quest had not been in vain.

Before the sun came up, even before dawn streaked the eastern sky, his meager, ill-cooked breakfast was bolted, and his morning scouting begun. First of all he slipped with coyote cunning down to the lower fork to see if Jake still kept his drunken stupor. The cold chimney of the miserable hut was the first eagerly sought-for sign, and every furtive visit awakened dread that a ribbon of smoke would meet his eye. A nearer approach made with the wariness of some hunted creature of the wild, let him sense the unnatural quiet of the little shack. A stealthy glance through a glassless opening, called a window, after the light made it possible, showed him morning after morning that his jug had not failed him. The unshaven, matted, unclean face of the stupefied man lay sometimes in a bunk, sometimes on the floor, and once the huge bulk was sprawled out inertly across the rough table amid a disarray of cracked, broken, and unwashed dishes. On the fifth morning the anxious prowler, fearing the lowered contents of the jug, had left a full bottle against the door of the hut and, slinking into the scanty cover, had run like a hunted thing back to the riven riffle and its unsightly ditch and crater.

Feverishly he worked, scorning food, unconscious of the glare of a molten sun rising to the zenith of its scorching heat. Shovel and bucket, trips without end from the ditch to a place above the steep bank where the carried sand grew rapidly higher and higher; panting, straining, frantic, worked Blascom. Foot by foot the ditch widened, foot by foot it lengthened, inch by inch it deepened, slide after sandy slide slipping to its bottom to be furiously, madly cursed by the prospector.

Then at last came the instant when the treasure was momentarily uncovered. Dropping the blunted, ragged-edged shovel, he plunged to all fours and thrust eager, avaricious fingers, bent like the talons of some bird of prey, into the storehouse of gold. Noiselessly responding to the jar and the impact of the groveling body, the great bank of sand had collapsed and slid down upon him, burying him without warning. The mass split and heaved, and the imprisoned miner, wild-eyed, sobbing for breath after his spasmodic exertions, burst through it and, raising quivering fists, cursed it and creation.

Hope had driven him remorselessly, but now that he had seen and felt the treasure, his efforts became those of a madman. More buckets of sand, jealous of each spilled handful, more punishing trips at a dogtrot, more frantic digging, and again he stared wildly at the pocket under his knees. Suddenly leaping erect, he cast anxious glances around him and a panicky fear gripped him and turned him into a wild beast. Yanking his coat from the rock riffle he spread it over the treasure and then, running low and swiftly, gun in hand, he scouted through the brush on both sides of the creek, and then bounded toward the lower fork. Approaching the hut on hands and knees, cruelly cut by rock and thorn, he studied the door and the open window. The bottle was where he had left it, the snores arose regularly, and once more he was reassured. Had there been signs of active life he would have murdered with the exultant zeal of a religious fanatic.

The day waned and passed. Night drew its curtains closer and closer, and yet Blascom labored, the treacherous sand turning him into a raving, frenzied fury. Higher and higher grew the sand pile on the bank, a monument to his mad avarice. With gold in lumps massed at the foot of that rock ridge, yet he must save the sand for its paltry yield in dust, pouring out his waning strength in a labor which, to save pence, might cost him pounds. At last he stumbled more and more, staggering this way and that, his tortured body all but asleep, forced on and on by his fevered mind, flogged by a stubborn will. Then came a heavier stumble, following a more unbalanced stagger and his numbed and vague protests did not suffice to get him back on his feet. When he awakened, the glaring sun shocked him by its nearness to the meridian, and the shock brought a momentary sanity; if he scorned the warning he would be lost--and another shadowy prompting of his subconscious mind was at last allowed to direct him. Calmly, but shakily, he weakly crawled and staggered toward his shack, from which came a thin streamer of smoke, climbing arrow-like into the quiet, heated air.

He stopped and stared at it in amazement, doubting his senses. Had he seen it the day before it would have enraged him to a blind, killing madness; but now, suspicious as he was, and deadly determined to protect his secret, the reaction of the high tension of the last six days made him momentarily apathetic. The abused body, the starved tissues and dulled nerves, now took possession of him and forced him, even though it was with gun in his hand, to approach the door of his squalid, disordered habitation erect and without hesitation. At the sound of his slowly dragging steps a well-known, friendly voice called out and a well-known, friendly face appeared at a window.

The marshal was nearly stunned by what he saw and then, surging into action, leaped through the door and caught his staggering friend.

The well-cooked, wholesome breakfast out of the way, a breakfast made possible only by the marshal's forethought in bringing supplies with him from town, he refused Blascom's request for a third cup of coffee and smilingly offered a glass of whiskey, over which he had made a few mysterious passes.

"Don't want none," objected the weary miner.

"But yo're goin' to overcome yore sudden temperance scruples an' drink it, for me," persuaded Tex. "A good shock will do you a lot of good--an' put new life into you. As you are you ain't worth a cuss."

The prospector held out his hand, smilingly obedient, and downed the fiery draught at a gulp. "Tastes funny," he observed, and then laughed. "Wonder I can taste it at all, after th' nightmare I've had since th' smoke of that blast rolled away. Where'd you think I was when you came?"

Tex chuckled and stretched. "I didn't know, but from th' glimpse I got of th' crick bed I was shore I wasn't goin' huntin' you, an' mebby get shot accidental. Did you find it, Blascom?"

"My G--d, yes!" came the explosive answer. "There's piles of it, all shapes an' sizes, layin' on a smooth rock floor. When that sand stops slidin' I can scoop it up with a shovel, like coal out of a bin. Half of it belongs to you, Jones: go look at it!"

"I don't want any of it," replied Tex with quiet, but unshakable, determination. "If you divide it, no matter how much there is, by th' number of years you've sweat an' slaved and starved, it won't be too much to pay you. You set here a little while an' I'll go on a scout in th' brush an' watch it till you come out. Better lay down a few minutes, say half an hour, an' give that grub a chance to put some life into you. I'll shake you if you fall asleep."

"Feel sleepy now," confessed the prospector, yawning and moving sluggishly toward his bunk. "Seein' as how yo're here, I'll just take a few winks--don't know when I'll get another chance. That sand shore is gallin' an' ornery as th' devil. Go up an' take a look at it--I'll foller in a little while."

Tex, closing the door behind him, slipped into the brush, where he made more than a usual amount of noise for Blascom's benefit, and as he worked up toward the ditch he chuckled to himself. There had been no need for a full dose, he reflected, and he was glad that he had not given one. Blascom's drink of whiskey had just enough chloral in it to deaden him and give his worn-out body the chance it sought; besides, he was not too certain of the effect of a full dose on a constitution as undermined as that of his friend.

The ditch, again slowly filling with sand, showed him nothing, and he stood debating whether he should disturb it for a look at the treasure, when he suddenly thought of Jake and the whiskey jug. He remembered that Jake had been almost senselessly drunk when he had left the hotel on the night of the blast and that he had not been seen by anyone since. It would do no harm to go down to the lower fork and see what there was to be seen. The thought became action, and he was on his way, down the middle of the creek bed, where the footing was a little more to his liking.

The hut appeared to be deserted and the bottle of whiskey outside the door brought a frown to his face, which deepened as a nearer approach showed him that the door was fastened shut by rope and wire on the outside, and that the snoring inmate virtually was a prisoner. There was a note in the snores that disturbed him and aroused his vague, half-forgotten professional knowledge. Hastening forward he pushed the bottle aside with an impatient foot and worked rapidly with the fastenings on the door. At last it opened, and gun in hand against any possible contingency, he entered the hovel and looked at its tenant, sprawled face down near the jumbled bunk. A touch of the drunken man's cheek, a tense counting of his pulse, sent Tex to his feet as though a shot had nicked him. Running back to Blascom's hut, where he had left his horse, he leaped into the saddle and sent Omar at top speed toward town.

His thundering knock on the doctor's door brought no response and, not daring to pause on the dictates of custom, he threw his shoulder against the flimsy barrier and went in on top of it. Scrambling to his feet, he dashed into the rear one of the two rooms and swore in sudden rage and disgust.

Doctor Horn lay on his back on a miserable cot and his appearance brought a vivid recollection to his tumultuous caller. Tex turned up a sleeve and nodded grimly at the tiny puncture marks and, with an oath, faced around and swept the room with a searching glance. It stopped and rested on a heavy volume on a shelf and in a moment he was hastily turning the pages. Finding what he sought he read avidly, closed the book, and hunted among the bottles in a shallow closet. Taking what he needed, he ran out, leaped into the saddle and loped south to mislead any curious observer, only turning west when hidden from sight of the town.

When night fell it found a weak and raving patient in the little hovel on the lower fork, roped in his bunk, and watched anxiously by the two-gun man at his side. The long dark hours dragged, but dawn found a battle won. Noon came and passed and then Tex, looking critically at his patient, felt he could safely leave him for a few minutes. Glimpsing the filled bottle of liquor at the door of the hut he grabbed it and hurled it against a rock.

Blascom was up and around when Tex reached the upper fork, dragging heavy feet by strangely dulled legs.

"Just in time to feed," he drawled. "Didn't sleep as long as I thought," he said dully, glancing at the sun patch on the floor. "Must be near two o'clock--an' I felt like I could sleep th' sun around."

Tex would not correct the mistake and nodded. "You must 'a' slept some last night," he suggested. "Looked like you had when I saw you from th' window this mornin'."

Blascom nodded heavily. "Near sixteen hours. I feel dead all over."

"A long sleep like that often makes a man feel that way," responded Tex. "Th' muscles are stubborn an' th' eyes get a little touchy, too," he added.

They ate the poorly cooked dinner and leaned back for a smoke, Blascom allowing himself to lose the time because he felt so inert.

"Have any visits from friend Jake?" carelessly asked the marshal.

Blascom laughed. "Not one. You see, Jake come home that night about as drunk as a man can get an' walk at all. I planted th' jug, a full bottle of gin, an' near half a quart of brandy in his cabin where he'd shore see it. He's been petrified for a week steady. To make shore I put another bottle of whiskey ag'in' his door."

Tex nodded. "I busted that, just now. You come near killin' him. I just about got him through. Don't give him no more. I sat up all last night with him, draggin' him back from th' Divide, an' only left him a little while ago. Get yore gold out quick an' you don't have no call to want him drunk. Cache it, an' then spend a week takin' things easy. You wasn't far behind Jake when I saw you."

Blascom was staring at him in vast surprise. "I never thought good likker would hurt an animal like him!"

"I didn't say it was good likker," rejoined Tex. "Even good likker will do it when drunk by th' barrel; an' there's no good likker in Windsor, if I'm any judge. Well," he said, arising and taking up his hat, "I'll drift along for another look at Jake an' then head for town. Seein' as how you got him that way, through my suggestion, I'll admit, you better look in at him once in awhile an' see he has what he needs. Take some of yore water with you: his stinks."

Chapter XVI
Buffalo Creek in the Spotlight

What instinct it is and how it operates, that leads vultures from over the horizon to a dying animal, has never been satisfactorily explained to a lot of people; no more than the instinct which led Sinful and Hank to go prowling around Buffalo Creek when by all rights they should have been hanging around their own camp or loafing in the hotel; but prowl they did, their cunning old eyes missing nothing, certainly nothing so new and shining and high as the sand heap above the creek bank.

Sinful saw it first and he nudged his companion, whose cud nearly choked him before he could cough it back where it belonged.

"Glory!" he choked. "Jest look at it! Come on, Sinful: we got to inwestigate. Nobody's diggin' all that out an' totin' it up there for th' fun of it. But why's he luggin' it so far?"

Sinful snorted scornfully. "Too busy totin' to pan it," he snapped. "Rain's due 'most any time an' he's workin' to beat it. I don't have to inwestigate it--anybody that's workin' like that knows what he's doin'; an' I ain't never heard it said that Blascom's any fool. If he didn't know it was rich, he wouldn't be workin' so hard in th' sun."

"Well, mebby," doubted Hank, always a cold blanket in regard to his companion's contentions. "Looks like he ain't got no water for pannin', like everybody else. He ain't lazy like you, an' instead of wastin' his time around th' hotel like us he's totin' sand so he can work while th' crick's floodin'. When th' floodin' comes everybody else'll have to set down an' watch it till it gets low enough. Me an' you would be doin' somethin' if we follered his example. Where you goin'?" he demanded as his sneering companion walked away.

Sinful flashed a pitying glance over his shoulder. "To git a handful of that sand an' prove you ain't got no sense, that's where. You keep yore eye open for Blascom while I raid his sand pile. Here's a can," he said, stooping to pick it up. "It'll mebby tell us somethin' when we gits it to some water. If you see him a-comin' out, throw a pebble at me. 'Twon't take me long, once I git my boots off."

Hank obeyed and scouted toward the hut, finally stopping when he could see its door. Watching it a few minutes he saw Blascom pass the opening, and after another few minutes, the watcher slipped away, hastening toward the sand pile. Reaching it, he saw no signs of his partner and backed into the brush to await developments. He no sooner had stopped behind a patch of scrub oak than he caught sight of Sinful carefully picking his way across the stony ground in his socks, one hand carrying the can, the other a pair of boots. On his leathery face was an expression of vast surprise and pious awe. He seemed almost stunned, but he was not so lost to his surroundings that he ignored a bounding, clicking pebble which passed across his path. Clutching can and boots in a firmer grip, he sprinted with praiseworthy speed and agility toward the somewhat distant railroad track. In his wake sped Hank, an unholy grin wreathing his face at the goatlike progress of his old friend over the rocky ground. To Sinful's ears the sound of those clattering boots spelled a determined pursuit and urged him to better efforts. At last, winded, a cramp in his side and his feet so tender and bruised that he preferred to fight rather than go any farther in his socks, he dropped the boots, drew his gun, and wheeled. At sight of Hank's well-known and inelegant figure a look of relief flashed over his face, swiftly followed by a frown of deep and palpitant suspicion.

"What you mean, chasin' me like that?" he shouted.

"Gosh!" panted Hank as he drew near. "That was shore close! An' for an old man yo're a runnin' fool. Jack rabbits an' coyotes can cover ground, but they can't stack up ag'in' you. Did you see him?"

Sinful, one boot on and the other balanced in his hand, looked up. "No, I didn't; did you?" he demanded, suspicion burning in his old eyes.

"Shore," answered Hank, lying with a facile ease due to much practice. "He suddenly busted out of th' door with a rifle in his hands an' headed for his sand pile. I dusted lively, heaved th' pebble; an' here we are." He cast an apprehensive glance behind him and then sharply admonished his friend. "Hustle, you! Yo're settin' there like there ain't no mad miner projectin' around in th' brush with a Winchester! Think I want to git shot?"

"I reckon mebby you ought to," retorted Sinful, struggling erect and trying each tender foot in turn. "Stone bruises, cuts, an' stickers, an' all because you git in a panic!" he growled. "Come on, you old fool: there's a pool of water in th' crick, t'other side of th' railroad bridge. Yo're too smart, you are. Mebby yore eyes'll pop out when you see what's in this here can. Great guns, what a sight I've seen!"

Panning gold in a tomato can might be difficult for a novice, but Sinful's cunning old hands did the work speedily and well. After repeated refillings and mystic gyrations he carefully poured out the last of the water and peered eagerly into the can, bumping his head solidly against his companion's, for Hank was as eagerly curious.

Sinful placed it reverently on the creek bank and looked at his staring friend.

"An' only a canful," he muttered in awe.

"Glory!" breathed Hank, and looked again to make sure. "Nothin' but dust--but Good Lord!" He packed a vile pipe with viler tobacco, lit it, and arose. "No wonder he grabbed his gun an' dusted for his sand pile! Come on, Sinful: we got a long walk ahead of us, some quick packin' to do, an' a long walk back ag'in. If we only could get a couple of mules, we'd load 'em with three-hundred pounds apiece an' go down th' crick a day's journey. It'd be worth it."

Sinful looked scornfully at his worrying companion and slowly arose. "No day's journey for me, mules or no mules," he declared, spitting emphatically. "I ain't shore it would be worth it, considerin' th' time an' th' trouble; but it's worth pannin' right where it is. I've jumped claims before in my life an' I ain't too old to jump another. When I looked over that bank an' saw that wallopin' big rock a-stickin' up in th' crick bed, from bank to bank; an' th' ditch he's put down on th' upstream side, I purty near knew what th' sand pile would show. I'm bettin' he's got *bushels* of gold at th' foot of that riffle. If his location don't run up that far, an' mebby it don't, we got somethin' to keep us busy. An' if it does, we've mebby got more to keep us busy. Come on, you wall-eyed ijut: we got to be gittin' back to camp. Great Jerus'lam!"

The marshal of Windsor, riding slowly toward town south of the railroad track after a long detour to mask his trail, saw two scarecrows bumping along the ties, bobbing up and down jerkily as they tried to stretch their stride to cover two ties and repeatedly fell back to one. They were well to the northeast of him and to his left, but he thought they looked familiar and he pushed more to the south to remain hidden from them while he rode ahead. When he finally had reached a point south of the station he turned and rode toward it, timing his arrival to coincide with theirs.

Sinful grinned up at the smiling rider, his missing teeth only making more prominent the few brown fangs he had left. Two dribbles of tobacco juice had dried at each corner of his mouth and reached downward across his chin, giving him an appearance somewhat striking. He mopped the perspiration from his face by a vigorous wipe of his soiled shirt sleeve and lifted each palpitating foot in turn.

"Been ridin' far?" he asked in idle curiosity and in great good humor, considering the aches in his body and the soreness of his feet.

"Oh, just around exercisin' Oh My," answered Tex. "I thought you two was located out on Antelope, west of town?"

"We are," replied Hank, ignoring his partner's furtive elbow. "Been gettin' sorta tired of it, though, not havin' nothin' to do but set around an' look at th' same things. Thought we'd take a look at th' Buffaler, south of th' track; but it ain't much better, though there is some water in th' pools. Anyhow, Antelope's kinda crowded. We may shift our camp. Jake's out on Buffaler som'er's, ain't he?"

Tex nodded and glanced at the can. "Been fishin'?"

"If we had enough bait to fill that can we'd 'a' ate it ourselves," chuckled Hank.

"Naw, there ain't no fish left now," said Sinful. "Hard-luck coffeepot, that's all it is. Good as anythin' else, an' shore plentiful. Punch a hole in each side of it an' shove in a piece of wire, an' she'll cook anythin' small. Ain't it hot?"

"Hot, an' close," replied the marshal. "Well, I reckon I'll be gettin' along. Feels like rain is due 'most any time, though I don't reckon we'll get any before th' moon changes. Still, you can't allus tell."

"Can't tell nothin' about it at all, this kind of weather," observed Hank, the can now against the other side of his body. "But one thing's shore--it's gettin' closer every day. So-long," and the grotesque couple went bobbing down the track toward their own camp.

Tex looked after them, humorously shaking his head. "'It's gettin' closer every day,'" he mimicked. "Shore it is. Pair of cunning old coyotes, an' entirely too frank about Buffalo Creek." Just then Sinful leaped into the air, cracked his sore heels together and struck his companion across the shoulders. This display of exuberance awakened a strong suspicion in the marshal. "I'll keep my eye on you two old codgers," he soliloquized, thoughtfully feeling of the handcuffs in his pocket. Wheeling abruptly he rode up to the station, where Jerry grinningly awaited him. "Let me know when those mossbacks go west, Jerry, if you see them," he requested. "They're too cussed innocent an' happy to suit me. How are things?"

Jerry shook his head. "I'll be cussed if I know. But I know one thing, and that is that I'm apologizing to you for the way Jane shut the door in your face. I don't know what's the matter with her lately."

"There's never any tellin' about wimmin," said Tex, smiling. "An' don't you ever apologize to anybody for anythin' she does. Wimmin see things from a different angle, an' they ain't got a man's defenses. A difference in structure is likely to be accompanied by differences in nature, in this case notably in the more delicate balance of th' nervous system. Their reactions are both more subtle an' more extreme. I wasn't insulted, but just folded my tents like th' Arabs, an' as silently stole away. Which I'm now goin' to repeat. See you later, mebby."

Jerry watched his visitor ride off and a puzzled frown crept over his face.

"Wish I knew more about you, Mr. Tex Jones," he muttered. "You're either as fine a human as I have seen, or the smoothest rascal: and I'm d--d if I can tell which."

The marshal rode to his office and sought the chair outside the door, his thoughts running back over recent events. Blascom's find and the physical condition of the man naturally brought to mind Jake's narrow escape. The latter bothered him, notwithstanding the certainty that Blascom would keep a good watch over the sick man. While he anxiously ran over his scant knowledge of Jake's illness and the remedies he had employed, he glanced up to see Doctor Horn nervously hurrying toward him. The doctor, in view of what he now knew of him, became a very interesting study for the marshal.

"Marshal!" cried the physician while yet a score of paces away, "somebody burst down my door during my absence and took some drugs which by their nature are not common out here and, consequently, hard to obtain. I am formally reporting it, sir."

"Doctor," replied Tex, "when a patient comes to you for help you naturally expect him to be frank and truthful. It is the same with a peace officer, who endeavors to cure not the ills of a single unit of society, but the ills of society as a whole. Here, as in your own field, a refractory or diseased unit may, and generally does, affect the body of which he is a part. So, as a social physician, I must ask of you that frankness so valuable to a medico. First, what drugs did you miss?"

"Your analogy, while clever, is sophistical and is entirely unwarranted," retorted the physician, taken somewhat aback by the words and attitude of a "cowhand," as he contemptuously characterized punchers. "Leaving it out of the argument, except to say, in passing, that your 'social physician' does not exercise a corrective influence, but rather a punitive one, I hardly see how the naming of the missing drugs will give any enlightenment to a layman. There still exists the forcible breaking into, and the unlawful entry of, my residence."

"For purposes of identification it might be well to know the drugs that were stolen; but I'll waive that. What time would you say this occurred?" asked Tex with professional interest.

"Some time yesterday," answered the physician.

"You certainly are not very specific, Doctor," commented Tex. "I'm afraid we must come closer to it than that. You say you were away at the time?"

"Yes: I did not return until quite late."

"In body or in spirit, Doctor Horn?"

"Sir, I do not understand you!" retorted the complainant, flushing slightly and gazing with great intensity into the marshal's eyes.

"There have been many others who did not understand me," replied Tex, calmly rolling and lighting a cigarette. "I'm mentioning that so you won't think you are an exotic variation of our large and interesting species. The study of man is the greatest of all, Doctor. The words were more of a joke than anything else. Have you ever suffered from hallucinations, Doctor? I've heard it said that too close confinement, too close an application to study, and too intimate relations with chemicals, volatile and otherwise, operate that way in these altitudes. Hothouse gardeners, for instance, notably those engaged in raising poppies, have slight touches of mental aberration. You are certain that your house was entered while you were away?"

The doctor, arms akimbo, was staring at this calm mind-reader as though in a trance, too stunned to be insulted.

Tex continued: "The value of the missing drugs and the damage to the door undoubtedly will be paid to you, Doctor, in a few days. In fact, I am so confident of that that I will pay you just damages now, taking your receipt in return. Do you agree with a great many people that a physician to the body has much the same high obligations as those belonging to a minister or a priest, who are physicians to the soul? That his work is of a humanitarian nature before it is a matter of remuneration; that he should hold himself fit and ready to answer calls of distress without regard to his own bodily comfort?"

Doctor Horn still stared at him, rallying his thoughts. He nodded assent as he groped.

"There are professional secrets, Doctor, which need not be divulged," continued Tex. "I understand that you have a horse?"

The physician nodded again.

"Then use it. I have reason to believe that a man named Jake, a miner, who is located on the first fork of Buffalo Creek, west of town, urgently needs your professional services. I understand that he has been brought back from death from alcoholic poisoning, but will be much safer if you look at him. Did you say you are going now? And by the way, before you start, let me say that the old idea of peace officers being corrective forces, in a punitive sense only, is rapidly becoming obsolete among the more intelligent and broader-minded men of that class. While punishment is undoubtedly needed as a warning to others, the cure's the thing, to paraphrase an old friend of mine. Is there any connection between the natures of the missing drugs and alcoholic poisoning, Doctor? But we are wasting time. This little problem can wait. Just now speed's the thing. Drop around again soon, Doctor: I always enjoy the companionship of an educated man," and the marshal, slowly arising, bowed and entered his little office, the door softly closing behind him.

Chapter XVII
The Rush

The marshal was leaving the hotel after breakfast the following morning when he saw Jerry walking briskly toward him from the station and he waited for the agent to come up.

"Those two old prospectors just passed the station, going west along the track," Jerry informed him. "From the way they were loaded down it looked as though they are moving their camp. And how men as old as they are can carry such packs is beyond my understanding."

"Thanks, Jerry," said the marshal. "Go back to th' station. I've got to take a ride. Trouble's brewin', I reckon."

Passing the hotel on his way to Carney's stable, Tex saw a running miner hurrying into it and in a moment an excited half-score of armed prospectors poured into the street, shouting and gesticulating. The little crowd picked up additions as it passed along the street and headed westward to strike the railroad at an angle. Some of them had partners with them and, when the tracks had been reached, quite a number turned and ran eastward toward their camps to pack up belongings and supplies.

"Mental telepathy?" murmured Tex, watching them in some surprise. "Hank and Sinful are too clever rascals to tell anybody anything of value that they might know. Huh! That's only a name, I guess, for subconscious weighing of facts subconsciously received: instinctive deductions from observations too vague to be definitely recognized. Instinct, I'm afraid you have more names than most people recognize. But it does beat the devil, at that! An animal does seemingly wonderful and impossible things because of the keenness of its scent, which passes our understanding; birds of prey have eyes nearly telescopic in power--but how the knowledge of this gold strike has spread about so quickly when everyone concerned in it naturally would be secretive, is too much for me. One thing is certain, however: it is known, and I have work to do, and quickly!"

Omar welcomed him and soon was stringing the miles out behind him as smoothly almost as running water. There was no need to urge the animal at its best speed, for it was doing two miles to the miners' one and easily would beat them to the scene of action.

When he reached the second fork, Blascom was not at the hut and, leading the roan into a brush-filled hollow, the marshal took his rifle from its scabbard and went up to the scene of the miner's operations. His hail was followed by a startled crouching on the prospector's part and a rifle barrel leaped up to the top of the ditch.

"Don't shoot: It's Jones," called the marshal, slowly emerging from his cover. "I come up to warn you that th' rush has started. Hank an' Sinful ought to get here in about half an hour, th' others a little behind them. I'm aimin' to be referee: th' kind of a referee I once saw at a turf prize fight: he had to jump in an' thrash both of th' principals--an' he did it, too. Get that bonanza cleaned out and cached yet?"

Blascom swore as he stood up again. "Yes: but nobody's goin' to git *this* without a fight! How th' devil did they find out I'd struck it rich?"

"Shore this claim is staked an' located?" demanded Tex.

"Yes; an' there's work enough done on it to make it stick. But how did they find out I'd struck it?"

"Don't know," answered the marshal. "You better climb out an' go off an' hide somewhere in th' brush from where yore rifle will cover th' cache. They're keen as hounds an' there's no use takin' chances of losin' th' greater to save th' less. I'll handle this end of it. If you hear a shot you better slip back an' look things over. Get a rustle on you--time's flyin'."

In a few minutes the creek bed and the little hut appeared to be deserted. Blascom lay on his stomach at a point from which he could see his cache and the ditch as well. After a short silence there came the sound of a snapping twig and a few minutes later Sinful's greedy eyes peered over the creek bank down at the big ditch. He slid a rifle over the edge and looked around eagerly. To his side crept Hank, who added his scrutiny to that of his partner. Sinful spoke out of one corner of his mouth as he gazed intently down the creek bed, where one corner of Blascom's hut could be seen through the scrawny timber on the little point. Hank nodded, crawled to the edge of the bank and was about to slip over it when a low warning from the brush at their side froze them both.

"Stay where you are," said a well-known voice, cold and unfriendly. "That claim's got one owner now, an' he ain't lookin' for no partners, a-tall. Better shove up yore hands an' face th' crick. You know me--an' so far you ain't seen me miss, yet."

Tex emerged from his cover, a Colt in one hand, a pair of shining handcuffs clinking from their short chains as they swung from the other. Snapping one over Sinful's wrist he curtly ordered Hank to his partner's side and linked the two together. Disarming them he unloaded the weapons, appropriated the cartridges, and searched them both to make certain they could do him no injury.

"Sit down," he said, "an' keep quiet. Th' real show is about to start. Who all did you chumps tell about this strike?"

Hank glared at Sinful, Sinful glared at Hank, and then both glared at their captor. "Nobody, so strike me blind!" snapped Sinful. "Hank ain't been out of my sight since we left here yesterday. Think we're fools?"

"Anything but that," grimly rejoined Tex. "Shut up, now: I want to listen. Any play you make that don't suit me will call for a gun butt bein' bent over yore heads. If I need you, I'll call: an' you come a-runnin'. Hear me?"

"We could come faster if we was loose from each other," whispered Sinful in bland innocence. "Couldn't we, Hank?"

"Can't come fast, a-tall, hooked up this way," said Hank earnestly.

"Shut up!" snapped the marshal in a low voice.

A winged grasshopper rasped up over the bank and rasped back again instantly. A few birds chirped and sang across the creek bed and chickadees flashed and darted in an endless search for food. Several birds shot suddenly into the air from the fringe of timber and brush on the farther bank halfway between the ditch and the cabin, quickly followed by vague movements along the ground. Then more than a half-score of men popped into sight and, leaping from the steep bank, landed in the bed of the creek and scurried to different points, fooled by the numerous sumps which Blascom had dug in his quest for water. None of them had the knowledge possessed by Hank and Sinful, and the weather conditions had been such that the ages of the various sumps could not be quickly determined. Each man, eager to grab a hole while there was one left to grab, and to become established, chose a mark and appropriated it without loss of time. No sooner had the scurrying crowd selected their grounds than the marshal, who had crept along the top of the high bank, jumped over it and held two guns on them, guns which they had good reason to respect.

"Han's up!" he roared. " *Pronto* an' high! You-all know me--don't gamble! I drop th' first man that makes a gunplay. *Hank! Sinful!* " he shouted. "Come a-runnin'!" Crouched, he faced the scowling crowd, his steady hands before his hips, his steady guns ready to prove his mastery. The handcuffed pair, squabbling as they came, shuffled up to him.

"You yank me any more an' I'll bust yore fool head!" growled Sinful to his bosom friend. "Just because yore laigs is longer is no reason for playin' kite with me! Knock-kneed old fool! Here we are, Marshal: what you want?"

"Hold yore han's close," ordered Tex, his left gun slipping into its sheath, his right becoming even more menacing. With the free hand he fished out the key, handed it to Hank and waited until he had made use of it. It went swiftly back into the pocket and the left hand again held a gun. "Slip around an' take their weapons!" he snapped. "Don't get between them an' me. Lively!"

"We ain't goin' to spoil yore aim, Marshal," Hank assured him with great fervor. "Come on, you bald-headed old buzzard--git them guns for th' marshal!" He gave his companion a shove forward. "He done us a good turn--an' one good turn deserves another. Come on!"

"Who you shovin'?" blazed Sinful, starting away.

"You ain't got no right, cuttin' in here!" shouted a red-faced, angry miner, his companions growling and cursing their hearty endorsements. "Yo're a town marshal, not a county sheriff! Turn them guns off us!"

"I got a wider range than marshal," rejoined Tex grimly and not for an instant relaxing his alertness. "Gus Williams said so when he 'pinted me; an', besides, I got th' very same authority out here as I have in town: twelve sections of th' Colt statutes as made an' pervided. Blascom has legally established his claim, drove his stakes, and done his work on it. When he comes he'll p'int out his boundaries. Hold still, you two! Git 'em all, Sinful; don't overlook nothin', Hank! No use turnin' this crick into a slaughter-pen."

"I ain't likely to overlook nothin'," replied Sinful, moving more rapidly, "though I'm shore bothered by these here cussed contraptions on my wrist. You'll notice Hank unlocked *his* end of 'em! D--d claim jumpers! A man's rights ain't safe no more these days. Hank an' me shore would 'a' planted some of this passel if they'd bothered us. How th' devil did they find out about it, *I* want to know?"

"What you reckon yo're goin' to do with us all?" sneered a wrathy prospector, his hands slowly coming down toward a harmless belt.

"I'll tell you that after I see Blascom," answered the marshal, firing a shot into the ground. He ordered Sinful and Hank to pile the weapons at his feet, locked them together again and ordered them to get closer to the rest of the miners. The shot brought Blascom as rapidly as he could get there with a due regard to caution. Obeying Tex's terse command he slid down the bank and went to him.

"Shore yore claim takes in th' ditch an' th' riffle?" asked Tex in a whisper.

"Th' new one does," answered Blascom. "I sent off th' papers with Jerry, like you said, th' day I got th' dynamite."

"Th' old one any good?"

"Not much; not much better'n day wages. 'Tain't no good without water; but neither is th' other, now."

"This crowd is fooled by yore old sumps," explained Tex hurriedly. "If we drive 'em off they'll be back ag'in, an' mebby add yore murder to th' rest of their crimes. I can't stay here day an' night; an' if I could, they'd get us both after dark, or at long range in daylight. You got to let 'em stay. By tomorrow there'll be twice as many. I'm scared some'll come slippin' up any minute an' turn th' tables on us. You let Sinful an' Hank divide a quarter of th' sand pannin' between 'em--they'll commit murder for half that, an' you've got to have partners in case of a rush. Besides, rain's due any day now, an' you need 'em to beat it."

"I hate like--" began Blascom stubbornly.

"We all has to do things we hate!" cut in his companion. "You can't do anythin' else. If you can, tell me quick!"

Blascom shook his head. He could do nothing else. He turned and faced the crowd, telling it to go ahead and stake out claims where each man had started to, on condition that there was to be no more jumping and that they join him in putting up a solid front against any newcomers other than partners. The scowls died out, heads nodded, and the hustle and bustle began again from where it had left off.

Tex called the Siamesed pair to him and they listened, with their eyes glowing, to Blascom's offer of limited partnership, Hank nearly swallowing his cud when asked if he was satisfied with the terms. Sinful smelled a rat and looked properly suspicious, his keen old mind racing along on the theory that no one ever gave away anything valuable. Suddenly he grinned so expansively that a generous stream of tobacco juice rolled down his sharp chin.

"Us three ag'in' that gang," he mused. "Huh! Fair enough, *I* says. Hank an' me can lick 'em by ourselves. Can't we, Hank?"

"Shore!" promptly answered the other weather-beaten old rascal. "We shore kin, Sinful!"

Tex smiled at the cheerful old reprobates, bound closer together now than ever they had been before. "I ought to dump th' pair of you in th' new jail," he said, "though it shore wouldn't get no benefit from it. Yo're a pair of land pirates an' you both ought to be hung from th' yardarm of some cottonwood tree. Hold out yore hands till I turn you loose. You two youngsters want to keep th' bargain, or I *will* hang you!"

"Glad to git shet of them cuffs," growled Sinful. "Hank takes sich long steps an' walks sideways, th' old fool. We'll play square, won't we, Hank? There; he said so, too. We allus has felt kind of friendly to Blascom, ain't we, Hank? Shore we has. An' he needs us to keep our eyes on them blasted claim jumpers. 'Sides, he's a friend of yourn, Marshal: an' we ain't forgettin' them few dollars we won from you t'other night-- *are* we, Hank?" His shrewd old eyes baffled Tex's attempt to read just what he thought about the poker game.

"We ain't!" emphatically replied Hank, spitting copiously and vehemently. "We'll make these claim jumpers herd close to home; yes, sir, by glory!" He paused a moment and leaned nearer to his companion's ear. " *Won't* we, Sinful?" he suddenly shouted.

"Who you yowlin' at that way?" blazed Sinful, and then his eyes popped wide open in frank surprise. "Cussed if th' doc ain't got th' fever, too!" he ejaculated. "Here he comes up th' crick! Beats all how news does spread! An', great Jerus'lam: if he ain't as sober as a watched Puritan!"

Nodding right and left Doctor Horn rode slowly among the busy claim jumpers and drew rein in front of Tex and his companions.

"How do you do, gentlemen?" he said, smiling. "I see you're quite busy, Marshal, which seems to be a habit of yours. I happened to have a patient out this way, down on the lower fork, and while I was in his vicinity I thought I would drop in and compliment Blascom for his care of Jake. While the efficient treatment he first received undoubtedly saved his life, Blascom's nursing comes in for well-earned praise. He is still a sick man, although out of danger. I hope you will disregard our former conversation, so far as my part of it is concerned, Marshal. Good day to you all," and wheeling, he rode up a break in the creek bank and slowly became lost to sight among the bowlders and timber.

Sinful had watched both men carefully while the doctor spoke, and now he covertly glanced at the marshal, who was gazing after the departing physician. Then he looked at Blascom, and from him to his own, disreputable partner.

"Come on, Hank," he said. "If any of these gold thieves start swappin' claims, we'll play 'em a smart tune for 'em to dance to. There's shore been a-plenty of lives saved on this crick plumb recent--our own, mebby, among 'em. An' who do you reckon yo're a-starin' at?"

"You, you pore ol' fool!" retorted Hank. He blew out a bleached cud, rammed in a fresh one, nodded at Blascom and the contemplative marshal, and followed his impatient partner toward their packs and guns.

Tex slowly turned and looked after them. "Hey, Sinful!" he called. "You still makin' coffee in old tin cans? If you are, you want to watch 'em close on account of sand gettin' in 'em!"

Sinful nudged his companion, stopped, scratched his head, and then grinned.

"Don't have to use 'em *now* . We got all our traps along, an' th' old coffeepot is with 'em, kivver an' all. Anyways, *we* don't mind a little sand once in awhile-- *do* we, Hank?"

"No, sir, by glory!" cried Hank. "Not no more, we don't, a-tall!"

Chapter XVIII
"Here Lies the Road to Rome!"

A few nights later Tex awakened to feel his little lean-to shaking until he feared it would collapse. A deafening roar on the roof made an inferno of noise, the great hailstones crashing and rolling. Flash after flash of vivid lightning seemed wrapped in the volleying crashes of the thunder. A sudden shift in the hurricane-like wind drove a white broadside against his front windows, both panes of glass seeming spontaneously to disintegrate. Another gust overturned a freight wagon in the road before the office and tore its tarpaulin cover from it as though it were tied on with strings, whisking it out of sight through the incessant lightning flashes like the instant passing of some huge ghost. The teamster, who saw no reason to pay for hotel beds while he had the wagon to sleep in, went rolling up the slatted framework and down again, bounced to his knees, and crawled frantically free, beaten by the streaking hail and buffeted by the shrieking wind. He was blown solidly against the lean-to, almost constantly in the marshal's sight because of the continuous illumination. Groping along the wall, he reached the shattered window and, desperate for shelter, promptly dived through it and rolled across the room.

Tex laughed, the sound of it lost to his own ears. "Yo're welcome, stranger!" he yelled. "But I'm sayin' yo're some precipitate! Better gimme a hand to stop up that window, or she'll blow out th' walls and lift off th' roof. Grab this table an' we'll up-end it ag'in th' openin'. I'll prop it with th' benches from th' jail. That's right. Ready? Up she goes."

After no mean struggle the window was closed enough to give protection against the raging wind, the two benches holding it securely. Then Tex struck a match and lit both of his lamps.

"We don't hardly need any light, but this is a lot steadier," he shouted, turning to look at his guest. His eyes opened wide and he stared unbelievingly. "Good Lord, man! You look like a slaughter-house! Here, lemme look you over!"

The teamster, cut, bruised, and streaked with blood, held up his hand in quick protest, shouting his reply. "'Taint nothin' but th' wallerin' I did when th' wagon turned over, an' th' beatin' from th' hail. I've seen it worse than this, friend. These stones are only big as hens' aigs, but I've seen 'em large as goose aigs, an' lost three yoke of oxen from 'em. I was freightin' in a load of supplies for a surveyin' party, down on th' old Dry Route, southwest of th' Caches. One ox was killed, his yokemate pounded' senseless, an' th' others couldn't stand th' strain an' lit out. I never saw 'em again. I was under th' wagon when they left, which didn't turn over till th' hail changed into rain, an' I wouldn't 'a' poked out my head for all th' oxen in th' country. This here's a little better than a fair prairie hail storm. Gosh," he said, grinning, as he glanced at the badge on his companion's vest. "I got plenty of nerve, all right, bustin' into th' marshal's office! Ain't got any likker, have you?"

Tex handed him a full bottle and packed his pipe. The deafening crashing of the hailstones grew less and less, a softer roar taking its place as the rain poured down in seemingly solid sheets. The great violence of the wind was gone and the lightning flashed farther and farther away.

"Feel better now," said the teamster, passing the bottle to his host and taking out his pipe. He accepted the marshal's sack of tobacco and leaned back, puffing contentedly. "Sounds a lot better, now. I'd ruther drowned than be beat to death, any time. There won't be a trail left tomorrow an' not a crick, ravine, or ditch fordable. Some of 'em with sand bottoms will be dangerous for three or four days. I once saw th' Pawnee rise so quick that it was fetlock deep when I started in, an' wagon-box deep before I could get across--an' a hull lot wider, too, I'm tellin' you. An' yet some fools still camp in dried crick beds!"

"That's just what I been thinkin' about," said the marshal, a look of worry on his face. "Out on Buffalo Crick there's near two dozen miners with claims staked out on th' dried bed. It shore would be terrible if this caught 'em asleep!"

"Don't you worry, Marshal," reassured his guest, laughingly. "Them fellers may have claims in a crick bed, but they don't sleep on 'em. They know too much!"

Tex related what a hail storm had done to a trail herd one night years before, and so they talked, reminiscence following reminiscence, until dawn broke, dull and watery, and they started for the hotel, to rout out the cook for hot coffee and an early breakfast.

All day it rained, but with none of the fury of the darker hours, and for the next ten days it continued intermittently. There was no special news from Buffalo Creek except that it had changed its bed in several places, and that two miners had been forced to swim for their lives. It was noteworthy, however, that the prospectors of the country roundabout began to spend dust with reckless carelessness. The hotel was well patronized during the day, and the nights were times of great hilarity. Drink flowed like water and old quarrels, fed by fresh fuel, added their share of turbulence to the new ones.

Sleeping late in the mornings, the marshal was on his feet until nearly every dawn, stopping brawls, deciding dangerous contentions, and once or twice resorting to stern measures. The little jail at one time was too full for further prisoners and had forced him to resort to fines, which brought his impartiality and honesty into question. He had been forced to wound two men and had been shot at from cover, all on one night. He grew more taciturn, grimmer, colder, wishing to avoid a killing, but fearing that it must come or the town would turn into a drunken riot. Then came the climax to the constantly growing lawlessness.

Busy in repairing washouts along the railroad and strengthening the three little bridges across the creeks of his section of track, Murphy and Costigan, reinforced by half a dozen other section-hands from points east, who had rolled into town on their own hand car, had scarcely seen the town for more than a week when they came in, late one Saturday afternoon. The extra hands were bedded at the toolshed and at Murphy's box car, and took their meals at Costigan's, whose thrifty wife was glad of the extra work for the little money it would bring her. Well knowing the feeling of the Middle West of that time against his race, the section-boss cautioned his crew to avoid the town as much as they could; but rough men are rough men, and wild blades are wild. Knowing the wisdom in the warning did not make it sit any easier on them, added to which was the chafing under the restraint and the galling sense of injustice.

Sunday morning found them quiet; but Sunday noon found them restless and resentful. The lively noise of the town called invitingly across the right-of-way and one of them, despite orders, departed to get a bottle of liquor. He drew hostile glances as he made his way to the bar in the saloon facing the station, but bought what he wanted and went out with it entirely unmolested. The news he brought back was pleasing and reassuring and discounted the weight of the section-boss' admonitions, and later, when the bottle had been tipped in vain and thirsts had only been encouraged by the sops given them, some wilder soul among the crowd arose and announced that he was going to paint the town. There was no argument, no holding back, and the half-dozen, laughing and singing, sallied forth to frolic or fight as Fate decreed.

The first saloon they entered served them and let them depart unharmed and without insult, raising their spirits and edging their determination to enjoy what pleasures the town might have for them. They were as good as any men in town, and they knew it, which was right and proper; but soon it did not satisfy them to know it: they must tell everyone they met. This, also, was right and proper, although hardly wise; but in the telling there swiftly crept a fighting tone, a fighting mood, a fighting look, and fighting words; yet they were behaving not one whit different from the way gangs of miners had behaved since the town was built. The difference was sharp and sufficient: The miners had been in the town of their friends; the section-gang was in the town of its enemies.

The half-dozen entered the hotel barroom, jostled and elbowed, jostling and elbowing in return, their tempers smoldering and ready to burst into flames. Calling for whiskey at the bar they drank it avidly and turned to look over the room, where all sorts and conditions of rough men and ready fighters were frowningly watching them. The frowns grew deeper, and here and there a gibe or veiled insult arose above the general noise. The gibes became more bitter, the insults less veiled, and finally a huge miner, belted and armed, stood up and shouted for silence. Sensing trouble the crowd obeyed him, waiting with savage eagerness to hear what he would say, to see what he would do.

"I'm goin' to tell you a story," he cried, and forthwith made good his promise. It was not a parlor story by any stretch of imagination, and it ended with St. Peter slamming shut the gates of heaven as he repeated one of the then popular slogans of the country along the roadbeds, "No Irish need apply." It was not couched in language that St. Peter would use, and suitable epithets of the teller's own gave added weight to the insult of the tale. Still swearing the miner sat down, an ugly leer on his face, while shouts, laughter, catcalls, and curses answered from every part of the room.

"Run 'em out of town!" came a shout, which swiftly became a universal demand.

The track-layer nearest the door, a burly, red-haired, red-faced fighting man, leaped swiftly to the miner's table, kicked the half-drawn gun from his hand, and went to the floor with him. "St. Peter will open no doors to th' like av ye!" he shouted. "I'm sendin' ye to h--l, instead!"

The bartender, fearing pistol work, whipped his own over the counter and yelled his warning and his demand for fair play. "I'll drop th' man that draws! Let 'em have it out, man to man!"

This suited the crowd as an appetizer for what was to follow, and chairs and tables crashed as it surged forward to better see the fight, the five section-hands, their broad backs against the bar, forming one side of the pushing, heaving ring, their faces set, their huge fists clenched, in spirit taking and giving the flailing blows of the rolling combatants, so intent, so lost in the struggle that consciousness of their own danger gradually faded from their minds. They had faith in their champion and were with him, heart and soul.

The miner could fight like the graduate he was of the merciless, ultra-brutal rough-and-tumble of the long frontier, biting, kneeing, gouging, throttling as opportunity offered, and he was rapidly gaining the advantage over his cleaner-fighting opponent until, breaking a throat hold, barely escaping the fingers thrust at his eyes and a wolflike snap of murderous jaws, the Irishman broke free, and staggered to his feet to make a fight which best suited him. Great gasps of relief broke from his tense friends, their low words of advice and encouragement coming from between set teeth.

"Steady, Mac, an' time 'em!" whispered his nearest friend. "He fights like a beast--lick him like th' man ye are. He's as open as a book!"

Panting, his breath whistling through his teeth, the miner scrambled to his feet, needlessly fearing a kick as he arose, and rushed, his great arms flaying before him as he tore in. Met by a straight left that caught him on the jaw a little wide of the point aimed at, he rocked back on his heels, his knees buckling, and his arms wildly waving to keep his balance. Before he could recover and set himself, a right flashed in against his chest and drove him back against the ring of men behind him. Gasping, he bent over and threw himself at his enemy's thighs, missing the hold by a hair. The Irishman retreated two swift steps and waited until his opponent had leaped up and then, feinting with his left at the swelling jaw, he swung his right shoulder behind a stiffening right arm and landed clean and squarely above the brass buckle of the cartridge belt. The crash shook the building, for the miner's feet came up as he was hurled backward and he struck the floor in a bunched heap.

The bruised and bleeding victor, filling his lungs with great gulps of foul air, started backing toward the bar to regain his breath among his friends, but he staggered sidewise on his course, coming too close to the first line of the aroused crowd and one of them leaped on him, the impact toppling him over, just as the five friends charged. Chaos reigned. Shouts, curses, the stamping of feet, bellows of rage and pain filled the dusty air with clamor as the crowd surged backward and forward, the storm center ever nearing the door. The valiant half-dozen, profiting by experience, resisted all efforts to separate them, keeping in a compact group, shoulder to shoulder, with their rapidly recovering champion in their middle. They had passed the end of the bar, which had been a sturdy bulwark against their complete encircling, and the crowd was pouring in to attack from that once-protected side when a hatless figure leaped through the deserted rear door, bounded onto the long bar without changing his stride, dashed along it and jumped, feet first straight at the heads bobbing nearest to the stout-hearted six. It was Costigan who, not finding Murphy, was acting on his own initiative and according to his lights. In his hand was a broken mattock handle and under its raining blows an opening rapidly grew in the crowd. Had he been given arm room, where his full strength could have been used, Boot Hill would have reaped a harvest. Audacity, that Audacity which is the fairest child of Courage, the total unexpectedness of his hurtling, spectacular attack won more for him and his friends than the deadly effectiveness of the hickory handle. The astonished crowd drew back in momentary confusion and Costigan, cursing at the top of his panting lungs, shoved the nearly exhausted handful through the door and into the street. As the last man staggered through and pitched to the ground, the club wielder leaped to the door, barring it with his body. He was about to tell the crowd what he thought of it when the situation changed again.

A hand clutched his shirt collar and yanked him back and he went striking with the club as he sprawled beside a battered friend. The change had been so sudden and the crowd just recovering from its surprise at Costigan's flaying attack that it looked like magic. One instant a red-shirted Irishman, his clothing torn into shreds, lovingly balancing his favorite weapon; the next, a calm, cold-faced, blue-shirted, leather-chapped gunman, bending eagerly forward behind the pair of out-thrust Colts, his thumbs holding back swift death in each hand.

"The devil!" growled a miner.

"Aye!" snapped Tex. "An' I'll find work for idle hands to do! *Why do you stop and turn away? Here lies th' road to Rome!* " he laughed, exultantly, sneeringly, insultingly; and never had they heard a laugh so deadly. It chilled where words might have inflamed. There was not a man who did not shrink instinctively, for before him stood a killer if ever he had seen one.

"I only got twelve handy--which dozen of you want to open th' way for th' rest?" asked the marshal. His quick eye caught a furtive movement in the crowd and the roar of his flaming Colt jarred the room. The offender-pitched forward before the paralyzed front line, rocking to and fro in his pain. "Th' next man dies!" snapped the marshal, his deadly intent fully revealed by his face.

The crowd gazed at impersonal Death, balanced in the two firm hands. They saw no hesitancy reflected between the narrowed lids of those calculating eyes, no qualifying expression on that granite face; and they were standing where Bud Haines had stood, facing the man he had faced. A restless surge set the mass milling, those behind pushing those in front, those in front frantically pushing back those behind. Tense and dangerous as the situation was, a verse of an immortal fighting poem leaped to the marshal's mind and a sneering smile flashed over his face. *Was none who would be foremost to lead such dire attack; but those behind cried "Forward!" And those before cried "Back!"* He seemed to tense even more, like some huge, deadly spider about to spring, and his clearly enunciated warning, low as it was spoken, reached the ears of every man in the room. "Go back to yore tables, like you was before."

The surge grew and spread, split following split, until the dragging rearguard sullenly followed its companions. The dynamic figure in the door slowly forsook its crouch, arising to full height. The left-hand gun grudgingly slid into its sheath, reluctantly followed by its more deadly mate. Casting a final, contemptuous look at the embarrassed crowd, each unit of it singled out in turn and silently challenged, the marshal shoved his hands into his pockets, turned his back on them with insolent deliberation and stepped to the street, where a bloody, battered group of seven had waited to back him up if it should be needed.

"Yer a man after me own--" began Costigan thickly between swollen lips, but he was cut short.

"That'll keep. Take these fellers back where they belong, an' *keep* 'em there," snapped Tex, the fighting fire still blazing in his soul. He watched them depart, proud of every one of them; and when they had reached the station he wheeled and went back into the hotel, had a slowly sipped drink, nodded to his acquaintances as though nothing out of the ordinary had occurred, and then sauntered out again without a backward glance, turning to go to the station.

When he reached the building he stopped and looked toward the toolshed where Murphy, just back from a run of inspection up the line, and Costigan, had turned the corner of the shed and stopped to renew their argument, which must have been warm and personal, judging from their motions. Finally Costigan, looking for all the world like a scarecrow, hitched up what remained of his trousers, squared his shoulders, and limped determinedly toward his little cottage, glancing neither to the right nor to the left. Murphy, hands on hips, gazed after him, nodded his head sharply, and was about to enter the shed when he caught sight of the motionless two-gun man. Snapping his fingers in sudden decision, he started toward his capable friend, his frame of mind plainly shown by the way his stride easily took two ties at once.

"God loves th' Irish, or 'twould be diggin' graves we'd now be doin'," he said. "An' me away! But they'll be mindin' their P's an' Q's after this. I was goin' to skin Costigan, but how could I after I learned what he did? It ain't th' first time he's tied my hands by th' quality av his fightin'. But 'twas well ye took cards, an' 'twas well ye played 'em, Tex."

"I have due respect for Costigan, but if he leaves th' railroad property he'll lose it quick," replied the marshal. "I turned that mob into a mop, but there's no tellin' what might happen one of these nights. Tim, I wish his family was out of town. It's no place for wimmin an' children these days, not with ten marshals. I can't be everywhere at once, an' I'm watchin' one house now more than I ought to."

"They're leavin' on tomorry's train east," said Murphy, breathing a sigh of relief. "I've Mike's word for it, an' if he can't get 'em to go without him, then he's goin' with 'em, superintendent or no superintendent! I'm sorry that it's my fault that ye had th' trouble, Tex; I should 'a' stayed close to them d--d fools."

"There's no harm done, Tim, as it turned out. It was comin' to a show-down, gettin' nearer an' nearer every day. Now that it's over th' town will be quiet for a day or two. I know of marshals who were paid from eight hundred to a thousand dollars a month--I'm admittin' that I've earned my hundred in just about five minutes today. For about fifteen seconds th' job was worth a hundred dollars a second--it was a close call."

"But look at th' honor av it," chuckled Murphy. "It's marshal av Windsor ye are, Tex--an' ye have yer Tower, as well!"

Tex laughed, glanced over the straggling town from Costigan's cottage to another at the other end of the street. "I'm not complainin'. I'm only contrastin' and showin' that Williams didn't pull any wool over my eyes when he offered me my princely salary. I agreed to it, and I'm paid enough, under th' circumstances."

"Aye," said Murphy, following his friend's glance, a sudden smile banishing his anxious frown. "Money ain't everythin'. Perhaps yo're not paid much now, Tex--but later, who can tell?"

Chapter XIX
A Lecture Wasted

That evening Tex had a caller in the person of Henry Williams, who seemed to be carrying quite a load of suspicion and responsibility. He nodded sourly, and nonchalantly seated himself on a chair at the other side of the door. His troubled mind was not hidden from the marshal, who could read surface indications of a psychological nature as well as any man in the West. No small part of his poker skill was built upon that ability. Should he lead his visitor by easy and natural stages to unburden himself; make a hearty, blunt opening, or make him blurt out his thoughts and go on the defensive at once? Having anything but respect and liking for the vicious nephew, he determined to make him as uncomfortable as possible. So he paid him the courtesy of a glance and resumed his apparently deep cogitations.

Henry waited for a few minutes, studying the ground and the front of his uncle's store and then coughed impatiently.

"'Tis that," responded Tex abstractedly; "but hot, an' close. I was thinkin'," he said, definitely.

Henry looked up inquiringly: "Yes?"

"Yes," said the marshal gravely. "I was." His tone repulsed any comment and he kept on thinking from where he had left off.

Henry shifted on the chair and recrossed his legs, one foot starting to swing gently to and fro. To put himself *en rapport* with his forbidding companion, he too, began thinking; or at least he simulated a thinker. The swinging foot stopped, jiggled up and down a few times, and began swinging more energetically. Soon he began drumming on the chair with the fingers of one hand. Presently he shifted his position again, recrossed his legs, grunted, and drummed alternately with the fingers of both hands. Then they drummed in unison, the nails of one set clicking with the rolling of the pads of the fingers of the other hand. Then he puckered his lips and began to whistle.

"Don't do that!" snapped Tex, and returned to his cogitations.

"What? Which?" asked Henry, starting.

"That!" exploded the marshal savagely and lapsed into intense concentration.

Henry's lips straightened and he looked down at the drumming fingers, and stopped them. Squirming on the chair, he uncrossed his legs and pushed them out before him, intently regarding the two rounded groves in the dust made by his high heels. Then he glanced covertly at his frowning companion, cleared his throat tentatively, and became quiet as the frown changed into a scowl.

The marshal thought that his visitor must have something important on his mind, something needing tact and velvety handling. Otherwise he would have become discouraged by this time and left. Was it about Jane? That would be the natural supposition, but he slowly abandoned it. Henry never had shown any timidity when speaking about her. It must be something concerning the riot in the hotel.

"I say it can't be nothin' else!" fiercely muttered the marshal, his chair dropping solidly to all fours as he rammed a fist into an open palm. "No, sir! It *can't!* " He glared at his companion. "What did you say?"

"Huh?" demanded Henry, his chair also dropping to all fours because of the impetus it had received from his sudden start. "What for?" he asked inanely.

"What for what?" growled Tex accusingly. "Who said: 'What for'?"

"I did: I just wanted to know," hastily explained Henry in frank amity.

"That's what you said!" retorted Tex, leaning tensely toward him; "but what did you mean?" he demanded.

"What you talkin' about?" queried Henry, truly and sincerely wondering.

"Don't you try to fool me!" warned Tex. "Don't pretend you don't know! An' let me tell you this. You are wrong, like th' ministers an' all th' rest of th' theologians. That's th' truest hypothesis man ever postulated. It proves itself, I tell you! From th' diffused, homogeneous, gaseous state, whirlin' because of molecular attraction, into a constantly more compact, matter state, constantly becomin' more heterogeneous as pressure varies an' causes a variable temperature of th' mass. Integration an' heterogeneity! From th' cold of th' diffused gases to th' terrific heat generated by their pressure toward th' common center of attraction. Can't you see it, man?"

Henry's mouth remained open and inarticulate.

"You won't answer, like all th' rest!" accused Tex. "An' what heat! One huge molten ball, changing th' force of th' planets nearest, shifting th' universal balance to new adjustments. 'Equilibrium!' demands Nature. An' so th' struggle goes on, ever tryin' to gain it, an' allus makin' new equilibriums necessary, like a dog chasin' a flea on th' end of his spine. Six days an' a breathin' space!" he jeered. "Six trillion years, more likely, an' no time for breathin' spaces! What you got to say to that, hey? Answer me this: What form of force does th' integration postulate? Centrifugal? Hah!" he cried. "You thought you had me there, didn't you? No, sir; not centrifugal--centripetal! Integration--centripetal! Gravity proves it. Centrifugal is th' destroyer, th' maker of satellites--not th' builder! Bah!" he grunted. "You can't disprove a word of it! Try it--just try it!"

Henry shook his head slowly, drew a deep breath and sought a more comfortable position. "These here chairs are hard, ain't they?" he remarked, feeling that he had to say something. Surely it was safe to say that.

Tex leaped to his feet and scowled down at him. "Evadin', are you?" he demanded. Then his voice changed and he placed a kindly hand on his companion's shoulder. "There ain't no use tryin' to refute it, Hennery," he said. "It can't be done--no, sir--it can't be done. Don't you ever argue with me again about this, Hennery--it only leads us nowhere. Was it Archimedes who said he could move th' earth if he only had some place to stand? He wasn't goin' to try to lift himself by his boot straps, was he, th' old fox? That's th' trouble, Hennery: after all is said we still got to find some place to stand." He glanced over Henry's head to see Doctor Horn smiling at him and he wondered how much of his heavy lecture the physician had heard. Had he expected an educated man to be an auditor he would have been more careful. "That was th' greatest hypothesis of all--the hypothesis of Laplace--it answered th' supposedly unanswerable. Science was no longer on th' defensive, Hennery," he summed up for the newcomer's benefit.

"Truly said!" beamed the doctor, getting a little excited. "In proof of its mechanical possibility Doctor Plateau demonstrated, with whirling water, that it was not a possibility, but a fact. The nebular hypothesis is more and more accepted as time goes on, by all thinking men who have no personal reasons strong enough to make them oppose it." He clapped the stunned Henry on the back. "Trot out your refutations and the marshal and I will knock them off their pins! Bring on your theologians, your special-creation adherents, and we'll pulverize them under the pestle of cold reason in the mortar of truth! But I never thought you were interested in such beautiful abstractions, Henry; I never dreamed that inductive and deductive reasoning, confined to purely scientific questions appealed to you. What needless loneliness I have suffered; what opportunities I have missed; what a dearth of intellectual exercise, and all because I took for granted that no one in this town was competent to discuss either side of such subjects. But he's got you with Laplace, Henry; got you hard and fast, if you hold to the tenets of special creation. Now that there are two of us against you, I'll warrant you a rough passage, my friend. 'Come, let's e'en at it!' We'll give you the floor, Henry--and here's where I really enjoy myself for the first time in three weary, dreary years. We'll rout your generalities with specific facts; we'll refute your ambiguities with precisions; we'll destroy your mythological conceptions with rational conceptions; your symbolical conceptions with actual conceptions; your foundation of faith by showing the genesis of that faith--couch your lance, but look to yourself, for you see before your ill-sorted array a Roman legion--short swords and a flexible line. Its centurions are geology, physics, chemistry, biology, astronomy, and mathematics. Nothing taken for granted there! No pious hopes, but solid facts, proved and re-proved. Come on, Henry--proceed to your Waterloo! Special creation indeed! Comparative anatomy, single-handed, will prove it false!"

"My G--d!" muttered Henry, forgetting his mission entirely. His head whirled, his feet were slipping so rapidly that he did not know where he was going. He stared, open-mouthed at Doctor Horn, dumbly at the marshal, got up, sat down, and then slumped back against his chair, helpless, hopeless, fearing the worst. Over his head hurled words he thought to be foreign, as his companions, having annihilated him, were performing evolutions and exercises of their verbal arms for the sheer joy of it. Finally, despairing of the lecture ever ending, he arose to escape, but was pushed back again by the excited, exultant doctor. Daylight faded, twilight passed, and it was not until darkness descended that the doctor, finding no opposition, but hearty accord instead, tired of the sound of his own voice and that of the marshal, and after profuse expressions of friendship and pleasure, departed, his head high, his shoulders squared, and his tread firm and militant.

Henry's sigh of relief sounded like the exhaust of an engine and he shifted again on the chair and tried to collect his scattered senses. Before he could get started the marshal sent him off on a new track, and his unspoken queries remained unspoken for another period.

"Seen Miss Saunders yet?" asked Tex, struggling hard to conceal his laughter.

Henry shook his head. "No; but I ain't goin' to wait much longer. I don't see no signs of her weakenin', an' that C Bar puncher is gittin' too cussed common around her house. For a peso I'd toss him in th' discard. I reckon yore way ain't no good with her, Marshal. I got to do somethin'--got to get some action."

"I know about how you feel," sympathized Tex. "I know how hard it is to set quiet an' wait in a thing like this, Hennery, even if action does lose th' game. Who was it you aimed to have perform th' ceremony?"

"Oh, there's a pilot down to Willow--one of them roamin' preachers that reckons he's found a place where he can stick. He'll come up here if th' pay's big enough, an' if I want any preacher. He'll only have to stay over one night to git a train back ag'in. Anyhow, if we has to wait a day or two it won't make much difference, as long as we're goin' to git hitched afterward."

Tex closed his eyes and waited to get a good hold on himself before replying. "He'll come for Gus, all right," he said. "Think you can hold out a few days more--just to see if my way will work? It'll be better, all around, if you do. Where was you aimin' to buy them presents for her?"

"Kansas City or St. Louie--reckon St. Louie will be better. Gus gets most of his supplies from there. You still thinkin' stockin's is th' proper idea?"

Tex cogitated a moment. "No; they're a little embarrassin': better try gloves. I'll find out th' size from her brother. Nice, long white gloves for th' weddin'--an' mebby a nice shawl to go with 'em--Cashmere, with a long fringe. They're better than stockin's. You send for 'em an' wait till they come before you go around. You shouldn't go empty-handed on a visit like that. An' you want th' minister with you when you go after her--you can leave him outside till he's needed. Folks'll talk, an' make trouble for you later. There's tight rules for weddin's; very tight rules. You don't want nobody pokin' their fingers at yore wife, Hennery. It'll shore mean a killin', some day."

"I ain't so cussed anxious to git married," growled Henry. "It's hard to git loose ag'in--but I reckon mebby I better go through with it."

"I--reckon--you--had," whispered Tex, his vision clouding for a moment. He grew strangely quiet, as though he had been mesmerized.

"A man can allus light out if he gits tired of it," reflected Henry complacently.

The marshal arose and paced up and down, thankful for the darkness, which hid the look of murder graven on his face. "Yes," he acquiesced; "a man--allus--can--do--that." This conversation was torturing him. Anything would be a relief, and he threw away the results of all his former talking. "What was on yore mind when you come down to see me today?"

"Oh!" exclaimed his companion a little nervously. "I plumb forgot all about it. You see," he hesitated, shifting again on the chair, "well, it's like this. Us boys admires th' way you handled things in th' hotel this afternoon, but somebody might 'a' been killed. 'Tain't fair to let a passel of Irish run this town--an' they started th' fight, anyhow. Th' big Mick kicked Jordan's gun out of his hand an' jumped on him. Then th' others piled in, an' th' show begun. We sort of been thinkin' that th' marshal ought to back up his town ag'in' them foreigners. Gus is mad about it--an' he's bad when he gits his back up. He thinks we ought to go down to th' railroad an' run them Micks out of town on some sharp rails, beatin' 'em up first so they won't come back. Th' boys kinda cotton to that idea. They're gettin' restless an' hard to hold. I thought I'd find out what side yo're on."

Tex stopped his pacing, alert as a panther. "I ain't on no side but law an' order," he slowly replied. "I told that section-gang to stay on th' right-of-way. They're leavin' town early tomorrow mornin', an' may not come back. A mob's a bad thing, Hennery: there's no tellin' where it'll stop. Most of 'em will be full of likker, an' a drunken mob likes bright fires. Let 'em fire one shack an' th' whole town will go: hotel, Mecca, an' all. It's yore best play to hold 'em down, or you an' yore uncle will shore lose a lot of money. Th' right-of-way is th' dead line: I'll hold it ag'in' either side as long as I can pull a trigger. You hold 'em back, Hennery; an' if you can't, don't you get out in th' front line--stay well behind!"

"Mob's do get excited," conceded Henry, thoughtfully. "Reckon I'll go see what Gus thinks about it. See you later."

Tex watched him walk away, silhouetted against the faintly illuminated store windows, and as the door slammed behind him the marshal shifted his heavy belts and went slowly up the street and into the hotel, where he received a cold welcome. Seeing that the room was fairly well crowded, accounting for most of the men in town and all of the afternoon crowd, he sat in a corner from where he could see both doors and everything going on.

In a few minutes Gus Williams and Henry entered and began mixing with the crowd, which steadily grew more quiet, but more sullen, like some wild beast held back from its prey. Henry sat at one table, surrounded by his closest friends, while his uncle held court at another. The nephew was drinking steadily and his glances at the quiet marshal became more and more suspicious. Around midnight, the temper of the crowd suiting him, Tex arose and went down the street toward his office, passed around it and circled back over the uneven plain, silently reaching the railroad near the box car.

Murphy quietly crept out of his bunk, gun in hand, and slipped to the door, pressing his ear against it. Again the drumming of the fingers sounded, but after what had occurred earlier in the day he wanted more than a tapping before he opened the door or betrayed his presence in the car. Soon he heard his name softly called and recognized the voice. As quietly as he could, he slid back the door and peered into the caller's face from behind a leveled gun.

"Don't let that go off," chuckled Tex, stepping inside. "Close th' door, Tim."

Murphy obeyed and felt his way to his visitor and they held a conversation which lasted for an hour. Tex's plans of action in certain contingencies were more than acceptable to the section-boss and he went over them until he was letter-perfect. To every question he gave an answer pleasing to the marshal and when the latter left to go up and guard the toolshed and its inmates he felt more genuine relief than he had known since he had become actively engaged in the town's activities. Things were rapidly approaching a crisis and the knowledge had filled him with dread; now let it come--he was ready to meet it.

Silently he chose a position against the railroad embankment close to the toolshed and here he remained until dawn. Murphy and Costigan passed him in the darkness on a nearly silent hand car, going west, but did not see him; and he did not know that they had returned until the sky paled. For some time he had heard a bustling in the building, and just as he was ready to leave he saw the section-gang roll out their own hand car and go rumbling up the line toward Scrub Oak.

Chapter XX
Plans Awry

For the next few days a tense equilibrium was maintained in the town, the marshal, grim, alert, and practically ostracized by nine-tenths of the population. He could feel the veiled hostility whenever he went up and down the street, and silence fell abruptly on groups of men conversing here and there whenever he was seen approaching. Hostile glances, sullen faces, shrugging shoulders greeted him on every side, and he felt more relieved than ever when he reviewed his arrangements with the section-boss.

Henry Williams was growing openly suspicious of him, impatiently awaiting the arrival of the presents from St. Louis, which he had ordered through Jerry's telegraph key, and he was drinking more and more and keeping more and more to himself, his only company being two men whom Tex had been watching since the death of Bud Haines. The marshal felt that with the coming of the presents trouble would begin, and he had asked Jerry to keep a watch for them, and let him know the moment they arrived. Fate tricked him here, for when they did come they were packed in a large consignment of goods for Gus Williams, and since he regularly was receiving shipments there was nothing to indicate to the station agent that Henry's gifts had passed through his hands.

Henry's suspicions of the marshal were cumulative rather than sudden. Never very confident about what Tex really thought and what he might do, certain vague memories of looks and of ambiguous words and actions recurred to the nephew. He was beginning to believe that the marshal would shoot him down like a dog if he pressed the issue as he intended to press it in regard to Jane Saunders, and he was determined that Tex should have no opportunity to go to her defense. Several methods of eliminating the disturbing marshal presented themselves to the coyote-cunning mind of the would-be lover. He could be shot from cover as he moved about in his flimsy office, or as he slept. He could walk into a rifle bullet as he opened his door some morning, or he could be decoyed up to Blascom's while Henry's plans went through. This last would taste sweeter in the public mouth than a coldly planned murder, but on the other hand the return of the marshal might end in cyclonic action. There was no doubt about Tex's feelings in regard to killing when he felt it to be necessary or justified. He would kill with no more compunction than a wolf would show. Then from the mutterings of rebellion and the sullen looks of discontent among the hotel habitues a plan leaped into the nephew's mind. It solved every objectionable feature of the other schemes; and Henry forthwith went to work.

The nephew was no occult mystery to a man like the marshal, who almost could see the mental wheels turning in any man like him. Tex was preparing for eventualities and part of the preparation was the buying of a pint flask of whiskey from Carney--a bottle locally regarded as pocket-size. When night fell he emptied into the liquor a carefully computed amount of chloral hydrate, recorked it, shook it well, and placed it among sundry odds and ends in a corner of the office, where it would be overlooked by any thirsty caller, whose glance was certain to notice the bottle of whiskey in plain sight on a shelf. Against the consciousness of sixteen men that innocent-looking flask would tip the scales to its own side with an emphasis; and the marshal not only knew the proper dose for horses but also how to shove it down their throats with practiced ease and swiftness. Buck Peters had paid him no mean compliment when he had said that Tex could dose a horse more expertly than any man he ever had known. Having put all of his weapons in order he marked time, awaiting the pleasure of the enemy.

He did not have long to wait. To be specific he waited two days more, which interval brought time around to the last day on the calendar for that month, the day which railroad regulations proclaimed to be the occasion for making out sundry and numerous reports, a job that kept many a station agent writing and figuring most of the night. Having sense and imagination, the agent at Windsor did what he could of this work from day to day and as a consequence saved himself from a long, high-tension job at the last minute; but he did not have imagination enough to know that a packing-case of formidable dimensions which he had received that noon from the west-bound train and later saw hauled to the Mecca, held the watched-for gifts that Henry Williams would eagerly present to Jane.

Contemptuous of any interference that Jerry might make in a physical sense, Henry nevertheless preferred to have him absent when he made his determined attempt. The brother doubtless would have great influence on Jane by his protests, and that would necessitate drastic measures which only would make the matter worse. If Jerry were detained by force, injured, or killed to keep him from the house it would cause a great deal of unpleasantness, from a domestic standpoint, to run through the years to come. There was only one night a month when the agent remained away from his house for any length of time, and this must be the night for the action to be carried through.

The mob was being slowly, but surely, inflamed by the nephew and his two friends, its anger directed against Murphy and Costigan since the section-gang had not returned to town. The section-boss and his friend came in every night while they worked along Buffalo Creek, and were careful not to give any excuse for a hostile demonstration against them. They were even less conspicuous because they walked in instead of rolling home on the hand car. But on this last night of the month the whole crew, rebelliously disobeying orders, came in on their crowded hand car, much to Henry's poorly concealed delight, and to Tex's rage. Murphy had promised otherwise.

Here was oil for the flames Henry had set burning! Here was success with a capital letter! The mob now would surely attack, divert Jerry's attention, and perhaps rid the town of its official nuisance. He would act on the marshal's kindly warning, for he would not be in the front rank of the mob; in fact, he would not be with the mob at all. He had other work to do.

The sudden look of joyous expectation, so poorly disguised, on Henry's face acted on Tex like the warning whirr of an angry rattlesnake and he quietly cleaned and oiled his guns, broke out a fresh box of cartridges, and dumped them into his right-hand pocket. The remaining chloral-filled shells he slipped in the pocket of his chaps. Shaking up the flask of whiskey to make certain of the crystals being dissolved and the drug evenly distributed throughout the fluid, he hid it again and, seating himself in his favorite place, awaited the opening number.

Darkness had just closed down when Tommy loped in from the ranch and stopped to say a few careless, friendly words, but he never uttered them, for the marshal's instructions were snapping forth before the C Bar rider could open his mouth.

"This is no time for pleasantries!" said Tex in a voice low and tense. "Turn around, ride back a way, circle around th' town an' leave yore cayuse a couple of hundred yards from Murphy's box car. Tell him trouble's brewin' an' to look sharp. Then you head for her house, actin' as cautious, an' go up to it on foot, an' as secretly as you know how. Lay low, outside. Don't show yourself at all--a man in th' dark will be worth five in th' light tonight. Stay there no matter what you hear in town. If she should see you, on yore life don't let her think there's any danger--on yore life, Tommy! Mebby there ain't, but there's no tellin' what drunken beast will remember that there's a woman close at hand. You stay there till daylight, or till I relieve you. Get-a-goin'--an' good luck!"

Tommy carried out his orders, gave Murphy the warning, and was gone again before the big Irishman, seething with rage at his crew's disobedience, could say more than a few words. Murphy had been forced to construct a plan of his own, and he wished to get word of it to the marshal's ears. Tommy having left so quickly, he could not send it. Convincing himself that it was not really necessary for the marshal to be told of it, and savagely pleased by the surprise in store for him and every man in town, the section-boss went ahead on his own initiative. Going to the toolshed he went in, frowning at the thoroughly cowed and humbled crew, blew out the lamps and with hearty curses ordered the gang to put their car on the rails and to start east for the next town.

"Roll her softly, by hand, till ye get out av th' hearin' av this hell-town, an' then board her, an' put yore weight on th' handles," he commanded. "An' don't ye come back till I send for ye. Costigan an' me are plannin' work for ourselves an' will not go with ye. Lively, now--an' no back talk. A lot depends on yer doin' as yer told. One more order disobeyed an' I'll brain th' pack av ye with a crowbar. Ye've raised h--l enough this night. Now git out av here, an' mind what I've told ye!"

The orders quickly obeyed and the car quietly placed on the rails, the gang went into the night as silently as bootless feet would take them, pushing the well-greased car ahead of them, and as gently as though it were loaded with nitro-glycerin. When far enough away not to be heard by anyone in town, they put on their boots, climbed aboard, and sent their conveyance along at an ordinary rate of speed. They hated to desert their two countrymen, and began to talk about it. Finally they made up their minds that Murphy's orders, in view of their recent disobedience, were to be followed, and with hearty accord they sent the car rolling on again, the greater part of the grades in their favor, toward the next town. The distance was nothing to become excited about with six husky men at the handles to pump off the miles.

Up at the station a single light burned in the little office where Jerry worked at his reports. Outside the building in the darkness Murphy lay on his stomach in a tuft of weeds, a rifle in his hand, and a Colt beside him on the ground. Within easy reach of his right hand lay a coatful of rocks culled from the road-bed, no mean weapons against figures silhouetted by the lamp-lighted windows of the buildings facing the right-of-way; and close to them were half a dozen dynamite cartridges, their wicked black fuses capped and inserted. Tim Murphy, like Napoleon, put his trust in heavy artillery.

Costigan was nowhere to be seen. Down the track lights shone under the cracks of the doors of the toolshed and the box-car habitation of the section-boss, and one curtained window of Costigan's rented cottage glowed dully against the night. Crickets shrilled and locusts fiddled, and there were no signs of impending danger.

In the hotel the tables were filled with lowly conversing miners in groups, each man leaning far forward, elbows on the table, his shoulders nearly touching those on either side. Gus Williams and his closest friends had pulled two tables together and made a group larger than the others. Henry and his two now inseparable companions were at a table near the back door, talking earnestly with Jake, who by this time had recovered from his recent sickness. The Buffalo Creek miner was quieter and more thoughtful than he had been before Blascom had nearly killed him, and his mind for several days had been the battle ground of a fiercely fought struggle between contending emotions, which still raged, but in a lesser intensity. He listened without comment to what was being said to him, swayed first one way and then another. His last glass of liquor was untasted, which was something of no moment to Henry's whiskey-dulled mind. Finally Jake nodded, tossed off the drink with a gesture of quick determination, hitched up his cartridge belt and, forgetting his sombrero on the floor, arose and slipped quietly out of the door. As he left, another man, peremptorily waved into the vacated chair, also listened to instructions and also slipped out through the rear door. He set his course toward the right-of-way, whereas Jake had gone in the other direction, toward Carney's saloon and the marshal's office.

The last man stopped when even with the line of shacks facing the railroad, noted the dully glowing shade in Costigan's house, the yellow strips of light around the rough board shutters of the box car, and the broader yellow band under the toolshed door. Satisfied by his inspection he slipped back the way he had come and made his report to Henry.

Jake crept with infinite caution toward the marshal's office, but when nearly to it he paused as the battle in his mind raged with a sudden burst of fury. The marshal had humbled him in sight of his friends and acquaintances and had boasted of worse to follow if his victim forced the issue; the marshal had saved his life in the little hut on the lower fork, laboring all night with him. Doctor Horn had said so, and Blascom, playing nurse at the marshal's request, had endorsed the doctor.

Ahead of him, plain to his sight, was the marshal's side window, its flimsy curtain tightly drawn; and silhouetted against it were the hatted head and the shoulders of the man he had been sent to kill. Again he crept forward, the Colt gripped tightly in his right hand. Foot by foot he advanced, but stopping more frequently to argue with himself. A few yards more and the mark could not be missed. He, himself, was safe from any answering fire. A heavy curse rumbled in his throat and he stopped again. He fought fair, as far as he knew the meaning of the term in its generally accepted definition among men of his kind. He never had knifed or shot a man from behind, and he was not going to do it now, especially a man who had no reason to save his sotted life, but who had done so without pausing. Jake arose, jammed the gun back into its holster and walked briskly to the door of the flimsy little office, which he found locked against him. He knocked and listened, but heard nothing. Again he knocked and listened and still there was no answer.

"Marshal!" he called in a rasping, loud whisper. "Marshal! Git away from that d--d window: th' next man won't be one that owes you for his life. I'm goin' back to Buffaler Crick. Look out for yoreself!" and he made good his words, striding off into the dark.

Back of the hotel, lying prone behind a pile of bleached and warped lumber, the marshal watched the rear door. He saw Jake leave, recognizing the man in the light of the opening door by certain peculiarities of carriage and manner. He smiled grimly when the man turned toward the north, and he waited for the sound of the shot which would drill the window, the shade, and the old shirt hanging on the back of a chair. He wondered if the rolled-up blanket, fastened to the broken broom handle, which made the head and held Carney's old sombrero, would fall with the impact. Then the door opened again and the second man hurried out, turning to the south. He came back shortly, left the door open behind him and with his return Henry's voice rang out in an impassioned harangue. The hotel was coming to life. The stamp of heavy boots grew more continuous; loud voices became louder and more numerous, and shouts arose above the babel. The protesting voice of Gus Williams was heard less and less, finally drowned completely in the vengeful roar. Sudden noises in the street told of angry men pouring out of the front door, simultaneously with the exodus through the rear door. Oaths, curses, threats, and explosive bursts of laughter arose. One leathern-lunged miner was drunkenly singing at the top of his voice, to the air of *John Brown's Body* , a paraphrase worded to suit the present situation.

The marshal leaped to his feet, secure against discovery in the darkness, and sprinted on a parallel course for an opening between the row of buildings facing the right-of-way. His sober-minded directness and his lightness of foot let him easily outstrip the more aimless, leisurely progress of the maudlin gang, which preferred to hold to a common front instead of stringing out. Drunk as they were, they were sober enough to realize, if only vaguely, that a two-gun sharpshooter by all odds would be waiting for the advance guard. In fact, their enthusiasm was largely imitation. Henry's mind had not been keen enough to take into consideration such a thing as anticlimax; he had not realized that the psychological moment had passed and that in the interval of the several days, while the once white-hot iron of vengeful purpose still was hot, it had cooled to a point where its heat was hardly more than superficial. The once deadly purpose of the mob was gone, thanks to Gus Williams' efforts, the ensuing arguments, and the wholesome respect for the marshal's courage and the speed and accuracy of his two guns. Instead of a destroying flood, contemptuous of all else but the destruction of its victims, the mob had degenerated into a body of devilish mischief-makers, terrible if aroused by the taste of blood, but harmless and hesitant if the taste were denied it.

Tex, sensing something of this feeling, darted through the alleyway between the two buildings he had in mind, dashed across the open space paralleling the right-of-way, crossed the tracks, and slipped behind the toolshed to be better hidden from sight. Its silence surprised him, but one glance through a knot hole showed the lighted interior to be innocent of inmates.

He forthwith sprinted to the box car and a warped crack in one of the barn-door shutters told him the same tale. A sudden grin came to his face: Murphy had done what he could to offset the return of his section-gang. He glanced at Costigan's house and its one lighted curtain, and at that instant he remembered that he had not noticed the gang's hand car in the toolshed. He brought the picture of its interior to his mind again and grunted with satisfaction. Its disappearance accounted for the disappearance of the gang.

The mob would now become a burlesque, having nothing upon which to act. Chuckling over the fiasco, he trotted toward the station to see that Jerry got away before the crowd discovered its impotence to commit murder as planned, and to stay on the west side of the main street in case the baffled units of the mob should head for Jerry's house. There was no longer any shouting or noise. He knew that it meant that the advance guard of rioters was cautiously scouting and approaching the lighted buildings with due regard to its own safety; and he reached the station platform before he saw the sudden flare of light on the ground before the toolshed which told of its doors being yanked open. Figures tumbled into the lighted patch and then milled for a moment before hurrying off to join their fellows on the way to attack the other two buildings.

"That you, Tex?" said a low voice close to him. "This is Murphy."

"Good!" exclaimed the marshal. "You've beat 'em, Tim. They're like dogs chasin' their tails; an' from th' beginnin' they didn't sound very business-like. But there's no tellin' what some of them may do, so you go up an' join Costigan while I take a look around Jerry's house. Where is he? His light's out."

"He went home when he heard th' yellin'," answered Murphy, "to git th' lass out av th' house an' to Costigan in case th' mob started that way. 'Tis lucky for them they didn't, an' pass within throwin' distance av me! 'Tis dynamite I'd 'a' fed 'em, with proper short fuses. Look out ye don't push that lighted cigar too close to th' darlin's!"

Tex stepped back as though he had been stung. "I'm half sorry they didn't give you a chance to use th' stuff," he growled. "Well, I reckon mobs will be out of style in Windsor by mornin'. This ain't no wolf-pack, runnin' bare-fanged to a kill, but a bunch of coyotes usin' coyote caution. We'll let Costigan stay where he is, just th' same. You better join him as soon as these fools go back to get drunker. Th' woman in this makes us play dead safe. I'll head up that way an' look things over. If I hear a blast I'll get back fast enough. Don't forget to throw 'em quick after you touch 'em to that cigar!"

"I'll count five an' let 'em go," chuckled Murphy. "I got 'em figgered close."

"Too close for me!" rejoined the marshal, moving off toward the Saunders' home.

"I'd like to stick one in Henry's pocket," said the Irishman, growling.

"D--n me for a fool!" snapped Tex, leaping into the darkness.

Chapter XXI
An Equal Guilt

Tommy Watkins, after delivering his message to Tim Murphy, hastened to the Saunders' home, where he carried out his orders, with but one exception; but the exception nullified all his efforts for a stealthy approach and a secret watch. The best cover he could find around the house was a little building near the back door in which firewood, kerosene, and odds and ends were kept. Despite the kindling and the darkness his entrance had been noiseless and he was paying himself hearty compliments upon the exploit when his head collided with a basket of clothespins which hung from a peg in the wall, and sent the basket and its contents clattering down on the kerosene can and a tin pan. He started back involuntarily and his spurred heels struck the side of a washtub which was nearly full of water, kept so against drying out and falling apart. Into this he sat with a promptness and abandon which would have filled the heart of any healthy small boy with ecstasies. Bounding out of the tub, he fell over the pile of kindling and from this instant his rage spared nothing in his way. Had he deliberately started out with the firm intention of arousing that part of Kansas he scarcely could have made a better job of it. While he cursed like a drunken sailor, and burned with rage and shame, the door was suddenly flung open and Jane, lamp in hand, stared at him in fright and determination, over the trembling muzzle of a short-barreled .38.

"Oh!" she exclaimed, the hand holding the gun now pressing against her breast. "Oh!" she repeated, and the lamp wobbled so that she tremblingly blew it out. For some moments she struggled to get back to normal, Tommy thankful that the lamp no longer revealed him in his present water-soaked condition. He felt that his flaming face would give light enough without any further aid.

He sidled out of the door, tongue-tied, crestfallen, miserable, and placed his back against the shed, intending to slip along it, and dash around the corner into the kindly oblivion of the black night.

"Wait!" she begged, sensing his intention. "Oh, my; how you frightened me! Whatever made you get into this shed, anyway? What were you trying to do?"

Here it was, right in his teeth. Tex fairly had hammered into him the warning not to frighten her--on his life he was to keep from her any thought of danger if she should see him. She had seen him, all right. She had seen entirely too much of him--and he was not to frighten her! Holy Moses! He was not to frighten her! He resolved that plenty of time should elapse before he allowed Tex Jones to see him. Not to frighten her--it was a wonder she had not died of fright.

"What on earth ever made you go in there?" she demanded, a little acerbity in her voice.

"Why, ma'am, I was hidin' from you," said the culprit. "Let me light th' lamp, ma'am, an' straighten things out in there. Everythin' slid that wasn't nailed fast. That tub, now: was you savin' th' water for anythin', ma'am? If you was I plumb spoiled it."

"No; it was only to keep the staves swelled tight--for heaven's sake, do you mean that you fell in it?" She reached out and grasped his coat, and suddenly collapsed against the building, shrieking with laughter. When she could speak she ordered him to feel for and pick up the lamp, and to lead the way into the house. "Go right into Jerry's room and change your clothes--I hope you can get his things on. But whatever made you go in there, anyway? What was it?"

"Like I done said, ma'am," he reiterated, flushing in the dark. "I was goin' to play a joke on Jerry when he came home--but I didn't aim to do no damage, ma'am, or scare you!" he earnestly assured her.

"Oh, but you were willing to scare Jerry!" she retorted.

"I don't reckon he'd 'a' been scared," he mumbled. "Here's th' lamp, ma'am, on th' step; I'll see Jerry at th' station. I'm fadin', now," and before she could utter a protest he had put down the lamp and disappeared around the house. But he did not go far. Wet clothes meant nothing to him, nothing at all in his present state of mind, and he intended to stay, and to keep his watch faithfully. And it was to his present flurried state of mind that he owed his more serious misadventure of the night, for he blundered around the second corner squarely into two figures hugging the wall and a descending gun butt filled his mental firmament with stars. He sagged to the ground without even a sigh and was quickly disarmed and bound. A soiled handkerchief was forced into his mouth and he was rolled against the wall, where he would be out of the way.

One of the two hirelings nudged the other as they stood up, putting his mouth close to his companions ear. "Hey, Ike!" he whispered. "This fool is wet as a drownded pup--wears a gun an' cowpunch clothes. He ain't the agent!"

"H--l, no!" responded Ike; "but he meant us no good, bein' here. We'll git th' agent, too. He'll be comin' soon, an' fast. Git over by th' path he uses."

Jane, somewhat vexed, had picked up the lamp and entered the house. The constantly re-peated "ma'am" and the stammering explanations, which she put but little stock in, made her suddenly contrast this big, overgrown boy with a man she knew, and to Tommy's vast discredit. She had hit it: one was no more than an overgrown boy, coarse, unlearned, clumsy, embar-rassed; the other, a grown man, cool, educated, masterful, unabashed. One was in his own way; the other, unobtrusive in manner but persistently haunting in his personality. She might not be able for good reasons to see Tex Jones in a room filled with people, but she could not fail to sense his presence. But the marshal was no longer to be thought of; he had taken a human life and was forever beyond the pale of her interest and affections. He had blood on his hands.

Suddenly she started and cast an apprehensive glance toward the window which faced the town. A low, chaotic roaring, indistinct in its blurred entirety, but fear impelling because of its timbre, came from the main street. A shot or two sounded flatly and the roaring rose and fell in queer, spasmodic bursts. Before she could move, a knock sounded on the door and, fearing bad news about her brother, she took a tight grip on herself and walked swiftly toward the summons, flinging the door wide open.

Henry Williams, a smirk on his face, bowed and entered, not waiting for an invitation. He forgot to remove his hat in his eagerness to place his packages on the table where she plainly could see them. Selecting the easiest chair, he seated himself on the edge of it, and tossed his sombrero against the wall.

"Nice evenin', ma'am," he said, flushing a little. "I was hopin' for more rain but don't reckon we'll git none for a spell. What we had has helped wonderful. You an' Jerry feelin' well?"

"It doesn't feel like rain, Mr. Williams," she replied, torn between fear and mirth at the presence of this unwelcome visitor. "Both my brother and myself are as well as we can expect to be. If you'll go to the station you'll find him there--this is report night and he may not be home until quite late."

"I ain't waitin' for Jerry," explained Henry, leering. "It's just as well if he is a little late. My call is shore personal, ma'am; personal between me an' you."

She was staring at him through eyes which were beginning to sparkle with vexation. She was now beginning to accept her first, intuitive warning.

"I am not aware that there is anything of a personal nature which concerns us both," she rejoined. "I believe you must be mistaken, Mr. Williams. If you will close the door behind you on your way out I will be duly grateful. Jerry is at the station." She stepped back to let him pass, but he ignored the hints.

There came an increase in the roaring from the direction of town and she started, casting an inquiring and appealing glance at her visitor.

"Th' boys are a little wild tonight," he said, smiling evilly. "They've got so much dust that they're bustin' loose to paint th' old town proper. There ain't nothin' to be scared about."

"But Jerry: my brother!" she exclaimed fearfully. "He's alone in the office!"

"No, he ain't ma'am," replied Henry with an air meant to reassure her. "I got four good boys, deputized by th' marshal, watchin' th' station in case some fool gets notions. Jones, hisself, is settin' on a bench outside, an' you know what *that* means. I allus look after my friends, ma'am." He smiled again. "'Specially them that are goin' to be real close to me. That's why I'm here--to look after you now--now, an' all th' time, now an' forever. Just see what I brought you--sent all th' way to St. Louie for 'em, an' shore got th' very best there was. Why," he chuckled, going to the table, and so engrossed in his packages that he did not see the look of revulsion on her face, a look rapidly turning to a burning shame and anger.

"These here gloves, now--they cost me six dollars. An' lookit this Cashmere shawl--you'd think I was lyin' if I told you what that cost. I told th' boys you'd show 'em off handsome an' proper. Put 'em on and let's see how they look on you." He held the gifts out, looking up at her, surprised by her silence, her lack of pleased exclamations, and paused, dumbfounded at her expression.

Mortification yielded place to shame and fear; shame and fear to anger with only a trace of fear, and then rage swept all else before it. The colors playing in her cheeks fled and left them white, her lips were thin as knife blades and her eyes blazed like crucibles of molten metal. She struck wildly at the presents, sending them across the room and raised her hand to strike him. Never in all her life had she been so furious.

"Why--what's th' matter?" he asked, not believing his senses. He put out a hand to pacify her. It touched her arm and turned her into a fury, her nails scoring it deeply as she struck it away.

"What's th' matter with you?" he demanded angrily, looking up from his bleeding hand. "Oh!" he sneered, his face working with anger. "That's it, huh? All right, d--n you! I'll cussed soon show you who's boss!" he gritted, moving slowly forward. "If you won't come willin'ly, you'll come unwillin'ly! Puttin' on airs like you was too good for me, huh? I'll bust yore spirit like you was a hoss!"

She flung a quivering arm toward the door, but he pressed forward and backed her into a corner, from where she struck at him again and again, and then felt his arms about her as he wrestled with her. Her strength amazed him and he broke loose to get a more punishing hold. "Ike!" he shouted. "George! Hurry up: she's worse'n a wildcat!"

Ike's head popped in through a window, George dashing through the door, and with them at his side Henry leaped for her. She clutched at her breast and crouched, as savage and desperate as any animal of the wild. He shouted something as he closed with her and then there came a muffled roar, a flash, and a cloud of smoke spurted from between them. Henry, his glazing eyes fixing their look of fear, amazement, and chagrin, spun around against his companions, his clutching hands dragging down their arms, and slid between them. For him the mob had been incited in vain.

His two friends, stupefied for an instant, gazed unbelievingly from Jane to Henry and back again, vaguely noticing that her horror and revulsion were unnerving her and that the short-barreled Colt in her hand was wobbling in ever-widening circles. Ike recovered his self-possession first and, reaching out swiftly, knocked the wavering weapon from her hand. Shouting savagely he leaped for her as a streak of flame stabbed in through the window he had entered by, the deafening roar filling the room. He stiffened convulsively, whirled halfway around and pitched headlong under the table, dead before he touched the floor. His companion's arms jerked upward with spasmodic speed.

"Keep 'em there! Sit down, Miss Saunders," came an even, unflurried voice from the window as the marshal, hatless and coatless, hoping that George would draw, crawled into the house behind a steady gun. "Good Lord!" he muttered, glancing over the room, his eyes passing the fallen .38 without betraying any recognition. "Steady!" he cried as Jane's knees buckled and she slid down the wall. "Keep 'em up!" he snarled at George as he swiftly disarmed him. "Face th' door!" As the frightened man obeyed, the marshal stepped quickly to a shelf on which stood a bottle of brandy and some glasses. He changed the gun to his left hand, snatched a cartridge from his chaps' pocket and, yanking out the lead with his teeth, emptied the shell into a glass. Quickly filling this and another he wheeled and thrust one out at the rigid prisoner. "Drink this," he ordered. "You shore need it; an' if you don't I'll blow you apart." George's stare of amazed incredulity changed to one of hope and relief and he downed the drink at a gulp. Tex slipped a pair of handcuffs over his wrists and ordered him to sit down. "Sit down in that big chair, an' close yore eyes. I got somethin' for you to do--relax!"

As he bent over Jane she stirred, opened her eyes, glanced at him, and then fixed them on the men on the floor, shuddering and shrinking from the sight; but she could not look away. "I killed him! I killed him!" she sobbed hysterically, over and over again.

"Drink this," ordered the marshal, forcing the glass between her lips. He nodded with quiet satisfaction. "Shore," he replied in an assumed matter-of-fact voice, as though it were an everyday occurrence. "Good job, too. I should have done it, myself, days ago." He held up the glass again. "Can you drink a little more of this, Miss Saunders? There are times when a little brandy is very useful." His low, even, unemotional tones were almost caressing, and she thankfully put herself in his capable hands. Slowly growing calmer she began to see things with a less blurred vision and the slow slumping of the sleepy man in the chair took her wondering attention.

"Why, is he--killed--too?" she asked shuddering.

"Oh, no; he's only half asleep," replied Tex, smiling. "Three more minutes an' he'll be sound asleep, for a dozen hours or more. Brandy has an hypnotic effect on some people, Miss Saunders, while it stimulates others. Will you please collect a small valise of your most valuable and indispensable possessions, all the money in the house, a good wrap of some kind, and allow me to escort you to Murphy and Costigan? You are leaving town, you know, never to return."

"But I've killed a man, and you are an officer of the law! Do you mean--" she paused unbelievingly.

"You shot a mad skunk in plain self-defense," he replied. "He has powerful friends and influence to avenge him. The jury would be packed and justice scorned. I'm marshal no longer, Miss Saunders. I accepted the appointment on the definite understanding that I would be marshal only as long as I could. The term has automatically come to an end. So far as this town is concerned I'm a rabid outlaw." He tore the badge from his vest and threw it on the table. "Ah! George is sleeping more soundly than he ever slept before. There's no need of gagging him, for he'll give no alarm. Please fill that satchel, Miss Saunders--time presses."

"You are a good friend, Mr. Jones; and I have wronged you," she said, her words barely audible. "My hands are as bloody as yours--and I scorned you for taking life! Take me away from here--please--please!"

"As fast as I can," replied Tex, soothingly. "You help me by filling a satchel and getting your wrap. Put your mind on your possessions, please; think what you wish to take with you, and then get them. Money? Jewels? Miscellaneous valuables, intrinsic or sentimental? Documents? Apparel? Please--you must aid me all you can if I'm to aid you. We have no time to lose!"

"But my brother--he is safe?"

"Waiting outside, tied, and gagged. I couldn't stop to free him," Tex answered. "Watkins, likewise. They laid their plans well, but the mob was a misfire and didn't keep me as busy as they counted on. Will you obey me, Miss Saunders, or must we leave bare-handed? I'll give you just three minutes by that clock--then we go."

A pious, shocked exclamation came from the window where Murphy stared suddenly into a magic gun before he was recognized. "Holy Mother!" he whispered, and then: "I found Tommy--where is Jerry?"

"Don't you ever do that again!" snapped Tex, a little white showing in his face. "I don't know how I kept th' hammer up! You look around by that clump of scrub oak, where the path goes around the big bowlder. I nearly fell over him. Take them both with you--we'll follow close. Any signs of anyone coming from town?"

"Not yet--but ye needn't stay here all night! Hurry, miss, or there'll be a slaughter that'll shake this country!"

As Jane obeyed, Tex walked over, drew up one of George's eyelids and smiled grimly. Then he placed a hand on each of the figures on the floor and nodded, a sneer flickering over his face. In a moment Jane, still a little unsteady, returned and found the ex-marshal pinning the nickeled badge on the lapel of Henry's coat, and while it meant nothing to her then in her agitated state of mind its significance came to her later. When that badge was found she would be freed of blame for Henry's death. Opening the door Tex blew out the light and led the way. They hurried over the uneven, hard ground and soon reached the railroad, where a hand car, with Murphy, Costigan, and Tommy at the handles, waited to run them over a trail where no tracks would tell any tales.

"Head for Scrub Oak, an' stop outside th' town till Jerry's party gets away," ordered Tex. "Th' grades are mostly against you an' all of you came from th' east, where Mike's family went. They'll figger you went th' same way, if they think of th' hand car at all. It ain't likely they will, because I'm aimin' to give them something plain to read, when they're *able* to read it. Got money? Got enough to buy three good cayuses with saddles, grub, an' everythin' you need? Good! Tommy, when you get to town, go in alone, get three outfits, an' take Miss Saunders an' Jerry to Gunsight as fast as they can travel. When you get there, ask for Nelson, an' tell him Tex Ewalt says to hold off h--l an' high water before givin' up these two. I'll join you there as soon as I can. Here, listen close," and he gave a description of Gunsight's location sufficient for a rider of the plains. "Off with you, now--let her roll gently near Buffalo Crick--she'll rumble deep crossin' that bridge an' Jake may be at home. So-long--get a-goin'!"

"But you?" cried Jane. "Where are you going? Surely not back into that town!" The distress and anxiety brought a smile to the ex-marshal's lips. "You must come with us! You must! You must!" she insisted almost hysterically. "You can't fight the whole town!"

"I'm bettin' he can," growled Murphy. "Here, Tex! Better take a couple av these little fire-crackers! Count five an' let 'em go; but *you* better count sorta fast."

"No, thanks, Tim," laughed Tex. "I can't go with you, Miss Saunders. I've got a pack of coyotes to make fools of--see you at th' SV in four or five days. Don't you worry--it was clean self-defense. He brought it on himself. All right, Tim: get a-goin'!"

He listened to the sounds of the cautiously propelled car, the clicks of the rail joints growing softer and softer. When they had died out, he walked swiftly back to the house, where he got his hat and coat and then went on to town. Going to where the roan patiently waited for him he led it to John Graves' stable and reconnoitered the building. John was not at home on this night of excitement.

Tex forced the door, and quietly saddled the sorrel and the gray, threw a sack of corn across the latter and, leading them forth, led the three animals back of a deserted building and then went toward the hotel.

Chapter XXII
The False Trail and the True

The maudlin crowd was ugly and did not accept the marshal's appearance with any enthusiasm. While he had not opposed them he had warned and sent away their hoped-for victims. Frank scowls met him wherever he looked. He stopped at the table where Gus Williams and a dozen cronies, the bolder men of the town, were drinking and arguing.

"Blascom's cussed sick," he announced. "Sick as a dog. I rode out to spend th' night with him, knowin' that when that coyote section-boss sent his pack out of town there wouldn't be no reason for me to stay here an' make myself unpopular. I got a good job in this town, an' I've got a right to have friends here. Anyhow, I told Murphy that if his men came back they'd have to do their own fightin'. Reckon that's why he sent 'em along. Him an' Costigan follered 'em on th' other hand car." He glanced over the room. "Where's Hennery?" he asked. "I heard he wanted to see me."

Williams roused himself and looked up through bloodshot eyes. "Th' fool's gone courtin', I reckon; an' on a night like this, when I needed him. Don't know when he'll git back. He mus' be enjoyin' hisself, anyhow."

John Graves chuckled and endorsed the sentiment.

Tex nodded. "I reckon mebby he is, his star bein' bright tonight. Much excitement in town after I left? Station agent make any trouble?"

"A lot of chances he'd 'a' had to make any of us any trouble," sneered a miner. "I reckon he cut an' run right quick. We've been figgerin' he's better off in some other town. Been thinkin' of chasin' him out. Any objections from th' marshal of Windsor?"

"Not a cussed one," answered Tex. "He's a trouble-maker, stayin' here. Chuck him on th' train tomorrow an' send him back East, where he come from. An' his sister, too, if you want."

Williams shook his head. "Not her," he said. "Henry'll never let her git away from him. He's aimin' to take care of her; an' he shore can handle her, *he* can."

"I reckon he can," agreed Tex. "I just come in to get th' doc to go out an' look at Blascom. Since he's struck it rich he's been feedin' like a fool. Them as live by canned grub, dies by canned grub, says I; an' he's close to doin' it. I got a bottle of whiskey for him, but I reckon gin will be better for his stummick. Yes, a lot better. Hey, Baldy!" he shouted. "Put me out a bottle of gin an' set up th' drinks for all hands. We'll drink to a better understandin' an' to Hennery an' his bride." He pulled the pint flask from his pocket and winked at his companions. "I got a little somethin' extra, here. Th' smoke of Scotch fires is in it. Might as well use it up," and he quickly filled the glasses on the table, discovering when too late that he had none left for himself. "Oh, well; whiskey is whiskey, to me. I'll take some of Baldy's with th' boys," and he swaggered over to the bar, tossing a gold piece on the counter.

"Where's yore badge, Marshal?" asked Baldy, curiously.

Tex quickly felt of his coat lapel and then of his vest. "Cuss it!" he growled. "I knowed I'd lose that star--th' pin was a little short to go far enough in th' socket. Oh, well," he laughed, holding up his glass, "everyone knows me now; an' they'll know me better as time goes on. Here's to Hennery!" he shouted. "Drink her standin'!"

The toast drunk to roaring jests, he took the gin and went back to Williams. "Goin' after th' doc," he remarked. "Lost my badge, too; but lemme say that anybody found wearin' it shore will have bad luck. See you all tomorrow. He's sick as a pup, Blascom is. Good night, an' sleep tight, as th' sayin' is!" he shouted laughingly and nodding at the crowd he wheeled and went out. Once secure from observation of any curious inhabitants of the town, he ran to the horses, mounted, and rode up to the Saunders' house, a home no longer. Entering it he quickly collected a bag of provisions and then, milling the horses before the door to start a plain trail, he cantered toward the station, where he crossed the tracks and struck south for the old cattle trail.

All night he rode hard, sitting the sorrel to keep his own horse fresh, and at dawn, giving them a ration of corn each, he ate a cold and hurried breakfast and soon was on his way again. During the forenoon he let the sorrel go, riding the gray with the depleted corn sack tied to the pommel. Several hours later he threw the still further depleted sack on the roan, changed horses again and turned the gray loose. After nightfall he came within sight of the lights of a small town and, waiting until the hour was quite late, rode through it casually to lose the tracks of his horse among the countless prints on its streets. He left it along a well-traveled trail leading westward, one which would take him, eventually, to Rawlins.

In the town of Gunsight, Dave Green was polishing glasses behind his bar when a dusty, but smiling, stranger rode up to the door and called out. Grumbling, Dave waddled forth to answer the summons.

"Which way to th' SV?" asked the stranger. "I'm lookin' for my friend Nelson."

"What is it--a house-raisin' or a christenin'?" asked Dave, grinning broadly. "Th' SV's gettin right pop'lar these days--as it ought to be." Dave cogitated a moment. This man said Nelson was a friend of his; but if not, there would be no harm done to anyone on the SV. Dave was quite certain of that, with Hopalong, Red, and the outfit at Johnny's back. Still, his curiosity was aroused. "Yore name Jones, or Ewalt?" he asked.

"Ewalt," replied Tex, grinning.

Dave left the door and gravely held out his hand. "Heard tell about you, long ago," he said. "We're good friends till you horn into a poker game that I'm settin' in. Heard about you this mornin', too. A tenderfoot, a cowpunch, an' a reg'lar picture in skirts stopped an' asked me what you did. Also wanted to know if I had seen Jones or Ewalt. You just foller that Juniper trail," and he gave a description tiresome, and needlessly detailed, to a man to whom compass points would have sufficed. "Jones comin', too? Don't know I ever heard of him."

"Jones is dead," said Tex with touching sorrow. "Th' pore ol' soul, we'll never see him more. He had buttons runnin' up his back, an' buttons down before."

"Too bad," replied Dave, but he was suspicious of the other's grief. He shook his head. "Life shore is uncertain. You tell Johnny if he's havin' a party that I ain't too fat to ride that far, not if I'm invited. I ain't much on dancin', but I'll do my best."

Tex nodded, thanked him for his information and went on, gradually becoming lost in introspective musings.

"Omar," he muttered, shaking his head sadly, "I ain't got no right. I'm hard-boiled, an' I've reached purty low levels th' last twenty years. There ain't no human meanness, no human weaknesses, hardly, that I ain't seen. My view of life is so cynical that it near scares me, now. I lost my illusions years ago, an' I'm allus lookin' for th' basest motives for a man's actions. Besides, I'm forty-odd years old--an' that's *too* old.

"Now you take Tommy Watkins. He's fresh, young, chock-a-block with illusions; trustin', ambitious, steady. He's clean, body an' mind. When he grows up, ten years from now, he'll be a purty fair sort of a young man. It shore does beat all, Omar."

A little farther along he drew a deep breath and patted the roan. "Omar, I've made up my mind: Youth should be for youth; illusions, for illusions; freshness, for freshness; innocence, for innocence. Her purity deserves better than my mildewed soul--if a man's got one." After a moment's silence he patted the horse again. "Omar, yore name brings somethin' back to me:

> *Ah Love! could you and I with Him conspire*
> *To grasp this sorry Scheme of Things entire,*
> *Would not we shatter it to bits--and then*
> *Remould it nearer to the Heart's Desire!*

Raising his head he saw a rattlesnake sunning itself on a rocky patch of ground near the trail and his gun leaped into crashing life. The snake writhed, trying in vain to coil. A second shot stretched it lifeless.

"There, d--n you!" shouted Tex, shaking his fist at the quivering body, "that's how I feel!" and, the burst of passion gone as quickly as it had come, he shook his head and rode on again, calm and determined. At last he came to the top of the last hill hiding the ranchhouse and drew rein as he looked down into the north branch of the SV valley. A boy was riding along the bottom of the slope and Tex hailed him.

"Hey, sonny!" shouted the ex-marshal. "I'm lookin' for Hopalong Cassidy. Know where he is?"

"He's at th' house!" replied the boy. "Yo're Tex Ewalt! Foller me, an' I'll beat you to him!"

"Bet yo're Charley!" responded Tex. "Yo're shore goin' to ride some, cowboy, if you aim to beat me!" and a race was on.

There came a flurry of movement at the ranchhouse door and three men ran to their saddled horses. A sudden cloud of dust rolled up and the three, bunched leg to leg, raced toward the galloping newcomer. Heedless of Charley's vexatious appeal they shot past him and kept on while he swung his pony around and saw them sweep up to the slowing roan and surround him and his rider. More soberly, after a hilarious welcome, the four, with Charley endeavoring to wedge into shifting openings not half large enough for his pony, they rode up to the ranchhouse, where Jerry had run out to meet them, Margaret Nelson at his heels. As soon as he could Tex asked for Jane and learned that she was resting.

"She has been under a very heavy strain, Mr. Ewalt," Margaret told him. "She asked that you see her as soon as you came; but she is sleeping, now, and it will be better for her if you wait. Her remorse is as great as her horror and fatigue."

"I suppose so," replied Tex. "That's the woman of it. She shot a beast in plain self-defense and now she's remorseful. Shucks--it's all my fault. I should have done it, myself, days before."

"I didn't say just what I think is causing her remorse," replied Margaret, smiling enigmatically; "but that is something a man should find out for himself," and, turning quickly, she entered the house.

Tex stared after her and then around the circle of happy, grinning faces. An answering smile crept to his own, a smile wistful, but shaded with pain.

The next few days were busy ones from a conversational standpoint, for there was a great deal to talk about. Tex learned the history of the SV's rejuvenation, and his friends eagerly listened to the news he brought from Montana, and to the messages he brought from their friends; while Jane, much better because of the rest she had had, sat by the cheerful group, smiling at the perfect accord between its units and rapidly changing her ideas of western men. Here she saw friendships which seemed to be founded on the eternal rock, unshakable, unquestioning. She found it almost impossible to believe that these thin-lipped, yet kindly and smiling men, whose trick of looking out through narrowed lids at first made her wonder, each had killed again and again, as Margaret had told her. To her they were gravely kind, courteous, and deferential, accepting her without question, their manner a soothing assurance as to her safety. Jerry and Tommy were unquestionably accepted and made part of the happy circle--they were friends of Tex Ewalt, whom she now knew by his right name. Johnny's boyish enthusiasm and mischievous smile made it hard for her to believe that he, single-handed, had overcome the odds against him and cleared this range of its undesirable inhabitants. Margaret's proud account of his deeds rang true, and Jane knew that they were true.

There they all sat on the front porch, telling anecdotes on each other which amazed Jane, speaking of remarkable exploits in matter-of-fact voices. She learned of Tex's part in the saving of Buck Peter's ranch, and gradually pieced together the story of his activities in Windsor. Prodded by Tex, at last Johnny and Hopalong gave a grudging exhibition of revolver shooting which made her catch her breath. Tex Ewalt had been right: these two cheerful men could ride into Windsor and wipe it from the map; and she no longer feared the appearance of any of Williams' friends. If they could find and follow the trail, let them!

Tex was the quietest man in the party, and she was pleased because he spoke only in the vernacular. She had not heard him deviate from it for one instant. He had no wish to "show off" at the expense of his roughly speaking friends. Tommy's garrulity, considering how little he really had to say, sounded like the prattle of a child among grown-ups; but he was a good, well-meaning boy. Daily he spoke of getting work on the Double X, where Lin Sherwood could use another rider; but he had made no attempt to go, preferring to stay where she was and to follow her about at every opportunity.

Then came the afternoon when Johnny volunteered to show his guests about the ranch and they had set out, Tex remaining behind. Jane had felt a restraint at the thought of how close she and the ex-marshal would be thrown together on this ranch, but soon found it to be groundless. Deferential, reserved, friendly, he had not obtruded, and apparently had not noticed Tommy's attentions. They rode off, Jerry with their host, Tommy at the side of Jane. When down in the main valley Johnny had turned off to look at the fenced-in quicksands, Jerry going with him to see the now harmless death trap, and Tommy remained behind with her; and when they returned they found a flushed Jane and a despondent Tommy. The following morning when she sat down to a late breakfast with Mr. Arnold, Johnny's father-in-law, she learned quite casually that Tommy had gone to the Double X and that the rest of the men, her brother included, had ridden up to the north wire to make some repairs. Arnold explained about the difficulty of keeping the posts up along the bottom of the ravine where he had suffered his broken leg, and he told her of the fondness of the cattle for the wilderness of brush and of the difficult task of running a round-up on that part of the ranch.

"Let me throw a saddle on yore horse, Miss Saunders," he suggested. "It will make a pleasant ride for you; an' you can take 'em up some lunch if you like. They've got a bigger task than they think, for th' ravine floor is solid rock. I'll send Charley with you--he's on th' rampage because he overslept and I wouldn't let him go up and bother them. But he might as well go."

She thought for a moment, and then turned a grave and pitiful face to him.

"I feel that I can ask you anything, Mr. Arnold; and I'm so upset."

"You certainly can, Miss Saunders," he replied, abandoning the vernacular in response to her way of speaking.

She hurriedly told him of the killing of Henry Williams, of the blood on her hands, but avoided the real appeal, the question she must find her own answer to. He heard her through, and, arising, placed a fatherly hand on her shoulder.

"Jane," he said, slowly shaking his head. "Environment, circumstances, change all things. There's not a man on this ranch that doesn't feel proud of what he knows about you. A woman has as much right, and often a greater need, to defend herself, as a man has. Don't you worry about that beast; and don't you worry about anyone coming down here after you. We can muster forty fighting men, if we need them, purely on Johnny's say-so. We're all proud of you. Now I'll saddle your horse while Peggy puts up the lunch. You and Charley can easily carry it between you. There's no place down here where you can't safely go; but please keep in the saddle while you're on the range. These cattle are dangerous to anyone afoot."

While the simple preparations were being made she heard Charley's exultant whoops and soon she rode with him toward the upper end of the small valley, listening to his worshiping chatter about his heroes. Now he had a new one, the man who could pull poker hands out of a fellow's nose, eyes, and ears.

"He'd 'a' got that Hennery feller, too," he averred, "only you beat him out. Gee, Miss Saunders! Wish I'd 'a' been there! I ain't never shot nobody yet--but you just wait, that's all! I heard Tex say he'd 'a' shot up th' whole d--d town if they'd tried to bother you--an' Hoppy said he could 'a' done it, *easy* ! Hoppy knows, too. Why don't you like Tex, Miss Saunders? I think he's aces-up!"

"Why, I do, Charley. Whatever made you ask me that?"

"Well, if you do, Tex don't think so," he grumbled. "You know that pile of rock, up on th' hill where th' Gunsight trail winds like a letter S?"

She nodded. She could see it plainly from her window.

"Well, I was layin' up there, keepin' watch for that Williams' gang, an' he never even reckoned anybody was near him!" he boasted. "Takes a good man to find me when I don't want him to, I tell you. Injuns can't, an' they're cussed cute, Hoppy says."

"Who was it who didn't see you?"

"Tex," chuckled the boy. "He come walkin' along like there wasn't nobody around, an' he sorta slammed hisself down on th' rock next to th' top one. You an' Tommy an' Jerry was ridin' back from th' main valley. We could just see you, me an' him, only he didn't know *I* was there. After awhile we could see plain. Jerry rode off to look at somethin', an kinda fell back, leavin' you an' Tommy goin' on without him. I was watchin' Tex, because he had a funny look on his face. He just looked steady, an' when he saw you two ridin' along together, he threw out his arms an' said somethin' about bein' like Jerry. Somethin' about falling back an' seein' you an' Tommy ridin' through life together--as if anybody would ride as long as that! Tell you what: These grown-ups say some cussed foolish things. There was tears in his eyes--him, a grown-up, gun-fightin' son-of-a-gun! Huh! An' they used to tease me when *I* cried! What you think about that?" He looked eagerly at her for the answer and then snorted in frank disgust. "Cuss it--an' yo're snifflin', too! I'll be a son-of-a-gun!"

"You mustn't tell anyone about it, Charley!" she pleaded. "They won't understand!"

"I won't," he promised. "Don't blame you for bein' ashamed. Tex would 'a' been, too, if he knowed I saw him. Then mebby he wouldn't go up there every night an' watch yore window till the light goes out, an' I wouldn't have nobody to trail. Reckon he's scared that Williams gang will trail you down here? Huh! With him settin' up there, me roamin' loose, an' with Johnny, Hoppy, an' Red in th' house, I shore wish they would come a-pokin' their noses around here! I tell you, things'd shore pop. If Tex could clean out their whole town all alone, they'd shore have a pleasant time down here ag'in' him an' his friends! Gee!"

After supper the nightly gathering on the porch passed a pleasant hour or two and then dwindled as its members retired, the two women and Charley going first. Jerry followed soon afterward and not much later Red and Hopalong left to go to the bunkhouse, where they now were berthed. Arnold soon went into the house, to the room which Tex stubbornly had refused to occupy, the latter preferring the bunkhouse with his old friends. After a cigarette or two Johnny said good night and left his companion alone. Tex arose, paced restlessly to and fro across the yard and, wheeling abruptly, went toward the corral. He had not been gone very long when Charley, noiselessly crawling out of the window of the room he shared with his father, froze in his tracks as he heard a noise beyond the summer kitchen. He had Red's Winchester, which he had taken from the gun rack in the dining-room, and he scouted cautiously toward the suspicious sounds. The moonlight let him see plainly, and he drew back behind the corner of the building as Jane rode away, leaving the light burning brightly in her room.

Charley frankly was puzzled. "Somethin's goin' on," he cogitated. "I was goin' to stalk Tex-
-now I dunno. Shucks! He can look out for hisself, but she might get lost. Reckon I'll foller
her." He suited action to the words and soon was riding after her, keeping out of her sight
with a woodcraft worthy of his elders.

She led him along the Gunsight trail, closer and closer to the S it made up the rocky hill,
and because of the view commanded by the rocky pile on the summit, he had to dismount,
picket his horse, and proceed on foot, working from cover to cover, often on hands and knees.

Tex had taken his time, buried in thought, oblivious to everything outside of himself. He
followed the well-marked trail instinctively and soon reached the top of the hill, where he sat
quietly in the saddle for a few minutes. Finally, shaking his head, he dismounted and listlessly
walked to the place of his nightly vigil. Seating himself on the top-most bowlder he gazed
steadily at the yellow light of the distant window and, like many men of his class, given to solitude, he argued his problem aloud. It seemed that often he could think more clearly that way.

This could not go on. Tomorrow he would start back to Montana, and he soon arose to
return to the SV, to spend his last night there. As he went back to his horse another verse
came to his mind, a verse of finality, and one fitting the present situation. He laughed bitterly
and flung out his arms:

> *And when like her, O Sákí, you shall pass*
> *Among the Guests Star-scatter'd on the Grass,*
> *And in your blissful errand reach the spot*
> *Where I made One--turn down an empty Glass!*

Suddenly he stiffened, his hands leaping instinctively to his guns. Then he let them fall to his
sides and stared unbelievingly: "Miss Saunders!" he exclaimed in amazement. "Why--what are
you--?" and ceased, tongue-tied.

"You are--going away?" she asked, her voice breaking, speaking so low he barely could hear
her words.

"Tomorrow."

She hung her head for a moment and then turned a wistful, anxious face up to him. "I--I
heard what you have been saying. O Tex--I--I am going with you!"

The Orphan

Chapter I
The Sheriff Rides to War

Many men swore that The Orphan was bad, and many swore profanely and with wonderful command of epithets because he was bad, but for obvious reasons that was as far as the majority went to show their displeasure. Those of the minority who had gone farther and who had shown their hatred by rash actions only proved their foolishness; for they had indeed gone far and would return no more.

Tradition had it that The Orphan was a mongrel, a half-breed, asserting that his mother had been a Sioux with negro blood in her veins. It also asserted that his father had been nominated and unanimously elected, by a posse, to an elevated position under a tree; and further, that The Orphan himself had been born during a cloudburst at midnight on the thirteenth of the month. The latter was from the Mexicans, who found great delight in making such terrifying combinations of ill luck.

But tradition was strongly questioned as to his mother, for how could the son of such a mother be possessed of the dare-devil courage and grit which had made his name a synonym of terror? This contention was well stated and is borne out, for it can be authoritatively said that the mother of The Orphan was white, and had neither Indian nor negro blood in her veins, but on the contrary came from a family of gentlefolk. Thus I start aright by refuting slander. The Orphan was white, his profanity blue, and his anger red, and having started aright, I will continue with the events which led to the discovery of his innate better qualities and their final ascendency over the savagely hard nature which circumstances had bred in him. These events began on the day when James Shields, for reasons hereinafter set forth, became actively interested in his career.

Shields, by common consent Keeper of the Law over a territory as large as the State of New Jersey and whom out of courtesy I will call sheriff, was no coward, and neither was he a fool; and when word came to him that The Orphan had made a mess of two sheep herders near the U Bend of the Limping Water Creek, he did not forthwith pace the street and inform the citizens of Ford's Station that he was about to start on a journey which had for its object the congratulation of The Orphan at long range. Upon occasions his taciturnity became oppressive, especially when grave dangers or tense situations demanded concentration of thought. The more he thought the less he talked, the one notable exception being when stirred to righteous anger by personal insults, in which case his words flowed smoothly along one channel while his thoughts gripped a single idea. To his acquaintances he varied as the mood directed, often saying practically nothing for hours, and at other times discoursing volubly. One thing, a word of his, had become proverbial-when Shields said "Hell!" he was in no mood for pleasantries, and the third repetition of the word meant red, red anger. He was a man of strong personality, who loved his friends in staunch, unswerving loyalty; and he tolerated his enemies until the last ditch had been reached.

He, like The Orphan, was essentially a humorist in the finest definition of the term, inasmuch as he could find humor in the worst possible situations. He was even now forcibly struck with the humor of his contemplated ride, for The Orphan would be so very much surprised to see him. He could picture the expression of weary toleration which would grace the outlaw's face over the sights, and he chuckled inwardly as he thought of how The Orphan would swear. He did his shooting as an unavoidable duty, a business, a stern necessity; and he took great delight in its accuracy. When he shot at a man he did it with becoming gravity, but nevertheless he radiated pride and cheerfulness when he hit the man's nose or eye or Adam's apple at a hundred yards. All the time he knew that the man ought to die, that it was a case of necessity, and this explains why he was so pleased about the eye or nose or Adam's apple.

With The Orphan popular opinion said it was far different; that his humor was ghastly, malevolent, murderous; that he shot to kill with the same gravity, but that it was that of icy determination, chilling ferocity. He was said to be methodical in the taking of innocent life, even more accurate than the sheriff, wily and shrewd as the leader of a wolf-pack, and equally relentless. The Orphan was looked upon as an abnormal development of the idea of destruction; the sheriff, a corrective force, and almost as strong as the evil he would endeavor to overcome. The two came as near to the scientists' little joke of the irresistible force meeting the immovable body as can be found in human agents.

So Shields, upon hearing of The Orphan's latest manifestation of humor, appreciated the joke to the fullest extent and made up his mind to play a similar one on the frisky outlaw. He could not help but sympathize with The Orphan, because every man knew what pests the sheepmen were, and Shields, at one time a cowman, was naturally prejudiced against sheep. He was exceedingly weary of having to guard herds of bleating grass-shavers which so often passed across his domain, and he regarded the sheep-raising industry as an unnecessary evil which should by all rights be deported. But he could not excuse The Orphan's crude and savage idea of deportation. The sheriff was really kind-hearted, and he became angry when he thought of the outlaw driving two thousand sheep over the steep bank of the Limping Water to a pitiful death by drowning; The Orphan should have been satisfied in messing up the anatomy of the herders. He did not like a glutton, and he would tell the outlaw so in his own way.

He walked briskly through his yard and called to his wife as he passed the house, telling her that he was going to be gone for an indefinite period, not revealing the object of his journey, as he did not wish to worry her. Accustomed as she was to have him face danger, she had a loving wife's fear for his safety, and lost many hours' sleep while he was away. He took his rifle from where it leaned against the porch and continued on his way to the small corral in the rear of the yard, where two horses whisked flies and sought the shade. Leading one of them outside, he deftly slung a saddle to its back, secured the cinches and put on a light bridle. Dropping the Winchester into its saddle holster, he mounted and fought the animal for a few minutes just as he always had to fight it. He spun the cylinders of his .45 Colts and ran his fingers along the under side of his belt for assurance as to ammunition. Seeing that the black leather case which was slung from the pommel of the saddle contained his field glass and that his canteen was full of water, he rode to the back door of his house, where his wife gave him a bag of food. Promising her that he would take good care of himself and to return as speedily as possible, he cantered through the gate and down the street toward the "Oasis," the door of which was always open. Two dogs were stretched out in the doorway, lazily snapping at flies. As the sheriff drew rein he heard snores which wheezed from the barroom.

"Say, Dan!" he cried loudly. "Dan!"

"Shout it out, Sheriff," came the response from within the darkened room, and the bartender appeared at the door.

"If anybody wants me, they may find me at Brent's; I'm going out that way," the sheriff said, as he loosened the reins. "Bite, d———n you," he growled at his horse.

"All right, Jim," sleepily replied the bartender, watching the peace officer as he cantered briskly down the street. He yawned, stretched and returned to his chair, there to doze lightly as long as he might.

Shields usually left word at the Oasis as to where he might be found in case he should be badly needed, but in this instance he had left word where he could not be found if needed. He cantered out of the town over the trail which led to Brent's ranch and held to it until he had put great enough distance behind to assure him that he was out of sight of any curious citizen of Ford's Station. Then he wheeled abruptly as he reached the bottom of an arroyo and swung sharply to the northeast at a right angle to his former course and pushed his mount at a lope around the chaparrals and cacti, all the time riding more to the east and in the direction of the U Bend of the Limping Water. He frowned slightly and grumbled as he estimated that The Orphan would have nearly three hours' start of him by the time he reached his objective, which meant a long chase in the pursuit of such a man.

To a tenderfoot the heat would have been very oppressive, even dangerous, but the sheriff thought it an ideal temperature for hunting. He smiled pleasantly at his surroundings and was pleased by the playful vim of his belligerent pinto, whose actions were not in the least intended to be playful. When the animal suddenly turned its head and nipped hard and quick at the sheriff's legs, getting a mouthful of nasty leather and seasoned ash for its reward, he gleefully kicked the pony in the eye when it let go, and then rowelled a streak of perforations in its ugly hide with his spurs as an encouragement. The ensuing bucking was joy to his heart, and he feared that he might eventually grow to like the animal.

When he arrived at the U Bend he put in half an hour burying the human butts of The Orphan's joke, for the perpetrator liked to leave his trophies where they could be seen and appreciated. Shields looked sadly at the dead sheep, said "Hell" twice and forded the stream, picked up the outlaw's trail on the further side and cantered along it. The trail was very plain to him, straight as a chalk line, and it led toward the northeast, which suited the sheriff, because there was a goodly sized water hole twenty miles further on in that direction. Perhaps he would find The Orphan fortified there, for it would be just like that person to monopolize the only drinking water within twenty miles and force his humorous adversary to either take the hole or go back to the Limping Water for a drink. Anyway, The Orphan would get awfully soiled wallowing about in the mud and water, and he would not hurt the water much unless he lacked the decency to bleed on the bank. Having decided to take the hole in preference to riding back to the creek, the sheriff immediately dismissed that phase of the game from his mind and fell to musing about the rumors which had persistently reiterated that the Apaches were out.

Practical joking with The Orphan and interfering with the traveling of Apache war parties were much the same in results, so the sheriff made up his mind to attend to the lesser matter, if need be, after he had quieted the man he was following. Everybody knew that Apaches were very bad, but that The Orphan was worse; and, besides, the latter would be laughing derisively about that matter concerning a drink. The sheriff grinned and rode happily forward, taking pains, however, to circle around all chaparrals and covers of every nature, for he did not know but that his playful enemy might have tired of riding before the water hole had been reached and decided to camp out under cover. While the sheriff was unafraid, he had befitting respect for the quality of The Orphan's marksmanship, which was reputed as being above reproach; and he was not expected to determine offhand whether the outlaw was above lying in ambush. So he used his field glass constantly in sweeping covers and rode forward toward the water hole.

Chapter II
Concerning an Arrow

The bleak foreground of gray soil, covered with drifts of alkali and sand, was studded with clumps of mesquite and cacti and occasional tufts of sun-burned grass, dusty and somber, while a few sagebrush blended their leaves to the predominating color. Back of this was a near horizon to the north and east, brought near by the skyline of a low, undulating range of sand hills rising from the desert to meet a faded sky. The morning glow brought this skyline into sharp definition as the dividing line between the darkness of the plain in the shadow of the range and the fast increasing morning light. To the south and west the plain blended into the sky, and there was no horizon.

Two trails met and crossed near a sand-buffeted bowlder of lava stone, which was huge, grotesque and forbidding in its bulky indistinctness. The first of the trails ran north and south and was faint but plainly discernible, being beaten a trifle below the level of the desert and forming a depression which the winds alternately filled and emptied of dust; and its arrow-like directness, swerving neither to the right nor left, bespoke of the haste which urged the unfortunate traveler to have done with it as speedily as possible, since there was nothing alluring along its heat-cursed course to bid him tarry in his riding. There was yet another reason for haste, for the water holes were over fifty miles apart, and in that country water holes were more or less uncertain and doubtful as to being free from mineral poisons. On the occasions when the

Apaches awoke to find that many of their young men were missing, and a proved warrior or two, this trail become weighted with possibilities, for this desert was the playground of war parties, an unlimited ante-room for the preliminaries to predatory pilgrimages; and the northern trail then partook of the nature of a huge wire over which played an alternating current, the potentials of which were the ranges at one end and the savagery and war spirit of the painted tribes at the other: and the voltage was frequently deadly.

The other trail, crossing the first at right angles, led eastward to the fertile valleys of the Canadian and the Cimarron; westward it spread out like the sticks of a fan to anywhere and nowhere, gradually resolving itself into the fainter and still more faint individual paths which fed it as single strands feed a rope. It lacked the directness of its intersector because of the impenetrable chaparrals which forced it to wander hither and yon. Neither was it as plain to the eye, for preference, except in cases of urgent necessity, foreswore its saving of miles and journeyed by the more circuitous southern trail which wound beneath cottonwoods and mottes of live oak and frequently dipped beneath the waters of sluggish streams, the banks of which were fringed with willows.

As a lean coyote loped past the point of intersection a moving object suddenly topped the skyline of the southern end of the sandhills to the east and sprang into sharp silhouette, paused for an instant on the edge of the range and then, plunging down into the shadows at its base, rode rapidly toward the bowlder.

He was an Apache, and was magnificent in his proportions and the easy erectness of his poise. He glanced sharply about him, letting his gaze finally settle on the southern trail and then, leaning over, he placed an object on the highest point of the rock. Wheeling abruptly, he galloped back over his trail, the rising wind setting diligently at work to cover the hoofprints of his pony. He had no sooner dropped from sight over the hills than another figure began to be defined in the dim light, this time from the north.

The newcomer rode at an easy canter and found small pleasure in the cloud of alkali dust which the wind kept at pace with him. His hat, the first visible sign of his calling, proclaimed him to be a cowboy, and when he had stopped at the bowlder his every possession endorsed the silent testimony of the hat.

He was bronzed and self-reliant, some reason for the latter being suggested by the long-barreled rifle which swung from his right saddle skirt and the pair of Colt's which lay along his thighs. He wore the usual blue flannel shirt, open at the throat, the regular silk kerchief about his neck, and the indispensable chaps, which were of angora goatskin. His boots were tight fitting, with high heels, and huge brass spurs projected therefrom. A forty-foot coil of rawhide hung from the pommel of his "rocking-chair" saddle and a slicker was strapped behind the cantle.

He glanced behind him as he drew rein, wondering when the sheriff would show himself, for he was being followed, of that he was certain. That was why he had ridden through so many chaparrals and doubled on his trail. He was now riding to describe a circle, the object being to get behind his pursuer and to do some hunting on his own account. As he started to continue on his way his quick eyes espied something on the bowlder which made him suddenly draw rein again. Glancing to the ground he saw the tracks made by the Apache, and he peered intently along the eastern trail with his hand shading his eyes. The eyes were of a grayish blue, hard and steely and cruel. They were calculating eyes, and never missed anything worth seeing. The fierce glare of the semi-tropical sun which for many years had daily assaulted them made it imperative that he squint from half-closed lids, and had given his face a malevolent look. And the characteristics promised by the eyes were endorsed by his jaw, which was square and firm set, underlying thin, straight lips. But about his lips were graven lines so cynical and yet so humorous as to baffle an observer.

Raising his canteen to his lips he counted seven swallows and then, letting it fall to his side, he picked up the object which had made him pause. There was no surprise in his face, for he never was surprised at anything.

As he looked at the object he remembered the rumors of the Apache war dances and of fast-riding, paint-bedaubed "hunting parties." What had been rumor he now knew to be a fact, and his face became even more cruel as he realized that he was playing tag with the sheriff in the very heart of the Apache playground, where death might lurk in any of the thorny covers which surrounded him on all sides.

"Apache war arrow," he grunted. "Now it shore beats the devil that me and the sheriff can't have a free rein to settle up our accounts. Somebody is always sticking their nose in my business," he grumbled. Then he frowned at the arrow in his hand. "That red on the head is blood," he murmured, noticing the salient points of the weapon, "and that yellow hair means good scalping. The thong of leather spells plunder, and it was pointing to the east. The buck that brought it went back again, so this is to show his friends which way to ride. He was in a hurry, too, judging from the way he threw sand, and from them toe-prints."

He hated Apaches vindictively, malevolently, with a single purpose and instinct, because of a little score he owed them. Once when he had managed to rustle together a big herd of horses and was within a day's ride of a ready market, a party of Apaches had ridden up in the night and made off with not only the stolen animals, but also with his own horse. This had lost him a neat sum and had forced him to carry a forty-pound saddle, a bridle and a rifle for two days under a merciless sun before he reached civilization. He did not thank them for not killing him, which they for some reason neglected to do. Apache stock was down very low with him, and he now had an opportunity to even the score. Then he thought of the sheriff, and swore. Finally he decided that he would just shoot that worthy as soon as he came within range, and so be free to play his lone hand against the race that had stolen his horses. His eyes twinkled at the game he was about to play, and he regarded the silent message and guide with a smile.

"If it's all the same to you, I'll just polish you up a bit"—and when he replaced it on the bowlder its former owner would not have known it to be the same weapon, for its head was not red, but as bright as the friction of a handful of sand could make it. This destroyed its message of plentiful slaughter and, he knew, would grieve his enemies. He touched it gently with his hand and it swung at right angles to its former position and now pointed northward and in the direction from which he expected the sheriff.

"It was d—-d nice of that Apache leaving me this, but I reckon I'll switch them reinforcements-the sheriff will be some pleased to meet them," he said, grinning at the novelty of the situation. "Nobody will even suspect how a lone puncher"–for he regarded himself as a cowman–"squaring up a couple of scores went and saved the eastern valleys from more devilment. If the war-whoops are out along the Cimarron and Canadian they are shore havin' fun enough to give me a little. But I would like to see the sheriff's face when he bumps into the little party I'm sending his way. Wonder how many he will get before he goes under?"

Then he again took up the arrow and carefully removed the hair and thong of leather, chuckling at the tale of woe the denuded weapon would tell, after which he placed it as before, wishing he knew how to indicate that the Apaches had been wiped out.

He rode to a chaparral which lay three hundred yards to the southeast of him and thence around it to the far side, where he dismounted and fastened his horse to the empty air by simply allowing the reins to hang down in front of the animal's eyes. The pony knew many things about ropes and straps, and what it knew it knew well; nothing short of dynamite would have moved it while the reins dangled before its eyes.

Its master slowly returned to the bowlder, where he set to work to cover his tracks with dust, for although the shifting sand was doing this for him, it was not doing it fast enough to suit him. When he had assured himself that he had performed his task in a thoroughly workmanlike manner he returned to his horse, and finally found a snug place of concealment for it and himself. First bandaging its eyes so that it would not whinny at the approach of other horses, he searched his pockets and finally brought to light a pack of greasy playing cards, with which he amused himself at solitaire, diligently keeping his eyes on both ends of the heavier trail.

His intermittent scrutiny was finally rewarded by a cloud of dust which steadily grew larger on the southern horizon and soon revealed the character of the riders who made it. As they drew nearer to him his implacable hatred caused him to pick up his rifle, but he let it slide from him as he counted the number of the approaching party, before which was being driven a herd of horses which were intended to be placed as relays for the main force.

"Two, five, eight, eleven, sixteen, twenty, twenty-four, twenty-seven," he muttered, carefully settling himself more comfortably. He could distinguish the war paint on the reddish-brown colored bodies, and he smiled at what was in store for them.

"I reckon I won't get gay with no twenty-seven Apaches," he muttered. "I can wait, all right."

Upon reaching the rock the leaders of the band glanced at the arrow, excitedly exchanged monosyllables and set off to the north at a hard gallop, being followed by the others. As he expected, they were Apaches, which meant that of all red raiders they were the most proficient. They were human hyenas with rare intelligence for war and a most aggravating way of not being where one would expect them to be, as army officers will testify. Besides, an Apache war party did not appear to have stomachs, and so traveled faster and farther than the cavalry which so often pursued them.

The watcher chuckled softly at the success of his stratagem and, suddenly arising, went carefully around the chaparral until he could see the fast-vanishing braves. Waiting until they had disappeared over the northern end of the crescent-shaped range of hills, he hurried to the bowlder and again picked up the arrow.

"Huh! Didn't take it with them, eh?" he soliloquized. "Well, that means that there's more coming, so I'll just send the next batch plumb west-they'll be some pleased to explore this God-forsaken desert some extensive."

Grinning joyously, he replaced the weapon with its head pointing westward and then looked anxiously at the tracks of the party which had just passed. Deciding that the wind would effectually cover them in an hour at most, he returned to his hiding place, taking care to cover his own tracks. Taking a chance on the second contingent going north was all right, but he didn't care to run the risk of having them ride to him for explanations. Picking up the cards again he shuffled them and suffered defeat after defeat, and finally announced his displeasure at the luck he was having.

"I never saw nothing like it!" he grumbled petulantly. "Reckon I'll hit up the Old Thirteen a few," beginning a new game. He had whiled away an hour and a half, and as he stretched himself his uneasy eyes discovered another cloud on the southern horizon, which was smaller than the first. He placed the six of hearts on the five of hearts, ruffled the pack and then put the cards down and took up his rifle, watching the cloud closely. He was soon able to count seven warriors who were driving another "cavvieyeh" of horses.

"Huh! Only seven!" he grunted, shifting his rifle for action. The fighting lust swept over him, but he choked it down and idly fingered the hammer of the gun. "Nope, I reckon not-seven husky Apaches are too much for one man to go out of his way to fight. Now, if the sheriff was only with me," and he grinned at the humor of it, "we might cut loose and heave lead. But since he ain't, this is where I don't chip in—I'll wait a while, for they'll shore come back."

The seven warriors went through almost the same actions which their predecessors had gone through and great excitement prevailed among them. The leaders pointed to the very faint tracks which led northward and debated vehemently. But the two small stones which held the arrow securely in its position against the possibility of the wind shifting it could not be doubted, and after a few minutes had passed they rode as bidden, leaving one of their number on guard at the bowlder. Soon the other six were lost to sight among the chaparrals to the west and the guard sat stolidly under the blazing sun.

The dispatcher noted the position of a shadow thrown on the sand by a cactus and laughed silently as he fingered his rifle. He could not think out the game. Try as he would, he could find no really good excuse for the placing of the guard, although many presented themselves, to be finally cast aside. But the fact was enough, and when the moving shadow gave assurance that nearly an hour had passed since the departure of the guard's companions, the man with the grudge cautiously arose on one knee.

After examining the contents of his rifle, he brought it slowly to his shoulder. A quick, calculating glance told him that the range was slightly over three hundred yards, and he altered the elevation of the rear sights accordingly. After a pause, during which he gauged the strength and velocity of the northern wind, he dropped his cheek against the walnut stock of the weapon. The echoless report rang out flatly and a sudden gust of hot wind whipped the ragged, gray smoke cloud into the chaparral, where it lay close to the ground and spread out like a miniature fog. As the smoke cleared away a second cartridge, inserted deftly and quickly, sent another cloud of smoke into the chaparral and the marksman arose to his feet, mechanically reloading his gun. The second shot was for the guard's horse, for it would be unnecessarily perilous to risk its rejoining the departed braves, which it very probably would do if allowed to escape.

Dropping his rifle into the hollow of his arm he walked swiftly toward the fallen Indian, hoping that there would be no more war parties, for he had now made signs which the most stupid Apache could not fail to note and understand. The dead guard could be hidden, and by the use of his own horse and rope he could drag the carcass of the animal into the chaparral and out of sight. But the trail which would be left in the loose sand would be too deep and wide to be covered. He had crossed the Rubicon, and must stand or fall by the step.

The Indian had fallen forward against the bowlder and had slid down its side, landing on his head and shoulders, in which grotesque position the rock supported him. One glance assured the "cowman" that his aim had been good, and another told him that he had to fear the arrival of no more war parties, for the arrow was gone. He was not satisfied, however, until he had made a good search for it, thinking that it might have been displaced by the fall of the Apache. He lifted the body of the dead warrior in his arms and flung it across the apex of the bowlder, face up and balanced nicely, the head pointing to the north. Then he looked for the arrow on the sand where the body had rested, but it was not to be found. A sardonic grin flitted across his face as he secured the weapons of the late guard, which were a heavy Colt's revolver and a late pattern Winchester repeater. Taking the cartridges from his body, he stood up triumphant. He now had what he needed to meet the smaller body of Indians on their return, ten shots in one rifle and a spare Colt's.

"One for my cavvieyeh!" he muttered savagely as he thought of the loss of his horse herd. "There'll be more, too, before I get through, or my name's not"– he paused abruptly, hearing hoofbeats made by a galloping horse over a stretch of hard soil which lay to the east of him. Leaping quickly behind the bowlder, he leveled his own rifle across the body of the guard and peered intently toward the east, wondering if the advancing horseman would be the sheriff or another Apache. The hoofbeats came rapidly nearer and another courier turned the corner of the chaparral and went no further. Again a second shot took care of the horse and the marksman strode to his second victim, from whose body and horse he took another Winchester and Colt.

"Now I am in for it!" he muttered as he looked down at the warrior. "This is shore getting warm and it'll be a d——-n sight warmer if his friends get anxious about him and hunt him up."

Glancing around the horizon and seeing no signs of an interruption, he slung the body across his shoulders and staggered with it to the bowlder, where he heaved and pushed it across the body of the first Apache.

"Might as well make a good showing and make them mad, for I can't very well hide you and the cayuses—I ain't no graveyard," he said, stepping back to look at his work. He felt no remorse, for that was a sensation not yet awakened in his consciousness. He was elated at his success, joyous in catering to his love for fighting, for he would rather die fighting than live the round of years heavily monotonous with peace, and his only regret was having won by ambush. But in this, he told himself, there was need, for his hatred ordered him to kill as many as he could, and in any way possible. Knowing that he was, single-handed, attempting to outwit wily chiefs and that he had before him a carnival of fighting, he would not have hesitated to make use of traps if they were at hand and could be used. Perhaps it was old Geronimo whose plans he was defeating and, if so, no precautions nor means were unjustifiable and too mean to make use of, for Geronimo was half-brother to the devil and a genius for warfare and slaughter, with a ferocity and cruelty cold-blooded and consummate.

He had yet time to escape from his perilous position and meet the sheriff, if that worthy had eluded the first war party. But his elation had the upper hand and his brute courage was now blind to caution. He savagely decided that his matter with the sheriff could wait and that he would take care of the war parties first, since there was more honor in fighting against odds. The two Winchesters and his own Sharps, not to consider the four Colt's, gave him many shots without having to waste time in reloading, and he drew assurance from the past that he placed his shots quickly and with precision. He could put up a magnificent fight in the chaparral, shifting his position after each shot, and he could hug the ground where the trunks of the vegetation were thickest and would prove an effective barrier against random shots. His wits were keen, his legs nimble, his eyesight and accuracy above doubt, and he had no cause to believe that his strategy was inferior to that of his foes. There would be no moon for two nights, and he could escape in the darkness if hunger and thirst should drive him out. Here he had struck, and here he would strike again and again, and, if he fell, he would leave behind him such a tale of fighting as had seldom been known before; and it pleased his vanity to think of the amazement the story would call forth as it was recounted around the campfires and across the bars of a country larger than Europe. He did not realize that such a tale would die if he died and would never be known. His was the joy of a master of the game, a virile, fearless fighting machine, a man who had never failed in the playing of the many hands he had held in desperate games with death. He was not going to die; he was going to win and leave dying for others.

Chapter III
The Sheriff Finds the Orphan

The day dragged wearily along for the man in the chaparral, and when the sun showed that it was still two hours from the meridian he leaped to his feet, rifle in hand, and peered intently to the west, where he had seen a fast-riding horseman flit between two chaparrals which stood far down on the western end of the Cimarron Trail. Without pausing, he made his way out of cover and ran rapidly along the edge of the thicket until he had gained its northwestern extremity, where he plunged into it, unmindful of the cuts and slashes from the interlocked thorns. Using the rifle as a club, he hammered and pushed until he was screened from the view of any one passing along the trail, but where he could see all who approached. As he turned and faced the west he saw the horseman suddenly emerge from the shelter of the last chaparral in his course and ride straight for the intersection of the trails, his horse flattened to the earth by the speed it was making. Waiting until the rider was within fifty yards of him, he pushed his way out to the trail, the rifle leaping to his shoulder as he stepped into the open. The newcomer was looking back at half a dozen Apaches who had burst into view by the chaparral he had just quitted, and when he turned he was stopped by a hail and the sight of an unwavering rifle held by the man on foot.

"A truce!" shouted The Orphan from behind the sights, having an idea and wishing to share it.

"Hell, yes!" cried the astonished sheriff in reply, slowing down and mechanically following the already running outlaw to the place where the latter had spent the last few hours.

By keeping close to the edge of the chaparral, which receded from the trail, The Orphan had not been seen by the Apaches, and as he turned into his hiding place a yell reached his ears. His trophies on the bowlder were not to be unmourned.

As he wormed his way into the thicket, closely followed by the sheriff, he tersely explained the situation, and Shields, feeling somewhat under obligation to the man who had refrained from killing him, nodded and smiled in good nature. The sheriff thought it was a fine joke and enthusiastically slapped his enemy on the back to show his appreciation, for the time forgetting that they very probably would try to kill each other later on, after the Apaches had been taken care of.

As they reached a point which gave them a clear view of the bowlder, The Orphan kicked his companion on the shin, pointing to the Apaches grouped around their dead.

"It's a little over three hundred, Sheriff," he said. "You shoot first and I'll follow you, so they'll think you shot twice–there's no use letting them think that there's two of us, that is, not yet."

"Good idea," replied the sheriff, nodding and throwing his rifle to his shoulder. "Right end for me," he said, calling his shot so as to be sure that the same brave would not receive all the attention. As he fired his companion covered the second warrior, using one of his captured Winchesters, and a second later the rifle spun flame. Both warriors dropped and the remaining four hastily postponed their mourning and tumbled helter skelter behind the bowlder, the sheriff's second shot becoming a part of the last one to find cover.

"Fine!" exulted the sheriff, delighted at the score. "Best game I ever took a hand in, d——d if it ain't! We'll have them guessing so hard that they'll get brain fever."

"Three shots in as many seconds will make them think that they are facing a Winchester in the hands of a crack shot," remarked The Orphan, smiling with pleasure at the sheriff's appreciation. "They'll think that if they can back off from the bowlder and keep it between them and you that they can get out of range in a few hundred yards more. That is where I come in again. You sling a little lead to let them know that you haven't moved a whole lot, but stop in a couple of minutes, while I go down the line a ways. The chaparral sweeps to the north quite a little, and mebby I can drop a slug behind their fort from down there. That'll make them think you are a jack rabbit at covering ground and will bother them. If they rush, which they won't after tasting that kind of shooting, you whistle good and loud and we'll make them plumb disgusted. I'll take a Winchester along with me, so they won't have any cause to suspect that you are an arsenal. So long."

The sheriff glanced up as his companion departed and was pleased at the outlaw's command of the situation. He had a good chance to wipe out the man, but that he would not do, for The Orphan trusted him, and Shields was one who respected a thing like that.

The outlaw finally stopped about a hundred yards down the trail and looked out, using his glasses. A brown shoulder showed under the overhanging side of the bowlder and he smiled, readjusting the sights on the Winchester as he waited. Soon the shoulder raised from the ground and pushed out farther into sight. Then a poll of black hair showed itself and slowly raised. The Orphan took deliberate aim and pulled the trigger. The head dropped to the sand and the shoulder heaved convulsively once or twice and then lay quiet. Leaping up, the marksman hastened back to the side of the sheriff, who did not trouble himself to look up.

"I got him, Sheriff," he said. "Work up to the other end and I'll go back to where I came from. They have got all the fighting they have any use for and will be backing away purty soon now. The range from the point where I held you is some closer than it is from here, so you ought to get in a shot when they get far enough back."

"All right," pleasantly responded Shields, vigorously attacking the thorns as he began his journey to the western end of the thicket. "Ouch!" he exclaimed as he felt the pricks. Then he stopped and slowly turned and saw The Orphan smiling at him, and grinned:

"Say," he began, "why can't I go around?" he asked, indicating with a sweep of his arm the southern edge of the chaparral, and intimating that it would be far more pleasant to skirt the thorns than to buck against them. "These d——d thorns ain't no joke!" he added emphatically.

The outlaw's smile enlarged and he glanced quickly at the bowlder to see that all was as it should be.

"You can go around in one day afoot," he replied. "By that time they"–pointing to the Apaches–"will have made a day's journey on cayuses. And we simply mustn't let them get the best of us that way."

Shields grinned and turned half-way around again: "It's a whole lot dry out here," he said, "and my canteen is on my cayuse."

"Here, pardner," replied The Orphan, holding out his canteen and watching the effect of the familiarity. "Seven swallows is the dose."

The sheriff faced him, took the vessel, counted seven swallows and returned it.

"I'm some moist now," he remarked, as he returned to the thorns. "It's too d———n bad you're bad," he grumbled. "You'd make a blamed good cow-puncher."

The Orphan, still smiling, placed his hands on hips and watched the rapidly disappearing arm of the law.

"He's all right-too bad he'll make me shoot him," he soliloquized, turning toward his post. As he crawled through a particularly badly matted bit of chaparral he stopped to release himself and laughed outright. "How in thunder did he get so far west? My trail was as plain as day, too." When he had reached his destination and had settled down to watch the bowlder he laughed again and muttered: "Mebby he figured it out that I was doubling back and was laying for me to show up. And that's just the way I would have gone, too. He ain't any fool, all right."

He thought of the sheriff at the far end of the chaparral and of the repeater he carried, and an inexplicable impulse of generosity surged over him. The sheriff would be pleased to do the rest himself, he thought, and the thought was father to the act. He picked up the Winchester he had brought with him and fired at the bowlder, only wishing to let the Apaches know his position so that they would think the way clear to the northwest, and so innocently give the sheriff a shot at them as they retreated. Dropping the Winchester he took up his Sharps, his pet rifle, with which he had done wonderful shooting, and arose to one knee, supporting his left elbow on the other; between the fingers of his left hand he held a cartridge in order that no time should be lost in reloading. The range was now five hundred yards, and when The Orphan knew the exact range he swore with rage if he missed.

His shot had the effect he hoped it would have, for suddenly there was movement behind the bowlder. A pony's hip showed for an instant and then leaped from sight as the outlaw reloaded. A cloud of dust arose to the northwest of and behind the bowlder, and a series of close reports sounded from the direction of the sheriff. The Orphan leaped to his feet and dashed out on the plain to where his sight would not be obstructed and saw an Apache, who hung down on the far side of his horse, sweep northward and gallop along the northern trail. He fired, but the range was too great, and the warrior soon dropped from sight over the range of hills. As The Orphan made his way toward the bowlder the sheriff emerged from his shelter and pointed to the west. A pony lay on its side and not far away was the huddled body of its rider.

As they neared each other the outlaw noticed something peculiar about the sheriff's ear, and his look of inquiry was rewarded. "Stung," remarked Shields, grinning apologetically. "Just as I shot," he added in explanation of the Apache's escape. "Wonder what my wife'll say?" he mused, nursing the swelling.

The Orphan's eyes opened a trifle at the sheriff's last words, and he thought of the war party he had sent north. His decision was immediate: no married man had any business to run risks, and he was glad that he refrained from shooting on sight.

"Sheriff, you vamoose. Clear out now, while you have the chance. Ride west for an hour, and then strike north for Ford's Station. That buck that got away is due to run into twenty-seven of his friends and relatives that I sent north to meet you. And they won't waste any time in getting back, neither."

Shields felt of his ear and laughed softly. He had a sudden, strong liking for his humorous, clever enemy, for he recognized qualities which he had always held in high esteem. While he had waited in the chaparral for the Apaches to break cover he had wondered if the Indians which The Orphan had sent north had been sent for the purpose of meeting him, and now he had the answer. Instead of embittering him against his companion, it increased his respect for that individual's strategy, and he felt only admiration.

"I saw your reception committee in time to duck," the sheriff said, laughing. "If they kept on going as they were when I saw them they must have crossed my trail about three hours later. When they hit that it is a safe bet that at least some of them took it up. So if it's all the same to you, I'll leave both the north and the west alone and take another route home. I have shot up all the war-whoops I care about, so I am well satisfied."

He suddenly reached down toward his belt, and then looked squarely into The Orphan's gun, which rested easily on that person's hip. His hand kept on, however, but more slowly and with but two fingers extended, and disappeared into his chap's pocket, from which it slowly and gingerly brought forth a package of tobacco and some rice paper. The Orphan looked embarrassed for a second and then laughed softly.

"You're a square man, Sheriff, but I wasn't sure," he said in apology. "So long."

"That's all right," cried the sheriff heartily. "I was a big fool to make a play like that!"

The Orphan smiled and turned squarely around and walked away in the direction of his horse. Shields stared at his back and then rolled a cigarette and grinned: "By George!" he ejaculated at the confidence displayed by his companion, and he slowly followed.

After they had mounted in silence the sheriff suddenly turned and looked his companion squarely in the eyes and received a steady, frank look in return.

"What the devil made you ventilate them sheep herders that way?" he asked. "And go and drive all of them sheep over the bank?"

The Orphan frowned momentarily, but answered without reserve.

"Those sheep herders reckoned they'd get a reputation!" he answered. "And they would have gotten it, too, only I beat them on the draw. As for the idiotic muttons, they went plumb loco at the shooting and pushed each other over the bank. To hell with the herders-they only got what they was trying to hand me. But I'm a whole lot sorry about the sheep, although I can't say I'm dead stuck on range-killers of any kind."

The sheriff reflectively eyed his companion's gun and remembered its celerity into getting into action, which persuaded him that The Orphan was telling the truth, and swept aside the last chance for fair warfare between the two for the day.

"Yes, it is too bad, all them innocent sheep drowned that way," he slowly replied. "But they are shore awful skittish at times. Well, do we part?" he asked, suddenly holding out his hand.

"I reckon we do, Sheriff, and I'm blamed glad to have met you," replied the outlaw as he shook hands with no uncertain grip. "Keep away from them Apaches, and so long."

"Thanks, I will," responded the arm of the law. "And I'm glad to have met you, too. So long!"

Chapter IV
The Second Offense

Bill Howland emerged from the six-by-six office of the F. S. and S. Stage Company and strolled down the street to where his Concord stood. He hitched up and, after examining the harness, gained his seat, gathered up the lines and yelled. There was a lurch and a rumble, and Bill turned the corner on two wheels to the gratification of sundry stray dogs, whose gratification turned to yelps of surprise and pain as the driver neatly flecked bits of hair from their bodies with his sixteen foot "blacksnake." Twice each week Bill drove his Concord around the same corner on the same two wheels and flecked bits of hair from stray dogs with the same whip. He would have been deeply grieved if the supply of new stray dogs gave out, for no dogs were ever known to get close enough to be skinned the second time; once was enough, and those which had felt the sting of Bill's leather were content to stand across the street and create the necessary excitement to urge the new arrivals forward. The local wit is reported as saying: "Dogs may come and dogs may go, but Bill goes on forever," which saying pleased Bill greatly.

As he threw the mail bag on the seat the sheriff came up and watched him, his eyes a-twinkle with humor.

"Well, Sheriff, how's the boy?" genially asked Bill, who could talk all day on anything and two days on nothing without fatigue.

"All right, Bill, thank you," the sheriff replied. "I hope you are able to take something more than liquid nourishment," he added.

"Oh, you trust me for that, Sheriff. When my appetite gives out I'll be ready to plant. I see your ear is some smaller. Blamed funny how they do swell sometimes," remarked the driver, loosening his collar.

The sheriff knew what that action meant and hurried to break the thread of the conversation. "New wheel?" he asked, eying what he knew to be old.

"Nope, painted, that's all," the driver replied, grinning. "But she shore does look new, don't she? You see, Dick put in two new spokes yesterday, and when I saw 'em I says, says I, 'Dick, that new wheel don't look good thataway,' says I. 'It'll look like a limp, them new spokes coming 'round all alone like,' says I. So we paints it, but we didn't have time to paint the others, but they won't make much difference, anyhow. Funny how a little paint will change things, now ain't it? Why, I can remember when——"

"Much mail nowadays?" interposed the sheriff calmly.

"Nope. Folks out here ain't a-helpin' Uncle Sam much. Postmaster says he only sold ten stamps this week. What he wants, as I told him, is women. Then everybody'll be sendin' letters and presents and things. Now, I knows what I'm talking about, because——"

"The Apaches are out," jabbed the sheriff, hopefully.

"Yes, I heard that you had a soiree with them. But they won't get so far north as this. No, siree, they won't. They knows too much, Apaches do. Ain't they smart cusses, though? Now, there's old Geronimo-been raising the devil for years. The cavalry goes out for him regular, and shore thinks he's caught, but he ain't. When he's found he's home smoking his pipe and counting his wives, which are shore numerous, they say. Now, I've got a bully scheme for getting him, Sheriff——"

"Hey, you," came from the office. "Do you reckon that train is going to tie up and wait for you, hey? Do you think you are so d——d important that they won't pull out unless you're on hand? Why in h–l don't you quit chinning and get started?"

"Oh, you choke up!" cried Bill, clambering up to his seat. "Who's running this, anyhow!" he grumbled under his breath. Then he took up the reins and carefully sorted them, after which he looked down at Shields, whose face wore a smile of amusement.

"Bill Howland ain't none a-scared because a lot of calamity howlers get a hunch. Not on your life! I've reached the high C of rollicking progress too many times to be airy scairt at rumors. Show me the feather-dusters in war paint, and then I'll take some stock in raids. You get up a bet on me Sheriff, make a little easy money. Back Bill Howland to be right here in seventy-two hours, right side up and smiling, and you'll win. You just bet you'll——"

"Well, you won't get here in a year unless you starts, you pest! For God's sake get a-going and give the sheriff a rest!" came explosively from the office, accompanied by a sound as if a chair had dropped to its four legs. A tall, angular man stood in the doorway and shook his fist at the huge cloud of dust which rolled down the street, muttering savagely. Bill Howland had started on his eighty-mile trip to Sagetown.

"Damnedest talker on two laigs," asserted the clerk. "He'll drive me loco some day with his eternal jabber, jabber. Why do you waste time with him? Tell him to close his yap and go to h–l. Beat him over the head, anything to shut him up!"

Shields smiled: "Oh, he can't help it. He don't do anybody any harm."

The clerk shook his head in doubt and started to return to his chair, and then stopped.

"I hear you expect some women out purty soon," he suggested.

"Yes. Sisters and a friend," Shields replied shortly.

"Ain't you a little leary about letting 'em come out here while the Apaches are out?"

"Not very much–I'll be on hand when they arrive," the sheriff assured him.

"How soon are they due to land?"

"Next trip if nothing hinders them."

"Jim Hawes is comin' out next trip," volunteered the clerk.

"Good," responded the sheriff, turning to go. "Every gun counts, and Jim is a good man."

"Say," the agent was lonesome, "I heard down at the Oasis last night that The Orphant was seen out near the Cross Bar-8 yesterday. He ought to get shot, d——n him! But that's a purty big contract, I reckon. They say he can shoot like the very devil."

"They're right, he can," Shields replied. "Everybody knows that."

"Charley seems to be in a hurry," remarked the agent, looking down the street at a cowboy, a friend of the sheriff, who was coming at a dead gallop. The sheriff looked and Charley waved his arm. As he came within hailing distance he shouted:

"The Orphan killed Jimmy Ford this morning on Twenty Mile Trail! His pardner got away by shootin' The Orphan's horse and taking to the trail through Little Arroyo. But he's shot, just the same, 'though not bad. The rest of the Cross Bar-8 outfit are going out for him; they've been out, but they can't follow his trail."

"Hell!" cried the sheriff, running toward his corral. "Wait!" he shouted over his shoulder as he turned the corner. In less than five minutes he was back again, and on his best horse, and following the impatient cowboy, swung down the street at a gallop in the direction of Twenty Mile Trail.

As they left the town behind and swung through the arroyo leading to the Limping Water, through which the stage route lay, Charley began to speak again:

"Jimmy and Pete Carson were taking a rest in the shade of the chaparral and playin' old sledge, when they looked up and saw The Orphan looking down at them. They're rather easy-going, and so they asked him to take a hand. He said he would, and got off his cayuse and sat down with them. Jimmy started a new deal, but The Orphan objected to old sledge and wanted poker, at the same time throwing a bag of dust down in front of him. Jimmy looked at Pete, who nodded, and put his wealth in front of him. Well, they played along for a while, and The Orphan began to have great luck. When he had won five straight jack pots it was more than Jimmy could stand, him being young and hasty. He saw his new Cheyenne saddle, what he was going to buy, getting further away all the time, and he yelled 'Cheat!' grabbing for his gun, what was plumb crazy for him to do.

"The Orphan fired from his hip quick as a wink, and Jimmy fell back just as Pete drew. The Orphan swung on him and ordered him to drop his gun, which same Pete did, being sick at the stomach at Jimmy's passing. Then The Orphan told him to take his dirty money and his cheap life and go back to his mamma. Pete didn't stop none to argue, but mounted and rode away. But the fool wasn't satisfied at having a whole skin after a run-in with The Orphan, and when he got off about four hundred yards and right on the edge of Little Arroyo, where he could get cover in one jump, he up and let drive, killing The Orphan's horse. Pete got two holes in his shoulder before he could get out of sight, and he remembered that his shot had hardly left his gun before he had 'em, too. Pete says he wonders how in h–l The Orphan could shoot twice so quick, when his gun's a Sharp's single shot."

Shields was pleased with the knowledge that it was not a plain murder this time, and fell to wondering if the other killings in which The Orphan had figured had not in a measure been justified. Hearsay cried "Murderer," but his own personal experience denied the term. Did not The Orphan know that Shields was after him, and that the sheriff was no man to be taken lightly when he had shown mercy near the big bowlder? The outlaw must be fair and square, reasoned the sheriff, else he would not have looked for those qualities in another, and least of all in an enemy. The outlaw had given him plenty of chances to kill and had thought nothing of it, time and time again turning his back without hesitation. True, The Orphan had covered him when his hand had streaked for his tobacco; but the sheriff would have done the same, because the movement was decidedly hostile, and he had been fortunate in not having paid dearly for his rash action. The Orphan had taken a chance when he refrained from pulling the trigger.

Charley continued: "Jimmy's outfit swear they'll have a lynchin' bee to square things for the Kid. They are plumb crazy about it. Jimmy was a whole lot liked by them, and the foreman is going to give them a week off with no questions asked. They are getting things ready now."

The sheriff turned to his companion, his hazel eyes aflame with anger at this threat of lynching when he had given plain warning that such lawlessness would not for one minute be tolerated by him.

"We'll call on the Cross Bar-8 first, Charley, and find out when this lynching bee is due to come off," he said, turning toward the northwest. Charley looked surprised at the sudden change in the plans, but followed without comment, secretly glad that trouble was in store for the ranch he had no use for.

After an hour of fast riding they rode up to the corral of the Cross Bar-8, and Shields, seeing a cowboy busily engaged in cleaning a rifle, asked for Sneed, at the same time making a mental note of the preparations which were going on about him.

The foreman, as if in answer to the sheriff's words, walked into sight around the corral wall and stepped forward eagerly when he saw who the caller was.

"I see that you know all about it, Sheriff," he began, hastily. "I've just told the boys that they can go out for him," he continued. "They're getting ready now, and will soon be on his trail."

"Yes?" coldly inquired the sheriff.

"They'll get him if you don't," assured the foreman, who had about as much tact as a mule.

"I'll shoot the first man who tries it," the sheriff said, as he flecked a bit of dust from his arm.

"What!" cried Sneed in astonishment. "By God, Sheriff, that's a d——d hard assertion to make!"

"And I hold *you* responsible," continued the sheriff, leaning forward as if to give weight to his words.

The cowboy stopped cleaning his rifle and stood up, covering the sheriff, a sneer on his face and anger in his eyes.

"If you're a-scared, we ain't, by God!" he cried. "The Orphan has got away too many times already, and here is where he gets stopped for good! When we gets through with him he won't shoot no more friends of ourn, nor nobody else's!"

Shields looked him squarely in the eyes: "If you don't drop that gun I'll drop you, Bucknell," he said pleasantly, and his eyes proclaimed that he meant what he said.

Sneed sprang forward and knocked the gun aside; "You d——n fool!" he cried. "You ornery, silly fool! Get back to the bunk house or I'll make you wish you had never seen that gun! Go on, get the h—l out of here before you join Jimmy!"

Then the foreman turned to Shields, feeling that he had lost much through the rashness of his man.

"Don't pay any attention to that crazy yearling, Sheriff," he said earnestly. "He's only feeling his oats. But we only wanted to round him up," he continued on the main topic. "We meant to turn him over to you after we'd got him. He's a blasted, thieving, murdering dog, that's what he is, and he oughtn't get away this time!"

"You keep out of this, and keep your men out of it, too," responded Shields, turning away. "I mean what I say. Jimmy started the mess and got the worst of it. I'll get The Orphan, or nobody will. As long as I'm sheriff of this county I'll take care of my job without any lynching parties. Come on, Charley."

"Deputize some of my boys, Sheriff!" he begged. "Let 'em think they're doing something. The Orphan is a bad man to go after alone. The boys are so mad that they'll get him if they have to ride through hell after him. Swear them in and let them get him lawfully."

"Yes?" retorted Shields cynically. "And have to shoot them to keep them from shooting him?"

"By God, Sheriff," cried Sneed, losing control of his temper, "this is our fight, and we're going to see it through! We'll get that cur, sheriff or no sheriff, and when we do, he'll stretch rope! And anybody who tries to stop us will get hurt! I ain't making any threats, Sheriff; only telling plain facts, that's all."

"Then I'll be a wreck," responded Shields, still smiling. "For I'll stop it, even if I have to shoot you first, which are also plain facts."

Sneed's men had been coming up while they talked and were freely voicing their opinions of sheriffs. Sneed stepped close to the peace officer and laughed, his face flushed with foolish elation at his strength.

"Do you see 'em?" he asked, ironically, indicating his men by a sweep of his arm. "Do you think you could shoot me?"

The reply was instantaneous. The last word had hardly left his lips before he peered blankly into the cold, unreasoning muzzle of a Colt, and the sheriff's voice softly laughed up above him. The cowboys stood as if turned to stone, not daring to risk their foreman's life by a move, for they did not understand the sheriff's methods of arguments, never having become thoroughly acquainted with him.

"You know me better now, Sneed," Shields remarked quietly as he slipped his Colt into its holster. "I'm running the law end of the game and I'll keep right on running it as I d——d please while I'm called sheriff, understand?"

Sneed was a brave man, and he thoroughly appreciated the clean-cut courage which had directed the sheriff's act, and he knew, then, that Shields would keep his word. He involuntarily stepped back and intently regarded the face above him, seeing a not unpleasant countenance, although it was tanned by the suns and beaten by the weather of fifty years. The hazel eyes twinkled and the thin lips twitched in that quiet humor for which the man was famed; yet underlying the humor was stern, unyielding determination.

"You're shore nervy, Sheriff," at length remarked the foreman. "The boys are loco, but I'll try to hold them."

"You'll hold them, or bury them," responded the sheriff, and turning to his companion he said: "Now I'm with you, Charley. So long, Sneed," he pleasantly called over his shoulder as if there had been no unpleasant disagreement.

"So long, Sheriff," replied the foreman, looking after the departing pair and hardly free from his astonishment. Then he turned to his men: "You heard what he said, and you saw what he did. You keep out of this, or I'll make you d——d sorry, if he don't. If The Orphan comes your way, all right and good. But you let his trail religiously alone, do you hear?"

Chapter V
Bill Justifies His Creation

Bill Howland careened along the stage route, rapidly leaving Ford's Station in his rear. He rolled through the arroyo on alternate pairs of wheels, splashed through the Limping Water, leaving it roiled and muddy, and shot up the opposite bank with a rush. Before him was a stretch of a dozen miles, level as a billiard table, and then the route traversed a country rocky and uneven and wound through cuts and defiles and around rocky buttes of strange formation. This continued for ten miles, and the last defile cut through a ridge of rock, called the Backbone, which ranged in height from twenty to forty feet, smooth, unbroken and perpendicular on its eastern face. This ridge wound and twisted from the big chaparral twenty miles below the defile to a branch of the Limping Water, fifteen miles above. And in all the thirty-five miles there was but a single opening, the one used by Bill and the stage.

In crossing the level plain Bill could see for miles to either side of him, but when once in the rough country his view was restricted to yards, and more often to feet. It was here that he expected trouble if at all, and he usually went through it with a speed which was reckless, to say the least.

He had just dismissed the possibility of meeting with Apaches as he turned into the last long defile, which he was pleased to call a cañon. As he made the first turn he nearly fell from his seat in astonishment at what he saw. Squarely in the center of the trail ahead of him was a horseman, who rode the horse which had formerly belonged to Jimmy of the Cross Bar-8, and across the cut lay a heavy piece of timber, one of the dead trees which were found occasionally at that altitude, and it effectively barred the passing of the stage. The horseman wore his sombrero far back on his head and a rifle lay across his saddle, while two repeating Winchesters were slung on either side of his horse. One startled look revealed the worst to the driver–The Orphan, the terrible Orphan faced him!

"Don't choke–I'm not going to eat you," assured the horseman with a smile. "But I'm going to smoke half of your tobacco–and you can bring me a half pound when you come back from Sagetown. Just throw it up yonder," pointing to a rocky ledge, "and keep going right ahead."

Bill looked very much relieved, and hastily fumbled in his hip pocket, which was a most suicidal thing to do in a hurry; but The Orphan didn't even move at the play, having judged the man before him and having faith in his judgment. The hand came out again with a pouch of tobacco, which its owner flung to the outlaw. After putting half of it in his own pouch and enclosing a coin to pay for his half pound, The Orphan tossed it back again and then moved the tree trunk until it fell to the road, when he dismounted and rolled it aside.

"You forget right now that you have seen me or you'll have heart disease some day in this place," warned the horseman, moving aside. Bill swore earnestly that at times his memory was too short to even remember his own name, and he enthusiastically lashed his cayuse sextet. As he swung out on the plain again he glanced furtively over his shoulder and breathed a deep breath of relief when he found that the outlaw was not in sight. He then tied a knot in his handkerchief so as to be sure to remember to get a half-pound package of tobacco. A new responsibility, and one which he had never borne before, weighed upon him. He must keep silent–and what a rich subject for endless conversations! Talking material which would last him for years must be sealed tightly within his memory on penalty of death if he failed to keep it secret.

After an uneventful trip across the open plain, which passed so rapidly because of his intent thoughts that he hardly realized it, he ripped into Sagetown with a burst of speed and flung the mail bag at the station agent, after which he hastened to float the dust down his throat.

When he met his Sagetown friends he had fairly to choke down his secret, and his aching desire to create a sensation pained and worried him.

"You made her faster than usual, Bill," remarked the bartender casually. "Yore half-an-hour ahead of time," he added in a congratulatory tone as he placed a bottle and glass before the new arrival.

"Yes, and I had to stop, too," Bill replied, and then hastily gulped down his liquor to save himself.

"That so?" asked old Pop Westley, an habitué of the saloon. Pop Westley had fought through the Civil War and never forgot to tell of his experiences, which must have been unusually numerous, even for four years of hard campaigning, if one may judge from the fact that he never had to repeat, and yet used them as his *coup d'état* in many conversational bouts. "What was it, Injuns?" he asked, winking at the bartender as if in prophecy as to what the driver would choose for his next lie.

"Oh, no," replied Bill, groping for an idea to get him out of trouble. "Nope, just had to lose twenty minutes rollin' rocks out of the cañon–they must have been a little landslide since I went through her the last time. Some of 'em was purty big, too."

"I thought you might a had to kill some Injuns, like you did when they broke out four years ago," responded the bartender gravely. "Tell us about that time you licked them dozen mad Apache warriors, Bill," he requested. "That was a blamed good scrap from what I can remember."

"Oh, I've told you about that scrap so much I'm ashamed to tell it again," replied the driver, wishing that he could remember just what he had said about it, and sorry that his memory was so inferior to his imagination.

"Bet you get scalped goin' back," pleasantly remarked Johnny Sands, who had not fought in the Civil War, but who often ferociously wished he had when old Pop Westley was telling of how Mead took Vicksburg, or some other such bit of history. Pop must have been connected to a flying regiment, for he had fought under every general on the Union side.

"You're on for the drinks, Johnny," answered Bill promptly, feeling that it would be a double joy to win. "The war-whoops never lived who could scalp Bill Howland, and don't forget it, neither," he boastfully averred as he made for the door, very anxious to get away from that awful gnawing temptation to open their eyes wide about his recent experience.

"Then The Orphan will get you, shore," came from Pop Westley. Bill jumped and slammed the door so hard that it shook the building.

He saw that his sextet was being properly fed and watered for the return trip, which would not take place until the next day. But a trifle like twenty-four hours had no effect on Bill under his present stress of excitement, and he fooled about the coach as if it was his dearest possession, inspecting the king-bolt, running-gear and whiffletrees with anxious eyes. He wanted no break-down, because the Apaches *might* be farther north than was their custom. That done he took his rifle apart and thoroughly cleaned and oiled it, seeing that the magazine was full to the end. Then he had his supper and went straight therefrom to bed, not daring to again meet his friends for fear of breaking his promise to The Orphan.

At dawn he drew up beside the small station and waited for the arrival of the train, which even then was a speck at the meeting place of the rails on the horizon.

The station agent sauntered over to him and grinned.

"I guess I will get that telegraph line after all, Bill," he remarked happily. "I heard that the division superintendent wanted to get word to me in a hurry the other day, and raised the devil when he couldn't. I've been fighting for a wire to civilization for three years, and now I reckon she'll come."

"I always said you ought to have a telegraph line out here," Bill replied. "Suppose that train should run off the track some day, what would they do, hey?"

"Huh, that train never goes fast enough to run off of anything," retorted the station agent. "She'd stop dead if she hit a coyote-by gosh! Here she comes now! What do you think of that, eh? Half-an-hour ahead of time, too! Must be trying to hit up a better average than she's had for the last year. She's usually due three hours late," he added in bewilderment. "She owes the world about a month-must have left the day before by mistake."

"Johnny Sands says he raced her once for ten miles, and beat it a mile," replied Bill, crossing his legs and yawning. Then he began one of his endless talks, and the agent hastily departed and left him to himself.

When the train finally stopped at its destination, after running past the station and having to back to the platform, three women alighted and looked around. Seeing the stage, they ordered their baggage transferred to it and gave Bill a shock by their appearance.

"Is this the stage which runs to Ford's Station?" the eldest asked of Bill.

Bill fumbled at his sombrero and tore it from his head as he replied.

"Yes, sir, er-ma'am!" he said, confusedly. "Are you Sheriff's sister, ma'am?"

"Yes," she answered. "Why do you ask? Has anything happened to him in this awful country?" she asked in alarm.

"No, ma'am, not yet," responded Bill in confusion. "He just didn't expect you 'til the next train, ma'am, that's all. He was going to meet you then."

"Now, *isn't* that just like a man?" she asked her companions. "I distinctly remember that I wrote him I would come on the twenty-fourth. How stupid of him!"

"Yes, ma'am, you did," interposed Bill, eagerly. "But this is only the twenty-first, ma'am."

She refused to notice the correction and waved her hand toward the coach.

"Get in, dears," she said. "I *do* so hope it isn't dirty and uncomfortable, and we have so far to go in it, too. Thirty miles-think of it!"

Bill thought of it, but refrained from offering correction. If Shields had said it was thirty miles when he knew it was eighty that was Shields' affair, and he didn't care to have any unpleasantness. He had offered correction about the date, and that was enough for him. Clambering down heavily he opened the side door of the vehicle and then helped the station agent put the trunks and valises and hat boxes on the hanging shelf behind the coach and saw that they were lashed securely into place. Then he threw the mail bag upon his seat, climbed after it and started on his journey with a whoop and rush, for this trip was to be a record-breaker. Shields had said it was thirty miles, and it behove the driver to make it seem as short as possible.

The unexpected arrival of the women had driven everything else from his mind, even The Orphan, and after he had covered a mile he had a strong desire to smoke. Giving his whip a jerk he threw it along the top of the coach and slipped the handle under his arm. Then he felt for his pouch, and as his fingers closed upon it he suddenly stiffened and gasped. He had forgotten The Orphan's half pound! Swearing earnestly and badly frightened at the close call he had from incurring the anger of a man like the outlaw, he pulled on the reins with a suddenness which caused the sextet to lay back their ears and indulge in a few heartfelt kicks. But the darting whip kept peace and he swung around and returned to town.

As he drove past the station Mary Shields, the sheriff's elder sister, poked her head out of the door and called to him.

"Driver!" she exclaimed. "Driver!"

Bill craned his neck and looked down.

"Yes, ma'am," he replied anxiously.

"Are we there already?" she asked.

"Why, no, ma'am, it's ei-thirty miles yet," he responded as he sprang to the ground.

"Then where are we, for goodness' sake?"

"Back in Sagetown, ma'am," he hurriedly replied. "I shore forgot something," he added in explanation of the return as he ran toward the saloon.

She turned to her companions with a gesture of despair:

"Isn't it awful," she asked, "what a terrible thing drinking is? A most detestable habit! Here we are back to where we started from and just because our driver must have a drink of nasty liquor! Why, we would have been there by this time. I will most assuredly speak to James about this!"

"Well, I suppose we may go on now!" she exclaimed as Bill bolted into sight again, holding a package firmly in his two hands. "I suppose he feels quite capable of driving now."

Bill, blissfully ignorant of the remarks he had called forth, tossed the tobacco upon the mail bag and climbed to his seat again. The long whip hissed and cracked as he bellowed to the team, and once more they started for Ford's Station.

The passengers had all they could do to keep their seats because of the gymnastics of the erratic stage. Bill, who had always found delight in seeing how near he could come to missing things and who was elated at the joy of getting over the worst parts of the trail with speed, decided that this was a rare and most auspicious occasion to show just what he could do in the way of fancy driving. The return to town had spoiled his chances for a record, but he still could do some high-class work with the reins. The weight of the baggage on the tail-board bothered him until he discovered that it acted as a tail to his Concord kite, and when he learned that he joyously essayed feats which he had long dreamed of doing. The result was fully appreciated by the terrified passengers who, choking with the dust which forced its way in to them, could only hold fast to whatever came to their grasp and pray that they would survive.

As he passed a peculiarly formed clump of organ cacti, which he regarded as being his halfway mark, he happened to glance behind, and his face blanched in a sudden fear which gripped his heart in an icy grasp.

He leaped to his feet, wrapping the reins about his wrists, and the "blacksnake" coiled and writhed and hissed. Its reports sounded like those of a gun, and every time it straightened out a horse lost a bit of hair and skin. Both of the leaders had limp and torn ears, and a sudden terror surged through the team, causing their eyes to dilate and grow red. The driver's voice, strong and full, rang out in blood-curdling whoops, which ended in the wailing howl of a coyote, wonderfully well imitated. The combination of voice and whip was too much, and the six horses, maddened by the terrible sting of the lash and the frightful, haunting howl, became frenzied and bolted.

Braced firmly on the footboard, poised carefully and with just the right tension on the reins, the driver scanned the trail before him, avoiding as best he could the rocks and deep ruts, and watching alertly for a stumble. His sombrero had deserted him and his long brown hair snapped behind him in the wind. Bill was frightened, but not for himself alone. With all his bravado he was built of good timber, and his one thought was for the women under his care. He unconsciously prayed that they might not be brought face to face with the realization of what menaced them; that they would not learn why the coach lurched so terribly; that the trunk which obstructed the back window of the coach would not shift and give them a sight of the danger. Oh, that the running gear held! That the king-bolt, new, thank God, proved the words of the boasting blacksmith to be true! He soon came to the beginning of a three-hundred-yard stretch of perfect road and he hazarded a quick backward glance. Instantly his eyes were to the front again, but his brain retained the picture he had seen, retained it perfectly and in wonderful clearness. He saw that the Apaches were no longer a mile away, but that they had gained upon him a very little, so very little that only an eye accustomed to gauging changing distances could have noticed the difference. And he also saw that the group was no longer compact, but that it was already spreading out into the dreaded, deadly crescent, a crescent with the best horses at the horns, which would endeavor to sweep forward and past the coach, drawing closer together until the circle was complete, with the stage as the center.

Another yell burst from him, and again and again the whip writhed and hissed and cracked, and a new burst of speed was the reward. Well it was that the horses were the best and most enduring to be found on the range. He was dependent on his team, he and his passengers. He could not hope to take up his rifle until the last desperate stand. Oh, if he only had the sheriff, the cool, laughing, accurate sheriff with him to lie against the seat and shoot for his sisters! Already the bullets were dropping behind him, but he did not know of it. They dropped, as yet, many yards too short, and he could not hear the flat reports. The wind which roared and whistled past his ears spared him that.

A stumble! But up again and without injury, for a master hand held the reins, a hand as cunning as the eyes were calculating. Could Bill's scoffing friends see him now their scoffing would freeze on lips open in admiring astonishment. If he attained nothing more in his life he was justifying his creation. He was doing his best, and doing it wonderfully well. Long since had fear left him. He was now only a superb driver, an alert, quick-thinking master of his chosen trade. He thrilled with a peculiar elation, for was he not playing his hand against death? A lone hand and with no hope of a lucky draw. All he could hope for was that he be not unlucky and lose the game because of the weakness of a wheel, or the traces, or that new king-bolt; that the splendid, ugly, terrorized units of his sextet would last until he had gained the cañon, where the stage would nearly block the narrow opening, and where he could exchange reins for rifle!

Within the coach three women were miserably huddled in a mass on the floor. Two would be more proper, because the third, a slim girl of nineteen, was temporarily out of her misery, having fainted, which was a boon denied to her companions. Thrown from side to side as if they were straws in weight, they first crashed into one wall and then into the other, buffeted from the edge of the front seat to that of the rear one. Bruised and bleeding and terrified, they dumbly prayed for deliverance from the madman up above them.

The driver's eye caught sight of the turn, which lay ten miles northeast of the cañon-then he had passed it.

"Only ten miles more, bronchs!" he shouted, imploringly, beseechingly. "Hold it, boys! Hold it, pets! Only ten miles more!" he repeated until the left-hand leader lurched forward and lost its footing. Another bit of masterly manipulation of the reins saved it from going down, and again the coyote yell rang out in all of its acute, quavering, hair-raising mournfulness. The blacksnake again and again mercilessly leaped and struck, and another wonderful burst of speed rewarded him.

His heart suddenly went out to his horses, as he realized what speed they were making and had been holding for so long a time, and he swore to treat them better than they had ever known if they pulled him safely to the mouth of the cañon.

A second backward glance, forced from him because of the awful uncertainty at his back, because if it was the last thing he ever did he must look behind him as a child looks back into the awful darkness of the room, caused his face to be convulsed with smiles, sudden and sincere. He shouted madly in his joy at what he saw, dancing up and down regardless of his perilous footing, bending his knees with a recklessness almost criminal, as he uncoiled the hissing blacksnake high up in the air. Again and again the whistling, hissing length of braided rawhide curled and straightened and cracked, faster and faster until the reports almost merged. He tossed his head and laughed wildly, hysterically, and danced as only a man can dance when eased of a terrible nervous tension; the rasping of the icy, grasping fingers of Death along his back suddenly ceased, and there came to him assurance of life and vengeance. Turning again he hurled the writhing length of his whip at the yelling Apaches, snapping the rifle-like reports at their faces, cursing them in shouted words; hot, joyous, cynical, taunting words fresh from the soul of him, throbbing with his hatred; venomous, contemptuous, scathing, too heartfelt to be over-profane.

"Come *on*, d——n you! Your slide to h–l is greased *now!* Come on, you wolves! You cheap, blind vultures! Come on! *Come on!!*" he yelled, well nigh out of his senses from the reaction. "Yes, yell! Yell, d——n you!" he shouted as they replied to his taunts. "Yell! Shoot your tin guns while you can, for you'll soon be so full of lead you'll stop forever! *Come on!* Come on!"

They came. All their energies were bent toward the grotesque figure that reviled them. They could not catch his words, but their eyes flashed at what they could see. Dust arose in huge, low clouds behind them, and they gained rapidly for a time, but only for a time, for their mounts had covered many miles in the last few days and were jaded and without their usual strength because of insufficient food. But they gained enough to drop their shots on the coach, although accurate shooting at the pace they were keeping was beyond their skill.

Puffs of dust spurted from the plain in front of the team and arose beside it, and a jagged splinter of seasoned ash whizzed past the driver's ear. A long, gray furrow suddenly appeared in the end of the seat and holes began to show in the woodwork of the stage. One bullet, closer than the others, almost tore the reins from the driver's hands as it hit the loose end of leather which flapped in the air. Its jerk caused him to turn again and renew his verbal cautery, tears in his eyes from the fervor of his madness.

"Hi-yi! Whoop-e-e!" he shouted at his straining, steaming sextet. "Keep it up, bronchs! Hold her for ten minutes more, boys! We'll win! We'll win! We'll laugh them into h–l yet! We'll dance on their painted faces! Keep her steady! You're all right, every d——d one of you! Hold her steady! Whoop-e-e!"

A new factor had drawn cards, and the new factor could play his cards better than any two men under that washed-out, faded blue sky.

Chapter VI

The Orphan Obeys an Impulse

When Sneed promised to try to restrain his men he spoke in good faith, and when he discovered that half of them were missing his anger began to rise. But he was helpless now because they were beyond his reach, so he could only hope that they would not meet the sheriff, not only because of the displeasure of the peace officer, but also because good cowboys were hard to obtain, and he knew what such a meeting might easily develop into.

The foreman knew that Ford's Station bore him and his ranch no love and that if the sheriff should meet with armed resistance and, possibly, mishap at the hands of any members of the Cross Bar-8, that trouble would be the tune for him and his men to dance to. Angrily striding to and fro in front of the bunk house he gave a profane and pointed lecture to several of his men who stood near, abashed at their foreman's anger. He suddenly stopped and looked toward the rocky stretch of land and hurled epithets at what he feared might be taking place in its defiles and among its rocks and bowlders.

"Fools!" he shouted, shaking his fist at the Backbone. "Fools, to hunt a man like that on his own ground, and in the way you'll do it! You can't keep together for long, and as sure as you separate, some of you will be missing to-night!"

Had he been able, he would have seen six cowboys, who were keeping close together as they worked their way southward, exploring every arroyo and examining every thicket and bowlder. Their Colts were in their hands and their nerves were tensed to the snapping point.

They finally came to the stage road and, after a brief consultation, plunged into it and scrambled up the opposite bank, where they left one of their number on guard while they continued on their search. The guard found concealment behind a huge bowlder which stood on the edge of the cañon above the entrance. He lighted a cigarette, and the thin wisps of pale blue smoke slowly made their way above him, twisting and turning, halting for an instant, and then speeding upward as straight as a rod. It was strong tobacco and very aromatic, and when the wind caught it up in filmy clouds and carried it away it could be detected for many feet.

Five minutes had passed since the searchers had become lost to sight to the south when something moved on the other side of the cañon and then became instantly quiet as the smoke streamed up. The guard was cleverly hidden from sight, but he felt that he must smoke, for time passed slowly for him. Again something moved, this time behind a thin clump of mesquite. Gradually it took on the outlines of a man, and he was intently watching the tell-tale vapor, the odor of which had warned him in time.

Retreating, he was soon lost to sight, and a few minutes later he peered through a thin thicket which stood on the edge of the cañon wall. As he did so the guard stuck his head out from the shelter of his bowlder and glanced along the trail. Again seeking his cover he finished his cigarette and lighted another.

"He won't look again for a few minutes, the fool," muttered the other as he dropped into the road and darted across it. After a bit of cautious climbing he gained the top of the cañon wall and again became lost to sight.

Still the smoke ascended fitfully from behind the bowlder, and the prowler gradually drew near it, at last gaining the side opposite the smoker. He crouched and slowly crawled around it, his left hand holding a Colt; his right, a lariat. As the guard again turned to examine the lower end of the cañon his eyes looked into a steady gun, and while his wits were rallying to his aid the rope leaped at him and neatly dropped over his shoulders, pinning his arms to his side. It twitched and a loop formed in it, running swiftly and almost horizontally. It whipped over his head and tightened about his throat, while another loop sped after it and assisted in throttling the puncher. Then the lariat twitched and whirled and loops ran along it and fastened over the guard's wrists, rapidly getting shorter; and when it ceased, its wielder was brought to the side of his trussed victim. The bound man was turning purple in the face and neck and his captor, hastily crowding the guard's own neck-kerchief into the open, gasping mouth, released the throat clutch of the rawhide and then securely fixed the gag into place.

Roughly dragging his captive to a mass of débris he tore it apart and dragged and pushed the man into it, after which he pushed the rubbish back into place and then ran to the bowlder, where he covered all tracks. Picking up the puncher's revolver he took the cylinder from it and hurled it far out on the plain, throwing the frame across the defile into a tangled mass of mesquite. Looking carefully about him, to be sure he had not overlooked anything, he disappeared in the direction from which he had come.

He again appeared in the cañon, and ran swiftly along it until he came to the tracks made by the guard's horse, which he followed into an arroyo and where he found the animal hobbled. Loosening the hobbles he threw them over the horse's neck and sprang into the saddle. He picked his way carefully until he had reached the level plain, when he cantered northward, keeping close to the rock wall of the Backbone to avoid being seen by the searchers. When he had put a dozen miles behind him he turned abruptly to the east, soon becoming lost to sight behind the scattered chaparrals.

The Orphan, surmounting a rise, looked to the southwest and saw something which almost caused his hair to rise, and raising hair was not the rule with him, which latter is mentioned to give proper emphasis to the seriousness of what he looked upon. He leaped to the ground and saw that the cinches were securely fastened, after which he vaulted back into the saddle, and, instead of offering prayer for success, sent up profanity at the possibility of failure.

Two miles to the southwest of him he saw six horses flattened almost to earth in keeping the speed they had attained and were holding. Back of them lurched and rocked and heaved the sun-bleached coach, dull gray and dusty, its tall driver standing up to his work, hatless and with his arm rapidly rising and falling as he sent the cruel whip cruelly home. Behind the stage whipped the baggage flap, a huge leathern apron for the protection of luggage, standing out horizontally because of the rush of wind caused by the speed of the coach. It flapped defiantly at what so tenaciously pursued it. A thousand yards to the rear, riding in crescent formation, the horns now far apart and well ahead of the center, were five arm- and weapon-waving bronzed enthusiasts whose war paint could just be discerned by The Orphan's good eyes and field glasses.

As yet, the reason for the lifting hair has not been disclosed, because The Orphan was proud in his belief that he had few nerves and a dormant sympathy, and this scene alone would not have aroused much sympathy in his heart for the driver, and neither would it have changed the malevolent expression which disfigured his face, an expression caused by the remembrance of six cowboys who had searched for him as if he was a cowardly, cattle-killing coyote. But the exuberant baggage-flap revealed two trunks, three valises and a pile of white cardboard boxes; and as if this was not enough for a man adept at sign reading, the door of the coach suddenly became unfastened and alternately swung open and shut as the lurching of the coach affected it. And through the intermittent opening he could see a mass of gray and brown and blue.

The Orphan had spent ten years of his life battling against the hardest kinds of odds, and his brain had foresworn long methods of thinking and had adopted short cuts to conclusions. His mental processes were sharp, quick and acted instantly on his nerves, often completing an action before he became clearly conscious of its need. He forgot the pleasant sheriff and the unpleasant, blundering cowboys who, very probably, were now engaged in wondering where their companion had gone; and he forgot his determination to return and free that puncher. He asked himself no questions as to why or how, but simply sunk his spurs half an inch into a horse that had peculiar and fixed ideas about their use, and that now bucked, pitched and galloped forward because its rider had suddenly decided to save those gray and brown and blue dresses.

The Apaches had passed the point immediately south of him and were now more to the west, going at right angles to the course he took. They were so intent upon gaining yard upon yard that they did not look to the side-their thoughts were centered on the tall, lanky man who stood up against the sky and cursed them, and whose hat they had passed miles back. As he turned and stole the look at them which had so pleased him, they only waved guns and wasted cartridges more recklessly, yelling savagely.

Down from the north charged a brown, a dirty brown horse, and it was comparatively fresh. It gained steadily, silently, and its gains were measured in yards to each minute it ran, since it was coming at a sharp angle. Astride of it and lying along its neck was a man whose spurs and quirt urged it to its uttermost effort. Soon the man straightened up in his saddle, the horse braced its legs and slid to a stand as a rifle arose to the rider's shoulder, and at the shot the animal leaped forward at its top speed. A puff of smoke flashed past the marksman's head to mingle with the dust cloud in his wake, and the nearest brave, who was the last in the crescent, dropped sprawlingly to the ground and rolled rapidly several times. His horse, freed of its burden, ran off at an angle and was soon left behind. The excitement of the chase and the noise of the hoofbeats of their own horses and of the reports of their own rifles effectually lost the report of the shot and soon another, and nearest, Apache also plunged to the plain. This time the freed horse shot ahead and ranged alongside the wearer of the head-dress, who turned in his saddle and looked back. His eyesight was good, but not good enough to see the .50 caliber slug which passed through his abdomen and tore the ear of another warrior's horse.

The rider of the horse owning the mutilated ear looked quickly backward, screamed a warning and war-cry all in one and began to shoot rapidly. His surprised companion followed suit as the coach came to a stand, and another rifle, long silent, took a hand in the dispute with a vim as if to make up for lost time. The first warrior fell, shot through by both rifles, and the other, emptying his magazine at the new factor, who was very busily engaged in extracting a jammed cartridge, wheeled his pony about and fled toward the south, panic-stricken by the accuracy of the newcomer and terrorized by the awful execution. But the Apache's last shot nearly cleaned the sheriff's slate, grazing The Orphan's temple and stunning him: a fraction of an inch more to the right would have cheated the Cross Bar-8 of any chance of revenge.

Bill, still holding the rifle, leaped to the sand and ran to where his rescuer lay huddled in the dust of the plain.

"I've got yore smoking," he exclaimed breathlessly, at last getting rid of his mental burden. Then he stopped short, swore, and bent over the figure, and grasping the body firmly by neck and thigh, slung it over his shoulders and staggered toward the coach, his progress slow and laborious because of the deep sand and dust. As he neared his objective he glanced up and saw that his passengers had left the stage and were grouped together on the plain like lambs lost in a lion country.

They were hysterical, and all talked at once, sobbing and wringing their hands. But when they noticed the driver stumbling toward them with the body across his shoulders their tongues became suddenly mute with a new fear. Up to then they had thought only of their own woes and bruises, but here, perhaps, was Death; here was the man who had risked his life that they might live, and he might have lost as they gained.

They besieged Bill with tearful questions and gave him no chance to reply. He staggered past them and placed his burden in the scant shadow of the coach, while they cried aloud at sight of the blood-stained face, frozen in their tracks with fear and horror. Bill, ignoring them, hastily climbed with a wonderful celerity for him, to the high seat and dropped to the ground with a canteen which he had torn from its fastenings. Pouring its contents over the upturned face he half emptied a pocket flask of whisky into The Orphan's mouth and then fell to chafing and rubbing with his calloused, dust-covered hands, well knowing the nature of the wound and that it had only stunned.

Soon the eyelids quivered, fluttered and then flew back and the cruel eyes stared unblinkingly into those of the man above him, who swore in sudden joy. Then, weak as he was and only by the aid of an indomitable will, the wounded man bounded to his feet and stood swaying slightly as one hand reached out to the stage for support, the other instinctively leaping to his Colt. He swayed still more as he slowly turned his head and searched the plain for foes, the Colt half drawn from its holster.

As soon as he had gained his feet and while he was looking about him in a dazed way the women began to talk again, excitedly, hysterically. They gathered around this unshaven, blood-stained man and tried to thank him for their lives, their voices broken with sobs. He listened, vaguely conscious of what they were trying to say, until his brain cleared and made him capable of thought. Then he ceased to sway and spread his feet far apart to stand erect. His hand went to his head for the sombrero which was not there, and he smiled as he recalled how he had lost it.

"Oh, how can we ever thank you!" cried the sheriff's eldest sister, choking back a nervous sob. "How can we ever thank you for what you have done! You saved our lives!" she cried, shuddering at the danger now past. "You saved our lives! You saved our lives!" she repeated excitedly, clasping and unclasping her hands in her agitation.

"How can we ever thank you, how can we!" cried the girl who had fainted when the chase had begun. "It was splendid, splendid!" she cried, swaying in her weakness. She was so white and bruised and frail that The Orphan felt pity for her and started to say something, but had no chance. The three women monopolized the conversation even to the exclusion of Bill, who suddenly felt that his talking ability was only commonplace after all.

Blood trickled slowly down the outlaw's face as he smiled at them and tried to calm them, and the younger sister, suddenly realizing the meaning of what she had vaguely seen, turned to Bill with an imperative gesture.

"Bring me some water, driver, immediately," she commanded impatiently, and Bill hurried around to the rear axle from which swung a small keg of three gallons' capacity. Quickly unsnapping the chain from it he returned and pried out the wooden plug, slowly turning the keg until water began to flow through the hole and trickle down to the sand. Miss Shields took a small handkerchief from her waist and unfolded it, to be stopped by Bill.

"Don't spoil that, miss!" he hastily exclaimed. "Take one of mine. They ain't worth much, and besides, they're a whole lot bigger."

"Thank you, but this is better," she replied, smiling as she regarded the dusty neck-kerchief which he eagerly held out to her. She wet the bit of clean linen and Bill followed her as she stepped to the side of the outlaw, holding the keg for her and thinking that the sheriff was not the only thoroughbred to bear the name of Shields. He turned the keg for her as she needed water, and she bathed the wound carefully, pushing back the long hair which persisted in getting in her way, all the time vehemently declining the eager offers of assistance from her companions. The Orphan had involuntarily raised his hand to stop her, feeling foolish at so much attention given to so trivial a wound and not at all accustomed to such things, especially from women with wonderful deep, black eyes.

"Please do not bother me," she commanded, pushing his hand aside. "You can at least let me do this little thing, when you have done so much, or I shall think you selfish."

He stood as a bad boy stands when unexpectedly rewarded for some good deed, uncomfortable because of the ridiculous seriousness given to his gash, and ashamed because he was glad of the attention. He tried not to look at her, but somehow his eyes would not stray from her face, her heavy mass of black hair and her wonderful eyes.

"You make me think that I'm really hurt," he feebly expostulated as he capitulated to her deft hands. "Now, if it was a real wound, why it might be all right. But, pshaw, all this fuss and feathers about a scratch!"

"Indeed!" she cried, dropping the stained handkerchief to the ground as she took another from her dress, plastering his hair back with her free hand. "I suppose you would rather have what you call a real wound! You should be thankful that it is no worse! Why, just the tiniest bit more, and you would have—" she shuddered as she thought of it and turned quickly away and tore a strip of linen from her skirt. Straightening up and facing him again she ripped off the trimming and carefully plucked the loose threads from it. Folding it into a neat bandage she placed the handkerchief over the wound after pushing back the rebellious hair and bound it into place with the strip, deftly patting it here and pushing it there until it suited her. Then, drawing it tight, she unfastened the gold breast-pin which she wore at her throat and pinned the bandage into place, stepping back to regard her work with satisfaction.

"There!" she cried laughing delightedly. "You look real well in a bandage! But I am sorry there is need for one," she said, sobering instantly. "But, then, it could have been much worse, very much worse, couldn't it?" she asked, smiling brightly.

Before The Orphan could reply, Bill saw a break in the conversation, or thought he did, and hastened to say something, for he felt unnatural.

"I got yore smokin', Orphant!" he cried, clambering up to his seat. "Leastawise, I had before them war-whoops–yep! Here she is, right side up and fine and dandy!"

Could he have seen the look which the outlaw flashed at him he would have quailed with sudden fear. Three gasps arose in chorus, and the women drew back from the outlaw, fearful and shocked and severe. But with the sheriff's younger sister it was only momentarily, for she quickly recovered herself and the look of fear left her eyes. So this, then, was the dreaded Orphan, the outlaw of whom her brother had written! This young, sinewy, good-looking man, who had swayed so unsteadily on his feet, was the man the stories of whose outrages had filled the pages of Eastern newspapers and magazines! Could he possibly be guilty of the murders ascribed to him? Was he capable of the inhumanity which had made his name a synonym of terror? As she wondered, torn by conflicting thoughts, he looked at her unflinchingly, and his thin lips wore a peculiar smile, cynical and yet humorous.

Bill leaped to the ground with the smoking tobacco and, blissfully unconscious of what he had done, continued unruffled.

"That was d—-n fine-begging the ladies' pardon," he cried. "Yes sir, it was plumb sumptious, it shore was! And when I tell the sheriff how you saved his sisters, he'll be some tickled! You just bet he will! And I'll tell it right, too! Just leave the telling of it to me. Lord, when I looked back to see how far them war-whoops were from my back hair, and saw you tearing along like you was a shore enough express train, I just had to yell, I was so tickled. It was just like I held a pair of deuces in a big jack-pot and drew two more! My, but didn't I feel good! And, say-whenever you run out of smoking again, you just flag Bill Howland's chariot: you can have all he's got. That's straight, you bet! Bill Howland don't forget a turn like that, never."

The enthusiasm he looked for did not materialize and he glanced from one to another as he realized that something was up.

"Come, dears, let us go," said Mary Shields, lifting her skirts and abruptly turning her back on the outlaw. "We evidently have far to go, and we have wasted *so* much time. Come, Grace," she said to her friend, stepping toward the coach.

Bill stared and wondered how much time had been wasted, since never before had he reached that point in so short a time. He had made two miles to every one at his regular speed.

"Come, Helen!" came the command from the elder, and with a trace of surprise and impatience.

"Sister! Why, Mary, how can you be so mean!" retorted the girl with the black eyes, angry and indignant at the unkindness of the cut, her face flushing at its injustice. Her spirit was up in arms immediately and she deliberately walked to The Orphan and impulsively held out her hand, her sister's words deciding the doubts in her mind in the outlaw's favor.

"Forgive her!" she cried. "She doesn't mean to be rude! She is so very nervous, and this afternoon has been too much for her. It was a man's act, a brave man's act! And one which I will always cherish, for I will never forget this day, never, never!" she reiterated earnestly. "I don't care what they say about you, not a bit! I don't believe it, for you could not have done what you have if you are as they paint you. I will not wait for our driver to tell my brother about your splendid act-he, at least, shall know you as you are, and some day he will return it, too."

Then she looked from him to her hand: "Will you not shake hands with me? Show me that you are not angry. Are you fair to me to class me as an enemy, just because my brother is the sheriff?"

He looked at her in wonderment and his face softened as he took the hand.

"Thank you," he said simply. "You are kind, and fair. I do not think of you as an enemy."

"Helen! Are you coming?" came from the coach.

He smiled at the words and then laughed bitterly, recklessly, his shoulders unconsciously squaring. There was no malice in his face, only a quizzical, baffling cynicism.

"Oh, it's a shame!" she cried, her eyes growing moist. She made a gesture of helplessness and looked him full in the eyes. "Whatever you have done in the past, you will give them no cause to say such things in the future, will you? You will leave it all behind you and get work, and not be an outlaw any more, won't you? You will prove my faith in you, for I *have* faith in you, won't you? It will all be forgotten," she added, as if her words made it so. Then she leaned forward to readjust the bandage. "There, now it's all right-you must not touch it again like that."

"You are alone in your faith," he replied bitterly, not daring to look at her.

"Oh, I reckon not," muttered Bill, scowling at the stage as if he would like to unhitch and leave it there. Then seeing The Orphan glance at the horse which was grazing contentedly, he went out to capture the animal. "D——d old hen, that's what she is!" he muttered fiercely. "I don't care if she is the sheriff's sister, that's just what she is! Just a regular ingrowing disposition!"

"You are kind, as kind as you are beautiful," The Orphan responded simply. "But you don't know."

She flushed at his words and then decided that he spoke in simple sincerity.

"I know that you are going to do differently," she replied as she extended her hand again. "Good-by."

He bowed his head as he took it and flushed: "Good-by."

She slowly turned and walked toward the coach, where she was received by a chilling silence.

Bill brought the horse to where The Orphan stood lost in thought, unbuckled his cartridge belt and wrapped it around the pommel of the saddle, the heavy Colt still in the holster. Then he clambered up for his rifle and tied it to the saddle skirt by the thongs of leather which dangled therefrom. Looking about him he espied the keg on the sand and, driving home the plug, slung it behind the cantle of the saddle where he fastend it by the straps which held the outlaw's "slicker." Jamming the package of tobacco into the pocket of the garment he stepped back and grinned sheepishly at his generous gifts. He turned abruptly and strode to the outlaw and shoved out his hand.

"There, pardner, shake!" he cried heartily. "Yore the best man in the whole d——d cow country, and I'll tell 'em so, too, by God!"

The outlaw came out of his reverie and looked him searchingly in the face as he gripped the outstretched hand with a grip which made the driver wince.

"Don't be a fool, Bill," he replied. "You'll get yourself disliked if you enthuse about me." Then he noticed the additions to his equipment and frowned: "You better take those things, I can't. The spirit is enough."

"Oh, you borrow them 'til you see me again," replied Bill. "You may need 'em," he added as he wheeled and walked to the coach. He climbed to his seat and wrapped the lines about his hands, cracking the whip as soon as he could, and the coach lurched on its way to Ford's Station, the driver grunting about fool old maids who didn't know enough to be glad they were alive.

The Orphan hesitated about the gifts and then decided to take them for the time. He mounted and rode past the coach door, keeping near to the flank of the last horse, where he listened to Bill's endless talk.

"How is it that you've got a Cross Bar-8 cayuse?" Bill asked at length, too idiotically happy to realize the significance of his question.

The Orphan's hand leaped suddenly and then stopped and dropped to the pommel, and he looked up at the driver.

"Oh, one of their punchers and I sort of swapped," he laughingly replied, thinking of the man under the débris. "Say, if I don't get as far as the cañon with you, just climb up above on the left hand side near the entrance and release a fool puncher that is covered up under a pile of rubbish, will you? I came near forgetting him, and I don't want him to die in that way."

As he spoke he saw a group of horsemen swing over a rise and he knew them instinctively.

"There's the gang now-tell them, I'm off for a ride," he said, dropping back to the coach door, where he raised his hand to his head and bowed.

Chapter VII

The Outfit Hunts for Strays

As the group of punchers and the stage neared each other Bill saw two horsemen ride out into view beside a chaparral half a mile to the northwest, and he recognized Shields and Charley, who were loping forward as if to overtake the cowboys, their approach noiseless because of the deep sand. As the cowboys came nearer Bill recognized them as being the five worst men of the Cross Bar-8 outfit, and his loyalty to his new friend was no stronger than his dislike for the newcomers. They swept up at a canter and stopped abruptly near the front wheel.

"Who was *that?*" asked Larry Thompson impatiently, with his gloved hand indicating the direction taken by The Orphan.

"Friend of mine," replied Bill, who was diplomatically pleasant. "Say," he began, enthusing for effect, "you should have turned up sooner-you missed a regular circus! We was chased by five Apaches, and my friend cleaned 'em up right, he shore did! You should a seen it. I wouldn't a missed it for——"

"Cheese it!" relentlessly continued Larry, interrupting the threatened verbal deluge. "Don't be all day about it, Windy," he cried; "who is he?"

"Why, a friend of mine, Tom Davis," lied Bill. "He just wiped out a bunch of Apaches, like I was telling you. They was a-chasing me some plentiful and things was getting real interesting when he chipped in and took a hand from behind. And he certainly cleaned 'em up brown, he shore did! Say, I'll bet you, even money, that he can lick the sheriff, or even The Orphant! He's a holy terror on wheels, that's what he is! Talk about lightning on the shoot-and he can hit twice in the same place, too, if he wants to, though there ain't no use of it when he gets there once. The way he can heave lead is enough to make——"

"Choke it, Bill, choke it!" testily ordered Curley Smith, whose reputation was unsavory. "Tell us why in h–l he hit th' trail so all-fired hard. Is yore friend some bashful?" he inquired ironically.

"Well," replied Bill, grinning exasperatingly, "it all depends on how you looks at it. Women say he is, men swear he ain't; you can take your choice. But they do say he ain't no ladies' man," he jabbed maliciously, well knowing that Curley prided himself on being a "lady-killer."

"Th' h–l he ain't!" retorted Curley, with a show of anger, preparing to argue, which would take time; and Bill was trying to give the outlaw a good start of them. "Th' h–l he ain't!" he repeated, leaning aggressively forward. "Yu keep yore opinions close to home, yu big-mouthed coyote!"

"Well, you asked me, didn't you?" replied Bill. "And I told you, didn't I? He's a good man all around, and say, you should oughter hear him sing! He's a singer from Singersville, he is. Got the finest voice this side of Chicago, that's what."

"That's *real* interesting, and *just* what we was askin' yu about," replied Larry with withering sarcasm. "An' bein' so, Windy, we'll shore give him all the music he wants to sing to before dark if we gets him. Yore lying ability is real highfalutin'. Now, suppose yu tell th' truth before we drag it outen yu-who is he?"

"You ought to know it by this time. Didn't I say his name is Tom Davis?" he replied, crossing his legs, his face wearing a bored look. "How many names do you think he's got, anyhow? Ain't one enough?"

"Look a-here!" cried Curley, pushing forward. "Was that th' d——d Orphant? Come on, now, talk straight!"

"Orphant!" ejaculated Bill in surprise. "Did you say Orphant? Orphant nothing!" he responded. "What in h–l do you think I'd be lying about him for? Do I look easy? He ain't no friend of mine! Besides, I wouldn't know him if I saw him, never having seen that frisky gent. Holy gee! is the Orphant loose in this country, out here along my route!" he cried, simulating alarm.

"Well, we'll take a chance anyhow," interposed Jack Kelly. "I can tell when a fool lies. If it *is* yore friend Tom Davis we won't hurt him none."

"Honest, you won't hurt him?" asked Bill, grinning broadly. "No, I reckon *you* won't, all right," he added, for the sheriff was close at hand now and was coming up at a walk, and Bill had an abiding faith in that official. He could be a trifle reckless how he talked now. He laughed sarcastically and hooked his thumbs in the armholes of his vest. "Nope, I reckon *you* won't hurt him, not a little bit. Not if he knows you're going to try it on him. And if it should be Mister Orphant, well, I hear that he's dead sore on being hunted-don't like it for a d——-n. I also hear he drinks blood instead of water and whips five men before breakfast every morning to get up an appetite. Oh, no, and you won't hurt him neither, will you?"

"Yore real pert, now *ain't* yu?" shouted Curley angrily. "Yore a whole lot sassy an' smart, *ain't* yu? But if we find that he is that Orphant, we'll pay yu a visit so yu can explain just why yore so d——-d friendly with him. He seems to have a whole lot of friends about this country, he does! Even the sheriff won't hurt him. Even th' brave sheriff loses his trail. Must be somethin' in it for somebody, eh?"

"You'd better tell that to somebody else, the sheriff, for instance. He'd like to think it over," responded Bill easily. "It's a good chance to see a little branding, a la Colt, as the French say. Tell it to him, why don't you?"

"I'm a-tellin' it to yu, *now*, an' I'll tell it to Shields when I sees him, yu overgrown baby, yu!" shouted Curley, his hand dropping to his Colt. "Everybody knows it! Everybody is a-talkin' about it! An' we'll have a new sheriff, too, before long! An' as for yu, if we wasn't in such a hurry, we'd give yu a lesson yu'd never forget! That d——-d Orphant has got a pull, but we're goin' to give him a push, an' plumb into hell! Either a pull or our brave sheriff is some ascairt of him! He's a *fine* sheriff, *he* is, th' big baby!"

"Pleasant afternoon, Curley," came from behind the group, accompanied by a soft laugh. The voice was very pleasant and low. Curley stiffened and turned in his saddle like a flash. The sheriff was smiling, but there was a glint in his fighting eyes that gave grave warning. The sheriff smiled, but some men smile when most dangerous, and as an assurance of mastery and coolness.

"Looking for strays, or is it mavericks?" he casually asked, a question which left no doubt as to what the smile indicated, for it was a challenge. Maverick hunting was at that time akin to rustling, and it was occurring on the range despite the sheriff's best efforts to stop it.

Curley flushed and mumbled something about a missing herd. He had suddenly remembered the scene at the corral, and it had a most subduing effect on him. The sheriff regarded him closely and then noted the bullet holes in the coach. The door of the vehicle was closed, the curtains down, and no sound came from within it. The baggage flap had settled askew over the tell-tale trunks and hid them from sight on that side.

"Oh, it's a missing herd this time, is it?" he inquired coolly. "Well, I reckon you won't find it out here. They don't wander over this layout while the Limping Water is running."

"Well, we'll take a look down south aways; it won't do no harm now that we've got this far," replied Larry. "Come on, boys," he cried. "We've wasted too much time with th' engineer."

"Wait!" commanded the sheriff shortly. "Your foreman made me certain promises, and I reckon that you are out against orders. I wouldn't be surprised if Sneed wants you right now."

Larry laughed uneasily. "Oh, I reckon he ain't losin' no sleep about us. We won't hurt nobody" –whereat Bill grinned. "Come on, fellows."

"Well, I hope you get what you're looking for," replied the sheriff, whereat Bill snickered outright and winked at Charley, who sat alert and scowling behind the sheriff, rather hoping for a fight.

Larry flashed the driver a malicious look and, wheeling, cantered south, followed by his companions. They rode straight for the point at which The Orphan had disappeared, Bill waving his arms and crying: "Sic 'em." The chase was on in earnest.

The stage door suddenly flew open with a bang and interrupted the explanations which Bill was about to offer, and in a flash the sheriff was almost smothered by the attentions showered on him. Laughing and struggling and delighted by the surprise, the peace officer could not get a word edgewise in the rapid-fire exclamations and questions which were hurled at him from all sides.

But finally he could be heard as he extricated himself from the embraces of his sisters.

"Well, well!" he cried, smiles wreathing his face as he stepped back to get a good look at them. "You're a sight to make a sick man well! My, Helen, but how you've grown! It's been five years since I saw you-and you were only a schoolgirl in short dresses! And Mary hasn't grown a bit older, not a bit," addressing the elder of the two. Then he turned to the friend. "You must pardon me, Miss Ritchie," he said as he shook hands with her. "But I've been looking forward to this meeting for a long time. And I'm really surprised, too, because I didn't expect you all until the next stage trip. I had intended meeting you at the train and seeing you safely to Ford's Station, because the Apaches are out. I couldn't get word to you in time for you to postpone your visit, so I was going to take Charley and several more of the boys and escort you home."

Then he looked about for Charley, and found that person engaged in conversation with Bill as the two examined the bullet-marked stage.

"Come here, Charley!" he cried, beckoning his friend to his side. "Ladies, this is Charley Winter, and he is a real good boy for a puncher. Charley, Miss Ritchie, my sisters Mary and Helen. I reckon you ladies are purty well acquainted with Bill Howland by this time, but in case you ain't, I'll just say that he is the boss driver of the Southwest, noted locally for his oppressive taciturnity. I reckon you two boys don't need any introducing," he laughed.

Then, while the conversation throbbed at fever heat, Bill suddenly remembered and wheeled toward the sheriff.

"The Orphant!" he yelled in alarm, hoping to gain attention that way.

The sheriff and Charley wheeled, guns in hand, and leaped clear of the women, their quick eyes glancing from point to point in search of the danger.

"Where?" cried the sheriff over his shoulder at Bill.

"Down south, ahead of them fool punchers," Bill exclaimed. "He's only got a little start on 'em. And they know he's there, too. That's why they're looking for cows on a place cows never go."

Then he related in detail the occurrences of the past few hours, to the sheriff's great astonishment, and also to his delight at the way it had turned out. Shields thought of his own personal experiences with the outlaw, and this put him deeper in debt. His opinion as to there being much good in his enemy's makeup was strengthened, and he smiled at the fighting ability and fairness of the man who had declared a truce with him by the big bowlder on the Apache Trail.

"Oh, I hope they don't catch him!" Helen cried anxiously. "Can't you do something, James?" she implored. "He saved us, and he is wounded, too! Can't you stop them?"

The sheriff looked to the south in the direction taken by the cow-punchers, and a hard light grew in his eyes.

"No, not now," he replied decisively. "They've had too much time now. And it's safe to bet that they rode at full speed just as soon as they got out of my sight. They knew Bill would tell me. They're miles away by this time. But don't you worry, Sis-they won't get him. Five curs never lived that could catch a timber wolf in his own country-and if they do catch him, they will wish they hadn't. And I almost hope they win the chase, for they'll lose their fool lives. It will be a lesson to the rest of the bullies of the Cross Bar-8—and small loss to the community at large, eh, Charley?"

"Yore shore right, Jim," replied Charley, smiling at Miss Ritchie. "Did you ever hear tell of the dog that retrieved a lighted dynamite cartridge?" he asked her. "No? Well, the dog left for parts unknown."

"That's good, Charley," Shields responded with a laugh. "The dog just wouldn't mind, and he was only a snarling, no-account cur at that, wasn't he?" Then he looked at the coach, and his heart softened to the hunted man. "I can see it all, now," he said slowly. "Those punchers must have forced him out of the Backbone, and he was getting away when he saw the plight you were in. By God!" he cried in appreciation of the act. "It wasn't no one man's work, five

Apaches! One man stopping five of those devils–it was no work for a murderer, not much! It was clean-cut nerve, and if I ever see him I'll tell him so, too! I'll let him know that he's got some friends in this country. They can say what they please, but there's more manhood in him to the square inch than there is in all the people who cry him down; and who are in a great way responsible for his being an outlaw. I'm ready to swear that he never wantonly shot a man down; no, sir, he didn't. And I reckon he never had much show, from what I know of him."

"Helen was real kind to him," remarked the spinster. "She bathed his wound and bandaged it. Spoiled her very best skirt, too."

"You're a good girl, Sis," Shields said, looking fondly at the beautiful girl at his side. His arm went around her shoulder and he affectionately patted her cheek. "I'm proud of you, and we'll have to see if we can't get another 'very best skirt,' too." Then he laughed: "But I'll bet he blesses the warrior who fired that shot–he's not used to having pretty girls fuss about him."

Mary looked quickly at her sister. "Why, Helen! You've lost your gold pin! Where do you suppose it has gone? I'll look in the stage for it before we forget about it. Dear me, dear me," she cried as she entered the vehicle, "this has indeed been a terrible day!"

Bill grinned and turned toward his team. "I reckon she'll find it some day," he said in a low aside as he passed the sheriff. "I'll just bet she does. It'll be in at the finish of a whole lot of things, and people, too, you bet," he added enigmatically.

Shields looked quickly at the driver, his face brightened and he smiled knowingly at the words. "I reckon it will; fool punchers, for instance?"

Bill turned his head and one eye closed in an emphatic wink. "Keno," he replied.

Mary bustled out again, very much agitated. "I can't find it. Where do you suppose you lost it, dear? I've looked everywhere in the stage."

"Probably back where we stopped before," Helen replied quietly. "We were so agitated that we would never have noticed it if it slipped down."

"Well–" began Mary.

"No use going back for it, Miss Shields," promptly interrupted Bill from his high seat. "We just couldn't find it in all that trampled sand, not if we hunted all week for it with a comb."

"You're right, Bill," gravely responded the sheriff. "We never could."

As they entered the defile of the Backbone the sheriff suddenly remembered what Bill had told him and he stopped and dismounted.

"You keep right on, Bill," he said. "I'm going up to hunt that fool puncher. Lord, but it's a joke! This game is getting better every day–I'm getting so I sort of like to have The Orphan around. He's shore original, all right."

"He's better than a marked deck in a darkened room," laughed the driver. "He shore ought to be framed, or something like that."

"You better go with them, Charley," the sheriff said as his friend made a move at dismounting. "There ain't no danger, but we won't take no chances this time; we've got a precious coachful."

"All right," replied Charley as he wheeled toward the disappearing stage. "So long, Sheriff."

The sheriff looked the wall over and then picked out a comparatively easy place and climbed to the top. As he drew himself over the edge he espied a pair of boots which showed from under a pile of débris, and he laughed heartily. At the laugh the feet began to kick vigorously, so affecting the sheriff that he had to stop a minute, for it was the most ludicrous sight he had ever looked upon.

Shields grabbed the boots and pulled, walking backward, and soon an enraged and trussed cow-puncher came into view. Slowly and carefully unrolling the rope from the unfortunate man, he coiled it methodically and slung it over his shoulder, and then assisted in loosening the gag.

The puncher was too stiff to rise and his liberator helped him to his feet and slapped and rubbed and chuckled and rubbed to start the blood in circulation. The gag had so affected the muscles of the puncher's jaw that his mouth would not close without assistance and effort, and his words were not at all clear for that reason. His first word was a curse.

"'Ell!" he cried as he stamped and swung his arms. "'Ell! I'm asleep all o'er! ——-! 'Ait till I get 'im! ——-! 'Ait till I get 'im!"

"Sort of continuing the little nap you was taking when he roped you, eh?" asked Shields, holding his sides.

"Nap nothing! Nap nothing!" yelled the other in profane denial. "I wasn't asleep, I tell yu! I was wide awake! He got th' drop on me, and then that cussed rope of his'n was everywhere! Th' air was plumb full of rope and guns! I didn't have no show! Not a bit of a show! Oh, just wait till I get him! Why, I heard my pardners talking as they hunted for me, and there I was not twenty feet away from them all the time, helpless! They're fine lookers, they are! Wait till I sees them, too! I'll tell 'em a few things, all right!"

"Well, I reckon you may see one or two of them, if they're lucky-and you can't beat a fool for luck," replied the sheriff. "They want to be angels; they're on his trail now."

"Hope they get him!" yelled the puncher, dancing with rage. "Hope they burn him at th' stake! Hope they scalp him, an' hash him, an' saw his arms off, an' cave his roof in! Hope they make him eat his fingers and toes! Hope——-"

"You're some hopeful to-day," responded the sheriff. "If you like them, you better hope they don't get him. That's hoping real hope."

"Wait till I get him!" the puncher repeated, grabbing for his Colt, being too enraged to notice its absence. "I'll show him if he can tie a man up an' leave him to choke to death, an' starve an' roast! I'll show him if he can run this country like he owns it, shooting and abusing everybody he wants to!"

"All right, Sonny," Shields laughed. "I'll shore wait till you gets him, if I live long enough. But for your sake I shore hope you never finds him. He wouldn't get any more reputation if he killed you, and your friends would miss you."

"Don't yu let that worry yu!" retorted the enraged man. "I can take care of myself in a mix-up, all right! An' I'm going to chase after my friends an' take a hand in th' game, too, by God! He ain't going to leave me high an' dry an' live to boast about it! But I suppose you reckon yu'll stop me, hey?"

Shields raised both hands high in the air in denial. "I wouldn't think of such a thing, not for the world," he cried, laughter shaking his big frame. "You can go any place you please, only *I'd* take a gun if I was going after *him*," he added, eyeing the empty holster. "You know, you *might* need it," he was very grave in his use of the subjunctive.

The puncher slapped his hand to his thigh and then jumped high into the air: "——-! ——-!" he shouted. "Stole my gun! Stole my gun!" Then he paused suddenly and his face cleared. "But I've got something better'n a Colt on my cayuse!" he cried as he leaped toward the edge of the cañon. "An' I'll give him all it holds, too!" he threatened as he bumped and slid to the bottom. The sheriff took more care and time in descending and had just reached the trail when he heard a heart-rending yell, followed by a sizzling stream of throbbing profanity.

"Where's my cayuse?" yelled the puncher as he rounded the corner of the cañon wall on a peculiar lope and hop. "Where's my cayuse, yu law-coyote?" he shouted, temporarily out of his senses from rage. "Where's my cayuse!" dancing up to the sheriff and shaking both fists under the laughter-convulsed face.

When the sheriff could speak, he leaned against the cañon wall for support and broke the news.

"Why, Bill Howland said as how The Orphan was riding a Cross Bar-8 cayuse-dirty brown, with a white stocking on his near front foot. It had a big scar on its neck, too."

"Th' d——-d hoss thief!" began the puncher, but Shields kept right on talking.

"There was a dandy Cheyenne saddle," he said, counting on his fingers, "a good gun, a pair of hobbles and a big coil of rawhide rope on the cayuse. Was they yours?"

"Was they mine! Was they mine!" his companion screamed. "My new saddle gone, my gun gone and my fine rope gone! Oh, h–l! How'll I hunt him now? How'll I get home? How'll I get back to th' ranch?" Words failed him, and he could only wave his arms and yell.

"Well, it wouldn't hardly be worth while chasing him on foot without a gun, that's shore," the sheriff said, grave once more. "But you can get home all right; that's easy."

"How can I?" asked the puncher, eyeing the sheriff's horse and waiting for the invitation to ride double on it.

"Why, walk," was the reply. "It's only about twenty miles as the crow flies-say twenty-five on the trail."

"Walk! Walk!" cried his companion, savagely kicking at a lizard which looked out from a crevice in the rock wall. "I never walked five miles all at once in my life!"

"Well, it'll be a new experience, and you can't begin any younger," replied Shields as he swung into his saddle. "It'll do you good, too-increase your appetite."

"I'm so hungry now I'm half starved," replied the other. "But I'll pay up for all this, you see if I don't! I'll get square with that d——d outlaw!"

"You don't know enough to be glad you were found," retorted the sheriff. "And if he hadn't told Bill where to look for you, you wouldn't have been, neither. You got off easy, Bucknell, and don't you forget it, neither. Men have been killed for less than what you tried to do."

The puncher wilted, for twenty-five miles in high-heeled boots, over rocks and sand, and with an empty stomach, was terrible to contemplate, and he turned to the sheriff beseechingly.

"Give me a lift, Sheriff," he implored. "Take me up behind you–I can't walk all the way!"

Shields looked at the sun, which was nearing the western horizon, and thought for a minute. Then he shrugged his shoulders.

"Well, I hadn't ought to help you a step, not a single, solitary step, and you know it. You tried your best to run against me. You tried to hold me up there by the corral, and then after I had warned you not to go out for The Orphan you went right ahead. Now you're asking me to help you out of your trouble, to make good for your fool stupidity. But I'll take you as far as the end of the cañon-no, I'll take you on to the ford, and then you can do the rest on foot. That'll leave you ten or a dozen miles. Get aboard."

Chapter VIII
"A Timber Wolf in His Own Country"

When The Orphan said good-by to Bill he sat quietly in his saddle for a minute watching the departing stage and wondered how it was that he had the decency to avoid a fight with the cowboys in the presence of the women. Then Helen's words came to him and he smiled at the idea of peace when he would have to fight the outfit before sundown. The heat of the sun on his bare head recalled him from his mental wanderings and he wheeled abruptly and galloped along the trail to where he remembered that a tiny, blood-stained handkerchief lay in the dust and sand. Soon he espied it and, swinging over in the saddle, deftly picked it up and regained his upright position, his head reeling at the effort. Unfolding it he examined the neat "H" done in silk in one corner and smiled as he put it in his chaps pocket where he kept his extra ammunition.

"Peace and war in one pocket," he muttered, grinning at his cartridges' new and unusual companion.

Then he espied a Winchester near a fallen brave, and he procured it as he had the handkerchief. Describing an arc he picked up another, discarding it after he had emptied the magazine, for ammunition was what he wanted. Two Winchesters were all right, but three were too many. As he threw it from him he glanced through a slight opening in the chaparral and saw the outfit approach the stage. Then he galloped to where his sombrero lay, picked it up and turned to the south for the Cimarron Trail. When thoroughly screened by the chaparral he pushed on with the swinging lope which his horse could maintain for hours, and which ate up distance in an astonishing manner. He had lost time in going for his sombrero and the handkerchief, and every minute before nightfall was precious. His thoughts now bent to the problem of how either to elude or ambush his pursuers, and the Winchesters bespoke his forethought, for up to six hundred yards they were not a pleasant proposition to face. If he eluded the cowboys in the darkness he was morally certain that they would take up his trail at dawn, and what distance he had gained would be at the expense of the freshness of his horse. While he would average ten miles an hour through the night, their mounts, freshened by a night's rest, might cut down his gain before the nightfall of the next day.

One of the Winchesters worked loose from its lashings and started to slide toward the ground. He quickly grasped it and made it secure, smiling at the number of rifles he had had and lost during the past three weeks.

"Funny how this country has been shedding Winchesters lately," he mused. "There was the five I got by the big bowlder, which I lost playing tag with that d——d Cross Bar-8 gang, and here's two more, and I just left three what I didn't want. Well, they're real handy for stopping a rush, and I reckons that's what I'm up against this time. If I can find a likely spot for a scrap before dark I may stop that gang in bang-up style, d——n them."

Half an hour later he caught sight of a moving body of horsemen to the southeast of him and his glasses enabled him to make them out.

"'Paches!" he exclaimed, and then he smiled grimly and continued on his way toward them, taking care to keep himself screened from their sight by rises and chaparrals. His first thought had been of danger, but now he laughed at the cards fate had put in his hand, for he would use the Indians to great advantage later on.

He counted them and made their number to be twenty-two, which accounted for the five warriors who had pursued the stage coach. The odds were fine and he laughed joyously, recklessly: "All is fair in love and war," he muttered savagely.

Before the Indians had come upon the scene he had been alone to face five angry and vengeful men, and whom he had every reason to believe were at least fair fighters. Had the positions been reversed they would not have hesitated to make use of any stratagem to save themselves-and here were two contingents, both of which would take his life at the first opportunity. He felt no distaste at the game he was about to play; on the other hand, it pleased him immensely to know that he was superior in intellect to his enemies. They both wanted blood, and they should have it. If they found too much, well and good-that was their lookout. And no less pleasing was the knowledge that he had sent them north and that now he could make use of them. He wondered what they had been doing for the last three weeks and why they were still in that part of the country, but he did not care, for they were where he wanted them to be.

"Twenty-two mad Apaches on the warpath against five cow-wrastlers!" he exulted. "More than four to one, and just aching to get square on somebody! That Cross Bar-8 gang will have something to weep about purty d——n soon! And I shore hope they don't get tired and quit chasing me."

He stopped and waited when he had gained a screened position from where he could look back over his trail, and he had not long to wait, for soon he saw five cowboys galloping hard in his direction. Another look to the southeast showed him that the war party was now riding slowly toward him, not knowing of his presence, and they would arrive at his cover at about the same time the cowboys would come up. Neither the Indians nor the cowboys knew of the proximity of the other, while The Orphan could see them both. He glanced at the thicket to the west of him and saw that it was thin, being a connecting link between the two larger chaparrals.

"I don't know how you are on the jump, bronch," he said to his mount, "but I reckon you can get through that, all right."

The cowboys disappeared from his sight behind the northern chaparral, and as they did so he sunk his spurs into his horse and rode straight at the prickly screen and, going partly over and partly through it, galloped westward as the war party and the ranch contingent met. The shots and yells were as music to his ears, and he bowed in mockery and waved his hand at the turmoil as he made his escape. The timber wolf had won.

Chapter IX
The Cross Bar-8 Loses Sleep

Sneed was angry, which could be seen by the way he talked, ate, moved and swore. He had many cattle to care for and they were strewn over six hundred square miles of territory. The work was hard enough when he had his full dozen punchers, but now it forced groans from the tired bodies of his men, who fell asleep while removing their saddles at night, and who worked in a way almost mechanical. The extra work was not conducive to sweetness of temper, and he was continually quelling fights among the members of the outfit. Where only argument formerly would have arisen over differences of opinion, guns now leaped forth; and the differences were multiplied greatly, and getting worse every day. Things which ordinarily would have provoked no notice, or a laugh at most, now caused hot words and surliness. And the reason for the extra work was the continued absence of five cow punchers.

Sneed, tired of cursing the missing men and of offering himself explanations as to why they had not returned, fell, instead, to planning an appropriate reception for them on their return to the ranch. He needed no rehearsing, for while he did not know in just what manner he would reveal his ideas concerning them, he knew what his ideas were and he had always been good at extemporizing when under pressure, and he was under pressure now if he had ever been.

The extra work was hard enough in itself to cause his anger to rise and to create sensitiveness and surliness on the part of his men, but it was only one factor of his discontent. Busy all day at driving the scattered cattle away from the Backbone and closer to the ranch proper where they would be less likely to fall prey to Apache raiders; working all day from the first sign of dawn to the prohibitive blackness of the night, they could have stood up under the strain, for these were men of iron, inured to hardships and constant riding. But hardy as they were there was one thing which they must have, and that was sleep. If they could have only four hours of unbroken sleep when they threw themselves, fully dressed with the exception of their boots, in their bunks, they could have endured the labor for weeks. But this was denied them, and constantly on their minds were thoughts of fire, slaughtered cattle and death.

For a week night had been a terror on the Cross Bar-8. No sooner had the exhausted outfit fallen asleep than bits of window glass would fly about them, cutting and stinging. There was not a whole window pane in the house and the door was so full of lead that it sagged on its half-shattered hinges. Cooking utensils were fast deserving premiums, for hardly an unperforated tin could be found on the premises. And their cook, a Mexican, who most devoutly believed in a personal devil and a brimstone hell, and who feared that he was living in uncomfortable proximity to both, stood the strain for just two nights and then, panic-stricken, had fled from the accursed place and left them to get their own meals as best they could. The protection of the saints was all very well and good under ordinary circumstances, but when they failed to stop the bullets which passed through his cook shack and which more than once had grazed him, it was time for him to find some place far removed from the Cross Bar-8, and where the devil was less strong. When the saints allowed a devil-sped bullet to completely shatter a crucifix it was time to migrate, which he did, but in broad daylight when the outfit had departed and when the devil was not in evidence.

The interiors of both the ranch house and the bunk house were wrecked. The clock, the pride of the foreman, stood with half its wheels buried in the wall behind it by a .50 caliber slug, its hands pointing to half-past one. Lead filled the interior walls, where opposite windows, and the holes and splinters were a disgrace. Sombreros, equipment and the few pictures the walls boasted were like tops of pepper shakers. No sooner was a light shown than it became the target for a shot, and more than one wound gave proof as to the accuracy of the perpetrator. So tired that they fell asleep at supper, the men were constantly awakened by the noise of devastation and the whining hum of the bullets. Pursuit was a failure, and was also hazardous, as proven by Bert Hodge's arm, broken by a .50 caliber slug from somewhere.

The two houses, wrecked as they were, were fortunate when compared to the condition of the other appurtenances of the ranch. Horses were found dead at all points, and always with a bullet hole in the center of the forehead. The carcasses of cows dotted the plain, and fire had half-destroyed the three corrals. The three new cook wagons, unsheltered, were denuded of bolts and nuts, and their tarpaulins were hopelessly ruined. A wheel was missing from each of them and their poles had been cut through in the middle, the severed ends being found on the roof of the ranch house three minutes after their crashing descent had awakened the foreman, who heard the hum and thud of a bullet as he opened the door. The best grass had been burned off and the outfit had fought fire on several nights when it should have slept. And the small water hole near the cook shack, which furnished water for the bunk house, had been cleared of a dead calf on two mornings. Scouting was of no avail, for the few remaining horses (which now spent the night in the bunk house) were as exhausted as their riders. Keeping guard was a farce, for it had been tried twice, and the guards had fallen asleep; and, awakened by their foreman at dawn, found that their rifles, sombreros and even their spurs were missing. With all his hatred for The Orphan, Sneed was fair-minded enough to give his enemy credit for being the better man. When the harassing outrages had first begun and the foreman and his men were comparatively fresh, he had given the matter his whole attention; and he was no fool. But he had gained nothing but a sense of defeat, which fact did not improve his peace of mind or cause him to lose a whit of his anger. Do what he could, plan as he might, he was beaten, and beaten at every turn. He had to deal with a man whose cunning and ingenuity were far above the average; a man who, combining a rare courage and a wonderful accuracy in shooting with devilish strategy, towered far above the ordinary rustler and outlaw. Sneed knew that he was absolutely at the mercy of his persistent enemy and wondered why it was that he did not steal up in the night and kill the outfit as it slept, which was entirely feasible. Finally, when the strain had grown too much for even his iron nerves the sheriff was implored to take command on the ranch and give it his personal protection. The relations between the sheriff and the ranch were not as cordial as they might have been, and the asking of this favor was gall and wormwood to the foreman and his outfit.

When Shields arrived to take charge of the trouble, accompanied by Charley and two others, he sought the foreman, for Charley had news of a grave nature for the Cross Bar-8.

The foreman ran out of the bunk house and met them near the corral, where the disagreement had taken place.

"By the living God, Sheriff!" he cried, white with anger. "This thing has got to stop if we have to call out the cavalry! We can't get a decent breakfast-not a whole plate or pan in the house! Our cayuses and cows are being slaughtered by the score! And as for the rest of our possessions, they are so full of holes that they whistle when the wind blows!"

"So I heard," replied the sheriff. "I'll do my best."

"We've been doing our best, but what good is it?" cried the foreman. "We are so plumb sleepy we go to sleep moving about! We dassent show our faces after dark without being made a target of! Our new wagons are wrecks, the corrals destroyed and the best grass made us fight for our lives while it burned! That cursed outlaw has got to be killed, d——n him!"

"We'll do our best, Sneed," responded Shields. "I reckon we can stop it; at least we can give you a good night's rest."

"Where are my five punchers?" Sneed asked; his words bellowed until his voice broke. "And Bucknell! D——n near dead before you found him above the cañon, tied up like a package of flour!"

"Well, Charley can tell you about your men," Shields responded, viewing the devastation on all sides of him.

"Well, what about them?" cried the foreman turning to the sheriff's deputy, anger flashing anew in his eyes.

"Well," Charley slowly began, "I was taking a short cut this morning, and when I got to a place about a dozen miles southeast of the mouth of Bill's cañon, I saw five bodies on the desert. They were your cow-punchers, and they was so full of arrows that they looked like big brooms. Apaches, I reckon," he added sententiously.

Sneed tore his hair and swore when he was not choking.

"And after I told them to let up on that blasted outlaw's trail!" he yelled. "Where will it end, between war-whoops and murders? What sort of a God-forsaken layout is this, anyhow? A man can't stick his nose out of his own house after dark without having it skinned by a slug! He's a h–l of a hefty orphant, he is! Poor thing, ain't got no paw or maw to look after his dear little hide! He needs a regiment of cavalry for a papa, that's what he needs, and a good strong lariat for a mamma! Orphant! He's a h–l of a sumptious orphant!"

"Have you trailed him?" asked the sheriff, having to smile in spite of himself at the execution on all sides of him, and at the foreman's words.

"Trailed him!" yelled Sneed, raising on his toes in his vehemence. "Trailed him! Good God, yes! But what good is it, what can we do when our cayuses are so dod-gasted tired that they can't catch a tumble bug? Trailed him! Yes, we trailed him, all right! We trailed him until we fell asleep in the saddles on our sleeping cayuses! And while we were gone, d——d if he didn't blow in and smash up our furniture! We trailed him, all right; just like a lot of cross-eyed, locoed drunken ants! We had to wake each other up, and he could-a killed the whole crowd of us with a club! And my punchers who were so cock-sure they'd get him! How in h–l did they go and mess up with Apaches? They wasn't no fool kids!"

"The last time we saw them they were leaving the stage to go south after him," Charley said. "They hadn't got more than ten miles south when they must have met the Apaches. I have a suspicion that The Orphan had a hand in that meeting, but how he did it I don't know. But I know that the spot was lovely for a head-on collision. Punchers riding south would turn the corner of the chaparral and run into the war party before they knowed it. And I didn't see The Orphant's body laying around all full of arrows, neither."

Sneed's rage was pathetic. He almost frothed, and tears stood in his blood-shot eyes. His neck and his face were red as fire and the veins of his neck and forehead stood out like whip-cords, while his face worked convulsively. He was incapable of coherent speech, his words being unintelligible growls, a series of snarls, and he could only pace back and forth, waving his arms and cursing wildly.

Shields glanced about the ranch and gave a few orders, his men executing them without delay. One man was to keep guard in the bunk house while Sneed and his woe-begone men slept. The sheriff and Charley rode away toward the north to begin the search for the outlaw; and there was to be no quarter asked or given if his deputies had anything to do with it.

The remaining deputy busied himself about the ranch in executing a plan the sheriff had thought out, and his actions were peculiar. First selecting a position from which a man could command an extensive view of the premises, he began to pace off distances in all directions. The place was about eight hundred yards west of the ranch house and bunk house, and formed one angle of a triangle with them; and from it it was possible to look in through the windows of both of them. Any one passing within good rifle range of either house would show up against the lights in the windows; and if a man had been covered over with sand on that particular outlying angle, he could pick off the intruder without being seen. The Orphan was due to meet with a surprise if he paid his regular visit the coming night.

The deputy, after completing his work to his satisfaction found three more positions where they respectively commanded the corrals, the wagons and the rear of the bunk house. Then he paced more distances and was careful that bulky objects interposed in the direct lines between the positions, this latter precaution being to make it impossible for the deputies to shoot each other. This done, he went into the house and consulted with his companion in arms, laughing immoderately about the joke they would play on the marauder.

While Shields and Charley vainly searched the plain and while the deputy paced and thought and paced, and while Sneed and his exhausted cow-punchers slept as if in death, safely under guard, two men were riding along the Ford's Station Sagetown Trail well to the east of the Backbone, chatting amicably and smoking the same brand of tobacco. One of them sat high up in the air on the seat of a stage coach, from where he overlooked his six-horse team. His face was wreathed in grins and his expression was one of beatific contentment. The other cantered alongside on a dirty brown horse which had a white stocking on the near front foot, keeping close watch of the surrounding plain, his mind active and alert.

Bill Howland laughed suddenly and slapped his thigh with enthusiasm: "Say, Orphant," he cried, "you are shore raising h–l with that Cross Bar-8 gang! You has got them so tangled up and miserable that they don't know where they are! If their brains was money they'd have to chalk up their drinks. They're about as dangerous as ossified prairie dogs. They remind me of the feller who kicked a rattlesnake to see if it was alive, and found out that it was. No, sir, they shore won't die of brain fever. Why, they ain't had any sleep for a week, have to work double hard, eat what they can cook in sieve tins, and can't say their soul's their own after dark. They could get rest if they quit working one day and all but one get plenty of sleep. Then the other feller could get his at night. But they don't know enough. Oh, it's rich: the whole blamed town is laughing at 'em fit to bust. It's the funniest thing ever happened in these parts since I've been out here."

Then he suddenly paused: "Say, Sneed sent a puncher to town this morning. It was that brass-headed, flat-faced Bucknell, what you tied up by the cañon. He begged the sheriff to swear in a dozen bad men and come out and protect his foreman and the rest of the outfit. And the pin-headed wart went and blabbed the whole thing right in front of the Taggert's saloon crowd, and he shore had to blow, all right. He shore did, and that gang's always thirsty."

The horseman flecked the ashes from his cigarette and smiled: "Well?" he asked, looking up.

"So Shields took Charley Winter and the two Larkin boys and went out to the ranch right after the puncher went back. So you want to go easy to-night or you'll touch off some unexpected fireworks and such. Shields and his men will stay out there for several days and nights. That'll give the crazy hens a chance to rest up a bit nights. But you be blamed careful about them pinwheels and skyrockets or you'll get burned some. Now, don't you even remember that *I* told you about it. I wouldn't-a said nothing at all, seeing as it ain't none of my business, only you went and got me out of a tight place, and Bill Howland don't forget a favor, no siree! You gave me a square deal and a ace full on kings with them animated paint shops, and I'll give you a lift every time I can. It wouldn't be a bad scheme to watch for me once in a while–I might have some news for you."

Bill's offer, plain as it was that he wished to help, not only because he was in debt to the outlaw, but also because he wished to have safe trips, touched the horseman deeply. Never in his life had The Orphan been offered a helping hand from a stranger; all he could hope for was to get the drop first. He rode on silently, buried in thought, and then, suddenly flipping his cigarette at a cactus, raised his head and looked full at the man above him.

"You play square with me, Bill, and I'll take care of you," he replied. "The less you say, the less apt you are to put your foot in it. I'll hold my mouth about your information, for if Shields knew what you've just said he'd play a tune for you to dance to. The Cross Bar-8 would shoot you before a day passed. Any time you have news for me, tie your kerchief to that cactus," pointing to an exceptionally tall plant close at hand. "Do it on your outward trip. If I see it in time I'll meet you somewhere on the Sagetown end of the trail on your return. I'm going back now, so by-by."

"So long, and good luck," replied Bill heartily. "I'll do the handkerchief game, all right. Be some cautious about the way you buzz around that stacked deck of a Cross Bar-8 for the next few days."

The Orphan wheeled and cantered back, making a detour to the south, for he had a plan to develop and did not wish to be interrupted by meeting any more hunting parties. Bill lashed his team and rolled on his way to Sagetown, a happy smile illuminating his countenance.

"They can't beat us, bronchs," he cried to his team. "Me and The Orphant can lick the whole blasted territory, you bet we can!"

Chapter X
The Orphan Pays Two Calls

Shortly after nightfall a rider cantered along the stage route, fording the Limping Water and rode toward the town, whose few lights were bunched together as if for protection against the spirits of the night. He soon passed the scattered corrals on the outskirts of Ford's Station and, slowing to a walk, went carelessly past the row of saloons and the general store and approached a neat, small house some two hundred yards west of the stage office. He appeared careless as to being seen; in fact a casual observer would have thought him to be some cowboy who was familiar with the town and who feared the recognition of no man. But while he had no fear, he was alert; under his affected nonchalance nerves were set for instant action. He was in the heart of the enemy's country, in the crude stronghold of the Law, and if anything hostile to him occurred it would happen quickly. And he was familiar with the town, because he had on more than one occasion ridden through and explored it, but never before at such an early hour.

Arriving at his destination he dismounted and, leaving his horse unrestrained by rope or strap, walked boldly up to the door of the sheriff's house and knocked. Soon he heard footsteps within and the door opened wide, revealing him standing hat in hand and smiling.

"Good evening, ma'am," he said uneasily.

The sheriff's wife stepped aside and the light fell full on his face. For an instant she was at a loss, and then the fresh scar on his forehead and her husband's good description came to her aid. She gasped and stepped back involuntarily, astonished at his daring. Her act allowed her companions to see him and the effect was marked. Miss Ritchie sat upright in expectation, her face beaming, for this was as romantic and unexpected as she could wish. Mary gasped and dropped her hands to her side, not knowing what to do or say, while Helen slowly laid her work aside and leaned forward slightly, regarding him intently, a curious expression on her face.

"I only called to ask how the ladies were," he continued slowly, turning his hat in his hands, apparently not noticing Mrs. Shields' surprise. "I was afraid they might have-that their recent experience might have bothered them some."

Evidently it was to be only a social call, and Mrs. Shields owed something to this fair-minded and chivalrous man. She smiled kindly, remembering that the caller was rather well thought of by her husband-he was not a man for women to fear, whatever else he might be.

"It is very kind of you," she replied. "Won't you come in?" she asked from the habit of politeness, hardly expecting that he would do so.

"Thank you, I will be glad to for a minute," he responded, slowly stepping into the room, where he suddenly felt awkward and not at all comfortable.

Helen picked up her work to fasten a thread, and he found himself marveling at the cleverness of her fingers. Again laying the work aside, she arose to meet him, a mischievous twinkle in her dark eyes. It was so unusual to have been saved by an outlaw whom her brother had tried to capture, and still more unusual to have him dare to call on her in her brother's own house, especially after her sister's direct cut at the coach.

"Won't you be seated?" she asked, indicating her own chair by the light and taking his hat. When the hat left him he suffered a loss, for he had nothing to twist and grip. He replied by dropping into the chair, not even seeing that it was out of range of the door as a compliment to his hostess. There was no sign of a weapon on him, his holster being empty; but his blue flannel shirt was unbuttoned, the opening hidden by his neck-kerchief. He had, however, only put his Colt there to have it out of sight, and not because he feared trouble. Habitual caution was responsible for the shirt being open, for he was not even sure that he would fight if trouble should come upon him, unless the women gave him a clear field.

Helen drew a chair from the wall and seated herself in the semi-circle which faced him.

"I am very glad that your wound has healed so nicely," she said with a smile. "We are very sorry that you were hurt in our defense."

"Oh, it wasn't anything," he quickly replied, smiling deprecatingly. "You fixed it up so nice that it didn't bother me at all-didn't hurt a bit."

"I am glad it was no worse," she replied, looking around the circle. "Grace, Mary, you surely remember Mr.–Mr.——"

"Please call me by the name you know me by-The Orphan," smiling broadly. "I've almost forgotten that I ever had any other name."

"Mr. Orphan-how funny it sounds," she laughed. "It's most original. Margaret, this is the gentleman to whom we certainly owe our lives. Oh! I know you don't like to be reminded of it," she went on, answering his deprecatory gesture, "no doubt you are accustomed to that sort of thing out here, but in the East such an experience does not often occur."

"I am glad indeed to know and thank you," said Mrs. Shields, impulsively extending her hand. "Your bravery has put me still deeper in your debt. My husband–" her feelings overcame her as she realized that this was the man who had spared to her that husband, her laughing, burly, broad-shouldered, big-hearted king of men. Was it possible that this handsome, confident stripling was his peer?

Helen relieved the tension: "Mr. Orphan, this is Miss Ritchie, the same Miss Ritchie who was so badly frightened when she first met you. Perhaps you'll remember it. And this——"

"I wasn't! I wasn't one bit frightened!" declared Miss Ritchie hotly, to The Orphan's great enjoyment.

"Now, Grace, don't fib-you can't deny it. And this is my sister who was mean enough to keep her senses when I didn't. We thought highly of you then, but even more so now. You see, my brother has been talking about you, he takes a keen interest in you, Mr. Orphan–I declare I can't help laughing at that name, it sounds so funny; but you will forgive me, won't you? I knew you would. Well, James has been saying nice things about you, and so you see we know you better now. He likes you real well, as well as you will let him, and I'm awful sorry that he is not at home," she dared, her eyes flashing with delight. "I am sure he would like to meet you very much; in fact he has said as much. Oh, he speaks of you quite often."

The caller flushed, but he was determined to let them think him perfectly at ease.

"I am glad that he remembers me," he responded gravely. "I have only met him once, but I thought he was rather glad to see me. We had a very enjoyable time together and I found him very pleasant." He was forced to smile as he recalled the six Apaches in the sheriff's rear.

"Helen was just saying what awful risks her brother ran," Miss Ritchie remarked, intently studying the rugged face before her. "But then, he's a man. If I was a man, I wouldn't be afraid of them!"

"My, how brave you are, Grace," laughed Mrs. Shields. "I heard quite to the contrary about the stage ride."

"Goodness, Margaret!" retorted Miss Ritchie, up in arms at the remark. "You would have been afraid in that old coach if you had been banged about in it as I was. The noise was terrible, and that awful driver!"

The caller smiled at her spirit and then replied to her, serious at once.

"Well, he does take chances," he said. "But for that matter every man out in this country has to run risks. Now, I've taken some myself," he added, smiling quizzically. "But, you know, we get used to them after a while-we get used to everything but hunger and thirst-and life. I've even gotten used to being lonesome, and I find that it really isn't so bad after all. And then, you know, lonesomeness does have its advantages at times, for it certainly promotes peace, and the cartridges that it saves are worth considerable. But it took me several years before I could accept it in that light with any degree of ease."

Helen laughed merrily, for she most of all appreciated this outcast's humor, and she liked him better the more he talked.

"Yes, in time I suppose one does become accustomed to danger," she replied, "although I'll be frank enough to admit that I don't believe I could," glancing at her friend. "You risked much by coming here to-night–just suppose that you had called last night!"

"The danger was only from a chance recognition in the street," he replied, smiling, "and it would have been equally dangerous for the man who recognized me, and perhaps more so, since I was on the lookout–that balances. I would be the last man anyone would expect to be in Ford's Station at this time, and once free of the town, I could elude the pursuers in the dark. And as for the sheriff, I knew that he was not at home to-night, and, had he been so, I doubt if it would have stayed me, for he is fair and square, and an unarmed man is safe with him in his own house. He understands what a truce means, and we had one before."

Mrs. Shields smiled at him in such warmth that he thanked his stars that he had played fair out by the bowlder.

"He told us of that!" Helen exclaimed, laughingly. "It was splendid of you, both of you. And, do you know, I liked you much better for it. And I wanted to meet you again and talk with you; I'm dreadfully curious."

"Helen!" reproved her sister, and, turning from the girl to him, she tried to explain away her sister's boldness. "You must excuse Helen, Mr.–Mr. Orphan, because she is not a day older than she was five years ago."

"Why, Mary!" cried Helen, reproachfully, "how can you say that? Just the other day you said that I was quite grown up and dignified. I am sure that Mr.–oh, goodness, there's that name again!" she bewailed. "Why don't you get another name–that one sounds so funny!"

The Orphan laughed: "I am not responsible for the name, I had no hand in it. But, let's see what we can do," he said, counting on his fingers. "There's Smith, Brown, Jones–Jones sounds well, why not say it?" he asked gravely. "I am sure that's easier to say and remember."

"Yes, that *is* better!" she cried. "Let's see," she said, experimenting. "Mr. Jones, Mr. Jones–oh, pshaw, I like the other much better. I trust that I'll get accustomed to it in time, and I certainly should, because I hear it enough; only then it hasn't that formal Mister before it. And it is the Mister that causes all the trouble. Now, I'll try it again: I'm sure that The Orphan (I said that real nicely, didn't I?) I'm sure that The Orphan doesn't think me lacking in dignity, does he?" she asked, regarding him merrily, and with a dare in her eyes.

"Well, now really," he began, and then, seeing the look of warning in her face, he laughed softly. "Why, really, I think that you must be much more dignified than you were five years ago."

"That's such a neat evasion that I hardly know whether to be angry or not," she retorted, and then turned to Miss Ritchie, who was smiling.

"Grace," she cried, "for goodness sake, say something! You don't want me to do all the talking, do you?" and before her friend could say a word she began a new attack, her eyes sparkling at the fun she was having.

"What have you done since I told you to behave yourself?" she asked, assuming a judicial seriousness which was extremely comical.

He laughed heartily, for she was so droll, her eyes flashing so with vivacity, and so rarely beautiful that he breathed deep in unconscious effort to absorb some of the atmosphere she had created. And he was not alone in his mirth, for Helen's audacity had caused smiles to come to Miss Ritchie and Mrs. Shields, who were content to take no part in the conversation, and even Mary forgot to be serious.

"Well, I haven't had time to do much," he replied in humble apology, "although I have been occupied in a desultory way on the Cross Bar-8 for a week, and before that I was quite busily engaged in traveling for my health. You see, this climate occasionally affects me, and I am forced to go south or west for a change of air. I was just starting out on my last trip when I first met you, and I have reason to believe that my promptness in leaving you saved me much annoyance. But I have cooked quite a few meals in the interim-and I've learned how mutton should be broiled, too. I'll have to confess, however, that I have been out late nights. But then, I'll have a better record to report next time, honest I will."

Helen leveled an accusing finger at him: "You spoiled all the cooking utensils on that ranch, and you scared that poor cook so bad that he fled in terror of his life and left those poor, tired men to get all their own meals. Now, that was not right, do you see? The poor cook, he was almost frightened to death. I am almost ashamed of you; you will have to promise that you will not do anything like that again."

"I promise, cross my heart," he replied eagerly, thinking of the five dead punchers she had been kind enough to overlook. "I solemnly promise never to scare that cook again," then seeing that she was about to object, he added, "nor any other cook."

"And you'll promise not to spoil any more tins, or terrorize that poor outfit, or burn any more corrals, and everything like that?" she asked quickly, for she detected a trace of seriousness in his face and wished to drive home her advantage. If she could get a serious promise from him she would rest content, for she knew he would keep his word.

He thought for an instant and then turned a smiling face to her. Seeing veiled entreaty in her eyes, he suddenly felt a quiet gladness steal over him. Perhaps she really cared about his welfare, after all, though he dared not hope for that. He grew serious, and when he spoke she knew that he had given his word.

"I promise not to take the initiative in any warfare, nor to harass the Cross Bar-8 unless they force me to in self-defense," he replied.

She hid her elation, for she had gained the point her brother had failed to win, and did not wish to risk anything by showing her feelings. As if to reward him for yielding to her, she led the conversation from the personal grounds it had assumed and cleverly got him to talk about the country and everything pertaining to it.

He was thoroughly at ease now, and for an hour held them interested by his knowledge of the trails and the natural phenomena. He told them of cattle herding, its dangers and sports; and his description of a stampede was masterly. He recounted the struggles of the first settlers with the Indians, and even quite extensively covered the field of practical prospecting, lightening his story with naïve bits of humor and witty personal opinions which had them laughing heartily. It was not long before they forgot that they were entertaining, or, rather, being entertained by an outlaw; and as for himself, it was the most pleasant evening he had ever known. There was such an air of friendliness and they were so natural and human that he was stimulated to his best efforts; the barriers had been broken down.

"Oh, James says that you are a wonderful shot!" cried Helen, interrupting his description of a shooting match at a cowboy carnival he had once attended in a northern town. "He says that no man ever lived who could hope to beat you with either rifle or revolver, six-shooter, as he calls it. Won't you let me see you shoot, some day?"

He laughed deprecatingly: "You ask the sheriff to shoot for you," he responded. "He can beat me, I'm sure."

"No, he can't!" she cried impulsively, "because he said he couldn't. That was why he couldn't get you-" she stopped, horrified at what she had said. Then, determined to make the best of it, and knowing that excuses or apologies would make it worse, she hurriedly continued: "He says that you are so fair and square that he just will not take any advantage of you. He likes square people, and he isn't afraid to say it, either."

The Orphan sat silently for half a minute, thinking hard, while Mrs. Shields looked anxiously at him. Here was peace and happiness. The sheriff could come and go as he pleased, and every good citizen was his friend. He had a home-a pleasant contrast to the man who spent his nights under the stars, not sure of his life from day to day, hounded from point to point, having no friend, no one who cared for him; he was just an outlaw, and damned by his fellow men. Then he remembered what Helen had said before leaving him at the coach. She had faith in him, for she had told him so-and she would not lie. Her kindness and faith in him, an outcast, had been with him in his thoughts ever since, and he had felt the loneliness of his life heavily from that day. He felt a strange gnawing at his heart and he slowly raised his eyes to her, eagerly drinking in her radiant beauty, a beauty wonderful to him, for never before had he seen a beautiful woman. To him women had always been repellent-and no wonder. He scorned those usually found in the cow towns. At their best they were only ornaments, and to The Orphan's mind ornaments were trash. But now he suddenly awoke to the fact that she was more, that she was all that was worth fighting for, that she was the missing half of his consciousness. And she herself had given him heart for the fight, slight as it was, for he was like a drowning man clutching at straws. But still his cynicism swayed him and made him fear that it would be a hopeless battle. Again he thought of her brother and suddenly envied him, and the liking he had felt for the sheriff became strong and clear. Shields was a white man, just and square.

He slowly raised his eyes to Mrs. Shields and smiled, which caused her look of anxiety to clear.

"The Sheriff is the whitest man in this whole country," he said quietly, a trace of his mood being in his voice, "and only for that did I play square with him. In confidence, just to let you know that I am not as bad as people say, I will tell you that I have had him under my sights more than once, and that I will never try to harm him while he remains the man he is. I do not exaggerate when I say that I am naturally a good judge of men, and I knew what he was in less than a minute after I met him.

"At this minute he is watching for me, he and Charley Winter and the Larkin brothers. They are lying quietly out on the plain, waiting for me to show up between them and the lights of the windows. This is not guesswork, for I know it. And if it was only the sheriff, and I did show up over his sights, he would call out and give me a chance to surrender or fight, and not shoot me down like a dog; the others wouldn't. And because of my faith in his squareness, and because I above all others can fully appreciate it at its highest value, I am going to ask you to remember this, Mrs. Shields: If he ever needs a man to stand at his back, and I can be found, he has only to let me know. He is compromising himself with certain people because he has been fair to me, so please remember what I said. He is the sheriff, and he only does his duty, for which I cannot blame him. Bill Howland may be able to find me if trouble should come upon you and yours.

"Others have hunted for me as if I was a cattle-killing wolf. They have tracked me and hounded me in gangs, determined to shoot me down at the first opportunity, and unawares, if possible. They have laid traps for me, tried to ambush me, and even stooped so low as to poison the water of a remote water hole with wolf poison-strychnine. They knew that I occasionally filled my canteen from it. Those who fight me foully I repay in kind-but never with poison! It is my wits and gunplay against theirs and against their cowardice and dirty tricks. When I fight, it is not because I want to, except in the case of Indians, but because I must. But your husband is a white man, madam, a thoroughbred. He stands so far above the rest of the men in this country that I have only respect and liking for him. Can you imagine the sheriff using poison to kill a man?

"Once when I had finally found a good berth punching cows, once when I had started out aright, I was discovered. They didn't get me, though they tried to hard enough. And they call me a murderer because I declined to remain inactive while they prepared for my funeral! Ever since I was a lad of fifteen I have fought for my life at every turn, and continually. I have no friends, not a living soul cares whether I live or die. There is no one whom I can trust, and no one who trusts me. I have to be ever on the lookout, and suspicious. Every man is my enemy, and all I have is my life, worthless as it is. But pride will not let me lose it without making a fight.

"I hope the time will come when you can see me shoot, Miss Shields, that the time will come when I can turn my back to my fellow men without fearing a shot. Only once have I done that-it was with your brother, and I enjoyed it immensely. And no one will welcome that day more devoutly than the outlawed Orphan-the many times murderer-but by necessity: for I never killed a man unless he was trying to kill me, and I never will. I know what is *said*, but what I say is the truth. I can only ask you to believe me, although I realize that I am asking much."

He arose and walked over to his sombrero, taking it up and turning toward the door.

"To-night is the first time in ten years that I have been in a stranger's house unarmed, and at ease. You have made the evening so pleasant for me, so delightfully strange, and you all have been so good to talk to me and treat me white that I find it impossible to thank you as I wish I could. Words are hopelessly inadequate, and more or less empty, but you will not lose by it," he said as he opened the door. "Good night, ladies."

The door closed softly, quickly, and the women heard the cantering hoofbeats of his horse as they grew fainter and finally died out on the plain.

His departure was seemingly unnoticed. They sat in silence for a minute or more, each lost in her own thoughts, each deeply affected by his words, staring before them and picturing each as her temperament guided, the hunted man's dangers and loneliness. Mrs. Shields sat as he had left her, her chin resting in her hand, seeing only two men in a chaparral, one of whom was the man she loved. She could hear the shooting and the war cries, she could see them meet, and clasp hands at the parting; and her heart filled with kindly pity for the outcast, a pity the others could not know. Helen, her face full in the light, her arms outstretched on the table before her and her eyes moist, wondered at the savage unkindness of men, the almost unbelievable harshness of man for man. Her head dropped to her arms, and her sister Mary, also under the spell, wondered at the expression she had seen on Helen's face. Miss Ritchie, who had scarcely given more than a passing thought to the sadness in his words, was picturing his fights, drinking in the dash and courage which had so exalted him in her mind. With all his loneliness, his danger, she almost envied him his devil-may-care, humorous recklessness and good fortune, his superb self-confidence and prowess. Here was a man who fought his own battles, who stood alone against the best the world sent against him, giving blow for blow, and always triumphing.

Mrs. Shields stirred, glanced at Helen's bowed head and sighed:

"Now I understand why James likes him so. Poor boy, I believe that if he had a chance he would be a different and better man. James is right; he always is."

"I think he is just splendid!" cried Miss Ritchie with a start, emerging from her dreams of deeds of daring. "Simply splendid! Don't you Helen?" she asked impulsively.

Helen arose and walked to the door of her room, turning her face toward the wall as she passed them: "Yes, dear," she replied. "Good night."

"Oh, why are men so cruel!" she cried softly as she paused before her mirror. "Why must they fight and kill one another! It's awful!"

The door had softly opened and closed and Miss Ritchie's arms were around her neck, hugging tightly.

"It *is* awful, dear," she said. "But they can't kill *him!* They can't hurt him, so don't you care. Come on to bed-I have *so* much to talk about! Don't put your hair up to-night, Helen-let's go right to bed!"

Helen impulsively kissed her and pushed her away, her face flushed.

"You dear, silly goose, do you think I am worrying about him? Why, I had forgotten him. I'm thinking about James."

"Yes, of course you are," laughed Miss Ritchie. "I was only teasing you, dear. But it *is* too bad that nobody cares anything about him, isn't it, Helen?"

Tears trembled in Helen's eyes and she turned quickly toward the bed. "Well, it's his own fault-oh, don't talk to me, Grace! Poor James, all alone out there on that awful plain! I'm just as blue as I can be, so there!"

"Have a good, long cry, dear," suggested Miss Ritchie. "It does one *so* much good," she added as she stepped before the mirror. "But I think he is just as splendid as he can be-I wish I was a man like him!"

And while they played at pretending, the man who was uppermost in their thoughts was playing a joke on the sheriff at the Cross Bar-8 which would open that person's eyes wide in the morning.

.....

On the ranch the darkness was intense and no sounds save the natural noises of the night could be heard. The sky was overcast with clouds and occasionally a drop of rain fell. The haunting wail of a distant coyote quavered down the wind and the cattle in the corral were restless and uneasy. A mounted man suddenly topped a rise at a walk and then stopped to stare at the dim lights in the windows of the houses nearly a mile away. He laughed softly at the foolishness of the inmates trying to plot for *his* death by doing something they had not dared to do for a week. Who would be so foolish as to ride up to those lighted windows unless he was a tenderfoot?

Leaping lightly to the grass, he hobbled his horse and then took a bundle from his saddle, which he strapped on his back and then went quietly forward on foot, peering intently into the darkness before him. Soon he dropped to his hands and knees and crawled cautiously and without a sound. After covering several hundred yards in this manner he dropped to his stomach and wriggled forward, his eyes strained for dangers. A quarter of an hour elapsed, and then he heard a sneeze, muffled and indistinct, but still a sneeze. Avoiding the place from whence it came, he made a wide detour and finally stopped, chuckling silently. Untying the bundle he removed it from his back and placed it upon a pile of sand, which he heaped up for the purpose, and, printing his name in the sand at its base, retreated as he had come and without mishap. After searching for a quarter of an hour for his horse he finally found it, removed the hobbles and vaulted to the saddle. Wheeling, he rode off at a walk, soon changing to a canter, in the direction of the Limping Water. When he had gained it he chanced the danger of quicksands and rode north along the middle of the stream. If he was to be followed, the probability was that his pursuers would ride south to find where he had left the water; and they must be delayed as long as possible.

An hour later daylight swiftly developed and a peculiarly shaped pile of sand quaked and split asunder as a man arose from it. He shook himself and spent some time in digging the sand from his pockets and boots and in cleaning his rifle of it. Then he walked wearily toward the bunk-house, whose occupants were still lost in the sleep of the exhausted. It was very tedious to stay awake all night peering at the lights in the distant windows; and it was very hard to keep one's eyes from closing when lying in that position, and without any sleep for twenty-four hours. The sheriff determined to crawl into a bunk as soon as he possibly could and be prepared for his next vigil.

As he glanced over the plain he espied something which caused him to stare and rub his tired eyes, and which immediately banished sleep from his mind. Running to it, he suddenly stopped and swore: "Hell!" he shouted.

His wife's blue flower pot sat snugly on the apex of a pile of sand and from it arose a geranium, which was tied to a supporting stick by a white ribbon. He had whittled that stick himself, and he knew the flower pot. Roughly traced in the sand at its base was one word–"Orphan."

"Margaret's geranium in its blue pot, by God!" cried the sheriff, his mouth open in amazement. "Well, I'll be d—-d!" he exclaimed, running toward the corral for his horse. "If that son-of-a-gun ain't been out here under my very nose while I watched for him!"

Chapter XI
A Voice from the Gallery

Matters were fast coming to a head as far as the sheriff and the Cross Bar-8 were concerned. The loss of the five men who had won the friendship of their fellows, the reign of terror caused by the outlaw, the loss of their cook, the devastation and the extra work had only deepened the hatred which the members of the outfit held for The Orphan; and it went farther than The Orphan.

Sneed was not long in learning what took place at the stage and of the driver's loyalty to the outlaw, because Bill would talk; and the working of his mind was the same as that of his men, for it followed the line of least resistance. Questions of the nature of arraignments, and which were answerable by the outfit in only one way, constantly presented themselves in the minds of the men. They asked themselves why it was that a man of the sheriff's proven courage, marksmanship and cleverness should fail to get the man who so terrorized the ranch. Why was the sheriff so apparently reluctant to take up the chase in earnest and push it to a finish? Why was he so firm against the assistance of the ranchmen? Why did he keep to his determination to allow no lynch law when the evil was so great and the danger so pressing? And he was prepared to go to great lengths to see that his orders were not disobeyed, as proven by the scene at the corral. Why could he not have overlooked one lynching party when property was being destroyed and lives in danger? And why had the outrages suddenly ceased when Shields took charge of the defense of the ranch?—there had been no molestation, not a shot had been fired, not a cow killed. And how was it that a flower pot, which Shields had admitted as belonging to his wife, had been placed at a point hardly two hundred yards in front of the peace officer as he lay on guard? It was true that it was out of line of him and the lights, but that could be explained by events. From whom did The Orphan learn of the trap set for him, and all of its details, even to the placing of the men, enabling him to avoid the eager deputies and choose the position occupied by the sheriff when he had so recklessly flaunted his contempt from a pile of sand?

The cowboys were naturally enough warped and prejudiced because of their blind rage and hatred, and the questions which ran so riotously through their minds found their answers waiting for them; in fact, the answers induced the questions, and each recurrence gave them added weight until they ceased to be questions and became, in reality, statements of facts. Bill had talked too much when he had told in careful detail of the attentions shown The Orphan by the sheriff's sister; and to minds eager for confirmation of their suspicions this was the crowning proof of the double dealing of the sheriff. And to make matters worse, Tex Williard, who was as unscrupulous a man as ever wore the garb of honesty, had tried to force his attentions on Helen when she rode for exercise. His ideas of women had been developed among those who frequented frontier bar-rooms, and he was enraged at his rebuff, which had been sharp and final. She actually preferred a murdering outlaw to a hardworking cowboy! His profane oratory as to the collusion, or at least passive sympathy between the sheriff and the outlaw found eager ears and receptive minds awaiting the torch of initiative, and it was not long before low-voiced consultations began to plan a drastic course of action. Credit must be given to Sneed, because he knew only of the natural discontent and nothing of what was in the wind. Had he known what was brewing he would have stamped it out with no uncertain force, for he was wise enough to realize the folly of increasing the antagonism which already was held by Ford's Station for his ranch.

At first the conspirators had hopes of undermining Shields among the citizens of the town, not knowing the feeling there as well as their foreman knew it, but they were wise enough to go about it cautiously; and the returns justified their caution, for they found the inhabitants of Ford's Station unassailably loyal to the peace officer. To accuse him, either directly or by suggestion, of double dealing would be to array the two score inhabitants of the town on his side in hot and belligerent partisanship, and this they wished to avoid by all means, for they had no stomach for such a war as might easily follow. They then hit upon what appeared to them to be an excellent plan, inasmuch as it was indirect and would give the results desired; and the medium was to be the driver.

The talkative one had shown more than passing friendliness for The Orphan, and they had his boasting words for it and he could not deny it, for Bill was very proud of the part he had played on that memorable day, and he took delight in recounting the conversation he had held with the outfit at the coach-and he had a way of adding to the tartness of his repartee in its repetition. Tex Williard reasoned from experience that it would not appear at all strange and unusual for Bill to be called to account for his friendliness and assistance to the outlaw and for his contemptuous words concerning the cowboys if it was done by some member or members of the ranch as a personal affair and without the appearance of being sanctioned by the foreman. And through the driver he hoped to strike at Shields, for the sheriff would not remain passive in such an event; and once he was drawn into a brawl, hot tempers or accident would be the plea if he should be killed. The apologies and remorse of the sorrowful participants could be profound. And thus was cold-blooded murder planned by the very men who reviled The Orphan because they claimed he was a murderer, and who cried aloud for his death on that charge.

Tex was the ringleader and in his own way he was not without cunning, and neither was he lacking in daring. He selected his assistants for the game with cool, calculating judgment. The three he finally decided upon were reckless and not lacking in intelligence and physical courage for such work. After having made his selection he sounded them carefully and finally made his plans known, going into minute rehearsal of every phase and detail of the game with thoughtful care and studied sequence. When he believed them to be well drilled he fixed upon the time and place and caused word to get to Bill that he might expect trouble for his assistance to The Orphan, and for having had a hand in sending the five cowboys to their deaths. The news immediately reached the ears of the sheriff, who determined to see that Bill received no injury at the hands of the Cross Bar-8. He quietly made up his mind to be near the stage route on the days when Bill drove through the defile of the Backbone, and to be within call if he should be needed. If he should think it necessary, he would even go so far as to become a regular passenger in the coach until the trouble died down. To the masterly driving and cool-headed courage of Bill no less than to the daring and accuracy of The Orphan was the sheriff indebted for the lives of his sisters; and the protection of Bill clove close to the line of duty, and not one whit less to the line of law and order.

Bill laughed and boasted and made a joke of the thought of any danger from the malcontents of the Cross Bar-8, and flatly refused to allow the sheriff to ride with him. He talked volubly until the agent profanely sent him on his journey, and he tore through the streets of the town in the same old way. He forded the Limping Water in safety and crossed the ten mile stretch of open plain without a sign of trouble. As he left the water of the stream the sheriff started after him from town, intending to be not far behind him when he entered the rough country.

When Bill plunged into the defile through the Backbone he began to grow a little apprehensive, and he intently watched each stretch of the road as each successive turn unfolded it to his sight. His foot was on the brakes and he was braced to stop the rush of his team at the first glimpse of an obstruction, or to tear past the danger if he could. One coyote yell and one snap of the whip would send the team wild, for they remembered well.

All was nice until he neared the place where The Orphan had held him up for a smoke, and it was there the trouble occurred. As he swung around the sharp turn he saw four cowboys bunched squarely in the center of the trail and at such a distance from him that to attempt to dash past them would be to lay himself open to several shots. They had him covered, and as he grasped the situation Tex Williard rode forward and held up his hand.

"Stop!" Tex shouted. "Get down!"

"What in thunder do you want?" Bill asked, setting the brakes and stopping his team, wonder showing on his face.

"Yu!" came the laconic reply. "Get down!"

"What's eating you?" Bill asked in no uncertain inflection. Had Tex been less imperative and kept the insulting tone out of his words Bill might have had time to become afraid, but the sting made him leap over fear to anger; and genuine anger takes small heed of fear.

Tex motioned to one of his men, who instantly leaped to the ground and ran to the turn, where he knelt behind a rock, his rifle covering the back trail. Then Tex returned to the driver.

"Curiosity is eating me, yu half-breed!" he cried. "Get down! d——n yu, get down!! Don't wait all day, neither, do yu hear? What th' h–l do yu think I'm a-talkin' for!"

"Well, I'll be blamed!" ejaculated Bill, wrapping the reins about the back of his seat. "Anybody would think you was the boss of the earth to hear you! You ain't no road agent, you're only a fool amature with more gall than brains! But I'll tell you right here and now that if you *are* playing road agent, I wouldn't be in your fool boots for a cool million. And if you are joking you are showing d——d bad taste, and don't you forget it. You're holding up a sack of U. S. mail, and if you don't know what that means——"

"Shut yore face! Yu talk when I ask yu to!" shouted Tex as the driver dropped to the ground. "But since yore so unholy strong on th' palaver, suppose yu just explains why yu are so all-fired friendly to Th' Orphant? Suppose yu lisp why yu take such a peculiar interest in his health and happiness. Come now, out with it-this ain't no Quaker meeting."

"Warble, birdie, warble!" jeered one of the cowboys. "Sing, yu —— ——!"

"We're shore waitin', darlin'," jeered another. "Tune up an' get started, Windy."

"Well, since you talks like that," cried Bill, stung to reckless fury at the cutting contempt of the words, "you can go to h–l and find out from your fool friends!" he shouted, beside himself with rage. "Who are you to stick me up and ask questions? It's none of your infernal business who I like, you hog-nosed tanks! Why didn't you bring some decent men with you, you flat-faced skunks? Why didn't you bring Sneed! White men would a told you just what you are if you asked them to help you in your dirty work, wouldn't they? Even a tin-horn gambler, a crooked cheat, would give me more show for my money than you have, you bowlegged coyotes! Ain't you man enough to turn the trick alone, Williard? Can't you play a lone hand in ambush, you bob-tailed flush of a bad man! You're only a lake-mouthed, red-headed wart of a two-by-four puncher, that's what——"

Tex had been stunned by surprise at such an outburst from a man whom he had always regarded as woefully lacking in courage. Then his face flamed with an insane rage at the taunting insults hurled venomously at him and he sprang to action as though he had been struck. It would have been bad enough to hear such words from an equal, but from Bill!

"Yu cur!" he yelled as he leaped forward into the tearing sting of the driver's whip, which had been hanging from the wrist.

"You're the fourth dog I cut to-day," Bill said, jerking it back for another try.

Tex shivered with pain as the lash cut through his ear, as it would have cut through paper, and screamed his words as he avoided the second blow. "I'll show yu if I am man enough! I'll kill yu for that, d——n yu!"

As Tex threw his arms wide open to clinch, Bill leaped aside and drove his heavy fist into the cowman's face as he passed, knocking him sidewise against the wall of the defile; and then struggled like a madman in the toils of two ropes. He was a Berserker now, a maniac without a hope of life, and he screamed with rage as he tore frantically at the rough hair ropes, wishing only to destroy, to kill with his bare hands. The blow had not been well placed, being too high for the vital point, but it had smashed the puncher's nose flat to his face and one eye was fast losing its resemblance to the other. Tex staggered to his feet and returned to the attack, striking savagely at the face of the bound man. Bill avoided the blow by jerking his head aside and snarled like a beast as he drove the heel of his heavy boot into his enemy's stomach. Then everything grew black before his eyes and a roaring sound filled his ears. The rope slackened and the men who had thrown him head-first on a rock leaped from their horses and ran to him.

When his senses returned he found himself bound hand and foot and under a spur of rock which projected from the bank of the cut. His face was cut and bruised and his scalp laid open, but through the blood which dripped from his eyebrows he vaguely saw Tex, bent double and rocking back and forth on the ground, intoned moans coming from him with a sound like that made by a rasp on the edge of a box.

As Bill's brain cleared he became conscious of excruciating pains in his head, as if hammers were crashing against his skull. Glancing upward he saw that a rope ran from his neck to the rock, over it and then to the pommel of a saddle, and his face twitched as its meaning sifted through his mind. Then he thought of the time The Orphan had held him up in the defile-how unlike these men the outlaw was! If he would only come now-what joy there would be in the flashing of his gun; what ecstasy in the confusion, panic, rout that he would cause. He was dazed and the throbbing, heavy, monotonous pain dulled him still more. He seemed to be apart from his surroundings, to be an onlooker and not an actor in the game. He wondered if that whip was his: yes, it must be . . . certainly it was. He ought to know his own whip . . . of course it was his. He regarded Tex curiously . . . there had been Indians, or was it some other time? What was Tex doing there on the ground? He struggled to think clearly, and then he knew. But the deadening pain was merciful to him, it made him apathetic. Was he going to die? Perhaps, but what of it? He didn't care, for then that pain wouldn't beat through him. Tex looked funny. . . . He closed his eyes wearily and seemed to be far away. He *was* far away, and, oh, so tired!

Tex finally managed to gain his feet and straighten up and revealed his face, bloody and swollen and black from the blow. His words came with a hesitation which suggested pain, and they were mumbled between split and swollen lips.

"Now, d—-n yu!" he cried, brokenly, staggering to the helpless man before him. "Now mebby yu'll talk! Why did yu help Th' Orphant? If yu lie yu'll swing!"

Bill swayed and his eyes opened, and after an interval he slowly and wearily made reply, for his senses had returned again.

"He saved my life," he said, "and I'll help-anybody for that."

"Oh, he did, did he?" jeered Tex. "An' why? That ain't his way, helpin' strangers at his own risk. Why?"

"There was women-in the coach."

"Oh, there was, hey?" ironically remarked Tex. "Mebby he wanted 'em all to himself, eh?"

"He's a white man, not a cur."

"He's a cub of th' devil, that's what he is!" Tex cried. "He ain't no orphant, not by a d—-d sight-th' devil's his father, an' all hell is his mother. Now, I want an answer to this one, and I want it quick: no lie goes. Why don't th' sheriff get busy an' camp on his trail? What interest has th' sheriff an' Th' Orphant in each other? Come on, out with it!"

"I don't know," replied Bill, wishing that the sheriff was at hand to make an appropriate answer. "Ask him, why don't you?" he asked, stretching his neck to ease the hairy, bristling clutch of the lariat.

"Oh, yu don't, an' yore still cheeky, eh?" cried the inquisitor. "An' yu want yore d—-d neck stretched, do yu?"

He motioned to the man on the horse at the end of the rope and Bill straightened up and daylight showed under his heels. As he struggled there was an interruption from the man who covered the back trail: "'Nds up!" he cried. "Don't move!"

Tex signalled for Bill to be let down and ran backward to the opposite side of the defile until he could see around the turn; and he discovered the sheriff, who sat quietly under the gun of the cowboy.

"Stop! Don't yu even wiggle!" cried the guard. "I'll blow yore head off at the first move!" he added in warning; and for once in his eventful life Shields knew that he was absolutely helpless, for the time, at least. His hands were clasped over his sombrero, for it would be tiresome to hold them out, and he felt that he might have need of fresh, quick muscles before long.

"All right, all right, bub," he responded in perfect good nature, apparently. "Don't get nervous and let that gun go off, for it's shore your turn now," he added, smiling his war smile. "Any particular thing you want, or are you just practicing a short cut to eternity?"

"I want yu to stay just like yu are!" snapped the man with the drop. "And yu keep yore mouth shut, too!"

"Since it's your last wish, why, it goes," replied the sheriff, ignoring the command for silence. "Got any message for your folks? Any keep-sakes you'd like to have sent back East? Give me the address of your folks and I'll send them your last words, too."

"That's enough, Sheriff," said Tex, moving cautiously forward behind his leveled Colt. "I'll do all th' talkin' that's necessary; yu just listen for a while."

"Well, well," replied the sheriff, grinning and simulating surprise. "If here ain't Tex Williard, too! What's your pet psalm, sonny? Good God, what a face!"

"What's that got to do with this?" asked Tex, intently watching for war.

"Oh, nothing, nothing at all," replied the sheriff. "But, Lord, that cayuse of yours can shore kick! Was you tickling it? They do go off like that some times. Any of your nose coming out the back of your head yet? But to reply to your touching inquiry, I'll say that the psalm might work in handy after while, that's all. If you'll only tell me, I'll see that it is sung over your grave. But, honest, how did you get that face?"

"That'll just about do for yu!" cried the cowboy, angrily. "An' sit still, yu!" he added.

"Say, bub," confidentially said Shields, "my stomach itches like blazes. Can't I scratch it, just once?"

"No! Think I'm a fool!" yelled Tex, his finger tightening on the trigger. "Yu sit still, d——n yu!"

"Well, I only wanted to see just how much of a fool you really are," grinned the sheriff exasperatingly. "Judging from your present position I must say that I thought you didn't have any sense at all, but now I reckon you've got a few brains after all. But suppose you scratch it for me, hey? Just rub it easy like with your left paw."

Tex swore luridly, too tense to realize what a fool the sheriff was making of him. He could think of only one thing at a time, and he was thinking very hard about the sheriff's hands.

"Tut, tut, don't take it so hard," jeered the sheriff, smiling pleasantly. "Now that I know that you are some rational, suppose you tell me the joke? What's the secret? Who skinned his shin? What in thunder is all this artillery saluting me for?"

"Since yu want to know, I'll tell yu, all right," replied Tex. "Why are yu an' Th' Orphant so d——d thick? Don't be all day about it?"

"You d——d excuse!" responded the sheriff. "You mere accident! As the poet said, it's none of your business! Catch that?"

"Yes, I caught it," retorted Tex. "I reckon we needs a new sheriff, an' d——d soon, too," he added venomously.

"Well, people don't always get what they need," replied Shields easily. "If they did, you would get yours right now, and good and hard, too," he explained, making ready to put up the hardest fight of his life. Three men had him covered, and he knew they would all shoot if he made a move, for they had placed themselves in a desperate situation and could not back out now. He knew that never before had he been in so tight a hole, but he trusted to luck and his own quickness to crawl out with a whole skin. If he was killed, he would have company across the Great Divide; of that he was certain.

"I reckon I'll take yore guns for a while, just to be doin' somethin'," Tex said as he advanced a step. "Mebby that itch will go away then."

"I reckon you'll be a d——n sight wiser if you don't force matters, for they are purty well forced now," Shields replied. "No man gets my guns' butts first without getting all mussed up inside. You'll certainly be doing something if you try it."

"Well, then," compromised Tex, "answer my question!"

"And no man gets an answer to a question like that in words," the sheriff continued, as if there had been no interruption. "But I'll give you and your white-faced bums a chance for your lives-and I don't wonder The Orphan shot up Jimmy, neither. Put up your wobbling guns and get out of this country as fast as God will let you! If you ever come back I'll fill you plumb full of lead! It's your move, Lovely Face, and the quicker you do it the better it'll be for your health."

"Oh, I don't know about that," replied Tex with a leer and swagger. "To a man up a tree it looks like yu are up agin a buzz saw this time."

"To a man on the ground it looks like your tin buzz saw has hit the hardest knot it ever struck, and you'll feel the jar purty soon, too," Shields countered, his hazel eyes beginning to grow red. "You put up that gun and scoot before I blow your d——-d head off!"

"I'll give yu 'til I counts three to answer my question," Tex said, ignoring the advice. "One!"

"The less you count the longer you'll live," said Shields, gripping his horse with his knees in readiness to jump it sideways.

"Two!"

"Afternoon, gents," said a pleasant voice up above them, and all jumped and looked up. As they did so Shields jerked his guns loose and laughed softly: "That itch has plumb gone away," he said. "It's a new deal," he exulted, his face wreathed in grins.

Chapter XII
A New Deal All Around

On the edge of the bank, thirty feet above them, a man squatted on his heels, his forearms resting easily on his knees. In each hand was a long-barreled Colt, held in a manner oppressively businesslike. One of the guns was leveled at the stomach of the man who guarded Bill, and who still held the rope; the other covered the man who had baited the sheriff. Shields took care of the remaining two. One of the newcomer's eyes was half closed, squinting to keep out the smoke which curled up from the cigarette which protruded jauntily from a corner of his mouth. If anything was needed to strengthen the air of pertness of the man above it was supplied by his sombrero, which sat rakishly over one ear. A quizzical grin flickered across his face and the cigarette bobbed recklessly when he laughed.

"Was you counting?" he asked of Tex in anxious inquiry. "And for God's sake, who stepped on your face?"

Tex made no reply, for his astonishment at the interruption had given way to the iron hand of fear which gripped him almost to suffocation. In the space of one breath he had been hurled from the mastery to defeat; from a good fighting chance, with all the odds on his side, to what he believed to be certain death, for to move was to die. Had it been anyone but The Orphan who had turned the scale he would have hazarded a shot and trusted to luck, for his gun was in his hand; but The Orphan's gunplay was as swift as light and never missed at that distance, and The Orphan's reputation was a host in itself. He had threatened the sheriff with death, he had used Bill worse than he would have used a dog, and now his cup of bitterness was full to overflowing. Above him a pair of cruel gray eyes looked over a sight into his very soul and a malevolent grin played about the thin, straight lips of the man who had killed Jimmy, who had led his five friends to an awful death, and who had instilled terror night after night into the hearts of seven good men. His mind leaped back to a day ten years before, and what he saw caused his face to blanch. Ten years of immunity, but at last he was to pay for his crime. Before him stood the son of the man he had been foremost in hanging, before him stood the man he had cruelly wronged. His nerve left him and he stood a broken, trembling coward, a living lie to the occupation he had made his own, an insult to his dress and his companions. Had he by some miracle been given the drop he could not have pulled the trigger. He now had no hope for mercy where he had denied it. He had played a good hand, but he had made no allowance for the joker, and no blame to him.

No sooner had The Orphan spoken and the sheriff discovered that he had things safely in his hands, than Shields had leaped to the ground and quickly disarmed his opponents, tossing the captured weapons to the top of the bank near the outlaw. Then he folded his arms and waited, laughing silently all the while.

As soon as Shields had disposed of the last gun, The Orphan gave his whole attention to the man who was guarding Bill, and that person changed the course of his hand just in time.

"No, I wouldn't try to use that gun, neither, if I was you," The Orphan said, still smiling. "You can just toss it up on the bank over your head-that's right. Now drop that rope-I'm surprised that you didn't do it before. When you get Bill all untangled from those fixings come right around here, where I can see how nice you all look in a bunch. It'll take you one whole minute to get out of sight around that turn, so I wouldn't try any running."

The Orphan was ignorant of the condition of Bill's face, since he had only seen the driver's back as he had crawled to the edge of the bank, and now the bend in the opposite wall just hid Bill from his sight. So he gave no great attention to the driver, but turned to the sheriff and laughed.

"I knew that you would pull through, Sheriff," he said, "but I couldn't help having a surprise party; I'm a whole lot fond of surprise parties, you know. And it's shore been a howling success, all right."

"You have a very pleasant way of making yourself useful," Shields replied. "From the holes you've pulled me out of within the past six weeks you must have a poor impression of me. But seeing that you have reason to laugh at me, I accept your apology and bid you welcome. It's all yours." Then he glanced quickly up the trail and his face went red with anger. "Hell!" he cried in amazement.

The Orphan looked in the direction indicated and he leaped to his feet in sudden anger at what he saw. A man, followed by a cowboy, staggered and stumbled drunkenly along the trail toward them, his face a mass of cuts and bruises and blood. His hair was matted with blood and dirt, and a red ring showed around his neck. His hands opened and shut convulsively and he made straight as he could for Tex, who shrank back involuntarily.

"My God! It's Bill!" cried The Orphan, hardly able to believe his eyes.

"You're the cur *I* want!" Bill muttered brokenly to Tex, straightening up and becoming rapidly steadier under the stimulus of his rage. "You're the —- *I* want, d—-n you!" he repeated as he slowly advanced. "It's my turn now, you cur! Lynch me, would you? Lynch me, eh? Tried to hit me when I was tied, eh? Sicked your dogs on me, eh? Keep still, d—-n you-you can't get away!" he cried as Tex moved backward.

"Stand to it like a man, or I'll blow your head off!" cried The Orphan from his perch. "Go on, Bill!"

"You said you wanted me, didn't you? Do you still want me?" he asked, not hearing The Orphan's words. "Are you still curious?" he asked, backing Tex into a corner.

"Hash him up, Bill!" cried the man above, and then, "Hey, wait a minute–I want to see this," he added as he slid down the bank. "Go ahead with the slaughter-push his head off!"

Bill's one hundred and eighty pounds of muscle and rage suddenly hurled itself forward behind a huge fist and Tex hit the bank and careened into the dust of the trail, unconscious before he had moved.

"I told you you wasn't man enough to play a lone hand!" yelled the driver as he leaped after his victim. But he was stopped by the sheriff, who sprang forward and deflected him from his course.

"That's enough-no killing!" Shields cried, regaining his balance and swiftly interposing himself between the driver and Tex.

Bill didn't hear him, for he had just caught sight of the man who had told him to warble, and he lost no time in getting to him. A few quick blows and the enraged driver left his second victim face down in the dirt and passed on to the man who had held the rope.

"Hurrah for Bill!" yelled The Orphan, hopping first on one foot and then on the other in his joy. "Set 'em up in the other alley! I didn't know you had it in you, Bill! Good boy!" he shouted as Bill clinched with the third cowboy. "Oh, that was a beauty! Right on the nose-oh, what a whopper to get on the jaw! Whoop her up! Fine, fine!" he laughed as Bill dropped his man. "'And subsequent proceedings interested *him* no more!' Next!" he cried as Bill wheeled on the last of the group. "Eat him up, Bill!-that's the way! Just above the belt for his-Good! All down!" he yelled madly as Bill, drawing his arm back from the stomach of the falling puncher, sent a swift uppercut hissing to the jaw. "You lifted him five feet, Bill," The Orphan exulted as Bill wheeled for more worlds to conquer.

"Where's the rest of the gang?" savagely yelled the driver, looking twice at The Orphan before he was sure of his identity. "Where's the rest of 'em?" he shouted again, running around the bend in hot search. "Come out and fight, you cowards!" they heard him cry, and straightway the outlaw and the guardian of the law clung to each other for support as they cried with joy.

As Bill hurried back to the field of carnage one of his victims was mechanically striving to gain his hands and knees, to go down in a quivering heap by a blow from the insane victor. As Bill drew back his foot to finish his work, Shields broke from his companion and leaped forward just in time to hurl Bill back several steps. "D——n you!" he cried, standing over the prostrate figure, "If you hit another man while he's down I'll trim you right! Cool down and get some sense before I punch it into you!"

The Orphan, leaning limply against the bank of the defile, was making foolish motions with his hands, which still held the Colts, and was babbling idiotically, tears of laughter streaming down his face and dripping from his chin. His eyes were closed and he was bent over, rocking to and fro against the wall.

"Oh, Lord!" he sobbed senselessly. "Oh, Lord, oh, Lord! Let me die in peace! Take him away, take him away! Let me die in peace!"

"I'm a fine sight to hit Sagetown, ain't I?" yelled Bill, keeping keen watch on the four prostrate punchers. "They'll think I was licked! They'll point to my face and head and swear that some papoose kicked the stuffing outen me! That's what they'll do! But I'll show them, all right! I'll just take my game with me and prove that I am the best man, that's what I'll do! I'll pile 'em in the coach and lug 'em with me!" grabbing, as he finished, one of the men by the foot and dragging him toward the stage. It took The Orphan and Shields several strenuous minutes to dissuade him from his purpose. Shields placed his fingers on the bones of Bill's hand in a peculiar grip, and the driver loosened his hold without loss of time.

"You go back to town and get fixed up," ordered the sheriff. "I'll take your team out of this and turn them around, and then come back for you. Charley can make the trip if you can't. I would do it myself, only I've got to tell Sneed that he's shy four more men."

"I'll turn 'em around myself–I ain't hurt," asserted Bill with decision. "And when I get patched up I'll make the trip, Pop Westley or no Pop Westley. And I'll lick the whole blamed town, too, if they get fresh about my face! I'm a fighter from Fightersville, I am! I'm a man-eating bad-man, I am! I can lick anything that ever walked on hind legs, I can!" and he glared as if anxious to prove his words.

After the cowboys regained consciousness and got so they could stand, the sheriff lined them up with their backs to the wall and gave them the guns which The Orphan had obtained for him. The outlaw held them covered while the sheriff told them what they were, and he wound up his lecture with instructions and a warning.

"Get out of this country and don't never come back!" he told them. "I don't care where you go, so long as you go right now. If you even show your faces in these parts again I'll shoot first and talk after."

"Same here!" endorsed The Orphan, frowning down his desire to laugh at the wrecks in front of him.

"I'll kill you next time!" shouted Bill, prancing uneasily.

"The cayuses are yours," continued the sheriff. "I'll settle with Sneed if he has the gall to ask about them. Now git!"

Tex stared first at the sheriff and then at The Orphan and Bill as if doubting his ears. He was ten years nearer the grave than he had been before The Orphan had interrupted his counting. In less than half an hour he had gone through hell, and now he suddenly burst into tears from the reaction and staggered to his horse, which he finally managed to mount, a nervous wreck. "Oh, God!" he moaned, "Oh, God!"

The others stared at him in amazement until he had turned the bend, and then his companions slowly followed him and were lost to sight.

"D——n near dead from fright!" ejaculated the sheriff. "I never saw anybody go to pieces so bad!"

"He shore lost his nerve all right, all right," responded The Orphan. Then he turned to where Bill stood looking after them: "Bill, you're all right-you can fight like h–l!"

Bill slowly turned and grinned through the blood: "Oh, that wasn't nothing-you should oughter see me when I get real mad!"

. . . . .

Two men rode side by side after a lurching coach on their way toward the Limping Water, both buried in thought at what the driver had told them. As they emerged from the defile and left the Backbone behind, the elder looked keenly, almost affectionately, at his companion and placed a kindly hand on the shoulder of the man who had turned the balance, breaking the long silence.

"Son, why don't you get a job punching cows, or something, and quit your d——d foolishness?" he bluntly asked.

The younger man thought for a space, and a woman's words directed his reply:

"I've thought of that, and I'd like to do it," he said earnestly. "But, pshaw, who will give me a try in this country?" he asked bitterly. Then he added softly: "And I won't leave these parts, not now."

"You won't have to leave the country," replied the sheriff. "Why not try Blake, of the Star C?" he asked. "Blake is a shore square man, and he's a good friend of mine, too."

"Yes, I reckon he is square," replied The Orphan. "But he won't take no stock in me, not a bit."

"Tell him that you're a friend of mine, and that I sent you to punch for him, and see," responded Shields, examining his cinch.

"Do you mean that, Sheriff?" the other cried in surprise.

"Hell, yes!" answered Shields gruffly. "I'll give you a note to him, and if you watch your business you'll be his right-hand man in a month. I ain't making any mistake."

"By God, I'll do it!" cried the outlaw. "You're all right, Sheriff!"

"Well, I don't know about that," replied Shields, grinning broadly. "Mebby I just can't see the use of us shooting each other up, and that is what it will come to if things go on as they are, you know. I'd a blamed sight rather have you behaving yourself with Blake than bothering me with your fool nonsense and raising the devil all the time. Why, it's got so that every place I go I sort of looks for flower pots!"

The Orphan laughed: "I shore had a fine time that night!"

When half way to the Limping Water the sheriff said good-by to Bill and wheeled, facing in the direction of the Cross Bar-8.

"Orphan, you wait for me at the ford," he said. "I'm going up to break the news to Sneed, and I'll get paper and pencil while I'm there, and write a note to Blake. I'll get back as quick as I can-so long."

"So long, and good luck," replied The Orphan, heartily shaking hands with his new friend.

Shields loped away and arrived at the ranch as Sneed was carrying water to the cook shack.

"Hullo, Sneed! Playing cook?" he said, pulling in to a stop.

"I'll play *on* the cook if I ever get my hands on him," replied Sneed, setting the pail down. "Well, what's new? Seen Tex and the other three? I'll play on *them*, too, when they gets home! Off playing hookey from work when we all of us aches from double shifts-oh, just wait till I sees 'em sneaking in to bed! Just wait!"

"You ought to give 'em all a good thrashing, they need it," replied the sheriff, and then he asked: "Got any paper, and a pencil?" He wanted his needs supplied before he broke the news, for then he might not get them.

"Shore as you live I have," answered the foreman, picking up the pail and starting toward the bunk-house. "Come in and wet the dust-it's hot out here."

420

"Let me have the paper first—I want to scrawl a note before I forget about it," the sheriff responded as he seated himself on a bunk and looked critically about him at the bullet-riddled walls and pictures.

Sneed handed him an ink bottle and placed a piece of wrapping paper and a corroded pen on the table.

"That paper ain't for love letters, the ink is mud, and the pen's a brush, but I reckon you can make tracks, all right," the host remarked as he pushed a bench up to the table for his guest. "And if them punchers don't make tracks for home purty lively, I'll salt their hides and peg 'em on the wall to cure," he grumbled, rummaging for a bottle and cup. When he placed the tin cup on the table he grinned foolishly, for it was plugged with a cork. "D——-d outlaw!" he grunted.

"There," remarked the sheriff, fanning the note in the air. "That's done, if it'll ever dry."

"Blow on it," suggested Sneed, and then smiled.

"Here, wait a minute," he said, stepping to the door, where he scooped up a handful of sand. "Throw this on it–it can't get no muddier, anyhow."

Shields carefully folded the missive and tucked it in his hip pocket, and then he looked up at the foreman.

"Sneed," he slowly began, "your punchers ain't never coming back."

"What!" yelled the foreman, leaping to his feet, and having visions of his men being cut up by outlaws and Indians.

"Nope," replied Shields with an air of finality. "Bill Howland gave them the most awful beating up that I ever saw men get, the whole four of them, too! When he got through with them I took a hand and ordered them to get out of the country, and I told them that if they ever came back I'd shoot on sight, and I will."

Sneed's rage was pathetic, and was not induced by the beating his men had received, nor by the sheriff's orders, but because it left him only three men to work a ranch which needed twelve. As he listened to the sheriff's story he paced back and forth in the small room and swore luridly, kicking at everything in sight, except the sheriff. Then he cooled down, spread his feet far apart and stared at Shields.

"Why didn't you kill 'em, the d——-d fools?" he cried. "That's what they deserved!" Then he paused. "But what am I going to do?" he asked. "Where'll I get men, and what'll I do 'til I do get 'em?"

"I'll send Charley and half a dozen of the boys out from town to stay with you 'til you get some others," replied the sheriff, walking toward the door. "And you might tell the three that are left that I'll kill the next man who tries that kind of work in this country. I'm getting good and tired of it. So long."

Sneed didn't hear him, but sat with his head in his hands for several minutes after the sheriff had gone, swearing fluently.

"Orphan h–l!" he yelled as he picked up the water pail and stamped to the cook shack.

Chapter XIII
The Star C Gives Welcome

The Limping Water, within a mile after it passed Ford's Station, turned abruptly and flowed almost due west for thirty miles, where it again proceeded southward. At the second bend stood the ranch houses and corrals of the Star C, in a country rich in grass and water. Its cows numbered far into the thousands and its horses were the best for miles around, while the whole ranch had an air of opulence and plenty. Its ranch house was a curiosity, for even now there were lace curtains in some of the windows, badly torn and soiled, but still lace curtains; and on the floors of several rooms were thick carpets, now covered with dust and riding paraphernalia. Oddly shaped and badly scratched chairs were piled high with accumulated trash, and the few gilt-framed paintings which graced the walls were hanging awry and were torn and scratched.

At one time an Eastern woman had tried to live there, but that was when the owner of the ranch and his wife had been enthusiasts. New York regained and kept its own, and they now would rather receive quarterly reports by mail than daily reports in person. The foreman and his wolf hounds reigned supreme, not at all bothered by the stiff furniture and lace curtains, because he would rather be comfortable than stylish, and so lived in two rooms which he had fitted up to his ideas. Carpets and two-inch spurs cause profanity and ravelings, and as for pictures, they have a most annoying way of tilting when one hangs a six-shooter on one corner of the frame, and they are so inviting that one is constantly forgetting. So the unstable pictures, the dress-parade chairs, bothersome curtains and clutching carpets were left under the dust.

The Star C, being in a part of the country little traversed and crossed by no trails, was removed from the zone of The Orphan's activities and had no cause for animosity, save that induced by his reputation. Several of its punchers had seen him, and all were well versed in his exploits, for frequently Ford's Station shared its hospitality with one or more of them; and in Ford's Station at that time The Orphan was the chief topic of conversation and the bone of contention. But the foreman of the Star C would not know him if he should see him, unless by intuition.

Blake was a man much after the pattern of Shields in his ideas, and the two were warm friends and had roughed it together when Ford's Station had only been an adobe hut. Their affection for each other was of the stern, silent kind, which seldom betrayed itself directly in words, and they could ride together for hours in an understanding silence and never weary of the companionship; and when need was, deeds spoke for them. The Cross Bar-8 would have had more than Ford's Station to fight if it had declared war on the sheriff, which the Cross Bar-8 knew. The three cleverest manipulators of weapons in that section, in the order of their merit, were The Orphan, Shields and Blake, which also the Cross Bar-8 knew.

The foreman of the Star C rode at a walk toward a distant point of his dominions and cogitated as to whether he could ride over to Ford's Station that night to see the sheriff. It was a matter of sixty miles for the round trip, but it might have been sixty blocks, so far as the distance troubled him. He had just decided to make the trip and to spend a pleasant hour with his friend, and drink some of the delicious coffee which Mrs. Shields always made for him and eat one of her prize pies, or some of her light ginger bread, when he descried a horseman coming toward him at a lope.

The newcomer was a stranger to Blake and appeared to be a young man, which was of no consequence. But the thing which attracted more than a casual glance from the foreman was a certain jaunty, reckless air about the man which spoke well for the condition of his nerves and liver.

The stranger approached to within a rod of Blake before he spoke, and then he slowed down and nodded, but with wide-eyed alertness.

"Howdy," he said. "Are you the foreman of the Star C?"

"Howdy. I am," replied the foreman.

"Then I reckon this is yours," said the stranger, holding out a bit of straw-colored paper.

The foreman took it and slowly read it. When he had finished reading he turned it over to see if there was anything on the back, and then stuck it in his pocket and looked up casually.

"Are you The Orphan?" he asked, with no more interest than he would have displayed if he had asked about the weather.

"Yes," replied The Orphan, nonchalantly rolling another cigarette.

"How is the sheriff?" Blake asked.

"Shore well enough, but a little mad about the Cross Bar-8," answered the other as he inhaled deeply and with much satisfaction. "He said there was some good coffee waiting for you to-night if you wanted it," he added.

"Did he?" asked Blake, grinning his delight.

"Yes, and some-apricot pie," added The Orphan wistfully.

Blake laughed: "Well, I reckon I've got some business over in town to-night, so you keep on going 'til you get to the bunk house. Tell Lee Lung to rustle the grub lively—I'll be there right after you. Apricot pie!" he chuckled as he pushed on at a lope.

Jim Carter was washing for supper, being urged to show more speed by Bud Taylor, when the latter looked up and saw The Orphan dismount. His mouth opened a trifle, but he continued his urging without a break. He had seen The Orphan at Ace High the year before, when the outlaw had ridden in for a supply of cartridges, and he instantly recalled the face. But Bud was not only easy-going, but also very hungry at the time, and he didn't care if the devil himself called as long as the devil respected the etiquette of the range. Besides, if there was to be trouble it would rest more comfortably on a full stomach.

"Give me a quit-claim to that pan, yu coyote," he said pleasantly to Jim. "Yu ain't taking no bath!"

"Blub-no I ain't—blub blub-but you will be-blub-if yu don't lemme alone," came from the pan. "Hand me that towel!"

"Don't wallow in it, yu!" admonished Bud as he refilled the basin. "Leave some dry spots for me, this time."

Jim carefully hung the towel on a peg in the wall of the house and then noticed the stranger, who was removing his saddle.

"Howdy, stranger!" he said heartily. "Just in time to feed. Coax some of that water from Bud, but get holt of the towel first, for there won't be none left soon."

The Orphan laughed and dusted his chaps.

"Where'll I find Lee Lung?" he asked. "Blake wants him to rustle the grub lively."

"He's in the cook shack behind the house a-doing it and trying to sing," replied Jim. "He's always trying to sing; it goes something like this: Hop-lee, low-hop yum-see," he hummed in a monotonous wail as he combed his hair before a broken bit of mirror stuck in a crack. "Hi-dee, hee-hee, chop-chop——"

"Gimme that comb, yu heathen Chinee," cried Bud, "and don't make that noise."

"Anything else yu wants?" asked Jim, deliberately putting the comb away in the box.

"I want to be in Kansas City with a million dollars and a whopper of a thirst," replied Bud as he filled the basin for the stranger. "It's all yourn, stranger. Grub's waiting for yu inside when yore ready."

"Do yu know who that feller is?" Bud asked in a whisper as they made their way to the table, from which came much laughter. "That's The Orphant," he added.

"Th' h–l it is!" said Jim. "Him? Him Th' Orphant? Tell another! I'm more than six years old, even if yu ain't."

"That's straight, fellers!" said Bud to the assembled outfit in a low voice. "I ain't kidding yu none, honest. I saw him up to Ace High last year. That's him, all right. Wait 'til he comes in and see!"

"Well, I don't care if he's Jonah," responded Jim. "Only I reckons you're plumb loco, all the same. But I'm too hungry to care if Gabriel blows if I can fill up before these Oliver Twists eats it all up," he said, revealing his last reading matter.

"He shore enough wears his gun plumb low-and the holster is tied to his chaps, too," muttered Jim as he seated himself at the table. "So would I, too, if I was him. Pass them murphys, Humble," he ordered.

"You has got to bust that piebald pet what you've been keeping around the house to-morrow, Humble," exulted the man nearest to him. "And it'll shore be a circus watching you do it, too!"

The blankets which divided the bunk house into two rooms were pushed aside and The Orphan entered, carrying his saddle and bridle, which he placed beside the others on the floor. Then he unbuckled his belts and hung them, Colts and all, over the pommel, which was etiquette and which gave assurance that the guest was not hunting anyone. Then he seated himself at the table in a chair which Humble pushed back for him. His entry in no degree caused a lull in the conversation.

"Well, you hasn't got no kick coming, has you?" asked Humble. "Hey, Cookie!" he shouted into the dark gallery which led to the cook shack. "Rustle in some more fixings for another place, and bring in the slush!" Then he turned to his tormentor: "You has allus got something to say about my business, ain't you, hey?"

"Sic 'em, Humble!" said Silent Allen. "Go for him!"

From the gallery came sounds of calamity and then a mongrel dog shot out and collided with the table, glancing off it and under the curtain in his haste to gain the outside world. A second later the cook, his face fiendish, grasping a huge knife, followed the dog out on the plain. Those eating sprang to their feet and streamed after the cook, yelling encouragement to their favorite.

"Go it, Old Woman!" "'Ray for Cookie!" "Beat him out, Lightning!" and other expressions met Blake as he came up from the corral.

"Cook got 'em again?" he asked, elbowing his way into the house. "I told you to keep liquor away from him."

"'Tain't liquor this time; it's th' kioodle," replied Docile Thomas as he led the way back to the table. "Him an' th' dog don't mix extra well."

Blake swept aside the blanket and saw The Orphan standing by the window and laughing. Turning, he disappeared into the gallery and soon returned with a tin plate, a steel knife, a tin cup and the coffee pot.

"Sit down-good Lord, they would let a man starve," he said, roughly clearing a place at the table for the new arrival. "I don't know how you feel," he continued, "but I'm so all-fired hungry that I don't know whether it's my back or stomach that hurts. Take some beef and throw those potatoes down this way. Here, have some slush," filling The Orphan's cup with coffee. "This ain't like the coffee the sheriff drinks, but it is just a little bit better than nothing. You see, Cook's all right, only he can't cook, never could and never will. But he's a whole lot better than a sailor I once suffered under."

"What's the matter between you and Lightning, Lee?" asked Bud as the cook passed by the table on his way to the shack.

"Wouldn't he drink yore slush? I allus said some dogs was smart," laughed Jack Lawson.

Lee's smile was bland. "Scalpee th' dlog," he asserted as he disappeared. "No dlamn good!" wafted from the gallery.

"Say, Humble," said Silent Allen in an aggrieved tone, "the beef will wag its tail some night if you don't shoot that cur!"

"That's right!" endorsed Jack. "I'll shoot him for a dollar," he added hopefully. "The boys will all chip in to make up the purse and it won't cost you a cent, not even a cartridge."

"Anybody that don't like that setter can move," responded Humble with decision. "He's a O. K. dog, that's what he is," he added loyally.

"Well, he's a setter, all right," laughed Silent. "He ain't good for nothing else but to set around all day in the shade and chew hisself up."

"He ain't, ain't he?" cried Humble, delaying the morsel on his fork in mid-air. "You ought to see him a-chasing coyotes!"

"I did see him chasing coyotes, and that's why I want you to have him killed," replied Silent, grinning. "His feet are too big. Every time he shoves his hind feet between the front ones he throws hisself."

"What did he ever catch except fleas and the mange?" asked Blake, winking at The Orphan, who was extremely busy burying his hunger.

"What did he ever catch!" indignantly cried Humble, dropping his fork. "You saw him catch that gray wolf over near the timber, and you can't deny it, neither!"

"By George, he did!" exclaimed Blake seriously. "You're right this time, Humble, he did. But he let go awful sudden. Besides, that gray wolf you're talking about was a coyote, and he would have died of old age in another week if you hadn't shot him to save the dog. And, what's more, I never saw him chase anything since, not even rabbits."

"He caught my boot one night," remarked Charley Bailey, reflectively, "right plumb on his near eye. Oh, he's a catcher, all right."

"He's so good he ought to be stuffed, then he could sit without having to move around catching boots and things," said Jim. "Why don't you have him stuffed, Humble?"

"Oh, yore a whole lot smart, now ain't you?" blazed the persecuted puncher, glaring at his tormentors.

"He can't catch his tail, Silent," offered Bud. "I once saw him trying to do it for ten minutes—he looked like a pinwheel what we used to have when we were kids. Missed it every time, and all he got was a cheap drunk."

Humble said a few things which came out so fast that they jammed up, and he left the room to hunt for his dog.

"Any particular reason why you call him Lightning, or is it just irony?" asked The Orphan as he helped himself to the beef for the third time. "I never heard that name used before."

"Oh, it ain't irony at all!" hastily denied the foreman. "That's a real good name, fits him all right," he assured. Then he explained: "You see, lightning don't hit twice in the same place, and neither can the dog when he scratches himself. And, besides, he can dodge awful quick. You have to figure which way he'll jump when you want him to catch anything."

"But you don't have to remember his name at all, Stranger," interposed Silent, who was not at all silent. "Any handle will do, if you only yells. Every time anybody yells he makes a crow line for the plain and howls at every jump. He's got a regular, shore enough trail worn where he makes his get-away."

Silence descended over the table, and for a quarter of an hour only the click of eating utensils could be heard. At the end of that time Blake pushed back his chair and arose. He glanced around the table and then spoke very distinctly: "Well, Orphan, get acquainted with your outfit." A head or two raised at the name, but that seemed to be all the effect of his words. "The boys will put you onto the game in the morning, and Bud will show you where to begin in case I don't show up in time. Better take a fresh cayuse and let yours rest up some. Don't hurt Humble's ki-yi and he'll be plumb nice to you; and if Silent wants to know how you likes his singing and banjo playing, lie and say it's fine."

The laugh went around and all was serene with the good fellowship which is so often found in good outfits.

"Joe, I'll bring the mail out with me, so you needn't go after it," continued the foreman as he strode towards the door. "That's what I'm going over for," he laughed.

"Lord, I'd go, too, if pie and cake and good coffee was on the card," laughed Silent.

"We'll shore have to go over in a gang some night and raid that pantry," remarked Bud. "It would be a circus, all right."

"The sheriff would get some good target practice, that's shore," responded Blake. "But I've got something better than that, and since you brought the subject up I'll tell you now, so you'll be good.

"Mrs. Shields has promised to get up a fine feed for you fellows as soon as Jim's sisters are on hand to help her, and as they are here now I wouldn't be a whole lot surprised if I brought the invitation back with me. How's that for a change, eh?" he asked.

"Glory be!" cried Silent. "Hurry up and get home!"

"Say, she's all right, ain't she!" shouted Jack, executing a jig to show how glad he was.

"Pinch me, Humble, pinch me!" begged Bud. "I may be asleep and dreaming–*here!* What the devil do you think I am, you wart-headed coyote!" he yelled, dancing in pain and rubbing his leg frantically. "You blamed doodle bug, yu!"

"Well, I pinched you, didn't I?" indignantly cried Humble. "What's eating you? Didn't you ask me to, you chump?"

"Hurry up and get that mail, Tom," cried Jim. "It might spoil–and say, if she leads at you with that invite, clinch!"

Blake laughed and went off toward the corral. As he found the horse he wished to ride he heard a riot in the bunk-house and he laughed silently. A Virginia reel was in full swing and the noise was terrible. Riding past the window, he saw Silent working like a madman at his banjo; and assiduously playing a harmonica was The Orphan, all smiles and puffed-out cheeks.

"Well, The Orphan is all right now," the foreman muttered as he swung out on the trail to Ford's Station. "I reckon he's found himself."

In the bunk-house there was much hilarity, and laughter roared continually at the grotesque gymnastics of the reel and at the sharp wit which cut right and left, respecting no one save the new member of the outfit, and eventually he came in for his share, which he repaid with interest. Suddenly Jim, catching his spurs in a bear-skin rug which lay near a bunk, threw out his arms to save himself and then went sprawling to the floor. The uproar increased suddenly, and as it died down Jim could be heard complaining.

"—-—-!" he cried as he nursed his knee. "I've had that pelt for nigh onto three years and regularly I go and get tangled up with it. It shore beats all how I plumb forget its habit of wrapping itself around them rowels, what are too big, anyhow. And it ain't a big one at that, only about half as big as the one I got for a tenderfoot up in Montanny," he deprecated in disgust.

The outfit scented a story and became suddenly quiet.

"Dod-blasted postage stamp of a pelt," he grumbled as he threw it into his bunk.

"The other skin couldn't 'a' been much bigger than that one," said Bud, leading him on. "How big was it, anyhow, Jim?"

"It couldn't, hey? It came off a nine-foot grizzly, that's how big it was," retorted Jim, sitting down and filling his pipe. "Nine whole feet from stub of tail to snoot, plumb full of cussedness, too."

"How'd you get it–Sharps?" queried Charley.

"No, Colt," responded Jim. "Luckiest shot *I* ever made, all right. I shore had visions of wearing wings when I pulled the trigger. Just one of them lucky shots a man will make sometimes."

"Give us the story, Jim," suggested Silent, settling himself easily in his bunk. "Then we'll have another smoke and go right to bed. I'm some sleepy."

"Well," began Jim after his pipe was going well, "I was sort of second foreman for the Tadpole, up in Montanny, about six years ago. I had a good foreman, a good ranch and about a dozen white punchers to look after. And we had a real cook, no mistake about that, all right.

"The Old Man hibernated in New York during the winter and came out every spring right after the calf round-up was over to see how we was fixed and to eat some of the cook's flapjacks. That cook wasn't no yaller-skinned post for a hair clothes line, like this grinning monkey what we've got here. The Old Man was a fine old cuss-one of the boys, and a darn good one, too-and we was always plumb glad to see him. He minded his own business, didn't tell us how we ought to punch cows and didn't bother anybody what didn't want to be bothered, which we most of us did like.

"Well, one day Jed Thompson, who rustled our mail for us twice a month, handed me a letter for the foreman, who was down South and wouldn't be back for some time. His mother had died and he went back home for a spell. I saw that the letter was from the Old Man, and wondered what it would say. I sort of figured that it would tell us when to hitch up to the buckboard and go after him. Fearing that he might land before the foreman got back, I went and opened it up.

"It was from the Old Man, all right, but it was no go for him that spring. He was sick abed in New York, and said as how he was plumb sorry he couldn't get out to see his boys, and so was we sorry. But he said as how he was sending us a friend of his'n who wanted to go hunting, and would we see that he didn't shoot no cows. We said we would, and then I went on and found out when this hunter was due to land.

"When the unfortunate day rolled around I straddled the buckboard and lit out for Whisky Crossing, twenty miles to the east, it being the nearest burg on the stage line. And as I pulled in I saw Frank, who drove the stage, and he was grinning from ear to ear.

"'I reckon that's your'n,' he said, pointing to a circus clown what had got loose and was sizing up the town.

"'The drinks are on me when I sees you again, Frank,' I said, for somehow I felt that he was right.

"Then I sized up my present, and blamed if he wasn't all rigged out to kill Indians. While my mouth was closing he ambled up to me and stared at my gun, which must 'a' been purty big to him.

"'Are you Mr. Fisher's hired man?' he asked, giving me a real tolerating look.

"Frank followed his grin into the saloon, leaving the door open so he could hear everything. That made me plumb sore at Frank, him a-doing a thing like that, and I glared.

"'I ain't nobody's hired man, and never was,' I said, sort of riled. 'We ain't had no hired man since we lynched the last one, but I'm next door to the foreman. Won't I do, or do you insist on talking to a hired man? If you do, he's in the saloon.'

"'Oh, yes, you'll do!' he said, quick-like, and then he ups and climbs aboard and we pulled out for home, Frank waving his sombrero at me and laughing fit to kill.

"We hadn't no more than got started when the hunter ups and grabs at the lines, which he shore missed by a foot. I was driving them cayuses, not him, and I told him so, too.

"'But ain't you going to take my luggage?' he asked.

"'Luggage! What luggage?' I answers, surprised-like.

"Then he pointed behind him, and blamed if he didn't have two trunks, a gripsack and three gun cases. I didn't say a word, being too full of cuss words to let any of 'em loose, until Frank wobbled up and asked me if I'd forgot something. Then I shore said a few, after which I busted my back a-hoisting his freight cars aboard, and we started out again, Frank acting like a d——n fool.

"The cayuses raised their ears, wondering what we was taking the saloon for, and I reckoned we would make them twenty miles in about eight hours if nothing busted and we rustled real hard.

"Well, about every twenty minutes I had to get off and hoist some of his furniture aboard, it being jolted off, for the prairie wasn't paved a whole lot, and us going cross-country. Considering my back, and the fact that he kept calling me 'My man,' and Frank's grin, I wasn't in no frame of mind to lead a religion round-up when I got home and dumped Davy Crockett's war-duds overboard for Jed to rustle in. I was still sore at Jed for bringing that letter.

"Davy Crockett dusted for the house and ordered Sammy Johns to oil his guns and put them together, after which he went off a-poking his nose into everything in sight, and mostly everything that wasn't in sight. When he got back to the house from his tour of inspection he found his guns just like he'd left them, and that was in their cases. Then he ambled out to me and registered his howl.

"'My man,' he said, 'My man, that hired man what I told to put my guns together ain't done it!'

"'Oh, he didn't?' I said, hanging on to my cuss words, for I was some surprised and couldn't say a whole lot.

"'No, he hasn't, and so I've come out to report him,' he said, looking mad.

"'My man!' said I, mad some myself, and looking him plumb in the eyes. 'My man, if he had I'd shore think he was off his feed or loco. He ain't no hired man, but he is a all-fired good cow-puncher, and I'm a heap scared about him not filling you full of holes, you asking him to do a thing like that! He must be real sick.'

"He didn't have no come-back to that, but just looked sort of funny, and then he trotted off to put his guns together hisself. I hustled around and saw that some work was done right and then went in to supper. After it was over my present got up and handed me a gun, and I near fell over. It was a purty little Winchester, and I don't blame him a whole lot for being tickled over it, for it shore was a beauty, but it oozed out a ball about the size of a pea, and the makers would 'a' been some scared if they had known it was running around loose in a grizzly-bear country.

"'I reckon that'll stop him,' he said, happy-like.

"'Stop what?' I asked him.

"'Why, game-bears, of course,' he said, shocked at my appalling ignorance.

"'Yes,' said I, slow-like, 'I reckon Ephraim may turn around and scratch hisself, if you hits him.'

"'Why, won't that stop a bear?'

"'Yes, if it's a stuffed bear,' I said.

"'Why, that's a blamed good rifle!'

"'It shore is; it's as fine a gun as I ever laid my eyes on,' I replied, 'for prairie dogs and such.'

"Then I felt plumb sorry for him, he being so ignorant, and so when he hands me a peach of a shotgun to shoot coyotes with I laid it down and got my breach-loading Sharps, .50 caliber, which I handed to him.

"'There,' I said, 'that's the only gun in the room what any self-respecting bear will give a d——n for.'

"He looked at it, felt its heft, sized up the bunghole and then squinted along the sights.

"'Why, this gun will kick like the very deuce!' he said.

"'Kick!' said I. 'Kick! She'll kick like a army mule if you holds her far enough from your shoulder. But I'd a whole lot ruther get kicked by a mule than hugged by a grizzly, and so'll you when you sees him a-heading your way.'

"'But what'll you use?' says he, 'I don't want to take your gun.'

"Well, when he said that I reckoned that he had some good stuff in him after all, and somehow I felt better. There he was, away from his mother and sisters, among a bunch of gamboling cow-punchers, and right in the middle of a good bear country. I sort of wondered if he was to blame, and managed to lay all the fault on his city bringing-up.

"'That's all right,' says I, 'I'll take an old muzzle-loading Bridesburg what's been laying around the house ever since I came here. It heaves enough lead at one crack to sink a man-of-war, being a .60 caliber.'

"Well, bright and early the next morning we started out for bear, and I knowed just where to look, too. You see, there was a thicket of berry bushes about three miles from the ranch house and I had seen plenty of tracks there, and there was a grizzly among them, too, and as big as a house, judging from the signs. The boys had wanted to ride out in a gang and rope him, but I said as how I was saving him for a dude hunter to practice on, so they left him alone.

"We footed it through the brush, and finally Davy Crockett, who simply would go ahead of me, yelled out that he had found tracks.

"I rustled over, and sure enough he had, only they wasn't made by no bear, and I said so.

"'Then what are they?' he asked, sort of disappointed.

"'Cow tracks,' said I. 'When you see bear tracks you'll know it right away,' and we went on a-hunting.

"We had just got down in a little hollow, where the green flies were purty bad, when I saw tracks, and they was bear tracks this time, and whoppers. It had rained a little during the night and the ground was just soft enough to show them nice. I called Davy Crockett and he came up, and when he saw them tracks he was plumb tickled, and some scairt.

"'Where is he?' he asked, looking around sort of anxious.

"'At the front end of these tracks, making more,' said I.

"'And what are we going to do now?' he asked, cocking the Sharps.

"'We're going to trail him,' said I, 'and if we finds him and has any accidents, you wants to telegraph yourself up a tree, and be sure that it ain't a big tree, too.'

"'"Be sure it ain't a big tree!" he repeated, looking at me like he thought I wanted him to get killed.

"'Exactly,' said I, and then I explained: 'The bigger the tree, the sooner you'll be a meal, for he climbs by hugging the trunk and pushing hisself up. A little tree'll slide through his legs, and he can't get a holt.'

"'I hope I don't forget that!' he exclaimed, looking dubious.

"'The less you forgets when bear hunting,' said I, 'the longer you'll remember.'

"We took up the trail and purty soon we saw the bear, and he was so big he didn't hardly know how to act. He was pawing berries into his mouth for breakfast, and he turned his head and slowly sized us up. He dropped on all fours and then got up again, and Davy Crockett, not listening to me telling him where to shoot, lets drive and busted an ear. Ephraim preferred all fours again and started coming straight at us, and Moses and all his bullrushers couldn't have stopped him. He was due to arrive near Davy Crockett in about four and a half seconds, and that person dropped his gun and hot-footed it for a whopping big tree. I yelled at him and told him to take a little one, but he was too blamed busy hunting bear to listen to a no-account hired man like me, so he kept on a-going for the big tree.

"I figured, and figured blamed quick, that the bear would tag him just about the time he tagged the tree, and so, hoping to create a diversion, I whanged away at the bear's tail, him running plumb away from me. I was real successful, for I created it all right. When he felt that carload of lead slide up under his skin he braced hisself, slid and wheeled, looking for the son-of-a-gun what done it, and he saw me pouring powder hell-bent down my gun. He must 'a' knowed that I was the real business end of the partnership, and that he'd have trouble a-plenty if he let me finish my job, for he came at me like a bullet.

"'Climb a *little* tree! Climb a *little* tree!' yelled Davy Crockett from his perch in his two-foot-through oak.

"I wasn't in no joyous frame of mind when a nine-foot grizzly was due in the next mail, but I just had to laugh at his advice when I sized up his layout. As I jumped to one side the bear slid past, trying awful hard to stop, and he was doing real well, too. As he turned I slipped on some of that green grass, and thought as how the Old Man would have to get another puncher.

"'I ain't never going to peter out with a tenderfoot looking on if I can help it!' I said to myself, and I jerked loose my six-shooter, shooting offhand and some hasty. It was just a last hope, the kick of a dying man's foot, but it fetched him, blamed if it didn't! He went down in a heap and clawed about for a spell, but I put five more in him, and then sat down. Did you ever notice how long it takes a grizzly to die? I loaded my gun in a hurry, the sweat pouring down my face, for that was one of the times it ain't no disgrace to be some scared, which I was.

"'Is he dead?' called Davy Crockett from his tree, hopeful-like and some anxious.

"'He is,' I said, 'or, leastawise, he was.'

"Davy was a sight. He was all skinned up from his clinch with the tree, though how he used his face getting up is more than I can tell. And he was some white and unsteady. He had all the hunting he wanted, and he managed to say that he was glad he hadn't come out alone, and that he reckoned I was right about his guns after all. So we took a last look at the bear and lit out for the ranch, where I told the boys to go out and drag our game home."

Jim knocked the ashes from his pipe and began to fill it anew, acting as though the story was finished, but Bud knew him well, and he spoke up:

"Well, what then?" he asked.

"Oh, the hunter left for New York the very next day, and I skinned the bear and sent the pelt after him as a present. When I wrote out my quarterly report, the foreman not being back yet, I told the Old Man that if he had any more friends what wanted to go hunting to send them up to Frenchy McAllister on the Tin Cup. I was some sore at Frenchy for the way he had cleaned me out at poker."

He threw the skin to the floor and began to undress.

"Come on, now, lights out," he said. "I'm tired."

Chapter XIV
The Sheriff States Some Facts

The foreman of the Star C impatiently tossed his bridle reins over the post which stood near the sheriff's door and knocked heavily, brushing the dust of his ride from him. Quick, heavy steps approached within the house and the door suddenly flew open.

"Hullo, Tom!" Shields cried, shaking hands with his friend. "Come right in–I knew you would come if we coaxed you a little."

"You don't have to do much coaxing–I can't stay away, Jim," replied Blake with a laugh. "How do you do, Mrs. Shields?"

"Very well, Tom," she answered. "Miss Ritchie, Helen, Mary, this is Tom Blake; Tom, Miss Ritchie and James' sisters. They are to stay with us just as long as they can, and I'll see that it is a good, long time, too."

"How do you do?" he cried heartily, acknowledging the introduction. "I am glad to meet you, for I've heard a whole lot about you. I hope you'll like this country-greatest country under the sky! You stay out here a month and I'll bet you'll be just like lots of people, and not want to go back East again."

"It seems as though we have always known Mr. Blake, for James has written about you so much," replied Helen, and then she laughed: "But I am not so sure about liking this country, although very unusual things seem to take place in it. The journey was very trying, and it seemed to get worse as we neared our destination."

"Well, I'll have to confess that the stage-ride part of it is a drawback, and also that Apaches don't make good reception committees. They are a little too pressing at times."

"But, speaking seriously," responded Helen, "I have had a really delightful time. James has managed to get me a very tame horse after quite a long search, and I have taken many rides about the country."

"Wait 'til you see that horse, Tom," laughed the sheriff. "It's warranted not to raise any devilment, but it can't, for it has all it can do to stand up alone, and can't very well run away."

"I see that The Orphan delivered my message, contrary to the habits of men," remarked the sheriff's wife as she took the guest's hat and offered him a seat. "I spoke to James about it several days ago, and asked him to send you word when he could, for you have not been here for a long time. And the wonderful thing about it is that he remembered to tell The Orphan."

"Thank you," he replied, seating himself. "Yes, he delivered it all right, it was about the second thing he said. But I just couldn't get here any sooner, Mrs. Shields. And I was just wondering if I could get over to-night when he told me. When he said 'apricot pie' he looked sort of sad."

"Poor boy!" she exclaimed. "You must take him one-it was a shame to send such a message by him, poor, lonesome boy!"

"Well, he ain't so lonesome now," laughed Blake.

Helen had looked up quickly at the mention of The Orphan's name, and the sheriff replied to her look of inquiry.

"I sent him out to punch for Blake, Helen," he said quickly. "If he has the right spirit in him he'll get along with the Star C outfit; if he hasn't, why, he won't get on with anybody. But I reckon Tom will bring out all the good in him; he'll have a fair show, anyhow."

"And you never told us about it!" cried Helen reproachfully.

"Oh, I was saving it up," laughed the sheriff. "What do you think of him, Tom?" he asked, turning to the foreman.

"Why, he's a clean-looking boy," answered Blake. "I like his looks. He seems to be a fellow what can be depended on in a pinch, and after all I had heard about him he sort of took me by surprise. I thought he would be a tough-looking killer, and there he was only a overgrown, mischievous kid. But there is a look in his eyes that says there is a limit. But he surprised me, all right."

"You want to appreciate that, Miss Ritchie," remarked the sheriff, smiling broadly. "Anything that takes Tom Blake by surprise must have merit of some kind. And he is a good judge of men, too."

"I do so hope he gets on well," she replied earnestly. "He was a perfect gentleman when he was here, and his wit was sharp, too. And out there on that awful plain, when he stood swaying with weakness, he looked just splendid!"

"Pure grit, pure grit!" cried the sheriff in reply. "That's why I'm banking on him," he added, his eyes warming as he remembered. "Any fellow who could turn a trick like that, and who has so much clean-cut courage, must be worth looking after. He's got a bad reputation, but he's plumb white and square with me, and I'm going to be square with him. And when you know all that I know about him you'll take his reputation as a natural result of hard luck, spunk, and other people's devilment and foolishness. But he's going to have a show now, all right."

"What did your men say when they saw him? Do they know who he is?" asked Mrs. Shields anxiously.

Blake laughed: "Oh, yes, they know who he is. They ain't the talking kind in a case like that; they won't say a word to him about what he has done. Besides, he was under their roof, eating their food, and that's enough for them. Of course, they were a little surprised, but not half as much as I thought they would be. He is a man who gives a good first impression, and the boys are all fine fellows, big-hearted, square, clean-living and peaceful. Reputations don't count for much with them, for they know that reputations are gossip-made in most cases. I asked him to stay, and they haven't got no reason to object, and they won't waste no time looking for reasons, neither. If there is any trouble at all, it will be his own fault. Then again, they know that he is all sand and that his gunplay is real and sudden; not that they are afraid of him, or anybody else, for that matter, but he is the kind of a man they like-somebody who can stand up on his own legs and give better than he gets."

"I reckon he fills that bill, all right," laughed the sheriff. "He *can* stand up on his own legs, and when he does he makes good. And as for gunplay, good Lord, he's a shore wizard! I reckoned I could do things with a gun, but he can beat me. He ain't no Boston pet, and he ain't no city tough, not nohow. And I'd rather have him with me in a mix-up than against me. He's the coolest proposition loose in this part of the country at any game, and I know what I'm talking about, too."

"You promised to tell us everything about him, all you knew," reproached Helen. "And I am sure that it will be well worth hearing."

"Well, I was saving it up 'til I could tell it all at once and when you would all be together," he replied. "There wasn't any use of telling it twice," he explained as he brought out a box of cigars. "These are the same brand you sampled last time you were here," he assured his friend as he extended the box.

"By George, that's fine!" cried the foreman, picking out the blackest cigar he could see. "I could taste them cigars for a whole week, they was so good. There's nothing like a good Perfecto to make a fellow feel like he's too lucky to live."

"Oh," said Mrs. Shields. "Then you won't care for the coffee and pie and gingerbread," she sighed. "I'm very sorry."

Blake jumped: "Lord, Ma'am," he cried hastily, "I meant in the smoking line! Why, I've been losing sleep a-dreaming of your cooking. Every time the cook fills my cup with his insult to coffee I feel so lonesome that it hurts!"

"You want to look out, Tom!" laughingly warned the sheriff, "or you'll get yourself disliked! When I don't care for Margaret's cooking I ain't fool enough to say so, not a bit of it."

"You're a nice one to talk like that!" cried his wife. "You are just like a little boy on baking day–I can hardly keep you out of the kitchen. You bother me to death, and it is all I can do to cook enough for you!"

After the laugh had subsided and a steaming cup of coffee had been placed at the foreman's elbow, Helen impatiently urged her brother to begin his story.

He lighted his cigar with exasperating deliberateness and then laughed softly: "Gosh! I'm getting to be a second fiddle around here. From morning to night all I hear is The Orphan. The first thing that hits me when I come home is, 'Have you seen The Orphan?' or, 'Have you heard anything about him?' The worst offenders are Miss Ritchie and Helen. They pester me nigh to death about him. But here goes:

"I reckon I'd better begin with Old John Taylor," he slowly began. "I've been doing some quiet hunting lately, and in the course of it I ran across Old John down in Crockettsville. You remember him, don't you, Tom? Yes, I reckoned you wouldn't forget the man who got us out of that Apache scrape. Well, I had a good talk with him, and this is what I learned:

"About twenty years ago a family named Gordon moved into northwestern Texas and put up a shack in one of the valleys. There was three of them, father, mother, and a bright little five-year-old boy, and they brought about two hundred head of cattle, a few horses and a whole raft of books. Gordon bought up quite a bit of land from a ranch nearby at almost a song, and he never thought of asking for a deed–who would, down there in those days? There wasn't a rancher who owned more than a quarter section; you know the game, Tom–take up a hundred and sixty acres on a stream and then claim about a million, and fight like the very devil to hold it. We've all done it, I reckon, but there is plenty of land for everybody, and so there is no kick. Well, he was shore lucky, for his boundary on two sides was a fair-sized stream that never went dry, and you know how scarce that is–a whole lot better than a gold mine to a cattleman.

"They got along all right for a while, had a tenderfoot's luck with their cattle, which soon began to be more than a few specks on the plain, and he was very well satisfied with everything, except that there wasn't no school. Old man Gordon was daffy on education, which is a good thing to be daffy over, and he was some strong in that line himself, having been a school teacher back East. But he took his boy in hand and taught him all he knew, which must have been a whole lot, judging from things in general, and the kid was a smart, quick youngster. He was plumb crazy about two things–books and guns. He read and re-read all the books he could borrow, and got so he could handle a gun with any man on the range.

"About five years after he had located, the ranchman from whom he bought his range and water rights went and died. Some of the heirs, who were not what you would call square, began to get an itching for Gordon's land, which was improved by the first irrigation ditch in Texas. There was a garden and a purty good orchard, which was just beginning to bear fruit. It was pure, cussed hoggishness, for there was more land than anybody had any use for, but they must grab everything in sight, no matter what the cost. Trouble was the rule after that, and the old man was up against it all the time. But he managed to hold his own, even though he did lose a lot of cattle.

"His brand was a gridiron, which wasn't much different from the gridiron circle brand of the big ranch. It ain't much trouble to use a running iron through a wet blanket and change a brand like that when you know how, and the Gridiron Circle gang shore enough knew how. Their expertness with a running iron would have caused questions to be asked, and probably a lynching bee, in other parts of the country, but down there they were purty well alone. They let Gordon know that he had jumped the range, which was just what they had done, that he didn't own it, and that the sooner he left the country the better it would be for his health. But he had peculiar ideas about justice, and he shore was plumb full of grit and obstinacy. He knew he was right, that he had paid for the land, and that he had improved it. And he had a lot of faith in the law, not realizing that he hadn't anything to show the law. And he didn't know that law and justice don't always mean the same thing, not by a long shot.

"Well, one day he went out looking for a vein of coal, which he thought ought to be there-abouts, according to his books, and it ought to be close to the surface of a fissure. He reckoned that coal of any quality would be some better than chips and the little wood he owned, so he got busy. But he didn't find coal, but something that made him hotfoot it to his books. When the report came back from the assay office he knew that he had hit on a vein of native silver, which was some better than coal.

"It didn't take long for the news to get around, though God Himself only knows how it did, unless the storekeeper told that a package had gone through his hands addressed to the assay office, and things began to happen in chunks. He caught three Gridiron Circle punchers shooting his cows, and he was naturally mad about it and just shot up the bunch before they knew he was around. He killed one and spoiled the health of the other two for some time to come, which naturally spelled war with a big W. Then about this time his wife went and died, which was a purty big addition to his troubles. As he stood above her grave, all broken up, and about ready to give up the fight and go back East, he was shot at from cover. He didn't much care if he was killed or not, until he remembered that he had a boy to take care of. Then he got fighting mad all at once, all of his troubles coming up before him in a bunch, and he got his gun and went hunting, which was only right and proper under the circumstances."

The sheriff flecked the ashes of his cigar into a blue flower pot which was gay with white ribbons, and poured himself a cup of coffee.

"I hate to think that it is possible to find a whole ranch of hellions from the owner down," he continued, "but the nature of the owner picks a dirty foreman, and a dirty foreman needs dirty men, and there you are. That fits the case of the Gridiron Circle to a T. There was not one white man in the whole gang," and he sat in silence for a space.

"Well, the boy, who was about fifteen years old by this time, took his gun and went out to find his daddy, and he succeeded. He cut him down and buried him and then went home. That night the shack burned to the ground, the orchard was ruined and the boy disappeared. Some people said that the kid took what he wanted and burned the house rather than to have it profaned as a range house by the curs who murdered his dad; and some said the other thing, but from what I know of the kid, I reckon he did it himself.

"Right there and then things began to happen that hurt the ease and safety of the Gridiron Circle. Cows were found dead all over the range-juglars cut in every case. Three of their punch-ers were found dead in one week–a .5O-caliber Sharps had done it. A regular reign of terror began and kept the outfit on the nervous jump all the time. They searched and trailed and searched and swore, and if one of them went off by himself he was usually ready to be buried. Ten experienced, old-time cowmen were made fools of by a fifteen-year-old kid, who was never seen by anybody that lived long enough to tell about it. When he got hungry, he just killed another cow and had a porterhouse steak cooked between two others over a good fire. He ate the middle steak, which had all the juices of the two burned ones, and threw the others away. Three meals a day for six months, and one cow to a meal, was the order of things on the ranges of the Gridiron Circle. He had plenty of ammunition, because every dead puncher was minus his belt when found and his guns were broken or gone; and early in the game the boy had made a master stroke: he raided the storehouse of the ranch one night and lugged away about five hundred rounds of ammunition in his saddle bags, with a couple of spare Colts and a repeating Winchester of the latest pattern, and he spoiled all the rest of the guns he could lay his hands on. Humorous kid, wasn't he, shooting up the ranch with its own guns and cartridges?

"Finally, however, after the news had spread, which it did real quick, a regular lynching party was arranged, and the U-B, which lay about sixty miles to the east, sent over half a dozen men to take a hand. Then the Gridiron Circle had a rest, but while the gang was hunting for him and laying all sorts of elaborate traps to catch him, the boy was over on the U-B, showing it how foolish it had been to take up another man's quarrel. By this time the whole country knew about it, and even some Eastern papers began to give it much attention. One of the punchers of the Gridiron Circle, when he found a friend dead and saw the tracks of the kid in the sand, swore and cried that it was 'that d——-n Orphan' who had done it, and the name stuck. He had become an outlaw and was legitimate prey for any man who had the chance and grit to turn the trick. For ten years he has been wandering all over the range like a hunted gray wolf, fighting for his life at every turn against all kinds of odds, both human and natural. And I reckon that explains why he is accused of doing so much killing. He has been hunted and forced to shoot to save his own life, and a gray wolf is a fighter when cornered. I know that I wouldn't give up the ghost if I could help it, and neither would anybody else."

"Oh, it is a shame, an awful shame!" cried Helen, tears of sympathy in her eyes. "How could they do it? I don't blame him, not a bit! He did right, terrible as it was! And only a boy when they began, too! Oh, it is awful, almost unbelievable!"

"Yes, it is, Sis," replied Shields earnestly. "It ain't his fault, not by any manner or means-he was warped." And then he added slowly: "But Tom and I will straighten him out, and if some folks hereabouts don't like it, they can shore lump it, or fight."

"Tell me how you met him, Jim," requested Blake in the interval of silence. "I've heard some of it, second-handed, or third-handed, but I'd like to have it straight."

"Well," the sheriff continued, "when he came to these parts I didn't know anything about him except what I had heard, which was only bad. He had a nasty way of handling his gun, a hair-trigger and a nervous finger on his gun, and he had a distressing way of using one cow to a meal, so I got busy. I didn't expect much trouble in getting him. I knew that he was only a youngster and I counted on my fifty years, and most of them of experience, getting him. Being young, I reckoned he would be foolhardy and hasty and uncertain in his wisdom; but, Lord! it was just like trying to catch a flea in the dark. He was here, there and everywhere. While I was down south hunting along his trail he would be up north objecting to the sheep industry in ingenious ways and varying his bill of fare with choice cuts of lamb and mutton. And by the time I got down south he would be-God only knows where, I didn't. I could only guess, and I guessed wrong until the last one. And then it was the toss of a coin that decided it.

"After a while he began to get more daring, and when I say more daring I mean an open game with no limit. He began to prove my ideas about his age making him reckless, though he was cautious enough, to be sure. One day, not long ago, he had a run-in with two sheepmen out by the U bend of the creek, who had driven their herds up on Cross Bar-8 land and over the dead-line established by the ranch. They must have taken him for some Cross Bar-8 puncher and thought he was going to kick up a fuss about the trespass, or else they recognized him. Anyway, when I got on the scene they were ready to be planted, which I did for them. Then I went after him on a plain trail north-and almost too plain to suit me, because it looked like it had been made plain as an invitation. He had picked out the softest ground and left plenty of good tracks. But I was some mad and didn't care much what I run into. I thought he had driven the whole blasted herd of baa-baas over that high bank and into the creek, for the number of dead sheep was shore scandalous.

"I followed that cussed trail north, east, south, west and then all over the whole United States, it seemed to me. And it was always growing older, because I had to waste time in dodging chaparrals and things like that that might hold him and his gun. I went picking my way on a roundabout course past thickets of honey mesquite and cactus gardens, over alkali flats and everything else, and the more I fooled about the madder I got. I ain't no real, genuine fool, and I've had some experience at trailing, but I had to confess that I was just a plain, ordinary monkey-on-a-stick when stacked up against a kid that was only about half my age, because suddenly the plainness of the trail disappeared and I was left out on the middle of a burning desert to guess the answer as best I could. I knew what he had done, all right, but that didn't help me a whole lot. Did you ever trail anybody that used padded-leather footpads on his cayuse's feet, and that went on a walk, picking out the hardest ground? No? Well, I have, and it's no cinch.

"I got tired of chasing myself back to the same place four times out of five, and I reckons that it wouldn't be very long before he had made his circle and got me in front of him. It ain't no church fair to be hunting a mad devil like him under the best conditions, and it's a whole lot less like one when he gets behind you doing the same thing. I didn't know whether he had swung to the north or south, so I tossed up a coin and cried heads for north-and it was tails. I cut loose at a lope and had been riding for some time when I saw something through an opening in the chaparrals to the east of me, and it moved. I swung my glasses on it, and I'm blamed if it wasn't an Apache war party bound north. They were about a mile to the east of me, and if they kept on going straight ahead they would run across my trail in about three hours, for it gradually worked their way. I ducked right then and there and struck west for a time, turning south again until I hit the Cimarron Trail, which I followed east. Well, as I went around one side of the chaparral six mad Apaches went around the other, and they hit my trail too soon to suit me. I heard a hair-raising yell and lit out in the direction of Chattanooga as hard as I could go, with a hungry chorus a mile behind me.

"I had just passed that freak bowlder on the Apache Trail when the man I was looking for turned up, and with the drop, of course. We reckoned that two was needed to stop the war-paints, which we did, him running the game and doing most of the playing. I felt like I was his honored guest whom he had invited to share in the festivities. He had plenty of chances to nail me if he wanted to, and he had chipped in on a game that he didn't have to take cards in; and to help me out. He could have let them get me and they would have thought that I had done all the injury and that there wasn't another man on the desert. But he didn't, and I began to think he wasn't as bad as he was painted."

Then he told of the trouble between The Orphan and Jimmy of the Cross Bar-8, and of the rage which blossomed out on the ranch.

"That shore settled it for the Cross Bar-8. They wanted lots of gore, and they got it, all right, when he played five of their punchers against the very war party he had sent north to meet me, while I was chasing him. That war party must have found something to their liking, wandering about the country all that time."

Blake interrupted him: "War party that he sent north to meet you?" he asked in surprise. "How could he do that?"

"That's just what I said," replied Shields, and then he explained about the arrow. "Any man who could stack a deck like that and use one danger to wipe out another ain't going to get caught by an outfit of lunkheads-by George! if he didn't work nearly the same trick on the Cross Bar-8 crowd! Oh, it's great, simply great!"

The foreman slapped his knee enthusiastically: "Fine! Fine!" he exulted. "That fellow has got brains, plenty of them! And he'll make use of them to the good of this country, too, before we get through with him."

Shields continued: "After he sic'd the chumps of the Cross Bar-8 on the Apaches he shore raised the devil on the ranch and I was asked to go out and run things, which I did, or rather thought I would do. Charley and I and the two Larkin boys laid out on the plain all night, covered up with sand, waiting for him to show up between us and the windows-and the first thing I saw in the morning was Helen's flower pot here-it used to be Margaret's—setting up on top of a pile of sand under my very nose where he had stuck it while I waited for him-and blamed if he hadn't signed his name in the sand at its base!" He suddenly turned to his sister: "Tell Tom about him calling on you while I was waiting for him out on the ranch, Helen."

Helen did so and the way she told it caused the women to look keenly at her.

Blake laughed heartily: "Now, don't that beat all!" he cried.

"It don't beat this," responded the sheriff, turning again to Helen. "Tell him about the stage coach, Sis."

"Well, I don't know much about the first part of it," she replied. "All I remember is a terrible ride –oh, it was awful!" she cried, shuddering as she remembered the tortures of the Concord. "But when we stopped and after I managed to get out of the coach I saw the driver carrying a man on his shoulders and coming toward us. He laid his burden down and revived him-and he was a young man, and covered with blood." Then she paused: "He was real nice and polite and didn't seem to think that he had done anything out of the ordinary. Then we went on and he left us."

The sheriff laughed and leveled an accusing finger at her:

"You have left out a whole lot, Sis," he said affectionately. "Helen acted just like the thoroughbred she is, Tom," he continued. "I guess Bill told you all about it, for he's aired it purty well. Why, she even lost her gold pin a-helping him!" and he grinned broadly.

Helen shot him a warning glance, but it was too late; Mary suddenly sat bolt upright, her expression one of shocked surprise.

"Helen Shields!" she cried, "and I never thought of it before! How could you do it! Why, that horrid man will show your pin and boast about it to everybody! The idea! I'm surprised at you!"

"Tut, tut," exclaimed Shields. "I reckon that pin is all right. He might find it handy some day to return it, it'll be a good excuse when he gets on his feet. And I'd hate to be the man to laugh at it, or try to take it from him. Now, come, Mary, think of it right; it was the first kind act he had known since he lost his daddy. And that pin is one of my main stand-bys in this game. I believe that he'll be square as long as he has it."

"Well, I don't care, James," warmly responded Mary. "It was *not* a modest thing to do when she had never seen him before, and he her brother's enemy and an outlaw!"

"How could I have fastened the bandage, sister dear?" asked Helen, her complexion slightly more colored than its natural shade. "It was so very little to do after all he had done for us!"

"Well, Tom and I have some business to talk over, so we'll leave you to fight the matter out among yourselves," the sheriff said, arising. "Come to my room, Tom, I want to talk over that ranch scheme with you. You bring the coffee pot and the cigars and I'll juggle the pie and gingerbread," he laughed as he led the way.

"Oh, Tom!" hastily called Mrs. Shields after good-nights had been said, and just before the door closed; "I promised you a dinner for your boys when Helen and Mary came, and if you think you can spare them this coming Sunday I will have it then."

"Thank you, Mrs. Shields," earnestly responded Blake, turning on the threshold. "It is awful good of you to put yourself out that way, and you can bet that the boys will be your devoted slaves ever after. If you must go to that trouble, why, Sunday or any day you may name will do for us. Gosh, but won't they be tickled!" he exulted as he pictured them feasting on goodies. "It'll be better than a circus, it shore will!"

"Why, it's no trouble at all, Tom," she replied, smiling at being able to bring cheer to a crowd of men, lonely, as she thought. "And you will arrange to have The Orphan with them, won't you?"

"I most certainly will," he heartily replied. "It'll do wonders for him." He glanced quickly at Helen, but she was busily engaged in threading a needle under the lamp shade.

"Good night, all," he said as he closed the door.

Chapter XV

An Understanding

Blake settled himself in the easy chair which his host pushed over to him and crossed his feet on the seat of another, and became the personification of contentment. One of the black Perfectos which a friend in the East kept Shields supplied with, was tenderly nursed by his lips, its fragrant smoke slowly issuing from his nose and mouth, yielding its delights to a man who knew a good cigar when he smoked it, and who knew how to smoke it. At his elbow stood a coffee pot, flanked on one side by a plate piled high with gingerbread; on the other by an apricot pie. His eyes half-closed and his arms were folded, and a great peace stole over him. He had the philosopher's mind which so readily yields to the magic touch of a perfect cigar. In that short space of time he was recompensed for a life of hardships, perils and but few pleasures.

They sat each lost in his own thoughts, in a silence broken only by the very low and indistinct hum of women's voices and the loud ticking of the clock, which soon struck ten. The foreman sighed, stirred to knock the ashes from his cigar, and then slowly reached his hand toward the pie. Shields came to himself and very gravely relighted his cigar, watching the blue smoke stream up over the lamp. He looked at his contented friend for a few seconds and then broke the silence.

"Tom," he said, "what I'm going to tell you now is all meat. I couldn't say anything about it while the women were around, for they shore worry a lot and there wasn't no good in scaring them.

"The Cross Bar-8 outfit got saddled with the idea that they wanted a new sheriff, and four of them didn't care a whole lot how they made the necessary vacancy. I got word that they were going to pay Bill Howland for the part he played, and on the face of it there wasn't nothing more than that. It was natural enough that they were sore on him, and that they would try to square matters. Well, of course, I couldn't let him get wiped out and I took cards in the game. But, Lord, it wasn't what I reckoned it was at all. He was in for his licking, all right, but *he* was the *little* fish-and *I* was the *big* one.

"They got Bill in the defile of the Backbone and were going to lynch him-they beat him up shameful. He wouldn't tell them that I was hand-in-glove with The Orphan, which they wanted to hear, so they tried to scare him to lie, but it was no go.

"Well, I followed Bill and, to make it short, that is just what they had figured on. They posted an outpost to get the drop on me when I showed up, and he got it. Tex Williard seemed to be the officer in charge, and he asked me questions and suggested things that made me fighting mad inside. But I was as cool as I could be apparently, for it ain't no good to lose your temper in a place like that. I suppose they wanted me to get out on the warpath so they could frame up some story about self-defense. It looked bad for me, with three of them having their guns on me, and Tex Williard had just given me an ultimatum and had counted two, when, d—-d if The Orphan didn't take a hand from up on the wall of the defile. That let me get my guns out, and the rest was easy. We let Bill get square on the gang for the beating he had got, by whipping all of them to the queen's taste. When they got so they could stand up I told them a few things and ordered them out of the country, and they were blamed glad to get the chance to go, too.

"The Orphan didn't have to mix up in that, not at all, and it makes the third time he's put his head in danger to help me or mine, and he took big chances every time. How in h–l can I help liking him? Can I be blamed for treating him white and square when he's done so much for me? He is so chock full of grit and squareness that I'll throw up this job rather than to go out after him for his past deeds, and I mean it, too, Tom."

Blake reached for another piece of pie, held his hand over it in uncertainty and then, changing his mind, took gingerbread for a change.

"Well, I reckon you're right, Jim," he replied. "Anyhow, it don't make a whole lot of difference whether you are or not. You're the sheriff of this layout, and you're to do what you think best, and that's the idea of most of the people out here, too. If you want to experiment, that's your business, for you'll be the first to get bit if you're wrong. And it ain't necessary to tell you that your friends will back you up in anything you try. Personally, I am rather glad of what you're doing, for I like that man's looks, as I said before, and he'll be just the kind of a puncher I want. He's a man that'll fight like h—l for the man he ties up to and who treats him square. If he ain't, I'm getting childish in my judgment."

"I sent him to you," the sheriff continued, "because I wanted to get him in with a good outfit and under a man who would be fair with him. I knew that you would give him every chance in the world. And then Helen takes such an interest in him, being young and sympathetic and romantic, that I wanted to please her if I could, and I can. She'll be very much pleased now that I've given him a start in the right direction and there ain't nothing I can do for her that is not going to be done. She's a blamed fine girl, Tom, as nice a girl as ever lived."

"She shore is-there ain't no doubt about that!" cried the foreman, and then he frowned slightly. "But have you thought of what all this might develop into?" he asked, leaning forward in his earnestness. "It's shore funny how I should think of such a thing, for it ain't in my line at all, but the idea just sort of blew into my head."

"What do you mean?"

"Well, Helen, being young and sympathetic and romantic, as you said, and owing her own life and the lives of her sister and friend, not to mention yours, to him, might just go and fall in love with him, and I reckon that if she did, she would stick to him in spite of hell. He's a blamed good-looking, attractive fellow, full of energy and grit, somewhat of a mystery, and women are strong on mysteries, and he might nurse ideas about having some one to make gingerbread and apricot pie for him; and if he does, as shore as God made little apples, it'll be Helen that he'll want. He's never seen as pretty a girl, she's been kind and sympathetic with him, and I'm willing to bet my hat that he's lost a bit of sleep about her already. Good Lord, what can you expect? She pities him, and what do the books say about pity?"

The sheriff thought for a minute and then looked up with a peculiar light in his eyes.

"For a bachelor you're doing real well," he said, still thinking hard.

"Being a bachelor don't mean that I ain't never rubbed elbows with women," replied the foreman. "There are some people that are bachelors because they are too darned smart to get roped and branded because the moon happens to be real bright. But I'll confess to you that I ain't a bachelor because I didn't want to get roped. We won't say any more about that, however."

"Well," said Shields, slowly. "If he tries to get her before I know that he is straight and clean and good enough for her, I'll just have to stop him any way I can. First of all, I'm looking out for my sister, the h—l with anybody else. But on the other hand, if he makes good and wants her bad enough to rustle for two and she has her mind made up that she'd rather have him than stay single and is head over heels in love with him, I don't see that there's anything to worry about. I tell you that he is a good man, a real man, and if he changes like I want him to, she would be a d——d sight better off with him than with some dudish tenderfoot in love with money. He has had such a God-forsaken life that he will be able to appreciate a change like that-he would be square as a brick with her and attentive and loyal-and with him she wouldn't run much chance of being left a widow. Why, I'll bet he'll worship the ground she walks on-she could wind him all around her little finger and he'd never peep. And she would have the best protection that walks around these parts. But, pshaw, all this is too far ahead of the game. How about that herd of cattle you spoke of?"

"I can get you the whole herd dirt cheap," replied the foreman. "And they are as hungry and healthy a lot as you could wish."

"Well," responded the sheriff, "I've made up my mind to go ranching again. I can't stand this loafing, for it don't amount to much more than that now that The Orphan has graduated out of the outlaw class. I can run a ranch and have plenty of time to attend to the sheriff part of it, too. Ever since I sold the Three-S I have been like a fish out of water. When I got rid of it I put the money away in Kansas City, thinking that I might want to go back at it again. Then I got rid of that mine and bunked the money with the ranch money. The interest has been accumulating for a long time now and I have got something over thirty thousand lying idle. Now, I'm going to put it to work.

"I ran across Crawford last week, and he is dead anxious to sell out and go back East-he don't like the West. I've determined to take the A-Y off his hands, for it's a good ranch, has good buildings on it, two fine windmills over driven wells, good grass and shelters. Why, he has put up shelters in Long Valley that can't be duplicated under a thousand dollars. His terms are good-five thousand down and the balance in installments of two thousand a year at three per cent., and I can get *over* three per cent, while it is lying waiting to be paid to him. He is too blamed sick of his white elephant to haggle over terms. He was foolish to try to run it himself and to sink so much money in driven wells, windmills and buildings-it would astonish you to know how much money he spent in paint alone. What did he know about ranching, anyhow? He can't hardly tell a cow from a heifer. He said that he knew how to make money earn money in the East, but that he couldn't make a cent raising cows.

"If The Orphan attends to his new deal I'll put him in charge and the rest lies with him. I'll provide him with a good outfit, everything he needs and, if he makes good and the ranch pays, I'll fix it so he can own a half-interest in it at less than it cost me, and that will give him a good job to hold down for the rest of his life. It'll be something for him to tie to in case of squalls, but there ain't much danger of his becoming unsteady, because if he was at all inclined to that sort of thing he would be dead now.

"This ain't no fly-away notion, as you know. I've had an itching for a good ranch for several years, and for just about that length of time I've had my eyes on the A-Y. I was going to buy it when Crawford gobbled it up at that fancy price and I felt a little put out when he took up his option on it, but I'm glad he did, now. Why, Reeves sold out to Crawford for almost three times what I am going to pay for it, and it has been improved fifty per cent. since he has had it. But, of course, there was more cattle then than there is now. You get me that herd at a good figure and I'll be able to take care of them very soon now, just as soon as I close the deal. But, mind you, no Texas cattle goes-I don't want any Spanish fever in mine.

"I'm thinking some of putting Charley in charge temporarily, just as soon as Sneed gets some men, and when The Orphan takes it over things will be in purty fair shape. I won't move out there because my wife don't like ranching-she wants to be in town where she is near somebody, but I'll spend most of my time out there until everything gets in running order. Oh, yes-in consideration of the five thousand down at the time the papers are signed, Crawford has agreed to leave the ranch-house furnished practically as it is, and that will be nice for Helen and The Orphan if they ever should decide to join hands in double blessedness. You used to have a lot of fun about the high-faluting fixings in your ranch-house, but just wait 'til you see this one! An inside look around will open your eyes some, all right. It is a wonder, a real wonder! Running water from the windmills, a bath-room, sinks in the kitchen, a wood-burning boiler in the cellar, and all the comforts possible. If Crawford tries to move all that stuff back East it would cost him more than he could get for it, and he knows it, too. It's a bargain at twice the price, and I'm going to nail it. I can't think of anything else."

"Well," replied Blake, "I don't see how you could do anything better, that's sure. It all depends on the price, and if you're satisfied with that, there ain't no use of turning it down. I know you can make money out there with any kind of attention, for I'm purty well acquainted with the A-Y. And I'll see about the cattle next week, but you better leave The Orphan stay with me a while longer. My boys are the best crowd that ever lived in a bunk-house, and if he minds his business they'll smooth down his corners until you won't hardly know him; and they'll teach him a little about the cow-puncher game if he's rusty.

"You remember the time we had that killing out there, don't you?" Blake asked. "Well, you also remember that we agreed to cut out all gunplay on the ranch in the future, and that I sent East for some boxing gloves, which were to be used in case anybody wanted to settle any trouble. They have been out there for two years now, and haven't been used except in fun. Give the boys a chance and they'll cure him of the itching trigger-finger, all right. They're only a lot of big-hearted, overgrown kids, and they can get along with the devil himself if he'll let them. But they are hell-fire and brimstone when aroused," then he laughed softly: "They heard about your trouble with Sneed and they shore was dead anxious to call on the Cross Bar-8 and make a few remarks about long life and happiness, but I made them wait 'til they should be sent for.

"They know all about The Orphan-that is, as much as I did before I called to-night. Joe Haines is a great listener and when he rustles our mail once a week he takes it all in, so of course they know all about it. They had a lot of fun about the way he made the Cross Bar-8 sit up and take notice, for they ain't wasting any love on Sneed's crowd. And it took Bill Howland over an hour to tell Joe about his experiences. So when The Orphan met the outfit they knew him to be the man who had saved the sheriff's sisters, which went a long way with them. Say, Jim," he exclaimed, "can I tell them what you said about him to-night? Let me tell them everything, for it'll go far with them, especially with Silent, who had some trouble with the U-B about five years ago. He was taking a herd of about three thousand head across their range and he swears yet at the treatment he got. Yes? All right, it'll make him solid with the outfit."

"Tell them anything you want about him," said the sheriff, "but don't say anything about the A-Y. I want to keep it quiet for a while."

Shields poured himself a cup of coffee and then glanced at the clock: "Too late for a game, Tom?" he asked, expectantly.

The foreman laughed: "It's seldom too late for that," he replied.

"Good enough!" cried his host. "What shall it be this time-pinochle or crib?"

The foreman slowly closed his eyes as he replied: "Either suits me-this feed has made me plumb easy to please. Why, I'd even play casino to-night!"

"Well, what do you say to crib?" asked the sheriff. "You licked me so bad at it the last time you were here that I hanker to get revenge."

"Well, I don't blame you for wanting to get it, but I'll tell you right now that you won't, for I can lick the man that invented crib to-night," laughed the foreman. "Bring out your cards."

Shields placed the cards on the table and arranged things where they would be handy while his friend shuffled the pack.

The foreman pushed the cards toward his host: "There you are-low deals as usual, I suppose."

"Oh, you might as well go ahead and deal," grumbled the sheriff good-naturedly. "I don't remember ever cutting low enough for you-by George! A five!"

Blake picked up the cards and started to deal, but the sheriff stopped him.

"Hey! You haven't cut yet!" Shields cried, putting his hand on the cards. "What are you doing, anyhow?"

Blake laughed with delight: "Well, anybody that can't cut lower than a five hadn't ought to play the game. What's the use of wasting time?"

"Well, you never mind about the time-you go ahead and beat me," cried the sheriff. "Of all the nerve!"

Blake picked up the cards again: "Do you want to cut again?" he asked.

"Not a bit of it! That five stands!"

"Well, how would a four do?" asked the foreman, lifting his hand. "It's a three!" he exulted. "All that time wasted," he said.

"You go to blazes," pleasantly replied the sheriff as he sorted his hand. "This ain't so bad for you, not at all bad; you could have done worse, but I doubt it." He discarded, cut, and Blake turned a six.

"Seven," called Shields as he played.

"Seventeen," replied Blake, playing a queen.

"No you don't, either," grinned the sheriff. "You can play that four later if you want to, but not now on twenty-seven. Call it twenty-five," he said, playing an eight.

Blake carefully scanned his hand and finally played the four, grumbling a little as his friend laughed.

"Thirty-one-first blood," remarked the sheriff, dropping the deuce.

While he pegged his points Blake suddenly laughed.

"Say, Jim," he said, "before I forget it I want to tell you a joke on Humble. He thought it would be easy money if he taught Lee Lung how to play poker. He bothered Lee's life out of him for several days, and finally the Chinaman consented to learn the great American game."

Blake played a six and the sheriff scored two by pairing, whereupon his opponent made it threes for six, and took a point for the last card.

"As I was saying, Humble wanted the cook to learn poker. Lee's face was as blank as a cow's, and Humble had to explain everything several times before the cook seemed to understand what he was driving at. Anybody would have thought he had been brought up in a monastery and that he didn't know a card from an army mule."

Blake pegged his seven points and picked up his cards without breaking the story.

"But Lee had awful luck, and in half an hour he owned half of Humble's next month's pay. Now, every time he gets a chance he shows Humble the cards and asks for a game. 'Nicee game, ploker, nicee game,' he'll say. What Humble says is pertinent, profane and permeating. Then the boys guy him to a finish. He'll be wanting to teach Lee how to play fan-tan some day, so the boys say. Lee must have graduated in poker before Humble ever heard of the game."

Shields laughed heartily and swiftly ran over his cards.

"Fifteen two, four, six, a pair is eight, and a double run of three is fourteen. Real good," he said as he pegged. "Passed the crack that time. What have you got?"

The foreman put his cards down, found three sixes and then turned the crib face up. "Pair of tens and His Highness," he grumbled. "Only three in that crib!"

"That's what you get for cutting a three," laughed the sheriff.

The game continued until the striking of the clock startled the guest.

"Midnight!" he cried. "Thirty miles before I get to bed-no, no, I can't stay with you to-night—much obliged, all the same."

He clapped his sombrero on his head and started for the door: "Well, better luck next time, Jim-three twenty-four hands shore did make a difference. Right where they were needed, too. So long."

"Sorry you won't stay, Tom," called his friend from the door as the foreman mounted. "You might just as well, you know."

"I'm sorry, too, but I've got to be on hand to-morrow—anyway, it's bright moonlight-so long!" he cried as he cantered away.

"Hey, Tom!" cried the sheriff, leaping from the porch and running to the gate. "Tom!"

"Hullo, what is it?" asked the foreman, drawing rein and returning.

"Smoke this on your way, it'll seem shorter," said the sheriff, holding out a cigar.

"By George, I will!" laughed Blake. "That's fine, you're all right!"

"Be good," cried the sheriff, watching his friend ride down the street.

"Shore enough good–I have to be," floated back to his ears.

Chapter XVI
The Flying-Mare

The Sunday morning following Blake's visit to Ford's Station found the Star C in excitement. Notwithstanding the fact that on every pleasant night after the day's work had been done it was the custom for the outfit to indulge in a swim, and that Saturday night had been very pleasant, the Limping Water was being violently disturbed, and laughter and splashing greeted the sun as it looked over the rim of the bank. Cakes of soap glistened on the sand on the west bank and towels hung from convenient limbs of the bushes which fringed the creek.

Silent, who was noted among his companions for the length of time he could stay under water, challenged them to a submersion test. The rules were simple, inasmuch as they consisted in all plunging under at the same time, the winner being he who was the last man up. Silent had steadfastly refused to have his endurance timed, which his friends mistook for modesty, and no sooner had all "ducked under" than his head popped up-but this time he was not alone. Humble, whose utmost limit was not over half a minute, grew angry at his inability to make a good showing and craftily determined to take a handicap. The two stared at each other for a space and then burst into laughter, forgetting for the time being what they should do. Other heads bobbed up, and the secret was out. Only that Silent was the best swimmer in the crowd saved him from a ducking, and as it was he had to grab his clothes and run.

After being assured that he was forgiven for his trickery he rejoined his friends and his towel.

More fun was now the rule, for dressing required care. The sandy west bank sloped gradually to the water's edge, and it was necessary to stand on one foot on a small stone in the water while the other was dipped to remove the sand. Still on one foot the other must be dried, the stocking put on, then the trouser leg and lastly the boot, and woe to the man who lost his balance and splashed stocking and trouser leg as he wildly sought to save it! Humble splashed while his foot was only half-way through the trouser leg, and The Orphan fared even worse. Then a race of awkward runners was on toward the bunk house, where breakfast was annihilated.

"Hey, Tom, what time do we leave?" asked Bud for the fifth time.

"Nine o'clock, you chump," replied the foreman.

"Three whole hours yet," grumbled Jim as he again plastered his hair to his head.

"I'll lose my appetite shore," worried Humble. "We got up too blamed early, that's what we did."

"Why, here's Humble!" cried Silent in mock surprise. "Do *you* like apricot pie, and gingerbread and *real* coffee?"

"You go to the devil," grumbled Humble. "You wouldn't 'a' been asked at all, only she couldn't very well cut you out of it when she asked me along. *I'm* the one she really wants to feed; you fellers just happen to tag on behind, that's all."

"Going to take Lightning with you, Humble?" asked Docile, winking at the others.

"Why, I shore am," replied Humble in surprise. "Do you reckon I'd leave him and that d——d Chink all alone together, you sheep?"

"I was afraid you wouldn't," pessimistically grumbled Docile, but here he smiled hopefully. "Suppose you take Lee Lung and leave the dog here?" he queried.

"Suppose you quit supposing with your feet!" sarcastically countered Humble. "I know you ain't got much brains, but you might exercise what little you have got once in a while. It won't hurt you none after you get used to it."

"How are you going to carry him, Humble-like a papoose?" queried Joe with a great show of interest.

Humble stared at him: "Huh!" he muttered, being too much astonished to say more.

"I asked you how you are going to carry your fighting wolfhound," Joe said without the quiver of an eyelash. "I thought mebby you was going to sling him on your back like a papoose."

"Carry him! Papoose!" ejaculated Humble in withering irony. "What do you reckon his legs are for? He ain't no statue, he ain't no ornament, he's a dog."

"Well, I knowed he ain't no ornament, but I wasn't shore about the rest of it," responded Joe. "I only wanted to know how he'd get to town. There ain't no crime in asking about that, is there? I know he can't follow the gait we'll hit up for thirty miles, so I just naturally asked, *sabe?*"

"Oh, you did, did you!" cried Humble, not at all humbly. "He can't follow us, can't he?" he yelled belligerently.

"He shore can't, cross my heart," asserted Silent in great earnestness. "If he runs to Ford's Station after us and gets there inside of two days I'll buy him a collar. That goes."

"Huh!" snorted Humble in disgust, "he won't wear your old collar after he wins it. He's got too much pride to wear anything you'll give him."

"He couldn't, you mean," jabbed Jim. "He's so plumb tender that it would strain his back to carry it. Why, he has to sit down and rest if more'n two flies get on the same spot at once."

"He can't wag his tail more'n three times in an hour," added Bud, "and when he scratches hisself he has to rest for the remainder of the day."

Humble turned to The Orphan in an appealing way: "Did you ever see so many d——d fools all at once?" he beseeched.

The Orphan placed his finger to his chin and thought for fully half a minute before replying: "I was just figuring," he explained in apology for his abstraction. Then his face brightened: "You can tie him up in a blanket-that's the best way. Yes, sir, tie him up in a blanket and sling him at the pommel. We'll take turns carrying him."

"Purple h–l!" yelled Humble. "You're another! The whole crowd are a lot of ——-!"

"Sing it, Humble," suggested Tad, laughing. "Sing it!"

"Whistle some of it, and send the rest by mail," assisted Jack Lawson.

"Seen th' dlog?" came a bland, monotonous voice from the doorway, where Lee Lung stood holding a chunk of beef in one hand, while his other hand was hidden behind his back. Over his left shoulder projected half a foot of club, which he thought concealed. "Seen th' dlog?" he repeated, smiling.

"Miss Mirandy and holy hell!" shouted Humble, leaping forward at sight of the club. There was a swish! and Humble rebounded from the door, at which he stared. From the rear of the house came more monotonous words: "Nice dlog-gie. Pletty Lightling. Here come. Gette glub," and Humble galloped around the corner of the house, swearing at every jump.

When the laughter had died down Blake smiled grimly: "Some day Lee *will* get that dog, and when he does he'll get him good and hard. Then we'll have to get another cook. I've told him fifty times if I've told him once not to let it go past a joke, but it's no use."

"He won't hurt the cur, he's only stringing Humble," said Bud. "Nobody would hurt a dog that minded his own business."

"If anybody hit a dog of mine for no cause, he wouldn't do it again unless he got me first," quietly remarked The Orphan.

Jim hastily pointed to the corner of the house where a club projected into sight: "There's Lee now!" he whispered hurriedly. "He's laying for him!"

There was a sudden spurt of flame and smoke and the club flew several yards, struck by three bullets. Humble hopped around the corner holding his hand, his words too profane for repetition.

Smoke filtered from The Orphan's holster and eyes opened wide in surprise at the wonderful quickness of his gunplay, for no one had seen it. All there was was smoke.

"Good God!" breathed Blake, staring at the marksman, who had stepped forward and was explaining to Humble. "It's a good thing Shields was square!" he muttered.

"Did you see that?" asked Bud of Jim in whispered awe. "And I thought *I* was some beans with a six-shooter!"

"No, but I heard it-was they one or six?" replied Jim.

"I didn't know it was you, Humble," explained The Orphan. "I thought it was the Chink laying for the dog."

"——- ——-! Good for you!" cried Humble in sudden friendliness. "You're all right, Orphant, but will you be sure next time? That stung like blazes," he said as he held out his hand. "I can always tell a white man by the way he treats a dog. If all men were as good as dogs this world would be a blamed sight nicer place to live in, and don't you forget it."

"Still going to take Lightning with you, Humble?" asked Bud.

"No, I ain't going to take Lightning with me!" snapped Humble. "I'm going to leave him right here on the ranch," here his voice arose to a roar, "and if any sing-song, rope-haired, animated hash-wrastler gets gay while I'm gone, I'll send him to his heathen hell!"

"Come on, boys," said Blake, snapping his watch shut. "Time to get going."

"Glory be!" exulted Silent, executing a few fancy steps toward the corral, his companions close behind, with the exception of The Orphan, who had gone into the bunk house for a minute.

As they whooped their way toward the town Blake noticed that a gold pin glittered at the knot of the new recruit's neck-kerchief, and he chuckled when he recalled the warning he had given to the sheriff. He shrewdly guessed that the apricot pie and the rest of the feast were quite subordinated by The Orphan to the girl who had given him the pin.

Bud suddenly turned in his saddle and pointed to a jackrabbit which bounded away across the plain like an animated shadow.

"Now, if Humble's bloodhound was only here," he said, "we would rope that jack and make the cur fight it. It would be a fine fight, all right," he laughed.

"You go to the devil," grunted Humble, and he started ahead at full speed. "Come on!" he cried. "Come on, you snails!" and a race was on.

.....

The citizens of Ford's Station saw a low-hanging cloud of dust which rolled rapidly up from the west and soon a hard-riding crowd of cowboys, in gala attire, galloped down the main street of the town. They slowed to a canter and rode abreast in a single line, the arms of each man over the shoulders of his nearest companions, and all sang at the top of their lungs. On the right end rode Blake, and on the left was The Orphan. Bill Howland ran out into the street and spotted his new friend immediately and swung his hat and cheered for the man who had helped him out of two bad holes. The Orphan broke from the line and shook hands with the driver, his face wreathed by a grin.

"You old son-of-a-gun!" cried Bill, delighted at the familiarity from so noted a person as the former outlaw. "How are you, hey?"

The line cried warm greeting as it swung around to shake his hand, and the driver's chest took on several inches of girth.

"Hullo, Bill!" cried Bud with a laugh. "Seen your old friend Tex lately?"

"Yes, I did," replied Bill. "I saw him out on Thirty-Mile Stretch, but he didn't do nothing but swear. He didn't want no more run-ins with me, all right, and, besides, my rifle was across my knees. He said as how he was going to come back some day and start things moving about this old town, and I told him to begin with the Star C when he did."

He looked across the street and waved his hand at a group of his friends who were looking on. "Come on over, fellows," he cried, and when they had done so he turned and introduced The Orphan to them.

"This ugly cuss here is Charley Winter; this slab-sided curiosity is Tommy Larkin, and here is his brother Al; Chet Dare, Duke Irwin, Frank Hicks, Hoke Jones, Gus Shaw and Roy Purvis. All good fellows, every one of them, and all friends of the sheriff. Here comes Jed Carr, the only man in the whole town who ain't afraid of me since I licked them punchers in the defile. Hullo, Jed! Shake hands with the man who played h—l with the Cross Bar-8 and the Apaches."

"Glad to meet you, Orphan," remarked Jed as he shook hands. "Punching for the Star C, eh? Good crowd, most of them, as they run, though Humble ain't very much."

"He ain't, ain't he?" grinned that puncher. "You're some sore about that day when I cleaned up all your cush at poker, ain't you? Ain't had time to get over it, have you? Want to borrow some?"

"You want to look out for Humble, Jed," bantered Bud. "He's taken a lesson at poker from our cook since he played you. Didn't you, Easy?" he asked Humble.

The roar of laughter which followed Bud's words forced Humble to stand treat: "Come on over and have something with the only man in the crowd that's got any money," he said.

When they had lined up against the bar jokes began to fly thick and fast and The Orphan felt a peculiar elation steal over him as he slowly puffed at his cigar. Suddenly the door flew open and Bill's glass dropped from his hand.

"Bucknell, by God! And as drunk as a fool!" he exclaimed.

The puncher whom The Orphan had tied up above the defile leaned against the door frame and his gun wavered from point to point unsteadily as he tried to peer into the dim interior of the room, his face leering as he sought, with a courage born of drink, for the man who had made a fool of him.

A bottle crashed against the wall at his side, and as he lurched forward, glancing at the broken glass, a figure leaped to meet him and with agile strength grasped his right wrist, wheeled and got his shoulder under Bucknell's armpit, took two short steps and straightened up with a jerk. The intruder left the floor and flew headforemost through the air, crashing against the rear wall, where he fell to the floor and lay quiet. The Orphan, having foresworn unnecessary gunplay, and always scorning to shoot a drunken man, had executed a clever, quick flying-mare.

As the sheriff stepped into the room Blake ran forward and lifted Bucknell to his feet, supporting him until he could stand alone. The puncher was greatly sobered by the shock and blinked confusedly about him. The Orphan was smoking nonchalantly at the bar and Bill had just given the sheriff the victim's gun.

"What's the matter?" asked Bucknell, rubbing his forehead, which was cut and bruised.

"Nothing's the matter, yet," answered Shields shortly. "But there would have been if you hadn't been too drunk to know what you was doing. I saw you and tried to get here first, but it's all right now. Take your gun and get out. Here," he exclaimed, "you promise me to behave yourself and you can go back to Sneed, for he needs you. Otherwise, it's out of the country after Tex for you. Is it a go?"

"What was that, and who done it?" asked Bucknell, clinging to the bar. "What was it?" he repeated.

"That was me trying to throw you through the wall," said the sheriff, wishing to give Bucknell no greater cause for animosity against The Orphan, and for the peace of the community; and also because he wished to help The Orphan to refrain from using his gun in the future. "And I'd 'a' done it, too, only my hand was sweaty. Will you do what I said?" he asked.

Bucknell straightened up and staggered past the sheriff to where The Orphan stood: "You done that, but it's all right, ain't it?" he asked. "You ain't sore, are you?" His eyes had a crafty look, but the dimness of the room concealed it, and The Orphan did not notice the look.

"It's all right, Bucknell, and I ain't sore," he replied. "I won't be sore if you do what the sheriff wants you to."

"All right, all right," replied Bucknell. "Have a drink on me, boys. It's all right now, ain't it? Have a drink on me."

"No more drinking to-day," quickly said the bartender at a look from Shields. "All the good stuff is used up and the rest ain't fit for dogs, let alone my friends. Wait 'til next time, when I'll have some new."

"That's too d——d bad," replied Bucknell, leering at the crowd. "Have a smoke, then. Come on, have a smoke with me."

"We shore will, Bucknell," responded Shields quickly.

As the cowboy started for the door the sheriff placed a hand on his shoulder: "You behave yourself, Bucknell," he said. "So long."

Chapter XVII
The Feast

Joyous whoops, loud and heartfelt, brought the women to the door of the sheriff's house in time to see their guests dismount. A perfect babel of words greeted their appearance as the cowboys burst into a running fire of jokes, salutations and comments. Even the ponies seemed to know that something important and unusual was taking place, for they cavorted and bit and squealed to prove that they were in accord with the spirit of their riders and that thirty miles in less than three hours had not subdued them. Bright colors prevailed, for the neck-kerchiefs in most cases were new and yet showed the original folding creases, while new, clean thongs of rawhide and glittering bits of metal flashed back the sunlight. Spurs glittered and the clean looking horses appeared to have had a dip in the Limping Water. Blake had hunted through the carpeted rooms of his ranch-house for decorations, and in the drawer of a table he had found a bunch of ribbons of many kinds and shades. These now fluttered from the pommels of the saddles and in one case a red ribbon was twined about the leg of a vicious pinto, and the pinto was not at all pleased by the decoration.

The sheriff led the way to the house closely followed by Blake, the others coming in the order of their nerve. The Orphan was last, not from lack of courage, but rather because of strategy. He thought that Helen would remain at the door to welcome each arrival and if he was in the van he would be passed on to make way for those behind him. Being the last man he hoped to be able to say more to her than a few words of greeting. As he mounted the steps she was drawn into the room for something and he stepped to one side on the porch, well knowing that she would miss him.

Bud poked his head out the door and started to say something, but The Orphan fiercely whispered for him to be silent and to disappear, which Bud did after grinning exasperatingly.

The man on the porch was growing impatient when he heard the light swish of skirts around the corner of the house. Sauntering carelessly to the corner he looked into the back-yard and saw Helen with a tray in her hands, nearing the back door. She espied him and stopped, flushing suddenly as he leaped lightly to the ground and walked rapidly toward her. Her cheeks became a deeper red when he stopped before her and took the tray, for his eyes were rebellious and would not be subdued, and the first thing she saw was the gold pin which stood out boldly against the dark blue neck-kerchief. She was rarely beautiful in her white dress, and the ribbon which she wore at her throat did not detract in its effect. Later her sister was to wonder if it was a coincidence that the ribbon and his neck-kerchief were so good a match in color.

She welcomed him graciously and he felt a sudden new and strangely exhilarating sensation steal over him as he took the hand she held out, the tray all the while bobbing recklessly in his other hand.

"Why aren't you in the house paying your respects to your hostess?" she chided half in jest and half in earnest.

"The delay will but add to my fervor when I do," he replied, "for I will have had a stimulus then. As long as the hostesses are four and insist on not being together, how can I pay my respects all at once?"

"But there is only one hostess," she laughingly corrected. "I am afraid you are not very good at making excuses. You probably never felt the need to make them before. You see, I, too, am only a guest."

"We two," he corrected daringly.

"I am very glad to see you," she said, leading away from plurals. "You are looking very well and much more contented. And then, this is ever so much nicer than our first meeting, isn't it? No horrid Apaches."

"I've gotten so that I rather like Apaches," he replied. "They are so useful at times. But you mustn't try to tempt me to subordinate that eventful day, not yet. It can't be done, although I've never tried to do it," he hastily assured her, making a gesture of helplessness. "Sometimes an unexpected incident will change the habits of a lifetime, making the days seem brighter, and yet, somehow, adding a touch of sadness. I have been a stranger to myself since then, restless, absentminded, moody and hungry for I know not what." He paused and then slowly continued, "I must beg to remain loyal to that day of all days when you bathed an outlaw's head and showed your love for fair play and kindness."

"Goodness!" she cried, for one instant meeting his eager eyes. "Why, I thought it was a terrible day! And you really think differently?"

"Very much so," he assured her as she withdrew her hand from his. "You see, it was such a new and delightful experience to save a stage coach and then find that it was a hospital with a wonderful doctor. I accused that Apache of being stingy with his lead, for he might just as well have given me a few more wounds to have dressed."

"Yes," she laughingly retorted, "it was almost as new an experience as starting on a long and supposedly peaceful journey and suddenly finding oneself in the middle of a desert surrounded by dead Indians and doctoring an Indian killer who was at war with one's brother. And that after a terrible shaking up lasting for over an hour. Truly it is a day to be remembered. Now, don't you think you should hurry in and greet my sister-in-law?"

"Yes, certainly," he quickly responded. "But before I lose the opportunity I must ask you if you will care if I ride over and see you occasionally, because it is terribly lonely on that ranch."

"You know that we shall always be glad to see you whenever you can call," she replied, smiling up at him. "We are all very deep in your debt and brother and all of us think a great deal of you. Are you satisfied on the Star C, and do you like your work and your companions?"

"Thank you," he cried happily, "I will ride over and see you once in a while. But as for my work, it is delightful! The Star C is fine and my companions-well, they just simply can't be beat! they are the finest, whitest set of men that ever gathered under one roof."

"That's very nice, I am glad that you find things so congenial," she replied in sincerity. "James was sure that you would, for Mr. Blake is an old friend of his."

"I'm very anxious about this pin," he said, putting his hand on it. "May I keep it for a while longer?" he asked with a note of appeal in his voice.

"Why, yes," she replied, "if you wish to. But only as long as you do not displease me, and you will not do that, will you? James has such deep confidence in you that I know you will not disappoint him. You will justify him in his own mind and in the minds of his acquaintances and prove that he has not erred in judgment, won't you?"

"If I am the sum total of your brother's trouble, he will have a path of roses to wander through all the rest of his life," he responded earnestly. "And I'm really afraid that you will never again wear this pin as a possession of yours. Of course you can borrow it occasionally," and he smiled whimsically, "but as far as displeasing you is concerned, it is mine forever. It will really and truly be mine on that condition, won't it? My very own if I do not forfeit it?"

"If you wish it so," she replied quickly, her face radiant with smiles. "And you will work hard and you will never shoot a man, no matter what the provocation may be, unless it is absolutely necessary to do it for the saving of your own life or that of a friend or an innocent man. Promise me that!" she commanded imperatively, pleased at being able to dictate to him. "Men like you never break a promise," she added impulsively.

"I promise never to shoot a man, woman, child or-or anybody," he laughingly replied, "unless it is necessary to save life. And I'll work real hard and save my money. And on Sundays, rain or shine, I'll ride in and report to my new foreman." Then a bit of his old humor came to him: "For I just about need this pin-knots are so clumsy, you know."

She glanced at the knot which held the pin and laughed merrily, leading the way into the house.

As they entered Humble was extolling the virtues of his dog, to the broad grins of his companions, who constantly added amendments and made corrections *sotto voce.*

"Why, here they are!" cried the sheriff in such a tone as to suffuse Helen's face with blushes. The Orphan coolly shook hands with him.

"Yes, here we are, Sheriff, every one of us," he replied. "We couldn't be expected to stay away when Mrs. Shields put herself to so much trouble, and we're all happy and proud to be so honored. How do you do, Mrs. Shields," he continued as he took her hand. "It is awful kind of you to go to such trouble for a lot of lonely, hungry fellows like us."

"Goodness sakes!" she cried, delighted at his words and pleased at the way he had parried her husband's teasing thrust. "Why, it was no trouble at all-you are all my boys now, you know."

"Thank you, Mrs. Shields," he replied slowly. "We will do our very best to prove ourselves worthy of being called your boys."

The sheriff regarded The Orphan with a look of approbation and turned to his sister Helen.

"He ain't nobody's fool, eh, Sis?" he whispered. "I'm wondering how you ever made up your mind to share him with us!"

"Oh, please don't!" she begged in confusion. "Please don't tease me now!"

"All right, Sis," he replied in a whisper, pinching her ear. "I'll save it all up for some other time, some time when he ain't around to turn it off, eh? But I don't blame him a bit for exploring the yard first-you're the prettiest girl this side of sun-up," he said, beaming with love and pride. "How's that for a change, eh? Worth a kiss?"

She kissed him hurriedly and then left the room to attend to her duties in the kitchen, and he sauntered over to where The Orphan was talking with Mrs. Shields, his hand rubbing his lips and a mischievous twinkle in his kind eyes.

"Did you notice the new flower-bed right by the side of the house as you ran past it a while ago?" he asked, flashing a keen warning to his wife.

The Orphan searched his memory for the flower-bed and not finding it, turned and smiled, not willing to admit that his attention had been too fully taken up with a fairer flower than ever grew in earth.

"Why, yes, it is real pretty," he replied. "What about it?"

"Oh, nothing much," gravely replied the sheriff as he edged away. "Only we were thinking of putting a flower-bed there, although I haven't had time to get at it yet."

The Orphan flushed and glanced quickly at the outfit, who were too busy cracking jokes and laughing to pay any attention to the conversation across the room.

"James!" cried Mrs. Shields. "Aren't you ashamed of yourself!"

"When you tickle a mule," said the sheriff, grinning at his friend, "you want to look out for the kick. Come again sometime, Sonny."

"James!" his wife repeated, "how can you be so mean! Now, stop teasing and behave yourself!"

"For a long time I've been puzzled about what you resembled, but now I have your words for it," easily countered The Orphan. "Thank you for putting me straight."

The sheriff grinned sheepishly and scratched his head: "I'm an old fool," he grumbled, and forthwith departed to tell Helen of the fencing.

Mrs. Shields excused herself and followed her husband into the kitchen to look after the dinner, and The Orphan sauntered over to his outfit just as Jim looked out of a rear window. Jim turned quickly, his face wearing a grin from ear to ear.

"Hey, Bud!" he called eagerly. "Bud!"

"What?" asked Bud, turning at the hail.

"Come over here for a minute, I want to show you something," Jim replied, "but don't let Humble come."

Bud obeyed and looked: "Jimminee!" he exulted. "Don't that look sumptious, though? This is where we shine, all right." Then turned: "Hey, fellows, come over here and take a look."

As they crowded around the window Humble discovered that something was in the wind and he followed them. What they saw was a long table beneath two trees, and it was covered with a white cloth and dressed for a feast. Bud turned quickly from the crowd and forcibly led Humble to a side window before that unfortunate had seen anything and told him to put his finger against the glass, which Humble finally did after an argument.

"Feel the pain?" Bud asked.

"Why, no," Humble replied, looking critically at his finger. "What's the matter with you, anyhow?"

"Nothing," replied Bud. "Think it over, Humble," he advised, turning away.

Humble again put his finger to the glass and then snorted:

"Locoed chump! Prosperity is making him nutty!" When he turned he saw his friends laughing silently at him and making grimaces, and a light suddenly broke in upon him.

"Yes, I did!" he cried. "That joke is so old I plumb forgot it years ago! Spring something that hasn't got whiskers and a halting step, will you?"

Jim laughed and suggested a dance, but was promptly squelched.

"You heathen!" snorted Blake in mock horror. "This is Sunday! If you want to dance wait till you get back to the ranch-suppose one of the women was here and heard you say that!"

"Gee, I forgot all about it being Sunday," replied Jim, quickly looking to see if any of the women were in the room. "We're regular barbarians, ain't we!" he exclaimed in self-condemnation and relief when he saw that no women were present. "We're regular land pirates, ain't we?"

"You'll be asking to play poker yet, or have a race," jabbed Humble with malice. "You ain't got no sense and never did have any."

"Huh!" retorted Jim belligerently, "I won't try to learn a Chinee cook how to play poker and get skinned out of my pay, anyhow! Got enough?" he asked, "or shall I tell of the time you drifted into Sagetown and asked——"

"Shut up, you fool!" whispered Humble ferociously. "Yu'll get skun if you say too much!"

"'Skun' is real good," retorted Jim. "Got any more of them new words to spring on us?"

Helen had been passing to and fro past the window and Docile Thomas here put his marveling into words, for he had been casting covert glances at her, but now his restraint broke.

"Gee whiz!" he exclaimed in a whisper to Jack Lawson. "Ain't she a regular hummer, now! Lines like a thoroughbred, face like a dream and a smile what shore is a winner! See her hair-fine and dandy, eh? She's in the two-forty class, all right!" he enthused. "Why, when this country wakes up to what's in it the sheriff will have to put up a stockade around this house and mount guard. Everybody from Bill up will be stampeding this way to talk business with the sheriff. No wonder The Orphan has got a bee in his bonnet-lucky dog!"

"She can take care of my pay every month just as soon as she says the word," Jack replied. "But suppose you look away once in a while? Suppose you shift your sights! You, too, Humble," he said, suddenly turning on the latter.

"Me what?" asked Humble, without interest and without shifting his gaze. "What are you talking about?"

"Look at something else, see?"

"Shore I see," replied Humble. "That's why I'm looking. Do you think I look with my eyes shut! Gee, but ain't she a picture, though!"

"She shore is, but give it a rest, take a vacation, you chump!" retorted Jack. "You're staring at her like she had you hoodooed. Come out of your trance-wake up and make a fool of yourself some other way. Don't aim all the time at her. Mebby Lee Lung has killed your dog!"

"If he has we'll need a new cook," replied Humble with decision.

"Come on, boys! Don't start milling!" cried the sheriff, suddenly entering the room. "Dinner's all ready and waiting for us. And I shore hope you have all got your best appetites with you, because Margaret likes to see her food taken care of lively. If you don't clean it all up she'll think you don't like it," he said, winking at Blake, "and if she once gets that notion in her head it will be no more invitations for the Star C."

There was much excitement in the crowd, and the replies came fast.

"I ain't had anything good to eat for fifteen long, aching years!" cried Bud. "When I get through you'll need a new table.

"Same here, only for thirty years," replied Jim hastily. "I just couldn't sleep last night for thinking about the glorious surprise my abused stomach was due to have to-day. I'll bet my gun on my performance if the track is heavy, all right. I'm not poor on speed, and I'm a stayer from Stayersville."

"Well, I won't be among the also rans, you can bet on that," laughed Silent. "I don't weigh very much, but I'm geared high."

"I'll bet it's good!" cried Humble, "I'll bet it's real good!"

"D——n good, you mean!" corrected Jack. "Hey, fellows!" he cried, "did you hear what Humble said? He said that he'd bet it was *real* good!"

"Horray for Humble, the wit of the Star C," laughed Docile.

"Me for the apricot pie!" exulted Charley. "Here's where I get square on Blake for rubbing it in all these months about the fine pie he gets over here."

"There ain't no apricot pie," gravely lied the sheriff in surprise.

"What!" cried Charley in alarm. "There ain't none for me! Oh, well, you can't lose me in daylight, for I'll double up on everything else. I ain't going to get left, all right!"

"Don't wake me up," begged Joe Haines. "Let me dream on in peace and plenty. Grub, real, genuine grub, grub what is grub! Oh, joy!"

Mrs. Shields hurried into the room and then paused in surprise when she saw that the outfit had not moved toward the feast.

"Land sakes!" she cried. "Aren't you boys hungry, or is James up to some of his everlasting teasing again!"

"You talk to her, Bud," whispered Jim eagerly. "I'm so scary I shore can't."

"Yes, go ahead, Bud!" came instant and unanimous endorsement in whispers.

"Well, ma'am," began Bud, clearing his throat, glancing around uneasily to be sure that the crowd was giving him moral backing, and feeling uncomfortable, "we was just getting up a—a——"

"B, C, D," prompted Jim in a whisper.

"We was just getting up a resolution of thanks, Mrs. Shields," he continued, stabbing his elbow into the stomach of the offending Jim. "You shut up!" he fiercely whispered. "I'm carrying one hundred and forty pounds now without the saddle!" Then he continued: "We all of us are plumb tickled about this, so plumb tickled we don't hardly know what to say——"

"That's right," whispered Jim, folding his arms across his stomach. "You're proving it, all right."

Silent and Jack hauled Jim to the rear and Bud continued unruffled: "But we want to thank you, ma'am, from the bottoms, the very lowest bottoms of our hearts for your kindness to a orphant outfit what ain't had anything to eat since the war, and very little during it. Joe Haines, here, ma'am, was just saying as how he was a-scared that it is all a dream——"

"I didn't neither!" fiercely contradicted Joe in a whisper, looking very self-conscious. He was whisked to the rear to join Jim and the speech went on.

"He is afraid it is a dream, ma'am, and I know we all of us have more or less doubts about it being really true. But, ma'am, we shore are anxious to find out all about it. We've rid thirty miles to see for ourselves, and I don't reckon you'll have any fears about our appetites being left at home when you sizes up the wreck left in the path of the storm after the stampede is over. The boys want to give you three cheers even if it is Sunday, ma'am, for your kindness to them, and I'm shore one of the boys!"

"Hip, hip, horray!" yelled the crowd, surging forward.

"Good boy, Bud!" they cried.

"I'm proud of you, Buddie!" exulted Charley, slapping him extra heartily on the back.

"I didn't know you had it in you, Bud!" cried Silent. "It was shore a dandy speech, all right."

"We'll send you to Congress for that, some day, Bud," cried Jack Lawson. "You're all right!"

"I once had a piece of pie, a piece of pie, a piece of pie,
I once had a piece of pie, when I was five years old,"

sang Charley as he pranced toward the door.

"Good! Go on, Charley, go on!" cried his companions joyously.

"Now I'll have another piece, another piece, another piece,
Now I'll have another piece, that's two all told.
Good bye, Lee Lung, good bye Lee Lung,
Good bye, Lee Lung, we're going to forget you now!"

"Again on that Lee Lung, altogether-it hits me right!" cried Bud, and the matter pertaining to the farewells to Lee Lung was promptly and properly attended to in heartfelt sincerity.

The ladies laughed with delight, and Mrs. Shields whispered to her husband, who nodded and escorted The Orphan to a seat near the head of the table, where he was flanked by Helen and Blake.

"Grab your partners, boys," the sheriff cried, pointing to the chairs. There was a hasty piling of belts and guns on the ground, and after much confusion all were seated.

The sheriff arose: "Boys, Mrs. Shields wants me to tell you how pleased she is to have you all here. She has felt plumb sorry about you and she shore has shuddered at the thought of a Chinee cook——"

"Which same we all do-it's chronic," interposed Jim to laughter.

"She wants you to make yourselves at home," continued the sheriff, "learn the lay of the land around this range and never forget the trail leading here, because she insists that when any of you come to town you have simply got to pay us a visit and see if there is a piece of pie or cake to eat before you go back to that cook. And Tom says that he'll fire the first man who renigs——"

"I'm going to carry the mail hereafter!" cried Bud, scowling fiercely at Joe.

"Not if I can shoot first, you don't!" retorted the mail carrier. "I was just a-wondering if it wouldn't be better to come in twice a week for it instead of once. We might get more letters."

"We'll bid for your job next year," laughed Silent.

"Before I coax you to eat," continued the sheriff, "I——"

"Wrong word, Sheriff," interposed Humble. "Not coax, but force."

"I am going to ask you to reverse things a little, and drink a standing toast to the man who saved the stage, to the man who saved Miss Ritchie and my sisters and who made this dinner possible. This would be far from a happy day but for him. I want you to drink to the long life and happiness of The Orphan. All up!"

The clink of glasses was lost in the spontaneous cheer which burst from the lips of the former outlaw's new friends, and he sat confused and embarrassed with a sudden timidity, his face crimson.

"Speech!" cried Jim, the others joining in the cry. "Speech! Speech!"

Finally, after some urging, The Orphan slowly arose to his feet, a foolish smile playing about his lips.

"It wasn't anything," he said deprecatingly. "You all would have done it, every one of you. But I'm glad it was me. I'm glad I was on hand, although it wasn't anything to make all this fuss about," and he dropped suddenly into his seat, feeling hot and uncomfortable.

"Well, we have different ideas about its being nothing," replied the sheriff. "Now, boys, a toast to Bill Halloway," he requested. "Bill couldn't get here to-day, but we mustn't forget him. His splendid grit and driving made it possible for our friend to play his hand so well."

"Hurrah for Bill!" cried Silent, leaping to his feet with the others. When seated again he looked quickly at his glass and turned to Bud.

"Real sweet cider!" he exulted. "Good Lord, but how time gallops past! I'd almost forgotten what it was like! It's been over twenty years since I tasted any! Ain't it fine?"

"I was wondering what it was," remarked Humble, a trace of awe in his voice as he refilled his glass. "It's shore enough sweet cider, and blamed good, too!"

Charley was romping with the mail carrier and he had a sudden inspiration: "Speech from Joe! Speech for the pieces of pie and cake he's due to get!"

"Now, look here, boy," Joe gravely replied. "I'm the mail carrier. I don't have to go on jury duty, lead religion round-ups, go to war or make speeches. As the books say, I'm exempt. All I have to do is punch cows, rustle the mail and eat pie and cake once a week," he said, glancing at Bud, who glared and groaned.

"Good boy, Joe!" cried Humble, waving his glass excitedly. "You're shore all right, you are, and I'm your deputy, ain't I?"

"No, not my deputy, but my delirium," corrected Joe.

"Glory be!" cried Silent as his plate was passed to him. "Chicken, real chicken! Mashed potatoes, mashed turnips and dressing and gravy! And here comes stewed corn, boiled onions and jelly and mother's bread. And stewed tomatoes? Well, well! I guess we ain't going to be well fed, and real happy, eh, fellows? My stomach won't know what's the matter-it'll think it died and went to heaven by mistake. Holy smoke! It hurts my eyes. What, cranberry jam? Well, I'm just going to close my eyes for a minute if you don't mind; I want to recuperate from the shock. This is where I live again!"

Humble stared in rapture at the feast before him and finally heaved a long drawn sigh of doubt and content.

"Gee!" he cried softly, a far-away look in his eyes. "Look at it, just look at it! Just like I used to get when I was a little tad back in Connecticut-but that was shore a long time ago. Well," he exclaimed, bracing up and bravely forgetting his boyhood, "there's one thing I hope, and that is that Lee beats my dog. Then I can shoot him and get square for all these years of imitation grub what he's handed out to me!"

"Hey, Tom!" eagerly cried Charley, "why can't we handle a herd of chickens out on the ranch, and have a garden? Why, we could have eggs every day and chickens on holidays!"

"No wonder Tom likes to ride to town," laughed Silent. "Gee whiz, I'd walk it for pie and cake and real genuine coffee!"

"Walk it!" snorted Jim. "Huh, I'd crawl, and stand on my head, knock my feet together and crow every half mile! Walk it, huh!"

Merriment reigned supreme throughout the meal and when the bashfulness had worn off the conversation became fast and furious, abounding in terse wit, verbal attacks and clever counters, and in concentrated onslaughts against the unfortunate Humble, who soon found, however, a new and loyal champion in Miss Ritchie, who took his part. Her assistance was so doughty as to more than once put to rout his tormentors, and before the dessert had been reached he was her devoted slave and admirer and was henceforth to sing her praises at every opportunity, and even to make opportunities.

At The Orphan's end of the table all was serene. He, Helen, Blake and the sheriff found much to talk about, and all the while Mrs. Shields regarded the four in a motherly way, and tempered the keenness of her husband's wit, for he was prone to break lances with The Orphan and to tease his sister, much to her confusion. She was very happy, for here at her side were her husband and the man she had feared would harm him, laughing and joking and the best of friends; and down the table a crowd of big-hearted boys, her boys now, were having the time of their lives. They were good boys, too, she told herself; a trifle rough, but sterling at the heart, and every one of them a loyal friend. How good it was to see them eat and hear them laugh, all happy and mischievous. The welding of the units had been finished, and now the Star C and The Orphan were one in spirit.

Chapter XVIII
Preparation

After the dinner at the sheriff's house, life meant much to The Orphan, for the dinner had done its work and done it well. Whatever had been missing to complete the good fellowship between him and the others had been supplied and by the time the outfit was ready to leave for home, all corners had been rounded and all rough edges smoothed down. With his outfit he was in hearty, loyal accord, and the spirit of the ranch had become his own. With the sheriff his already strong liking had been stripped of any undesirable qualities, and he felt that Shields was not only the whitest man he had ever met, but also his best friend. He had become more intimate with the sheriff's household, and for Mrs. Shields he had only love and respect.

With Helen his cup was full to overflowing, for he had managed to hold several long talks with her during the afternoon, and to his mind he had heard nothing detrimental to his hopes. His eyes had been opened as to what it was he had been hungering for, and the knowledge thrilled him to his finger-tips. He was a red-blooded, clean-limbed man, direct of words and purpose, reveling in a joyous, surging, vigorous health, in tune with his surroundings; he was dominant, fearless, and he had a saving grace in his humor. To him came visions of the future, golden as the sunrise, rich in promise and assurance as to a happiness such as he could only feebly feel. Himself he was sure of, for he feared no failure on his part; as far as he was concerned it was won. Helen, he believed from what the day had given him, would not refuse him when the time came for her to decide, and his effervescent spirits sent a song to his lips, which he hurled to the sky as a war-cry, a slogan of triumph and a defiance.

As yet he knew nothing of the sheriff's plans, and his thoughts concerning his future position in the community did not dare to soar above that of foreman of some ranch. To this end he would bend his energies with all the power of his splendid trinity-heart, mind and body. He was far too happy to think of failure, because there would be none; had the word passed through his mind he would have laughed it into oblivion. His experience gave him confidence, for he was no weakling sheltered and protected by any guiding angel; to the contrary, he was the survivor of a bitter war against conditions which would have destroyed a less strong man; he was victor over himself and his enemies, a conqueror of adverse conditions, a hewer of his own path; his enemies had been his best friends, and his long fight, his salvation. For ten years he had constantly fought a bitter fight against nature and man; hunger and thirst, plots and ambushes had all played their parts, and he had won out over all of them. He was young, hopeful and unafraid, and now that he was on the right trail he would bend every energy to stay there, and he would stay there, be the opposition what it might; and if the opposition should be man, and of a strength dangerous to him, he would destroy it as he had destroyed others before it. While now scorning to use his gun on every provocation he would depend upon it as on a court of last resort-and its decision would be final.

He held ill wishes against no man save one, and that one was the man who had placed the rope about the neck of his father. He did not know that man's name, and he did not know that he might not be among those who had already paid for that crime. But should he ever learn that he lived he would take payment in full be the cost what it might.

But he had no thoughts for strife, he only knew that the sun had never been so bright, the sky so blue and the plain so full of life and beauty as it was on this perfect day. Only one other day rivaled it-the day he had swayed weakly by the side of a dusty coach and had felt warm, soft fingers touching his forehead. But, he told himself with joy, there would be days to come which would eclipse even that.

He was aroused from his reverie by the approach of the foreman, who gave him a hearty hail and smiled at the happy expression on the puncher's face.

"Well, you look like you had struck it rich!" cried Blake. "What is it, gold or silver?"

"Gold or silver!" cried The Orphan in contempt at such cheapness. "By God, Blake, I wouldn't sell my claim for all the gold and silver in this fool earth! Gold or silver! Why, man, I know where there is plenty of both. Here," he cried, plunging his hand into his chaps pocket, "look at this!"

The foreman looked and whistled and took the object into his hand, where he examined it critically. "By George, it's the yellow metal, all right, and blamed near pure!" He returned it to its owner and added: "That's the real stuff, Orphan."

"Yes, it is," replied the other as he pocketed the nugget. "And I know where it came from. There's plenty left that's just like it, but I wouldn't go after it if it was diamonds."

"You wouldn't!" exclaimed Blake in surprise. "By George, I'd go to-morrow, to-night, if I knew. Gold like that ain't to be sneered at. It spells ranches, ease, plenty, anything you want. And you wouldn't go for it?"

"No, I wouldn't, and I won't," replied the puncher. "I'm going to stay right here on this range and make good with my hands and brains. I'm going to win the game with the cards I hold, and when I say win I mean it. There are times when gold is a dangerous thing to have, and this is one of them, as you'll understand when I disclose my hand. When I win I won't need gold bad enough to go through hell and hot water for it and risk not getting back to my claim, and it's one hundred to one that I wouldn't get back, too. And if I lose, mind you, *if,* I won't have any use for it. I picked that nugget up in the middle of the damnedest desert God ever made, and when I got off it I was loco for a week. I won't tell any friend of mine where it is because I want my friends to go on drawing their breath. I need my friends a whole lot, and that's why I don't tell you where it is. I was saving that for my enemies. Two have gone after it already, and haven't been heard of since."

"Well, you are the first man who ever told me that gold isn't worth going after, and you have convinced me that in your case you are right," laughed the foreman.

"You wouldn't have to be told if you knew that desert as I do," replied The Orphan.

"How was the sheriff last night?" asked Blake. "Or didn't you notice, being too much occupied in your claim?"

The Orphan looked at him and then laughed softly: "He was the same as ever-the best man I ever knew. But how in thunder do you know about my claim? How did you know what I meant? I thought that I had covered that trail pretty well."

Blake put his hand on his friend's shoulders and gravely looked at him: "Son, having eyes, I see; having ears, I hear; having brains, I think. If you have been fooling yourself that you are on a quiet trail, just listen to this: There ain't a man who knows you well that don't know what you're playing for, even Bill had it all mapped out the second time he saw you. And most of us wish you luck. You're not a man who needs help, but if you *do* need it, you know where to come for it."

"Thank you, Blake," replied The Orphan, eagerly filling his lungs with the crisp air. "That's why I ain't hankering for that gold–I'm too blamed busy making my own."

"Well, what I wanted to speak to you about is this," said the foreman, thinking quickly as to how to say it. "Old man Crawford got me to promise that I'd pick up a herd of cows for him before fall. Now, I would just as soon do it myself as not, but if you want to try your hand at it, go ahead. He wants about five thousand, to be delivered in five herds, a thousand each, at his corrals. He won't pay any more than the regular price for them, and the more you can drop the price the better he will like it, of course. They must be good, healthy cattle and be delivered to him before payment is made. What do you say?"

"I say that it's a go!" cried The Orphan. "I've had some great luck lately!" he exulted. "I'm ready to go after them whenever you say the word, to-night if you say so. And I'll get the right number and kind or know the reason why. And I'll take a hand in driving the last herd to him myself. Good Lord, what luck!"

Blake talked a while longer about the trip, giving necessary instructions about prices and where he would be likely to find the herd, and then rode off in the direction of Ford's Station for a consultation with his friend, the sheriff.

"Hullo, Tom!" came from the stage office as he rode past. He quickly turned his head and then stopped, smiling broadly.

"Why, hullo, Bill," he replied. "Glad to see you. How are things? Had any trouble lately?"

"Nope, times are real dull since that day in the defile," Bill answered with a grin. "I saw Tex once at Sagetown, but he ain't talking none these days, he's too busy thinking. You see, I've got a purty strong combination backing me and nobody feels like starting it a-going, because there ain't no telling just where it'll stop. The Orphant and the sheriff make a blamed good team, all right."

"None better at any game, Bill," replied Blake. "And you used the right word, too. They're going to pull together from now on, in fact, the Star C will be in harness with them."

"That's the way to talk!" cried Bill enthusiastically. "I always said that Orphant was a white man, even before I ever saw him," he said, forgetting much that he might be in hearty accord. "He can call on me any time he needs me, you bet. He cheated the devil twice with me, and I ain't a-going to forget it. But say, what do you think of the sheriff's sister, Helen? Ain't she a winner, hey? Finest girl these parts have ever seen, all right, and her friend ain't second by no length, neither."

"Why, Bill," exclaimed Blake, a twinkle coming to his eyes, "you are not allowing yourself to get captured, are you? That's a risky game, like starting up The Orphan and the sheriff, for there's no telling just where it will stop."

"No, I ain't letting myself get captured," sighed Bill. "I ain't no fool. Bill Howland knows a thing or two, which he learned not more than a thousand years ago. I've got it all sized up. And since then I've seen a certain bang-up puncher hitting the trail for the sheriff's house some regular twice a week. Nope, I'm a batchler now and forever, long may I wave."

"Say," he continued, suddenly remembering something. "What's the sheriff up to now? Is he going to have a picnic out on Crawford's ranch? He asked me if he could have the lend of the stage on an off day some time soon. Wants me to drive it for him out to the A-Y and back. I don't know what his game is, and I don't care none. I'll do it, all right. But what's he going to do out there, anyhow?"

Blake laughed: "Oh, nothing bad, I reckon. You'll probably learn all about it as soon as the rest of us. How do you expect me to know anything about it? Mebby he is going to have a picnic out there for all we know. The A-Y is a good place for one, ain't it?"

"You just bet it is," cried Bill. "Your ranch is all right, Blake, but I like the A-Y better. It's got windmills and everything. Finest grove near the ranch-house that I ever saw, and I've seen some fine groves in my time. Old man Crawford knew a good thing when he saw it, all right. Here comes Charley Winter like he had all day to go nowhere-he's got a good job with the Cross Bar-8, but I wouldn't have it for a gift-no, sir, money wouldn't tempt me to be one of that outfit. But I reckon it's some better out there than it once was since the sheriff and The Orphant amputated its inflamed fingers. Hullo, Charley," he cried as the newcomer drew rein. "I was just telling Blake what a good job you have got with Sneed."

"Hullo, you old one-hoss driver," grinned Charley. "Hullo, Tom," he cried. "Looking for the sheriff?"

"Hullo, Charley," said the foreman, shaking hands with Sneed's substitute puncher. "Yes, I am. Do you know where he is?"

"He's out at the Cross Bar-8, giving Sneed a talking to," Charley answered. "Bucknell went and got loaded again last night, raised h–l in town and out of it all the way home. He thought he wanted to shoot up The Orphan, so he was some primed. Jim is telling Sneed to hold him down to water and peace unless he wants to lose him. He'll be in soon, though. How's The Orphan getting on out at your place?"

"Fine!" answered Blake, his face wearing a frown. "But I'm some sorry about that fool Bucknell, though. He may get on a spree some day and *find* The Orphan. I don't want any more gunplay, and if that idiot does find him and gets ambitious to notch up his gun another hole, there'll shore be some loose lead. If he ever gets on Star C ground, and I catch him there, I'll shore enough wipe up the earth with him, and when you see him, just tell him what I said, will you? It ain't no joke, for I will."

"Shore I'll tell him," replied Charley. "When will that bunch of cattle be on hand–I'm anxious to swap jobs."

Blake flashed him a warning glance and tried to ignore the question by changing the subject, but it was too late, for Bill was curious.

"What cattle is that, Charley?" asked the driver in sudden interest.

"Oh, some cattle that I'm going to get of Blake for Sneed," lied Charley easily.

"What in all get out does Sneed want with any Star C cows?" Bill asked in surprise. "He's got plenty of cows of his own, unless The Orphant shot a whole lot more than I thought he did."

"I don't know, Bill," replied Charley. "I didn't ask him, it being plainly none of my business."

Bill scratched his head: "No, I reckon not," he replied doubtfully.

"Here comes Shields now," said Blake suddenly. "I reckon I'll ride off and meet him. So long, Bill."

"So long," replied Bill. "Be sure to tell The Orphan I was asking about him. So long, Charley." He turned abruptly and entered the stage office: "I don't understand it," he muttered. "There's something in the wind that I can't get onto nohow. He has shore got me guessing some, all right."

The clerk tossed aside the paper and stared: "Well, that's too d——d bad, now ain't it?" he asked sarcastically. "You ought to object, that's what you ought to do! What right has anybody to keep quiet about their own business when you want to know, hey? If I wanted to know everybody's business as bad as you do, I'd shore raise h–l, I would. Why don't you choke it out of him, wipe up the earth with him? Go out right now and give him a piece of your mind."

"Oh, you would, would you! You're blamed smart, now ain't you? You work too hard-your nerves are giving away," drawled Bill as he picked up the paper. "Sitting around all day with your feet on the table and a pipe in your mouth that you're too lazy to light, working like the very devil trying to find time to do the company's business, which there ain't none to do. Ain't you ashamed to go to bed?–it must take a lot of gall to hunt your rest at night after finding it and hugging it all day. What would you do for a living if I forgot to bring the paper with me some day, hey? You ain't got enough animation to want to know what is going on in this little world of ours, you——-"

"You get out of here, right now, too!" yelled the clerk. "I don't want you hanging around bothering me, you pest! Get out of here right now, before I get up and throw you out! Do you hear me!"

Bill crossed his legs, pushed back his sombrero, turned the page carefully and then remarked, "I licked four husky cow-punchers, real bad men, last month. One right after the other, and I was purty near all in, too." He glanced at the next page disinterestedly, spat at a fly on the edge of the box cuspidor and then added wearily and with great deprecation, "I'm feeling fine to-day, never felt so good in my life, but I need more exercise–I'm two pounds over weight right now."

The clerk showed interest and awe: "Weight?" he asked. "What is your fighting weight?"

Bill looked up aggressively: "Fighting weight?" he asked, raising his eyebrows. "My *fighting* weight is something over nine hundred pounds, when I'm real mad. Ordinarily, one hundred and eighty. Why?"

"Oh, nothing," replied the clerk, staring out of the window.

Chapter XIX
The Orphan Goes to the A-Y

The A-Y had been a very busy place for the past two weeks because of the cattle which had to be re-branded and taken care of, and of other things which had to be done about the ranch. The sheriff had taken title and had persuaded Crawford to remain in nominal charge for a month at the most so as to keep the sale a secret until the new owner would be ready to make it known. So word went around that Crawford had hired the sheriff to put things on a paying basis and that half of the old outfit had left, their places being filled by Charley, the two Larkin brothers and two men from a northern ranch.

Shields had been very much pleased with the cattle which The Orphan had bought for him and had asked Blake if he could borrow the new puncher to help him get things in good running shape. Blake had told The Orphan of the sheriff's request and had advised him to accept, which the puncher was very glad to do. So this is how the former outlaw became temporary foreman of the A-Y under the sheriff. Only the sheriff's most intimate friends knew his plans, one of whom was Charley Winter, who found food for mirth in the unique position things had taken. The sheriff's deputies who had lain out-doors all night on the Cross Bar-8 waiting to capture or kill the outlaw were now working under him, and the best of feelings prevailed. The man who had hunted The Orphan now employed him as the bearer of the responsibilities of the new ranch. Truly, a change!

While The Orphan was busy with his duties on the A-Y the sheriff rode to the Star C and sought out the foreman, whom he finally found engaged in freeing a cow that had become mired in a quicksand. As the terror-stricken animal galloped wildly away from the scene of torture and indignities to its person Blake mopped his face and began to scrape the quicksand from him.

"Playing life-saver, eh?" laughed the sheriff.

The foreman looked up and smiled sheepishly: "Yes," he replied as he shook hands with the sheriff. "One cow more or less won't make nor break no ranch, but I just can't see 'em suffer. The boys and I were passing, so we stopped and got to work. But cows ain't got no gratitude, not nohow! That ornery beast will be all ready to charge me the first time he sees me afoot. Did you see him try to horn me when I let go?"

His friend laughed, and when they had ridden some distance from the others he turned in his saddle:

"Well, The Orphan is working like a horse, and he likes it, too," he said. "You ought to hear him giving orders-he just asks a man to do a thing, don't order it done. When he talks it sounds like the puncher would be doing him the greatest possible favor to do the work he is paid to do, but there is a suggestion that if any nastiness develops, hell will be a peaceful place compared to the near vicinity of the foreman of the A-Y. He sizes up a thing with one look, and then tells how it should be done. Everything has gone off so fine that I'm going to ask you to lose a good man, and real soon, too. What do you say, Tom?"

Blake laughed: "Why, we were a-plenty before he came and we'll be a-plenty after he goes. That's for your asking me to turn him over to you. The boys will be both sorry and glad to have him leave, because they like him a whole lot. But of course they want to see him land everything that he can, so they'll give him a good send-off. That reminds me to say that I know they will want to be on hand when you break the news to him. It'll be a circus for your Eastern friend, Miss Ritchie."

"Now you're talking!" enthused the sheriff. "I want to have as many fireworks at the ceremony as I can possibly get. Oh, it'll be a great day, all right. We are all going out and take a bang-up lunch, just like we're going on that picnic that Bill's been so worried about, and Bill is going to drive the women over in his coach. The first surprise will be the announcement of the new ownership of the A-Y, and right on top of it I'm going to fire the second gun. I hope none of your boys know anything about it," he added with anxiety.

"Not a thing," hastily replied the foreman. "You have your wife send a message to me by Joe when he rustles our mail to-morrow and ask us to come to the picnic at the A-Y on the day which you will decide on. They'll go, all right, no fear about that. Nothing more than your wife's cooking is needed to attract them," and he laughed heartily at how suddenly they would come to life at such a summons.

Shields thought intently for a few seconds and then slapped his thigh: "I've got it!" he exulted. "I'll ride over to your place with you and write a letter to my wife telling her just what to do. Joe can deliver it and bring back the invitation. You see, I won't be home to-night, but that will do the trick, all right. Now, what do you say to this coming Saturday?–this is, let me see: Wednesday. Will that be time enough for you to make any arrangements you may want to make?"

"Shore, plenty of time," Blake laughed. "It's good all the way. Joe will be delighted to have a real good excuse to call at your house. He's a bashful cuss, like all the rest. They talk big, but they're some bashful all the same. He's been worrying about it, for one day he came to me with a funny expression on his face and acted like he didn't know how to begin. So I asked him what was troubling him, and he blurted out like this, as near as I can remember:

"'Well, you know Mrs. Shields said we was to go to her house when any of us hit town?' he asked.

"'I shore do,' I answered, wondering what was up.

"'Well, I go to town a lot, and it takes a h–l of a lot of gall to do it,' he complained, looking so serious that it was funny.

"'Gall!' said I, surprised-like, and trying to keep my face straight. 'Gall! Well, I can't see that it takes such a brave man to call at a friend's house when he's been told to do it.'

"'Oh, that part of it is all right,' he replied. 'But she'll think I only call to get my face fed, and it makes me feel like a–I don't know what. You see, I always get away quick.'

"'Well, stay longer, there ain't no use of being in a hurry,' I said. 'Stay and talk a while.'

"'Then they'll think I ain't got enough and push more pie at me, like they did once,' he complained.

"'Suppose I give Silent your terrible ordeal to do,' I suggested tentatively, 'or Bud, he's dead anxious for your job.'

"'Oh, it ain't as bad as that!' he cried quickly. 'I only thought that I'd speak to you about it. I thought you could suggest something.'

"'Well,' I replied, 'every time you call you say I sent you over to ask about the sheriff's health. How'll that do?'

"He grinned sheepishly and then swore: 'H–l, that would make a shore enough mess of it,' he cried. 'I'd be a royal American idiot to say a thing like that, now, wouldn't I?'"

The sheriff laughed heartily, and they talked about the picnic until they had reached the ranch-house, where he wrote the note to his wife. Bidding his friend good-by, he rode out past the corrals and headed for the A–Y.

When about half-way to his own ranch, and on A–Y ground, he surmounted a rise and saw a figure flit from sight behind a thicket, and his curiosity was immediately aroused. Not knowing who the man might be, he stalked his quarry and finally found Bucknell standing beside his horse.

"Well, what's the trouble now?" the sheriff asked as he came out into sight. He was dangerously near angry, for Bucknell was on forbidden ground and was flushed as if from liquor. "What's the trouble?" he repeated.

Bucknell looked confused: "Nothing, Sheriff. Why?" he asked, evading the searching gaze of the peace officer.

"Oh, I thought something might have gone wrong on the Cross Bar-8, and that you were looking for me," Shields coldly replied.

Bucknell looked at the ground and coughed nervously before he replied, which only made the sheriff all the more determined to get at the matter in a true light.

"No, nothing's wrong," replied the puncher. "I was just riding out this way–I was some nervous, that's all."

"That don't go with me!" the sheriff said sharply. "I've lived too long to bite on a yarn like that. Why, you can't look at me!"

The puncher did not reply and the sheriff continued:

"Now, look here, Bucknell, take some good advice from me-stay on your ranch, mind your own business and let liquor alone. As sure as you monkey around the Star C Blake will give you a d——n sound licking, and he's man enough to do it, too, make no error. And as for the A–Y, well, the temporary foreman of that ranch is the cleverest man with a gun that I ever saw, and I've seen some good ones in my time. If you go up against him you'll get shot, for he'd think you were about the easiest proposition he ever met. As sure as you drink you'll get drunk, and as sure as you get drunk you'll work up an appetite for a fight, and if you pick a fight with him you'll never know what hit you. You stick to water and the Cross Bar-8."

"Oh, I reckon I can take care of my own business," sullenly replied Bucknell. "I can come out here drunk or sober if I wants to, I reckon."

"You can do nothing of the kind," rejoined the sheriff. "And you certainly ought to be able to take care of your own business, as you say," he retorted, holding his temper with an effort. "But in the past you didn't, and you may not in the future. And when your business gets too big for you to handle it gets into my hands, and if you make any trouble I'll d——n soon convince you that I can handle your surplus. Now, get out of here and think it over."

Bucknell swung into his saddle and then turned, the liquor making him reckless.

"D——n it!" he cried. "The Orphant killed Jimmy and a whole lot more good cow-punchers! He's nothing but a murdering thief, a d——d rustler, that's what he is! And you are his best friend, it seems!"

The wan smile flickered across the sheriff's face, but still he refrained, for such is the foolish consideration given by brave men to liquor. A drunkard may do much with impunity, for the argument states he is not responsible, forgetting that in the beginning he was responsible enough to have left liquor alone, and that injury, whether unintentional or not, is still injury.

"There is no seem about it!" he retorted. "I *am* his best friend, and he needs friends bad enough, God knows. But speaking of murder, those four good cow-punchers that stopped me in the defile tried hard enough to qualify at it, and The Orphan not only saved me, but also some of them, for I'd a gotten some of them before I cashed. You're a h–l of a fine cub to talk about murders, you are!"

"That's all right," retorted Bucknell, "he's just what I said he was. And a side pardner of our brave sheriff, too!"

"D——n you!" shouted Shields, his face dark with passion. "You have said enough, any more from you and I'll break your dirty neck! Just because I felt sorry for you when you got half killed in the saloon and let you stay in the country don't think you are the boss of this section. When I saw what a pitiful, drunken wreck you were, I felt sorry for you, but not any more. You don't want decent treatment, you want to get clubbed, and you're right in line to get just what you need, too! Now, I'm not going to stand any more of your d——d foolishness-my patience is played out. And if you were half a man you wouldn't sit there like a bump on a log and swallow what I'm saying-you'd put up a fight if you died for it. You are no good, just a drunken, lawless fool of a puncher; just a bag of wind, and it's up to you to walk a chalk line or I'll give you a taste of what I carry around with me for bums of your kind. What in h–l do you think I am? No, you don't, you stay right where you are 'til I get good and ready to have you go! You've come d——d near the end of your rope and there is just one thing for you to do, and that is, get out of this country and do it quick! You stay on your own side of the Limping Water, for if I catch you riding off any nervousness off of Cross Bar-8 ground without word from your foreman, I'll shoot you down like I'd shoot a coyote! And for a dollar I'd wipe up the earth with you right now! You d——d, sneaking, cowardly cur, you tin-horn bully! Pull your stakes and get scarce and don't you open your mouth to me-come on, lively! Pull your freight!"

Bucknell slowly rode away, his eyes to the ground and not daring to say what seethed in his heart. He swore to himself that he would get square some day on both, not realizing in his anger that when sober he feared them both.

The sheriff stared after him and then returned to the point where he had left his horse. As he mounted he shook his head savagely and swore. Glancing again after the puncher he struck into a canter and rode toward the ranch.

Chapter XX
Bill Attends the Picnic

The picnic aroused quite a stir for so frivolous a thing. When Blake read Mrs. Shields' invitation to the outfit they acted like schoolboys dismissed for a vacation. Grins of delight were the style on the Star C, and the overflow of bubbling happiness took the form of practical joking against Humble, whose life suddenly held much anxiety. In Ford's Station there was an air of expectancy, and Bill spent all of Saturday morning from daylight until time to start in cleaning his stage and grooming the horses, whose astonishment quickly passed into prohibitive indignation. After narrowly escaping broken bones and chewed arms Bill decided that the sextet could go as it was.

"Serves 'em right!" he yelled to his friendly enemy, the clerk, after he had barely dodged a vicious kick, wildly waving a curry comb. "Let the ignoramuses go like they are! Let 'em show how cheap and common they are! They never was any good for anything, anyhow, eating their heads off and kicking their best friend!"

"How about the time they beat out them Apaches?" asked the clerk, settling back comfortably against the coach.

"You get out!" yelled Bill pugnaciously. "Who asked you for talk, hey? And get away from that coach, you idiot, you'll dirty it all up!"

"Sic 'em, Tige!" jeered the clerk pleasantly. "Chew 'em up!"

"What!" yelled Bill, swiftly grabbing up the pail of water which stood near him. "Sic 'em, is it!" he cried, running forward. "Chew 'em up, hey!" he continued, heaving the contents of the pail at the clerk, who nimbly sprang inside the vehicle and slammed the door shut behind him as the water struck it. He leaped out of the other door and was safely away before Bill realized what had happened. Then the driver said things when he saw the mess he had made of the coach, upon which he had spent two hard hours in polishing.

"Suffering dogs!" he shouted, dancing first on one foot and then on the other. "Now look what you've done! You're a h–l of a feller, you are! After me rubbing the skin off'n my hands and breaking my arms a-polishing it up! You good for nothing, mangy half-breed! Wait till I get a hold of you, you long pair of legs, you! Just wait! I'll show you, all right!"

The clerk twiddled his fingers from afar and jeered in his laughter: "Serves you right! Sic 'em, Towser! Eat 'em up, Fido! Sic 'em, sic 'em!" he shouted joyously, and forthwith ran for his life.

Bill returned to the coach and worked like mad to undo the evil effects he had wrought and finally succeeded in bringing a phantom glow to the time-battered wood. Then he hitched up and drove to the sheriff's house, where he saw huge baskets on the porch.

"Good morning, Mrs. Shields," he said as he stamped to the door. "Good morning, ladies."

"Good morning William," replied the sheriff's wife as she hurried to collect shawls and blankets. "Will you mind putting those baskets on the coach, William? We will soon be ready."

"Why, certainly not, ma'am," he answered, recklessly grabbing up the two largest. "Jimminee!" he exulted. "These are shore heavy, all right, all right! Must be plumb full of good things! To-day is where your Uncle Bill Halloway gets square for the dinner the company froze him out of. Wonder if there's apricot pie in this one?" he mused curiously. He gingerly raised the cover and a grin distorted his face. "Must be six, yes, eight-mebby ten!" he soliloquized as he placed it on the stage. "Hullo, bottles of some kind," he whispered as he picked up another basket. "Hear the little devils clink, eh? Must be coffee and tea, hey? Yes, shore enough it is. Good Lord, how hungry I am-wish I had eaten that breakfast this morning-how in thunder did I know we was going to be so late? I'll be the strong man at this picnic, all right!"

"Here are some blankets, William," called Mrs. Shields. "Helen, would you mind showing him how to carry that box?–he's sure to turn it upside down if you don't."

"Next!" he cried, returning from the trip with the blankets. "I put them blankets up on top, Mrs. Shields, is it all right? How do you do, Miss Helen, any more freight?"

"How do you do," she replied. "This box is to go, please. Now, do be very careful not to turn it up, or jar it!" she warned. "And put it on the seat inside the coach where we can steady it."

"Gee, what's in it?" asked Bill, nearly dying from his curiosity. "Must be the joker of the feast, eh?"

"Three layer cakes," she laughingly replied. "Chocolate, cocoanut and lemon."

"Um!" he said. "I'll carry this one high up, it deserves it."

"Oh, do be careful!" she cried as he swooped it up to his shoulder. "Oh!" she screamed as it thumped against the top of the door frame.

"Whoa! Back up!" cried Bill, executing the order. "Easy, boy-all right, off we go!"

"Grace, Mary," cried Helen, "we are all ready to go!"

"Ain't there any more boxes?" asked Bill from the coach.

"Come, girls," cried Mrs. Shields as she stepped into the coach. "Close the door after you, and lock it, dear."

Bill gallantly helped the ladies into the coach, grinned at the cake box and started toward the front wheel when he was called back.

"Now, William," cautioned Mrs. Shields, laughing. "We will not be pursued by Apaches to-day, and this cake must not be shaken!"

"You won't know you're riding, ma'am, you shore won't," he assured her as he danced toward the front wheel again.

"Wake up there, you!" he yelled from the box. "Come on, Jerry, think you're glued to the earth? Come on, Tom! Easy there, you fool jackrabbit! —haven't you learned that you can't reach this high!"

When they had arrived at the A-Y the baskets were carried into the ranch-house and the women became very busy getting things ready for the feast. Bill took care of his team and then carried the blankets to the grove.

While the picnic was being prepared there arose a series of blood-curdling whoops off to the south where the outfit of the Star C made the air blue with powder smoke. As they came nearer something peculiar was noticed by Helen. It appeared to be a sort of drag drawn by a horse and supported by two long, springy poles, one end of which rested on the ground, and the other fastened to the saddle. While she wondered Bill came up and she turned to him for light.

"What have they got fastened to that horse?" she asked him.

He looked and then smiled: "Why, it is a travois," he said. "But what under the sun have they got on it? They must be bringing their own grub!"

The travois dragged and bumped over the uneven plain and soon came near enough for its burden to be made out. A man and a dog were strapped to it.

At this point Blake joined Helen and Bill, and as he did so he espied the travois.

"Thunder!" he cried, running forward. "Somebody is hurt! What's the matter, Silent?" he shouted.

"Matter?" asked Silent, in surprise as the outfit drew near. "There ain't nothing the matter. Why?"

"What's that travois doing with you, then?" Blake demanded.

Silent's face was as grave as that of an owl. "Travois?" he asked. Then his face cleared: "Oh, yes—I near forgot about it," he added, apologetically. "You see, Humble he shore wanted his dog to come to the picnic, so we reckoned we'd let it come along. Bud and Jim was for slinging it at the end of a rope and dragging it over, but I said no. We ain't got any ropes to have all frayed out and cut a-dragging dogs to picnics, and I said so, too. So we built the travois and strapped Lightning to it. When Humble saw what we had done he acted real unpolite. He said as how he wasn't going to have no dog of his'n toted twenty miles in a fool travois. Said that he'd make it stay home first, which was some mean after inviting the dog to come along. He said that he'd go in a travois himself first before he'd let the setter be made a fool of. Well, we simply had to subdue him, and he got so unreasonable that we just had to tie him with his dog. He shore does get awful pig-headed at times."

"Take off the gag, Jim," requested Silent, turning to the grinning cow-puncher. "Let him loose now, we've arrived."

Jim leaned over and whispered in Humble's ear, the information being that there were ladies about, and that all swearing must be thought and not yelled. Then he slipped the gag, and untied the ropes. Gales of laughter met the angry and indignant puncher when he had leaped to his feet, and he flashed one quick glance at the women and then, boiling with wrath and suppressed profanity, fled toward the corrals as swiftly as cramped muscles would allow. The dog snarled at its tormentors and then set off in hot pursuit of its discomfited master, whose waving arms kept time with his speeding legs.

"That's all the thanks we get," grumbled Bud, "but then, he don't know any better anyhow."

Blake laughed and regarded his grinning and expectant outfit, and the longer he looked at them the more he laughed. They had paid their respects to the women while Silent explained about the travois and now they cast many longing glances at the blankets and cloths spread out on the grass and at the baskets which Bill was busy over. They had tried to coax the driver to them to give information as to what they might expect in the way of edibles, but he had haughtily and disdainfully refused to enlighten them, taking care, however, to arouse their curiosity by looking fondly at the box and the baskets and even showed his elation by taking several fancy steps for their benefit.

"Well, get rid of the cayuses," said Blake, "and square things with Humble. Bring him back with you or you don't get any pie. You're such a darn fool crowd that I can't get mad this time, but don't ever drag a man in a travois again."

"Did he come, or was he kidnapped?" murmured Bud. "What we did once we can do again, and Humble will be on hand when the feast begins."

Jim had been scowling at Bill, whose manners were most aggravating. "You just wait, you heathen," threatened Jim. "You're ace high with the grub, all right, but just you wait 'til we get you alone!"

"Yah!" laughed the driver. "I shore can handle the best cow-wrastler that ever lived."

"Bill seems to be running this here festival," Bud complained to Helen.

"Oh, he is our right-hand man," she replied with enthusiasm. "We couldn't possibly get along without him, now. He has charge of the pie and cake."

Bill's chest expanded: "I'm foreman of the pie and cake herd," he exclaimed proudly. "You can't get ahead of me."

Bud looked at the driver and then significantly waved his hand at the travois: "And you'll shore travel in style, just like a real pie foreman, too, when we gets a chance to honor you like we wants to."

"You'll get no pie if you acts smart, little boy," retorted the driver. "Run along and play till lunch is ready, and don't dirty your hands and face."

"Well, we've got fine memories," Bud suggested as he led the way to the corrals, where he found The Orphan.

"Hullo, Orphan!" he cried enthusiastically as he gripped the outstretched hand. "Plumb glad to see you. How's things?"

"Glad to see you, boys," cried the temporary foreman, who was all smiles. "One at a time!" he laughed as they crowded about him. "Make yourselves right at home-that smallest corral is for your cayuses. And you'll find plenty of soap and water and towels by the bunk-house, and there's a box of good cigars, a tin of tobacco, and a jug on the table inside. Help yourself to anything you want, the place is all yours."

"Gee, this is a good game, all right," Bud laughed as he turned to put his horse in the corral. "The sheriff shore knows how to deal."

"Leave a cigar for me, Silent," jokingly warned Jim as his friend turned toward the bunk-house. "Too many smokes will make you sick."

"Well, you've got a gall, all right!" retorted Silent. "You better let me bring yours out to you and keep away from the box, for I'm always plumb suspicious of these goody-goody, it's-for-your-own-good people."

A crafty look came to Jack Lawson's face and he turned to The Orphan: "Has Bill Howland got his cigars yet?" he asked, winking at his friends.

"Why, I don't know whether he has or not," replied The Orphan. "But I don't believe that he has been out of sight of the pies since he came. They've got him in a trance."

"Guess I'll take him one," continued Jack, grinning broadly. "He likes to smoke."

"Shore enough, go ahead," endorsed the foreman of the A-Y as he turned toward the grove. Then he stopped, and with a knowing look added: "If you want to see Humble, he just went in the bunk-house."

A yell of dismay arose as the outfit started pell-mell for the house. Silent entered it first and his profanity informed his companions that their fears were well grounded. Neither Humble, cigars, tobacco nor jug were to be seen, and a search was forthwith instituted. Jack looked at a distant corral and saw Lightning as the dog disappeared from sight into it.

"Hey!" he cried. "He's in the big corral-I just saw his dog go in, and it was wagging its tail a whole lot. Come on, we'll surround it and show that frisky gent a thing or two!"

No more words were wasted, and in a very short time figures were creeping around the corral. Then there was a scramble as most of the searchers scaled the wall at different points while two of them ran in through the gate. The first thing they saw was the dog, and his tail was still wagging as he curiously followed, nose to the ground, a huge horned toad. He looked up at the sudden disturbance and backed off suspiciously, looking for a way to escape.

"—- —-!" chorused the fooled punchers, who discovered that deductions don't always deduct, and then they returned to the bunk-house to "slick up." When finally satisfied about their appearance they made their way to the grove and the sight which greeted their eyes as they entered it almost made them drop in their tracks.

Humble and Bill sat cross-legged on a blanket, which was surrounded with guns. The jug, tobacco and cigars were flanked by pies and a cake, while each of the conspirators held a lighted cigar in one hand while they took turns at the jug. A huge piece of pie rested in a plate at Humble's side, while Bill's knee held a piece of cake.

"Hands up!" shouted Humble, grabbing a gun. "Don't you dare to raid the gallery! You stay right where you are!"

Bill's blacksnake whip leaped from point to point experimentally, picking up twigs and leaves with disturbing accuracy.

The invaders halted just beyond the range of the whip and consulted uneasily, not noticing that the driver had shortened his weapon by twice the length of its handle. Finally Jim and Docile ran back toward the corral while their friends waited impatiently for their return, grinning at the enemy with an I-told-you-so air.

Bill suddenly leaned forward, the whip slid down into his hand to the end of the handle and cracked viciously. Joe Haines, who had grown a little careless, leaped into the air and yelled, grabbing at his leg.

"Keep your distance, you!" warned the driver, trying to look ferocious. "Twenty feet is the dead-line, children."

Jim and Docile returned apace and brought with them half a dozen lariats, which ranged in length from thirty to forty feet.

"Hey, you!" cried Humble in alarm. "That ain't fair!"

Grim silence was the only reply as the invaders each took his rope and surrounded the two. Then, suddenly, the air was full of darting ropes and in less time than it takes to tell of it the pair were hopelessly and helplessly trussed. Silent ran in and hurled the whip away and then squatted before the prisoners, throwing their cigars after the whip as he took up the pie and cake, which he tantalizingly munched before their eyes.

"I like a hog, all right, but you suit me too blamed well!" asserted Bud, grabbing at Silent's pie.

"Gimme some of that," demanded Jim, trying for the cake. And when the disturbance had ceased there were no signs of either pie or cake.

"It's the travois for you, Humble dear!" softly hummed Charley Bailey. "And to the ranch, by the way of town!"

"And Bill will be pleased to explore the Limping Water on the bottom," amended Jim. "One of us can drive the women home!"

Chapter XXI
The Announcement

About thirty people sat in a circle on the grass in the grove on the A-Y, engaged in taking viands from the well-filled plates which made the rounds. Keen humor from all sides kept them in roars of laughter, Humble and Bill provoking the greater part of it. Humble sat next to Miss Ritchie, while The Orphan and Bill flanked Helen, the sheriff next to his new foreman.

Humble's face had a look of benign condescension when he allowed himself to bestow perfunctory attentions on the members of his outfit, whom he graciously called "purty fair punchers in a way."

Crawford, the former owner of the A-Y, sat next to Shields, and when the lunch had reached the cigar stage he arose and cleared his throat.

"Ladies and Gentlemen, Bill and Humble," he began amid laughter. "I have been regarded as the host of this picnic, and the false position embarrasses me. But any such momentary feeling is compensated by the importance of what I have to tell you.

"When I took up the A-Y it was with a determination to keep it and to spend the rest of my days on it in peace. This I have found to be impossible, and in consequence I have turned it over to a better man. The energy which I have seen applied in the right way for the last few weeks has assured me that the A-Y will soon be second in importance and wealth to no ranch in this country. I have seen order, system, emerge from chaos; I have seen five thousand cattle re-branded and taken care of in such dispatch as to astonish me and be almost beyond my belief. The sheriff has been as economical in the use of his energy as he can be in the use of his words. By that I don't mean in the way that is causing you to smile, but simply that he knows how to accomplish the most work with the least possible expenditure of effort and time, as witnessed by the condition of this ranch to-day. But while he has been the guiding spirit in the work of putting the ranch on its proper footing, he has had as good assistants as it is possible to find.

"I don't wish to tire you with any long speech, for brevity is the soul of more than wit, so I will close by telling you that the A-Y is in new and better hands-our sheriff is now its owner, and I extend to him my heartiest wishes for his success in his new venture. I must thank him and all of you for a very pleasant day and a memory to take East with me."

For an instant there was intense silence, and then a small battle seemed to be taking place. The noise of the shooting and cheering was deafening and smoke rolled down like a heavy fog. The sheriff met the rush toward him and put in a very busy few minutes in shaking hands and replying to the hearty congratulations which poured in upon him from all sides. Everybody was happy and all were talking at once, and Bill could be heard reeling off an unbroken string of words at high speed.

The Orphan fought his way to his best friend and gripped both hands in his own.

"By God, Sheriff!" he cried. "This is great news, and I'm plumb glad to hear it! I hope you have the very best of luck and that your returns, both in pleasure and money, far exceed your fondest expectations. Anything I can do is yours for the asking."

"Thank you, son," replied the sheriff, looking fondly into his friend's eyes. "I'm going to call on you just as soon as I can make myself heard in all this hellabaloo. Just listen to that!" he exclaimed as Silent let loose again.

"Glory be!" yelled he of the misleading name, slapping Humble across the back. "For this you ride home like a white man, Humble-all your sins are forgiven! Hurrah for the sheriff, his family and the A-Y!" he shouted at the top of his lungs, and his cheer was supported unanimously with true cowboy enthusiasm and vim.

"Hurray for me, too!" shouted Bill in laughter. Then he fled, with Silent in hot pursuit.

The sheriff tried to speak, and after several attempts was finally given silence.

"Thank you, everybody!" he cried, his face beaming. "I am happy for many reasons to-day, but foremost among them is the fact that I have so many warm and loyal friends. The A-Y is always open to all of you, and I'll be some disappointed if you don't put in a lot of your spare time over here."

He paused for a few seconds and then looked at The Orphan, who stood at Helen's side.

"Mr. Crawford did his part a whole lot better than I can do mine, I'm afraid, but I'm going to do my best, anyhow. The news has only been half told-the name of the new foreman of the A-Y henceforth will be The Orphan! Whoop her up, boys!" he shouted, leading a cheer which was not one whit less a cheer than those which had gone before.

The Orphan stared in astonishment, for once in his life he had been surprised. The sheriff at last had the drop on him. He looked from one to another, started to step forward and then changed his mind and looked appealingly at Helen, who smiled in a way to double the speed of his heart-beats.

Her eyes were moist, and the sudden consciousness that she formed half of the objective of all eyes caused her cheeks to go crimson. Her hand impulsively went to his shoulder and without thought on her part, and his incredulous questioning was answered by her.

"It's all true," she said earnestly. "I've known of it for a whole week now. You are the real foreman of the A-Y, and I most earnestly hope for your success."

He suddenly seemed to be above the earth and his voice broke in his stammered reply. For a fraction of a second her eyes had told him what he had dreamed of, what he had hoped for above all things, and he grasped her hand for a second as he stepped forward toward his new employer, whose hand met his with a man's grasp.

"Thank you, Sheriff," he said, his head whirling from the surprises of a minute. "You've been squarer and fairer with me than any man I've ever known, and hell will look nice to me if I don't make good with you.

"Thank you, boys; thank you, Bill: you're all right, every one of you!" he cried as his friends crowded about him. "What the sheriff said about warm friends was the truth-thank you, Bud and Jim! Thank you, Blake-you're another brick! Good God, what I have gained in two months! I can scarcely believe it, it seems so like a dream. That's a real warm grip, all right, though," he exclaimed as he shook hands with Humble, "so I reckon it's all true. Two months!" he marveled. "Two glorious, glorious months! A new start in life, a loyal crowd of friends, a–and all in two months! And there is the man I owe it all to," he suddenly cried, pointing to the sheriff. "There's the whitest man God ever made, and I'll kill the man who says I lie!"

"Good boy!" shouted Bill in enthusiastic endorsement. "You two make a pair of aces what can beat any full-house ever got together, and *I'll* lick the man who says *I* lie!" he yelled pugnaciously. "The Orphant may be an orphant, all right, but he's got a whole lot of brothers."

Mrs. Shields walked over to The Orphan and placed a motherly hand on his shoulder as he recovered.

"You won't be an orphan any longer, my boy," she said, smiling up at him. "You're one of us now–I always wanted a son, and God has given me one in you."

Chapter XXII
Tex Williard's Mistake

During the month which followed the picnic things ran smoothly on the A-Y, and the rejuvenated ranch was the pride of the whole contingent, from the sheriff down to the cook. The Orphan had taken charge with a determination which grew firmer with each passing day and the new owner was delighted at the outcome of his plans. The foreman, elated and happy at his sudden shift in fortune, radiated cheerfulness and consideration. His men knew that he would not ask them to do anything which he himself feared to do, which would not have been much consolation to a timid man, since he feared nothing; but to them it meant that they had a foreman who would stick by them through fire and water, and a foreman who commands respect from his outfit is a man whose life is made easy for him. He had known too much of unkindness, harshness, to become angry at mistakes; instead, he set diligently at work to undo them, and mistakes were rare. The very men who had once wished for his life would now fight instantly to save it. They were proud of him, of the owner, the ranch and themeselves; and proudest of all was Bill, once driver of the stage, but now a cowboy working hard and loyally under the man who had once held him up for a smoke.

Visitors were numerous, and every man who called became enthusiastic about the ranch, and after he had departed marveled at the complete change in the man who was its foreman, and felt confidence in the good judgment of the sheriff. Ford's Station was openly jubilant, for the town exulted in the discomfiture of the Cross Bar-8 and in the proof that their sheriff was right. And Ford's Station chuckled at the news it heard, for the foreman of the Cross Bar-8 had called twice at the A-Y and was fast losing his prejudice against The Orphan. Sneed had found a quiet, optimistic foreman in the place of his former enemy, and the laughter which lurked in The Orphan's eyes closed the breach. He had seen the man in a new light, and when he had said his farewell at the close of his second visit the grip of his hand was strong. As for the Star C, a trail had been worn between the two ranches and hardly a day passed but one or more of its punchers dropped in to say a few words to their former bunkmate, and to stir up Bill. The Star C, no less than his own men, swore by The Orphan.

One bright morning the sheriff left for a trip to Chicago and other packing cities to arrange for future cattle shipments, and announced that he would be away for a week or two. On the night following his departure trouble began. The ranch and bunk houses of the Cross Bar-8 were fired into, and when Sneed and his men had returned after a fruitless search in the dark the foreman stared at the wall and swore. Was it The Orphan again? In the absence of the sheriff had he renewed the war? First thought cried that he had, but gradually the idea became untenable. Why should The Orphan risk his splendid berth on the A-Y, his prospects now rich in promise, to work off any lingering hatred? When Sneed had shaken hands with him he found apparent sincerity in the warm clasp. He would ride over at daylight and have the matter settled once and for all. And if satisfied that The Orphan was guiltless of the outrage he would turn his whole attention to the imitator of the former outlaw.

The Orphan was mending his saddle girth when he saw Sneed cantering past the farthest corral. The latter's horse bore all the signs of hard riding and he looked up inquiringly at the visitor.

"Good morning, Sneed," he said pleasantly, arising and laying aside the saddle. "What's up, anything?"

"Yes, and I came over to find out about it," Sneed answered. "I hardly know how to begin-but here, I'll tell it from the beginning," and he related what had occurred, much to the wonder of The Orphan.

"Now," finished the visitor, "I want to ask you a question, although I may be a d—-n fool for doing it. But I want to get this thing thrashed out. Do you know who did it?"

The foreman of the A-Y straightened up, his eyes flashing, and then he realized that Sneed had some right to question him after what had occurred in the past.

"No, Sneed, I do not," he answered, "but in two guesses I can name the man!"

"Good!" cried Sneed. "Go ahead!"

"Bucknell?"

"No, he was with me in the bunk-house," replied the foreman of the Cross Bar-8. "It wasn't him-go on."

"Tex Williard," said The Orphan with decision.

"Tex?" cried Sneed. "Why?"

"It's plain as day, Sneed," The Orphan answered. "He's sore at me, but lacks nerve."

"But, thunderation, how would he hurt you by shooting at us?" Sneed demanded, impatiently.

"Oh, he would scare up a war during the sheriff's absence by throwing your suspicions on me. He reckoned you would think that I did it, get good and mad, fly off the handle and raise h–l generally. He figured that I, according to the past, would meet you half way and that you or some of your men might kill me. If you didn't, he reckoned that the sheriff would kick me out of this berth, and that one or both of us might get killed in the argument. He could sit back and laugh to himself at how easy it was to square up old scores from a distance. It's Tex as sure as I am here, and unless Tex changes his plans and gets out of this country d—-n soon he won't be long in getting what he seems to ache for."

Sneed pushed back his sombrero and smiled grimly: "I reckon that you're right," he replied. "But you ain't sore at the way I asked, are you? I had to begin somewhere, you know."

"Sore?" rejoined his companion, angrily. "Sore? I'm so sore that I'm going out after Tex right now. And I'll get him or know the reason why, too. You go back and post your men about this-and tell them on no account to ride over my range for a few days, for they might get hurt before they are known. Put a couple of them to bed as soon as you get back-you need them to keep watch nights."

He turned toward the corral and called to a man who was busy near it: "Charley, you take anybody that you want and get in a good sleep before nightfall. I will want both of you to work to-night."

"All right, after dinner will be time enough," Charley replied. "I'll take Lefty Lukins."

The Orphan went into the ranch house and returned at once with his rifle, a canteen of water and a package of food. As he threw a saddle on his horse Bill galloped up, waving his arms and very much excited.

"Hey, Orphant!" he shouted. "Somebody's shore enough plugged some of our cows near the creek! I lost his trail at the Cottonwoods!"

"All right, Bill," replied the foreman, "I'll go out and look them over. You take another horse and ride to the Star C. Tell Blake to keep watch for Tex Williard, and tell him to hold Tex for me if he sees him. Lively, Bill!"

Bill stared, leaped from his horse, took the saddle from its back and was soon lost to sight in the corral. In a few minutes he galloped past his foreman and Sneed swearing heartily. His quirt arose and fell and soon he was lost to sight over a rise near the ranch-house.

The foreman of the A-Y rode over to Charley: "Charley, in case I don't get back to-night, you and Lefty keep guard somewhere out here, and shoot any man who don't halt at your hail. If I return in the dark I'll whistle Dixie as soon as I see the lights in the bunk house, and I'll keep it up so you won't mistake me. So long."

Sneed and he cantered away together and soon they parted, the former to ride toward his ranch, the latter toward the Cottonwoods near the Limping Water and along the trail left by Bill.

When near the grove The Orphan saw five dead cows and he quickly dismounted to examine them.

"Not dead for long," he muttered as he examined the blood on them. He leaped into his saddle and galloped through the grove. "Now, by God, somebody pays for them!" he muttered.

Here was a sudden change in things, positions had been reversed, and now he could appreciate the feelings which he had, more than once, aroused in the hearts of numerous foremen. He emerged from the grove and rode rapidly along the trail left by the perpetrator, alert, grim and angry. Soon the trail dipped beneath the waters of the creek and he stopped and thought for a few seconds. If it was Tex, he would not have ridden toward the Cross Bar-8 and the town, and neither would he have ridden south toward the Star C, nor north in the direction of the A-Y. He would seek cover for the day if he was still determined to carry on his game, and would not emerge until night covered his movements. That left him only the west along the creek, and more than that, the creek turned to the south again about five miles farther on and flowed far too close to the ranch-houses of the Star C for safety. He must have left the water at the turn, and toward the turn rode The Orphan, watching intently for the trail to emerge on either bank. His deductions were sound, for when he had rounded the bend of the stream he picked up the trail where it left the water and followed it westward.

The country around the bend was very wild and rough, for ravines between the hills cut seams and gashes in the plain. The underbrush was shoulder high, and he did not know how soon he might become a target. The trail was very fresh in the soft loam of the ravines and the broken branches and trampled leaves were still wet with sap. Soon he hobbled his horse and proceeded on foot, but to one side of and parallel with the trail. He had spent an hour in his advance and had begun to regret having left his horse so early, when he heard the report of a gun near at hand and a bullet hissed viciously over his head as he stooped to go under a low branch.

He threw up his arms, the rifle falling from his hands, pitched forward and rolled down the side of the hill and behind a fallen tree trunk which lay against a thicket. As soon as he had gained this position he glanced in the direction from whence the shot had come and, finding himself screened from sight on that side, quickly jerked off his boots and planted them among the bushes, where they looked as if he had crawled in almost out of sight. That done, he crawled along the ground under the protection of the tree trunk and then squirmed under it, when he pushed himself, feet first, deep into a tangled thicket and waited, Colt in hand, for a sign of his enemy's approach.

A quarter of an hour had passed in silence when a shot, followed by another, sounded from the hillside. After the lapse of a like interval another shot was fired, this time from the opposite direction. He saw a twig fall by the boots and heard the spat! of the bullet as it hit a stone. Two more shots sounded in rapid succession, and then another long interval of silence. Half an hour passed, but he was not impatient. He most firmly believed that his man would, sooner or later, come out to examine the boots, and time was of no consequence: he wanted the man.

Whoever he was, he was certainly cautious, he did not believe in taking any chances. It was almost certain that he would not leave until he had been assured that he had accomplished his purpose, for it would be most disconcerting at some future time to unexpectedly meet the man he thought he had murdered. Another shot whizzed into the place where the body should have been, according to the silent testimony of the boots. It sounded much closer to the thicket, but in the same direction of the last few shots. Then, after ten minutes of silence, a twig snapped, and directly behind the thicket in which The Orphan was hidden! The foreman's nerves were tense now, his every sense was alert, for his was a most dangerous position. He quickly glanced over his shoulder into the thicket and found that he could not penetrate the mass of leaves and branches, which reassured him. He was very glad that he had forced himself well into the cover, for soon the leaves rustled and a pebble rolled not more than four feet off, and in front of him, slightly at his right. More rustling and then a head and shoulder slowly pushed past him into view. The man moved very slowly and cautiously and was crouched, his head far in advance of his waist. The Orphan could see only one side of the face, the angle of the man's jaw and an ear, but that was enough, for he knew the owner. Slowly and without a sound the foreman's right hand turned at the wrist until the Colt gleamed on a line with the other's heart. The searcher leaned forward and to one side, that he might better see the boots, when a sound met his ears.

"Don't move," whispered the foreman.

The prowler stiffened in his tracks, frozen to rigidity by the command. Then he slowly turned his head and looked squarely into the gun of the man he thought he had killed.

"Christ!" he cried hoarsely, starting back.

"I don't reckon you'll ever know Him," said The Orphan, his voice very low and monotonous. "Stand just as you are–don't move–I want to talk with you."

Tex simply stared at him in pitiful helplessness and could not speak, beads of perspiration standing out on his face, testifying to the agony of fear he was in.

"You're on the wrong side of the game again, Tex," The Orphan said slowly, watching the puncher narrowly, his gun steady as a rock. "You still want to kill me, it seems. I've given you your life twice, once to your knowledge, and I told you with the sheriff that I would shoot you if you ever returned; and still you have come back to have me do it. You were not satisfied to let things rest as they were."

Tex did not reply, and The Orphan continued, a flicker of contempt about his lips.

"You were never cast for an outlaw, Tex. If I do say it myself, it takes a clever man to live at that game, and I know, for I've been all through it. As you see, Sneed and I didn't shoot each other, for the play was too plain, too transparent. You should have ambushed one of his men, burned his corrals and slaughtered his cattle, for then he might have shot and talked later. And he might have gotten me, too, for I was unsuspecting. I don't say that I would kill an innocent man to arouse his anger if I had been in your place, I'm only showing you where you made the mistake, where you blundered. Had you killed one of his men it is very probable that his rage would have known no bounds, but as it was the provocation was not great enough."

Tex remained silent and unconsciously toyed at his ear. The Orphan looked keenly at the movement and wondered where he had seen it before, for it was familiar. His face darkened as memory urged something forward to him out of the dark catacombs of the past, and he stilled his breathing to catch a clue to it. He saw the little ranch his father had worked so hard over to improve, and had fought hard to save, and then the picture of his dying mother came vividly before him; but still something avoided his searching thoughts, something barely eluded him, trembling on the edge of the Then and Now. He saw his father's body slowly swinging and turning in the light breeze of a perfect day, and he quivered at the nearness of what he was seeking, its proximity was tantalizing. The rope!–the rope about his father's neck had been of manila fiber; he could never forget the soiled, bleached-yellow streak which had led upward to Eternity. And manila ropes were, at that time, a rarity in that part of the country, for rawhide and braided-hair lariats had been the rule. And on the day when he had given Tex his life in the defile he had noticed the faded yellow rope which had swung at the puncher's saddle horn. As he strained with renewed hope to catch the elusive impression another scene came before him. It was of three men bent over a cow, engaged in blotting out his father's brand, and instantly the face of one of them sprang into sharp definition on his mental canvas.

"D—-n you!" he cried, his finger tightening on the trigger of the Colt which for so many years had been his best friend. "I know you now, changed as you are! Now I know why you have been so determined for my death. On the day that I cut my father down I swore that I would kill the man who had lynched him if kind fate let me find him, and I have found him. You have just five minutes to live, so make the most of it, you cowardly murderer!"

Tex's face went suddenly white again and his nerve deserted him. His Colt was in his hand, but oh, so useless! Should he fight to the end? A shudder ran through him at the thought, for life was so good, so precious; far too precious to waste a minute of it by dying before his time was up. Perhaps the foreman would relent, perhaps he would become so wrapped up in the memories of the years gone by as to forget, just for half a second, where he was. The watch in The Orphan's hand gave him hope, for he would wait until the other glanced at it–that would be his only hope of life.

The foreman's watch ticked loudly in the palm of his left hand and the Colt in his right never quivered. The first minute passed in terrifying silence, then the second, then the third, but all the time The Orphan's eyes stared steadily at the man before him, gray, cruel, unblinking.

"They told me to do it! They told me to do it!" shrieked the pitiful, unnerved wreck of a man as he convulsively opened and shut his hand. "I didn't want to do it! I swear I didn't want to do it! As God is above, I didn't want to! They made me, they made me!" he cried, his words swiftly becoming an unintelligible jumble of meaningless sounds. He stared at the black muzzle of the Colt, frozen by terror, fascinated by horror and deadened by despair. The watch ticked on in maddening noise, for his every sense was now most acute, beating in upon his brain like the strokes of a hammer. Then the foreman glanced quickly at it. The gun in Tex's hand leaped up, but not quickly enough, and a spurt of smoke enveloped his face as he fell. The Orphan stepped back, dropping the Colt into its holster.

"The courage of despair!" he whispered. "But I'm glad he died game," he slowly added. Then he suddenly buried his face in his hands: "Helen!" he cried. "Helen-forgive me!"

Chapter XXIII
The Great Happiness

The town was rapidly losing sharpness of detail, for the straggling buildings were becoming more and more blurred and were growing into sharp silhouettes in the increasing dusk, and the sickly yellow lights were growing more numerous in the scattered windows.

Helen moved about the dining-room engaged in setting the table and she had just placed fresh flowers in the vase, when she suddenly stopped and listened. Faintly to her ears came the pounding hoofbeats of a galloping horse on the well-packed street, growing rapidly nearer with portentous speed. It could not be Miss Ritchie, for there was a vast difference between the comparatively lazy gallop of her horse and the pulse-stirring tattoo which she now heard. The hoofbeats passed the corner without slackening pace, and whirled up the street, stopping in front of the house with a suddenness which she had long since learned to attribute to cowboys. She stood still, afraid to go to the door, numbed with a nameless fear-something terrible must have happened, perhaps to The Orphan. The rider ran up the path, his spurs jingling sharply, leaped to the porch, and the door was dashed open to show him standing before her, sombrero in hand, his quirt dangling from his left wrist. He was dusty and tired, but the expression on his face terrified her, held her speechless.

"Helen!" he cried hoarsely, driving her fear deeper into her heart by his altered voice. "Helen!" She trembled, and he made a gesture of hopelessness and involuntarily stepped toward her, letting the door swing shut behind him. He stood just within the room, rigidly erect, his eyes meeting hers in the silence of strong emotion. Breathlessly she retreated as he advanced, as if instinct warned her of what he had to tell her, until the table was between them; and a spasm of pain flickered across his face as he noticed it, leaving him hard and stern again, but in his eyes was a look of despair, a keen misery which softened her and drew her toward him even while she feared him.

The silence became unbearable and at last she could endure it no longer. "What is it?" she breathed, tensely. "What have you to tell me?"

His eyes never wavered from her face, fascinated in despair of what he must read there, much as he dreaded it, and he answered her from between set lips, much as a man would pronounce his own death sentence. "I have broken my word," he said, harshly.

"Broken your word-to me?" she asked.

"Yes."

Her face brightened and was softened by a child-like wonder, for she felt relieved in a degree, and unconsciously she moved nearer to him. "What is it-what have you done?"

He regarded her without appraising the change in her expression and his reply was as harsh and stern as his first statement, accompanied by no excuses nor words of extenuation. "I have killed a man," he said.

A shiver passed over her and her eyes went closed for a moment. The great choice was at hand now, and in her heart a fierce, short battle raged; on one side was arrayed her early training, all her teachings, all regard for the ideas of law and order which she had absorbed in the East, where human life was safeguarded as the first necessity; and on the other was the Unwritten Law of the range as exemplified by The Orphan. Blood, and human blood, was precious, and her early environment fought bitterly against this regime of direct justice, so startlingly driven into her mind by his bold, cold admission. And then, he had sinned in this way again after he had promised her not to do so. The last thought dominated her and she opened her eyes and looked at him hopefully.

"Perhaps," she said, eagerly, "perhaps you could not avoid it-perhaps you were forced to do it."

"No."

"Oh!" she cried. "You did not-you did not shoot him down without warning! I *know* you didn't!"

"No, not that," he said slowly. "And, besides, this was his third offense. Twice I have given him his life, and I would have done so again but for what I discovered after I faced him." He paused for a moment and then continued, with more feeling in his voice, a ring of victory and an irrepressible elation. "I found that he was the man for whom I have been looking for fifteen years, and whom I had sworn to kill. He killed my father, killed him like a dog and without a chance for life, hung him to a tree on his own land. And when I learned that, when he had confessed to me, I forgot the new game, I forgot everything but the watch in my hand slowly ticking away his life, the time I had given him to make his peace with God-and I hated the slow seconds, I begrudged him every movement of the hands. Then I shot him, and I was glad, so glad-but oh, dear! If you-if you——-"

His voice wavered and broke and he dropped to his knees before her with bowed head as she came slowly toward him and seized the hem of her gown in both hands, kissing it passionately, burying his face in its folds like a tired boy at his mother's knee.

Her eyes were filled with tears and they rimmed her lashes as she looked down on the man at her feet. Bending, she touched him and then placed her hands on his head, tenderly kissing the tangled hair in loving forgiveness.

"Dear, dear boy," she murmured softly. "Don't, dear heart. Don't, you must not-oh, you must not! Please-come with me; get up, dear, and sit with me over here in the corner; then you shall tell me all about it. I am sure you have not done wrong-and if you have-don't you know I love you, boy? Don't you know I love you?"

He stirred slightly, as if awakening from a troubled sleep, and slowly raised his head and looked at her with doubt in his eyes, for it was so much like a dream-perhaps it was one. But he saw a light on her face, a light which a man sees only on the face of one woman and which blinds him against all other lights forever. Then it was true, all true-he had heard aright! "Helen!" he cried, "Helen!" and the ring in his voice brought new tears to her eyes. He sprang to his feet, tense, eager, all his nerves tingling, and his quirt hissed through the air and snapped a defiance, a warning to the world as he clasped her to him. "I *knew*, I *knew!*" he cried passionately. "In my heart I *knew* you were a thoroughbred!"

He tilted her head back, but she laughed low with delight and eluded him, leading him to a chair, the chair he had occupied on the occasion of his first visit, and then drew a low, rough footrest beside him and seated herself at his feet, her elbows resting on his knees and her chin in her hands. He looked down into the upturned face and then glanced swiftly about the homelike room and back to her face again. She snuggled tightly against his knees and waited patiently for his story.

He sighed contentedly and touched her cheek reverently and then told her all of the story of Tex Williard, from the very beginning to the very end, from the time he had seen Tex bending over one of his father's cows to the last scene in the thicket. When he had finished, Helen took his head between her hands, pressing it warmly as she nodded wisely to show that she understood. He looked deep into her eyes and then suddenly bent his head until his lips touched her ear: "Helen, darling," he whispered, "how long must I wait?"

"Why, you scamp!" she exclaimed, teasingly, threatening to draw away from him. "You haven't even told me that you love me!"

He pressed her hands tightly and laughed aloud, joyously, filled with an elated, effervescent gladness which surged over him in waves of delight: "Haven't I? Oh, but you know better, dear. Many and many times I have told you that, and in many ways, and you knew it and understood. You never doubted it, and I hope," he added seriously, "that you never will."

"I never will, dear."

They did not hear Grace Ritchie in the kitchen, did not hear her quiet step as it crossed the threshold and stopped, and then tiptoed to the rear door and sped lightly around the house to the street, and down it to where Mrs. Shields and Mary were walking toward the house. They did not know that half an hour had passed since the coming of the quiet step and the three women, and that the supper was hopelessly ruined. They knew nothing-and Everything: they had learned the Great Happiness.

Footnotes

1. The boy and girl history of David Jones (Black Jack) and his sister, Veia (called Jill) was well known to some of the old timers who went to Montana in the first gold rush and stayed there. It was difficult to get them to tell it and one was sorry to have heard it, if successful.